ROSIE MEADOWS REGRETS . . .

Rosie Meadows regrets . . .

Catherine Alliott

HEADLINE

First published in 1998 by
HEADLINE BOOK PUBLISHING

10 9 8 7 6 5 4 3 2 1

British Library Cataloguing in Publication Data

Alliott, Catherine
Rosie Meadows regrets
I.Title
823.9'14[F]

Hb ISBN 0 7472 2020 4
Sb ISBN 0 7472 7701 X

Typeset by
Letterpart Limited, Reigate, Surrey

Printed and bound in Great Britain by
Mackays of Chatham plc, Chatham, Kent

HEADLINE BOOK PUBLISHING
A division of Hodder Headline PLC
338 Euston Road
London NW1 3BH

For my parents

Chapter One

'So anyway, Charlie here turned to me and said, "Okay, Charlotte, if you're such a crack shot, how about a game of strip shooting in the field!" – expecting me to swoon and reach for the vapours or something. So I said all right, you bastard, you're on!'

I took a sip of wine to steady my nerves and gazed at my raconteuring hostess over the mahogany dining table. I certainly couldn't look at Charlie's wife, Lavinia, down the other end.

'So out we all went with our shotguns,' Charlotte went on, 'drunk as skunks – well, Charlie and I certainly were – into the paddock, and someone managed to focus long enough to send up the clays and I hoisted Daddy's Purdey up into my shoulder and – well!' She paused, suspending animation just long enough to draw a few dutiful gasps of admiration from her guests. 'Blow me if I didn't get every single one of those clays and these bastards didn't get a dicky bird!'

Raucous laughter and much table thumping greeted this, particularly from my husband who was going to put his fist through his side plate in a minute. I watched as he roared away, his round, moon-like face gleaming as red as the foppish hanky sticking out of his breast pocket, upper lip perspiring freely, eyes gleaming lasciviously.

'And did they?' he bellowed. 'Strip?'

'You bet they did!' came back the retiring Charlotte. 'Stark bollock naked every single one of them *and* I had them standing to attention presenting arms – amongst other things – before I moved along the ranks inspecting them with a riding crop – ha ha!'

'Oh, Charlotte, you *didn't*!' shrieked a horsy girl to my left. 'You are a *scream*!'

Yes, wasn't she just? I didn't notice Lavinia screaming too much though. I glanced at her flushed face. She'd just about managed to bare her teeth in a brave semblance of a smile as she pushed a piece of Brie around her plate. I sipped my wine and flashed a look at Charlotte's husband Boffy, wondering how he was taking all this. On

1

what passed for his chin, apparently, judging by the way he was doubled up with mirth, spluttering Stilton down his red braces. Clearly he couldn't have been more pleased that his wife took such a keen interest in other men's anatomy.

As I gazed around the table at the assembled port-swilling, braying throng, it did occur to me to wonder, though, whether I was being entirely fair here. Wasn't I being just a little bit jaundiced on account of the company? A little bit partisan? If this had been a dinner party at one of *my* friends' houses for instance, and had it been Kate, say, or Alice doing the story-telling, might I not have found it amusing? Wasn't it just the fact that it was one of Harry's friends that made it all so puerile?

'Rosie, get that port moving,' bellowed my shy hostess. 'I've got a hell of a thirst on over here!'

'Oh, sorry.' I dutifully shoved along the ship's decanter which had obviously been stuck in front of me for some time and cleared my throat which was dry from lack of use.

'Actually,' I said bravely, trying to catch Harry's bloodshot eye, 'I think we'd better be making a move soon. I told the baby-sitter midnight and it's half past already . . .'

'Is it?' Charlotte flashed up her Rolex. 'Christ! I've got a bridge lesson first thing in the morning. Come on, you lot, get out of here. Go on, bugger off. I'll get the Hoover out in a minute!'

There was a great deal of laughing and scraping back of chairs but not many bottoms were off the tapestry seat covers quite as smartly as mine. Two seconds later I had my coat on and my bag firmly over my shoulder. Five minutes went by and I was still smiling fixedly, waiting patiently as Harry did his usual protracted round of leave-taking, slapping backs heartily and collecting prospective engagements wherever he could.

'Charlie! It's been far too long, we must get together again soon . . . Oh, really? On Thursday? No, not a thing, yes, we'd love to come, wouldn't we, darling? Hey, Rosie, social secretary – wake up! Drinks party on Thursday night all right?'

'Charlie and Lavinia live in Hampshire, Harry,' I said quietly.

'So what? Won't take long, we'll be there in an hour, won't we, Charlie? Charlie?'

Charlie broke off from talking to someone else. He turned to Harry as if he couldn't quite remember him. 'Hour and a half from central London, old boy.'

'Much as that, eh? Can't think why you live out there in the sticks, takes me eight and a half minutes to get to Sloane Square!'

Charlie raised his eyebrows. 'Eight and a half minutes? I'm only halfway down my drive.'

Much guffawing greeted this, with Harry promising, nonetheless, that we'd be there come hell or high water, eh, Rosie?

'Fine,' I said nodding, grinning, and wishing to God Harry wouldn't do this. If Charlie had wanted us there in the first place he'd have sent us an invitation. I gave a tight little smile. 'We'd love to come, Charlie.'

Finally we were at the door, planting more kisses, making more false promises.

'Rosie, *do* come and make up a bridge four some time,' insisted Charlotte. 'I know you're crap but it doesn't matter in the least, no one minds, really!'

'You're sweet,' I lied. 'And I'll ring you, really I will. Thanks so much, Charlotte, it was a lovely evening, delicious supper. 'Night, Boffy.' I pecked their cheeks.

''Bye, darlings!' Charlotte carolled as we went off into the night. 'And don't forget to ring, Rosie!'

'I won't!' I waved back to the light of the hall, keeping a bright smile going at the two figures silhouetted within it. At last the blue front door closed on them, shutting us out, leaving us to the welcoming cold night air. I gave a sigh of relief as it enveloped us and huddled down into my coat, breathing the icy wind in gratefully as I made my way along the slippery pavement to the car.

I got in quickly and waited, hand poised on the ignition, watching in the rear-view mirror as Harry made his habitually slow, stumbling progress round the back to his side. He fumbled with the handle, missed, tried again, opened it, and then with a great grunt lowered himself into the passenger seat. His huge bulk spilled out over the handbrake, his knees ending up somewhere near his nose. He sank back happily and sighed.

'Ahhh . . . well done, darling,' he patted my hand. 'Very well done indeed. I think that went extremely smoothly. Nine and a half, I'd say.'

I ground my teeth and turned the ignition. 'Good,' I murmured, wisely keeping my counsel. Gone were the days when I'd upbraid Harry for his loathsome habit of giving an evening marks out of ten when we'd just been to supper with someone who owned a grouse moor, or a salmon river, or a chalet in Switzerland, or any other sort of action that Harry might want a slice of. No, the last thing I wanted was a heated row on the way home, only to crawl into bed with a raging headache, tossing and turning all night as Harry snored for England beside me.

As we purred slowly down the narrow, lamp-lit Fulham street, Harry settled his head back on the rest and closed his eyes.

'Just one teeny point though, darling,' he murmured. 'You were a bit sort of – quiet tonight. Bit mousy. You must try to loosen up with my friends, you know. I know you find them intimidating but they won't bite. It's all a question of confidence.' There was a pause. 'Oh, and one other thing.' He turned his head towards me. 'I overheard you talking to Boffy about going horse racing. It's racing actually, sweetie. A small point, but one worth remembering, eh?'

I didn't answer, just ground my teeth some more. Don't rise, Rosie, just don't rise.

'All right to drive, my love?' he went on sleepily. 'Not sure I'm up to it tonight, feeling a bit kippy.'

'Of course I'm all right,' I muttered, wondering why he even bothered to ask. I always drove home; in fact these days it was nip and tuck whether Harry could actually drive *to* a party depending on how many pre-dinner whiskies he'd sunk in his bath beforehand. I sighed and shunted up a gear. Oh, so what, Rosie, let him drink, at least it puts him to sleep, doesn't it? I glanced hopefully across at his slumbering profile but – hello, the eyelids were flickering again. He'd obviously remembered something crucial. He blinked his pale blue eyes and grinned into the night.

'I say, Charlotte's an awfully good sort, isn't she?'

Sort of what? I was tempted to ask. Sort of witch? Sort of trollop? But I knew better than that. I gave a twisted smile. 'Yes, isn't she.'

'Sound quite fun, these little bridge parties of hers. Why don't you go along? Do you good.'

I gripped the steering wheel hard, thinking I'd rather haemorrhage from the navel. 'Don't be ridiculous, Harry, how can I possibly play bridge when I've got Ivo to look after? What d'you expect him to do, sit in his high chair and count the rubbers?'

'Rubbers?' He looked startled. 'Aren't they – condoms or something?'

I grinned. 'No, Harry, it's a bridge term, although actually it wouldn't surprise me if condoms did make an appearance soon. If Charlotte's giving nude shooting parties it won't be long before she spices up her bridge afternoons too, turns them into Ann Summers parties or something.' I smiled to myself. Privately I'd always thought the C was silent in Charlotte's name.

Harry frowned, confused. 'Ann Summers? Don't think we know her, do we? Ah yes, got it, pretty little red-head, met her at the Compton-Burnetts' – father's a bishop?'

'Well, if he is, he's bitterly disappointed,' I muttered as I swerved dangerously round a midnight cyclist with an apparent death wish. 'No, forget it, Harry, you don't know her, but the point is I can't do anything remotely social during the day until Ivo goes to nursery school, can I? And that won't be for ages.'

'Well, get a nanny, everyone else has got one,' he said petulantly.

I dug my nails fiercely into the mock leather trim of the wheel. This was an age-old bone of contention.

'Everyone that *you* know has got one, everyone that I know either looks after their children or has a nanny because they go to work, they don't fiddle-fart around at bridge parties and coffee mornings. But look, darling,' I said quickly, seeing him bridle, 'let's not discuss it now, okay? I'm tired and I just want to get home and go to bed.'

'Fine,' he said tersely. 'Fine. All I'm saying, Rosie, is don't expect invitations to shoot in Northumberland to fall into your lap, okay? You have to be prepared to put in a bit of groundwork first, you know!'

I smiled. Ah, so that's what this was all about. Shooting in Northumberland. Yes, well, I'd had such a terrific time there last year, no doubt I'd be round at Charlotte's first thing tomorrow, sharpening my pencils, turning in my tricks and singing for my supper with the rest of the gang. I sighed. Last year, due to the fact that one of the husbands couldn't keep his hands off the cook, goosing her every time she bent down to put the roast pork in the oven and then lying prostrate on her bed, naked but for a wooden spoon in his mouth and a strategically placed oven glove, the poor girl had finally collapsed in a heap and walked out, leaving muggins here to pick up the pieces and cook for fourteen. Well, it was either that or starve.

'Where are we going to find another one?' they'd all squeaked hysterically, looking around the room as if by chance they might find a stray cook hiding behind the sofa. 'We'll never get one from an agency at such short notice!'

'Of course we won't,' I'd said shortly, making my way to the kitchen. 'We'll have to do it ourselves.'

'Oh, good old Rosie,' they'd all chorused, 'she'll take the helm! Thank goodness someone knows what they're doing. I couldn't boil an egg!' Which left me to wonder, as they tore off to the tennis courts gaily swinging their rackets again, how it was that they were all so hale and hearty. You'd think they'd all have wasted away by now, wouldn't you?

'Yes, well, I'm not altogether sure I want another busman's holiday,' I said as lightly as possible.

5

'You said you didn't mind,' Harry said huffily. 'I distinctly remember, you said you quite enjoyed it.'

'I didn't particularly mind,' I said levelly, 'I just don't want to do it again, that's all.'

There was a long pause.

'I was very proud of you,' he said abruptly. 'Stepping in like that.'

I sighed. 'Yes, I *know* you were.'

God, yes, I remembered his face when everyone had patted me on the back and said what a little star I was, how he'd glowed and glowed with pride until I thought he was going to explode. And then, when everyone had disappeared to the courts, how he'd trotted off after them, last as usual, his thick legs rubbing together in his too-tight white shorts. I remembered watching him go, standing at the kitchen window, surrounded by eight uncooked lobsters and not a single offer of help from anyone.

'I just wonder if you should have been quite so proud,' I said quietly. 'I felt as though – well, as though somehow we were paying our way.'

'Oh, don't be ridiculous,' he scoffed. 'Charlotte and Boffy are my oldest friends! I don't have to buy my way into their house!'

Have to attend a few bridge parties though, make the right noises at the right social events, don't we? I thought privately.

Actually I hadn't minded doing the cooking that weekend. I'd put on my apron and rolled up my sleeves with alacrity, anything to get away from this hearty, bellowing crowd who did nothing but shriek about what a good time they were having and guffaw at unfunny jokes. In the beginning, when Harry and I were first married, I'd thought perhaps I was missing the point. They were, after all, a good ten years older than I was and so naturally more sophisticated. In time, I thought, I'd get the jokes. But then I realised there was nothing to get. 'Having fun' was simply what they did, it was their raison d'être, and if something wasn't funny they'd roar with laughter anyway. These were rich, aimless people, buoyed up by trust funds, daddies in the City and the most exclusive educations money could buy. From a very early age they'd taken a long, cool look at themselves, found themselves to be utterly flawless and with that conviction ringing soundly in their ears had marched off from the nursery to shout as loudly as they could and do as they blinking well liked. Not for the likes of Charlotte and Boffy the anxiety and shyness most mortals suffer. Not for them the anxious words in the car on the way home from parties – 'You know when I said Amanda had lost weight, you don't think she thought I meant she was grossly

6

overweight before, do you?' Or, 'When I said their Tommy was a quiet little thing, did it sound like I thought he was retarded?' No, no, Harry's friends were all imbued with the utmost self-confidence. They lacked for nothing in their lives, except humility.

I sighed and swung the wheel into the Wandsworth Road. And I'd tried, I really had. In the beginning I'd been so keen to get on with Harry's crowd, to find a girlfriend, a kindred spirit, one who perhaps wasn't as boisterous and outrageous as the rest, but they were all the same, and whereas at first I'd been in awe of them, thinking them such a fast, zany bunch, now they just made my head ache. And Harry too? I glanced across at him sitting next to me, head back, mouth open, pudgy hands clasped limply across his pinstriped waistcoat, snoring soundly. I smiled ruefully. The real irony was that when I'd first met Harry I'd thought him so different from the rest. What I hadn't known was that this wasn't by choice.

We'd met in Ireland, also at a house party, but this time it was very much a legitimate working weekend for me, as the cook, the hired help. It wasn't the sort of thing I usually did, I mostly cooked in London, working with a friend who had her own catering business, but an agency had rung at the last minute and begged me to take the job because some other girl had dropped out and the clients were apoplectic with rage. This, in itself, should have been enough to set alarm bells ringing, but instead I said, 'Oh all right, I'll do it,' and the following morning saw me setting off across the Irish Sea singlehand-edly to cook breakfast, lunch, tea and dinner for fifteen guns and their wives.

Now under normal circumstances I wouldn't be nearly such a mug, but the truth was I was dying to get away from London and any excuse would do. I badly needed to bolt. You see, I'd just come to the end of a very one-sided relationship – heavy on my side and feather-light on his – with an extremely attractive landscape gardener called Rupert, who for the last nine months I'd considered to be the most delectable thing in faded corduroy trousers. Twinkly-eyed, tousled-haired, fatal sexy grin – he was the whole delicious package and I was smitten. True, I only managed to see him on Tuesday, Thursday and Sunday nights but that was because pressing tree surgery business took up the other evenings. He was a very busy man. Wednesday evenings therefore found me at a comparatively loose end, and if there was nothing on the telly, I tended to while away the hours pumping iron in the local gym.

One particular Wednesday I was down at my club as usual, keeping one eye out for royalty and another on the rampant cellulite, pounding away on my immobile bike, when the girl on the adjacent bicycle, with whom I'd previously only been on smiling terms, suddenly struck up a conversation.

'Fancy a break?' she puffed, pink leotard dark with perspiration.

'Oh – yes!' I gasped back piteously.

Needing no further prompting, we shot off to the cafe together. As we sat there in a window seat, basking in the beams of hazy evening sunshine which bounced off our sweaty heads, happily guzzling our high-calorie hot chocolates, we naturally, as strangers do, swapped our most intimate details. Fat, of course, was first and foremost on the agenda. Fat on thighs, fat on bottoms, fat on tummies and amid cries of 'Oh, don't be silly, my bottom's *much* bigger than yours!' we struck up a cosy camaraderie. Hair removal came next – waxing on my part, electrocution on hers – and then, of course, men. And, strangely, it transpired she had a similar problem. You see, it turned out that my new friend was also in love with a man she could only pin down to certain nights of the week, namely Monday, Friday and Saturday. Coincidentally, this man was also a tree surgeon and funnily enough . . . he was also called Rupert. I remember us staring at each other incredulously, skins forming on our cooling hot chocolates as slowly the respective pennies dropped with a resound-ing 'clunk'. Leg warmers tightened, trainers creaked, headbands shrank with horror until at last we found our voices and shrieked –

'No!'

'I don't *believe* it!'

'How *could* he!'

'He *couldn't*!'

'He bloody *has*!'

'The BASTARD!'

Quite a lot more outraged screaming and shouting took place before we stood up as one, threw our coats over our damp leotards and strode out into the night.

Tight-lipped we hailed a taxi and trundled round to Draycott Terrace where, of course, being Wednesday, we found him in, having his one night of the week off games. His bemused flatmate let us in and there was Rupert, stretched out on a sofa, watching EastEnders, eating an Indian takeaway and quietly picking his nose. Together we stood over his astonished form and told him, in graphic detail, where exactly he could put his trees and what sort of surgery we thought he really needed. Pink Leotard even went so far as to tip his Vindaloo into his corduroy crutch, which I thought was a nice touch.

That was the Wednesday. On Thursday I was still incensed, but by

Friday the misery had well and truly set in. It was the end of me and Rupert and it was also, I determined, the end of my flirtation with the main squeeze of the species. You see, up until now I'd always eschewed these fast, glamorous men as being far too dangerous for me, my predilection always being for the sidekicks of life. Why, even at school, whilst other girls lusted after Napoleon Solo, I went for Ilya Kuryakin, while some screamed for Le Bon, I guitared with Taylor, and whilst some yearned for Bodey, I dreamt of Doyle. I'd felt happier that way, more comfortable, more at ease with my ever so slightly upper hand, and that's how it should have stayed. Until Rupert. The main attraction, the sublime tree surgeon who'd felled me at the knees.

Well, never again, I told myself firmly as I sobbed into the sofa in my flat that Friday night. Never, never again. It was back to the bargain basement for me, back to riffling through the rails hoping to find something more suitable, something someone else had cast aside maybe. Something a little bald, a little short, a little fat, a little thin – something I could *do* something with. And that's where I found Harry.

The agency had telephoned as I sobbed out my resolve into my cushion and I took the job out of sheer desperation.

'It's in Ireland,' they pointed out.

'I don't care!' I sobbed.

'You'd have to leave tonight.'

'Even better!'

'You'll be rushed off your feet.'

'It'll numb the pain!'

And that was how it came to pass that the following day I found myself on the west coast of Ireland, standing at a vast wooden table in the middle of a huge old kitchen that looked like something out of Mrs Beeton, staring miserably at a dozen woodcock that all needed plucking, gutting and cooking, and with the firm promise of a dozen more to follow shortly.

An hour and a half later with only three birds plucked, covered in feathers, guts and blood, and feeling decidedly ill and close to tears, I heard the crunch of tyres on the gravel outside. Glancing up, I saw a dirty old Land Rover draw up alongside the window. I remember thinking with horror – and a certain amount of mutiny – that if this was the other dozen birds appearing I'd either burst into tears or take the first ferry home, when out of the cab jumped Harry. He was wearing a rather smart lovat green shooting ensemble and bearing not six brace of woodcock but a bottle of champagne.

9

He was a huge blond man, six foot five at least and very broad, but without the weight he's carrying now. As he strode into the kitchen brandishing his bottle, it seemed to me the whole room went dark. I paused in mid-pluck, gazing up at this giant, waiting for yet more orders from on high. Instead, he took one look at my wobbly face and the feather-strewn kitchen, told me to go and wash my hands and face and he'd do the rest. True to his word, he sat down on a stool, dragged a bin between his knees and set about expertly de-fluffing the smelly beasts while I sat beside him sniffing and sipping my chilled champagne. I could have kissed him. And of course that's all I should have done. Instead, I married him. Not just like that, of course, it was a few more months before I actually became Mrs Harry Meadows, but it was a fairly snap decision for such a momentous one.

Looking back, I'm not at all sure it didn't have a lot to do with my condition at the time of that very first meeting. I was so emotionally exhausted and pathetically grateful to this enormous, kindly – or so I thought – bear of a man, that I think I decided there and then that I'd been treated too shabbily for too long by too many smooth-talking handsome bastards – one, actually, for all of nine months – and that this straightforward, capable, decent man would do very nicely, thank you. Let's face it, I was rebounding like a cannon ball and I was flying faster than the speed of light. Someone had to catch me; it happened to be Harry.

I told myself I liked his eyes – blue, can't go wrong, Rosie – and his reassuring broad shoulders, and as far as I remember he made me laugh, which is strange, because he hasn't since. If I'm honest, I also liked the fact that I was better looking than he was, which was saying something actually, because at the time I was a good stone over-weight and had just had an ambitiously short 'elfin' haircut which, considering I have neither the 'elfin' face nor the figure to back it up, resulted in me looking like a fat little pixie. But Harry saw none of this. I was blonde, I had beautiful green eyes – his words, not mine – my skin was peachy (ditto), I was voluptuous (the less said about that the better) and I was all his heart desired. Well. What could I say? If he was smitten then I could be too, and I sank back into the whole cosy relationship with a monumental sigh of relief. I didn't have to try too hard, didn't have to be too witty, too amusing, too beautiful, didn't have to jump through any more hoops. It was like landing on a feather mattress after all those years of being Out There.

He was older than I was (by about ten years), taller than me (by about a foot) and yes, okay, maybe he was a bit pompous, a bit pleased with himself and a teensy bit on the dull side, particularly when he'd drunk too much, which was more than occasionally, but my goodness who *didn't* have their faults and he was, after all, a basically nice man, wasn't he?

I bit my lip and shifted angrily down to third as I took the bend too sharply at the Wandsworth roundabout. Harry lolled sleepily to one side, his head propped up against the window, mouth wide open, a tiny trace of dribble appearing at the side of it.

Mummy, of course, had been delighted. She'd opened the front door, taken one look at the whopping great sapphire on my left hand and almost gone down on her knees and kissed the hem of his Barbour, she was so excited. Beaming widely, she'd taken him firmly by the arm and marched him straight into the sitting room to draw up a guest list for the wedding, and from then on it was like a bobsleigh ride to the altar. Mummy was at the helm and the telephone was rarely out of her hand.

'He's some sort of relation of Lord Something-or-other-of-Somewhere!' I heard her squeak excitedly down the phone to her friend Marjorie Burdett. 'Imagine, if *he* dies, and then his *cousin* dies and then someone a bit further down the *line* dies, Rosie might even end up being a lady! She might end up doing even better than Philippa!' This was almost too orgasmic for words and she dropped the telephone with a clatter on the reproduction hall table, because Philippa's marriage, frankly, was hard to beat.

Philippa was my elder sister. She was not only a beautiful, willowy, swan-like creature but also highly intelligent to boot. Some years back she'd taken time out from her hectic schedule at a London teaching hospital where she worked as an anaesthetist – oh yes, seriously intelligent – to come home for a local dance. It was here that she'd met, captivated, and consequently married – or 'bagged' as my mother so tastefully put it – an extremely rich local landowner who, according to Mummy, lived in 'the only house in Gloucestershire really worth having, Marjorie!'

Harry then, with his pretensions to nobility, summoned up all the latent suburban snobbery in my mother's heart, and she went into overdrive the minute the engagement was announced. One day I was being whisked around Peter Jones to assemble my wedding list, the next she had me scrambling in and out of wedding dresses in Harrods, bullying the staff, reducing assistants – and sometimes me – to tears, dragging me into travel agents to check out the arrangements for the honeymoon, so that for one awful moment I was so confused I thought I was marrying my mother. All of this enthusiasm

11

is perfectly normal in the mother of the bride, of course, but I couldn't help thinking there was an element of about-bloody-time about it too, for as she never failed to remind me, I was in my late twenties. As late as you can get, in fact.

The more the plans rolled on, the more she and Harry got on famously, with Mummy dribbling into her soup as snippets of well-connected friends and family fell from his lips. It didn't seem to matter that Harry didn't actually have a job, that he didn't have much money, and that all he owned was a couple of small houses in Wandsworth and some mythical stocks and shares; the fact that he could mention Michael Heseltine in the same breath as the Duchess of Devonshire had my mother practically writhing on the carpet, kicking her heels and begging for more. I remember going upstairs with her one night after supper when Harry had regaled us with yet another close encounter with the late Laurens Van Der Post – so much easier for Harry if these friends were 'late', incidentally – and she actually squeezed my waist on the landing as she said goodnight.

'You've done it, Rosie,' she breathed, 'you've really done it!'

I stared at her in amazement, and I remember thinking, how odd. After all those years of disapproval, all those years of scruffy clothes and unsuitable friends and no ambition, of giving her nothing but disappointment, in one fell stroke I'd pulled it off. I'd won her approval and maybe even her love. And by what? By bringing home a complete stranger. I blinked at her and, funnily enough, I didn't recoil, I didn't scoff, I didn't bolt in horror. I just looked into her excited shining eyes and basked contentedly in their glow. It was so easy, you see, and it made such a change not to be fighting her, not to be the rebel. I never thought it had bothered me that I hadn't managed to please her as much as Philly had, or my brother Tom, Philly's twin, but that night I went to bed feeling ridiculously, some would say pathetically, happy.

My father of course was another matter. His love had always been strong, upfront and unconditional and when he heard the news, he went very quiet.

'Well, if you're happy, love, then that's all that matters,' he said at length.

'But you do like him, don't you, Daddy?' I asked anxiously.

'Of course I do. Of course.'

We'd been sitting together on the old bench by the greenhouse and I remember sensing the tone of his voice, turning quickly, guiltily almost, for more reassurance. But he'd already stood up. He gathered up his gardening gloves, his secateurs, tapped his battered old hat smartly down on his head and moved on, down to the vegetable patch at the bottom of the garden. His tall frame moved as quickly and deliberately as ever, but was it my imagination or was there a slight droop to those shoulders, a drag in his step?

That was the first time I can recall being uncertain. The second time was just before I walked down the aisle. As I stood at the door of our village church on my father's arm, I suddenly had this overwhelming urge to rip my headdress off and run like crazy for the nearest number 9 bus. I gritted my teeth and told myself it was just pre-match nerves, and a second later 'The Queen of Sheba' struck up and I raised my chin and swept down the aisle. The third wave of uncertainty came an hour or so later, at our wedding reception in my parents' garden. It was the charmless Charlotte actually, who, incredibly tight and looking flushed and hot in a God-awful pink hat, had swayed up to me and brayed, 'Gosh, I *do* think you're marvellous to take on dear old Humpty, Rosie! How incredibly brave of you! Lord only *knows* what you're in for!'

'H-Humpty?' I stuttered.

'Yes,' she laughed gaily. 'An old nursery name. I expect you had one, didn't you?'

I didn't, and I was tempted to add I hadn't had a nursery either, but something more galling than this deprivation struck me smack between the eyes with all the force of a runaway truck. Good God. I'd married Humpty Dumpty. I'd married the stooge, the fat boy of the gang, and not only that, I'd been brave, selfless, done something no one else in their right mind had wanted to do. I remember standing there in my cream silk gown, staring blankly after Charlotte as she sauntered away, gripping my glass, the champagne already feeling flat in my hand.

After that my world went slowly darker as little by little the truth emerged. I'd married a man who, at thirty-nine, was desperate to marry. I was the fourth cook in a row he'd come back to help pluck the woodcock. It was the fourth bottle of champagne, the fourth mop-up-your-tears-Cinderella routine. It was a standing joke, how Humpty tried to get his leg over. But this time – get this – *this* time, not only had he got it over, I'd actually *married* him too! Cue raucous laughter, howling mirth, hysteria, and – cut. Because, wait a minute. How were they to know that I didn't love him? How were they to know that it wasn't a marriage made in heaven, eh?

Sadly, though, I didn't, and it wasn't, so the joke was firmly on me. Because no sooner had I shaken the confetti from my hair than it became clear that Harry was not the man I'd imagined him to be.

13

He wasn't just harmless, he was foolish. He wasn't solid, he was stationary – mostly lengthwise on a sofa with his eyes shut – and he wasn't just a heavy drinker, he was – well, the less said the better. Instead, let's move smartly on to the good news. My son, Ivo, precisely two years, two months old now, conceived on our honeymoon in India and born, funnily enough, nine months later. My darling boy – I smiled fondly over the steering wheel as I thought of him. My bright, blond, shining light who got me through my days, my marriage. The very epicentre of my world. For him, Harry – I glanced at him sideways – I thank you from the bottom of my heart. For him, I should be able to forgive you anything.

As we drew up alongside our house in Meryton Road, I sat there in the dark, willing myself to feel something, to bring back, if not the love, at least the tenderness. Quietly I slipped my seat belt off and turned sideways in my seat. I gazed upon my sleeping husband. Try, Rosie. Try to summon up something. For Ivo. There must have been something there in the beginning, surely, some sort of magic. I reached out and stroked his hand.

'Darling?' I whispered.

Not a flicker. On he snored.

'Harry, darling, we're home.'

He smacked his huge chops and turned his face the other way.

'Harry.' I shook him. 'Come on, it's cold out here, wake up.' I shook him a bit harder. 'Come on, my love.'

'Bugger off,' he muttered.

My hand froze on his.

'Well, bugger off too, you stupid fat git!' I roared.

I slumped back in my seat. Yes, well, that had really brought back the magic, hadn't it? Really summoned up the tenderness. I sighed. God, if only I'd married Mel Gibson, I'm sure I wouldn't have had all this trouble. I looked at Harry, biting my thumbnail. I was sorely tempted to leave him there, to let him fight his own way out of the car at four in the morning, let him stagger up the frosty path, search hopelessly for his door key, wrestle with the latch, but I knew it was counterproductive. I'd only have to leap out of bed in the middle of the night to intercept him, to stop him crashing around and waking Ivo. I leaned over and found his ear.

'Harry,' I shouted, 'if you stay here you'll freeze to death!' My eyes sparkled briefly in their tired old sockets at this, but I bade them dim. No, no. Only in your dreams, Rosie. On he snored.

'Right!' I screeched importantly. 'That's *it*!'

I scrambled out of the car and ran round to Harry's side. I flung open his door with a flourish. It was time for the Last Resort, a method thus far used only on a handful of occasions due to its inherent danger, but tonight was going to be one of them. I ran back to my side, got up on to my seat on all fours like a dog and began pushing Harry towards his open door. It was like moving a mountain. I put my shoulder against his and shoved for all I was worth, swearing and cursing, puffing and panting, when into my line of vision came an elderly man and his dog. They came along the pavement, stopped, and watched with interest, taking a moment out of their late-night constitutional to witness this piece of street theatre. I ignored them and pushed on regardless.

'He's going to fall on the pavement and crack his head open,' the man observed at length.

'That's the idea,' I muttered through clenched teeth.

There was a pause.

'Ah.' He nodded. Reassured, he moved on up the street.

Interesting exchange that, I thought, panting away. Obviously it was all right for me to inflict wilful bodily harm on my husband, it was accidental bodily harm that had bothered him. Finally, I gave one last superhuman push and Harry began to roll, and roll, and then j-u-s-t at the last minute as he was about to hit the pavement, he stuck his leg out and saved himself. Yes, well, he always *did*, didn't he? I sat panting, marvelling as he swung the other leg round and somehow stumbled to his feet, like a dazed elephant coming round from a drugged dart. Extraordinary, I thought, that inherent instinct for survival. It seemed that Harry, like the poor, would always be with us.

As he started to weave his way precariously up the garden path to the front door, I locked the car and quickly nipped past him, beating him to it. It was important at this juncture to stop him rapping on the knocker and hollering 'What-shall-we-do-with-the-drunken-sailor?' through the letter box, as was his wont.

'Well done,' he muttered as I opened the door and hustled him through. 'Well done, old thing.' Oh yes, I forgot to mention that. When I married Harry, I'd been lucky enough to lose my Christian name as well as my surname. I was no longer Rosie Cavendish, but Old Thing Meadows.

As I breathlessly steered him through to the sitting room, Alison, our baby-sitter, was already getting up from her chair, tucking her magazine in her bag and turning off the television.

'Had a good evening?' she asked shyly.

'Lovely, thanks, Alison, how about you? Has Ivo been all right, everything okay?'

'Oh yes, he's been an absolute angel as usual. He woke up at about ten o'clock so I gave him a drink and he went straight back down again. I hope that was all right?'

This was quite a long sentence for Alison and she went a bit pink. She was a sweet, shy girl of about seventeen from across the road who adored children, particularly Ivo.

I smiled. 'Of course, that's exactly what I would have done. Well done.' I had some money ready in my hand and I quickly slipped it into hers. 'Sorry we were a bit late, by the way.'

'Oh no, you weren't really – oh! No, that's far too much, Rosie.' She looked at the notes in her hand.

'No, please, take it.'

Alison was the eldest of five children and money was tight across the road. I knew that this was her way of getting a few nice clothes; in fact I knew for certain that her shiny black sixties-style mac which she'd proudly shown me when she'd arrived had been bought with her baby-sitting money.

'Thanks.' She beamed. 'I can get that mini skirt from Top Shop now.'

'Oh good,' I rejoined enthusiastically, and as I watched her glow with pleasure it occurred to me that perhaps that was what was missing from my life. A mini skirt from Top Shop.

'Well, I'll be off then,' she said. ''Night, Rosie. Goodnight, um, Mr Meadows.' She looked nervously at Harry. She never knew quite what to call him or what to say to him. He stood swaying in the sitting-room doorway, blocking her path to the hall. She edged towards him but he didn't move aside to let her through, instead he looked her up and down, his eyes running blatantly and rather mockingly over her youthful figure in her cropped Lycra top.

'Ah, you're off then, are you, um—'

'Alison,' I put in quickly. He never remembered her name and she'd been our baby-sitter for over a year now.

'Ah, yes, Alison. Son and heir been behaving himself?'

'Perfectly,' she said, trying to edge past him.

'Good, good.' He shut his eyes and swayed dangerously. Oh God. He wasn't just pissed, he was catastrophically drunk.

''Scuse me a minute,' he muttered. 'Must have a slash.'

He turned and stumbled from the room, but instead of turning right to the loo, he turned left, and opened the cupboard where we keep the coats. Without turning on the light and before I could open my mouth to speak, he'd unzipped his flies and started peeing. Noisily. At length. Against the coats. As I stood there frozen with

16

horror, I heard the unmistakable sound of water on plastic, and I just knew. I knew because I'd hung it there not a few hours ago. He was peeing all over Alison's shiny new mac.

Alison and I stood shoulder to shoulder, waiting, aghast, until the tinkling torrent subsided. There was a pause. Then a muffled, and slightly confused 'Bugger'.

A moment later, he staggered out.

'I say, I'm awfully sorry, Abigail old thing, I appear to have pissed in your coat pocket.'

It was at that moment that I knew for certain. I could no longer live with this man, he simply had to go.

Chapter Two

In case you think I'm the sort of girl who'd divorce her husband on the strength of a pissed indiscretion after a party, I'd like to say I'm not. It was simply the straw that broke the camel's back and one way and another my back was getting pretty humpy. It wasn't as if we were in uncharted waters either, oh no, I'd been here before. Leaving Harry was nothing new. I'd packed twice, got to the end of the road twice, I'd even – after he'd prodded me in the middle of the night and mumbled, 'Come on, pig, off to market,' got as far as my parents' house once, but never Right Away. Never For Good. It was with a certain amount of trepidation, therefore, that I opened my eyes the following morning and tested my resolve. I explored it fairly tentatively at first, expecting it to cave in under the slightest pressure, but to my surprise it held firm, even after seven hours' sleep. In fact it came to me with such startling clarity that this was the day that I, Rosie Meadows, was destined to leave her husband, that I bounced out of bed with an alacrity I hadn't shown in years.

I tiptoed over to my dressing-table mirror and gazed at my reflection, hooking my straight blonde hair back behind my ears. Did I look different? Did I look determined, decisive, as if I meant business? A pair of troubled green eyes stared anxiously back at me. Well, no, probably not, but the important thing was, I did mean it. This time I was certain. This time I was off.

I crept around the bedroom pulling on jeans and a jumper, being careful not to wake Harry, then stole from the room, shutting the door gently behind me.

'Mu-mmy . . . Mu-mmy . . . Mu-mmy . . .'

The steady chant that had originally woken me was getting louder now, and as I hastened across the landing I felt like a footballer trotting out from the tunnel to the roar of his fans on the terraces. 'Mu-MMMY!' it crescendoed as I opened his door.

'Iv-O!' I responded enthusiastically as I reached into his cot, picking him up for our first clinch of the day. But not too clinchy, I decided hastily, dropping to my knees and wrestling him to the floor, he was always pretty pongy first thing. I struggled with a stinking nappy, a wriggling child, and a hermetically sealed box of baby wipes – some manufacturer's joke – then snapping him into a clean nappy – I'd yet to summon up the courage to put him into pants – I hurried him into his clothes. Ivo's big blue eyes gazed at me in amazement. Pyjamas were usually perfectly acceptable at the breakfast table.

'Sorry, darling,' I muttered, thrusting his legs into trousers and hoisting him on to my hip, 'got to get out of here this morning. Got to get a wiggle on, as they say.'

We hurried downstairs and Ivo watched from his high chair as I whizzed around the kitchen, snapping machines on as I went. Toaster, kettle, microwave and washing machine whirred into action as I buttered toast, warmed milk, washed clothes and threw coffee down my neck. I badly wanted to go and break the news to Alice and I was keen to leave before Harry had a chance to intercept me. I didn't particularly want him to spot the marital meltdown message that I felt sure was written all over my face.

But no such luck. Ten minutes later, just as I was spooning the last of the Ready Brek into Ivo's mouth with one hand and unloading the dishwasher with the other, the doorway suddenly filled up with stripy blue pyjama. Harry yawned, stretched, and scratched his head like a great bear.

'Oooh, dear me. Feel a bit liverish this morning.' He patted his tummy tentatively. This was Harry's usual euphemism for a stonking great hangover. He looked me up and down and frowned. 'You're dressed early.'

'Am I?' I said guiltily. 'Oh well, I just thought – you know, it's such a lovely morning, I thought I'd take Ivo to the park.'

He gave an incredulous grunt and lowered himself slowly down at the kitchen table. There he sat, waiting to be served. I made a mug of coffee and set it in front of him.

'Nasty feeling I'm in disgrace,' he muttered as he stirred it. 'Seem to remember I was out of order last night.'

'No more than usual,' I said lightly.

'Tell the girl I'm sorry, would you? Spastic colon.' For a moment I thought he was insulting Alison again but then he went on, 'Doctor says it's quite common in chaps of my age. You know, with my levels of stress.'

Stress! I boggled quietly into the washing-up.

'Says it's all linked up with my irritable bowel.'

19

'Ah, right.' Personally I couldn't see what his irritable bowel had to do with peeing in the coat cupboard, but I let it pass. 'You should get that seen to then,' I said, humouring him. 'Go and see a specialist. I seem to remember I booked an appointment for you once, someone Tom recommended in Harley Street. Did you ever go?'

'Certainly not,' he growled. 'Don't want some fellow peering up my arse.'

'It was a woman actually.'

'Christ!' Harry spat his coffee across the table. 'Jesus, the lengths some women will go to to get their hands on a fellow!'

I considered this, elbows deep in suds. 'You mean, you think she spent five years at medical school purely in the hope that she might one day peep up the male backside?'

'Don't joke, Rosie,' he growled. 'Believe me, there are some desperate women out there.'

I looked round at his glowering form hunched over his coffee in his M&S extra large pyjamas, his fair hair flopping over his forehead. 'Oh, I don't doubt it, Harry, and you're right, it's no joke. It's not safe for a man like you to walk the streets these days with so many predatory women lurking about. I'm amazed you even venture out of the house.'

Harry gave me a quick, suspicious look. 'What's up with you this morning anyway?' he said sharply. 'You're being very pert. Very . . . puckish.'

'Am I? Sorry.' I instantly dropped the puckishness and reverted to doormat mode, hiding my guilty face in the sink and scrubbing a pan vigorously. God, I mustn't get too carried away here, mustn't get overconfident. The last thing I wanted was for Harry to suspect anything. There was no point in muddying the waters with rows and recriminations when what was called for was a swift, clean break. Happily, Ivo caused a diversion.

'He's dribbling again,' Harry said suddenly. 'Look, Rosie, it's disgusting, it's all over his chin. For God's sake do something!'

I took a cloth from the sink and wiped Ivo's face as Harry sat there, mute with horror. I lifted Ivo out of the high chair. 'It's just a bit of milk,' I muttered. 'For heaven's sake, Harry.'

When Ivo was born, Harry had been delighted. A son, an heir to the Harry Meadows throne, the Meryton Road semi-detached dynasty – what more could a man want? He'd been euphoric with joy, toasting his genes, his manhood, his marvellous equipment, congratulating himself – even congratulating me, once – but when the grim reality of bringing up a child had dawned, he'd taken a very dim view of the whole thing. Harry's idea of parenthood was to have

a clean, bathed child with neatly parted hair in scaled down gentleman's pyjamas presented to him at six o'clock in the evening to
dangle on his knee for a few minutes. He might even warble, 'This is
the way the ladies go, nimble, nimble, nimble,' but when the first
signs of up-chuck appeared at 'gallop-a-gee, gallop-a-gee', he'd hand
him straight back to his mother.

The irony was, though, that Harry's relationship with Ivo had up
to now been my stumbling block to throwing in the towel and
re-joining the free world. Call me old-fashioned but I'd firmly
believed a boy needed a father and, good, bad, or indifferent,
preferably his *own* father. And so I'd stayed. But recently a creeping
realisation had begun to persuade me that surely, if I knew in my
heart I'd never stick it out for ever, wasn't it better to go now? Before
Ivo knew too much about it? Before he was six, ten, fourteen, when it
would be that much harder? I experienced a brief pang of regret as I
pushed Ivo's arms into his corduroy jacket, but I gulped it down,
hardening my heart. As I hoisted him on to my hip, I turned a bright
smile on my husband.

'We'll be off then,' I said, hopefully not too portentously.

'Where are you going?' he mumbled through the propped up
Telegraph.

'Oh, just round to Alice's. Are you going to do some work today?'

'Don't I always?'

'Yes, of course,' I murmured, although this was debatable.

Doing 'some work' in Harry's case generally meant having a long,
leisurely breakfast, changing his clothes – three or four times
sometimes, our Harry was very sartorial – before slowly making his
way to the top of the house where, as he walked through the study
door, he suddenly became – abracadabra – a property developer.
Now since Harry owned precisely two properties, one of which we
lived in and one of which he rented out, you can imagine this was
stressful stuff. Little wonder this pressure cooker of a job was playing
fast and loose with his bowels. Little wonder he had to relieve the
tension by making a series of morning phone calls to his friends –
most of whom were called things like Bunky, Munky and Spunky
and had similarly stressful jobs – and little wonder that finally, when
it all got too much for him, he had to lie prostrate on the sofa till
lunchtime. The rest of the day would go something like this. At
precisely twelve o'clock the telephone would disturb him, he'd
stagger to the desk and the conversation would go:

'Humpty?'

'Boffy!'

'How's tricks?'

'Surprisingly sluggish actually' – I loved that 'surprisingly' – 'fancy a spot of lunch?'

'Why not? See you there at one.'

And off he'd go to his club, always optimistically taking the car, and always returning without it, the worse for wear in a taxi. After a few attempts at getting the key in the door, he'd stagger upstairs again, collapse on the sofa, surface at five, have a bath, drink heavily, eat supper, drink even more heavily, and go to bed. Oh, it was a full-time job.

I glanced at the clock as I made for the front door. 'See you at the end of play then,' I called.

I stopped dead in my tracks. *See you at the end of play?* Had I really said that? God, I was even beginning to *talk* like him now! I shuddered and hurried off down the path.

'Where did you say you were going?' Harry's voice suddenly halted me. I turned back, guilty. He was standing in the doorway.

'To the park and then on to Alice's.'

'At this hour? People like that don't get up till about ten o'clock. They'll still be snoring in their pits, hallucinating into their bean-bags.' He frowned. 'And anyway, I thought I told you I didn't like Ivo going on that bike.'

'He's got a helmet on, Harry,' I said patiently as I loaded Ivo into the baby seat of my pushbike. 'And anyway, he loves it, and we're only going through the park.'

What Harry actually meant was he didn't like to see either of us on the bike. Image was all with Harry and this one was far too Bohemian for him. What he'd really like was for me to be dressed from head to toe in navy blue with the odd touch of minimalist white – pants and pearls – and for Ivo to be dressed as a sailor. Then he'd like us both to be strapped firmly into a dark green Range Rover with Ivo clutching a black-market copy of *Little Black Sambo*. Thankfully, funds at Mery-ton Road stretched only to the pants for me and the sailor suit for Ivo, which I had actually put him in once for a visit to Alice's, only to be met by her horrified face at the door as she squealed, 'Oh God, you've got him in a uniform! You'll be pinning medals on him next. Quick, get him out of it before he becomes anally retentive!'

I gave Harry a winning smile as I pushed a beaming Ivo to the gate. 'See, he loves it, look.'

'Hmph,' he grunted. 'Well, just be careful. Don't want to break the son and heir's neck.' (Just as I had relinquished my Christian name, so, incidentally, had Ivo.)

'Don't worry, he'll be fine.'

'And don't take any drugs!' was his parting shot as I pushed off down the road.

I clenched my teeth to prevent me from yelling obscenities back and pedalled on.

Alice was an artist. She was also my dearest friend, I'd known her since I was fourteen and to the best of my knowledge she'd never even smoked a cigarette let alone taken drugs. Harry, of course, knew better. The fact that she wore fairly eccentric second-hand clothes and had been known to tie scarves round her head while she wielded her paintbrush suggested all manner of depravities to him.

Still, as I cycled through the Wandsworth streets and into the sunny park, I suddenly felt as if I was leaving Harry and all his prejudices behind me. It was a glorious winter morning, a crisp, cold, blue-sky day, and the birds who hadn't upped sticks and gone south were delighted at this unexpected pleasure. They sang their little hearts out, as did Ivo, who was having a jolly good go at 'Puff the Magic Dragon' behind me. I smiled and breathed deeply as I whizzed along the narrow path with the cold breeze stinging my cheeks and ears. Suddenly I felt lighter and happier than I had done for ages.

'We thee Alice?' yelled Ivo.

'Yes, darling.'

'And Molly and Lou?'

'Of course.' These were Alice's daughters.

'And shops?' he added hopefully. Shops might mean sweets.

I laughed. 'Perhaps.'

'An' then wot?'

Yes, and then what, Rosie? What would happen next? Where would we go? Where would we live? What would we do? I had no money and I hadn't worked for two years. Where did women who left their husbands go? Was there a convenient runaway wives' home located handily about, somewhere to take refuge for a while and collect one's thoughts, or did one just go Straight Home To Mother without passing Go and without collecting £200? I shuddered at the thought. No, that I couldn't contemplate. I'd almost rather stay put in the frying pan, but maybe – maybe I could rent a room. Share a flat like I used to. You mean, like you used to before you had a child, a small voice in my head said. Like you used to when you had a full-time job and earned the money to pay the rent. Before you were a single parent. I bit my lip. A single parent. God, I was about to become a statistic, wasn't I? A burden

23

on the state, one of those people that needed housing, looking after, one of the Needy. I swallowed hard. No, I couldn't do that either, I'd find something. I'd work part-time, I'd find *some* way of supporting us without being a pain in the neck to anyone. Something would turn up.

As I turned a corner, the low morning sun shone straight into my eyes, dazzling me. I lowered my lashes, filtering the light and enjoying the blurred effect it had on my senses. I didn't want to think too deeply right now, get too bogged down in the logistics. I'd made the decision to leave and that was the main thing. I'd find somewhere to go, and wherever it was would have to be better than where I'd been, wouldn't it? Of course it would. A far, far better place. I smiled confidently as I turned out of the park and freewheeled down the hill towards Alice's street.

Alice's house was at the end of a grim, redbrick Victorian row, but it was completely different to all the others. For one thing it was much smaller, almost a cottage – as if someone had tacked it on at the end as an afterthought – and it was painted pale pink with a dark blue front door. Crawling all over the paintwork were various evergreen creepers which in summer had a dusting of clematis and roses over them, and instead of the usual dismal patch of dusty London grass at the front, she'd grown a cottage garden with a brick path snaking through the middle of it. Cynics might say that a parody of country life in the middle of Wandsworth was too whimsical for words, but Alice somehow carried all her cottage gardening and bread-making off with an elegance and aplomb that dared anyone to mock it.

I parked the bike against the wall, followed the path to the door and rang the bell. A moment later I heard singing, then the door swung back. Alice gazed at me. She was barefoot in her ancient blue silk dressing gown, her red-gold hair falling around her face like a lion's mane, a half-eaten piece of toast in her hand. She blinked her confident blue eyes in surprise.

'God, you're early, I thought we said ten o'clock.'

'I know, we did, but I wanted to get away. Sorry, are you up to your eyes?'

'No more than usual. Come in – if you can get past the pushchairs. Sorry, it's like Mothercare in here – oh, hello, angel-baby!' She paused as she ushered me into the long narrow hallway, crowded with baby paraphernalia, to take Ivo's face in her hands. She gave him a resounding kiss on the cheek and he rewarded her with one of his very best smiles.

24

'No, no, back! I'm coming through, I'm afraid!' At the other end of the hall Alice's husband Michael, looking late and harassed in a double-breasted suit, waved us back with his briefcase as he came squeezing down towards us. 'For God's sake, Alice, we've got to do something about this sodding double buggy!' He aimed a kick at it. 'Can't they learn to walk or something?'

'Only when they've learnt to run,' said Alice firmly. 'First things first, you know how I aspire to talented children.'

'Whilst I just aspire to a life of peace and plenty away from this madhouse. I really wouldn't go in there, Rosie,' he said, jerking his head kitchenwards. 'Someone's forgotten to buy the Cheerios and they're staging a rebellion. It's not far removed from the Boston Tea Party.'

'Thanks for warning me,' I grinned.

He went to move on, then did a double take as he edged past me. 'I say, you're looking wonderfully pulchritudinous this morning, Rosie. There's an almost pre-pubescent glow to your cheeks and a light in your eyes that suggests – have you just had sex?'

'Certainly not! I've just had a cycle ride.'

'Ah, yes, those slim little bicycle saddles.' He grinned. 'Too, too thrilling, followed, of course, by a close encounter in a darkened hallway with the husband of your best friend – just the thing to get the old heart pounding, the blood rushing to the cheeks, the—'

'Oh, stop being such a revolting old flirt and get to work!' ordered his wife, ushering him out. 'And don't come back until you've earned a fortune!'

He grinned and swept her off her feet as he reached her at the front door. He kissed her rather thoroughly on the mouth and I noticed they looked right into each other's eyes. Harry never looked at me like that. Not deep into me. I suddenly realised that they probably *had* just made love.

'She beats me, you know,' he whispered with a smile, not taking his eyes off his wife. 'Nightly.'

'In your dreams,' she responded, giving him a little shove. 'Now go on, get out there. Get hustling!'

He went, and she watched him go off down the street, leaning on the doorpost, her arms folded, a slight smile on her face.

Michael was an account executive in an advertising agency and Alice had met him when she'd worked in the business as an art director. He was a handsome, urbane man, and a surprising contrast to her with his fine line in patter, his suave wardrobe and his conscious charm. If we were being really picky I'd say he was a touch

25

too double O seven for me, but hell, who was I to criticise a happy marriage?

'Right,' Alice said decisively, shutting the door behind him. 'Lead on, McMeadows, let's go and sort out the revolting natives.'

We went down to the kitchen where the clatter of spoons on bowls was getting louder and louder, accompanied by shrieks of laughter. Alice's small daughters were chanting away, high on momentum, and Alice had to suck right down to her boot straps, curl back her tongue and expand her chest to bring up a resounding, 'ALL RIGHT, THAT WILL DO!'

Instant silence, then giggles, then sulks. I sank happily down into the cushion-strewn window seat and watched as Alice placated and scolded her brood, selling Weetabix on the grounds that Xena the Warrior Princess ate them regularly and shaking the cereal into bowls amidst howls of protest. I quietly stroked the cat who'd usurped Ivo from my lap and gazed around the small, chaotic kitchen with its eclectic collection of painted wooden furniture. It really was like something out of Hänsel and Gretel's cottage. There were chests that fell apart if you touched them, wobbly tables with bits of newspaper stuffed under the short leg, cupboards that didn't shut, nothing that matched and nothing that had ever been designed for practical cooking purposes, but then, since most of the surfaces were over-flowing with toys and books and ancient magazines anyway, it didn't really make much difference.

Amongst all this clutter and confusion, on the plain whitewashed walls above, were Alice's pictures; bold, strong strokes of gouache colour shone bravely out, resolutely creative amidst the grind of everyday family life. The table we sat at was only half devoted to cereal packets and Peter Rabbit crockery, the other half was taken up with Alice's silk screens, sketchpads, and marmalade jars stuffed full with brushes and calligraphy pens. A compromise had been reached in Alice's life. It was comfortable, and it showed. I also happened to know that much of this seeming confusion was artfully arranged, and that Alice, if pressed, could lay her hands on a gym shoe, a car key, or a cleaning ticket at a moment's notice – albeit under that mouldy pear festering away on top of A.S. Byatt on the dresser. For Alice was a secretly organised woman. What we were witnessing here was art-directed, organised chaos.

For all its semi-conscious style, though, whenever I left here and went back to my own house I always felt the repression there more keenly. Walking into 63 Meryton Road with its determinedly striped wallpapers and fleur-de-lys borders, its regimented ranks of silver photo frames, its snuffboxes lined up with blinding symmetry on highly polished tables, its overstuffed cushions on even more over-stuffed sofas so that anyone who dared to sit on them simply perched, like a pea, on top – this, after a morning at Alice's, seemed like a house with a cucumber right up its basement.

And that of course was how Harry liked it; stiff, formal, intimidating and with pretensions to grandeur. What he actually wanted, I'd come to realise, was a scaled-down version of a stately home, but when the huge ancestral portrait of his Uncle Bertram took up the entire sitting-room wall, and the pendulous chandelier hung so heavily – and perilously – from the thin dining-room ceiling, it looked to my mind more comical than stately. When I'd first moved in we'd had heated rows about re-decoration and I couldn't believe I wasn't going to be allowed to be let loose with the steam stripper, but Harry was adamant, and although I'd made efforts to loosen the place up a bit, these days I limited myself to scattering cushions on the sly and riffling the snuffbox arrangement whenever I passed. But even these minor protests didn't go unnoticed and Harry was quick to restore order with a pseudo-mild reproach like, 'I see yesterday's newspaper saw fit to stay a day longer than was absolutely necessary, Rosie?' Or, 'You're happy with those coats slung over the banisters like that, are you?' Or, 'Rosie, any idea what your best shoes are doing by the back door?'

Making a run for it, came to mind, but lately I simply bit my tongue and quietly put the shoes back in the wardrobe, threw away the old newspaper and hung up the coats.

On the odd occasion when we were invited to Alice and Michael's for dinner, Harry would be rendered almost speechless with horror by his surroundings. When he finally found his tongue on the way home, he'd mutter something like, 'Rum couple, that, very rum indeed. Beats me how people can live like that. What are they, druids?'

I smiled to myself now as I sank back into the tapestry cushions, waiting patiently for Alice's undivided attention. She sloshed orange juice into cups for the children and brought some coffee to the table for us, but then suddenly, inexplicably, just as she went to settle down opposite me, I felt my intent begin to waver. Hang on a minute. Exactly how receptive was Alice going to be to my grand plan? How highly was she going to think of me for breaking up the home, for taking Ivo from his father, for throwing in the towel after, what, barely three years of marriage? I gazed around at the cosy domestic scene, the Lego on the floor, the headless dolls in the fruit bowl, the laundry basket under the table with one of Michael's shirt sleeves hanging reproachfully over the side. Alice had often said she envied me my orderly household, just as I envied her chaotic one, and this was so often the way with home life, wasn't it? It wasn't always perfect, but other people's often looked more so. How could I possibly tell her what I planned to do to mine? How could I ask her to condone the destruction of what she, like every other mother I knew, spent every waking moment trying to hold together? Juggling the commitments – the children, the husband, the painting, the garden – keeping all those balls in the air, how could I tell her I just wanted to walk away from them and let them fall to the ground with a dull thud?

'So?' she demanded. 'What's up?'

'Hmmm?' I stroked the cat distractedly, pretending I hadn't heard.

'What's going on, why did you have to get away at the crack of dawn?'

'Oh, no reason really.' I sipped my coffee miserably. 'Just the usual four walls and a baby thing, I expect. Thursday morning blues, nothing special.'

'Don't give me that, you had a bee in your bonnet when you arrived, even Michael noticed it. Where's it gone?'

I shrugged and looked down, feeling tears pricking my eyes. It's done a bunk, I thought. Bugger, bugger, bugger. It was slipping away like sand through my fingers, I could feel it. I absently picked a piece of dried egg off the tablecloth, aware that she was watching me and that, being Alice, she wouldn't be fobbed off so easily. I sighed.

'Oh, I don't know, it was just something I decided to do last night. A brave, late-night decision that seemed to make perfect sense after a horrific dinner party with the red wine still storming furiously in my blood, but that actually, in the cold light of a Thursday morning here in your kitchen, seems – ridiculous.' I gazed at the egg stain on the cloth. 'It was madness,' I said softly. 'I see that now.' I looked up and forced a bright smile. 'Forget it. How's the painting going? Did you get hold of that guy who was keen to share an exhibition with you?'

She was staring at me across the table, her hands cupping her coffee mug very still. Suddenly she put it down, reached across the table and seized my hand.

'Do it,' she breathed.

I blinked. 'What?'

'Do it. You're going to leave him, aren't you? You decided last night, I can tell. God Almighty, bloody well *do* it, Rosie!'

I stared at her in amazement. Her face was alive, her red hair blazing in the sun, her eyes shining.

'But . . . how did you know I—'

'Oh, for heaven's sake, Rosie, it was obvious! You had to do it sooner or later, it was just a question of when!'

'No! Really?'

'Of course! No sane woman could have stood it as long as you have, it's only because you're such a flaming pushover you've managed it this long!'

I gazed at her incredulously. 'You mean . . . you really think I should leave him?'

'Of course you bloody should!' she thundered. 'You should never have married him in the first place! The man's a prat and you know it!'

'Alice!' I was aghast.

'Well, it's true.'

'But . . . you . . . you've never said!' I spluttered. 'I had no idea!'

'Well, of course I've never said, I'm hardly likely to have told you, am I? I'm hardly likely to have taken you to one side and said, congratulations, Rosie old bean, you've married a prize dickhead there, now am I?'

'A prize . . .' I boggled. 'Jesus, it's all coming out now, isn't it!' I said angrily. 'Why didn't you say all this when I was going out with him then?'

'What, for two minutes? If you recall, Rosie, you brought him round for supper precisely once before you got married. As I remember, he spent the entire evening telling me how to decant my wine, how to rearrange my furniture, how to bring up my children, how to cook coq au vin properly – while simultaneously eating the very same dish – and as a parting thrust informed me that my pictures weren't real paintings at all but merely "decorative art". Naturally I shut the door and wrote him off as the biggest jerk I'd met in a long time but I thought, no, now don't go and open your big mouth, Alice Feelburn. We all make mistakes and Rosie's made a huge one here but let her find that out for herself, okay? I then went off to Italy for a few weeks on that painting course and when I came back you met me for lunch in the Pitcher and Piano with a silly grin on your face and a rock the size of Gibraltar on your finger and then about two weeks later you were waltzing down the aisle, dewy-eyed in a sea of silk organza! I mean, where exactly did you expect me to stick my oar in? Before, during or perhaps even *after* the nuptials, like when you were instantly pregnant with Ivo perhaps? Maybe I should have mentioned it then? Popped round with a pair of bootees and had a word in your ear about the total ghastliness of the father of your unborn child?'

'Total . . . God, the gloves are really off now, aren't they?' I blustered. 'Don't hold back, will you, Alice!'

'Sorry,' she gulped, reaching for her coffee, 'I can't help it. I've been holding back for too long, bottling it all up, and now it's all coming out in a rush like last night's dodgy curry.'

'But you never even hinted!'

'Well, would you have listened?' she hissed, leaning across the table. 'Of course you wouldn't, because actually, Rosie, marrying Harry was so bloody typical of you. The more I thought about it afterwards, the more I realised you were running totally true to form. You waft along, gloriously vague most of the time, not knowing if it's Tuesday or Wednesday, and then every now and then you get a rush of blood to the head and a fixed idea about something and WHAM!' She slammed her hand down on the table. 'That's it, you're like a guided missile and no amount of persuasion will deter you from some lunatic course. It was just the same at school. There you were, cruising serenely towards your A levels with consummate ease and then suddenly, with projected straight As and stupendous gall, you announce you're not going to Oxford after all, you're going to be a cook – a move which, if not actually calculated to piss your mother off, was certainly guaranteed to do so. It's just so *like* you, Rosie!'

I gaped at her in amazement. 'But I *wanted* to be a cook, it was nothing to do with pissing Mum off!'

'Fine, marvellous, be a cook, marry Harry, but it's the abruptness of it all that takes everyone around you by surprise. You don't think anything through, Rosie, it's always a spur-of-the-moment decision that makes absolute sense to you but not to anyone else. A bolt comes from above, you're temporarily blinded and – SHAZAM! – that's it, off you go, generally from the sublime to the ridiculous, which was certainly the case with Rupert and Harry.'

'There was nothing sublime about Rupert,' I snapped. 'He was a rat of the first order.'

'Yes, well, all right, maybe he did turn out to be a bit rodent-like but there were plenty of other sublime ones circling predatorily around you before *he* came along, although most of the time, I'll grant you, you didn't seem to notice. Didn't seem to realise that when you lost your car keys at the end of a party and were standing about helplessly there were at least four men overturning sofas and hurling chairs out of the window in an effort to find them for you. I'll give you that, you've always been blissfully unaware of your seductive powers, but take it from one who watched with envy, those guys were *there*, Rosie, panting to get at you.'

'Bollocks.'

'Trust me, as one who's suffered in silence.' She cradled her mug, narrowing her eyes. 'But to get back to Rupert, or rather what happened *next*, after Rupert. D'you remember, Rosie?'

'Oh, spare me,' I muttered.

'Can't do that, I'm afraid, it's too crucial to my argument. No, no, *next* is far too interesting. *Next*, you put on a teensy bit of weight, Rupert comes out of the closet as a double-dater and knocks your confidence for six and suddenly the whole world goes black. Suddenly you're incredibly ugly and no one will ever fancy you again. Suddenly you're going to be alone for the rest of your life. Suddenly the only solution is to marry a fat git like Harry with a diametrically small brain.'

'Alice!'

'No, no, you're right, maybe he wasn't so fat when you married him, that came later, didn't it, when you both got pregnant together, the only difference being that you shed your load nine months later and he carried on parading his around, filling out those maternity smocks, billowing around like a ship in full sail. His mind was always small, though, you can't argue with that.'

I stood up. 'Alice, how *dare* you! This is outrageous, this is my husband you're talking about!'

There was a pause. Suddenly she felt her forehead, went a bit pale. 'God, you're right, you're right,' she muttered. 'I don't know what came *over* me.' She stretched out an arm. 'God, I'm so sorry, Rosie. Sit down, please, I'm sorry.'

I stood over her for a moment, then sat, shaking slightly. There was a silence.

'I must be mad,' she muttered at length. Her hand went to her mouth, then it flew to her forehead in horror as another thought struck her. 'Oh God, Rosie, I'm not going to have to take all this back, am I? You're not going to ask us round for supper next week and I'll have to back-pedal like mad and say how much I've always admired him? How I adore cuddly men? You are going to leave him, aren't you?' she said, aghast.

I stared at her for a moment. Then I got shakily to my feet and went to the window. I rested my hot cheek on the cold glass, staring out at the dull winter grass, the swings, the climbing frame, wet and abandoned for the duration. My God, she hated him. Despised him. My best friend and I never knew. I felt slightly sick.

31

'I don't know,' I said without turning round. 'I was, and then I wasn't. When I came here and saw you in your nest, I thought I couldn't go through with it, but now . . .' Oh God, what now? Why should it matter what Alice thought? What anyone thought? Why should that have any bearing on anything?

I stayed like that for a while with my face pressed to the windowpane. Its coldness was something of a comfort. I could hear Molly and Lou behind me, pretending to read nursery rhymes to Ivo, their shrill little voices ringing out, confident and sure. Wee Willie Winkie was being rattled through now, a character I'd always regarded with the utmost suspicion. Quite apart from his spectacularly pervy name his penchant for running around in his nightie questioning people on the whereabouts of their children would have been enough for me. I'd have had him up for harassment. Ivo, though, was entranced. I turned to look as he gazed adoringly at Molly, open-mouthed with wonder as she pretended to read from an upside-down book, her small rosy mouth bossily forming the words. She flipped over the page and took a deep breath.

'Humpty Dumpty—'

'I think I am,' I said quickly, suddenly. 'I mean, yes. I am leaving him. Definitely.'

Alice had been watching me intently. Her face relaxed visibly. She sank back in her seat and sighed. Then she beamed. 'Good for you. Go for it, Rosie. Go for it like you go at your mistakes, single-mindedly, blinkered and purposefully!' She raised a clenched fist in salute.

I blinked. 'Wow, thanks,' I muttered. Blimey, with friends like these . . . I shook my head. 'I honestly had no idea you felt so strongly about him.'

'Oh, never mind about all that,' she said quickly. 'I said much too much and got carried away by the momentum. In all probability he's not nearly that bad.'

'He's not,' I said earnestly. 'He's honestly not a bad man at all, Alice, he's—'

'Yes, okay, but he's not a particularly good one either, is he?' she snapped back. I stared at her. My lip wobbled, tears threatened. I threw my head back to keep them at bay.

'So why did I marry him then?' I blurted out to the ceiling.

She sipped her coffee thoughtfully and eyed me over the rim. 'Well, I've got a pretty shrewd idea. How about you were twenty-nine, slightly desperate, all your friends were married and your mother pushed you into it?'

I opened my mouth to protest, but suddenly couldn't be bothered. I blinked away the tears and silently sipped my coffee.

'So,' I said at length, forcing a smile. 'Tell me, Alice, how does a girl go about getting a divorce these days?' There. It was out. I'd said it. And it wasn't so bad.

'Well, the first thing you do,' she got up and went to the fridge, 'is have a drink.' She brandished a bottle with a grin.

'Steady on, it's only half past nine.'

'I know, but it's a momentous decision and not one to be taken without alcohol. And anyway, it's either this or a Mars Bar and if you're going Out There again,' she jerked her eyes expressively to the window, 'better to ruin your liver than your thighs. Here.' She poured me a glass. 'Apart from anything else,' she went on more gently, 'I can tell you're a bit shaken.'

'Thanks.' I took a slug gratefully. 'I am a bit.' I grimaced. 'God, you didn't make this, did you?'

She looked surprised. 'I did actually. It's rhubarb and elderflower, why?'

'Oh, Alice, it's filthy. Throw it away and give me some of that Sainsbury's wine box I spotted nestling in there.'

She tasted it, pretended to look hurt but couldn't help screwing her own nose up. 'Yeuch.' She threw it down the sink and poured a couple of fresh ones from the wine box.

'Now,' she said, setting the glass in front of me. 'First things first. Have you got a solicitor?'

'Er, no, not to my knowledge. Harry uses Boffy – Edmund Boffington-Clarke – but they're best buddies, I can't possibly go to him.'

'Edmund Boffington-Clarke,' she muttered. 'That's not a name, that's a sentence. No, well quite, if he's a buddy he's definitely out. I think the best thing you can do is to go to a Citizens' Advice Bureau or – no, I know, we'll look up a few local solicitors in the Yellow Pages, but when you get there, for heaven's sake don't forget to ask about legal aid. I'll come with you,' she said quickly, seeing my face go pale.

'But shouldn't I, you know, tell Harry first? Ask him how he feels about it, that sort of thing? Aren't we supposed to drag it out a bit, toddle off to Relate together, discuss our most intimate sexual problems with a complete stranger? Cry on some busybody's shoulder? It all seems a bit deceitful somehow to go off and do it on my own, like a backstreet abortion or something. And so final. It's the end, isn't it?'

'Or the beginning,' she said briskly. 'A new life. One you want, too. That's how you should look at it, Rosie. No good looking back.'

God, those phrases. They sounded so tired, so hackneyed out in the open like that. But then it was a mistake that had been made many times before, wasn't it? There was nothing trail-blazing about extracting oneself from a rotten marriage, so inevitably the advice became hackneyed. Go forward, don't go back. Look to the future, not to the past. I sank into my wine and Alice got up from the table, knowing it was necessary for me to plunge into some serious gloom now. Knowing it was necessary for me to go down before I could come up. And there was probably nothing very revolutionary about that, either. I watched morosely as she moved around the kitchen, tidying up, picking up toys, wiping Lou's nose, handing round biscuits, getting on with normal life. She began shoving a pile of dirty washing into the machine, cramming it too full as usual.

'Speaking of Sainsbury's,' she said, slamming the door and straightening up. She fixed me with a beady eye.

'Were we?' I said warily.

'The wine box. I was in there yesterday and that bloke was asking after you again.'

'What bloke?'

'That totally gorgeous one with the blond hair and the strangely educated accent. Wanted to know if I'd seen you lately. Quite heartening, don't you think?'

I stared at her in disbelief. Finally I found my voice. 'Alice, my marriage is over. I'm leaving my husband, the father of my child. My life as I've known it for the past three years is coming to an abrupt halt. Do you really think I want to hear that some toy boy of a shelf-stacker has got the hots for me?'

'He's not a shelf-stacker, he's a Cambridge graduate doing a holiday job and all I'm trying to do here, if you must know, is instil a little confidence. Let you know that people notice you, that you're still very attractive to the opposite sex!'

'Oh, right. Well, stroll on down. Someone in Sainsbury's fancies me, glory hallelujah. I'll get shot of my husband right away then, shall I? Quick, give me a decree nisi and I'll sign it now, why hang about?'

'Okay, okay,' she muttered, 'that was pretty ham-fisted, I admit. I just . . . well, I just feel that someone like you, Rosie, should have the world at your feet, but for some reason you never have. You've gone from a domineering mother to a domineering husband—'

'To a domineering friend.'

'Oh!' She looked startled.

'I'm joking,' I laughed, seeing her shocked face. I stood up and hugged her. 'You couldn't have been a better friend, actually.'

'I've said too much,' she said unhappily.

'No, you haven't.' I bent down and scooped Ivo up off the floor. 'You've been brilliant. Made me see I've got to do it. Made me see sense. Come on, Ivo.'

'Are you going?'

'I've got to get him back for his nap. Thanks, Alice. I mean it.' I hugged her again and she squeezed me very hard back.

'Those things I said,' she said anxiously. 'It's because I care, you know that, don't you?'

'I know.'

We released each other and she trailed me thoughtfully to the front door.

'What was it that finally pushed you over the edge then?' she asked, opening the door.

'What d'you mean?'

'What made you decide to leave?'

'Oh! Oh, nothing really, he just – well, if you must know, he peed in the baby-sitter's coat pocket.'

Her eyes grew round with horror. 'You mean he just strolled up, got it out – and *peed* on her?'

'Oh no,' I said quickly, 'no, she wasn't wearing it. Happily, even Harry's not that gross. No, it was in the cloakroom and he took a wrong turning in the dark, that's all.' I shrugged and put Ivo on my bike. 'These things happen, I suppose,' I ventured hopefully.

Alice raised her eyebrows. 'I suppose they do,' she said slowly. 'Mostly at nursery school, though, I believe.'

I sighed in weary acknowledgement as I got on my bike, then pushed off down the road, giving her a backward wave as I went.

Chapter Three

The following day was Friday, which in the normal run of things meant packing up the car after breakfast and going down to my parents for the weekend – Harry always took an official break on Friday as opposed to the unofficial break he took the rest of the week. Never in my life had I seen so much of my parents until I married Harry. Oh, I used to pop down for the odd weekend, mostly to have a chat with Dad or see my sister Philly who lived close by, but since I'd got married it seemed to me we practically lived with them, and all at Harry's instigation. As far as he was concerned, it was social death to be seen in London at the weekend and since his parents were dead and his only living relative, Uncle Bertram, lived miles away in a huge baronial hall in a godforsaken spot on the Yorkshire moors – a house, incidentally, that Harry was destined to inherit on Bertram's death, yet another good reason for breaking the marital contract, as far as I was concerned – and since we didn't get asked away to house parties nearly as much as Harry pretended, we invariably found ourselves on the M40 of a Friday morning, beetling off to Oxford again. A strange twist of fate really, considering how desperate I'd been to get away from home.

But it wasn't just the stigma of weekends in London that made Harry head for the wide open spaces, there were other, more cynical factors at play here. Money was tight in the Meadows household and our Harry had very expensive tastes. The obvious answer was to indulge them at his in-laws', where everything was free. Here the wine flowed, the roast beef appeared as if by magic and there was a far more obliging waitress, in the shape of my mother, than the one he was used to at home (who, frankly, had got a bit mutinous lately).

Ah yes, Mum. Amazingly enough, three years spent in close proximity to her son-in-law had not diminished the dazzle that shone from his backside, and she was only too delighted to accommodate him on a full board and lodging basis with morning coffee and afternoon tea thrown in too. The latter of these rituals Harry liked to take in the drawing room, so while Dad and I slunk off and slurped our mugs of tea in the potting shed or the kitchen, Harry would be presented with the full scones and crumpet complement by the fire. At this hallowed hour my mother was lucky enough to take off her pinny and join him, and then *what* a happy time was had by all. The two of them would sit for hours discussing titles, nobility, acreage, lineage, cheerfully dissecting the social pages of *The Times* or the *Tatler* and dropping names so thick and fast the carpet must have been knee-deep in peers of the realm. At length, though, exhausted by all this social climbing and having scaled heights so dizzy he practically needed crampons and an oxygen mask, Harry would give a subtle little flicker of the eyelids to indicate that the audience was over, and that my mother was free to leave him. Balancing a tray of teacups and empty plates, she'd tiptoe from the room, a finger to her lips, whispering to anyone who was interested, 'Shhh . . . Poor lamb, let him sleep, he's *quite* worn out. Works so hard during the week, you see. Quite exhausted.'

Well, that suited me fine, and although it amused me that Harry insisted on spending his weekends in the country but never stuck his nose outside the back door, I was very happy to put Ivo in my backpack and take him for long walks over the hills or help Dad in the garden. Together we'd weed our way round the beds or slowly pick fruit from the canes, chatting a bit, but mostly in companionable silence, with Ivo at our heels, trailing a miniature trowel or a bucket. But not today, I thought as I packed a changing bag for Ivo on the kitchen table in London. Today, the walks and the weeding could wait, because today I had a different agenda. I crammed a few bibs and muslins in the side and zipped the bag up with a flourish.

'There.' I smiled at Harry who was eating his breakfast. 'That's all Ivo's things ready. I've put loads of nappies in, don't forget to change him when you get down there, will you?'

Harry looked up from his double candelabra of soft-boiled eggs and blinked his pale blue eyes in surprise. He'd never changed a nappy in his life, and there seemed to be a puzzling lack of the plural in that sentence.

'What d'you mean, when "I" get down there. What are you doing?'

'Oh, didn't I say?' I said airily. 'I'm coming on later, after lunch. I desperately need to go shopping this morning, there's loads of things we need for the house and I must get to John Lewis. I rang Mum this morning and told her.'

'Well, you might have told me!'

'Sorry, I forgot. Anyway, it doesn't matter, does it? You can take my car with Ivo in his seat and I'll see you later, okay?' I swung my handbag over my shoulder and gave him a dazzling smile, feeling braver by the minute.

'You're going shopping now?'

'Might as well. The sooner I get started, the sooner I'll be down – oh, and don't forget to take his Blinky Bill koala, will you? Otherwise we'll never get him to sleep tonight.'

I bent down to kiss my son who'd abandoned his wooden bricks on the floor and was beginning to look aghast at the prospect of being left with Daddy, who was looking equally aghast at being left with his son. I had to make a speedy exit now or tears would surely follow.

''Bye then!'

'But he's not even dressed! Where are his clothes?'

'In his cupboard, of course.'

I exited swiftly by the back door. Harry was behind me, but I had the advantage of being dressed while he was still in his pyjamas.

'What the hell is it you need to buy so urgently that can't wait till Monday?' he yelled after me from the doorway.

'Oh, you know, tea towels, some new mugs, a few pairs of tights, that kind of thing,' I said airily as I got into his car. And a solicitor of course, I added privately as I snapped my seat belt on with a smile. Usual weekend shopping list.

I had actually managed to have a quick flick through the Yellow Pages last night as Alice had suggested, but they'd all had ghastly sounding names like Sharpe and Dimm, or Dolally and Donothing and it was impossible to tell who were the expensive ones who charged like wounded rhinos and who were the dodgy ones who operated out of a broom cupboard over a chip shop. The only thing to do, I'd decided, was to check out the various establishments at first hand and then make an appointment. The one I'd circled in the phone book as sounding reassuringly solid and English was Barker and Barker, at 101 Wandsworth High Street, an old-established family firm, no doubt. Either that or a couple of dogs.

Round and round the Wandsworth one-way system I went, peering in vain for 101 until finally I found it. In a broom cupboard over a chip shop. The fact that it was a family firm, though, was in no doubt. After I'd parked, yelled into a squawking entry phone, scaled four flights of cracked lino stairs and arrived panting with fatigue, I was greeted by Mrs Barker – a dead ringer for Mrs Patel – beaming in her sari in the doorway. Round her knees swarmed three or four junior Pat— Barkers, all of whom were suspiciously overjoyed to see me, and all of whom seized my hands and begged me to sit on a greasy looking sofa in 'reception' and wait for Mr Barker. Mr Barker, it transpired, was 'incommoded with a client' at present. I glanced nervously at the sofa and chose to stand, a mistake, as it happened, because a moment later a loo chain flushed noisily in my ear and the door to my right flew open, banging me on the head and almost knocking me senseless. As I reeled from the pain, Mr Barker materialised, beaming widely, doing up his flies and then offering me the very same hand in greeting.

I gazed at his hand. I felt sorry for them, really I did, but not as sorry as I felt for me. 'Oh, um, I'm terribly sorry, I've just realised I'm – badly parked. Double yellow.'

'No problem,' he beamed. 'My wife will move it for you.'

'Oh, except that she's not insured.'

'My wife's insured to drive any car.'

'Ah, but this one is – automatic.'

'No problem.'

'And it's got no – tax.'

'No prob—'

'Or brakes,' I put in quickly.

'No brakes? How do you stop?'

'Well, quite,' I agreed. 'It's possible, of course – steep hills, brick walls, that kind of thing, but it's quite a skill.' I started backing towards the door. 'So sorry, won't be a mo.'

The beaming smiles dropped and they glared at me as I turned, took to my heels, raced down the lino staircase and out into the hazy sunshine again.

Oh no, I thought as I fled to my car, no, I wasn't ending my marriage like that. Not in some backstreet dive, not when it had started so auspiciously on a sunny afternoon in Oxfordshire in a church filled with orange blossom. I may not have very much money but I'd beg, borrow or steal to end it in a more dignified fashion than that.

I pointed the car purposefully in the direction of the more expensive part of town, wishing to God I'd thought to bring the phone book with me and thinking what an idiot I'd been to assume solicitors just sprang up in the high street like NatWest Banks or Pizza Huts. And why did they have to have such discreet little itty-bitty signs, for heaven's sake? What was wrong with a socking great neon light?

Eventually I reached Knightsbridge and my heart sank. This was crazy. This was where ambassadors and film stars got divorces, not suburban housewives. What was I doing here? I swung the car round, teeth gnashing now at the thought of all the time I'd wasted, and headed for home with a vengeance. I overtook a lorry at the Albert Hall, zipped past Kensington Gardens in seconds, plunged down into the High Street, screamed 'Bastard!' at a particularly pushy Fiesta, when suddenly – hang on, that looked rather promising – I skidded to a halt. A blare of horns went up around me but I was too busy peering out of the window to notice. A brass plaque on the door of a redbrick Georgian building declared 'Thompson and Cartwright, Solicitors'. It wasn't too ritzy but neither was it too downmarket, and conveniently to my right was an NCP. Encouraged, I swung a very hairy right through the oncoming traffic – more blaring horns – and disappeared down the ramp and into the gloom to park in the bowels of the earth.

Two minutes later I emerged into the fresh air again, optimistic, confident, and heading purposefully for Thompson and Cartwright. I stood outside for a second, gazing up at the redbrick. Yes, perfect. Very sort of Jane Austen. My hand went to the large brass handle – but then I hesitated. Hang on a minute, what was I going to say? Should I pretend I'd been recommended by someone or something? Or could one just enrol on the list like one did at the doctor's? Was it all right just to barge into a professional establishment like this without an appointment? I cleared my throat and practised a bit in my head. Good morning, I wonder, do you engage in matrimonial disputes? No, disputes was too strong, sounded like the gin bottles were already flying. Good morning, I'd like to make an appointment with a solicitor regarding a delicate—

'Look, are you going in or not?' said an irritated voice behind me.

I swung round to see a devastatingly attractive man with thick tawny hair swept back off his forehead, the remains of a tan and golden eyes to match his mane standing behind me. I looked up in awe, which was high. About six foot three.

'Um, going in, I think,' I muttered.

'Marvellous, so am I, so let's get this show on the road, shall we?' He had a distinct transatlantic drawl. 'Only I've been doing a kind of Fred Astaire soft shoe shuffle around you for the last few minutes. You through jigging about?'

'Oh! I'm so sorry.' I moved aside to let him go on ahead, but he held the door open for me and waited.

'In then?'

'Oh, er, yes. In.' I scuttled through to a marble hall, then hung back, hugging my handbag.

'You still don't look very convinced,' he said with a smile.

'Well, it's just . . . I couldn't decide if I had the time or not.'

'Oh yeah, the winged chariot. Runs away with you if you're not careful, doesn't it, but don't worry, you won't be here long.' He grinned. 'If you are, you'll be in the bankruptcy courts before you know it.'

Fear must have flashed through my eyes because he looked at me more kindly.

'Hey, it's okay, there's no one that terrifying here and Marcia will look after you.' He indicated the icy-cool blonde at the icy-cool marble reception desk in the middle of the hall.

I just managed to stammer out a thank you as he strode past me and took the sweeping staircase two at a time. He looked like a man going for an assault course. I caught a last glimpse of his dark flannel jacket as he reached the top and headed off down a corridor, presumably to his office.

In the distance, Marcia looked up from her book. She smiled with her mouth but not with her eyes. 'Can I help you?' she called.

'Oh, yes.' I scurried to her desk. 'I was just passing and I wondered, do you by any chance specialise in matrimonial law?'

'We do, along with commercial, property and litigation, madam.'

'Ah, well, could I possibly see someone about a matrimonial—' don't say dispute – 'sort of . . . thing?'

'Did you have anyone in mind? We have twenty-three solicitors here.'

'Do you really? Gosh, what a lot. Er, no, not really, except – well, does that American gentleman I just met specialise in, you know, the sort of family law side of things?' I jerked my head stairwards, feeling a deep blush unfurl. 'By any chance?'

She looked at me pityingly. 'That gentleman is a client, madam. He's not a solicitor.'

'Ah! Ah, right, yes, of course, it's just—' I could feel the blush spreading like a water mark now. 'Well, it's just he looked like someone I could talk to. That's all.'

She gave a sly smile and flicked through a directory. 'Really.'

Bitch. 'Yes, really.'

'Yes, well, I'm afraid we don't have anyone with *quite* that gentleman's magnetism, but Miss Palmer is free for an hour next Thursday afternoon. How would that suit?'

'Perfect,' I muttered.

'I'll pop you in for four o'clock then, shall I? Oh, and here's a copy of our fees.' She handed me a piece of paper with figures so exorbitant they made my eyes rotate, but I took it, forced a thank you and scurried from the building.

As I made my way to the car park, I glanced at the piece of paper again. Feeling sick, I stuffed it hastily in my bag. I sighed. Oh well, perhaps Dad would help me out, or Philly even. Yes, Philly would lend me some money, I was sure, but what a waste! God, if only I hadn't married the bugger in the first place! This was one of my favourite fantasies and I indulged in it for a moment as I went down the car park steps, dreaming of being Rosie Cavendish again without a ring or a marriage licence to my name. The problem with this scenario was that if I was still Rosie Cavendish I wouldn't have Ivo, and since this was unthinkable I'd recently started another line in fantasies which I'm ashamed to say involved Harry's death. Dreadful, I know, and I do feel incredibly guilty about it but, God, I found it hard to resist.

At first I'd gone in for the usual motorway pile-ups and fatal diseases, but faced with Harry's careful driving and excellent health – despite his hypochondria he was in peak condition – I'd recently taken to scouring the newspapers to find a more appropriate annihilation for him. One in particular that had caught my eye was a bizarre story about a man who'd tilted a vending machine to get the last drop of Coca Cola into his cup but had tipped it so far that it had toppled over and crushed him to death. I thought that was absolutely marvellous, and the greed was so apposite! Why, Harry had fights all over London with vending machines reluctant to give up their Toffee Crisps and I reckoned it was only a matter of time before he had a fight to the death with one. Another quite delicious story was the tale of an overweight property developer (well, exactly) who, while demonstrating the toughness of a high-rise windowpane to his clients, had shoulder-barged it with machismo, crashed through the glass and plummeted eighteen storeys to his death. Again, it was so neat, and so absolutely Harry. The bluff, the bluster, the excess weight carrying him through – ah, yes, I mused dreamily, it had all the qualities I was looking for. Of course I was always thoroughly ashamed of myself after such an indulgence and swore blind I'd never do it again, but the trouble was, it was just so moreish and I found my mind fleeing that way at the slightest provocation.

I wandered along the rows of parked cars, lost in macabre reverie, when suddenly I stopped for a moment and looked back. How odd. I could have sworn I'd left the car around here somewhere. I retraced my steps, glancing all around, but it wasn't long before I got that awful sinking feeling in the pit of my stomach. It quite clearly wasn't here. The bloody car was missing. Good God, it had been *nicked*. I launched one last frenzied search before hurtling up two flights of stairs to find the man on the turnstile. Another futile search, as it turned out, because after dashing about a bit it soon became clear that Turnstile Man had ceased to exist and had been replaced by a slot, a button and a voice box which failed to respond to my call.

Furious now, I made a frantic search of the car park only to find that the only human being in the entire place was a chauffeur, quietly eating a fish-paste sandwich behind the wheel of his master's Jaguar. I rapped on the window.

'Can you help me, please?'

He buzzed it down. 'What's the matter, luv?'

'My car's been stolen!' I wailed as I simultaneously spotted a mobile phone on the seat next to him. 'Could I possibly borrow your phone to ring the police?'

'Course you can, 'ere.' He passed it over and I punched out, rather importantly and for the first time in my life, 999, whereupon I was promptly transferred to the local nick. The desk sergeant there sounded bored and lethargic and made it quite clear he was loath to get up a search party.

'Just give me the details, dear, and I'll log it in the computer.'

'Certainly not,' I snapped. 'I pay my taxes and I happen to know this car park is bang next door to your station. Would it be too much to ask you to walk a hundred yards and attend the scene of the crime?'

Reluctantly he agreed to send someone round.

'God, they can't even be bothered to come out these days!' I fumed as I handed the phone back to my new friend the chauffeur.

'Yeah, well, they've already written it off, see,' he informed me. 'They know that car's halfway to Essex and they can't be fagged to do anything about it.'

'We'll soon see about that,' I said furiously. 'Thanks very much, I've got to go back to where I left the car and wait for them.'

'Good luck, luv. You give 'em hell.'

I bloody will, I thought, as I leaned against a car, waiting for the police to deign to show up. I'd probably interrupted their tea and biscuit break. Well, excuse me!

Ten minutes later a bored looking constable came ambling round the corner. I'd have put money on it that it was the same one I'd spoken to a minute ago. I slid off the bonnet.

'Marvellous, isn't it?' I said as he approached. 'You can't even leave your car in a car park these days without getting it pinched.'

'Third one this week,' he said languidly. 'Notorious hot spot, this.' He looked around. 'Oh yeah, level four again too. Leave your ticket in the window, did you? Nice and convenient like?'

'Yes, I did actually. I suppose that makes it my fault, does it?'

He sucked his teeth. 'Well, it's a bit of an open invitation, isn't it? These young lads, see, they love these multistoreys. Nice and dark, plenty of other cars to hide behind while they do their thieving, and *then* when you've gone and left the ticket for them too, well, you've more or less made their day. And the thing is, all around it's written up as clear as day – take the ticket *with* you!' He pointed to the admittedly abundant signs and eyed me witheringly. It was enough to take me from controlled annoyance to full-throttled rage. I drew myself up mightily to my full five foot four.

'Oh, that's just typical, isn't it! It's never the villain's fault, is it? No, no, it's *my* fault for putting temptation in the poor lad's way! Let's not blame the perpetrator, eh? Let's not blame the criminally insane because, after all, he probably comes from a broken home, poor mite!'

The policeman wearily got out his notebook. 'Make of car, madam?'

'Volvo 405. And I suppose if my house had been burgled you'd be telling me it was my fault for not putting proper locks on the windows, wouldn't you? And if I'd been raped, no doubt my skirt would have been too short. God, it's no wonder the police force has got such a bad name when you alienate people like this!'

'Registration?'

'N128 UBY. And if this is such a notorious hot spot and you've had three cars stolen from level four this week, would you mind telling me why you're not doing a bit more about it? Why you aren't patrolling the area with Alsatians straining at the leash? God, you haven't even radioed in my details yet, haven't even sent out an APB!' (My *Miami Vice* viewing days had left their mark.) 'They could be in the Blackwall Tunnel by now and you haven't done a thing about it!'

'Madam, I can assure you every effort will be made to retrieve your car and—'

'Oh, don't give me that. I can tell you've written it off already. You don't think I stand a hope in hell of getting it back, you're just going through the motions, trotting out the flannel to fob me off and—' I broke off abruptly. Something had caught my eye. I froze.

'What?' he looked around.

'Nothing,' I gasped, my eyes flitting back to him. Nothing, except that four cars down from us was a little green Peugeot. Harry's little green Peugeot. Just four cars down, where I'd left it.

'Believe it or not we have quite a high success rate and once I've got all this on the computer – did you say a 405, madam?'

'Um, yes.' Shit. I'd been looking for the wrong car.

'And provided it hasn't been resprayed, you stand an eighty per cent chance of getting it back.'

'That's . . . tremendous,' I breathed. God what a *moron*, all this time I'd been looking for the Volvo and I'd come in the Peugeot!

'We like to think we're making progress,' he said huffily. He eyed me carefully. 'You all right?'

'Yes, yes, I'm fine, and thank you so much, officer,' I whispered. 'You've been very helpful. Very – supportive.'

He regarded me cautiously, not quite sure how to take this massive capitulation. 'As I say, we do our best.' He shut his notebook.

I nodded. 'Oh, you do, you do, and more. You're a marvellous example to us all, the boys in blue, out there patrolling our streets. Don't let me take up any more of your precious time, officer. I'm sure you need to get all that logged on the computer, don't you? Hooray for the computer, eh? Who'd be without it these days?' I gazed at him fearfully, my smile frozen. Just go. Go away. Why was he still standing there? Did he suspect? Suddenly I realised he was waiting for *me* to make a move. After all, I had no business in the car park now, did I?

'Oh – and I'll come with you! Crikey, let's go!'

Just managing to resist taking his arm, I frogmarched him away, shutting my eyes as I went past my car, up the steps, up some more and out into the daylight. I couldn't tell him. I simply couldn't tell him. I know I should have done and I nearly did for a moment back there, I promise, but not now.

''Bye then! Off to the Tube!' I set off purposefully down the High Street.

'It's the other way.'

'So it is!' I swung round and set off in the other direction, blushing as I passed him.

He watched me go and I could feel his eyes boring suspiciously into my back as I went. On and on I walked, past Marks and Spencer, past the library, staring straight ahead, going absolutely nowhere, until finally I slid round the corner into Waterstone's and collapsed against a convenient wall of books. I moaned low as I sank down on my heels. Oh, you pillock, Rosie, you complete and utter *pillock*.

A few people turned to stare at the moaning nutter in the corner, so I picked myself up and pretended to browse around the shop for a bit. After a while I decided I'd given him enough time to get back to his tea and biscuits so I slipped furtively back down the High Street, hugging the shop windows as I went, and down into the car park. I put my sunglasses on as I hurried head down to the car. Once inside I kept my head low, drove speedily to the turnstile, slipped in the ticket, roared up the ramp and headed for home. Only when I'd negotiated the Hammersmith roundabout did I breathe a monumental sigh of relief and take my glasses off.

As I slumped back in my seat I thought about what Alice had said yesterday. Perhaps she was right, perhaps I was a bit, sort of, not with it. And I seemed to be getting worse. Why, only the other day I'd walked out of the local butcher's without paying for my lamb chops. Harry had been horrified.

'Well, I hope you took them back!' he'd said, appalled.

'No, actually, I ate them right there in the street, raw. Yes, of course I took them back, Harry. I'm not a thief, I'm just a bit vague!'

Vague enough to lose a car without really losing it and vague enough to slip into a career or a marriage without really thinking it through either, although actually I'd take issue with Alice on the career front. I didn't regret becoming a cook one little bit, but I did remember how staggered everyone else had been. How many hands had gone up in horror.

It was strange, really, because if a woman cooked, it wasn't seen as a good career move, just an extension of the housework. It was like saying you wanted to specialise in ironing or dusting or something, but if a man did it, hell's teeth, stand well back! Because a *man* at the stove was no simple cook, he was a creative genius! He could shout abuse at his staff, bellow at his customers, refuse to put salt on the tables, throw tantrums on a regular basis – oh, he was to be treated with the utmost respect. I smiled to myself. One day, though, I'd engender that respect too, and not by throwing my weight around or smashing plates, but just by opening the most fabulous restaurant serving the most beautifully prepared dishes in a stunningly different way; dishes that over the years I'd perfected in my head, even down to the minutest amount of seasoning in the merest soupçon of sauce.

I sighed as I swung the car into my road. Dreams again, Rosie, dreams dreams dreams. Yes, well, I was aware of that. I was also aware that over the last couple of years I'd retreated into my head rather too much and I had a feeling it wasn't all that healthy. Real life had become an unwelcome intruder, butting in when it was least wanted. Well, not any more, I determined as I pulled up outside my house. From now on my dreams would become reality and, let's face it, I was well on the way, wasn't I? I'd booked an appointment with a solicitor. I'd at least made a start.

I stared up at the house. Really and truly I should just pick up a few things and set off again. On the other hand, what was the rush? Ivo would be fine with his grandparents and Harry certainly wouldn't miss me, so why dash down just yet? Why hare down to Oxfordshire like I did every flaming weekend of my life? Why not do something that *I* wanted to do for a change, cook on my own perhaps, with the radio on, peacefully in the kitchen. Yes, why not? I was dying to try out a recipe I had in my head for aubergines with a caper and sesame seed sauce and if I could do it without Harry sticking his finger in and declaring, 'A touch more salt I think, Old Thing,' so much the better. And if it was a success, I thought with a little rush of excitement, I could add it to my book. Ah, yes, I forgot to mention that. As well as my restaurant I had a best-selling cookery book in my head. Delia Meadows. More dreams.

As I locked the car, I felt that thrill of pleasure I always got when I embarked on something creative and I eagerly set off on foot to buy the ingredients. One of the good things – well, no, actually, the *only* good thing – about living in Meryton Road was that we were right behind the supermarket so one could forgo the battle of the car park and literally trolley home to the back garden.

Being Friday, it was packed to the gunnels but I knew exactly where to pick up the sesame seeds, the capers and everything else I needed. I added some tea towels, tights, mugs and bubble bath just in case Harry should bother to check up on me, and then, on an impulse, headed for the alcohol section. I had a feeling they did mini bottles of champagne or – yes, here we go, one glass in a can, perfect. If the recipe was a success, I could toast it, toast the beginning of the rest of my life. I grabbed a packet of Phileas Fogg just for good measure and headed cheerfully for the checkout. As I stood dreamily in line waiting my turn, on the point of loading my goodies on to the conveyor belt, a low voice in my ear said, 'Where's the party?'

I swung round. It was Alice's friend, the bag packer, and supposedly my friend too, but despite, or perhaps because of, the blond good looks – he was very ornamental, the sort of thing you might want in miniature next to your Delft figurine above the fireplace – he wasn't really my type. A bit too pink-cheeked and pastoral for me, although I had to admit the lopsided grin was fairly hard to resist.

'The party?'

He eyed my mini can of champagne with mock alarm. 'Looks like being quite a bender, really letting your hair down, aren't you?'

I laughed, and normally I would have blushed too, and hastened out clutching my bags, but I suddenly felt emboldened by my new status. Yes, I was very nearly a merry divorcée, for heaven's sake, why shouldn't I trade some idle banter with this attractive and extremely cheeky young whippersnapper?

'It's at my place,' I said with a confident smile as he caught my goods at the other end and popped them into bags. 'And it's a private party, for one, I'm afraid.'

'You mean I'm not invited?'

'Certainly not.'

'Ah, a solitary drinker. I've heard about women like you, dancing round the sitting room sipping your bevvy, singing into the vacuum cleaner nozzle. It's the slippery slope, you know. Tomorrow you'll be in here for two cans, then three, and then before you know it you'll be getting stuck into the Carlsberg straight from the can in the car park.'

I grinned. 'Thanks for the warning. You're obviously quite an authority.'

'Well, I've packed a few bags, you see. It's a marvellous insight into the life of the middle-class housewife. I've turned it into an anthropological study to while away the hours of tedium in here.' He paused for a moment to enlighten me. 'You, for example, have a very sophisticated palate – capers, groundnut oil, champagne – very upmarket, and I'd hazard a guess you know your way around a kitchen too, but there are some women who look like the model of bourgeois respectability, all Armani jackets and Gucci heels, who live almost exclusively on Pot Noodles and Diet Coke. And then there's one woman,' he looked about furtively to check no one was listening, 'who comes in here every single day for a Cadbury's Cream Egg and an extra large pack of lavatory paper!' His eyes widened. 'Now what sort of a problem d'you suppose she's got?'

I suppressed a smile. 'I haven't the faintest idea and I really *don't* want to think about it, thank you.'

He grinned. 'Me neither, so let's get back to your party. Anything I can bring? Nibbles, peanuts – I see we're all right for aubergines.'

I giggled. 'We're fine, I mean I'm fine, and that's it, actually, just me and the aubergine.' I really wish I hadn't said that. I blushed as soon as it was out. Blondy's eyes lit up with delight.

'Ah, yes, I should have known,' he breathed. 'I've seen the way you squeeze the peaches in the fruit and veg, and the way you bulk buy bananas. Silly old me.'

'Idiot,' I muttered, paying the check-out girl and hiding my blush in my handbag as I took my change. 'Is he always like this?' I muttered to her as she grinned at me.

'He's not, actually. Seems to have made a bee line for you though.'

'Can't think why, I'm old enough to be his mother.'

'Perhaps that's it then,' she said with a wink.

I thanked her and hurried towards the exit, aware that he was still watching me and wishing I had the confidence to turn round and say, 'Right, young man, you're on. Trousers down and I'll give you a good seeing to in the frozen food section' – or something equally assertive.

As it was I threaded my way through the car park towards the gate on the opposite side, but I wasn't too surprised when after a minute I heard the patter of size nine trainers behind me.

'Carry your bags, ma'am, carry your bags?' he wheedled, tugging his forelock beside me.

'Aren't you supposed to be working?'

'Oh, it's Mr Sainsbury's policy to encourage us to escort harassed housewives to their cars. All part of the service, you see.'

'It's Lord Sainsbury actually, and I'm not at all sure he'd encourage you to escort the housewife home.' I stopped abruptly and bestowed a glittering smile on him. 'I walked, you see.'

He grinned, took the bags from me and marched on. 'Well, I may as well take them anyway. It's only round the corner, isn't it?'

'How the hell do you know where I live?'

'I believe I might have forced it out of your friend at some point.' He smiled back at me disarmingly.

'Alice? How remarkably indiscreet of her.'

'Oh, you can't really blame her. I tied her to a railway track and put a gun to her head.'

I glanced at him. Why me? I was tempted to ask. Why single me out from all the women who must shop in Sainsbury's?

'Do you make a habit of this?'

'I don't actually,' he said with what sounded like an element of truth. 'But I fell victim to your soft green eyes and your dazzling smile and the way you chat to your little boy in the trolley as you push him round and don't scream, "Oh, for God's sake, Wayne, put it back or I'll fump you!" And the way you've always got time to chat to the check-out girls and the fact that you're obviously totally oblivious of your charms.'

I really did have to blush now. 'And the way I squeeze the peaches,' I reminded him.

'Naturally.'

'And the way that I'm so obviously married?'

'Well, I can't argue with that.'

I smiled. 'No, you can't. Well, thank you so much for carrying my bags. As I'm sure you're aware, this is my house so I'll take them in now.'

'I could help you unpack?' he said hopefully.

'I'll manage.'

'Quick cup of coffee? Before I begin my next six-hour shift back at the conveyor belt?'

I hesitated. He was obviously so thoroughly 'all right', but even so, to let him into my house . . . The telephone rang inside.

'Your phone's ringing.' He walked up the path towards the door.

'I know.' I hastened after him. 'Look, thanks for your help. If you could just pop those down on the front step I'll—' I opened the front door and reached inside to lift the receiver off the hook. 'Hello?'

'My name's Tim by the way,' he said as he sailed past me, through the open door, carrying the bags down the passage to the kitchen.

'Rosie? It's Alice, how did it go?' said a voice in my ear.

'Wh-what?' I stammered, watching dazed as Tim unpacked the bags at my kitchen table, putting champagne in the fridge, Phileas Fogg on the side.

'The solicitor, did you find one?'

'Yes, I did . . . amongst other things . . .' Good grief, he'd put the empty bag in the bin and was unpacking another one now.

'Listen,' said Alice, 'I was thinking, you could use the cottage.'

'What cottage?' I watched in amazement as he got the Badedas out and the shampoo and came back towards me in the hall. He surely wasn't thinking of taking them—

'In Pennington, our weekend place. You could live there for a bit, it's just up the road from Philly and we only use it at the weekends.'

'Oh, Alice, you're an angel, but—' I gazed, speechless, as he walked round me at the foot of the banisters and then on *up the stairs*!

'Oi!' I called after him. 'Come back!'

'What?' said Alice in my ear.

'Look, Alice, can I ring you back? Only I've got someone here.'

'Who?'

'That supermarket chappie, if you must know,' I hissed. 'And he's just gone upstairs!'

'No! Wow, quick work, Rosie. God, how thrilling! Ring me back immediately!'

I crashed down the receiver and bolted up after him, two at a time.

'Excuse me, what the hell d'you think you're doing?' I swung round on the empty landing. Where was he?

'Just putting the Badedas in the cabinet. I presume that's where you keep it?' came a voice.

God, he was in my bathroom, which meant – he'd gone through my *bedroom*!

I ran through. 'Now look here—'

'Funny, I had you down as more of a Radox girl myself. Shampoo in here too?'

I folded my arms, watching as he made room among Harry's shaving things for the shampoo. 'You've got a nerve, haven't you?'

He grinned. 'So I've been told.'

'As a general rule I don't allow strange men into my bathroom, you know.'

'Oooh, come on now, I don't believe that. Have you never had a plumber? Never had your S bend attended to? And who hung all this spriggy Laura Ashley wallpaper? Grouted the tiles? I wouldn't mind betting all manner of blue-collar workers have toiled away in the cause of your *en suite*, Rosie.'

'How d'you know my name?'

'It's on your credit card. Tights in the bedroom?' He slid past me back into my bedroom.

Suddenly I began to feel panicky. 'Look,' I said quietly, moving towards the doorway and hovering there. 'Thanks, you've been a great help, but I'd really like you to go now.'

'Oh, look, here's your little boy.' He picked up a photograph of Ivo from my dressing table. The hairs on the back of my neck began to feel a bit prickly.

'Nothing like your husband, is he?'

'How d'you know what my husband looks like?' I breathed.

'There's a picture of him here, on your wedding day.' He picked up our wedding photo and turned round. 'At least, I presume that's him.'

'Yes, that's him. Look, I'd really, *really* like you to go now. He'll be home very soon and to be honest he won't be too thrilled to find you here.' I began hopping nervously from foot to foot, keeping one eye on the open front door and thinking I could actually make a mad dash down the stairs and run straight out into the street shouting like billyo if need be. What the hell was this guy up to?

'It's okay,' he grinned. 'I'm not the mad axeman or anything, don't look so worried. I was just interested, that's all.' He glanced at Ivo again. 'Yes, he's very like you.'

'Yes, isn't he just, and now that we've established the dominant characteristics from the gene pool, I wonder, would you be kind enough to put that picture back on the dressing table and get the hell out of my bedroom before I—'

'Sshh . . .' Tim put his finger to his lips and crossed quickly over to the window. He looked out.

'What is it?'

'There's someone here, just arrived.'

'Where?' I hurried to the window and looked down.

Sure enough, outside the house, behind Harry's Peugeot was parked – my Volvo. Which was odd really, because Harry had it in the country. Just as my brain had assimilated this information I heard the front door slam. Then footsteps came slowly up the stairs. My heart stopped.

'Oh, dear God,' I whispered.

'Who is it?' hissed Tim.

'It's my husband!'

Chapter Four

'Rosie!' Harry called as he came up the stairs.

Paralysed, I shut my eyes and prayed. Oh, dear God, how does one explain away a strange man in the marital bedroom? Particularly, dear God, a twinkly-eyed shelf-stacker like the one I've got here, and particularly to someone like Harry who doesn't even speak to the proletariat let alone allow them in the house? Tim, luckily, was more alive than the Almighty to the compromising nature of the situation and inquired by means of an urgent jerk of his head whether he should hide in the bathroom.

I nodded, panic-stricken, just as the footsteps came across the landing. A second later, as Tim disappeared behind the bathroom door, Harry appeared in the bedroom. I managed not to faint.

'Oh, there you are. Why didn't you answer when I called?'

'Sorry, I – didn't hear you,' I gasped.

'And why the hell was the front door wide open?'

'Oh, because I – I came in in a hurry. Had to go to the loo, emergency, you know how it is. Um, what are you doing here, Harry?'

'I forgot that blasted Blinky Bill, bloody child wouldn't stop crying! I tried to get hold of you to tell you to bring him down but you weren't here and I thought you were probably on your way. Would you believe it, I've just driven thirty-five miles back down the sodding M40 to get a stuffed koala bear!'

'Oh! Right.' I eyed the bathroom door nervously. 'Yes, well, he is rather crucial and I did remind you.'

'Yes, and I forgot, so come on, let's find the wretched thing and get going again. I presume you've done all the titivating you need to do this morning. Done all the spurious errands you invented to get you out of a morning's childcare?'

'Er, yes, although—'

'Right, let's get back on the road. Your mother's got roast pheasant for lunch and I'm damned if I'm missing that. No point taking two cars down, is there?'

'Um, no.'

'Well, come on then.'

'Yes. Right. Listen, Harry, Blinky's probably in Ivo's bed. If you could just go and get him I'll grab a few things I need from the bathroom – make-up, sponge bag, that kind of thing . . .'

'Well, hurry up. I'm bloody hungry and I could do with a drink. All I need now is to miss lunch, that would really make my day!'

Harry exited angrily and I hastened to the bathroom. I stuck my head round the door. Tim was sitting up on the loo seat, hugging his knees to his chest like a little gnome.

'We're going,' I hissed. 'You'll have to climb out of a window or something. Okay? Make sure you shut it behind you!'

The fact that I was leaving a strange man alone in my house, and that there would then be a window conveniently left unlocked for any other strange man who happened to be passing, was nothing, let me tell you, to being discovered with a toy boy in the *en suite*.

'Will do,' he whispered with a grin. 'Quite fun this, isn't it? I could get used to all this subterfuge.' He winked. 'Quite a turn-on.'

'Don't be ridiculous,' I spluttered, shutting the door. Harry reappeared in the bedroom.

'Right, you get in the car and I'll set the alarm.'

I stared at him aghast. 'You're going to . . . set the alarm?'

'Yes, of course. Why not?'

'Well, I never bother!'

'I know you never bother, Rosie, but that's one of the curious differences between you and me. If I invest in a burglar alarm I make damn sure I use it, unlike you who can't even be bothered to find out how the ruddy thing works.'

I gulped in horror. Oh God, Tim would be stuck in the bathroom all weekend. Either that or he'd make a run for it and the place would be crawling with police in seconds.

'But, Harry, we can't!' I croaked, finding my voice at last.

'Why not?'

'Well, because – it's broken.'

'Broken? Since when?'

'Since – yesterday. When I broke it. By mistake. I thought I'd have a go, you see, and I punched in all the wrong numbers. The whole thing went berserk, blew up in my face!'

'Oh, don't be ridiculous, Rosie, it's working perfectly. Punching in the wrong numbers doesn't make any difference. Come on, I'll show you.'

He made to lead me away when suddenly, to our left, someone

started whistling the theme tune to *The Guns of Navarone*. Very loudly and very tunelessly. I stiffened. Harry stared at me. The whistling stopped. There was a silence, then it began again. Only this time it was *633 Squadron*.

Harry spoke slowly. 'Rosie, would you mind telling me who, in the name of God, is whistling Second World War theme tunes in my bathroom?'

'Ah,' I croaked. 'Yes. Well, now that would be, um, that's . . .'

Without waiting for an explanation, Harry kicked open the bathroom door as if it was the saloon at the OK Corral. Tim was revealed, on his knees, with his hand thrust down the lavatory, shoulder deep in water, whistling away furiously.

'That's all right now, missus,' he announced cheerfully, withdrawing his arm. 'I've located the problem, that's your S bend unblocked!'

'That's the plumber!' I finished triumphantly. Oh, bless him, bless him! My, what astounding ingenuity, King's College Cambridge watch out, this boy was destined for great things.

Tim stood up and grinned, wiping his arm on a towel. 'All in perfect working order now.'

Harry gawped.

'I forgot to tell you, darling,' I gabbled. 'That's what the emergency was. You see, when I came back from shopping, there was water everywhere, the upstairs loo was overflowing, so I had to call out an emergency plumber!'

'Twenty-four-hour service and if we're not there in five minutes you get a year's supply of free loo paper. Crapper's the name and plumbing's the game – you won't have any more trouble with that little darling, missus,' said Tim nodding knowledgeably at our low-level flush. 'I've sorted her elementary canal out good and proper. Nothing serious, mind, just a bit of overenthusiasm with the quilted Andrex.' He stepped forward and lowered his voice confidentially. 'A little tip. I recommend only four sheets per wipe, see?' He pulled four pieces off the roll to demonstrate. 'And only three wipes. One up, one down and one to polish. Any more than that and you're in trouble. Oh, and if it's going to take more than three wipes,' he tapped his nose, 'flush in between, that's what I say. Have a mid-crap flush.'

Harry was puce, speechless.

'Er, excellent, thank you so much,' I stammered, wishing he wouldn't throw himself into the role-playing quite so enthusiastically. 'Um, this is my husband, by the way,' I added, and then experienced a moment of social unease as I wondered if one normally introduced one's husband to the plumber.

'Good morning to you, sir. Mr Crapper at your service!' He gave a dinky little bow. Oh God, he was really playing the cheeky chappie, any minute now he'd turn into Dick Van Dyke, leap up on the loo seat and do the plumber's equivalent of Chim-chimeney. Tim peered at Harry's incredulous face.

'Haven't we met before, sir?'

I groaned inwardly. Did he have to push his luck?

'Certainly not!' spluttered Harry.

Tim cocked his head to one side. 'Funny, I never forget a lavvy and I never forget a face.' He frowned. Then his face cleared. 'Ah yes, got it. White's Club, St James's, January ninety-six. Bit of trouble with the overflow in the gents there, a nice white Viceroy Standard, as I recall. I remember passing you on the way out, snoozing on the library sofa, ha ha! Anyway, I'll be off now – oh, and I wouldn't perform on that for a day or two, missus, let it settle down a bit before you have a motion, all right? Want me to mop up in here first?'

I looked down at the flood he'd had the presence of mind to create on the floor. 'No, no, I'll do that.'

'Righto. Cheerio then.'

'I'll, um, see you out.' I followed him quickly downstairs.

As he went through the front door he gave me a broad wink. 'Didn't I do well?' he whispered.

'Too well,' I muttered as I shut the door firmly in his face.

I turned round – and jumped. Harry was standing right behind me. He looked rather pale.

'Plumber, eh?'

'Er, yes!'

'Curiously devoid of a tool bag, a spanner, a widget, a whatnot, or even, dare I say it, a plunger.'

'Ah. He must have left them . . . in his van.'

Even as I spoke we both turned to see Tim through the hall window, skipping merrily up the road, hands in his pockets, very much on foot, very much back to Sainsbury's.

Harry gazed at me for a moment, a strange, twisted expression on his face. Then he turned and went into the sitting room. He made straight for the drinks cupboard. Without even bothering to get out a glass, he unscrewed the top of the whisky bottle, held it to his lips, tipped his head back and glugged hard. Then he set it down. He wiped his mouth and turned back to me, staring. For once I almost felt sorry for him. Oh God, he thought I was having an affair. Thought he'd surprised us, done a coitus interruptus.

I sighed. 'Look, okay, you're right, Harry, he wasn't a plumber, actually he works in Sainsbury's. He carried my bags home and for some obscure reason saw fit to take the bubble bath upstairs to the bathroom. Rather cheeky, I agree, but he's bigger than me so I decided not to wrestle him downstairs again. When we heard you come in, I knew you were going to think the worst so he hid in the bathroom, and when you said you were going to put the alarm on he pretended to be a plumber. Ridiculous, I know, but that's all there is to it, I swear.'

His pale eyes bored into mine for a long moment. 'Get in the car, Rosie,' he said quietly.

I stared at him for a second, and suddenly I couldn't be bothered to argue. Oh God, I was off anyway, wasn't I, so why try to convince him? So what if he thought I was playing fast and loose with boys young enough to be bob-a-jobbing for me? So what if he thought I'd begun the extramarital activity already? I went back upstairs to get the few things I needed for the weekend and then went silently out to the car.

The drive down to Oxfordshire was slow, silent and tense. The traffic was very heavy and I was aware that Harry, now on his third leg of the journey and sandwiched firmly between two juggernauts, was simmering away quietly beside me. He finally came to the boil somewhere around High Wycombe.

'Of course you realise you've condemned us to Friday afternoon traffic now, don't you? While you've been canoodling with underage gippos, half the planet has seen fit to hit the M40!'

'You were the one who forgot Blinky,' I reminded him mildly.

'Only because you were too busy dreaming about getting your leg over that bit of rough to pack the bloody thing in the first place! It's going to take all afternoon to get down there now. Look at all these ghastly people in their revolting little cars!' He ground his teeth at an innocuous looking couple in a Metro beside us. They looked away in alarm. 'Quadruple the price of petrol, that's what I say. That would keep these proles off the road! Make it twenty quid a gallon, thirty even. That'll make them think twice before they nip down to Auntie Maureen's in the Fiesta. When I come to power I shall push that through as a matter of urgency. We'll use superior purchasing power to out-manoeuvre these bastards and go back to the days when only gentlemen drove on the highways!'

'Yes, and you could live at Toad Hall.'

'There are too many people on this island, Rosie,' he seethed. 'Too many common people. I'd like to round up at least ninety per cent of them, march them all off to the white cliffs of Dover and—'

'Push them off the edge, yes, I know, you've told me before. Harry, I want a divorce.'

I hadn't meant to say it so soon. In fact, I hadn't planned exactly when I was going to say it, but at that particular moment, as he launched into his habitual Nazi diatribe on the great unwashed, which I'd heard so many times before, I truly hated him. We were crawling along in the slow lane of the motorway at the time, which required little in the way of driving skill, so he was able to turn almost ninety degrees to look at me. His mouth dropped open, his blue eyes popped, but at the same time a police siren wailed abruptly behind us. He glanced up into his rear-view mirror.

A panda car was advancing at speed towards us up the hard shoulder, lights flashing. A moment later it had slowed to a crawl alongside us. The driver leaned out of his window and by means of an eloquent gesture invited us, unequivocally, to join him.

Harry touched his chest. 'Me?' he mouthed back, incredulous.

Both policemen nodded firmly in unison.

Shaking his head in disbelief, Harry pulled over, watched gleefully, I might add, by the massed ranks of the great unwashed, including the couple in the Metro.

Now from the moment when I'd reached an age when I could sit behind a wheel, my father had impressed upon me the importance of getting out of the car when stopped by the police. Not only is it polite, he'd stressed, but it also subliminally predisposes them towards you. Harry, of course, knew better. He sat firm, arrogant and unamused as they approached. As the policeman crouched into view in Harry's window, I suddenly had a nasty feeling I knew what this was all about.

'This your car, sir?'

'Of course it's my car. What the devil have you pulled me over for?'

'Well, according to our records, this car was stolen this morning. Would you happen to know anything about that?'

'Stolen! Don't be ridiculous, this is my car and I'm driving it, how can it have been stolen? You've got the wrong vehicle, officer.'

My tongue seemed to have got entangled with my tonsils. I unwound it and leaned across.

'Er, no,' I stammered, 'you're right, officer, it was this car. You see, I thought I'd lost it in a car park this morning and reported it missing, but actually I hadn't lost it at all because my husband was driving it and I was driving his. I'm afraid it was just a silly misunderstanding and totally my fault.'

Harry turned to me, momentarily dumbstruck. But only momentarily. 'Do you mean to say you reported this car stolen and didn't even bother to tell me?'

'Harry, so much has happened this morning and there simply wasn't time. I meant to ring the police station and tell them it was all a silly mistake but I just forgot. I'm terribly sorry.' I addressed this last remark to the policeman, blushing furiously.

He pushed his cap back and scratched his head. He looked baffled, but not murderous like Harry. 'I see. Right, well, I suppose that explains it. Can I see your documentation and your licences please?'

I produced mine from my handbag but Harry hadn't got his on him.

'It's at home in my study. Good God, I'm so sorry about all this, officer, quite frankly I'm *appalled* at my wife's behaviour. What a perfectly bloody stupid thing to do. Talk about wasting police time, you ought to be ashamed of yourself, Rosie! These people have got better things to do than charge around looking for fictitious cars!'

'Yes, I know,' I muttered.

'That's okay, sir,' said the policeman kindly. 'No harm done. We'll just check with London though. Which police station was it, madam?'

'Kensington.'

'Kensington!' brayed Harry. 'What the hell were you doing in Kensington!'

'Shopping,' I muttered. 'I told you.'

'Ha! All the way to Kensington for a pair of knickers and some shampoo – women, I ask you, eh?' He turned jovially to the policemen for solidarity, but one of them was looking at Harry rather carefully.

'Have you been drinking, sir?'

A horrid silence fell. Harry went very pink. 'Of course not, officer,' he spluttered at last. 'I haven't even had lunch yet!'

What that had to do with the price of eggs, I've no idea.

'Well then, you won't mind stepping from the car and blowing into the bag for me, will you? Just a formality.'

'I don't think there's any need for that.'

'Probably not, but all the same, sir, we can't be too careful.'

Harry stared at him belligerently, and for a moment I thought he was going to refuse. Then he got out and slammed the door furiously. As he walked off towards the panda car, I heard him berating them.

'This is just the sort of easy crime you enjoy, isn't it, officer?

You've lost control of the streets, you can't catch the real criminals, but by golly you'll nail the middle classes as they go quietly about their business!'

I sank down in my seat with a low moan, watching with trepidation as the equipment was produced from the police car. Oh God, this was really going to send him into orbit. Forget the divorce, if Harry lost his licence I might as well emigrate. I watched fearfully through my fingers as Harry stood in the wind by the panda car, trouser legs flapping, hair standing on end, blowing into a bag. The two policemen regarded the result grimly. Then one of them approached my car again. He crouched down at the window.

'I'm afraid we're going to have to ask your husband to accompany us to the station. Would you like to follow on behind?'

I did. And then I sat for what seemed like an age in a cold, grey waiting room, decorated with lots of stern posters with dire warnings about the dangers of not locking your car or protecting your property, while Harry was taken away to be tested again. Surprise, surprise, this test also proved to be extremely positive, at least that's what I assumed when Harry finally emerged from a little back room with a face like thunder.

'Don't speak to me,' he hissed as we walked out. 'If you value your life, don't even utter. This is all your fault, Rosie!'

I knew better than to argue and got back in the car.

'Move over,' he snarled.

'But, Harry, surely I should drive. You can't—'

'I'm perfectly entitled to drive until my case comes up in a month's time, when I will, in all probability and thanks to you, be banned from driving a vehicle for at least a year, but until such time I am quite within my rights to sit behind a wheel. Now MOVE OVER!'

Crazy not to. I shifted into the passenger seat and he drove away at top speed. The motorway was clearer now and we zipped along it in silence. No mention was made of the divorce and I felt it was almost as if I'd never said it. I wondered if this was a deliberate ploy on his part, or if actually, in the light of this massive blow to his morale, it was simply of no importance. After all, what was the dissolution of a marriage compared to this restriction of Harry's liberty? Lost your wife and child, Harry old boy? Jolly bad luck, have another glass of port. Lost your *licence*? Good God, how on earth will you get to Cheltenham? To Goodwood? I sank back in my seat with a sigh and wondered if I'd ever have the nerve to say it again. Or perhaps I wouldn't have to, I thought hopefully. Yes, perhaps it didn't matter, perhaps I could just serve him with the relevant papers and when he expressed surprise say, oh, don't you remember, Harry? I mentioned it a few Fridays ago, just before we took the scenic route to my parents' via the police station.

As we careered off the motorway at the appropriate exit I glanced at his set, angry face. I knew that look and gripped my seat hard as he began to take his aggression out on the narrow lanes that led to my parents' house. My knuckles were white and my eyes shut as we flew along at breakneck speed, but I knew better than to say anything. As we zipped past the farm at the end of my parents' road we suddenly had to screech to a halt within centimetres of a car trying to pass in the opposite direction. The woman driver buzzed down her window.

'Pig!' she screamed.

Harry buzzed down his. 'Cow!' he roared back, and we sped off again, a mistake as it happened, because just round the next bend we crashed into – a pig.

We sat for a moment in shocked silence. The huge Tamworth sow was laid out cold on the road in front of us. I turned to look at Harry.

'Oh God,' I gasped, my mouth twitching. 'She meant—'

'Yes, I know what she meant, thank you!'

Suddenly I felt ridiculously, uncontrollably giggly. Snorting a bit, I scrambled from the car. 'D'you think it's all right?'

'Never mind the bloody pig, what about my car!'

Actually it was my car, a wedding present from my parents. As Harry got out to survey the damage, I attended to the pig. It was a huge ginger sow which I recognised as belonging to the farmer down the road from us. It blinked a bit, but as I prodded it, it gave a snort and staggered woozily to its feet.

'I think it's okay!' I cried. 'Get that chocolate bar out of the glove compartment, Harry.'

For once Harry obliged. I took the chocolate, broke it up and threw it into the field. The pig turned, crashed back through the hole in the hedge where it had come through and tucked into the Toblerone. Then I ran along the hedgerow and found some willow branches to mend the hole.

'We've got to patch this up or she'll get out again!' I yelled, dragging half a ton of hedgerow back, puffing, panting, sweating, while Harry got back in the car.

As I wrestled with ten-foot branches I spotted him through the windscreen, glancing at his watch. Suddenly I realised he was still thinking about lunch. After all that had happened – underage Lotharios, divorce threats, breathalyser tests, flattened pigs – he was still thinking about his groaning stomach and wondering if the Cavendishes were holding the roast pheasant for him. This tickled me somewhat, and as I went about my business, I couldn't resist making rather a meal of it. Glancing at him occasionally out of the corner of my eye, I wove an elaborate tapestry of branches in and out, this way and that way, doing a spectacular darning job, watching as he tapped his fingers impatiently on the dashboard, glanced at his watch, wondering how long it would take him to lose his—

'OH, FOR GOD'S SAKE, GET BACK IN THE SODDING CAR!'

Not long. Suppressing a smile, I ran back and jumped in. His word was my command. For the moment anyway. We sailed past my newly woven hedge and a few minutes later turned left into the private road where my parents live. We drove silently past the rows of immaculately manicured lawns with their dinky little chain link fences, past the identical tubs of winter pansies, over the sleeping policemen, and finally turned and came to a halt in the gravel drive.

I breathed a sigh of relief as I looked up at the house I'd grown up in. For once I was glad to be home. It was a large but fairly hideous 1930s redbrick, red-tile affair with strange extensions sticking out here and there and dark leaded windows. Thanks to my father, though, the garden was always fabulous. Even this late in the year it knocked spots off any other garden in the neighbourhood, and today the Christmas roses were out to greet us in style. Also on the welcoming committee was my mother, who came running down the front steps, resplendent in some sort of green silk ensemble that looked more suitable for going to a wedding in than cooking Sunday lunch for her family. I climbed weakly out of the car.

'Darlings, you're here! Where on earth have you been? We've been so worried!'

Harry slammed his door and strode rudely past her.

'Harry?' She turned and stared after him.

I put a restraining hand on her arm. 'Leave him, Mum. He was breathalysed. It was positive.' At least I presumed that was the problem.

Mummy turned back to me in horror. 'Well, for pity's sake, why weren't you driving? Did you know he'd had a drink?'

I shrugged. 'Harry's always had a drink. I can't see why he's so fussed, actually. He spends his life lolling around in the back of taxis, why does he need a car?'

She stared at me. 'Oh, you stupid girl!' She stormed after him into the house.

I wearily climbed up the steps after her and encountered my father in the hall.

'What's happened?'

'Harry failed the breath test.'

'Ah. Oh well, it had to happen sooner or later, didn't it? Probably just as well. Never mind, come and see what I've been doing in the garage.'

He turned me round and led me firmly outside, right away from the fray. As far as he was concerned, that was it on the sympathy front for Harry. My mother would no doubt be sitting by the fire with him even now, commiserating, tutting, handing him a micro-waved plate of roast pheasant, sympathising, blaming me. I wasn't hungry, and the last thing I needed was re-heated game and Mum. I squeezed Dad's arm gratefully as we walked round the side of the house.

'Where's Ivo?'

'Tucked up in bed. Havin' a bit o' shut-eye,' he said with his flat, Mancunian vowels, which despite years of living in the south and intense pressure from my mother he'd never bothered to lose. 'He cried for Blinky for a bit, but next time we peeped in he was out like a light. Come on, come and look at this.' He opened the garage door, went over to the far corner and pulled off a dustsheet. I blinked, adjusting my eyes to the gloom. Underneath was a miniature version of a convertible Bentley, dark shiny blue with red leather upholstery.

I gaped. 'Oh Dad, it's wonderful! Where did you get it?'

'Had it for years. It was mine when I was a boy, actually, but it's been in a terrible state for a long time. I've been doing it up for months.'

'Who for?'

'For Ivo of course.'

I flushed with pleasure. My sister Philly had three children too.

'The others can use it too of course,' he said magnanimously, 'but they've got toys coming out of their ears. I thought Ivo would appreciate it more. He's a bit young at the moment but in a year or so when his feet can reach the pedals – look at this.' He reached inside with his hand, turned a key, pushed the pedals and sure enough it shot off down the garage.

I laughed. 'You're a genius. It must have taken ages to get the old motor going again.'

He shrugged. 'Oh well, I quite enjoy tinkering around in here, as you know.'

Of course he did. It was his bolt hole, his way of escaping my mother, and it always had been. Not that my parents were unhappy, they rubbed along pretty amicably most of the time, just as long as my father toed the line. Just as long as he'd done all his jobs in my mother's domain, the house. Oh yes, after he'd fetched in the wood, cleared the grates, laid the fires and done a certain amount of skivvying in the kitchen he was free to go out to his garden, or his potting shed and, if he'd been very good, his garage. Philly and I had been quietly alarmed at the thought of Dad retiring, thinking he'd be under Mum's feet and that she'd be at his throat, but actually it worked better than when he used to come home exhausted from the City every day and she'd nagged and bullied him relentlessly when all he wanted to do was collapse in front of the nine o'clock news. She still nagged and bullied of course, but if he wasn't tired, he didn't mind so much, and if he didn't mind so much, she didn't do it so much. Funny, that.

'Still got a lot of work to do on it of course,' he said, reaching for a rag.

'I'll give you a hand.'

I took a duster off the shelf and started polishing the back bumper while he rubbed away at the front. Like him, I felt safe in here and I didn't want to go back inside. Didn't want to go and face the music. In here, the Armchair Symphony on Dad's old Roberts radio provided a serene background hum and the smells of oily rags and spilled petrol were comforting and familiar. I remembered how I'd sat in here as a little girl, watching him fix a bicycle or polish hubcaps. It was always a sanctuary for me too.

'Dad?' I ventured after a while.

'Hmmm?'

'Harry and I. We're not . . . we're not getting along so well at the moment.'

He sat back on his heels. 'You'll need a bit of Brasso on your duster to really bring that up, love. This rust takes some shifting.'

'What?' I glanced down at my duster. 'Oh, right.' I added some Brasso. 'To be honest it hasn't really been right for ages. Well, almost from the beginning actually.'

'That and elbow grease, of course. There's no substitute for elbow grease.'

I sat back and stared at him as he polished away, head bent. He didn't want to talk about it. He was ignoring me. For a moment I was hurt, offended, but then I realised this wasn't so unexpected really. Dad had never talked emotionally to any of his children, but so far that hadn't mattered. I'd never needed it. But I did now. I wanted to say to him, look, Dad, I do now, so please? I waited. Nothing. I bit my lip and carried on polishing, in what gradually became a companionable silence. Finally he stood up.

'There. That looks a lot better, you can almost see your face in it.'

I grinned and chucked my duster back on the shelf. 'Until Ivo gets his sticky little fingers on it of course.'

'Ah, well, that's all part of the fun. Come on, love, we'd better go in.'

We went out into the sunshine and he shut the door behind us. We both knew our time in that little retreat was over for the moment. Mum took a very dim view of the garage and would bustle down to drag us out if we didn't show ourselves back at the house soon. We chose the long way back though, spinning out the walk, going via the greenhouse where Dad picked up his secateurs, then across to the herbaceous border to check out his euphorbias, then on up the slope of the lawn, where suddenly he took my arm. He squeezed it, then let it go. I looked up in surprise. He was still gazing straight ahead. I smiled. I knew that was his way. His way of saying, look, love, I can't talk about it, but it's okay, I'll back you all the way. You're doing the right thing. It was all there, in that little squeeze. Suddenly, my heart felt lighter than it had done for ages. I smiled in recognition.

The low winter sun shone straight into our eyes as we approached the house and at first I didn't see Harry. Then all at once he was bearing down on us, coming down the grassy slope from the terrace, walking back on his heels and bearing his weight before him like a huge bag of groceries that might spill at any moment, as fat men do. As he came to a halt he swayed slightly, reeking of whisky.

'I'd like a word with my wife, Gordon, if you don't mind.'

'By all means, dear boy,' murmured Dad, moving quietly away into the shadows.

As Harry took a step towards me, his body blotted out the sun. He fixed me with bleary, bloodshot eyes. 'The answer to your question, Rosie, is no. Absolutely, unequivocally, no. No, I do not want a divorce and no, I would not give you one should you seek it, and be assured that if you continue to pursue this unsavoury tack, I'll make life very difficult for you.'

'Harry, you know as well as I do the marriage is over,' I said in a low voice.

He smiled mockingly. 'Over? Good heavens, it never really began, did it? Any man would find it hard to make a success of being married to you, Rosie.'

I caught my breath sharply. 'And what's that supposed to mean?'

'Simply that you're a bore and a drudge. You know as well as I do your life centres round your domestic territory. You think only of your home, your hearth and your offspring and not once, in all the years I've known you, have you ever uttered a remotely interesting thought or ventured an opinion that you hadn't borrowed from someone else. Frankly, I'm embarrassed by the narrowness of your mind.'

Don't rise, I told myself, although I could feel myself seething inwardly, wanting to smack his fat face, just don't rise. This was very normal, very Harry, very calculated. He never balked at hitting below the belt and this was his way of turning the screw, hoping to provoke a scene, a volatile reaction so that he could throw up his hands and walk away saying, see? She's hysterical! I mean what *is* a man to do? She's *so* unreasonable.

I calmly met his eye. 'And where do you get your opinions from, Harry? Sniffing at the heels of your friends in high places, picking up a few crumbs from the master's table, eh?'

'Perhaps,' he said evenly, 'but they certainly don't have their origins in the kitchen sink. You're swamped in domesticity, Rosie. You're socially awkward, you contribute nothing to sophisticated gatherings other than an update on your son's teething situation or your latest recipe for tiramisu. You have neither political nor social savvy, no lively debate, you're gauche, ignorant, giggly and frivolous and you're unimaginative both in and out of bed.' He gave a twisted smile. 'I'm perfectly aware, my dear, that during any recent sexual encounter of ours, you've clearly been faking it.'

'Oh, I don't fake it, Harry. I really am asleep.'

'Don't be flippant,' he snapped. 'You're just proving my point.'

'So why did you marry me then?'

'Because I needed a wife. Because I wanted children, and because Bertram approved of you.'

You had to hand it to Harry. None of this 'your body was a temple, one touch and I was in ecstasy' lark for him. Oh no. I looked like a good breeder and his uncle had given me the thumbs up.

'Also,' he went on charitably, 'I thought you were reasonably decorative. You had an open, friendly disposition and I thought I might be able to do something about your mind. Thought I might be able to mould you, but I now see the folly of that. There wasn't enough raw material there for me to work with.'

The audacity of the man was phenomenal. This was a man without an A level to his name. This was a man who talked a good

Oxford but had never actually been there, except as a tourist, and yet he thought he could mould my mind. And the funny thing was that all this time I'd been thinking I could mould *his*, which is ironic really when you think about it. There we'd both been, three years ago at that altar, both plighting our troths and both secretly thinking he'll/she'll do. I'm sure I can do something with him/her.

'So why stay married to me, Harry? Why prolong the agony?'

'Because I don't believe in divorce. It's common and degrading and not for the likes of us. It's tantamount to admitting the biggest, grossest mistake of one's life and I don't make mistakes. But I do have a proposition for you.'

'I'm all ears.'

He drew himself up to his full height and girth. 'Separate bedrooms, separate lives. But to all intents and purposes, to the outside world, we carry on as man and wife.'

I blinked. To the outside world? What, our public? Anyone would think we were Charles and Diana, and even they, with all their vast estates and acreage, hadn't managed the sort of modus vivendi he was suggesting, to live together but not to live together. How on earth did he think we'd manage it in a Wandsworth semi?

'But why, Harry? What's the point?'

'I've told you,' he said coldly. 'I don't believe in divorce. I won't interfere with your life, you can come and go as you please – although I draw the line at you screwing that plumber johnnie, he really was the end. We can't have types like that about the place, you'll catch all manner of sexual diseases, one only had to look at his fingernails to see that. No, he'll have to go – imagine if any of my friends should see him!' Suddenly he swooped, his pale eyes big and popping. 'He didn't ask about me, did he? Didn't try to find out anything about me, where I worked or anything?'

'Harry, even I don't know the answer to that, and no, he didn't mention you. Why should he, for God's sake? We only chatted for a few minutes. I've told you, nothing happened!'

'Well, just make sure you keep it that way. You're still my wife, Rosie, and standards must be upheld. You stay with me for the duration and I'll see you're all right. But if you should cross me, if you should file for a divorce, be assured I'll fight you all the way. You'll get no money and no share of the house, I'll see to that. Neither will you get Ivo.'

'Don't be ridiculous, of course I'll get Ivo!'

'Not if I demonstrate to the courts what an unfit mother you are.'

'What do you mean?' I breathed.

'Not if I document your cruelty. Your neglect.'

I stared at him, totally flabbergasted. 'But that's not true!'

'So what? I'll lie. And I'll get others to lie too, to back me up. I can do that, you know, Rosie, my friends will do that for me. We're very close and I know some very influential people.'

Clearly he thought he was Lord Lucan now. Nevertheless I started to tremble. 'Don't threaten me, Harry.'

'No threats,' he said cheerfully, 'just food for thought. Something for you to think about before you make any rash moves.'

I looked him in the eye. 'But I already have. The ball is already in motion. I'll see you in court, Harry.'

He regarded me coldly. 'And I'll see you in hell.'

With that he turned and walked away.

Chapter Five

I sat down on the low terrace wall for a long while. I could feel myself
trembling still and Harry must have been gone five minutes. I
shivered, huddling down into my coat, hands thrust deep in my
pockets. At my feet a few dead leaves rustled around in the dank
lustrous winter lawn. I watched them blow this way and that, back
and forth, all dark and shrivelled, until they came to rest at my feet.
How strange, I thought as I stared at them, how one notices a thing
like a couple of dead leaves at a moment like this. I'd probably
remember them for ever. After a while I stood up. I took a deep
breath. Philly. Yes, that was it, I'd go and see Philly.

I went into the house and stole up the back stairs into the spare
room where Ivo slept. He was awake, but only just, sitting up in his
cot sucking his thumb, hair askew, eyes bright and cheeks rosy with
sleep.

'Hello, darling!' I whispered, my voice catching.

'Out! Out! No bed!' he demanded, raising his arms and clenching
and unclenching his chubby fists.

'No more bed,' I agreed, lifting him out and holding him close. He
smelled divine. I nuzzled into his hair and neck, breathing him in
deeply. My heart beat against his. Over my dead body, Harry. Over
my dead body. I quickly changed his nappy, then carried him
downstairs, sticking my head round the kitchen door.

'I'm just popping over to Philly's, Mum, okay?'

My mother turned round from the kitchen sink, an apron protecting her silk shirtwaister, Cabouchon bracelets clinking above her
Marigolds. She raised her gloves like a surgeon preparing to operate,
eyes wide. 'But she's coming over for lunch tomorrow, I told you!
You'll see her then.'

I shrugged. 'Okay, so I'll see her now and then.'

'Will you be back for supper?'

'I shouldn't think so, I'll probably stay over.'

'But I've asked the Burdetts and the Palmers! I thought we'd have some of those little cucumber mousses you do so beautifully and a bit of stuffed pork.'

My mother had a happy knack of inviting all her friends over for dinner when I was around to do the catering.

'I'm sure they'll love that, Mum. My recipes are in my blue folder in the drawer.'

'Oh, but the girls will be *so* disappointed.'

The only reason 'the girls' – Marjorie Burdett and Yvonne Palmer were both pushing sixty-five – would be disappointed was because they'd be getting the cucumber without the mousse, and the pork without the stuffing. Unless of course she stuffed the cucumber up the pork.

'Give them my love,' I said sweetly. 'And my regrets.'

I could almost hear my mother's teeth grinding as I went out to the car, but cooking a four-course meal for Marjorie Burdett was not top of my list of priorities at the moment. The only priority I have right now, I determined as I strapped Ivo into his seat and paused to regard him squarely, is you, mate.

Popping over to Philly's was not as easy as I'd deliberately and nonchalantly made it sound. She didn't exactly live next door, but in the next county, in deepest, rural Gloucestershire, some thirty-five minutes away, but that suited me fine. I needed time on my own, time to think. I set off down the lanes and reflected on my little debacle with Harry, which, in retrospect, although harrowing, had actually been extremely illuminating, particularly with regard to what he'd said about Bertram. Deep down I suppose I'd always known that his uncle's approbation of me had increased Harry's ardour, but it was a revelation actually to hear him say it. I remembered how I'd dreaded going up to Yorkshire to meet this mythical figure, Harry's only living relative, his benefactor, from whom Harry expected to inherit the earth. I remembered Harry's nerves too, how he'd made me change at least twice before we set off and given me a whole list of instructions about what to say and what not to say as we drove up there, and I remember how, finally, as we reached the craggy hills which led to Bertram's estate, I gasped as this colossal Gothic greystone pile came looming into view.

As I walked slowly up the ancient stone steps, the solid oak door swung back and I braced myself for a gouty, gin-soaked, cantankerous ex-general with a ruddy complexion, a brace of smelly Labrador and a monocle – only to discover that this wasn't Bertram at all. To my surprise the man who greeted us cheerfully at the door was an extremely spry, energetic little octogenarian with a fine line in wit and an even finer eye for the ladies. I'd never actually been chased around a kitchen table by a man of eighty-six before, but there's always a first time, and once I'd got the hang of it and made a few rules of my own – like for instance that even if he *did* catch me, his hand would get a smart slap if it so much as touched my bottom – he settled down and confined himself to leering at me over the breakfast table. After that, he and I, much to Harry's surprise, got along famously.

He lived almost entirely on his own, apart from an equally aged retainer named Parkinson, a stooped, white-haired old fellow, who lived in a grace and favour flat at the back of the house. As far as I could make out, Parkinson's main duty was to shuffle around the house dusting ornaments, dropping them, and then leaving the mess on the floor for a few days while he pottered outside to the garden to dig up daffodils instead of onions. Bertram had apparently sacked the cook and all the rest of his staff long ago on the grounds that they'd lusted after him too voraciously – although I suspect the reverse to be true – and now did all the catering himself, which in reality meant that he lived almost exclusively on corned beef, Branston pickle, claret and Curly Wurlys. I regarded this diet as thoroughly slothful, and told him so in no uncertain terms, but I also regarded it as a challenge. I set to work trying to teach him how to make an omelette, a shepherd's pie and how to stew the fruit that grew so abundantly in his orchards, instead of just leaving it to rot on the grass. He did actually have a stab at some cooking, although I think the only reason he bothered to learn was that he liked to stand extremely close to me at the stove, gazing at my breasts as I taught him.

For all his lechery he was actually very entertaining and bright, making it quite clear – at least to me – that he knew exactly how Harry's mind worked. He teased him mercilessly and apropos of nothing, was quite likely to look up from his newspaper at breakfast and say something like: 'I say, Harry, I forgot to mention. I had those Guide Dogs for the Blind chappies up here the other day. Very nice people, very nice indeed. Marvellous things they do. Seemed very interested in the house for some reason, said it would make an ideal training centre. Can't imagine what they meant.'

As Harry turned puce and spat his Cornflakes across the room, Bertram would disappear behind his paper again. A moment later, though, he'd slyly peek out and give me a huge wink.

Yes, he and I saw eye to eye on a lot of things, so much so that by the time we finally left, Harry was almost speechless I think with envy. When he eventually found his voice on the drive home he leaned across and patted my hand, saying incredulously, 'Well *done*, my dear. Very well done indeed. Good heavens, you charmed the pants off him!'

'Heaven forbid,' I'd muttered back.

But Bertram had indeed taken a shine to me, so much so that were Harry and I to divorce . . . ah yes, I thought grimly as I shunted down a gear to take the sharp bend into Philly's village, yes, it was all becoming very clear now. Very clear indeed. No wonder Harry wouldn't entertain the idea, he didn't want to upset Bertram. Didn't want to upset the inheritance apple cart. But wasn't it also very telling that in the latter stages of our conversation Harry had said, 'Stay with me for the duration, Rosie, and I'll see you're all right.' For the duration of what? For the duration of Bertram's life, that's what, because you can bet your greystone Gothic manor that as soon as Bertram turned up his toes, Harry would be only too delighted to be shot of me. He was hanging on to me as an insurance policy for his inheritance. Well, no dice, Harry, I thought as I drove slowly down the lane to Philly's farm, sorry, no dice at all.

I gazed out across the patchwork of fields to Philly's beautiful old farmhouse nestling just round the copse by the river. It was long, low, shaped in an L round a gravel courtyard and, like everything around here, built in the distinctive mellow Cotswold stone, which at this time of year was covered with gnarled branches of bare wisteria. Philly wasn't expecting me, of course, and could easily have been out, but somehow I wasn't surprised when I drove into her valley – and I mean that in the proprietorial sense since husband Miles did actually *own* the valley – to see her bending down in her vegetable garden behind the house, picking her winter greens and putting them in a wicker basket.

Philly always looked the part and today was no exception. She had on an old felt hat of Miles's and her hair hung down her back in a thick dark plait, quite a lot escaping in wisps around her face. As she worked, she occasionally paused to flick the plait back impatiently as it fell in her way. She wore faded cords, boots and a Barbour, but although it was *de rigueur* country gear, it all seemed to fit beautifully so that her long legs, long hair and nipped-in little waist did not go unnoticed. Two of her three children, Bertie and Chloe, who were blond and dark and six and four respectively, were playing at her feet, digging up stones from the ground and piling them up into a neat little pyramid, quietly and diligently. The perfection of the scene made me smile. It was like a Medici greeting card in its sentimentality, but then that had always been the way with Philly. You could have taken snapshots of her unawares at any stage of her life and never once found her to be anything other than perfect. At two years old you would have found her gurgling happily in her playpen, at six having nice little make-believe tea parties with her dollies, at twelve winning the best turned-out pony at the local gymkhana, at fifteen diligently doing her homework in her bedroom, at twenty swirling round an Oxford University ballroom looking drop-dead gorgeous, at twenty-five sailing through a hospital ward with a stethoscope round her neck and now, finally, at thirty-three, baking scones at her navy blue Aga in her farmhouse kitchen for her landowning husband with three small children at her feet. She was enough to make you puke, unless you loved her, which I did, unreservedly, but she was a very hard act to follow.

Not that I'd ever tried, actually. And I'm not saying it could never have been me in any of those photographs, it could. I was never a particularly naughty child, but by the same token if the candid camera had done its homework, it could also have glimpsed me being sick in my pram, scribbling on my bedroom walls, smoking in the woods at school, groaning with my head down the loo at a teenage party, snogging an undesirable yobbo behind McDonald's, and generally dropping a bollock, as Uncle Bertram would say. Not Philly. She'd never dropped a bollock in her life. I daresay if she hadn't been so nice I would have hated her, but I never had. Envied her, yes, but not in a dangerous, deep-seated smouldering sort of way, just a nice healthy upfront 'God, you old cow, why do you have to be so bloody perfect?' sort of way, which she took on the chin as her lot.

She turned her head now as she heard the car, shading her eyes and screwing them up against the sun, but that didn't stop any fool seeing that she had the face of an angel. It cleared into a broad grin and she raised her hand in recognition as I swept into the courtyard.

'I thought we were seeing you tomorrow!' she exclaimed, dropping her gardening gloves and striding over to greet me.

'You are.' I got out and lifted Ivo from his seat. 'But I just felt like coming to see you today too, is that a problem?'

'Not in the least.' She hugged my shoulders. 'We're pretty chaotic as usual, the house is a tip and I haven't got much in the way of food but I'll get a bottle of wine out and – oh, Rosie, what's wrong!'

I'd held myself together until she hugged me; now I collapsed in tears on my big sister's shoulder.

Philly held me for a moment, then turned to the gawping children at our feet.

'Bertie, take Ivo into the playroom and show him the new train set, there's a good boy, and find Anna and ask her to give you all a biscuit. Chloe, go with them.'

'But what's wrong with Aunt Rosie?' demanded Chloe, fascinated by adult tears, which doubtless she'd never seen in her life before. Certainly not in her own home.

'Nothing.' Philly gave her a little push. 'Go on, darling, I'll be along in a moment.'

At the mention of a train set and a biscuit Ivo had already ignored his sobbing mother and set off at a trot for the back door. His cousins reluctantly turned and followed.

Philly led me back to the vegetable garden where there was an old stone bench by the runner bean canes. We sat down together and I quickly got control, blowing my nose volubly into a hanky she'd passed me, wiping my eyes and stuffing it up my sleeve. We sat in silence for a moment.

'They're late,' I said eventually, nodding at the basket of cabbages on the ground.

'Mmm, I know. It was the wet autumn, I think. Keeps them going longer. What's wrong, Rosie?'

I sighed heavily. 'Oh, everything. Harry. Me. Harry and me.'

She nodded, as if she'd been expecting it.

I smiled sardonically. 'No one's surprised of course. In fact most people are delighted.'

'Who's most people?'

'Well, only Alice actually, but she nearly leapt for joy. And Dad, but I only hinted to him. Didn't want to upset him. You know what he's like, he'll burst into tears if you tell him the cricket season's over.'

'So it is over?'

'Yes. I hate him, Philly, and happily he hates me too, so that's marvellous, isn't it?' I laughed hollowly. 'Everyone's happy.'

She patted my hand. 'Of course he doesn't hate you. People say terrible things in the heat of the moment.'

'Oh no, he does, he loathes me, and he told me precisely why in no uncertain terms.' I screwed up my eyes to think. 'And the funny thing is, Phil, the things he accused me of are actually all quite true. It's just I'd never really thought of them as being particularly loathsome traits in my character before.'

'Such as?' she demanded, bristling loyally.

'Oh, he said I was ignorant and domesticated and had no firm views on anything outside the kitchen. Said I had no opinions on anything that really mattered, and to a certain extent I think he's right.'

'What sort of things does he think matter?'

'Oh, you know, politics, religion, anything topical, I suppose. And he's right, I can't get too excited about Maastricht and the ERM and global warming and whether the Hootsies are shooting the Tootsies in the footsies, because it all seems too remote and far removed from my life.'

'Yes, but you care about other things.'

'Like what?'

'Well, like education, health – matters that are closer to your heart. We all do.'

'Yes,' I said slowly, 'I suppose I do. I certainly get concerned about class sizes and whether there are enough helpers at the playgroup Ivo's going to, but that's just selfish, isn't it? It's because it affects me.' I struggled to think what else I cared about. 'And I suppose I get concerned that old people don't turn their heating on in the winter for fear of a stonking great gas bill and that the reason so many children wreak havoc in schools is because they aren't getting enough love at home, and occasionally I even pause to think about the planet and wonder if I should use terry towelling nappies to save it as I chuck another hundredweight of rainforest into the nappy bin, but it's all just cosy *Woman's Own* stuff, isn't it? To be honest my sphere of political interest doesn't get much beyond my own back door.'

'Well, neither does mine!'

'Oh, it does though, Phil. You know jolly well that if you were shelling peas on your doorstep with a toddler at your feet and some smart alec political columnist approached and asked for your views on the budget deficit, you'd have an intelligent response, and most probably put him firmly in his place. I wouldn't, and that must make me ignorant.'

'No, it doesn't, it just makes you disinterested. Ignorant is like Mum, who thought the ozone layer was in her armpit and what business was it of anyone else's if she destroyed it with deodorants?'

I giggled. 'All right, disinterested. But then, the thing is, when I realise people *do* expect a view on something, I panic and borrow someone else's.'

'But in reality that's all anybody does, and to be honest as long as it isn't Harry's it's fine. The man's a raving fascist.'

'You see,' I said gloomily, 'you know that. You've probably always

75

known that, and the awful thing is I've only recently realised how prejudiced and arrogant he is. It's only now that I've made myself stand back and look at him dispassionately, as an individual and not as my husband and the father of my child, that I can see it.'

'Of course,' she said staunchly. 'You were blinded by loyalty before.'

'And by wanting it to be right. Needing not to see his faults. Kidding myself we were the perfect, nuclear, happy family.'

'For goodness' sake, you don't have to have compatible political views to make a marriage work. Look at me and Miles. He'd vote for a donkey with a blue ribbon on it and I'm as woolly Liberal as they come. So what? What about the things that matter? What about love, what about passion? Whatever happened to all of that?'

'I'm not sure there ever was any of that,' I said quietly.

She stared. 'Rosie, are you telling me you never loved him?'

I sighed. 'I thought I did. I told myself I did. It was convenient.' I struggled to remember what I'd felt. 'Relief,' I said finally. 'There was a lot of that. On both sides. I think we both interpreted that as love. As for passion,' I made a face. 'Harry's always been a lights out and up with the nightie man.'

'But that's so unlike you, so untrue to form! You thrived on grand passion prior to him, all those gorgeous men – it was meat and drink to you!'

'I know,' I said gloomily, 'and I reckon I overindulged, binged, gorged myself. By the time I met Harry I was emotionally bulimic, sick of the very smell of the stuff. I thought being fond of a man was just what I needed.'

She made a face. 'I think it's called the rebound.'

'I believe it is.'

We were quiet for a moment.

'So,' she said at length, sitting up straight. 'It's divorce, is it?'

'That would be pleasant. Sadly, though, it's looking unlikely.'

'Why?'

'Harry doesn't want one.'

'So what? What can he do about it?'

'Take Ivo away from me.'

'Oh, don't be ridiculous,' she scoffed. 'How can he possibly do that? You're the mother, you're bound to get custody!'

'He says he'll tell the court what an unfit mother I am. Cite my cruelty. Say I pinch Ivo in his sleep, burn him with cigarettes, that kind of thing.'

Philly went pale. 'That's absurd, no one would ever believe him!'

'I agree, they probably wouldn't, but there's always a chance, isn't there? He says he'll get his friends in high places to corroborate and, believe me, he's got quite a few. Harry believes himself to be minor aristocracy, Phil, thinks all his cronies will come out of the ancestral woodwork to cloak him in lies, support him.'

'Of course they won't, no one would compromise themselves like that, perjure themselves in court. He's living in cloud-cuckoo-land!'

I shrugged. 'So perhaps he'll be more devious. Fabricate the evidence, mock up some photos of Ivo looking distressed with felt pen bruises on his arms, I don't know.'

'Don't!' She sprang up sharply from the bench. 'Don't, I can't bear it!'

She walked quickly to her vegetables, stooped down, wrenched up cabbages and flung them in her basket like a thing possessed. Her cheeks were pink with anger. For some reason it suddenly reminded me of a time long ago, when we were little, staying with our grandmother in Cheltenham. Opposite Granny's townhouse was a hairdresser's which could be seen from a bedroom window, and one morning my brother Tom and I telephoned the number on the shop front and in false, grown-up voices booked an entire day's worth of fictitious appointments. We watched, convulsed with laughter, clutching each other, as the young receptionist wrote them diligently in her book. When we confided our guilty, giggly secret to Philly, she clapped her hands over her ears in horror, crying, 'Don't! Don't, I can't bear it! That poor girl, it's too dreadful!'

Harry's deceit was of course on a much grander scale, but it reminded me that Philly couldn't take cruelty in any denomination.

'I'm exaggerating, Phil,' I said gently. 'I'm sure he wouldn't stoop to that.'

When she turned round she had two bright spots of colour burning high in her cheeks.

'He's a pig, isn't he?' she whispered.

I smiled. This was as vile as Philly could get.

'Oh, yes,' I agreed. 'No doubt about that.'

She nodded. I got up and we wandered slowly back towards the house, arm in arm.

'Anyway,' she said suddenly, stopping as we crossed the yard, 'he works all day, how could he possibly look after a child?'

'Ah, but that's where you're wrong. He doesn't actually work at all. He makes a big show of going upstairs to his office but that's as far as it goes. In reality he makes a few phone calls, farts a lot and snores on his sofa.'

77

'Which makes him totally unfit to look after a two-year-old!' she snorted.

'Well, you and I both know that, but some like-minded judge might think him a fine upstanding fellow with both time and money at his disposal to care for his only begotten child.'

She swung me round to face her. 'You're not going to let this put you off, are you? You're surely still going to go through with it?'

'Yes, I am. I'm certainly moving out, Alice says I can borrow her cottage for a bit, but I've got to see a solicitor, Philly. I've got to take advice. If there's any chance at all that I might lose Ivo, I couldn't do it. He's my whole life.' Tears welled up in my throat, my eyes, my nose. I swallowed them down hard.

'That won't happen,' she said staunchly. 'Any solicitor worth his salt will tell you Harry hasn't got a hope in hell.' She frowned. 'Did you say Alice's cottage?'

'Yes, it's not far from here actually, just over the other side of the valley.'

'Yes, I know, I went there once.' She made a face. 'It's pretty primitive, you know, Rosie. It's barely got indoor plumbing and electricity. Why don't you stay here with us?'

'Thanks, you're sweet, but I'd rather be on my own. No offence, but I just want to sort myself out. It'll be great having you so close, of course,' I added, not wanting to sound ungrateful. 'When did you see the cottage?'

'Oh, ages ago,' she said vaguely. 'Some friends of ours rented it before Alice. It's the old gardener's place on a big estate.'

'I know, I thought I might go and have a look tomorrow morning. Can I stay the night, Phil? I don't feel like going back and facing Harry and the parents.'

'You mean he's still there? After all that's been said?'

'Oh, of course. Don't forget, we're happily married. There'll be no more silly talk of divorce, Old Thing.'

She shuddered. 'Of course you can stay,' she squeezed my arm, 'and I'll come and look at the cottage with you in the morning. I'm sure we can do something with it, paint the walls, put a few rugs down . . .'

'A few fresh flowers?' I inquired.

She laughed. My mother's answer to life's rich tapestry was always to 'put a few fresh flowers about the place'.

'You don't want to let her anywhere near it, incidentally,' Philly warned. 'She'll be wrinkling her nose in disgust and smelling rats in the attic and damp in the mattresses and God knows what in the cellar. She'll have you out of there in no time.'

'I don't think she'll want to come anywhere near it anyway,' I said quietly.

'What d'you mean?'

I shrugged. 'I just have a hunch that when she knows the lie of the land, her sympathies will be firmly in her son-in-law's camp rather than mine.'

'Oh, don't be ridiculous,' she said warmly. 'Mum's pretty asinine at the best of times but even she knows blood's thicker than water.'

'Depends what colour the blood is,' I said grimly. 'Anyway, time will tell.'

Chapter Six

'Congratulations!' Philly's husband Miles boomed at me over his breakfast the following morning. 'That's the best news I've heard all winter!'

I blinked. 'Miles, I think you're supposed to say something along the lines of how sorry you are and how the break up of a marriage is always a cause for regret and have I really thought through the implications?'

'Could do,' he agreed, wiping some bread around his eggy plate, 'just to satisfy your middle class sensibilities, but the fact remains that it's the best decision you've made for years and far better to make it now while you're still young and you've got a good chance of re-marrying and giving Ivo the chance of a half decent father.' He popped the bread in his mouth and grinned at me disarmingly.

I couldn't help grinning back. I'd always found Miles's propensity to say what everyone else was thinking but daren't articulate rather refreshing.

'Oh, for heaven's sake, Miles, a little tact could be engendered just for once, couldn't it?' admonished Philly, who didn't always find it so refreshing.

'Why?' Miles turned round to face her as she cooked at the Aga. 'Tact might cloud the issue, force her to take her eye off the ball. She knows she's made a mistake and everyone else knows she's made a mistake. The man's a fat oaf and he needs marginalising in the nicest possible way, that's all there is to it.'

'He wasn't that fat when I met him,' I said defensively, although quite who I was defending here I wasn't sure.

'Well, he's certainly making up for it now. The last time I saw him wobbling towards me in that ridiculous Paisley dressing gown of his at your parents' house I seriously thought it was Demis Roussos in a kaftan, thought he was going to break into one of those Greek bandannas – ever and ever for ever and ever you'll b-eeeeeee the one,' he warbled, rising up from his chair and waving his arms evangelically.

I giggled but Philly wasn't amused. I'd noticed recently that she was irritated by some of his antics sometimes. She slammed the dishwasher door shut as she passed it.

'Miles, Rosie is not divorcing Harry because of his weight problem, okay? Believe it or not there's a little more to it than that.'

'Oh, I'm sure there is.' He turned his chair round and swung a leg over it, straddling it backwards. 'All the same, it'll be a relief to give up the night shift, eh Rosie?' He winked at me. 'All that rib crushing, all that gasping for air, all that tantric sex because you haven't got any choice, you simply can't move; all those secret fears about dying on the job and being found squashed like a pancake by the paramedics and—'

'Miles!' Philly's face was pink. 'Why is it that you constantly feel impelled to cross the bounds of good taste?'

'Sorry, sorry.' Miles scratched his head sheepishly. 'Just a joke, darling. Rosie doesn't mind, do you?'

'Not in the least, and if you must know Miles, it was more like being laid on by a large wardrobe with a very small key.' I grinned as Miles stifled a guffaw from his wife. No, I didn't mind my brother-in-law's banter, but then I didn't have quite the broad stroke of gentility that Philly had. I could roar with laughter at dirty jokes and sexual innuendo with the best of them, but Philly had always had a problem on that score. It made her uncomfortable, just as unlined drawers and milk bottles on the table did too. I'm not saying she'd ever put blue water down the loo or have lavender air fresheners in the bathroom, but in many respects she was very much our mother's daughter.

Miles, actually, had been terribly good for her. Everyone waxed lyrical about what a lucky man he was to have her, but Miles's slightly earthy, vulgar streak and his ability to air a prejudice without inhibition was just what Philly needed to stop her being prissy and priggish. I watched them now: Miles, tall, broad shouldered with curly dark hair, Viyella checked shirt and balding cords, very much the Gloucestershire farmer, getting up to cajole his pretty pouting wife at the Aga, deliberately patting her bum in front of me; and Philly, blushing, swatting his hand away, trying not to laugh, then laughing anyway as he restored her good humour. Despite their differences, or perhaps because of them, they made a good team and they knew it. And if Miles was a little lacking in the cerebral department, he certainly made up for it in the affable, hail-fellow-well-met department, qualities which were far more useful in his line of work down here. Miles was at his happiest propping up the bar in the village pub, talking crop yields and winter wheat and set-asides with the labourers and farmers or anyone, in fact, who cared to share a pint with him, buying everyone within hollering distance a drink and generally relaxing into his role of the country squire who had no problems remaining a man of the people. Miles had inherited the thousand-acre farm from his father, and his father before him. He knew everyone in the community, was well liked and well respected. He had eased gracefully into his place in life. His was an unshakeably happy lot.

'Lovely arse,' he murmured, still patting away.

'Oh, Miles!'

'Sorry.' He abandoned his wife's behind and hugged her shoulders instead.

'She's a terrible prude, you know,' he confided to me. 'Still gets undressed in the dark.'

'Who said anything about getting undressed?' Philly gave him a playful shove, but then, no doubt remembering Harry and the nightie lifting, shot me a sudden, guilty look. I sent her a placatory one back but I'm not sure she intercepted it.

'I bought her a vibrator for her birthday this year, for a joke,' said Miles, 'and she opened it just as your mother came walking through the front door bearing flowers and presents.'

'No!' I gasped.

'Oh yes, I couldn't stop her. I was quietly tiptoeing from the room to go and dig a hole in which to die, when I was suddenly halted by Philly saying, "What is it, darling?" I slowly turned round, looked solemnly into two pairs of wide, puzzled eyes and told them it was a cordless egg whisk.'

'Don't tell me they believed you!'

'Of course they did. "Oh isn't that marvellous!" trilled your mother, and, "Gosh, how handy – no cord!" from your sister, and then off they scurried to the kitchen to whisk up some double cream with it.'

'Did it work?' I gasped.

'I've no idea, Rosie, but I certainly didn't have cream with my apple pie that day. I'm thinking of getting your mother one for Christmas actually. I'd love to see it hanging up in her kitchen – you know, on her implement rack, next to the potato masher and the fish slice. A nice big black one, I thought.'

I giggled. 'Imagine if it caught on!'

'Well quite. Imagine if Marjorie got one, and Yvonne, and every other middle-aged housewife in West Oxfordshire. Imagine all their exhausted husbands coming home from work to be confronted with their sixty-plus wives, strapped into their pinnies, all gripping huge black phalluses, furiously whisking away at the egg whites and wondering why it was taking so long to form soft peaks.'

We fell about laughing and Philly sank helplessly into her husband's shoulder. I watched as he hugged her to him, laughing into each other's eyes. Suddenly a huge wave of self-pity threatened to engulf me. I stood up, shaking it off determinedly, but my mirth had evaporated.

'Right then,' I said decisively. 'I'm going to drag Ivo away from his cousins upstairs and then I'm off to see this cottage. Coming, Phil?'

'What cottage?' Miles grinned up at me, still holding on to his wife.

'Alice Feelburn, a friend of mine, owns it – well, rents it, actually. She's lending it to me, it's over on the Basswater estate.'

'I know,' he nodded. 'We've met the Feelburns, haven't we, Phil?'

'Yes, of course,' said Philly shortly.

She made no further comment but I remembered that she and Alice had never exactly hit it off. A couple of years ago, when Alice had suddenly announced that she was taking a weekend cottage in a village literally ten minutes from my sister, I'd been absolutely delighted and had promptly instigated a dinner party at Philly's place so they could all meet. It hadn't been the greatest social success. Philly and Alice had irritated each other from the word go, with Philly, probably because of nerves, coming across as more than usually Mrs Perfect, and Alice, on the defensive, more aggressively Bohemian than usual, eulogising about backpacking in Istanbul and the joys of orgies on the beaches – something I'm quite sure she'd never indulged in. Philly had been duly horrified and to change the subject had mentioned Bertie getting a place at a school that was known to be fiercely academic, whereupon Alice, thinking she was bragging, had launched an attack on pushy mothers. Philly had then produced some delicious profiteroles and Alice had remarked that M&S did some marvellous puddings too and had Philly ever tried them. Philly, genuinely astounded that anyone might even consider it, had said no, of course not! Alice, believing herself to be patronised, had bristled furiously. As the evening limped on, Philly had started raving about some terrific new power shower she'd just had installed, and said it was so marvellous she used it twice a day, whereupon Alice had said, what a ridiculous waste of water, people washed far too much these days and three times a week was really quite sufficient. Philly had said, oh, don't be silly, anyone who only washed three times a week would start to smell, and Alice had said, actually *she* only took a bath three times a week, and Philly had said, yes, well, there you go. Hmmm. More profiteroles anyone?

The men, meanwhile, sensing that the women weren't exactly hitting it off, had proceeded to overcompensate by getting quietly but spectacularly drunk, and Miles had ended the evening by insisting that Philly should climb on a chair and show everyone her Father Christmas knickers. 'Cummon, darling, don't be sush a shpoilshport, everyone wants to seeee! Oh cummon, dar-*ling*!'

Philly had eventually stormed from the room in tears. It had been a memorable evening and remained a salutary reminder that just because one loves two people dearly, it doesn't necessarily mean that they themselves will automatically bond. In fact, it rarely happens.

I sighed as I recalled, and went to the phone on the dresser to ring Alice. I needed to discover where the key to the cottage was. There was no answer, but I left a message on her machine, knowing she was probably sipping coffee at her kitchen table but wanted to hear who was ringing her first.

'You'll have some breakfast before we go, won't you, Rosie?'

I turned to see Philly brandishing a spatula at the stove. 'Oh, er, what is it?' I looked nervously at Miles's plate. The funny thing about Philly was that she was a marvellous dinner party cook but very hit or miss on an everyday basis. This was chiefly because she insisted on using up absolutely everything in the fridge before she went shopping again, which of course is very laudable, and can be quite delicious if the leftovers happen to be eggs, smoked salmon and cream for instance, but when it's haddock, salami, baked beans and yoghurt – which Philly was quite capable of chucking into the liquidiser and whisking up into a heave-making soup – I tended to pass and make myself a sandwich. I'd once, in a very giggly moment, sellotaped a piece of cold, cooked macaroni to a postcard and sent it to her saying, Philly, what on earth can I do with this? I've run out of ideas.

'Sausage and courgette omelette is on the menu today,' murmured Miles as at that moment the phone rang.

'That'll be Alice,' I said gratefully, launching myself at it.

'Saved by the bell,' he muttered drily.

'The key to the cottage?' said Alice when I asked her. 'Oh, you'll have to call in at the house for that. I used to leave it under a geranium pot but it went walkabout once, so now Joss has the spare.'

'Joss?'

'Jocelyn Dubarry, you know, the sculptor. He's on the telly a lot, does all those highbrow arty programmes on BBC 2, bit of a modern Michelangelo. You've heard of him, surely?'

I hadn't, but then the programmes I watched were decidedly middle brow, verging on the low.

'Oh well, anyway, he lives at the manor, our cottage is in his grounds. You'll see when you get there, you have to go past his house to get to us. Don't be put off by him by the way, his bark is much worse than his bite, it's just that being an artist and all that he hates being disturbed.'

'Hadn't you better ring him first and tell him I'm coming?' I said nervously, not really relishing the barking.

'Oh, I will, don't worry, I'll do that now. Listen Rosie, I've um, I've been talking to Michael about you having the cottage.' She sounded embarrassed.

'Oh, right. Is he not keen?'

'Oh no, it's not that, it's just rather than us lend it to you and then come down at weekends, we wondered – well he wondered actually – if you'd be able to take over the whole thing. Then we'd give it up, as it were. It's just that, to be honest, it's always been a bit of an extravagance and we hardly ever use it these days and Michael says we can't really afford to let you, sort of, have it for free . . .' she trailed off sheepishly.

'No, no, that's fine,' I said quickly. 'I'll take over the rent and there's no reason why you can't still come down at weekends if you want to. I wasn't expecting to have it for nothing. How much is it?'

She mentioned a sum so exorbitant it made my eyes water and my knees buckle, but I needed this house badly. I'd find the rent somehow. If I was making a break for it I wanted to get right out of London and a cottage near Philly was perfect.

'That's okay,' I said faintly.

'Oh, great,' she sounded relieved. 'Only you know what Michael's like, I can't really argue with him over something like this.'

This was true. For all Alice's breast-beating about feminist enlightenment, at the end of the day it was the man in the natty pinstriped suit with the chiselled chin and the fine line in charm who wore the trousers in that house.

'But I thought he still worked quite a lot in Cheltenham? Won't he need the cottage during the week?'

'He still goes down there about once a week but to be honest he'd much rather stay in a hotel with a decent bathroom and a hot meal in the dining room which the company pays for anyway. He's been doing that recently because, apart from anything else, in the winter it takes about a day to get the cottage warm and to air the beds, and then just when it's all cosy, he's off again.'

'Well, tell him he's welcome to come and stay any time, and listen, don't forget to clear all this with the sculptor chappie, will you? He might not take kindly to a new tenant just pitching up and moving in.'

'Oh, yes, I'll ring him now, but don't worry, as long as I recommend you, he'll be fine. Joss is the last person to worry about that sort of thing,' she promised. 'He's pretty cool.'

When Philly and I arrived at Farlings Manor an hour or so later, minus the children who'd stayed with Miles, it soon became clear that this man was anything but cool. As we stood on the steps of his gorgeous, crumbling Cotswold manor house for what seemed like an eternity, the door was finally flung back and a tall, well built, angry looking man with tawny hair and heavy lidded eyes glowered down at us.

'Yes?' he said irritably.

Philly nearly fell off the step in alarm.

'Oh, um, I'm sorry to bother you,' I stammered. 'We're friends of Alice Feelburn.'

'And who the hell is Alice Feelbum?' he drawled.

'Burn,' I corrected, stifling an immature giggle. 'She's, er, your tenant. In the cottage? Didn't she telephone to say we were coming?'

'If she did it's still on the answer machine. I don't take calls when I'm working if I can help it and as a rule I don't answer the door either.' As he spoke he stared fixedly at Philly, as most people do. His evident distraction gave me a little steel.

'I'm so sorry, we've clearly interrupted you,' I said smoothly. 'Let's start again. I'm Rosie Meadows and this is my sister Philippa Hampton.' I held out my hand, smiling determinedly.

His eyes came back to me. He took my hand. 'We've met.'

I blinked. 'We have?'

'Outside a solicitor's office in Kensington. You're a little more decisive today than you were then, Mrs Meadows.'

'Oh!' I was taken aback, but yes, of course, those eyes, that subtle American drawl. I gaped. 'Gosh, how strange that we should both be—'

'Seeing divorce lawyers? I agree, except that mine was a purely social call. My brother-in-law runs the joint and he keeps a very fine malted Scotch in his bottom drawer. What's your excuse?'

'I – don't have one,' I stammered, feeling myself blush.

God, this man was rude. Rude and intrusive, and actually not nearly as good looking as I'd originally thought. His face, though tanned, was tense and drawn and he was older than I'd imagined too. His baggy navy jumper and cords were strangely covered in dust, and without the Savile Row suit he'd lost that urbane suaveness.

'So what can I do for you?' he demanded briskly.

Apart from not ask us in, of course, I thought, but I stifled my annoyance. I needed this cottage. I took a deep breath and explained Alice's offer.

'So you want to take over the rent from her, is that it?'

'Please. If you don't mind.'

He considered us as if we were a couple of urchins touting for a car wash or something.

A telephone rang from inside the house. He glanced back. 'I'll have to take that. It's probably my wife calling from the States. Come in a minute.'

Marvelling at how he could distinguish between the time-wasting calls that took him from his work and important ones from America, we followed him into a large, honey-coloured hall, two walls of which were lined from top to toe with books. Underfoot, deep red Turkish rugs took the chill off the ancient grey flagstones and a fire burned brightly in the grate, completing the glowing red and gold effect. I sighed. It was the ultimate in luxury, I thought, to have a fire burning just to take your coat off in front of. He answered the telephone on an antique bureau in the corner.

'Hello? Annabel! Where the hell have you been, I've been calling you all morning . . . Oh, okay, okay, well, at least I've got you now. I take it you'll be back on Tuesday, at least that's the message I got from some lackey of yours . . . Thursday, I see.' He sounded grim. 'Amazing how it creeps up and up, isn't it? We'll be into the millennium soon.'

Poor Annabel, I thought, joining Philly by the fire and warming the backs of my legs. He must be hell to live with. I turned round to warm the fronts and surreptitiously gazed at the photographs on the stone mantel in front of me. There was a family group in a silver frame of him, his wife – presumably Annabel – and three rather beautiful children, a boy and a brace of identical girls, all with blonde hair, creamy skins and bright blue eyes. I gazed at their mother. She was absolutely stunning too but in contrast to her children, sleekly dark with a strong, intelligent face, large brown eyes and swift dark strokes for eyebrows. Suddenly I realised I recognised her. Gosh, yes, of course, she was one of those American health Hitlers, wasn't she? Very young, tremendously successful and wrote all those books about how to run your life, your diet, your lover, and God knows what else. Of course, Annabel Johnson. God she looked far too young to have those strapping school-age children flanking her, must have slipped them out when she was about eighteen, in between best-selling books and TV appearances. I sighed. Made you realise some people didn't waste any time making a success of their lives, did they? And look how long I'd fannied around making a complete mess of mine.

I turned back to look at Joss, studying him as he finished his conversation with his wife. He looked slightly mollified now, barking marginally less and smiling occasionally. His face, as it softened, was undoubtedly handsome if a little haughty for my taste. As he half turned, giving us the benefit of his profile, the light from an artfully poised lamp on the bureau fell on him, highlighting the lines around his eyes and the few flecks of dust in his hair. Presumably he had quite a job keeping up with Annabel. He put the receiver down.

'Sorry about that.' He stared at us for a moment as if he couldn't quite remember what we were doing there. I saw him divert his gaze to Philly again. 'Oh, okay, the cottage.' He opened the bureau drawer and brought out a bunch of keys. 'Well, if the Feelburns want to pass it over, that's fine by me. You'd better come and see it first though, before you get excited. It's a helluva dump. Come on.'

Well, whose fault is that, O landlord? I thought as he ushered us out through the ancestral porch. He banged the door shut behind us and set off at a cracking pace down the gravel drive. Philly and I scampered after him. The drive forked at some trees and we followed the right hand curl as it swept round and down, behind the back of the house, heading for the garden. Beyond the garden were some paddocks, then meadows which dipped down into a valley and were crossed by a stream, before soaring up the hill on the other side, far away into the distance. I caught my breath at the sheer beauty of the vista, then turned round and looked back at the house, perched on the brow of the hill behind us. It was certainly huge, but very mellow and totally in tune with the surrounding landscape and the picture perfect village below. It was almost as if a spontaneous natural eruption of Cotswold stone had risen up from the ground hundreds of years ago, settled there, and then been given the finishing touches by a sympathetic human hand which had sketched in a collection of Gothic windows, a few doors, some arches, and a smattering of pinnacles and gargoyles, before nature had returned once again, lavishly coating the whole edifice with a web of wisteria, vines and honeysuckles, softening the whole effect.

'Gorgeous house,' I muttered shyly.

He glanced back over his shoulder. 'Could be, but it's going to rack and ruin inside. It's too goddam big – costs a fortune to run. I'd like to pull half of it down to tell you the truth, it would certainly save on the heating bills.'

I'd got to the stage in my own disastrous life when I was faintly irritated by people who belly-ached about their own good fortune. If you were going to complain about living in a pile, give it away to the local peasants for God's sake. Go and live in a caravan.

'You might try turning some radiators off,' I suggested lightly. 'It's a little less extreme.'

He had the grace to smile. We strode through a stable yard and out the other side at breakneck speed, then he turned to look at me quizzically.

'It'll just be you in the cottage, will it?'

'And my little boy, Ivo. He's two and a bit.'

'Oh, okay. So where's the father?'

'We're not living together any more.' I looked him in the eye. 'That's what I was doing in the solicitor's office yesterday.'

'Ah. Sorry. I don't mean to pry but I guess I have to vaguely know the set up.' It was a genuine apology and I accepted it as such.

'That's all right, I understand. Oops!' I steadied myself as I tripped over some huge lumps of stone in the yard.

'One of the hazards of living here I'm afraid,' he remarked. 'That's my debris from the workshop. Any bits I don't need I just chuck out here. That's where I work.' He nodded over at a large barn, the huge black doors bolted and barred. 'Where I mould and tap away. Quite a lot of it joins the crap out here.' He kicked at a boulder.

Ah so that's where all his precious sculptures were. A barn full of bronzes and bits of old rock no doubt. I wondered what they were like. Alice had said he was an Associate Professor at the Royal College of Art, so I supposed he must be pretty good.

'Are these yours too?' I asked, nodding at the herd of hairy cattle gazing at us over the fence.

'Yeah, they're Longhorns. I only keep a very small herd, but animal sculptures are pretty popular at the moment so I use them for models. I'm only interested in ancient breeds though – Belted Galways, that type of thing.'

'My husband's a farmer,' said Philly with a smile. 'You probably know him. Miles Hampton?'

He looked at her. 'You know, I don't believe I do.' It was said politely, but coldly. Philly blushed, unused to getting such a chilly reception.

He stopped suddenly and Philly and I, slightly behind, almost cannoned into him like a couple of cartoon characters. 'Here we are then,' he said, 'and don't say I didn't warn you.'

I looked around in surprise. We'd been passing a row of what I'd assumed were just farm outbuildings, but I now saw that tacked on to the end of one of the barns was a tiny stone cottage, almost a lean-to, an afterthought.

Joss jingled his bunch of keys, peering for the requisite one. 'Annabel usually deals with all this, I haven't been in here for years so – Christ, these keys all look the same, ah, wait a bit, here we go.' He separated a key from the rest and stuck it in the lock. 'Like I say, I haven't a clue what it's like inside. Oh hell. The damned door's stuck.'

He stood back, put his shoulder to the flaky blue paint and as it flew open he flew with it, disappearing into the gloom. Philly and I followed rather more cautiously under the low doorway. It was very dark, very musty and from what one could determine extremely small.

'Can't see a damn thing,' said Joss.

'That's because there are shutters,' I said eagerly. I ran across to fling them open. Cold winter light streamed in through dirty windows.

'Oh look,' I cried, spinning round. 'It's sweet!'

'It's not sweet at all, it's a disgrace,' he said, gazing about him. We took in the threadbare green carpet, the sofa exploding with rusty, exposed springs, the faded rose wallpaper curling at the corners where it met the low ceiling which was sprinkled with suspiciously pale brown water marks, the general air of mustiness and neglect.

'It's damp,' said Philly, wrinkling her nose in disgust.

'Nonsense, it just needs a good airing. No one's been here for a while, that's all.' I crossed the room – in about three strides – and flung open the shutters at the other window, letting in more light. I tried to open the window too, but hastily shut it again as it threatened to come right off its hinges. I looked around, ignoring my disapproving companions. I, too, could sense neglect, the decay, but I could also see an encouragingly large open fireplace and a pretty bay window with a wooden window seat which looked out on the most marvellous view across open Gloucestershire countryside. I gazed far away into the dark green winter fields, all parcelled up and neatly tied with low, grey, drystone walls and sprinkled liberally with sheep.

'Oh, it's bliss!' I breathed.

'Rosie, you can't possibly live here,' Philly's angry voice called from elsewhere. 'Come and look at the kitchen. This place is *much* worse than I thought.'

I had to admit, the kitchen took a bit of laughing off. There was a cooker of sorts, but it looked decidedly pre-war and the cracked enamel sink defied anyone to fill it with water. The white paint was peeling off the walls and the red lino floor was more than cracked, it was erupting all over the place like teenage acne.

'Superficial,' I said defiantly. 'A lick of paint, a few nails in the floor, some rush mats, a bowl in the sink and it'll be fine. I can fix this place up in no time.'

'Your sister's right,' said Joss, walking in looking grim. 'I've just been inspecting the plumbing, there's no way you can live here with a little kid. I don't know what Annabel was thinking of letting it out in the first place. Even as a weekend cottage it's a disgrace.'

'Please,' I put a hand on his arm. 'Please don't say that. Don't say I can't have it. It's fine, honestly, I can make it fine.'

He regarded me through his tawny lion's eyes. 'You'd have to be desperate to live here.'

'I am desperate.'

There was a silence.

'Don't be silly, of course she's not!' said Philly hotly. 'You know very well you can come and live with us, Rosie!'

I swung round to her. 'I know I can, Philly, but I don't want that, I want . . .' I struggled. 'I need,' I corrected, 'something of my own.'

I had a rather panicky feeling that if I did go to Philly and Miles's place I might never get out. That it would all be too cosy, that Ivo and I would sink down into their sumptuous, ragged and swagged Colefax and Fowler spare rooms for ever, become part of my big sister's nest, just a couple of extra beaks that needed feeding. I had to start again on my own, repair my life on my own terms, and this rickety old cottage in need of a certain amount of repair itself fitted the bill. We could get sorted out together.

'All this place needs,' I said, turning to Joss, 'is a jolly good clean, a lick of paint and some new curtains and I can make those. I can do all that sort of thing myself, really, I'm a demon with a needle.'

He was watching me closely. I knew he'd seen my need and I saw him hesitate.

'Let's take a look upstairs,' he said finally.

Upstairs, happily, was slightly better. The paper was at least still clinging to the walls, the carpets were not overtly worn and the fittings in the bathroom, although clearly old, were at least clean and operational.

'See?' I said triumphantly. 'It's perfect!'

'It's marginally better than downstairs but it's far from perfect,' said Joss grimly. 'Most of this furniture is hopeless, it's falling to bits.'

He bent down to examine an old pine chair that had clearly lost a leg and was only balancing because the fourth one had been propped into position. He kicked it and it duly collapsed.

'Why Annabel sees fit to stuff the place with garbage like this is beyond me. All this folksy old pine rubbish is riddled with wood-worm when she buys it in the first place, it probably all comes from car boot sales.'

'I like it,' I said smiling. 'I like old things.'

I sat down on the ancient iron bed, happily patting the mattress. Yes, this really could be home for a bit. I could see us living here, could see Ivo in that sweet little room next door where the eaves dropped down almost to the floor and the two windows poked out like beady eyes. I'd do that room first, I decided, paint it in a day, put a border up for him, clean the carpet, hang curtains, put all his toys around. He'd love it. Become a real country child. Joss looked down at me sitting on the bed. He frowned.

'Do you have a problem with reproduction?'

I was startled. 'Er, no! At least, not with Ivo, I conceived straight away actually. Why?' God, what sort of question was that? Was the squire into breeding from his tenants or something? Was this some sort of archaic tithe?

'Furniture,' he said gently. 'We were talking about furniture, weren't we? I was going to send you off to John Lewis with my account card, that's if you don't have any qualms about sitting in new chairs. Annabel will only deign to park her backside if generations of gentry have done so before her.'

'Oh!' I flushed, feeling stupid but mightily relieved. 'No, I don't have a problem with that at all, in fact that would be great!' Crikey, let loose in a department store with someone else's credit card? My eyes began to shine. 'You mean – I can have it? Can I? Can I really? Oh, thank you so much!' I tried to resist kissing him.

'On one condition.'

'What's that?'

'That you have someone come in and sort out the plumbing, fix it up with a half decent kitchen and then go and buy some proper furniture. I don't want to be taken to court because a waif and a baby have contracted diphtheria from living in unsanitary conditions in my back yard.'

'Oh, I will, I will, I'll do all that – oh, Philly, I can have it!' I yelled over the banisters to my sister, who hadn't followed us up.

She shivered and disappeared into her coat collar, thrusting her hands into her pockets. 'Lucky you,' she said grimly.

'Let's say we'll halve the rent while the place is being fixed up,' Joss said, moving towards the top of the stairs. 'You'll be doing me a favour by simply being here and overseeing all the work.'

'You mean I can have it for half of what Alice said?'

'For the moment. Although I have to say, when Annabel gets back . . .' he hesitated. 'Sure, yes. For the moment.'

'Oh, thank you! Thank you so much!' My eyes, inexplicably, filled with tears.

He frowned and looked at me carefully. 'Do you always get so excited about derelict cottages?'

I shook my head, blinking. 'No, I'm sorry, I'm a bit emotional today. It's just – well, I'm not used to getting breaks, that's all.'

'You've had a bad time,' he said simply.

'A bit,' I admitted.

He regarded me a moment longer. Then he straightened up. 'Well, come on,' he said abruptly. 'Let's go. I think your horrified sister would like to get the hell out of here.'

Chapter Seven

When I arrived back at my parents' house in time for lunch, my mother was waiting for me. She was ominously stationed, pale-faced and erect, with her back to the drawing-room fire, the scene of many a showdown. Her chin was high, her lips pursed but trembling, and she was fingering her pearls manically. All bad signs.

'How does it feel to make a grown man cry!' she demanded theatrically as I walked in. 'How does it feel, Rosie, hmm? He's out there,' she pointed a quivering finger gardenwards, 'sobbing, yes, *sobbing* his heart out. It's pitiful!' Her voice rose to a tortured cry.

Philly and Miles, who'd followed my car, came in behind me now, their children and Ivo in tow.

'Do you know what she's done?' Mummy cried. 'Hmm? Have you heard, Philly? Miles? She's divorcing him! Leaving him for some common little loose-limbed lout she found shelf-stacking in the supermarket!'

'Oh, Mum, no, that's bollocks. Did he tell you that?'

'Don't you use that foul language with me, young lady,' she rounded on me fiercely, 'and no, he wasn't that graphic, mercifully. He said he found you both incontrovertibly together – those were the very words he used – in the marital bedroom, and I deduced the rest of the distasteful details for myself, thank you very much!' She wrapped her pale blue Pringle cardigan round her tightly and sniffed. 'Oh, I may not be a woman of the world,' she quavered. 'I may not have smoked pot and had free love on beanbags like your generation, but I do know a little hussy when I see one!'

Philly put a restraining hand on her arm. 'Calm down, Mum, and incidentally,' she jerked her head in the direction of four gaping children, '*pas devant les enfants*, okay?'

Miles turned them all round and hustled them out of the door. 'Come on, kids, let's go and find Grandpa in the garden, shall we?'

'You'll get nothing,' she whispered, 'nothing! No money, no house, no Stockley Hall!' Her voice cracked at this and she frantically ferreted up her sleeve for a crumpled tissue, burying her nose in it. 'No one's going to want you either, you realise that, don't you? A thirty-something woman with a child – you've got a past now, you're shop-soiled! You'll never find anyone else to take you on, and just when I thought you were finally beginning to amount to something! You'll never amount to anything now!'

'Thanks, Mum, for that vote of confidence,' I muttered wearily. 'It's just what I need right now. Look, I made a mistake. I should never have married him and I simply can't live with him any longer, that's all there is to it. In his heart I think Harry knows that too.'

'Harry knows nothing!' she spat, drawing the pearls tighter and tighter round her neck for comfort. 'The poor man is distraught!'

'I'll go and see him.'

'Oh no, it's too late, he's gone,' she said, shaking her head frenziedly and turning wild eyes in the direction of the French windows. 'He's out there, walking blindly, gone for miles, I shouldn't wonder!' She gazed out to the manicured lawn and herbaceous border beyond as if it was a blasted heath and Heathcliff himself was staggering around out there, demented with grief. In truth, Harry had probably just waddled down the path, past the lavender bushes and just about made it to the summerhouse for a kip.

'God *knows* where he'll finally rest his head. In a ditch maybe. He's probably fallen in a stream already, but what do you care!'

My mother, when she felt like it, could be very amateur dramatic.

'Mum, the only water around here is in the Turners' swimming pool next door and I'm quite sure they'd have heard if he'd fallen in. Look, don't worry, I'll go and find him.'

She seized my arm. 'Tell him you've changed your mind,' she urged. 'Tell him it was all a terrible mistake, say you were hallucinating, say it was PMT, you know how unreasonable it makes you!'

'I can't do that, Mum, it's not true.'

She turned away. 'But what will everyone say?' she wailed. 'The Burdetts, the Fosters – I've told them all you're going to inherit Stockley Hall. What will I tell them now?'

My mother was nothing if not disingenuous. I rounded on her. 'That's all you're worried about, isn't it? Bloody Stockley Hall. You haven't even mentioned Ivo!'

'Because I can't bear to!' she whispered, raising her chin defiantly. 'Can't bear to think about what you're doing to that poor child, foisting a broken home on him, taking him from the arms of a father who dotes on him, who *adores* him!'

'Rubbish, Harry never has anything to do with Ivo, as you well know, and anyway he can see him whenever he likes. Every weekend if he wants, which is probably more than he sees him now.'

'You're cruel and heartless,' she said, and then to my alarm began to cry. 'You always were,' she sobbed. 'You never think of anyone but yourself. You certainly never think of me.'

'Good God, Mum,' snorted Philly, 'the only reason Rosie's in this diabolical mess is because she probably thought far too much about you in the first place!'

Suddenly I couldn't bear it any longer. I bolted from the room, ran upstairs, tore along the passage to my old bedroom and threw myself down on the bed, sobbing into my ancient, balding candlewick bedcover. After a while I wiped my eyes and flipped over. I stared at the bookshelves in the alcove in front of me. Enid Blyton, E.Nesbit and Noel Streatfeild were still in alphabetical order, and beneath them was the little blue desk I used to sit at to do my homework. Tucked neatly under it was the blue chair with its gingham cushion I'd made by hand. When I was a child, that chair always had to be tucked in like that, never pulled out or sprawling at an angle. Everything in here had to be in its place and perfect. Pencils then were lined up on the desk in regimental rows, next to my ruler, my rubber and my lucky gonk. Dolls from around the world in their national costumes had stood sentry-like on the now bare mantelpiece – Serbia next to Syria next to Thailand. I didn't know where these places were but I jolly well knew where they were on my shelf. Clothes were always folded with geometric precision and put away in piles, and rosettes and certificates marched neatly across a now bare cork notice board. Only I was allowed to clean my room, no one else did it to my satisfaction, no one else lined up my rug with absolute symmetry to my bed. Mum used to laugh, said I'd make a terrific little soldier, probably go on to run an army, she said. I bit my lip.

After a while, Philly came up. She sat on the side of the bed and took my hand.

'She doesn't mean it, you know. She's just upset.'

'She does. She'd rather I lived in abject misery for the rest of my life than disturb the status quo. Not to mention abandoning Harry's bloody inheritance.'

Philly considered this. 'You're probably right, but she'll get over it, you'll see. And Dad's as happy as Larry.'

'Really?'

'Well, he hasn't said as much, but you should see him charging around the garden with Miles and all the children playing football, he's like a new man.'

I sat up. 'Ivo's okay out there, is he?'

'Of course, he's on Dad's shoulders, they're key strikers.'

I smiled. 'He'll be all right, won't he? I mean, with Dad as a father figure?'

'Course he will,' she said staunchly. She gave me a sideways glance. 'For a bit. That was utter drivel Mum was touting down there, you know that, don't you? You'll find someone else.'

I blew my nose. 'I'm not sure I want to, Phil. I'm quite happy just with Ivo, and I can't wait to get started on that cottage. I'm better off on my own now.'

The telephone began to ring somewhere downstairs. Philly sighed and got off the bed. 'Well, we'll see. For the moment you're probably right, but later on . . . Listen, I could easily take Ivo off your hands for you for a week or two while you sort that dreadful cottage out.'

'Thanks, but I think I'll keep him close for the moment. I sort of – feel the need.'

'Sure.' She understood immediately. 'By the way, we're not having a proper lunch, it's just help yourself from the fridge – oh, for God's sake, would someone answer that bloody phone!' She went next door to Mum's bedroom and I heard her answer.

'Hello? . . . Oh, yes, she is.' Her voice went suddenly cold. 'Just a minute.' I waited for her to come back. 'It's for you. It's Alice.'

'Oh!' I sprang off the bed in surprise and went next door. Philly disappeared downstairs.

'Alice!'

'God, Rosie, I'm so sorry, what must you think of me!'

'What?'

'Leaving the cottage like that, in such a mess! It suddenly occurred to me, the last time I was there I left in a terrible hurry and I didn't have a chance to clean it up. I was quietly painting a bowl of oranges in the kitchen just now when my brush suddenly froze, I nearly died of embarrassment as I thought of it. Did Philly go with you too?' she asked anxiously.

'She did, but don't worry, we didn't notice a thing,' I lied.

'God, how appalling, but you know me, I don't really notice mess. Michael says I only change the sheets when they start to look like the Turin Shroud.'

'We didn't inspect the sheets and it all looked fine,' I soothed. 'And anyway, it's such a dear little place.'

'Well, it's pretty basic but then we were only there at weekends and we mostly just went in the summer for the garden. What did you think of Joss, by the way?'

'Well, he gradually loosened up, I suppose, but he's a bit prickly on first encounter, isn't he?'

'I don't think he means to be, it's just that he's incredibly busy and in another world most of the time. He's got loads of commissions now, the great and the good are all lining up for his pieces, so his dealer's constantly bullying him to produce. He's always dashing off to Italy to inspect pieces of marble too, has to see the raw material for himself apparently, and then he's all over the place with his exhibitions. So I think he's pretty stressed out one way and another. I have a suspicion he's a complete softy at heart actually. He certainly lets Annabel get away with murder. Did you meet her?'

'No, she's away at the moment, she rang from America while we were there though. What's she like?'

'Beautiful, successful and devastatingly charming but personally I'm not convinced.'

'What d'you mean?'

'Oh, I don't know. Perhaps I'm just being a bitch because I'm not beautiful, successful or remotely charming, but she's a touch too saccharine for my liking. You know who she is, don't you?'

'Yes, she writes all those self-help books.'

'Quite, and lives them too.'

'Really? In what way?'

'Well, I know people think I'm a bit alternative but she really is wacko. She's a Buddhist okay, so there's lots of chanting and meditating and all that, which is fine, but I wouldn't put it past her to dance naked in the moonlight either. She's a bit like that, our Annabel. Any fad going she embraces it.'

I giggled. 'Well I hope she doesn't do it in my garden. So who looks after the children then? You know, if she's away chanting at an ashram or something?

'Oh, they have a mother's help. She's absolutely hopeless but that doesn't bother Annabel because they're not her children anyway.'

'What d'you mean? Whose are they then?'

'They're from his first marriage. His wife died about six years ago, having the twins.'

'No! God, how tragic! I didn't think people died in childbirth any more?'

'Don't you believe it,' she said grimly. 'I heard on *Woman's Hour* the other day that one woman a second still dies of it, and you can bet your life they're not all squatting in bushes in the Third World but quietly expiring in some dodgy English cottage hospital. She had appalling pre-eclampsia so they were born much too early and her whole system collapsed. She died a few days later. He was devastated.'

'I can imagine. God, how awful! So when did he marry Annabel?'

'About two years ago. She made a bee line for him at one of his exhibitions, swept him right off his feet.'

'Why? I mean, she's gorgeous, isn't she? And famous too. Presumably she could have had anyone. It seems an odd choice somehow, a sad man with three small children in tow.'

'Ah, but think of the kudos, Rosie. He's revered in the art world. And if you ask me she fancies herself as his muse. And then of course there's that huge, terribly English manor house of his.'

'I saw, quite a place.'

'Could be, but it needs a lot of work inside, although I don't suppose he asked you in. He doesn't like visitors much.'

'So we gathered. Oh well,' I sighed, 'I won't have much to do with them down at the cottage, will I?'

'Very little. They're actually very good at not poking their noses in, and as long as you don't, it works both ways.'

'Well, I certainly won't. Thanks, Alice, this is such a lifeline for me at the moment.'

I said goodbye and sat for a moment on Mum's bed, hugging my knees to my chest. After a while I got off and stole across to her cheval mirror in the corner by the chintz curtains. So often in the past I'd got dressed in my own bedroom and then, lacking a full-length mirror, had hastened in here to get the full effect. In those days the Full Effect had always been the same: glowing with good health, optimism and shiny blonde hair but too pudgy by half, and I'd spend the next five minutes furiously re-angling the mirror as if that was the problem, tugging away at my clothes trying to reduce the bulges and putting talcum powder on my cheeks to minimise the bucolic Nell Gwyn effect. I was almost shocked by what I saw today. Huge green eyes gazed back at me out of an almost thin face. My hair was still blonde but had lost all its shine and my clothes hung off me. God, I must have lost about two stone in as many years without even noticing it. I sighed and ran my fingers down my pale cheeks, thinking how I would have loved this gaunt look a few years ago. Pale and interesting, it was all I'd ever wanted, but now I'd got it, it just depressed me. I gulped hard. Depressed me? Rubbish, Rosie, this is the way forward. Buck up, no good looking back, we're going onwards and upwards, remember? I nodded firmly at my reflection. Right. That's more like it. And first thing next week I'd get a decent haircut, have a few sizzling highlights put in and borrow a pair of Philly's jeans which would at least fit me and, let's face it, I used to fantasise about borrowing her jeans.

The next time I encountered my family again was at supper that evening. Philly had cooked roast lamb since Mummy had apparently been rendered incapable of even lifting a potato peeler, and as she brought the vegetables through to the hotplate in the dining room, I slipped in and took the seat beside her. Harry was absent. I tried to ignore Mummy who was doing a lot of stagy sniffing opposite me, dabbing at her nose with her napkin and shooting me hurt, vengeful glances. Daddy was standing at the head of the table carving the joint and Miles, always oblivious of any sort of atmosphere, was in the throes of telling a supposedly hilarious story about a friend of his called Tarquin – Miles's friends were always called things like Tarquin – who, after a few too many jars in the local pub, had apparently felt unwell and hastened to the loo in order to chuck it all up.

'Unfortunately,' snorted Miles, 'he barged into a cubicle that was already occupied, some bald guy was sitting there having a crap, but, too late, old Tarquin throws up anyway, all over his head!' Miles's sides began to split. We waited patiently as he tried to gain control, to pick himself up from the parquet floor and continue, because clearly there was more.

Spluttering into his parsnips he went on, 'This guy, okay, the one on the loo, he can't believe it, right, and Tarquin said his face literally changed before him. First he's incredulous, then furious and finally he looks murderous, at which point old Tarquers, sensing a smack in the mouth is more or less due, has the presence of mind to punch him first, before turning round and legging it!' Tears fled down Miles's face. 'God, just imagine!' he gasped. 'There you are, just popping in for a quiet dump and a read of *The Sun* and the next minute – puke – wallop!'

My father paused in his carving, head to one side in a bemused fashion, genuinely willing to accept there was humour in this tale but struggling to deduce where it lay.

'But not funny from his point of view, surely, dear boy? The bald enthroned one? Vomit on head? Punch in the face?'

Mummy laughed politely. 'Oh, I don't know.' She didn't, actually. Hadn't the faintest idea what Miles was talking about and rarely did, but anyone who owned a thousand acres of prime Gloucestershire farmland deserved to have their jokes laughed at in her book. 'How very amusing. Mint sauce, anyone?'

'Well, no, all right, Gordon,' spluttered Miles, 'perhaps not funny from *his* point of view, but certainly—'

'Ah! Dear friends.' A voice cut through the proceedings.

We swung round as one to behold – Harry. He was standing in the open doorway, as I suspect he had been for some time, beaming benignly and swaying ominously. I swallowed hard. I'd rather assumed that Harry's tortured state had precluded his joining us, that he was still languishing grief-stricken in a woodshed somewhere, but I'd reckoned without his keen sense of smell and his ever demanding stomach. His hair was wet and neatly combed to one side like a small boy's, and underneath his jumper I noticed he'd even bothered to put a tie on, but that didn't disguise the fact that his cheeks were unnaturally flushed and his eyes over-bright. As he passed slowly round the table, he caught the back of my father's chair to steady himself. He was dangerously drunk.

'Or should I say,' he said quietly, 'dear family.' He paused unsteadily behind a vacant chair. 'I see I'm just in time. Elizabeth, may I?'

'Of course!' She pulled the chair out for him. 'Philly, lay a place for Harry, quick, and a napkin. No, not that one, darling, a pink one, with a nice lacy edge . . . well, in the drawer, of course!'

Harry lowered himself cautiously into his seat as Philly bustled around him with knives and forks.

'Now.' He beamed round the table. 'Where were we? Ah yes,' he raised a deliberate finger. 'Miles, you were in full flow, I believe, recounting a humorous tale in your own inimitable, rugger-bugger style. Pray continue, it sounded unmissable. Finally managed to get a lavatory, some vomit and a punch-up all in one story, eh? Congratulations, old man. Surprised you didn't manage to sneak in some anal sex too.'

There was a nasty silence. My mother cleared her throat. Smiled brightly. 'Lot of silly fuss made about that, if you ask me. Gordon and I do it at least once a year, if not more, don't we, darling?'

A horrified silence followed this little revelation.

'Mum!' gasped Philly, who'd gone very pale.

Daddy laid down his carving knife carefully. 'I think, my love, that you mean annual sex. I'm afraid what Harry suggested is rather different.'

Miles gave a Neanderthal snort. 'Just a bit! Oh God, poor old you, Gordon – annual sex! High days and holidays, eh? Oh, Elizabeth, you are priceless – ha ha! No, no, *anal* sex is completely different, it's when—'

'MILES!' Philly and I both shrieked together.

Miles stopped. 'I wasn't going to say,' he said in an injured tone. 'I was just going to explain that—'

'Yes, well, just *don't* explain, okay?' cried Philly, rising to her feet. 'Don't you lot ever know when to stop!' She turned furiously to the hotplate behind her on the pretext of getting more vegetables. There was a silence.

'Oh Lord,' said Harry in a low but perfectly audible voice, winking at Miles behind her stiff back, 'you've done it now, old chap. Got her in a right little tizzy.'

When Philly sat down again, Harry inclined his head towards her solicitously. 'Good evening, fair Philippa. Let's begin again. Please accept my sincere apologies for all lewd and vulgar behaviour, the blame for which must surely be laid at my door. I'm quite sure I speak for all of us here when I say that from now on we will all endeavour to behave in accordance with your own saintly code of conduct. Such an example to us all.'

'Just eat your supper, Harry, and bloody well shut up,' said Philly between clenched teeth.

'Ooh, language, dear girl, the old halo slipped a bit then, I think. Prop it up a bit, eh, give it a shine . . . that's it. What, no smile, fair Philippa? Do I detect a shimmer of frost from our favourite head girl? I'm not in for a spanking, am I? Or are you saving that for Miles? Lucky man!'

'Harry,' I said warningly.

He spun round to me like a machine gun, hand cupped to ear. 'Sorry?' He craned his neck. 'Was that a little mouse squeaking? Was that my own little wifelet I heard, muttering something?' He dropped his hand and opened his eyes wide. 'Ah, yes! It's dear little Rosie mouse! What a delight. I didn't spot you lurking over there in the corner, nibbling your cheese. Such a shy little thing usually, but perhaps not so shy these days, eh? Almost, dare one say it – yes, almost bold! Oh, incidentally,' he turned back to the table and went on in hushed, confidential tones, 'speaking of dear little wifelets, some of you gathered here this evening may be under the mistaken impression that there be trouble afoot in the house of Meadows. That our marriage,' he looked around furtively as if others might be listening, 'is no more. Is deceased!' His eyes were wide with shock. Then he shook his head vehemently. 'Not so, dear friends, not so. May I be the first to reassure you that any reports of its death are *greatly* exaggerated. Isn't that right, Rosie?'

'Harry, this is neither the time nor the—'

'Oh, I know, I know, I'm a difficult bastard to live with, but shit, who isn't, eh, Miles? I bet you've been known to pick your nose in public, fart under the duvet and commit other heinous, bottom-spanking offences, and all, no doubt, incurring appropriate punishments at the hand of fair Philippa.' He winked. 'And I hold my hand up with you – yes, I too am a sinner, *mea culpa*! But now that I'm *enlightened*, now that Rosie mouse has come out of her hole and wagged her little claw at me, well, I stand corrected, and I can assure you that from now on, all will be well. I've seen the light, I'll take my punishment like a man, and my dear little wifelet can get back to preening her whiskers, isn't that right, my love?'

'No, Harry, it isn't, and I certainly don't wish to discuss it now.'

'Oh, come, come,' he insisted, 'we're all family here! A little kiss and make up over the roast lamb isn't going to embarrass anyone, is it, Elizabeth?'

'Of course not, Harry,' said Mummy warmly, her eyes shining. 'Oh, Harry, I'm *so* delighted, I was so afraid that you and Rosie were going to go your separate ways and that we'd never see you again!'

Harry's jaw dropped. He let his knife and fork clatter noisily on to his plate. 'Never see me again? Good Lord, what an idea! How on earth could I leave this happy fold? How on earth could I leave *you*, dear Elizabeth? Why, there's so much I'd miss! Do you really think I could give up our cosy little fireside chats?'

'Well, no, I can quite see that would be hard . . .' Mummy demurred.

'Hard? It would be impossible! Good heavens, dear lady, if I couldn't hear just one more time how Mrs Parker-Bowles came to the Cancer Relief Bring and Buy Sale and bought not just one but *two* of your very own dried-flower arrangements, why, I think I'd go insane! If I couldn't hear you speculate on whose royal eyes must have *feasted* on those very same arrangements – and I think you and I both know who I mean – why, I think I'd go into a terminal decline! Oh, no, no, to be expunged from your exclusive salon, no longer to be a party to your witty, razor-sharp repartee would be much too much to bear.' He shuddered.

'Harry,' I said warningly.

'Imagine,' he went on with wide eyes, 'if I could no longer hear about the day Lady Fairclough came trolleying round the aisle in Waitrose and knocked you flying into the Kitekat display? About how you sprained your ankle – remember, Elizabeth? And how she couldn't have been nicer? Bringing fresh flowers round in the Daimler the very next day and being so kind as to Step Inside For A

Coffee and, wait for it, admire your dried-flower displays? Imagine not hearing *that* quaint little anecdote again, or, for that matter, any other of your wild social successes. Why, I think I'd just faint clean away.' He shook his head mournfully. 'And then the salon itself.' He looked around wistfully, lovingly even. 'Ah, yes,' he sighed, 'this delightful house, and the charming way you've disguised the fact that it isn't – well, it isn't exactly period, is it, Elizabeth? More, shall we say, *fin de siècle?* The glorious abundance of onyx ashtrays on dainty nests of tables, the doilies on every conceivable plate, the way you rest your pretty pale blue head back on the antimacassars and the charming way you make all your visitors *so* welcome, always *so* pleesto meecho, the—'

'Harry, that will do!' I snapped. Philly was also looking furious. She may be a joke but she was our mother. Mummy, of course, was looking enchanted, patting her lavender locks delightedly.

'What?' Harry raised his eyebrows innocently. 'Can't I compliment your dear mama?'

'Of course you can, Harry,' Mummy purred.

'Just keep your compliments to yourself, there's a good chap.' Daddy spoke softly but he looked strangely pale. For a man who at his most antagonistic was little short of benign, these were strong words. He pushed his half-eaten plate of food aside, propped his leather-clad elbows on the table and began to fill his pipe, keeping his eyes firmly fixed on Harry the while.

'Ah, Gordon.' Harry smiled. 'I was just coming to you. Last, but by no means least. Solid, dependable Gordon. No skeletons lurking in your cupboard, are there, old chap? Shall we take a peek? Just in case? No, no, just as I thought, just the golf clubs and the Rotary tie, jolly, jolly good. Nothing grubby, nothing sinister, and heavens, why should there be? You have, after all, led a blameless, honest-to-goodness Home Counties life, haven't you? You've mown the lawn, you've cleaned the car, you've worked your little socks off and come home night after night to dear Elizabeth's girlish chatter, loyally ploughing your way through her chicken cordon bleu – maybe just helping yourself to an extra thimbleful of wine when she disappears to the kitchen to get the trifle, you old dog! And then there's the splendid way you look after your grandson so handsomely at the weekends. Yes, my goodness, you've fixed that little car up a treat for him, haven't you?' Suddenly he paused. Frowned as if a thought had just struck him.

'I say, you'll miss him, Gordon, won't you? Young Ivo? Did Rosie tell you that if she goes ahead with all this nonsense, I'm going to fight her for custody? No? Oh yes, yes I will.' He nodded soberly. 'Stand a damn good chance, too, I'm afraid, bearing in mind – well, you know. Or perhaps you don't?' He raised his eyebrows. Sighed. 'Not that I blame Rosie, of course. I mean, hell, who wouldn't have a short fuse with a truculent two-year-old at one's feet all day, eh? And I certainly don't relish having to spill the beans either, but then, why should I have to? After all, it doesn't have to be like that, does it? If you, Gordon, could just persuade young mousy-poo here to change her mind, tell her what a splendid chap I am – not as splendid as *you* of course, I'm but a student at your knee – but tell her how determined I am to mend my dissolute ways, well, then I really think she might listen. She's got a lot of time for you, Gordon old boy.' He looked around at the silent, shocked assembly. Suddenly he clapped his hand to his forehead. 'Good God, I nearly forgot the best bit! What an ass I am!' He smiled exultantly. 'Hold on to your hats, good people, I forgot to tell you – I intend to get a job!'

'Oh Harry!' Mummy's face cleared and she clasped her hands with delight. 'What a marvellous idea!'

He swung round to her. 'Isn't it just, Elizabeth? Or may I call you Lizzie? Like Gordon does? I've always wanted to.'

'Of course!'

'Yes, a job. I say, would you be able to help with that, Gordon? Put the word about the City for me? See if there's a spot of banking or stockbroking in the offing? Nothing too serious, just a bit of tinkering about on a computer screen all day, hmmm? How about that, Rosie? You'd like that, wouldn't you? Like to see me go off to the station every morning in a pinstriped suit, briefcase in hand, straighten my tie at the door, brush a few flecks from my collar, trill, "Toodle-oo, my darling!" just like your dear mama?'

'Harry, whether or not you get a job is a matter of complete indifference to me,' I said in a barely controlled voice.

'Oh, come now, I might earn a few pennies, and a little extra housekeeping never goes amiss, does it? Got to stock up on those silky undies for your young friend, don't forget, and I gather they don't come cheap these days, do they?'

Philly was on her feet. 'Harry, this is obscene! How dare you speak to Rosie like that!'

Harry cringed back in mock terror. 'Ooh, I say, look out, it's fair Phil on the warpath! Being a bit spunky now, sticking up for little sis – take a house point, that girl! And might I say, incidentally,' he leaned forward, 'how marvellously attractive you look with a touch of fire in your belly, my dear? I know your looks are much admired but personally I've always found them a little insipid, but that's probably got more to do with your Madonna-like disposition than your actual physiognomy. Yes, a bit of righteous indignation suits you down to the ground, puts some colour in your cheeks, some fire in your eyes, and I wouldn't mind betting those plucky little breasts of yours are heaving around like nobody's business in your M&S undies, eh? Getting a bit hot and monkeyish in there, is it? D'you know, I wouldn't mind stretching across the table right here and now and giving them—'

Whatever it was that Harry had in mind was lost, as a fist came flying out of nowhere, catching him hard and square on the jaw, and sending him and his chair flying backwards. He hit the floor with a crash. Miles stood over him, panting.

'Sorry, folks, should have let him stand up first.'

'Not at all, dear boy,' murmured my father. 'Marquess of Queensberry rules went out with the Ark. Anyway, long overdue. Had half a mind to do it myself.'

Dad got up and went round the table. He stooped, peering down at Harry, who was lying like a huge starfish, arms and legs akimbo, mouth open, eyes firmly shut.

'Good shot,' he murmured. 'Looks like he's out cold. Of course, the alcohol gave him a head start. Give me a hand, Miles, and we'll lug him upstairs, then with any luck we can finish our supper in peace. I've been looking forward to my apple crumble.'

'But shouldn't we get a doctor?' twittered Mummy, standing over him, twisting her hanky about in dismay. 'Suppose he's concussed?'

'Of course we shouldn't,' snapped Daddy. 'Now for heaven's sake, stand clear while we pick him up, and when I come back downstairs, Elizabeth, I want my bloody pudding!'

Mummy's jaw dropped in shock. Then it shut. To my amazement she turned and began hurriedly clearing the plates. The men picked up Harry, put his arms round their shoulders and between them lugged him heavily upstairs. I looked at Philly beside me. For a moment I thought I was about to burst into tears, but then I saw her face twitch. I could have gone either way, but as the waves of laughter came tearing up my throat, I was powerless to stop them, and clutching my sister I broke into helpless, hysterical giggles.

Chapter Eight

Sadly, Harry's concussion couldn't run to days, just a mere fourteen hours of heavy sleep, and he graced us with his presence at around ten thirty the following morning. I was alone in the kitchen making Yorkshire puddings for lunch when he staggered in, his Paisley dressing gown seductively agape to the navel, scratching his tousled head, blinking sleep from his eyes and yawning widely. There was a large blue bruise on the underside of his chin which he touched gingerly as he approached.

'Damn great bruise on my chin,' he said in surprise. 'Know anything about that, Rosie? Didn't get up to any horseplay last night, did we? Can't help thinking I must have been a bit too blitzed for all that malarkey.' He frowned. 'You didn't suck my face, did you?'

I ground my teeth. 'Why, in God's name, would I want to do that?'

'Well, you know, to practise love bites or something. Now that you're consorting with adolescents again and all that.'

'No, Harry, I did not. You earned that bruise after a series of character assassination attempts on various members of my family. Miles socked you in the jaw during supper last night.'

His eyes cleared. Memory flooded in. 'Ah, yes, right. It's all coming back now. Had a few too many bevvies, didn't I? Got a bad attack of the frankies. Imagine I'm in disgrace. Sorry about that.'

'It's not a problem,' I muttered into the batter, whisking hard. It's not a problem, Harry, because in precisely twenty-four hours from now I shall be leaving you. Packing my bags and loading them, Ivo, the gerbils and the black and white guinea pig into the Volvo just as soon as you've piled into your Monday morning taxi and trundled off to the club for lunch with Boffy.

'I really am sorry, Rosie posy.'

I turned. He hadn't called me Rosie posy for ages. In his eyes I noticed something else I hadn't seen for ages either. A drop of humility. A smidgen of contrition. A very small plea for forgiveness even. I swallowed.

107

'It's okay, Harry. You really were over the top, though, you know.'
'I know.'

There was a pause. He filled the kettle and put it on the hob. The batter was ready now but I carried on stirring it with the balloon whisk, knowing he was moving around behind me, sensing he hadn't quite had his say yet. He cleared his throat.

'Rosie?'
'Hmm?'

'I was thinking. Why don't we go away on holiday or something? Just the two of us, leave Ivo with your parents. We haven't been away together since our honeymoon and it would do us both the world of good.'

I sighed heavily.

'You're always saying we ought to get away without all the hangers-on, without Boffy and Charlotte and the rest of the crowd. Well, why not? We could go to Scotland or – no, even better, go somewhere *you'd* like to go for a change, away from the midges and the heather and the boring old shooting, go somewhere hot, like – oh, I don't know, Spain, Majorca. Have a bit of a here-we-go-here-we-go. You'd like that, wouldn't you?'

I had to smile. This was Harry's idea of pleasing me. Except that it was so long since he'd tried, he couldn't remember what I liked. Clearly he thought a kiss-me-quick hat and a few calamaris would do the trick.

'Harry, it's no good,' I said quietly. 'I've told you. I've made my decision.'

There was a silence. I thought, hoped, he was going to slip back into his usual venomous polemic which was much easier to deal with than this wheedling appeasement. But he didn't.

'Don't give up on me, Rosie.'

I caught my breath. This was wheedling appeasement gone wild. This even had the merest smack of sincerity to it. And I could see why. I mean, when all was said and done and the decree nisi was on the doormat, who else would want him? Who else was going to take him on?

He laughed, hollowly. 'I mean, let's face it, who else would take on an old sod like me, eh?'

I almost turned round, but managed not to. I didn't want to look at his eyes. Even Harry had the capacity to make himself, not loveable, but vulnerable, and it was something I didn't want to see right now.

He came round the breakfast bar, forcing me to face him. 'We could make a fresh start,' he urged. 'I could change, I really could. Give up the booze, be a proper husband to you, and I meant what I said about getting a job. I know I said a lot of stupid things last night, but I did mean that. I'll go into the City, earn an honest crust. And I'm sure you could forget all about that silly young teenager, couldn't you? Forget whatever line it was he was spinning you. Filling your head with lies. Come on, Rosie, don't let him come between us.'

I looked up from the batter. 'Harry, I'm sorry, but I'm not changing my mind. I'm going. I'm leaving you, and it has nothing whatever to do with anyone else. I just want a divorce. That's it.' I held his eyes but I also held on hard to the side of the glass mixing bowl, aware of the bubbles in the batter popping one by one. His eyes hardened.

'Is it, by Jove?' he said slowly. 'Well, well, well. Look at you getting all pink-faced and forceful. Quite the little tough nut now, aren't we?' He smiled darkly. 'Well, we'll soon see about that. We'll soon see who's got the real nuts around here. Meanwhile, I suppose it's too much to ask you to make me some breakfast. I mean technically speaking I am still your husband, tedious though that clearly is.'

I heaved a sigh of relief. Thank God for Harry's empty stomach. Thank God for his priorities.

'Not too much trouble at all,' I said sweetly, reaching for the frying pan. 'One egg or two?'

'Two, and since I don't believe in going to war on an empty stomach, I shall adjourn momentarily to the garden to gather some mushrooms to go with them.'

'Nice to see you haven't lost your appetite, Harry.'

'Oh, it would take more than a shot across the bows from you for that to happen. You don't know what you've let yourself in for, Rosie.'

And with that don't-mess-with-me missive hanging in the air, he turned round and flounced out, bound for the bottom of our garden where the woods met the fields and, even at this time of year, the wild mushrooms grew in abundance. I moved to the window above the sink and watched him go. He hastened across the lawn, slippers lapping the damp grass, his dressing gown flapping round his knees, bottom swaying heavily from side to side, a large man in a hurry. For all Harry's supposed love of the country, he only showed any alacrity in it when he ventured out to hunt for food to fill his belly. Whether it be grouse, salmon or mushrooms, the great outdoors was only ever a means to the great indoors and thence his stomach.

As he scurried along, my father and Miles came up the slope of the garden towards him, deep in conversation. I held my breath, wondering how this little encounter would go, wondering whether I'd suddenly be called upon to act as Harry's seconder as he and Miles arranged pistols at dawn, but as they passed, the two men acknowledged each other with an economic but not altogether hostile nod of the head. I breathed again and turned back to the Yorkshire pudding, pouring it out into a roasting pan. The front door clicked as Daddy and Miles came in. I heard them discussing crop rotation or low rain yields or some such other crucial topic in low voices. Through the open kitchen door I saw them go into the drawing room to join Mummy and Phil who were kneeling on the carpet with the children, showing them how to make paper-chain dollies out of the business section of *The Sunday Times*. I smiled. There'd always been this strong sexist demarcation in our house, the men pairing off to do something macho like polish hub caps and clear gutters while the women made fairy cakes, and it occurred to me that Harry had never really fitted into either of these camps, being too lazy to clear gutters and, well, too lazy to make fairy cakes either come to that.

He returned a few minutes later, wheezing with the uncharacteristic exertion and clutching his bounty – two great handfuls of beautifully fresh mushrooms. As he dropped them on the kitchen table, my father came in.

'Ah, Harry, you're up. No hard feelings, I hope?'

'None at all, Gordon, just a bruised ego and sincere apologies. Can't think what got into me.'

'The best part of a bottle of whisky, I should imagine. Speaking of which, I'm about to have one myself.'

I glanced up at the clock. 'It's only quarter to twelve, Dad.'

'So I'm fifteen minutes early, but this is my house and I need a drink, so I'm having one. I see you're about to tuck into your breakfast, Harry, so I won't offer you one.'

Harry watched him go, torn between two loves, like a little boy watching the opening credits of his favourite television programme and being told a trip to the zoo is in the offing, but only if he departs now. Liquor won.

'Check the mushrooms over for me, would you, Rosie old girl, and then give them a quick fry. Churlish to let your dear papa drink on his own. I won't be a minute.'

He scurried after Daddy. I smiled, knowing, as Harry did, that in this house, it was now or never. Aware of Harry's predilection for excess, Daddy kept a stern eye on the drinks cupboard and I don't think Harry had ever recovered from an occasion, early on in our marriage, when he'd swaggered over to Daddy's decanter, an empty glass in his hand, and said casually, 'Would it be very rude to help myself, Gordon?' To which Daddy had replied mildly, 'Yes, I believe it would, Harry.' Even Harry, with his thermal sensibility, had not had the gall to overturn this.

I cracked the eggs into the pan, prodding them despondently with a spatula. It was all going to turn incredibly nasty now, wasn't it? Harry was definitely not going to let me go quietly. Bugger, bugger, bugger. I sighed and picked the mushrooms over, peering at the gills. By sheer fluke we grew the most spectacular wild fungi here, but some had been known to be just a bit too spectacular and they needed checking carefully. On one famous occasion when Mummy had made wild cep and porcini soup for supper, we'd all come down the following morning boggle-eyed at the lasciviousness of our erotic dreams. Over the breakfast table we'd swapped in hushed, awed tones tales of orgies, donkeys, Negro slaves, satsumas – oh, it had all come out, and got incredibly giggly too, especially when Mummy kept saying, 'But what on earth was I *doing* with all those naked midgets?'

Diverting though this had been, there was always the chance one might pick something a little more than merely hallucinogenic, and since somewhere in my distant cookery past I'd once done a course with Antonio Carluccio, mycologist supremo, it was my job to ascertain that there were no life-threatening spores among them.

No such luck with today's little clutch, I thought gloomily, prodding them about. Quite a lot of ordinary field, a couple of cep, a few chanterelles and one or two other varieties, but nothing that was going to make Harry choke, turn purple, clutch his throat, gasp 'Poison!' and fall to the floor in a heap, sadly. I left the pan on a low heat, put some ice in a glass and wandered out to the hall where the drinks cupboard lived under the stairs. Since there was no embargo on my intake, I helped myself to a hefty gin and tonic. I sat on the bottom stair for a moment, swirling the ice around, savouring my flight of fancy. Yes, wouldn't that be wonderful? I mused dreamily. A dodgy mushroom. With no known antidote. A couple of days in intensive care, a brief coma, then – lights out. Pull that curtain round that bed. I smiled and sipped my drink. How marvellously convenient that would be. No divorce, no court case, no tug of love over Ivo. It would be much less messy, infinitely more final and altogether more satisfying somehow.

And if not a mushroom, well then, why not something else? As my three years of research had shown, there were plenty of other ways of dying these days. I slipped happily back into one of my familiar old fantasies, the one about the car with the faulty brakes, the momentary loss of concentration, the perilous coast road and – AAAaarggh! – the sea. 'Death would have been instantaneous, Mrs Meadows,' the coroner would assure me sympathetically over his half-moons as I sat, white-faced and black-suited, at the back of his court. 'He really wouldn't have felt a thing.' I'd nod sadly, and gripping Ivo's tiny hand, turn and walk, head bowed, through a throng of sympathetic relatives. As I got into the car I'd acknowledge the sombre condolences of the mourners, drive slowly down the road and then just round the next bend, YA-HOOO! Off would come my black hat, out would tumble my blonde hair and with Ivo bouncing excitedly beside me I'd put my foot down and zoom over the horizon with 'Born To Be Wild' blaring from the stereo. I sighed. Bliss.

I sucked an ice cube thoughtfully. The problem with this particular whim, though, was that it relied heavily on various components coming together simultaneously, like dodgy brakes and a clifftop drive, and since Harry's car was in peak condition and we lived nowhere near the sea, that seemed unlikely. However, there were plenty of other annihilations closer to home, weren't there? I mean, what about a gas leak? In Meryton Road? With me, Ivo and the guinea pig tiptoeing safely out of the back door leaving Harry upstairs, horizontal on his sofa – comatose anyway, for God's sake, so halfway there already – in his habitual, *après déjeuner* position? He wouldn't feel a thing, would he? Just snore gently, soporifically and peacefully into the next world. Except that we didn't have any gas. Ah. I chewed thoughtfully on a piece of lemon. Well, crikey, gas wasn't everything, how about a rucked-up paving stone outside his club in St James's? Out he comes, pie-eyed as ever, trips over the slab, cracks his head on the pavement and falls into an irreversible coma on the spot? Or, okay, say there was no handily ricked pavement, how about he just falls down the club steps, cuts his knee, contracts gangrene, has his leg cut off, then his other one, then all the other bits connected to it, until there are no bits left to cut off? Or how about – blimey Rosie, what are you on, for heaven's sake? I blinked and peered at my drink. Amazing what a generous slug of gin did for one's imagination mid-morning.

I frowned. No, no, this was all getting much too far-fetched. Something altogether more subtle and believable was called for to do the job properly. His diet, for instance. The last time Harry had visited his doctor he'd been told that if he carried on eating and drinking at his present rate he'd be dead in five years. Promises, promises, I'd thought bitterly at the time, but what if it was true? And how about if we speeded that process up a bit? How about if, instead of just giving him eggs for breakfast, I made it eggs Benedict, added a bottle of port, a packet of Marlboro and a banoffi pie with double cream for pudding? Surely he'd be dead within the year? I hesitated. For all the good doctor's assurances, I somehow thought it would take more than a cream sauce and a few fags to see Harry off. I could just see him getting more and more colossal, so huge in fact that he filled the house, cigarette smoke and port fumes belching from every orifice like some horrific suburban Caliban, so that in the end I'd just slit my own throat instead.

So that just left the mushrooms then. I stared down into my almost empty glass. Frowned. What, are you serious, Rosie? You mean, nip down to the woods, pluck out one of those greenish-yellow ones that we'd always thought looked a bit suspicious, steal back and add it to the pan? Well, why not? a little voice in my head said. Who on earth would be any the wiser? Who on earth would suspect you? I mean, let's face it, Harry gathered the bounty himself, didn't he? You didn't have anything to do with that, and the fact that he asked you to check them over is between you and him, isn't it? No one else was party to that conversation, and since he won't be there to spill the beans, what on earth have you got to lose?

My heart began to beat wildly. Think of it, Rosie. No court case. No nasty smear campaign. No ghastly aspersions on my character as an unsuitable mother. No grief for Ivo. No appalling grief for me. I stared down at the ice slowly melting at the bottom of my glass. Then I glanced next door. Mummy was talking loudly and ostentatiously to someone on the telephone, probably Marjorie. Daddy and Miles were both in armchairs, hidden behind broadsheet newspapers. Philly was playing on the floor with the children, showing them how to draw round saucers now. Harry was at the fireplace. He had his back to me and was slowly supping his whisky, still in his dressing gown, one arm outstretched and propping up the mantelpiece. He was staring intently into the flames. It would be the work of a moment to slip out, unnoticed. Do a little harvesting. And I'd be back in a trice to fry it up. Slowly, very slowly, I stood up. Suddenly Harry spun round. He caught my eye like barbed wire.

'Isn't my breakfast ready yet?'

I flushed, started guiltily, and as I did I spilled the remains of my drink on my skirt. 'Oh! Yes, probably. Sorry, I'll go and see.'

'No, don't worry, I'll go.' He set his whisky down and glared.

'Good grief, Rosie, it'll be lunchtime before you get your act together.'

Philly looked up and gave me an outraged glance, but I was pleased to see him go. Pleased to let him sort that frying pan out for himself. I brushed down my wet skirt and noticed my hand was trembling. Before I went to join the others in the drawing room, I stood for a moment, holding on to the banisters. I felt decidedly shaky. I touched my forehead. It was damp. Good God, how extraordinary. For a moment there, I think I'd been about to kill my husband.

Chapter Nine

Of course I didn't kill him. But I awoke in London the following morning with a mixed sense of excitement, guilt and trepidation. Because today was the day for the softer option. Today was Monday, and I was off. All I had to do was wait for Harry to leave the house to go to the club, and then a few minutes later swiftly follow suit in the opposite direction. Oh, he knew I was going, of course, Harry's a fool but he's not a complete fool, but what he didn't know was that I was jumping ship today.

Or did he? As he sat, slumped in his pyjamas at the kitchen table that morning, I could sense him watching me as I stood at the stove frying his usual side of pig. Perhaps it was the way my hand shook slightly as I manoeuvred the pan to the table, or the way I couldn't quite catch his eye as I slid the bacon on to his plate. Whatever it was, I could tell he was suspicious. He pushed the bacon around with his fork in a sulky, desultory manner, keeping his eye on me the while.

'I'm not hungry,' he said suddenly, and pushed his plate away like a petulant child.

This, of course, was highly unusual and Harry knew it.

'Oh. Really?' I hovered nervously. 'What's wrong?'

'I don't know, I just don't feel too good this morning.' He shot me a hurt, pitiful glance. 'Feel distinctly unwell actually.'

'Oh dear. Oh well, never mind.' I took his plate, and shovelled the bacon guiltily into the bin, turning my back so he couldn't see me redden. Suddenly I had an awful thought. I stared intently into the rubbish.

'Think you'll be able to manage lunch at the club?'

'Of course,' he said instinctively. Then he remembered. He pouted. 'Well, I think so. I'll see how I feel.'

I straightened up from the bin and turned round to look at him. 'I'm sure you'll be fine, Harry,' I said gently. 'Really, you will.'

I meant it. I honestly believed that if Harry employed a house-keeper, which I'd strenuously urged him to do, he wouldn't even know I'd gone. As long as there was someone around to cook his meals, clean the house and iron his shirts, I couldn't see how his life would change. Of course, if she could also see her way clear to taking off her apron, adopting a horizontal position and thinking of England once in a blue moon, so much the better, but if she didn't, well, I really didn't think he'd miss that either. It was only ever done out of a dreary sense of obligation on both our parts these days, a sort of unspoken, 'Oh, come on, the sooner we get this started, the sooner we can get it over with,' as Dame Edna would say. No, Harry wouldn't really miss me. He was congenitally unsuited for marriage and he'd realise that the moment I'd gone. What's more, he wouldn't even have to get re-married, he'd have the dignity of being a cool divorcé, not an ageing Lothario still roaming around looking desperately for a wife. He could say he'd been there, done all that, sired the son and heir, and now what better than to get back to the bachelor life he was really suited to? Think of all the dinner parties he'd be invited to as the 'spare man', think of the jealousy he'd inspire in like-minded men friends who longed to be shot of their spouses on golfing holidays or shooting weekends. Oh yes, I was doing him a huge favour if he did but know it.

Elbow deep in suds at the sink, I watched out of the corner of my eye as he got up from the table. He held on to the back of a chair for a second, manufactured a groan and looked piteously at me.

'I think I'll go and have a little lie down.'

So what's new? 'Okay, Harry.'

'I'm really not feeling so good.' Just in case I hadn't got the message.

'Righto. Shall I wake you when it's time to go to lunch?'

'Of course!' Ah, too quick again, you see, much too quick. I stifled a smile.

'See you later then.'

'Okay.'

He shuffled bravely out, bound for his study, and the moment his back was turned, I leapt into action. I snatched a plastic bag from a drawer and quickly filched a few things from under the sink – J Cloths, washing-up liquid, Domestos, etc. I wasn't going to clean Harry out but I didn't want to arrive at the cottage without a few basic items. Then I unstrapped Ivo from his high chair, wiped it down and quietly collapsed it, ready for sneaking it out to the hall and thence to the car with the rest of my belongings. I glanced around. Now, what else? Funnily enough, my instinct was to scrub the place from top to bottom, which I think says less about me and more about the ritualistic chains of female enslavement, etc., etc., but happily I resisted the temptation – shook the chains off with a little shimmy – and set about dragging suitcases and boxes up from the cellar. Quietly, stealthily, I filled them with mine and Ivo's clothes and bedding, tiptoeing from room to room, quietly sliding drawers in and out and then stashing everything back in the cellar until the appointed hour. Then I found a black bin liner and stole around the house like a burglar, taking very little but choosing wisely. A tin opener here, a hairdryer there, a clock here, a radio there, a packet of loo rolls, a jar of marmalade, marvelling as I merrily pilfered and pillaged how simple my needs had become. When I'd first got engaged, I remembered marching around Peter Jones, wedding list in hand, insisting in a loud voice that I couldn't possibly *live* without a pair of china Herond candlesticks with butterflies on them, but now I could see that I could exist without them quite easily. I was embarking on a new life and the goalposts had shifted somewhat; making sure I had a bit of Lifebuoy to splash under my arms was slightly more crucial than fine bone china.

I didn't take any furniture, mainly because it was Harry's, but also because I'd always hated it – mostly oak, mostly huge, and mostly with barley twist legs. I did take a couple of wedding presents though, a pretty pen and ink drawing that Philly and Miles had given us and a patchwork quilt that Alice had made, on the basis that my friends or family had donated them and Harry had never liked them anyway, sniffily dismissing Philly's gift as 'naive' and Alice's as 'arts and crafts whimsy'. Well, I could only think I was doing him a favour by taking them out of his line of vision.

Finally it got to eleven thirty, my bin liner was full, and Harry was still asleep, or pretending to be, upstairs. Who knows, I thought as I sat on the bottom stair nervously biting my thumbnail, perhaps he was lying there wide awake, listening to me playing Burglar Bill, plotting his revenge. I glanced upstairs. I could take a chance, start packing the car – the one large luxury item I was insisting on taking – and just hope he wouldn't come roaring out at the eleventh hour, Uncle Bertram's Napoleonic sword in hand, and drag me forcibly back by the hair in front of all the neighbours, or I could, more sensibly and stoically, just sit it out and wait until he stirred. Suddenly I had an idea. I picked up the phone, dialled a number, and when I heard a car pull up outside ten minutes later, went upstairs to Harry's room. He was snoring soundly on the sofa.

'Harry. Harry!' I shook his shoulder. 'Your taxi's here.'

'Hmmm? What taxi?' He opened his eyes and peered at me blearily.

'The one I ordered for you. Because you weren't feeling well I thought you'd better not drive. It's sitting outside, waiting to take you to the club.'

The mention of the club galvanised him slightly, as I knew it would, and when he stood up I managed to pour him into his jacket and tie, turn him round and hustle him downstairs. I propped him up with one hand as I opened the front door with the other, and all the time whispered magic words like 'Boffy', 'lamb cutlets', 'large gin', 'another large gin', subliminally predisposing him towards the throbbing taxi at the bottom of the path. He went like a lamb, very groggy, still half asleep, but he went. I opened the taxi door, manoeuvred him in, gave the driver instructions, pushed Harry's wallet into his pocket then waved him off like a small evacuee.

As I watched the taxi trundle round the corner and out of sight, a huge grin threatened to split my face. It was quite hard to resist the temptation to leap up, punch the air and shout 'YES!' but I managed not to. Instead, I hastened quickly back inside and seized the phone.

'Alice? It's me. Listen, I'm all packed up and I'm just about to go!' Impossible to keep the excitement from my voice this time.

'Brilliant!' she squeaked. 'Good for you, Rosie, you've done it, you've made your break for freedom, you've got your wooden horse! God, how thrilling. D'you know, I feel just like a member of the Colditz escape committee, probably that shadowy little man who always forged the papers and made civvy clothes out of old underpants.'

'Yes, well, never mind about the underpants, how about furnishing me with a key? Or do I have to call at the house and disturb the irascible sculptor again?'

'Oh no, I've got one here, pop round and – oh! Hell.'

'What?'

'I've just remembered. Michael's got it, damn him. He's down in Cheltenham today and he always takes it off the dresser, just in case he can't get a hotel room. Oh! Hang on, even better, he can meet you at the cottage and help you move in.'

'Oh no, Alice, I couldn't possibly ask him to do that, he'll be busy. Honestly, I'm fine, if I could just pick it up from him in Cheltenham maybe, or—'

'Nonsense,' she said briskly. 'He's never that busy and you'll be there in his lunch hour. I'll ring him now and tell him to meet you at – what, half past one? If you're leaving now?'

'Yes, I suppose so,' I said doubtfully, 'but won't he mind?'

'Of course not, he'll only be in the pub, and anyway, how are you supposed to unpack, chase a toddler, turn on the water and all the rest of it all on your own?'

'Well, quite. Thanks, Alice.'

I put the phone down thinking she had a point, but all the same I couldn't help feeling slightly uneasy that my first great foray into the big bad world without a man at my side had resulted in me instantly enlisting the services of another.

I doodled nervously on the pad by the phone. Now. A note. To Harry. Fifty ways to leave your lover and all that. I sucked the end of the pencil. I could think of many, many reasons but few ways of expressing it. Dear Harry. Sorry I couldn't stomach you any more? Sorry I grew to hate you? Sorry you turned out to be a cross between Pol Pot and Pigling Bland? In the end I simply told him I'd gone, wrote the address of the cottage, told him there wasn't a telephone there but that I would be in touch soon and that he could always reach me via my parents. Love Rosie.

With a shaky hand I folded the note in half, wrote Harry's name on it and put it on top of the telephone. Suddenly I glanced down. 'Shit!' Ivo, taking advantage of my distraction, had quietly unpacked my handbag, scribbled on my driving licence, scattered paracetamol on the floor and was now pretending to smoke one of my tampons. I scooped him up, made a quick detour to the larder for a packet of Hula Hoops and ran outside. I strapped him and the monosodium glutamate firmly into the car to keep him quiet. Then puffing and panting I dragged the cases and boxes up from the cellar, grabbed the bin liner, the high chair, the travel cot, and, aware that quite a few neighbouring curtains were twitching feverishly, packed up the car.

Five minutes later I was racing back up the path and shutting the front door for the very last time. My heart was pounding now, but then, inexplicably, I paused. Come on, Rosie, I thought nervously, don't hang about, don't blow it. Suppose the club is shut for redecoration or something and he comes home? You don't want to be standing here on the doorstep with your trousers down, now do you? Still, I hesitated. I looked up at the house. My house. It was no good, I just needed, very quickly, to search my conscience. It would only take a moment, really. Any regrets? I needed to know. Any last-minute changes of heart? I waited. No, I thought with a great surge of relief, no regrets at all. Just the merest pang about the break-up of the old order perhaps, but then I'd felt that when I'd left boarding school, which I'd loathed. I remembered packing up my trunk in the dormitory, wandering around the old classrooms, taking my last glance around the gym, going into the changing room and thinking how odd it would be never to get changed in there again. Of course there was always going to be a sense of loss, but it was more to do with a sense of lost time, the passing of youth because, let's face it, I'd hated that bloody freezing cold changing room with its pong of ripe socks and other people's rotting verrucas, just as I'd come to hate the house I was staring up at now. In fact – yes, I could almost smell the stale socks and the plimsolls again. I smiled, satisfied, and made my way back down the path. I was ready. I got in the car, turned the ignition and set off for the country.

I got to Pennington at bang on half past one and as I drove slowly through the village, I looked around with interest. This was, after all, to be my stamping ground now, my new patch. It was pretty, but not overly cute, and it certainly wasn't picture-postcard land. More an orderly, functional village in which people lived and shopped rather than one in which tourists stopped to ogle and feed the ducks on the village green. On one side of the lane was a post office, a butcher and a pub, and on the other a general store, a small Saxon church and another pub. And that was it. No chemist, I noticed, and no deli of course, I thought nervously, but then what on earth did I need with a deli? What need did I have now for sun-dried tomatoes, gravlax and balsamic vinegar? No, no, from now on my life was going to be streamlined and very natural. I was cutting out all that urban dross and concentrating on the good life, the rural life. Hell, I might even grow my own vegetables, keep a few chickens, maybe even a pig – no, not a pig, I'd had one of those. Anyway, I'd get back to the land and all that. Who knows, in a few months from now I might not even need shops at all!

With a growing sense of excitement I turned up the little lane by the church, then swung round the huge stone gateposts that led into Farlings Manor. The big house looked down at me sternly as I approached, huge, benign and quiet, and with no obvious signs of life, although one never quite knew, I thought nervously, who was watching out of one of those upstairs Gothic windows. As I crunched slowly up the drive, two or three frisky, expensive-looking horses trotted towards the post and rail fence to check me out, arching their necks and carrying their tails high in the air like banners. I hadn't noticed them before and wondered who they belonged to. Joss didn't strike me as a man who rode hard to hounds somehow, so perhaps they were Annabel's. Not content with being merely beautiful, talented and successful, she was no doubt a marvellous horsewoman too. I swept round the side of the house, keeping an eye out for children and dogs as a small sign instructed me, through the workshops, down past the barns and parked outside the little flint cottage. My cottage, I thought with a smile.

Sure enough, Michael's car was parked just round the corner. I glanced over my shoulder. Ivo was fast asleep, snuggled cosily into his snowsuit. His long eyelashes brushed his cheeks, his lips, cherry red and damp, were parted and one hand lay next to his chin with his thumb sticking up as if he'd been sucking it. I stroked his cheek, but he didn't stir. I could see no point in disturbing him so I left him there and went towards the cottage. Michael seemed to have left the front door wide open so perhaps he was out gathering wood. I did hope he'd managed to light a fire or at least turn the heating on if there was any, it really was getting pretty chilly now.

In fact, Michael had worked out how to turn the television on, and was sprawled full length on the exhausted old sofa in front of the rugby, huddled into his overcoat, controls in his hand. He just about managed to tear his eyes away as I came in, though, and glanced up, giving me a huge smile and what I imagine he thought was an endearing wink.

'I say, this is marvellous, Rosie. Thought I was going to have to miss this game!'

'Glad to be of service,' I said, looking around. The carpet was covered in leaves, blown in through the open door which he hadn't quite had time to close in his haste to flop, prostrate, on the sofa. It was freezing cold.

'D'you think you might have shut the door?' I inquired.

'Didn't seem much point. It's as cold in here as it is outside and of course there's no heating so – ooohh! *How did he miss!*' he roared, clutching his head in despair as a goal kick sailed wide of the posts.

I sighed and turned back to the car. Michael was undeniably amusing but totally useless and I did wonder how Alice put up with him at times. It occurred to me that there were precious few men of my acquaintance – and by this I suppose I meant my friends' husbands – who appealed to me at all, and there was certainly none that I'd want as a husband of my own. This was vaguely comforting somehow, and I cheerfully set about lugging my cases and boxes in, setting them down just inside the front door. After a while it began to get rather overcrowded, especially since Michael was occupying what would have been prime dumping ground.

'These two boxes need to go upstairs but I'll just leave them here for the minute, they're a bit heavy,' I said loudly.

'Okay. Oh, come *on*, Guscott, you great fairy!'

I eventually unpacked the entire car myself, with Ivo thankfully asleep all the while. I was halfway upstairs with a ton of bedding in my arms when the final whistle blew.

'Hopeless, hopeless!' Michael groaned, getting up and flicking the switch off. 'Don't know why we bother.' He turned and saw me struggling on the stairs. He stretched and yawned widely. 'Anything I can do, Rosie? You look a bit overloaded there.'

'I'm absolutely fine, Michael,' I said through gritted teeth, 'but if you wouldn't mind rubbing a couple of sticks together and getting a bit of heat going in here I'd be eternally grateful.'

'All right, all right,' he said, finally catching the edge in my voice. 'Gosh, you only have to ask.'

'Shouldn't really have to though, should I?' I muttered under my breath as I shouldered open a bedroom door, dragging the duvets inside.

The heating, as Michael had so cheerfully pointed out, was non-existent, but I'd brought a heater for Ivo's room, a radiator for the sitting room and there was of course the open fire, next to which, I noticed, someone had thought to put logs in the basket. The place had also been cleaned since I was last here. Was that Joss, I wondered, or had he tasked someone else to do it? Either way, it was thoughtful.

It was beginning to snow now and I paused at the landing window, gazing out as a flurry of flakes whirled past. I felt that same excitement I'd never got over from childhood, but also a sense of foreboding. It wouldn't be hard to get snowed in here and I was sure no one would think of us for days. Thank God, in a way, for Farlings Manor; I was pretty sure I could crawl up there with Ivo between my teeth if need be.

Downstairs, Michael's pathetic attempt at a fire had withered and died and he now seemed to be on his way upstairs with my radio to his ear, fiddling with the controls as he went, no doubt trying to tune in to some other unmissable sporting event. I crouched down at the grate, poking around at the logs, desperately trying to rekindle a spark and wishing I'd thought to bring firelighters with me, when a voice behind me made me jump.

'You have to scrumple up some paper first, uverwise it won't work.'

I stood up and swung round to see three adorable but dirty children gazing up at me. The boy was about eight with blond hair, large blue eyes and a sulky expression, and the speaker, a girl, was about six, with darker blonde curls and the same brilliant blue eyes. Her sister, an absolute mirror image, stood beside her, grinning from ear to ear.

'We did scrumple up paper,' I informed them, 'but it's all burnt away now and I don't have any more.'

'I got some.' One of the girls produced a dirty tissue and a sweet wrapper from her pocket.

I took them and crouched down. 'Thank you. And who are you?'

'I'm Lucy and this is Emma, we're twins.'

'I can see that,' I grinned, spotting a large freckle on the end of Emma's nose which was about all that came between them. 'And who's this then?' I smiled at the boy.

'This is our brover Toby. He's going to big school soon.'

Toby lowered his beautiful blue eyes and scuffed the carpet with his toe.

'I see. Shouldn't you be at some sort of school now?' I asked gently.

'Don't like it,' he muttered.

'He pretends he's sick,' piped up Emma, 'and Daddy believes him. Marfa doesn't but she says she can't be bovered to take him anyway 'cos it's fucking miles away and she has to get up at the crack of dawn.'

I blinked. 'Right. And who exactly is Martha?'

'Our pear. She's all right, isn't she, Tobe? She doesn't mind what we do. We can do anything we like, can't we, Tobe?'

The taciturn Toby nodded, eyes still on the carpet.

'I see. So, does she know you're here now?'

Emma shook her head and the girls moved off around the room, bored with this conversation now. Lucy stuck her finger up her nose and dug deep, gazing curiously into my boxes, picking up my belongings, turning them over with interest. Then she heard a noise. She looked upstairs.

'Is that your baby up there? Marfa said you had a baby.'

'No, my baby's asleep in the car. I'll wake him up soon and you can see him. That's a friend of mine. He's helping me unpack.'

'Your lover?' she asked eagerly, making for the stairs, Emma and Toby at her heels.

'No, it's not my lover,' I said, aghast. 'Why did you say that?'

'Marfa said you'd left your husband so you probably had a lover. Said you were probably a bit of a mympho.'

Did she indeed. Marfa really was sounding more and more peachy. It was entirely possible she was destined to be my new best friend

123

down here. I listened as they found Michael, whom they obviously knew, and then discovered beds to jump on and duvets to hide under. There were shrieks of glee as Michael pretended he didn't know they were there and went to sit down on them.

'Ahhh, good . . . a nice comfy bed . . .'

'No! Arhh, no! MICHAEL, GEDDOFF!'

After a deal of rough and tumble and hilarious horseplay, Michael stuck a rumpled head over the banisters.

'I forgot to tell you, these three come free with the cottage. It's one of the perks. They're completely unchaperoned and undisciplined as far as I can see and they spent most of their time as part of our extended family when we were here.'

I went to the bottom of the stairs. 'But doesn't anyone come and look for them?' I hissed. 'Does anyone know where they are?'

'Oh, there's a terrible, swearing, gum-chewing nanny who lets them do what the hell they like just so long as she's left alone to lie in a heap eating chocolates and watching *Neighbours*.'

'But why on earth do they employ someone like that?'

'Because she's been with them since the twins were born and anyway Annabel likes to think she's frightfully right-on and forward thinking. She doesn't believe in formal education and can't bear pushy mothers with over-organised children trotting off to tennis and ballet after school. Thinks they should be running naked in meadows picking wild flowers and all that. What she'd really like is a one-legged black lesbian with an alternative approach, but she has to make do with Martha, and Martha's not alternative, she's just bone idle and uninterested. They could be snorting coke up their noses for all she cares, and probably will be in a few years' time.'

'But what about Joss? Doesn't he care?'

'Yes, I think he does actually, but he's a soft touch where Martha's concerned. Her father was the gardener here ages ago but he had to retire when he got sick, and I think Joss still feels a certain loyalty to the family. Anyway Annabel organises things so he doesn't see too much and Martha lies through her teeth about what they're up to. I've heard him ask where they are and she says, "Oh, they're climbing trees in the woods," when in fact they're glued to the Disney channel. Between them, those women run rings round him and he's too busy to twig. Not that my heart exactly bleeds for him. You've met him, haven't you?'

'Briefly.'

'Well, briefly's enough.'

124

The door swung open and I spun round to see the man himself, framed in the doorway with Ivo in his arms.

'I hate to tell you,' Michael went on from upstairs, 'but your landlord is a self-satisfied, pompous old fart.'

The word 'fart' hung jauntily in the air, echoing around the room. I swallowed. Joss's face turned to stone. Gosh, he really did look like Charles Dance, didn't he? It must be those hooded eyes.

'Your baby, I presume,' he said icily, handing Ivo over.

'Oh! Yes, thank you.'

'He was crying and getting pretty cold in the car.'

'Oh, yes, well, I was just trying to get the fire going before I brought him in. It's a bit chilly.' I blushed, feeling like a terrible mother. 'Um, Michael, Mr – Joss is here,' I said loudly, before any more indiscretions were bellowed down the stairs. I wasn't quite sure what to call him, he wasn't a man instantly to inspire first-name terms.

'Joss will do fine,' he said as Michael came down the stairs.

'Joss! How are you!' Michael cried jovially, clearly oblivious of his *faux pas*. He thrust out his hand blokeishly. 'Good to see you again,' he added. I cringed.

'You too, Michael,' said Joss drily, briefly taking his hand. He turned to me. 'I came to see if I could be of any assistance, but I see you have all the help you require.'

I could see why Michael had said he was pompous, his Bostonian accent was peculiarly pedantic.

'Er, yes, we're, um, I'm fine really,' I mumbled, in a fairly unpedantic way.

'I still think you're crazy to take this place on with a child,' he said abruptly, looking around. 'You're aware it has virtually no heating?'

'Yes, I am, and I've brought a radiator for Ivo's room and another one for down here. Once the fire's alight, we'll be fine,' I said smoothly.

Out of the corner of my eye I saw Lucy's little face come round the top of the banisters. She put her finger to her lips then shot back again.

'That won't be enough, you'll want one for your room. I'll bring another radiator down from the house, it's going to be freezing tonight. Why haven't you lit the fire?'

'Well, I tried, but—'

'Here,' he took the matches from me, rearranged the sad little tangle of sticks in the grate and set fire to them annoyingly expertly. 'You'll need a fireguard too of course,' he said as Ivo, entranced by

125

the flames, staggered eagerly towards them.

'I'll get one,' I muttered, dragging Ivo back and wondering why Joss made me feel like a grubby fifth-former caught with ten Number Six in my gymslip pocket. 'I've ordered a few things from John Lewis already so I'll add it to the list.'

'Well, see that you do. I don't want to be held responsible for any horrific accidents.'

I bridled in fury, thinking that there were one or two things I could tell *him* about childcare, seeing as his foul-mouthed, truant-playing children were even now on the premises, but the memory of Lucy's white, alarmed little face stopped me.

'Otherwise everything okay? The wood pile is just around the back of the barn so just help yourself, and don't bring up a huge empty basket, fill it to the brim and then discover you can't stagger back with it. Try to keep it topped up as you go along. Think you can manage that?'

'Perfectly,' I snapped. I was beginning to see why Annabel spent so much time abroad. He really was the end with his patronising chauvinism, and the more I thought about it, the less like Charles Dance he looked. Well, all right, just a tiny bit around the eyes perhaps, but zero rating on the charm front. No, no, give me Michael's laid-back sangfroid any day. On the other hand, a little voice inquired, who was it who'd got the fire going? And who'd stocked up the log basket? Not charming Michael. I sighed. Oh well, just give me a break from men full stop then. That was clearly the answer.

'Right, well, I'll be off then. Let me know if there's anything else you need.' He turned to go, nodding briefly at us both by way of dismissal, bending his head low to get under the tiny cottage door. A couple of border terriers who'd been waiting patiently outside sprang to attention, tails wagging eagerly the moment they saw him. Michael and I watched him go from the doorway, a tall, thin figure with his head slightly bowed, his dogs at his feet.

When he was out of sight, Michael clicked his heels smartly together and gave a Nazi salute. '*Jawohl mein Fuehrer!*' He dropped his arm. 'Arrogant shit,' he muttered. 'He's enjoying himself, you know. Having a waif and a baby in one of his cottages makes him feel like a feudal lord. He'll be riding down here on his horse tomorrow with a basket of turnips and a rabbit for you to skin, expecting you to run from your hut, barefoot in your shawl, baby at your breast, seize his jewelled hand and press it to your lips in gratitude. If you were a virgin he'd probably hump you by way of rent.'

I giggled, but his vehemence surprised me. Michael didn't get worked up about anything as a rule, he was far too lazy. 'You don't like him much, do you?'

'No. And let's hope you don't find out why.'

I would have questioned him further, but the children came creeping downstairs.

'Has he gone?' whispered the one with the freckle.

'Yes, he's gone.'

'Thank God. He would have *killed* us!' She rolled her eyes expressively at her sister and pressed her small hands to her heart.

'Surely not. I mean, he must know you're all at home, why would it matter if you came down here?'

'Oh, well, he may not, sort of, know.' She averted her eyes shiftily.

Good God, what sort of house was this that the children could skive off school without their father even noticing?

'Come on, you two, we'll go home the back way.' She tugged at Toby's sleeve and they all crept off together, slinking round the side of the cottage and up through the trees, zigzagging through like a tribe of Red Indians.

Michael looked at his watch. 'Actually, Rosie, I think I'd better be off now too, if you don't mind. I've got a meeting with the Superglue clients at three o'clock.' He peered at me anxiously. 'D'you think you'll be all right on your own?'

I blinked. What, without the benefit of his invaluable, superhuman help, did he mean?

'Oh yes, Michael, I'll stagger on. But thanks, you've been a tower of strength.'

'It's an absolute pleasure.' He beamed magnanimously and bent down to kiss my cheek and I realised he reeked of aftershave. It wasn't something I'd ever cared for myself, and I wouldn't have thought it was Alice's cup of tea either.

'Now have fun, little Rosie,' he tapped my cheek playfully, 'and don't get up to too much mischief, will you!'

I bared my teeth in a parody of a smile and watched as he went to his car. He eased himself into his dinky little sports car, checked his rear-view mirror – couldn't be for traffic, must have been for hair – and as Ivo and I waved and smiled, he revved up like nobody's business and turned his car round on a sixpence in an ostentatious spray of slush and mud. Thanks, I thought, screwing up my nose from the fumes and brushing myself down.

'Be good, won't you!' was his parting shot from his car window.

I couldn't quite bring myself to reply, and as he tore up the back drive much too fast, it occurred to me to wonder exactly how good

Michael was. Oh well, I thought carrying Ivo back inside, thankfully that wasn't my problem.

The snow was coming down thick and fast now, swirling past the windows and settling on the damp grass as the afternoon got steadily colder. I built the fire up, grateful for the huge pile of logs, and turned the radiator on full in Ivo's room. The cottage was still cold but being so small I knew it wouldn't take long to heat up. When I'd got the fire roaring, I ventured upstairs to the tiny bathroom, propped open the door and stuck my other radiator just outside to heat that up a bit too. Then I turned the radio on and charged around the cottage with Ivo on my hip giggling away – I didn't dare put him down because of the fire – and between us we put up the travel cot, made the beds and unpacked the suitcases. Ivo, in supremely good heart and obviously finding the whole thing a huge adventure, sang away at the top of his voice. As we sat together by the fire an hour or so later, mopping up baked beans and fried eggs with slices of Mother's Pride, I couldn't help feeling ludicrously, absurdly happy. I knew this was early days and we'd just moved into a freezing cottage in the middle of winter and I knew I had precious little money and no job and no prospects either, but still, I thought as I looked around at the roaring fire, the cosy little room and the snow falling heavily outside while we were snug and warm within, still, not bad, Rosie. So far, so good.

After our picnic supper I went upstairs and tested the bath water pessimistically. I snatched my hand back sharply. Blimey! It was boiling. It came out in little more than a trickle, but mixed with a splash of cold it didn't take long to fill up a small bath for Ivo. I hastily undressed him to minimise the cold and plopped him in, watching as he splashed around happily.

'In! In, Mummy!' He flicked water at me.

'No, Ivo, not yet. I'll have one later.'

'Yeth! In!'

Oh God, why not? He did love me having a bath with him and apart from anything else there was always the prospect of the hot water running out later on. I quickly undressed and joined him and we splashed about for a bit.

'Right, out,' I said firmly. 'Come on, quick, before it gets too cold.'

I looked around. Ah, right. Towels. Bugger, had I really forgotten to steal some towels from Harry? It appeared I had. Improvising wildly, I found Ivo's towelling dressing gown and wrapped him in that, then ran dripping to the bedroom and grabbed – what? Oh, look, a spare duvet cover, that would do. Wrapped in thin cotton sheeting and feeling decidedly chilly now, I picked up Ivo, grabbed his pyjamas and hurried him down to the fire. At least we could sit here and dry off, and in a minute I could borrow his dressing gown and give myself a quick rub down with that. When he was dry, I shook out his pyjamas and tried to cajole him into them.

'Come on, Ivo, quickly, put your legs in.'

'No.' He shook his head. 'Chicken fing.'

'No, darling, not tonight, not the chicken thing, Mummy's freezing. Come on, just get dressed.'

'No! Want chicken fing!'

What he actually meant was the 'funky chicken', a ridiculous squawking dance I'd once done out of desperation to rouse him from a bathtime tantrum, but which I'd prudently renamed the 'chicken thing' on account of Ivo's pronunciation of funky, which rendered the n silent. We did, after all, live in a semi-detached house in London with paper-thin walls, and I didn't particularly want Social Services knocking on the door demanding to know what sort of depraved poultry fancying I was into and whether it was suitable viewing for a two-year-old.

'Yeth, Mummy, yeth!'

'No, Ivo, now come on.' I shivered violently, eyeing his few square inches of towelling enviously.

'Yeth!'

'Oh GOD!' I gave a quick squawk and flapped my wings under my sheet. 'There.'

'No!' His eyes filled up ominously. He knew he'd been short-changed. 'NOOO!' he roared.

Now I'm sure there are mothers out there who've never once resorted to pulling silly faces, standing on their heads, or even dishing out sweets to stop a child going critical. Me, I'll resort to anything, and anyway it was bloody freezing and it might warm me up a bit. I flung off my sheet and strutted up and down, elbows bent as I flapped my wings and squawked loudly, wondering, as Ivo roared with laughter, if the Queen had ever had to sink to this with Charles and the gang, and deciding on balance probably not, as bottom out, bosom bare, crowing away, I suddenly heard something. I froze, mid-flap. Shit, there it was again! I dived for my sheet, horrified. Yes, there was a crunch in the snow outside. There was someone out there!

I held my breath, staring fixedly at the black windowpane, cursing myself for not drawing the curtains, straining to see, to hear. After a while I crawled across the carpet in my sheet and came up under the window. I peered out. Nothing. Just blackness. Steeling myself, I reached across for the latch and opened the door, just a crack. My heart was pounding. All around was thick, white snow, and above, a dark, starry night. There was nobody out there, nobody at all. Hugely relieved, I went to shut the door when down at my feet I saw – a radiator and a fireguard. I stared at them, sitting together on the doorstep. Slowly it dawned. I gasped with horror and slammed the door shut. Oh God, he must have seen me! Stark naked! And not only that but impersonating a chicken! He must have glanced through the window, seen me flapping and clucking and thought, blimey, she's barking, she's laying eggs or something, I'm getting out of here, dumped the radiator and legged it. He was probably sitting in his kitchen even now, a large whisky in his shaking hand, wondering what sort of nutcase he'd allowed into his cottage. I sank on to my bottom with a groan, covering my face with my hands.

After a while I heard a little shuffle towards me. Two small hands pulled my fingers from my face and Ivo's bright blue eyes peeped in. He smiled.

'More chicken, Mummy. More!'

I narrowed my eyes to resemble two tiny bits of flint, clenched my teeth, and without a flicker of wavering intent said, 'NO!'

To my surprise he drew back. In fact he almost looked impressed. I snatched up his pyjamas and buttoned him into them in silence. Now why couldn't I have done that in the first place? Just said no and looked as if I meant business? I hoisted him furiously on to my hip and took him up to bed, still hot with shame at the thought of Joss's shocked face at the window. Oh well, I reasoned as I tucked Ivo into his cot, I suppose it could have been worse. I straightened up and frowned. Really, Rosie? How so, exactly? I turned out the light and trudged wearily downstairs.

Later that night when Ivo was fast asleep I pottered around the cottage putting china away in cupboards, folding clothes into drawers, and then I made myself a cup of coffee and sank into the chair by the fire. I sighed happily, enjoying the sweetness of solitude as it wrapped around me. Gosh, this was bliss, and so what if Joss thought I was mad, from now on he'd probably just give me an extremely wide berth, which suited me fine. I wanted to be left alone. Wanted the world to go away. Oh, I wasn't naive enough to suppose that this Hänsel and Gretel cottage existence would do forever; friends, a job, a lifestyle of sorts, maybe even a man might one day enter the equation, but at the moment my equation was small. I wanted to shrink my world so that I, and I alone was in control and only when I felt comfortable would I consider expanding. But only on my terms. Never again would I be at someone else's beck and call, never again would I agree to a takeover.

I stretched out my legs to the hearth, luxuriating in the heat and the deep, country silence, like a cat about to embark on a long, lazy afternoon on a sunny length of wall. A delicious evening stretched ahead of me with no three-course dinner to get, no washing-up to do, no one's mood to determine and no one to please but myself. I drained my coffee, got up from my chair and eschewing the television, which I somehow felt would intrude on my rural idyll, pottered across to the groaning bookcase. I crouched down to look. There were plenty of classics: the Brontës, Austen, Dickens, quite a lot of children's books, sports books and a general smattering of good holiday reads – Agatha Christie, Dick Francis and Ruth Rendell. I was tempted by a Ruth Rendell but as I pulled it out, I spotted an ancient copy of Elizabeth David. I fell on it eagerly. To me, this was comfort reading in the extreme. Her wonderful descriptions of the Mediterranean, her marvellously evocative recipes – God, I'd be in the south of France in minutes. I tottered back to my chair in my thick socks, baggy jumper and jeans and curled up with my find. I threw another log on the fire, settled back, read a few chapters, and then I suppose at some point I must have shut my eyes.

I obviously slept, because the next thing I knew there was a tremendous banging at the door. I woke up with a start. The fire was almost out, it must be very late. I glanced at my watch. Quarter to two. God, it was the middle of the night, who the hell was out there? I went towards the door, but as I did, a face came to the window. I gasped and jumped back in fright. Then I realised it was Joss. Except he looked very strange, very pale. He tapped on the window. 'Open up!' he mouthed. I stared at him. The last time he'd seen me I'd been dancing around this room stark naked, and now here he was, back again in the middle of the night. What did he want? What could he possibly want that couldn't wait until morning? Suddenly, the exchange with Michael came back to me. 'You don't like him much, do you?' I'd said. 'No, and let's hope you don't find out why,' had been his ominous reply.

Joss was still watching me through the window. I crept to the front door and stared at the white paint, knowing he was just on the other side. My heart was pounding. Don't be a fool, Rosie, a voice said, you're just frightening yourself because you're here on your own. You're running typically true to female form. He's perfectly all right,

131

he's your landlord, for heaven's sake, and he's a respected sculptor. Good God, he's practically famous!

Steeling myself, I reached up and shot back the bolt at the top of the door, but before I could turn the handle, Joss had pushed the door open himself. He barged inside, bareheaded, covered in snow, and a blast of cold air came in with him. He shut the door behind him. As he turned to face me, I stepped backwards, instinctively clutching at the neck of my jumper, thankful at least that I hadn't gone to bed and wasn't standing here in my pyjamas.

'What is it?' I whispered. 'What d'you want?'

He gazed down at me from his great height. He looked pained, as if he was about to do something he didn't want to do, something that was against his better judgement. My mind whirled. He's got a knife, I thought wildly, or a gun. Or maybe it'll be just his bare hands, they look big enough. My eyes flitted to the poker by the fire.

'Sit down, Rosie.'

'No!' I squeaked. I began to inch towards the poker. If I could just get one blow, one good blow. My heart was pounding.

'Rosie, I'm afraid I've got some very bad news. Your sister would have delivered it but the snow was too bad for her to reach you.'

One more step and I'd be able to reach out and – suddenly I stopped. Bad news? What bad news? It was then that I realised his face was not so much white with anger as white with shock. I stared at him, frozen with a different sort of fear.

'What?' I whispered. 'What is it?'

'Rosie, I'm terribly sorry to have to tell you this, but your husband is dead.'

Chapter Ten

I gazed at him, stupefied. 'My husband?'

'I'm so sorry, Rosie.'

'Well, no, no, don't be. I mean, he can't possibly be dead, you must have got it wrong. I saw him this morning.'

He led me to the chair I'd just vacated by the fire and I remember thinking, gosh, what a terrible mistake to make. What a thing to say. I mean, imagine if I'd loved him or something?

Joss sat me down in the chair and perched in the one opposite. He leaned forward, elbows resting on his knees, hands tightly clasped. His face was still strangely pale. Shock, I suppose, imagining he had a horrific message to convey.

'He collapsed in his club, apparently. He was taken straight to hospital but he died sometime around midnight. There was nothing they could do.'

I stared at him. Something in this rang true. What was it now? Ah, yes, the club. But no. No, it still couldn't be. I shook my head.

'Your sister Philly called. She tried to get here to break it to you herself but had to turn back on account of the snow, and of course there's no phone down here.'

Philly rang? Well, why would Philly do a thing like that, unless – I stared. Suddenly it struck me, right between the eyes with all the force of a runaway truck. Good God, it was true. He was dead. Harry was *dead*.

As I gazed at Joss, I realised I was curious to know exactly how I felt. Shocked of course, but that was more disbelief than anything else, but now that I believed, I felt very – yes, grown up. Something momentous, the sort of thing that only happened to other people, had happened to me, and everyone would talk about it. They'd say, there goes Rosie Meadows, of course you know her husband died. How strange. And I didn't feel sad either, just – rather numb. Rather cold. I kept looking at Joss, but I wasn't really seeing him, just using his face as a screen, staring through it, beyond any consciousness of

133

him. He didn't say anything either. Just watched me in silence.

'Was it – was it his heart, or something?' My voice sounded odd. Out of practice. Yes, it must have been his heart. Too much weight. Too much pressure.

'No, it wasn't his heart, it was food poisoning apparently.'

'Food poisoning! But – where, in the club?'

'That's unlikely. It wouldn't have affected him as quickly as it did. No, they reckon it was something he ate the day before. They're pretty sure it was some kind of fungi, a mushroom of sorts.'

It seemed to me that the world stood still for a minute. There was a terrible silence. My arms went rigid in the chair. 'A . . . mushroom?'

'Yes. You don't happen to know if he ate anything like that, do you?'

'Yes,' I whispered. 'At my parents' house. He collected them from the field.'

'Oh, okay. Well, apparently there's something called the Panther Cap which is deadly poisonous. They think he may have eaten that by mistake, thinking it was just a lousy field mushroom or something. I gather there's no known antidote.'

I stood up very quickly. I paced about the room, twisting my hands together, this way and that. I felt hot, sweaty. My mind was whirring frantically. The Panther Cap. Yes, I'd heard of it, uncommon but very deadly. Oh my God, the Panther Cap!

'But I checked them,' I whispered. 'I really did! He asked me to, and I always do, just in case and – well, I thought they were fine! They seemed fine to me, honestly they did!'

'Sure, of course. And how were you to know? Jeez, I wouldn't have a clue either.'

'But I do have a clue, I'm a cook, I've done a course, I've—' Suddenly I stopped. I swung round. 'I didn't do it, Joss!' I gasped.

He stared. 'Don't be silly, no one's suggesting you did.'

'But they will!' I insisted, aware of how awful and self-seeking I sounded but unable to stop myself. 'They will, won't they, because I checked them, told him to go ahead and eat them! I said, "Oh sure, Harry, those are fine, just a few jolly old mushrooms, there might be a bit of a heart stopper in there too, but you go right ahead and gobble them up, with any luck you'll be stone cold dead in the morning!" '

I sank down in a chair and hid my face in my hands. I wanted to cry, knew I should, but I couldn't. That release wouldn't come. I tried to remember exactly what had happened in that kitchen. I remembered him coming in with them, dropping them on the table, and me poking at them with a spatula, thinking, a few field, a couple of cep, one or two chanterelles and – what else? I racked my brains, desperately. What else had been in the pan? And did I turn them over? Did I check both sides? I couldn't remember, because actually I hadn't really been concentrating at the time, I'd been thinking of something else. Thinking how much I hated him and how convenient it would be if he could just shuffle off and die. Yes, that was it, I'd been so busy wishing he was dead I hadn't actually noticed I was killing him.

I was aware that Joss was still watching me. I brought my face up through my fingers and met his eyes.

'Is the Panther Cap very distinctive?' I breathed. 'Is it green or yellowish or something? Should I have recognised it?'

'Christ, Rosie, I haven't the faintest idea, and how the hell should you know either? You're not a goddam mycologist, are you? For Chrissake, it was just an accident. *He* collected them and *he* ate them, that's all there is to it. Period. Stop blaming yourself!'

'But I *do* blame myself!'

There was a pause. 'Sure, of course you do,' he nodded, and his voice seemed to come from far away. From a place locked in memory. 'And that's totally natural. When someone dies we instantly think, okay, this is my fault, it must be, because they're dead and I'm not. I'm still here. You're feeling guilty for being alive, not for killing someone.'

I gave this due consideration but thought, no, no, you're wrong actually. I'm not thinking that. That's what happens if you love someone. I'm just thinking, oh bloody hell, was it my fault?

I hung my head in shame. 'This is awful,' I muttered. 'Harry's dead, lying on some slab in a morgue somewhere and all I'm thinking about is how it affects me, whether I was to blame. I'm not even thinking about Harry, I can't even conjure up any grief. Oh God!' I burst into tears and it was a welcome relief. I couldn't tell where the tears were coming from and who they were for, but I wept them anyway, with my head hidden in my hands, and thankfully, Joss didn't comfort me. I wasn't sure I wanted that, or even deserved it. As the tears flooded through my fingers, I gazed at his boots opposite, big black wellingtons that he hadn't bothered to take off, with ice still clinging to the side of them in chunks. Some of it was melting now, dripping on to the carpet, disappearing. It must be colder than I thought out there, below freezing probably, minus six or seven. I must remember to check Ivo's blankets and – oh! God, now I was thinking about the *weather*! How appalling! Horrified, I tried to concentrate my mind. I sniffed hard and wiped my nose with the back of my hand.

'Was he – was he in a lot of pain?'

'I doubt it. Once they got him to hospital I'm sure he was made very comfortable.'

I nodded, aware that he didn't have a clue and was lying through his teeth, but I was grateful. Poor Harry. Ah, that was better, poor Harry. Suddenly I remembered he hadn't felt well this morning. That must have been the start of it. And I hadn't believed him. I'd bundled him heartlessly into a taxi, brushed him off like a dirty old fly. I cringed guiltily as I imagined him arriving at the club, stumbling in to meet Boffy, slightly puzzled no doubt as to why he was feeling so off colour but convinced it was nothing a steak and kidney pie and a decent bottle of claret couldn't sort out. I saw him ploughing gamely through lunch, struggling with his food, not talking much, while Boffy, relishing the sound of his own uninter-rupted voice for a change, would be loud and clear, not even noticing. But Harry would be pale and sweating now and perhaps the waiter would notice his pallor as he came to clear the plates. 'Are you all right, sir?' quietly. 'Yes, yes, fine, thanks, peak condition.' A brave smile, because it didn't do to whine, especially here. Boffy might glance up now that he'd cleaned his plate and notice his friend, wipe his mouth with his napkin, frowning. 'You all right, Harry? Look a bit sort of pasty.' 'Fine, fine. Couldn't be better. Might just trouble the gents for a moment, though. Back in a jiffy.' He'd stand up, stumble, clutch the table for support, and sway for a moment. There'd be a clatter of china as he knocked a plate off, and other diners would look up in time to see him lurch forwards on to the table, then roll off sideways, pulling the table cloth with him, his huge bulk crashing to the floor, china and silver following ear-splittingly in his wake.

After a shocked silence, Boffy would spring up in alarm and a swarm of waiters would gather, bending down, one, grim-faced, catching another's eye at the door, who'd pick up the phone. Outside, on a cold, winter afternoon, sirens would blare and an ambulance would pull up in St James's. A small, ghoulish crowd would gather, and after a while a huge, white-faced man, uncon-scious now, would be stretchered out, a red blanket over him, people jostling to see. Some old buffer no doubt, they'd mutter, who'd finally had one port too many. I saw Harry being rushed into the hospital, hurried down a corridor on a trolley to a room full of equipment, tubes going in fast and furiously, wires coming out, blood pumping, nurses shouting, and then I saw that rather good-looking blond doctor from *Casualty*, or is it *E.R.*, shouting 'Stand back!' as he clamped some huge earphones on to Harry's chest. His inert body would jump up and jerk around but clearly not enough, because the nurses would all look grim and the doctor would say, 'Right, are we all agreed it's pointless?' Sombre nods all round. 'Okay. Time of death . . .'

I bit my lip. In all probability food poisoning didn't result in a cardiac arrest, but my experience of casualty was limited and in my fuddled state my imagination was as parochial and mediocre as ever. Yes, forever afterwards I could say that at one of the most momentous, and some would say tragic, moments in my life, my thoughts inexorably turned to TV medical drama.

'Was anyone with him, when he died?'

'The guy he had lunch with, I believe. And his wife.'

For a moment I thought he meant Harry's wife, but that was me. 'Charlotte?'

'If that's her name.'

I nodded. Boffy and Charlotte. Well, that was something.

There was a silence. Joss broke it.

'Have you anything to drink around here?'

I started. 'Oh, no, sorry, I'm not very organised yet. Um, would you like a coffee or . . .' I got up politely.

'Don't be silly, I meant for you. I'll fetch some brandy.'

'No, no, really, I don't need it, I—' But he was gone, the door closing softly behind him. I sat down again and stared into the fire, at the logs smouldering in the grate. So. Harry was dead. I'd wanted a divorce and he'd gone one step further. Some might say he'd accommodated me. Obliged me.

A moment later Joss came back with a blast of cold air and a bottle of brandy. He kicked the door shut behind him with his boot, shaking the snow off his hair. Then he sat down and poured out the amber liquid, balancing two glasses in one hand.

'Here,' he passed one to me.

'Thanks.'

'Do you smoke?'

'No.'

'Me neither, as a rule.'

Clearly rules were to be broken tonight because he took out a Marlboro packet, tapped the bottom and pulled one out with his mouth, lighting it and inhaling right down to his boots. He blew the smoke up to the ceiling in a thin stream. His face was pale, troubled. Our eyes met.

'I lost my wife,' he said suddenly, by way of explanation almost.

Of course. Yes, of course, just after the twins were born. But – oh God, this wasn't anything like that, I wasn't . . .

I struggled to explain. 'Joss, I don't want you to be under any illusions. I'm shocked of course but, well, I was leaving him anyway, you knew that, didn't you? I didn't – we didn't love each other any more . . .' I tailed off miserably. It sounded so tacky. My husband was dead and I was trying to explain why I wasn't in a heap on the floor, but I had to tell him. I straightened up and looked him in the eye. 'I want you to know that I fantasised about my husband dying. Regularly,' I added firmly.

He smiled.

'Why are you smiling?'

'Sorry. You just sound like something out of Alcoholics Anonymous. My name is Rosie Meadows and I'm a dead husband fantasist.'

'Does it sound terrible?'

'No, it sounds like the truth.'

'And I feel—' oh God, I couldn't stop now, the valve had been loosened and I was metaphorically on my feet, wanting to share with my hug-me-hug-you group, '—well, I feel fine, actually. I mean, I feel strange, unhinged, and sad too, but sad because it's so weird to think that he's not asleep in London right now, in our bed, about to get up in the morning, potter blearily down to the kitchen, and it's strange to think that I'll never ever see him again, or hear his voice or his footsteps, hear him call my name. But I don't feel that awful raw haemorrhaging pain that I'm sure – well, I'm sure you must have felt.' I looked at him and instantly wished I hadn't said it. He flinched, as if I'd added to his pain by reminding him. His eyes darkened in his pale face. He rested his head back on the chair, cradling his brandy.

'Yeah, well, no one's saying you have to,' he said softly. 'There's no formula for grief. And anyway, I'm pleased to hear it. I wouldn't wish that shit on anybody.' He drained his glass quickly.

'You must have loved her very much.' Silly question, but I wanted to know. Suddenly I wanted to hear about true, pure, unsullied grief.

There was a pause. When he spoke his voice was low and measured. 'When Kitty died, I felt as if my own life blood had coursed out of me. Drained away. I felt limp. Helpless. I felt – not that part of me had gone with her, as some people say, because that would have been comforting somehow, but that whatever it was that gave me my life, my energy, my vitality had been sucked away into some deep, fathomless void. My soul, I guess.' He stared down at his empty glass. 'Not convinced I've ever got it back.' His face, for a moment, was unguarded, vulnerable and so sad. It was as if for a second a window had flown open and I'd got a glimpse of something beyond the dark façade. It slammed shut as he looked up abruptly.

'But life goes on and any other crummy cliché you care to mention. And I had Toby and the twins to worry about, so it had to. But one's always . . . damaged. Never quite the same.' He smiled gently. 'But this is your tragedy, Rosie. Why are we talking about me?'

'Because I feel guilty that I don't feel like you did, I suppose. Like a wife should feel when her husband dies.'

'Ex-husband to be.'

I smiled wanly.

'Look,' he went on, 'no one expects you to go into deep mourning, no one expects wailing and widow's weeds, or for you to flee to the nearest nunnery singing "The Hills Are Alive", but regardless of what you might think at the moment, take it from me, you're in shock, and you're gonna feel pretty wobbly about this for some time.'

I nodded. This I could conceive of. Wobbly was pretty normal for me anyway. I took a sip of brandy. I'd never really liked it, but strangely enough I found its strong, unpleasant taste rather comforting. It was something to contend with. I looked at him gratefully.

'People say you're arrogant and fierce,' I blurted out, 'but you're not at all. You're a lovely, decent man.'

He threw his head back and laughed. It was the first time I'd seen him so much as smile. 'Decent I'll accept, it sounds like I've never been had up for evading my TV licence, or pinching butts in lifts – which I haven't, incidentally – but lovely . . . few people are lovely.' He looked at me, still smiling slightly. 'Are you going to be okay, Rosie?'

'Yes. Yes, I'll be fine.'

'I mean on your own? Or do you want me to stay?'

'Oh! God, I'm so sorry.' I glanced around for a clock. 'It's probably the middle of the night, is it?'

'It's around four fifteen. You should try and get some sleep if you can.'

I nodded. 'I will. I'll try.'

He got up to go and looked down at me. 'Well, goodnight then. I'll leave the brandy, you might want another.'

139

'Thank you.' I smiled, and felt my eyes begin to water at his kindness.

He patted my shoulder, briefly, awkwardly, and left.

When he'd gone I stared into the dying flames, cradling my brandy. I stayed like that for some time, thinking, drinking a bit, until I realised it was beginning to get light outside. I gazed out at the dawn. It was that sharp, early, bright light that can be so unkind to insomniacs in the early hours, but which I welcomed now, wanting time to move on, wanting it to be another day. I looked at my watch. It was six fifteen. I'd sat here practically all night. I got up and stretched, took the brandy and glasses into the kitchen. There was no point going to bed now, Ivo would be up soon. Instead I had a hot bath, dressed in as many layers as I could and made a pot of tea. When Ivo woke up I gave him a quick breakfast, bundled him into his snowsuit and then, to his delight, went out into the snow. The sky was bright blue and under it, as far as the eye could see, all was white and soft, as if the clouds had sunk down to rest on the earth.

Ivo gasped. He'd never seen snow before. 'Mummy, look!'

I laughed. 'I know.' It was too deep for him to walk in so I picked up a handful and handed it back to him in a ball. 'Snow.'

'Thnow!' He watched, fascinated as he scrunched it in his gloved hand and it turned to water.

'Gone!' he said in surprise.

I laughed. 'Try it.'

He licked his glove. 'Cold!' Another surprise. Two revelations in as many seconds.

I took his hand and we set off, heading into the white light of the fields which stretched before us, rippling on and on, a hint of blue in their undulations. We followed what I knew to be a track round the fields, with Ivo pulling at snowy branches along the way, giggling as the snow fell on his hat. The silence and the whiteness enveloped us and I felt as if we were the only two people in the world that morning, and in a way, with Harry gone, in our own little world, we were. It wasn't a sobering thought, though; on the contrary, it filled me with determination. And I'd be a hypocrite if I didn't admit it made things easier. I walked for miles, thinking, planning, remembering quite a bit too, but Ivo was on my shoulders by now and no lightweight. I knew we had to go home soon or I'd collapse in the snow. On the horizon I could still see Farlings, which I'd deliberately kept in view for fear of getting lost, so I made my way back across country towards it. Our circuitous route meant I approached it from the front this time, and as I trudged up the front drive, I noticed a

Land Rover parked halfway up. On the other side of the post and rails fence, a man in a flat cap and a Barbour was putting a head collar on a grey mare and leading her over to the gate. She was dreadfully lame. He smiled as I approached.

'Morning!'

'Morning. It's beautiful, isn't it?'

He patted the mare's neck. 'Magical, but not so good for this poor old girl, I'm afraid. She's too old to find snow exciting, unlike that little chap on your shoulders.' He regarded me for a moment. He was tall with wavy auburn hair that curled out from under his cap to rest on his collar, and his eyes were the colour of moss. They crinkled up when he smiled at me. He slipped off his glove and stuck out his hand.

'I'm Alex Munroe, the local vet around here. You must be the new tenant in the cottage.'

'Gosh, news travels fast. Yes, I'm Rosie Meadows.' I shook his hand and noticed his grin was rather lopsided and sexy. I imagined it could be fatal if deployed properly. I quickly looked down at the horse's leg. 'What's wrong with her?'

'Oh, just a touch of arthritis, she gets it every year, especially when it's as cold as this. She'll be all right, but she needs to have her legs bandaged and go inside for a bit. I'm going to pop her into the stable opposite your cottage. Think you could keep an eye on her for me?'

'Of course I will. I'm afraid I don't know much about horses though.'

'Oh, she'll be happy if you just lob her a carrot every now and then.'

'I think I can manage that.'

He brought her slowly through the gate and we set off together back to the cottage, the mare limping painfully beside him. I glanced up at him, intrigued. 'Do you always pop round in the early hours, just on the off chance that some horse might be limping? It's jolly early to start making your house calls, isn't it?'

He laughed. 'No, I didn't wake up in the small hours and think – golly, it's snowing, I do hope old Sasha's okay, better go and see. No, he called me. He always worries about this one, she was Kitty's favourite.'

He jerked his head up towards the house and to my surprise I noticed a light on in the workshop. Silhouetted in the window was the unmistakable profile of Joss, head bent, chisel in hand, tapping at what looked like a large boulder. So he was still awake too.

'He rang me on my mobile to say he could see her limping and that she looked in pain, which she was, but you sometimes wish the guy would sleep a bit and then he wouldn't notice these things. Actually, I was out on a night call anyway so it didn't matter.'

'Doesn't he sleep then?' I said, going back to Joss.

He shrugged. 'I suppose he must at some point but whenever I'm out at night and driving past he's always out there, hammering away.'

'At least he cares about the horses,' I said loyally.

'Maybe, though God knows why he hasn't got rid of them, they never get any exercise. But I suppose because they were Kitty's he feels sentimental about them, and of course Annabel likes them because they give the place the air of an upmarket stud farm or something. She likes them to come trotting arrogantly over to the fence when people drive up.'

'You know them well, do you?' I said lightly. 'Joss and Annabel?'

'A bit, but only on a professional basis. He's pretty aloof and supercilious when he can bring himself to talk to you, but she's charming. And drop-dead gorgeous of course, which always helps.' He grinned at me sideways and I wondered how aware he was of his own rakish good looks. Can't imagine it could have escaped him. 'You've met her, I take it?' he asked.

'Annabel? No, I only arrived yesterday.'

'Ah.' He deposited Sasha in her stable, turning her round so that her head stuck over the door. He took her head collar off and watched as I stroked her nose. 'She likes that.'

'I can see.'

'She likes her back tickled too.'

'Don't we all.' I really wished I hadn't said that. He grinned, and his eyes lit up as if he'd just had a little brush with possibility.

'Well, quite,' he said softly.

Bugger. I concentrated hard on giving Sasha some intensive nose stroking, but could feel a blush unfurling and knew he was watching me with interest.

'Bit early to be out tramping around the fields, isn't it?' he said. 'It's not even eight o'clock yet.'

'I know, but Ivo woke up and it was such a beautiful morning I just thought, why not?'

'Why not take the noisy brat out for a breath of fresh air and give the other half a bit of a lie-in. Jolly noble of you.'

'Er, no. There isn't another half, actually.'

'Ah. I'm sorry. Divorced?'

'No.' I took a deep breath. 'Widowed.'

'Gosh, I *am* sorry.' He looked it too. 'I really am.' He frowned and squeezed Ivo's leg which was hanging over my shoulder. 'Golly. Poor little chap.'

There was a silence. I could tell he was moved.

'Was it . . . recent?'

I cleared my throat. Hell. 'Um, yes. Quite recent,' I said, hoping to goodness he wouldn't pin me down.

'So, did he know him?' He nodded up at Ivo.

'His father? Yes. Yes, he did.'

'Ah. Well, that's something. A few memories.'

'Well, quite.' I swallowed hard.

Luckily, at that moment we both heard a car. We swung round. Its tyres were muffled by the snow, but it was revving noisily and slowly weaving its way precariously round Farlings and down the back drive towards us. We watched as little by little it slid along, another Land Rover, presumably the only vehicle able to move an inch in these conditions. As it got closer, I recognised Miles at the wheel, with Philly beside him, and sliding around in the back of what was primarily an agricultural vehicle used for humping bales of hay or sheep were my parents. My heart sank. Oh God, it had started. The grieving merry-go-round had begun. It was time for lots of noisy mourning, funeral planning and breast beating, with my mother firmly at the helm.

As the car came to a slippery halt beside us, Mum literally fell out of the back in her old mink coat, matching hat and black patent high-heeled shoes. She steadied herself against going head first in the snow, then came tottering perilously through the deep drifts towards me, her face crumpled with grief, arms outstretched, hanky in one hand, handbag in the other. I quickly went to meet her and she fell on my neck, sobbing copiously.

'Oh, my poor darling! My poor darling! And Ivo, my poor fatherless boy. What will become of you both? What will you do? Oh, my poor, poor girl – a widow!'

Out of the corner of my eye I saw Alex's eyes widen in astonishment.

'Er, yes, come on, Mum, let's go inside.'

'A widow! And he looked so *well* on Sunday. Who would have thought that the very next day – ooohh! And now you've got to bury him!' She stuffed her hanky in her mouth and I half led, half carried her, distraught, into the cottage, with the rest of my family following sheepishly behind. This particular contingent had their heads bowed and their eyes cast well down. Hands were thrust deep into pockets and there was much concentrated stamping of snow from feet as they negotiated the doorstep. One by one they caught my eye as they came in, but there wasn't a tear amongst them. As I went to close the cottage door behind us all, I caught a last glimpse of Alex's shocked face, watching us. I cringed deeply and shut the door.

Chapter Eleven

Inside the cottage my mother tottered to the nearest armchair and collapsed in a heap.

'Ooooh, Harry!' she moaned.

The rest of my family stood around her in an uncertain huddle. Dad squeezed my shoulder.

'All right, love?' he asked gruffly.

'Yes, fine, Dad.'

'Jolly bad luck,' commented Miles ruefully. 'Occupational hazard though, I'm afraid. Goes with the territory. All part of country life really.'

By that I supposed he meant death by fungi. Well, that was one way of looking at it, I supposed, a bit like death by combine harvester, just one of those rural things.

Philly gave him an incredulous glare and hugged me showily, murmuring, 'Rosie, darling, how simply dreadful,' but she let go rather too quickly, as if she couldn't quite bring herself to prolong the sympathy.

We stood about awkwardly for a moment, then there was a collective shuffle for some chairs and we sat down, still huddled in our coats from the cold and consequently looking rather temporary. Ivo sat on the floor and solemnly untied my father's shoe laces, oblivious of the atmosphere. Mummy sobbed on.

'Dreadful business,' muttered Daddy at length.

'Hmmm,' I agreed.

'Spoken to Bertram?'

'Not yet.'

'Plenty of time. Poor fellow. Boffy?'

'No, not yet.'

'Ghastly for him too.'

Silence again. No one seemed to know what to say. Occasionally Philly would pass Mummy a tissue, or I'd reach out and pat her hand. I felt humbled by her grief actually, ashamed I couldn't even begin to match it and unable to pretend. A deep silence descended and apart from Mummy's choked sobs, we all fell to contemplating the carpet. My eyes began to glaze over but I couldn't look up. I was terrified I might catch someone's eye and not have a suitably sorrowful expression on my face. I gazed intently at the frayed end of a rug, and the awful thing was that the more the silence prevailed, the more I could feel myself getting faintly giggly. I breathed deeply, clenching my teeth. There seemed to be a terrible tenseness in the air. Mummy sniffed hard.

'Such a good, kind man,' she muttered.

I stared at my shoes, marvelling at this flagrant untruth.

'So young,' she moaned, 'and so brave!'

I gulped. Blimey. You'd think he was a Chaucerian knight or something.

'Cut down in his prime!'

I bit the inside of my cheek. I daren't look at Philly, fought with my face muscles and then just when I thought I was out of the woods –

'Just like Our Lord,' Mummy breathed.

That did it. Head bowed, I scuttled from the room and fled to the kitchen. I flung open a cupboard, desperate to hide my shameful mirth in its depths. Just like Our Lord! I boggled hysterically at a jar of pickled onions. Crikey, same sex perhaps, but there the similarity ended surely.

Someone came hurrying in behind me. I turned guiltily to see Philly, puce with suffused giggles.

'Rosie, I'm so sorry,' she snorted, 'can't help it!'

'Neither can I – oh Philly, this is dreadful!'

'Shhh!' she gasped, clutching me, tears rolling down her cheeks. We stood for a moment, hanging on to each other, convulsed.

'Philly, this is appalling!'

'It's nerves,' she whispered sternly. 'This sort of thing happens after shock.'

'Sure?' I wiped my eyes. 'I'm not a callous heartless bitch?'

'No, no, quite normal. Reflexes. It's like cutting off a chicken's head.'

I struggled with my face, not convinced this analogy helped at all.

'Right,' she breathed at last. 'I said I was getting some drinks. I see you've got some brandy, so you bring that and I'll take out the glasses.'

We composed ourselves and shuffled out, pouring out Joss's brandy, faces hidden. Dad downed his in one. He contemplated the bottom of his glass for a moment, then put it aside decisively. He stood up.

'Right. Well, seeing as you're all right, Rosie, I think we'll be off.'

'Oh! Oh, well, yes, I am. I'm fine.' I got up quickly.

'Excellent,' he rubbed his hands together as if we'd just compared diaries and settled on dates for a jolly boating holiday or something. 'Well, I think that's the best plan then. Only I'd like to get Mum back, get her into bed with a few aspirin.' He glanced over at his distraught wife. 'Oh, and by the way, love, the police have been over to us already, just a few routine questions. Been to Philly and Miles too but couldn't get here because of the snow. They said they'd pop in here this afternoon or tomorrow, depending on the weather, is that okay?'

'Fine.'

He tied up his shoe laces and turned to Philly and Miles. 'All right, my party?'

With undisguised relief the others got to their feet and gently heaved Mummy up between them. I gave them a hand.

'We're going? So soon?' she murmured, as if coming round from a private, tragic dream.

'I think Rosie wants to be on her own,' said Philly.

'Of course she does,' sniffed Mummy, 'alone with her grief. My dear, *dear* child.' She reached out and squeezed my wrist. Her face buckled again. 'Sure you don't want to come back with us?'

I hugged her. 'No, Mummy, honestly. I'll be fine, really.'

She nodded bravely, clamping her hanky to her mouth.

Philly hung back as the others went out to the car. 'Shall I come back?' she whispered. 'When we've taken Mum home?'

'No, no, I'll be all right. I'll ring you later, we'll have a chat then.'

'Okay. Oh, and listen, Mum wants to organise the funeral, do you mind?'

'Not at all, go ahead.'

'We thought it would give her something to do. Take her mind off everything.'

'Absolutely.'

As I stood at the door watching them go, I heaved a guilty but heartfelt sigh of relief. Daddy, bless him, had deliberately kept the visit as short as possible, but even so it could never have been short enough.

The next few days passed in something of a blur. Ivo and I stayed put in the relatively snowbound cottage and people left us alone. My only visitors were a horribly nervous pair of young constables who sat on the edge of their chairs sipping tea and very gently asked me a few questions about the morning of Harry's death. Satisfied that it was a genuine mistake on his part, they said that of course a coroner's inquiry had been opened, with a date for the inquest to be fixed, but that this was strictly routine and I'd hear more about it in due course. In the meantime, the coroner was releasing the body for burial.

I then rang Cartwright and Thompson to cancel my appointment with my solicitor, Miss Palmer. I recognised the receptionist's icy cool tones. 'Ah, so do I take it the problem's been resolved?'

'Er, you could say that,' I muttered, deciding on balance not to go into the spectacular nature of the resolution.

During that time, the only people I saw were the occasional farm workers when I trudged around the snowy fields, or, when I ventured out on the icy roads in my car, the people in the village. I had the feeling they knew exactly who I was and what had happened, but although they stared openly, they said nothing.

One morning, I picked up a copy of *The Times*, which informed me on the court and social page that Harry Meadows had passed away, and that a funeral would be taking place in London on Thursday, 16 November. No flowers please, family and close friends only, donations to the Poppy Day Appeal.

I shut the paper feeling very far removed from it all. All I had to do, it seemed, was brush down my old black jacket, buy a new hat, get to London and put in an appearance. Mummy and Philly had done the rest. In many ways it reminded me of my wedding.

The day the funeral dawned I drove up early, deposited Ivo with Alison, our erstwhile baby-sitter of the plastic mac fame, and then went on to the little chapel next to the West London Crematorium, where much to my surprise a small, sombre crowd had already gathered. I didn't recognise any of them. God, it just went to show, I thought with a gulp, the kind of separate lives we'd led when I didn't even know the people at my husband's funeral. I parked the car, and with a very dry mouth walked across to join them. It had suddenly dawned on me that this was very much my show and I was supposed to take the helm. I shook hands with a couple of elderly men and their wives who, it transpired, were cronies of Harry's from his club. I asked them, sotto voce, if they'd be kind enough to take a seat inside while I positioned myself at the door. I was pretty sure this was where my duty lay, and apart from anything else I was intrigued to see who else would turn up.

A few mates of Harry's from the wine trade followed, one or two school friends, a smattering of pin-striped chaps from the City: in fact I was relieved to see that, on the whole, Harry's crowd pretty much turned out in force. As they passed through, the girls clutching their hankies and their Ray-Bans, they all seized my hand, proffered cheeks and murmured appropriate sentiments as I murmured appropriate ones back.

'Rosie, darling, how dreadful. How simply *terrible* for you.'

'Charlie, Lavinia. Thank you so much for coming.'

On and on went the dark-suited trickle, with all sorts coming out of the woodwork, actually. There was that rather dubious doctor friend of Harry's, for instance, very much of the glistening moustache and bow tie brigade, firmly in the Terry Thomas mould.

'Ghastly thing to happen, my dear,' he murmured with a glint in his eye as it roved up and down me. 'If ever you want any help, any advice of any kind—'

'Yes, thank you so much,' I said quickly. 'I'll remember that.'

I remembered him all right. I'd met him at a drunken cocktail party when I was about three months pregnant. Having fed me the 'trust me I'm a gynaecologist' line, he'd gazed lustfully at my admittedly burgeoning bosom and proceeded to pitch for the business of overseeing my pregnancy. 'And you don't want to worry about me being a friend of Harry's and seeing your woo-woo,' he'd brayed. 'When you've seen as many as I have you've seen them all!' I remembered giving a tight little smile and thinking I'd rather have my baby in a public convenience than let this man anywhere near my woo-woo. He squeezed my hand sympathetically as I hustled him through.

'Hello Rosie.'

I turned as another vaguely familiar drinking pal of Harry's loomed.

'Rum do this. Where's Harry?'

'Er . . . he's dead.'

'*Dead*. Good God. There's a thing. I thought this was Reggie's funeral.'

'Um, no. It's not.'

'Well, that's a relief. Reggie's still with us is he? Okey-doke. Mustn't linger.'

As I blinked in astonishment at his departing back, someone else sidled up. It was our erstwhile next-door neighbour in Meryton Road, an earnest young churchgoer called Adrian who'd always tried to convert us over the garden fence, waving evangelical pamphlets across the wisteria and informing us about the next Bible-reading class. I smiled as I recalled. It was one of the few things Harry and I had ever had a laugh about.

'Adrian, how sweet of you to come,' I murmured.

His glasses steamed up in consternation as he took my hand and I noticed, rather nervously, that he seemed to be clutching a guitar and a Ralph McTell song book.

'What d'you think?' he asked anxiously. 'At the end of the service maybe? Just to lighten it up a bit, and not too ecumenical either? I thought "Go Tell It On The Mountain" might not have been quite Harry's thing.'

'Er, no, you're right, it probably wouldn't have been, and it's a kind thought, but actually, Adrian, he was a bit more of a Jerusalem man really, and they're doing that on the organ. Thanks so much anyway, though.'

I watched, dazed, as they all trooped through, this motley crew, to take their seats; upper lips nice and stiff and not a glimmer of a tear in sight. In fact the lack of tears was beginning to depress me somewhat. It was all right for me to be stoical, but hell, these were his friends, for God's sake. I tried hard to squeeze a few out just for form's sake and wished I'd thought to pop an onion in my pocket, but the realisation that I was actually faking it horrified me, and I switched to an expression of frozen gaiety just as Charlotte and Boffy came sailing through the door.

'Smiling through the tears,' murmured Boffy, taking my hand in both of his. 'Harry would have been so proud of you.'

'Thank you, Boffy,' I said guiltily. 'And thank you both so much for all you did for Harry . . . at the end.'

Charlotte seized my shoulders and clasped me firmly to her very considerable bosom. 'Come and see me soon,' she whispered urgently. 'We'll talk!'

'I'd like that,' I lied, face squashed into her mammoth cleavage. Oh dear, so many lies, so much guilt!

Some of my own friends came quietly by, including Alice and Michael, and then a few of my relatives. It amused me to think how horrified Harry would have been to see the Northern contingent, whom he'd actually banned from our wedding, saying, 'Rosie, my love, we can't possibly have those ghastly cousins on your father's side. Good God, one of them packs turkeys for Bernard Matthews!' With the turkey packer came his wife Hilda, who according to Harry was a loathsome creature who always put the milk in first. I'd once asked Harry why he always took such an instant dislike to people. 'Saves time,' he'd growled.

Then came my immediate family, with Mummy weeping silently, supported by Daddy, and Philly and Miles looking grave. I watched them troop down to the front of the chapel, accompanied by the gloomy organ music – and then someone goosed me from behind.

I swung round. 'Bertram!' I gasped. 'For heaven's sake!'

He kissed me noisily on both cheeks. 'Sorry, my dear, something about the hang of that sexy little black skirt. So how about that then, eh? The old bugger's up and died on you now, has he? Full of surprises, isn't he?' There was an alarming twinkle in his eye.

'Yes, it's – terribly sad.'

'Of course it is, of course. Still, won't be long before you'll be pulling through, eh? Living to fight another day and all that. Perhaps even playing the merry widow? Can't wait! Shall we say sometime after tea?' He chuckled roguishly, dug me hard in the ribs and headed for a pew at the back of the chapel.

I hurried after him. 'Bertram, no, you should be at the front. There's a special seat saved for you there.'

'No, no, I'm fine here, my dear. I can see more from here, monitor the grief. I've always been a bit of a back row boy anyway.' He settled down and stretched his arms out along the back of the pew, gazing around. 'Not a bad turn-out really. Considering.'

I hastened back to the door before he could elucidate on 'considering', and since there seemed to be a temporary lull in the stream of mourners coming through I busied myself by looking for some more service sheets.

'How long do I have to stand here before I get a kiss then?' inquired a familiar voice behind me.

I turned and found myself looking into the equally familiar face of my brother.

'Tom!' I fell on him in delight. He hugged me back, then held me at arm's length, looking at me as I gazed at him. Dark, floppy-haired, blue-eyed, suede-jacketed, cowboy-booted, the absolute personification of cool. He grinned as he saw me taking all this in. 'Sorry about the clothes, I've come straight from the airport and I didn't particularly want to fly the Atlantic in a black suit.'

'Doesn't matter at all, at least you're here! How are you?'

'Oh, I'm fine, but how are you, Rosie?' He peered carefully, looking for telltale signs of grief. 'Holding up all right?'

'Yes, I'm fine actually. It's . . .' I struggled. 'Well, it's sad, of course, but I'm absolutely fine.'

He nodded, satisfied. 'Good.'

'My gosh, Tom, you've come a long way though, I didn't even know you were coming! You honestly didn't have to, you know. I mean, you and Harry were never exactly bosom—'

'I came to see you,' he said firmly.

Right from the beginning, Tom had been a vigorous and outspoken opponent of my marriage, deploying such subtle sobriquets as 'tosser' and 'complete prat' on my husband-to-be.

'Whatever I thought of him, he was my brother-in-law, remember. And Ivo's father.'

'Yes, of course,' I said, recovering. It was so lovely to see him, so tall and handsome with his LA poolside tan. Suddenly I felt very close to tears. 'Oh, Tom, I'm so glad you're here. I've been so mixed up about all this, I don't know what to think, don't even know how I'm supposed to feel, how to react, I—'

'Shhh . . .' He put his fingers to his lips as the organist crescendoed to a mighty, quavering chord. It soared ominously up to the ceiling. I turned to see the vicar beside me, poised in the doorway in his voluminous white gown, head held high, half-moons perched on nose, Bible clasped to breast ready for the solemn march down the aisle.

Tom led me quickly to the front pew and I sat down, sandwiched between him and Philly. I glanced back for a moment and caught Bertram's eye. He winked lewdly. I froze, then swivelled quickly to the front.

'Dearly beloved, we are gathered here together today . . .'

We were off. At quite a rate, actually. I don't know whether the vicar was a bit behind with his services and had another one to fit in after this, but we cantered through the readings, a couple of hymns – 'Jerusalem' and 'I Vow To Thee My Country' (naturally) – at an incredible rate. Then the vicar said a little homily about how sad it was Harry had left us, and then Boffy did a little piece to camera about what a good chap he was, and then just when I was thinking it must be nearly over and wondering how the hell all these people would fit into the sitting room back at Meryton Road, he joined us. Harry, I mean. Down the aisle he came, carried high and slow in his coffin, and since I'd never actually been to a funeral before, I was totally unprepared. God, there he was, in that box. It came as a bit of a shock to realise that in these days of sanitising everything they still buried real bodies, and to my intense relief I took one look and burst into a flood of entirely genuine tears. It seemed to act like a Mexican wave upon the rest of the female congregation, because within seconds a sea of weeping was well and truly under way. As the pallbearers moved slowly down the aisle, I couldn't resist turning my tear-stained face rather defiantly in Bertram's direction, but as I did, I saw that he was standing up on his pew with a video recorder trained on the coffin.

'He's videoing it!' I hissed, horrified, to Tom.

Tom turned round and looked. But Tom lived in America. He

shrugged. 'Had to happen, I suppose. Weddings, christenings, why not funerals?'

The coffin came slowly to rest behind the lectern where it was laid on a platform, centre stage, as it were. I stared at it. About ten feet in front of it was a deep red curtain. There was a silence. What now? I thought, gripping my hanky tightly. Where was he off to now? Suddenly there was a low, mechanical whirring noise and the coffin began to move. It seemed to be on a sort of *Generation Game*-style conveyor belt and was heading towards the curtain, behind which was God knows what. Except that suddenly, I did. The flames, the furnace, the pyre and – Omigod! My hand suddenly shot to my mouth. Harry had always wanted to be buried! I froze. Of course! In the churchyard in Yorkshire, beside Bertram's house, he'd got his plot mapped out and everything – God, he'd even shown me the exact spot, next to someone, who was it now . . . Oh! His *parents*!

I tugged Tom's sleeve. 'Tom, I forgot,' I gasped. 'He wanted to be buried!'

He looked at me in alarm. 'Bit late now, Rosie.'

'But can't we stop it or something?' I hissed. 'Press a button?'

'This isn't a supermarket, you know,' he muttered, 'you can't just stop the thing and put back the carrots, he's on his way!'

I gazed in horror as the box continued to advance, but short of throwing myself on top of it and sailing off into the flames with him – which you must admit would have looked like a pretty selfless act – there was nothing I could do except watch as the curtain gently rose to accommodate the coffin, then fell back into place. He was gone.

'*Ooooh nooooo!*' I sobbed aloud.

A sympathetic murmur went up and many hands reached across pews to clutch mine.

Oh God! I thought, sobbing guiltily into my hanky. I couldn't even get that right for him, his final request! In all the confusion and with Mummy and Philly taking over the whole proceedings I'd completely forgotten, but I remembered now, he'd had very firm views on his demise. He was on no account to be left to medical science, on the basis that he didn't want his dick to end up in some medical student's pocket and pulled out in the pub as a joke – well, thank God I hadn't gone down that route – but neither had he wanted to be cremated, because he was damned if he was going to be sprinkled on some unscrupulous vicar's roses and have his casket refilled with a bit of old wood ash. I gulped guiltily into my hanky. Tom found my ear.

'You can bury the casket,' he murmured.

I glanced up in relief. 'Sure?' I breathed.

153

'Positive.'

'So – it'll almost be the same! I can take it up to Yorkshire and – he'll never know the difference!'

He smiled wryly. 'I think we can safely say you'll get away with it.'

This was a relief, but I was still in a state of quite genuine shock as we all stumbled out of the chapel. Naturally this helped my demeanour and invited lots of sympathy and hand squeezing from everyone assembled on the steps. After that there was a bit of uncertain hanging about, then a gradual trickle of cars started back to 63 Meryton Road, with me, as chief mourner, I supposed, glancing nervously through the rear window, in the lead.

As I put the key in the door of my old house, I had severe misgivings. The venue had been Mum and Philly's idea, but I wasn't at all sure I liked it. No, I didn't like it at all, I decided as I smiled hesitantly at the two waitresses stationed like sentries by the door to the drawing room. I took a glass of white wine from a proffered tray, gulped it down and went through. Why had I let them do this? Have it here? Why hadn't I asked for somewhere anonymous, like a room in a hotel or something? I gazed around at the familiar, heavy oak furniture, the huge dark paintings of Harry's forebears who glared accusingly down at me from the walls. I shivered. It had only been a week or so since I'd lived here but already I felt like a stranger. I certainly could never make this my home again, I knew that for sure. I felt as if the ghost of Harry was already around me, and it wasn't a particularly benevolent ghost either.

As I sipped my wine, I resolved there and then to put the house on the market at the very first opportunity; tomorrow, in fact. I'd hand over the keys to the nearest estate agent and tell him to do his damnedest, get as much as he could for it. I wondered, as I moved around the room, if I ought to give the place a good clean first. I hadn't been here for over a week so it was probably thick with dust. I ran my finger over a table. Spotless. I smiled. Philly, no doubt. She'd taken care of everything. She'd even got caterers to come in to do all the food; there were waitresses whizzing around with plates of food even now.

The room began to fill up. It was hot, oppressive. I tried to slip away and get out into the garden for some air but was cornered by an old school friend of Harry's. I nodded and accepted his sympathies, flying on automatic pilot now. It wasn't as if I had to say much anyway, just 'thank you', 'yes, dreadful', and 'you're very kind'. As I made polite conversation, I surreptitiously glanced around. Mummy had recovered enough to talk intently to Bertram who had his head bent low, listening. Daddy was chatting to his cousin Hilda, Philly was giving orders in the kitchen and the only other people I wanted to speak to were Tom and Alice who were over by the fireplace talking animatedly to one another. I watched as they chatted away, Alice, looking rather glamorous in a long, navy blue suit, throwing back her red hair and roaring with laughter at something Tom said, forgetting for a moment she wasn't at a drunken drinks party, then guiltily stopping her mouth with her hand, glancing around, remembering where she was. I smiled. They'd always got on well and they couldn't have seen each other for years, probably since Alice and I were at school. I tried to escape from my earnest, balding accountant to go and join them, but even as I made my polite excuses and turned away, I was boxed into another corner, by Bertram.

'My dear, I have to leave soon and I simply must talk to you for a moment.'

I was surprised by his subdued, rather perturbed tone, expecting to have to deal with his habitual innuendo, swatting away his wandering old hands.

'Of course, what is it?'

'Sit down.' He gestured to the unoccupied sofa and sat, patting a space next to him. He looked tired. 'For all my pretence, the old legs aren't what they used to be, Rosie, and I can't take all this standing up. It seems to be the vogue at these sort of events nowadays, nobody wants to sit any more.'

I perched obediently.

'Now, my dear. What I really want to talk about is Stockley Hall. D'you want it?'

I blinked, surprised. 'Well, I hadn't really thought about it, Bertram . . . Oh, I see. You mean now that Harry's gone.'

'Precisely. I'd left it to him in my will, of course, so technically I should make it over to you and then in turn to Ivo, but that would mean that if I should turn up my toes in a couple of years – which frankly is looking more and more likely the way my dicky heart's playing up – you'd have to go and live in the place.'

'Oh.'

'Exactly, oh. Or sell it.'

'Ah.' I brightened.

'Ah. Yes, much more appealing, I can see. But the thing is . . .' he hesitated.

'What?'

'Well, call me a sentimental old fool, but I've lived there all my life, as my father did before me, and I'm not convinced I want the old place sold the moment my back's turned, as it were.'

'Well, no. I can understand that.'

'Shall I tell you what I had in mind then?'

I smiled, knowing he would anyway. 'Do.'

'Well, I know you think it's a terrible old pile of crumbling rock and granite stuck out in the middle of nowhere, but you know, there's something about all that ruggedness that probably appeals more to a male sensibility than a female one. And you never know, Ivo, when he's older, might quite like the place.'

I nodded. 'Yes, you may be right. So?'

'So what I had in mind, if you don't feel too hard done by, is to put the place in trust for Ivo until he gets to an age when he can make up his own mind about it. Say about twenty-five. It may be he'll agree with you and think it's a ghastly old mausoleum, in which case he can sell it and buy himself a flashy pad in Mayfair and a Ferrari, and good luck to him, but he may, on the other hand, decide to keep it up. Live in it, shoot, hunt, maybe even raise a family.' He paused for a moment. 'I'd like him to have that option.'

I watched his face. It was soft, tender almost, for a moment. I felt for him. It was all he had left. I squeezed his hand.

'I'd like that too, Bertram, and I think it's a marvellous idea. Thank you, on Ivo's behalf. And you're absolutely right, I'd never live in it and I suppose in a few years' time I might decide to sell it, and then, who knows, Ivo might never forgive me.'

He smiled and patted my hand. 'Good. That's settled then. In the meantime I'll drum up some suitable trustees, make sure the place is looked after properly and get it all sorted out.' He sighed, leaned his head back on the sofa. 'You know, it's funny, Rosie. I was delighted when Harry married you, thought you'd be good for him, even imagined that one day you might all come up and live at Stockley. Thought I could take the granny flat in the attic, or maybe even one of the cottages. But it wouldn't have worked, would it? I mean, even if he hadn't died, I don't think you'd have stuck it out with him, would you?'

I swallowed. He didn't know I'd already left him. I licked my lips. 'Bertram, I'll tell you all about it some day. But – not here. Not now.'

He nodded. 'You're right. Neither the time nor the place.' He folded his arms and sat up straight. 'Well, now, to other things. How are you off for money, for instance? Did he see you all right?'

'D'you know, I'm not really sure. I'm seeing Harry's solicitor tomorrow to find out how he left things, but I expect I'll be fine.' I wasn't too certain at all, actually. Harry's solicitor, alias Boffy, hadn't given me much of an indication about Harry's estate but had suggested, rather tentatively after the funeral, that I might 'pop in'.

'Well, if there's any sort of hiccup, you come and see me. I wouldn't put it past the old fool to have left his affairs in a right bugger's muddle. He had no idea how to make money, or to hang on to it either, for that matter. Hadn't got much idea about a lot of things actually, God bless him,' he observed gloomily. He looked at me sideways. 'Can't imagine why you married him in the first place. Must have been the sex, I suppose, hmmm?'

I sighed. 'Bertram—'

'No, you're right, neither the time nor the place, I know.' He pursed his lips and sighed. 'Oh well, since there's to be no talk of sex, and since we've sorted out the money and the chattels, I think I should be getting myself back to Yorkshire.' He went to stand up but the sofa was very deep. I helped him up, much to his annoyance.

'How are you getting back?'

'Parkinson's in the kitchen. He's got the car outside. As soon as he's hoovered up as many egg sandwiches as he can stuff in his mouth, we'll be off.'

I smiled as he limped away to recover his chauffeur, barking 'Parkinson!' loudly, like something out of Jeeves and Wooster. Parkinson materialised and stood obediently by, helping him into his hat and coat in the hall. As I kissed his wrinkled old cheek, it occurred to me that Bertram hadn't come down here to pay his respects to Harry at all. He'd come down to settle his business affairs. Bertram was a very wily old man. I walked down the path to the car with him, folding my arms against the cold in my thin black suit and shivering as Parkinson opened the door to let him in. Once he'd settled himself, he buzzed down the window and leaned out.

'Now don't forget, my dear, if there's any problem financially, you come and see me. I don't want you to think I've cut you off without a penny.'

'I'll do that, Bertram, thank you.'

'Don't lie,' he snorted as the car moved off. 'You'd rather starve in a garret than come cap in hand to me!'

I laughed and stood waving on the pavement until the car was out of sight.

As I turned to go back inside I saw Mummy, waiting for me in the open doorway.

'Well?' she said eagerly, eyes alight.

'Well what?'

'Well, have you got it?'

'Got what?' I walked up towards her.

'Stockley Hall, of course! Has he left it to you?'

'Oh, right.' I shut the door behind me. 'Well, no, not really. He sort of offered it to me but I could tell he knew I didn't really want it, so no. But he's left it to Ivo.'

'Now?'

'No, not now, it's going to be held in trust.' I wandered through to the kitchen and picked absently at a smoked salmon pin wheel. 'Ivo can inherit when he's about twenty-five.'

'But – but that's ages away!'

'I suppose so, but it's in safe hands until then.'

'But it could have been in your hands!'

I frowned. 'What would I have done with it, Mum? I don't want to live there, I'd only have sold it and Bertram didn't want that.'

'Well, he wouldn't know, would he?' she hissed. 'He'd be dead!'

I stared in surprise.

'You could have made a fortune! Don't you realise that?'

I gazed at her incredulous face. Gosh, it meant so much to her, didn't it? I wondered if that's what she'd been bending Bertram's ear about earlier.

'Well, I'm sorry, Mum, I didn't want it and I thought it unscrupulous to take it and pretend I wouldn't sell it when in fact I probably would, especially when that was clearly what he didn't want, okay?'

'No, it's not okay, it's never bloody well okay when you do anything! Oh *God*, when will you ever get anything right!'

A few people around us stopped talking and turned to look.

'Mum, listen—'

'No, *you* listen! I'm sick of it, Rosie, the one chance you had to claw something back out of this God-awful mess and you can't even do that! You just muddle on through letting other people pick up the pieces of your life, letting me and Philly shoulder the entire load of this funeral while you take a back seat as usual and pitch up at the eleventh hour. It's all so typical! The trouble with you, my girl, is you've got no spunk!'

There were a few muffled titters around us, but my mother still referred to 'gay' curtains and wasn't to know that people didn't really shout about spunk these days.

Philly came zooming through the throng like a heat-seeking missile and seized Mummy's arm.

'What's going on?' she hissed. 'We can hear you in the drawing room, Mummy. Why are you shouting at Rosie? Everyone's listening!'

'D'you know what she's done?' Mummy raised her voice defiantly.

'Hmmm? She's let Stockley Hall go. Said she didn't want it, said, no thanks, she'd rather live in a two-up two-down rented gardener's cottage actually. It's pathetic, Philly!' She was shaking with emotion now. 'And after all the work I put in for you with that ghastly old man. I don't know where I've gone wrong with you, Rosie, I really don't.'

'Stop it right now,' warned Philly fiercely.

Mummy slumped down in a chair in defeat. 'The one chance this family had of finally being somebody somewhere. The Cavendishes of Stockley Hall. And you let it slip right through your fingers.' She shook her head. 'I don't believe it. I just don't believe it.'

Philly and I gazed at her. The Cavendishes of Stockley Hall? God, what planet was she on? Which century? Philly shook her head sadly.

'You're just tired, Mum,' she said softly. 'That's all it is. This has all been too much for you.'

Tom popped his head round the door. 'What's going on? Everyone's waiting for the crockery to start flying in here.'

'Nothing,' Philly said firmly. 'Mum's just a bit overwrought, that's all. She's overdone it. Tom, be an angel and help her upstairs, would you? I think she needs to lie down.'

'Sure.' He helped her up and she instantly fell on him, clinging like a barnacle.

'Tom, oh Tom, my dear boy, my only boy. When are you going to get married, Tommy, hmmm? Produce some heirs?'

'Heirs!' he muttered, rolling his eyes. 'What, to my rented, downtown, condominium dynasty?' He glanced ruefully over his shoulder at us as he helped her away. 'And you wonder why I live in America.'

Later, when everyone else had gone home, Miles and Philly stayed behind to help me clear up. I had to see Boffy and the estate agent in the morning so I was staying the night at the house, but part of me wished I'd arranged to stay at Alice's. I looked around the kitchen warily as I tidied up. It just seemed so peculiar now that Harry wasn't here. Philly wiped the table down as I rinsed some glasses. She paused for a moment, dishcloth in hand, then apropos of absolutely nothing said, 'You know that guy you were talking to when we came down to the cottage?'

'Which one?'

'You know, outside, as we drove up.'

'Oh. Alex Munroe?'

'That's it.' She folded her arms and beamed widely. 'Gosh, he's *so* nice.'

'Yes, he seemed it.'

'He's the local vet, you know.' She started scrubbing again. 'Miles and I know him quite well, what with all our animals and everything. He's always popping in, and he's been to dinner once or twice too. He had a girlfriend for years, a really sweet girl, but they broke up, I don't quite know why, and now he's absolutely hot property. Hottest, in fact, and that's saying something in our neck of the woods. Plenty of handsome young farmers about.'

'Really,' I said drily.

'Yes. In fact Miles went to a drinks party the other night – I couldn't go, couldn't get a baby-sitter – and he said it was amazing, there were all these bits of blonde totty from Cirencester with their Verbier tans circling him like piranhas. Said their puffas were practically squeaking with excitement, velvet hairbands bristling – you know how Miles exaggerates. But Milly Thomas was there too and she said her younger sister – who's absolutely knock-out looking, Michelle Pfeiffer but dark – was in a complete lather over him, dribbling into her dry white wine and flicking back her hair like her life depended on it. He's obviously got something.'

'Has he indeed? I really can't imagine why you're telling me all this, Philly.'

'Well, I'm just mentioning it, Rosie, that's all. It's no big deal, it's just—'

I flung the sponge in the water. 'Oh, you're *so* like Mummy, Phil! I know, I know, you're just casually mentioning it, just gently floating the idea, waiting to see if I'll take the bait, see if I'm interested, and even if I was – which I'm not, incidentally, seeing as I've just this minute buried my husband – but even if I was, d'you know something, Phil? It spoils it. All your so-called casual, well-meaning asides, it's downright scheming actually, and it sours it all from the word go.'

'I don't see why.'

'Because I feel watched, that's why. I don't *want* the telephone wires buzzing between you and Mummy the moment you get home from shopping because you've seen me "talking to a nice man" in the high street. I don't *want* pressure and I don't *want* to be pushed into anything, ever again!'

'I did not push you into marrying Harry!' she declared hotly.

'I know, I know, I got myself into that mess, but I'm very

160

conscious that I don't want to screw up again. I don't want any helpful advice, thank you very much, don't want any cosy candlelit foursome dinner parties,' I eyed her beadily, 'and I'm sorry if that thwarts your social arrangements and throws water on all your matchmaking skills but I just want to be left alone, if that doesn't sound too ungracious.'

'It does.'

'Well, I'm sorry.'

She sulked for a moment, then shrugged and picked up her J Cloth again. 'Oh well,' she said cheerfully, rubbing away at a wine stain on the table, 'it was worth a try.'

Later that evening, when I'd assured Philly and Miles for the millionth time that I was perfectly all right on my own, I finally shut the door on them and had the house to myself. I shivered in the hall for a moment, crossing my arms and rubbing my shoulders. I glanced quickly into the dining room. It was so odd. It was as if in every room, in every chair, I could still see him. Watching me. I shook myself mentally. Now stop it, Rosie, you're just being ridiculous, you're working yourself up into a right little tizz. Just go and get Ivo, put him to bed and then have a nice hot bath and get to bed yourself. Then first thing in the morning, get the hell out of here as fast as you can. Right. Absolutely. Good plan. I pulled on my coat and set off across the road to Alison's house to get Ivo.

It was nine o'clock now so he was fast asleep when I got there. Alison popped upstairs to get him and handed him to me on the doorstep, wrapped in a blanket. I took my bundle, whispered my thanks and gently carried him home. As I went I thought, how odd, there was someone, Alison, whom I'd known pretty well for two whole years now but whom I'd probably never see in my life again. Because for all our promises to keep in touch, what were the chances of our paths ever crossing? What were the chances of her coming down to Gloucestershire or me ever coming back to this road? Life had to be like that, though, didn't it, I mused as I walked, constantly changing tack, ebbing and flowing and – hello, here was someone else I thought I'd never see again! Coming round the corner, head bent, hands deep in his pockets, probably on his way back from a late shift at the supermarket, was Tim. He was heading straight towards me, but it was dark and he was whistling away at the pavement, clearly miles away. He hadn't seen me. I smiled as he got closer, remembering the ludicrous farce in the bathroom, his antics as the mad plumber. As he approached, he looked up and caught my eye. I stopped.

'Tim! How are you? D'you know, I was just thinking how funny it was—' I swung round, staring incredulously at his back as he sailed straight past me and walked on, for all the world as if he'd never seen me before in his life.

Chapter Twelve

I have to admit, despite my protestations I spent a fairly sleepless night in the old marital bed. Harry's things were very much in evidence around the house, but never more so than in the bedroom where I hadn't had the nerve to touch anything. His dressing gown hung limply on the back of the door, his hairbrush lay abandoned on the dressing table, and his socks, I knew, were festering at the bottom of the linen basket even now. Consequently he felt ever-present. I slept fitfully and at one point opened my eyes to see – aaaargh! There he was! Standing at the end of the bed! I sat bolt upright, only to realise it was just his Corby trouser press with a jacket thrown over the back, but that was enough for me. I seized the duvet, thundered downstairs and spent the rest of the night tossing and turning on the sofa. The following morning, as soon as Ivo was dressed and breakfasted, I got out of that house like a bat evicting hell, pedalled off furiously on my faithful old bicycle and arrived at Alice's house where I was dropping Ivo off for the day.

'Sure you don't mind?' I said anxiously as she came to the door in her working gear – baggy trousers, paint-splattered fisherman's jersey – and dragging a child on each ankle like a ball and chain.

'Of course I don't. You know jolly well I take my easel up to the attic, lock the door and yell "I'm not here!" when they bang on the door. He'll have a lovely time drinking bleach with Molly and Lou in the kitchen, won't you, darling? Come on, my love!' She held out her arms and he leapt on to her eagerly, instantly becoming her neck brace.

'Thanks, it's just – well, I seem to be leaving him all over the place at the moment, and I never used to.'

'Well, that's because you've had a funeral to go to and now you've got a solicitor to see, neither of which are particularly child-friendly venues. It's all right, Rosie, he won't grow up resenting you because you dropped him off with your best friend in your hour of need.'

163

I bit my lip. 'Might have to drop him off at a nursery or something when I get a job though.'

'Well, that's all right, he's over two now and you're only planning on doing a few mornings a week, aren't you?'

'Hopefully. Depends how the money goes really. Depends how much I need.'

'What are you going to do anyway?' She shifted Ivo on to her hip.

'Cook, if I can, but if not,' I shrugged, 'clean, I suppose.'

'What, people's houses?'

'Why not?' I bridled. 'People do, you know.'

'Yes, but my God, can you just see your mother's face? "A char!" she'll cry. "My daughter's a char!" She'll have the vapours and faint clean away on the spot. Good heavens, she'd rather you starved to death than scrubbed someone else's floor.'

'Well, I will if I don't work,' I said grimly. 'Anyway, you never know, I might be an incredibly rich widow.' I glanced at my watch. 'I must go and find out, Alice. I said I'd see Boffy at nine. 'Bye.' I kissed her quickly, then Ivo. 'You're an absolute star, by the way,' I threw over my shoulder as I hurried off down the path.

'Will you be back by two?' she called. 'Only I've got to take Molly to the doctor's.'

'I'll make sure I am. What's wrong with her?'

'Worms.'

'Oh, yuk!'

She grinned. 'There speaks a pre-school mother. Quite common amongst the three to fives, you know, along with head lice and a few other disgusting conditions I won't scare you with yet. Just so long as you don't get them yourself you're all right. Doesn't do much for your sex appeal.'

'I can imagine,' I said faintly. 'Thanks, I'll look forward to it.' I waved and pedalled off down the road.

The meeting with Boffy did not begin auspiciously. When I arrived at his office he came out to reception to meet me, looking very pink and nervous, his face clashing horribly with an eye-searing fuchsia shirt. Why was it, I wondered, that the people with the smallest brains always felt impelled to buy the most luminous shirts? I averted my eyes to his face. Boffy was actually quite good-looking in a dark and burly sort of way, but he had many small imperfections which taken in isolation might have been acceptable, but in conjunction with each other rendered him, to my mind, physically repulsive. For one thing he was so hirsute his chest hair peeked out above his collar, and it was clear that however much he shaved, he'd still always need another. In fact at one stupendously dull dinner party when he'd bored for Britain beside me, I became convinced I could actually see his stubble growing. He also had one of those tongues that was too big for his mouth and you could see it lolling around all pink and wet in its cave as he talked. Talking was something he did quite a lot, and always in a rather camp, theatrical way, peppering his conversation with lots of 'my dears' and 'my darlings', a strange affectation in a man who was undoubtedly as straight as a Roman road. I have to admit I'd never really seen the point of Boffy.

'Rosie, my dear,' he clasped both my hands anxiously and bore down on me for a kiss, jowls flapping. I had to stop myself wiping my cheeks with the back of my hand. He was a bit sweaty.

'Hello, Boffy, how are you?'

'Oh, I flourish, I flourish.' He hopped about stupidly from foot to foot. 'Come in, come in!' He gestured gallantly to his office. 'Sherry?' He indicated an array of bottles on a trolley in the corner.

I blinked. 'It's nine fifteen, Boffy.'

'Is it? Good Lord, so it is.' He glanced at his watch in surprise. 'Um, oh well, a couple of coffees then please, Karen, if you would.'

A peroxide blonde sitting outside his door nodded wordlessly and I thought a trifle contemptuously, and got up from her chair. We went inside and he sat down opposite me, looking uncomfortable behind his vast, leather-topped desk.

'We'll wait for the coffee then, shall we, Rosie? Don't want to go off half-cocked and get interrupted – ha ha!'

What was funny about that? 'Yes, fine,' I replied.

We sat in silence, Boffy gnawing away at the end of his pencil, frowning down at some papers on his desk, swivelling about in his chair. Suddenly I felt sorry for him. He clearly had bad news to impart and was desperately trying to find the most tactful way of doing it. Finally the coffee arrived and the door was shut. He looked up.

'It's bad news, I'm afraid, Rosie.'

What did I tell you? I cleared my throat. 'How bad?'

'We-ll . . . Harry's affairs, when he died, were not exactly in what one might call apple pie order.'

'I see.'

'Which is hardly surprising really. I mean one wouldn't expect a man of that age to be preparing for his death, now would one?'

'No, one wouldn't,' I agreed politely, accepting that little plea of mitigation on Harry's behalf. There was a silence. 'So . . . what sort of order were they in then, Boffy?'

'Hmmm?' He raised his eyebrows.

'His affairs,' I said gently. God, who was helping whom here?

'Ah, yes.' Boffy pursed his lips.

'A bugger's muddle?' I offered, borrowing Bertram's terminology.

He sucked his teeth, considering. 'Y-e-s,' he agreed finally, nodding. 'Yes, I think that would be fair.'

I sighed. Oh God. This was going to be hard work. Twenty questions with a man who presumably had passed some sort of exam to become a solicitor but who had nonetheless taken the inside track into Daddy's firm on the strength of his genes rather than his grey matter.

'Did he leave a Will?'

'He did actually, but I don't think it necessitates a formal reading. Such as he had he left to you and Ivo, it's just . . .' he tailed off, biting his pencil.

'There was nothing to leave,' I finished.

'Quite.'

'Well, did he have any life insurance?'

'Yes, yes he did, but, um, he didn't keep up with the payments, so it's lapsed. It's void, I'm afraid.'

'So, no provision was made for Ivo and me at all, is that it?'

'Not . . . as such.'

'Well, what about the houses? Our house, and the one Harry rented out. There were no mortgages on those, were there?'

'Fairly sizable ones actually, Rosie.'

'But they were a present from Bertram.'

'Ye-s, true, but just before the life insurance lapsed he, er, he remortgaged them.'

'No! Why?'

'To pay his debts.'

'What debts?'

'Oh, the usual. You know.' He squirmed.

'No, I don't.'

He leaned back in his chair. 'Well, the club of course is terribly expensive.' He laughed nervously and raked his hand through his hair. 'God, I should know. To be honest even I have a job paying their bills sometimes. They charge a fortune just for a simple gin and tonic, the bastards.'

'Yes?'

'Oh, and, er, one or two wine suppliers. Their accounts tend to mount up without one even realising it. It's amazing how much liquor one seems to get through without it even touching the sides. Oh, and, ah, one or two gambling debts too, I'm afraid.' He studied his fingernails, frowning hard.

'Gambling debts? From where?'

'Oh, just the odd game of blackjack at the Claremont Club, nothing serious. We all do it, but if it's not your lucky night – and to be honest it was rarely Harry's – it gets . . . well, expensive.'

'The Claremont Club! I didn't even know he was a member!'

'No, and to be honest neither does Charlotte, so mum's the word on that front, eh, Rosie?' Boffy blushed nervously.

The Claremont Club. I sat back, stunned. Good God, I could just see the pair of them sitting there at the roulette table in black tie like a couple of period pieces, imagining they were minor aristocracy or something, puffing away on huge cigars and discussing how many pheasants they'd put down on their imaginary shoots.

'I see,' I said faintly. 'And are there any debts outstanding?'

He nodded, eyes down. 'One or two, I'm afraid.'

I gazed at him. Well might he look ashamed. And neither should he bank on my discretion either. Charlotte had never exactly been my best buddy but even I felt a degree of sisterhood on this one.

'Tell me something, Boffy, if I sell both of the houses, will there be enough to cover the mortgages and Harry's debts?'

'Ah, well, that all depends on how much you get for the houses,' he said, glancing up. 'I really couldn't say, Rosie. The housing market is a law unto itself at the moment, you'd have to ask your estate agent.' He brightened visibly, clearly delighted to pass the buck.

'I see. So how much exactly will I need to make?'

He mentioned a sum so colossal, I thought for a moment he must be talking in lire or ecu. I nearly choked on my coffee but gulped it down grimly, trying to look as if that wouldn't be a problem since of course I had two huge imperial palaces to sell.

'Right.' I got to my feet and smiled broadly. No, I would not play the impoverished widow in front of Harry's friends, however much the situation demanded it. 'I'll let you know how the sales go, Boffy. The properties are going on the market this morning so it shouldn't be a problem. I think that's all we need to discuss for the moment.'

He nearly knocked his chair over, so keen was he to get to his feet. His face cleared with relief, overjoyed that this horrendous interview appeared to be over. But as he walked me to the door, he looked genuinely worried again. 'But you have got some money of your own, haven't you, Rosie? I mean, I don't want to pry but I'm sure Harry wouldn't have left his affairs like this if you hadn't got some private means.'

Ah, so that was how Charlotte managed. Squirrelled away her own little trust fund from Daddy, kept it for a rainy day, popped it in her knicker drawer, no doubt.

'Oh yes,' I assured him airily. 'I'm rotten with private means, Boffy. Don't you worry about me, Swiss bank accounts all over the shop.'

'Ha ha, excellent! Excellent news.' He laughed nervously, not quite sure how to take this. But then Boffy had never been quite sure how to take me ever since I'd once mentioned that Alice and I had been to a Save the Rainforest rally dressed as tropical rubber plants. 'You're joking, surely, my dear,' he'd kept saying. 'Having old Boffy on?' Clearly he'd found it more unbelievable than dressing up as Viscount Many-Acres and gambling the housekeeping.

I kissed his jowly cheeks at the front door. He peered at me anxiously, hopping from foot to foot again. 'Rosie, have we really covered everything? Anything else you want to ask? Any more questions?'

Yes, we've covered everything, I thought dismally. I'm as poor as a church mouse on account of you and my late husband behaving like complete and utter prats, and no, I have no other questions, other than to ask why you feel the urge to wear a shirt the colour of a baboon's anus.

I smiled. 'No, Boffy, you've been an absolute angel, thank you so much.'

'Not at all,' he beamed. 'Glad to be of service! Always happy to see your pretty face! Sorry about the Will and all that, but it could be worse. One of my clients left his wife four red light bulbs and a photograph of herself in the nude! Ha, ha!'

Pillock.

'Oh, a bike!' he chortled as I mounted it. 'How charming!'

Yes, charming and cheap, I thought grimly as I dutifully waved goodbye. ''Bye, Boffy.'

'Chow for now, my love!' He hurried gratefully inside and shut the door.

My heart sank as I cycled back over Battersea Bridge. God, Harry was a fool, I'd always known that, but *gambling*, for God's sake! And with what? No wonder he'd always been so tight with money and no wonder we'd had such stupid rows over the Peter Jones account and the supposedly exorbitant price of things like a Le Creuset frying pan or a Thomas the Tank Engine duvet cover, when all the time his money was going down the Claremont Club's lavatory. What a bastard! Don't think ill of the dead, don't think ill of the dead, I muttered as I pedalled away, but it was no good, the man was an imbecile of the highest order and actually it helped enormously knowing this. If he'd left me an incredibly rich widow I might have shuffled out of there feeling rather guilty about taking his money, particularly since I was leaving him, but as he clearly hadn't given a monkey's about Ivo and me, I could think as ill of him as I liked. I mean, how many normal married men let their *life* insurance lapse, for God's sake! I bet even Boffy, even Charlie, wouldn't do that, but not Harry, oh no. Eat, drink and be merry, for tomorrow you may die, I thought bitterly.

I got off my bike in the Wandsworth Bridge Road and wheeled it along the pavement, past the parade of shops, up to the estate agent's window. I peered in at the pictures of houses for sale. There were certainly plenty of them, but most seemed to have 'Sold' stickers slapped across them and not many seemed to be for sale. Perhaps he'd be glad of the business. Promise me an absolute fortune for them. I parked my bike and – 'bing-bong' – went in.

A Mr Mendleson (Bear-with-me) was delighted to be of service and nearly foamed at the mouth when I suggested that not one but *two* crumbling little semis at the wrong ends of Battersea and Fulham respectively might find their way on to his books. Business was clearly bad, but Mr Mendleson (Shan't-keep-you-a-moment) avidly wrote down the details, murmuring 'Tragic, tragic' as he learned of the reason for the sales. Beaming widely, he then assured me that these two des-reses were all he needed to get half of London beating a path to his door. I left him happily jangling both sets of keys, and as I mounted my bike felt hugely relieved that they were someone else's responsibility now, and that frankly the only 'tragic' thing about it would be if he didn't get a zonking great amount of money for them.

Pedalling away again, I glanced at my watch and – oh hell! – I was going to be late for Tom! He'd pinned me down yesterday to having lunch with him before he jetted back to America, and I had precisely ten minutes to cycle back into the West End and meet him at some rarefied watering hole at the fashionable end of the King's Road. I rose up in the saddle and pedalled away like billyo, wondering, at the same time, why on earth I couldn't just go at a more leisurely pace and arrive ten minutes late, which, let's face it, is exactly what he would do if the roles were reversed. Why was I always so pathetically eager not to let people down when all they did was let me down? I shook my head grimly. Things were going to have to change, Rosie Meadows, things were really going to have to change.

But not yet. I crashed into the elegant chrome and leather eatery hot, bothered, and probably even a little fragrant under the arms, but by golly I was only two minutes late.

'Hi!' I panted triumphantly, kissing Tom damply and flopping down opposite him.

'Well, hello.' He folded his *New York Times* languidly and regarded me with ironic amusement. 'Did you jog here or something?'

'No, I cycled.'

'Ah. Drink?'

'Please,' I gasped.

He leaned back slightly and caught the waiter's eye without having to stand on a chair and do semaphore like I usually do. I watched him as he waited for our man to come over. His hair was longer than usual and bleached by the sun, but its trendy floppiness suited his still boyish face, particularly with that tan and those piercing blue eyes. I settled back happily, admiring him. Like Philly, he still had the ability to turn heads, and far from being jealous, I'd always enjoyed it. I liked having good-looking siblings because I think I felt, in a pathetic sort of way, that if I hung around with them long enough, some of the magic might rub off on me. The waiter arrived and Tom raised his eyebrows quizzically at me.

'Beer? Wine?'

'No, just a squash or something please, I've got to pick Ivo up later.'

'A squash.' He grinned. 'You mean an orange juice?'

'Yes, fine.'

The waiter disappeared. Tom regarded me over the top of his Pils. 'Glad to see my little sister is still bouncing around drinking orange squash and riding bicycles. It rather restores my faith in human nature.'

I bridled. 'What, you mean like some hopeless case in the lower fourth or something?'

Tom looked startled. 'No, I didn't mean that.'

'And only round things "bounce" really, don't they, Tom?'

'Oh, for heaven's sake, Rosie!'

'Well, I'm sorry, but honestly, you and Philly are so flipping superior sometimes. Can't I ride a bike and have a soft drink? Or does it have to be all Porsches and champagne?'

He held up his hands. 'All right, all right, I'm sorry. Just an innocent little observation on your ever endearing nature but I take it right back, okay?'

I glared, still feeling a bit heated, but when he started dodging bullets behind his arm I caved in.

I grinned. 'Okay, I overreacted. I'm sorry. I'm just – well, I'm just a bit overwrought at the moment, that's all.'

Tom lowered his arm cautiously. 'Well, I'm not surprised. It's not every day you bury your husband.' He watched me closely to see how this would go down, but I quickly changed tack before he could interrogate me.

'So how are you, Tom? How's LA suiting you? Still doing lots of lounging around swimming pools in your shades being the swanky film director? Making lots of dosh as usual? Mum tells everyone you're loaded.'

He grimaced. 'God, hardly. Art house films are not exactly box office sensations, but it doesn't matter how often I explain that to Mum, she still doesn't take any notice. Last time I was over she took me to some ghastly sherry party and introduced me to a blue rinse crony of hers as "My son the mogul". We then had this ridiculous conversation, with Blue Rinse asking me how I liked India and which dynasty was I from and weren't their curries frightfully hot and was I a Muslim or a Hebrew. It didn't matter how often I shrieked "I'm a frigging film director!" in her ear, she didn't take a blind bit of notice.'

I laughed. 'Oh well, that'll teach Mum to brag. She's got you down as the next Stephen Spielberg, thinks it's only a matter of time before she can put on her best frock and come and view your latest oeuvre at the Royal Gala performance. She's already practising her curtsey and rehearsing "Yes, *very* proud" for the moment when she bobs to Prince Charles.'

Tom paled. 'Oh God, thanks for warning me. That's enough to put me off making films for life.'

'Oh, don't worry, you're still not quite flavour of the month. I mean, after all, you're still only a film director, aren't you? You're not a neurosurgeon or a tax lawyer like Marjorie Burdett's boy – Marjorie Burdett's boy is fifty-two, by the way – and of course she won't be totally enamoured with you until you settle down with a nice little wifey and have some children.'

'You think I don't know? It's all she's banged on about since I've been back.'

'And?' I grinned.

'And, since you're clearly as nosy as she is, no. There's no one remotely on the cards at the moment.'

'Why not? I thought LA was crawling with beautiful women. You're not gay, are you?'

He spat his drink over the table. 'No, I'm not gay, since you ask, although I'd be having a much better time of it if I was. Far more choice.'

'Rubbish, I bet there are millions of knock-out girls there absolutely gagging to sleep their way into the movies.'

'Of course there are, but not so many you'd want to face over the breakfast table the following morning.' He lit a Gauloise and frowned, blowing the smoke out thoughtfully in a thin blue line. 'It's hard to explain without sounding patronising, Rosie, but there are very few proper people out there. You go to parties and you know damn well it's just going to be one gorgeous silicone implant after another, and if a girl so much as mentions she's got a degree, or that she does something remotely interesting aside from "wanning to be in the moo-vies", you can't get near her for bees swarming round the honey pot. An intelligent woman is such a bloody novelty in California. It's one of the things that depresses me about the place, actually.'

'So you might come back?'

He grinned disarmingly. 'Don't be silly, I make far too much money to do that. But having said that, being here has made me realise what it is I miss about this place.'

'Ah, yes, the dewy English roses with their brilliant minds and their original floppy tits. You can't beat 'em, can you? I have a job swatting the bees off myself actually, I'm sick to death of being such a flaming honey pot.'

He laughed, but as his laughter faded there was a silence. He dragged on his cigarette, regarding me intently.

'So how are you really then?' he said quietly.

'Me? Oh God, I'm fine, fine! Couldn't be better.' I smiled brightly but could tell by his eyes he wasn't convinced. I sighed. 'Look, Tom, d'you mind awfully if we don't talk about Harry? For what it's worth, you were right about him and I was going to divorce him. That doesn't mean I'm glad he's dead, I'm not, but I can't play the grief-stricken widow.'

He nodded. 'And why should you? I don't expect you to, I'm just relieved it hasn't hit you too hard.' He paused. 'Ivo all right?'

'He's fine. He's so young and, well, to be honest, Harry didn't have much to do with him.'

'So . . . everything's worked out for the best then?'

'In a manner of speaking, I suppose,' I said guardedly.

'What about money?'

I hesitated. For all his protestations, Tom was pretty well off and it would be very easy to come clean, admit to being impoverished and accept a loan, maybe even a gift. But somehow that smacked of taking a room in Philly's house. The under-achiever forever being bailed out by her more successful, affluent siblings.

I smiled. 'Money's fine. Harry provided for us.'

'Really? Gosh, well, I underestimated him then. I thought he'd leave you up to your neck in debt.'

'No. No, he took care of us.'

'So you don't need to work?'

'Oh, well, I might anyway,' I hedged. 'Something to do, you know.'

'Good idea. In fact I know a production company in Soho that's desperate for a good PA. A friend of mine works there. D'you want me to give her a ring?'

'I'm not staying in London, Tom. I'm going back to Gloucester-shire, and anyway, I'm a cook, not a production assistant.'

'Ah, I see.' He smiled. 'Going back to the country to hide behind your pots and pans.'

'What's that supposed to mean?'

He leaned forward. 'Come on, Rosie, you're free again now, you need to be in London. You'll never meet anyone in a little mousehole in the Cotswolds.'

'Now who's sounding like Mum!'

'And you need a more buzzy job. I know you like cooking but it's so solitary, isn't it? You need to be around people.'

'There are people in Gloucestershire.'

'Yes, but—'

'You mean "happening" people, is that it? Bright young thingy people who go to parties, the ones you were telling me about just now who were so shallow? So silicone implanted? Plenty of "proper" people in the Cotswolds you know, Tom.'

He narrowed his eyes and regarded me quizzically. 'What is it you're afraid of, Rosie?'

'I'm not afraid of anything!'

'Yes you are, you're afraid of competing, you always have been. Afraid of standing up to be counted in case you topple over again. Well, that's the risk you have to take, Rosie, otherwise you're not really living.'

'I haven't the faintest idea what you're talking about.'

'Yes you have. You're by far the brightest of the three of us, you always were, so how come Philly and I went further? How come you dropped out of school just before your A levels when you were due to sit Oxbridge, suddenly announcing you didn't want to take them because you wanted to cook instead?'

'I did want to cook!'

'And how come you married Harry when you could have married a perfectly decent, normal sort of bloke?'

'Listen, Tom, I made those choices because I wanted to make them, there was no subversive, underlying motive behind them.'

'I disagree. I think you opted out. Whether you did it consciously or unconsciously I'm not sure, but you did it.'

There was a silence. I played with the stem of my glass, trying not to get angry, trying rationally to consider what he'd said. I seemed to remember Alice saying something along the same lines.

'Maybe you're right,' I said softly. 'I don't like competition. I find it faintly repulsive, if you must know. All those little egos struggling to get ahead of each other.'

'Like me and Philly.'

'Well, of course I don't find *you* two repulsive, but . . .' I hesitated. I thought back to the two of them studying in their rooms night after night, revising, testing each other, learning whole plays by heart, great chunks of history books, and then going up to Cambridge together in a blaze of glory, both with scholarships. The marvellous twins.

'It was the effort you put into it,' I said slowly. 'It was as if . . . as if nothing else mattered. As if academic success was the be all and end all.'

'As opposed to?'

'I don't know. But I remember thinking – well, I couldn't help thinking there must be something else.'

He sighed. 'But the point is, Rosie, we *had* to put all that effort in, whereas you could have done it so frigging effortlessly!'

I shrugged. 'Maybe, but maybe not. I might have flunked it at the last moment.'

He banged his glass down. 'You *see*! That's just so *like* you, Rosie. Yes, okay, you might have flunked it, but you've got to take that chance, accept the fact that you might fail. Don't be a coward! Stick your head above the parapet and if it gets knocked off, well, so be it, at least you'll know you've tried!'

I thought back, remembering the fear. The fear that took hold of me when it was my turn, my turn to take those crucial exams that were all-important in our household. For weeks the place would go silent, Mum would creep around delivering trays of food to bedrooms, softly closing doors, a finger to her lips. Quiet, please. Studying In Progress. And then after it was all over, we'd all wait with bated breath for the little bits of paper to come fluttering through the letter box with straight As on them. Or not, as the case may be. And what if I didn't make it? What if I failed? What would Mum say, what would she tell her friends? 'Poor little Rosie, she tries so hard, poor love, but she just isn't quite the calibre of Philly and Tom.'

I shifted in my seat. 'And how exactly does this relate to my present circumstances? You want me to do my A levels again, is that it? Be a mature student with a baby?'

'No, I just want you to take your chances. *Try*, Rosie. There's no shame in it. The real shame is if you waste your life because of some ridiculous embarrassment factor about ambition being too egotistical. When you're going for a job, for God's sake go for the best one around, and don't shoot yourself in the foot at the interview by telling them how your soufflés sometimes collapse, or your sauces curdle. Puff yourself up a bit, tell them how terrific your crème brûlées are. Don't sabotage your chances. And likewise with men. If there's some gorgeous guy lurking about in the shadows looking interested, for God's sake don't back off, don't shuffle back to your hole in your bobbly cardigan mumbling something about having to wash your hair tonight.'

Suddenly I smelt a rat. 'Lurking about? Where?'

'What?'

'You said if there was some man lurking about.'

'Yes, I just meant hypothetically.'

'No you didn't.'

He coloured up. 'I did, Rosie.'

'You bloody didn't! I know you, Tom, come on, out with it!'

He sighed. 'Oh God, all right. It was just – well, Phil said something. Something about a vet, bit of a dude, I don't know.'

I gaped at him speechless for a moment. Finally I found my voice. 'Oh!' I breathed. 'Oh, I do not *believe* this! This is what this is all about, isn't it? This is what you've been leading up to! Go for it, Rosie, *go for the sexy vet*! That's what you've been primed to say, isn't it?'

'Don't be silly, I just—'

'Oh! Oh yes, I see it all now, this whole softly-softly character analysis bit, this whole "Don't hang back, Rosie, must try harder, take your chances" – it's all a smoke screen to pair me off with yet another man! Another man who incidentally I talked to for all of five minutes. Yes, you're in on it too!'

'Rosie, will you just calm down, I'm not in on anything, it's just that Mum mentioned—'

175

'Mum! Oh, *Mum's* involved too, is she?' I was boiling now. 'God, just a few days ago she was blubbing inconsolably over her son-in-law's ashes and now she's trying to force another man down my throat!'

'Figuratively speaking, of course,' he murmured.

'NOT NECESSARILY!' I roared. 'That woman would stop at nothing!'

'Shh, shh, steady, Rosie.' He glanced around nervously. People were looking at us.

'Have a word with Rosie,' I seethed, nodding knowingly. 'Have a little word, that was it, wasn't it, Tom?'

'Yes, but only because they worry about you, my love, only because you're on your own.'

'Ten days!' I squeaked. 'Ten bloody days I've been on my own and already they're setting up Dateline! Already they're getting together, having little powwows, mapping out my life, having a word in my ear, giving me a nudge in the right direction. God, I feel like issuing a bloody statement. To all members of my family. Hear this! From now on, Rosie Meadows regrets that she will *not* be running true to form! From now on she will not be bullied or pushed into anything she doesn't want and will be pursuing her happiness regardless of the demands of others! She will be accountable to no one, and certainly to no man that her family sees fit to pimp and hustle in her general direction, because in actual fact she may be on her own for some considerable time! If not forever! She may never look at a man again. In fact, shall I tell you something, Tom?' I glared at him over the table. 'The way I'm feeling at the moment, I may NEVER HAVE SEX WITH A MAN AGAIN! DO I MAKE MYSELF CLEAR!'

This, shouted at a million decibels, more or less brought the wine bar to a standstill. There was a deathly hush and all heads turned to view me and my brother, whose face was flaming. A few titters made it through the silence, and at an adjacent table a party of office girls stared open-mouthed. One of them raised her glass.

'Hear hear!' she said loudly.

Her friend opposite followed suit. 'Yeah, hear bloody hear. I'll drink to that!'

All over the wine bar girls laughed and raised their glasses.

'Yeah, nuke the bastards. Hear hear!'

The men all looked sheepishly into their beers, giving the occasional nervous smile in our direction, but none more nervous than Tom.

'Well?' I demanded, not finished with him yet. The bar waited, spellbound.

'Yeah, well?' shouted a heckler.

'Shit, well what?' he muttered, glancing around, looking terrified. 'Do I make myself clear?'

'Yes, bloody hell, yes, Rosie, crystal clear!'

'Good.'

A great cheer greeted this and applause rang out. Amidst the clapping I smiled at him over my orange juice, sipping it with my eyes still on him. Eventually the noise subsided and the bar resumed its usual low hum again.

'Jesus Christ, Rosie,' he muttered, running his hands through his hair. 'That was a bit unnecessary, wasn't it?'

'I don't think so. I had a point to get across.'

'Yes, but blimey, I'm just on the receiving end of a load of bloody Chinese whispers. I just do as I'm told. Don't shoot the messenger, all right?'

I grinned. 'All right.'

'I mean, you don't have to tell *me* what those women are like, I've *lived* with them, for God's sake! And like I told you before, why d'you think I live in America? I'm on your side, Rosie, you shag who you like, shag a tortoise if you want, it doesn't bother me.'

I laughed. 'Okay, okay, I'm sorry. I just wanted to make my position clear, and you might pass *that* message back along the line.'

'What, and be bollocked by them at the other end as well? No bloody fear, I'm keeping right out of this, I'm on the next plane back to America.' He downed his drink in a heartfelt gulp and looked at his watch.

I grinned, then glanced down at mine. 'Bugger!' I shot out of my seat.

'What?'

'God, I've got to go! I said I'd pick Ivo up at two – oh gosh, Tom, all I've done is yell at you and now I won't see you again for ages, will I?' Suddenly I felt contrite. I scrabbled around on the floor, picking up my handbag, finding my purse and my keys which had spilled out. 'When d'you go back?'

'Tonight, and yes, you have yelled at me, and no, I didn't deserve it, and yes I do hope you lose sleep over it, and no, you won't see me, ever again.' He smiled. 'Not unless I fly back as planned in a few months' time to do some business in London. I might pop down to the country to see you, actually.' He paused for effect. 'I gather you're living in Annabel Johnson's cottage.'

177

I stopped packing my bag. Stared. 'How the hell d'you know her?'

'Met her in LA, promoting her new book like mad.' He smiled, wagged a finger. 'Now there's a real trier for you. She tried to talk us into making one of her dreadful videos for her, you know, one of those ghastly, smug, I-know-how-to-be-happy-and-healthy-and-you-don't jobbies.'

'Oh! Right. God, I had no idea you knew her. So I take it you don't like her?'

'Oh I wouldn't say that, Rosie. She's something else actually.'

'Really?'

'Well, she's breathtakingly gorgeous, extremely talented, terribly charming and incredibly, *incredibly* . . . pleased with herself.'

'Ah.' I smiled. 'Good. A pain in the tubes.'

'You're happy about that, aren't you?'

'Of course.' I stood up, pecked him on the cheek and swung my bag over my shoulder, ready to go. 'You see, Tom,' I gave him a broad wink, 'that's what comes of trying too hard.'

Chapter Thirteen

I pedalled furiously to Alice's and arrived to find her bundling all three children into the car in their coats.

'I'm so sorry!' I yelled, as I leapt off my bike and flung it in the hedge.

'It's okay, I was going to take him with me, but you can have him back now.'

Ivo ran along the pavement to meet me, I picked him up and hugged him.

'Thanks for having him, Alice. Was he all right?'

'He was an angel, as ever,' she said disappearing into the car to belt her girls in. 'I keep waiting for him to turn into the demonic little fiend mine were at that age, but he's not showing any of the symptoms yet, damn him! I think you drug him. So come on, what did Boffy say?'

'Oh, this and that.' I bit my thumbnail.

Her head reappeared. 'Oh. Bad news?'

'Well, put it this way, I shan't be chartering a private jet and flying all my friends off to Mustique next summer like Mr Branson.'

'Oh, shame, I was rather counting on that. Oh well, never mind, Cornwall for us again as usual,' she said lightly, seeing my face and sensing I didn't want to talk about it. 'So how was Tom then?'

I grinned. 'Dreadful. Rich, successful, handsome, dynamic, just about to fly back to New York and then on to LA, positively oozing glamour.'

'God, poor devil. Ah well,' she sighed, 'just the doctor's surgery and then on to Sainsbury's for me, there's no end to the glamour in my life. Honestly, Rosie, when I was talking to Tom at Harry's funeral I found myself practically having to invent a life for myself. He said, "The last time I saw you you were playing Miranda at Durham," and I seriously thought he'd got the wrong person. It seemed so long ago, I felt it couldn't really have been me at all!'

'I know what you mean,' I agreed wistfully, remembering taking

Tom to watch Alice in her university production of *The Tempest* as a very beautiful Miranda. Red hair tumbling Pre-Raphaelite style down her back, blue eyes sparkling with intensity, her heart-shaped face pale and ethereal.

'Speaking of Sainsbury's,' I said coming back down to earth, 'I ran into Tim the packer yesterday.'

'Oh yes? Still got the hots for you?'

'No, quite the opposite. He completely ignored me. I said hello and he just looked straight through me as if he'd never seen me in his life before.'

'How strange.' She shrugged. 'Oh well, perhaps it was seeing you out of context like that, I mean not in the supermarket. It happens, you know, like seeing your postman on the Tube or something.'

'I suppose,' I said doubtfully.

She jumped in the car. 'Anyway, I must go, Rosie, we're late already, but I thought I'd come down and see you next week when Michael's in Cheltenham. Thought we could all go out to dinner.'

'Oh yes, I'd love that.' I brightened instantly.

'Good. See you then, then. 'Bye!' She waved cheerily out of her window, but Alice was a terrible driver and needed two hands. The car performed a series of violent kangaroo jumps before lurching dangerously round the corner.

I took Ivo back to Meryton Road to pick up our things and did a quick whip round the house, taking some curtains, rugs and cushions for the cottage, then as quickly as possible bundled everything into the car and set off back to Gloucestershire. It occurred to me that all Harry's paintings and furniture could go back to Yorkshire. They'd be happy there.

The first thing I did when I arrived in the little village was to pop into the general stores. I bought some blank postcards then hastened back to the car. Balancing a card on my knee I scribbled: 'Cook available to cater for dinner parties or lunches. Anything considered.' Then I added my address at the bottom. I was just about to dash back into the shop, when I glanced down at the card again. I set it aside slowly and reached for another one. I gazed out of the window, sucking the end of my pencil thoughtfully. Finally I wrote:

'Qualified cordon bleu chef (Pru Leith, Jean-Phillippe du Fort and Albert Roux trained) available for dinner parties, luncheons, buffets etc. First-class French cuisine in your own home at affordable prices. Inquire within.'

'Okay Tom,' I muttered, hastening back to the shop, 'I *will* try. I'll try really hard, but I'll try what I'm good at first, all right?'

The woman behind the counter was round, smiley and apple-cheeked. She read the card with interest.

'Oh, you're a cook, are you deary? And you trained with that Albert Rooks fellow? The one on the telly? Oooh yes, I like him, he's got ever such a lovely face, hasn't he? And that funny French accent, although to my mind you can't beat that Johnny Craddock fellow, old Fanny's husband. He was a one, wasn't he! I'll never forget that day when she'd done a bit o' baking and he turned to the camera and said, "Well, I hope all your doughnuts turn out like Fanny's!" ' She threw her head back and roared. 'How we laughed! Anyway,' she chortled, wiping her eyes, 'enough vulgarity, I'll put this in the window for you, luv, and you never know, there are plenty of posh women round here who live in big houses and 'aven't got the time nor the inclination to dirty up their fully fitted kitchens. I should think they'll snap up a Cordon Blair like you. Too busy selling knickers in pyramids or whatever it is they do to make their own volley-vonts.' She sniffed.

'Well, that's rather what I thought,' I said eagerly, 'and I thought in time I could set up my own catering company. A sort of dinner parties on wheels for stressed-out gentlefolk.'

'That's a very good idea, my duck, I'll put the word about for you.' She clucked her tongue sympathetically and shook her head. 'Ooh yes, what with you being on your own an' that now, and with the kiddie an' all. Shocking, that was, shocking. Don't know how you manage.'

Ah, so word had obviously got about. 'Yes, well, thanks so much, I'd really appreciate it.'

'No trouble at all, my dear, anything I can do to help. I'll get you a job, you see if I don't!' She wagged my card cheerfully and bustled off to put it in the window.

You see, I thought, driving back to the cottage with a much lighter heart, things were looking up already. You just wait, Tom, I won't need bailing out, the Rosie Meadows world famous catering company might be offering you a loan soon!

The cottage was freezing and smelled musty as I pushed open the door, but at least I'd left it tidy, and once I'd lit a fire and arranged the things I'd brought from London, it immediately felt like home. The furniture I'd ordered from John Lewis had arrived recently and a small gate-leg table and a couple of wooden chairs were now in situ. I sank back happily into the armchair, swinging my legs up, while Ivo pottered about obviously pleased to be back. Gosh, this was great, I thought, basking in the solitude. I could eat cheese on toast in front of the fire, listen to whatever music I pleased, have a gin and tonic in the bath, pick my feet, read till midnight, go to bed whenever I felt like it and – good heavens, look at that. A phone!

I sat up and stared. Sure enough in the corner of the room on my new table, sat a telephone. With a note on top. I swung my legs round and hastened over.

'You can't possibly live down here without some form of telecommunication so I had this installed for you. Joss.'

I smiled. Pedantic, short, but very sweet, and yes, actually, what a huge difference that would make. I gave Ivo a biscuit to keep him quiet and then immediately settled down to ring Mr Mendleson the estate agent. He wasn't so sweet. In fact, if anything, he was curt and abrupt and without so much of a glimmer of his old toadying manner.

'It's bad news I'm afraid, Mrs Meadows,' he said grimly. 'I can't get you anything like the amount you expected to make on those houses.'

My heart sank. 'Oh, really? Why ever not?'

'Well, the one you were living in wasn't too bad, although I have to say it's riddled with damp and the decor's looking a bit tatty—' rude bastard, I thought, fuming inwardly, that's my home you're talking about, let's have a look at *yours*, matey, poke around behind the back of your sofas '—but the *other* one. My dear Mrs Meadows!'

'What? My dear Mrs Meadows what?'

'Well, have you been there recently?'

'Um, no, not for – well, I suppose not ever actually. At least, not inside. It's always had tenants in it, you see.'

'Well, it shouldn't have had really. I'm afraid it's an absolute disgrace. There's no central heating, precious little plumbing, the water's pouring down the walls and in one bedroom the roof has completely fallen in, the occupants had taped plastic sheeting up in an effort to stop the rain getting in. The whole place stinks of rotting carpets and then there's the rats!'

'Rats?' I echoed faintly, the phone slipping a bit from my hand.

'Well, I didn't actually see any but I can only assume that's what the traps were for in the kitchen. I'm very sorry but I'll have to put it on the market as a complete overhaul job.'

'I see.'

'You had no idea?'

'No, I – I didn't take a very keen interest,' I mumbled. 'I mean, my husband always dealt with that side of things, you know, the rental.' God, this was ghastly, appalling. A drunk, a gambler and now a Rackman-style landlord prising money out of people for unsanitary living accommodation. Had I really been married to this man for three whole years?

'I really think all I can suggest is that you let me get what I can for it. Obviously I'll do my best but under the circumstances . . .'

'Of course, of course,' I muttered, embarrassed. 'Thank you so much, Mr Mendleson, just . . . do whatever you can.'

I put the phone down feeling slightly sick. I made a few mental calculations, felt even sicker and ran for a pen and paper. I sat down and worked it all out carefully. First Harry's debts, then the rental on this place – half price for the first few months – then the bare minimum for living expenses plus gas and electricity bills. I slightly overestimated what Mr Mendleson expected to get for the houses, subtracted one from the other and found . . . I was heavily in debt. I desperately added on what I might hope to earn from a few decent cookery jobs, a couple of mornings cleaning, scrubbing, flaying, *any*thing, and found I might just keep my head above water except . . . I hadn't got a job, and it could be weeks, months, before I got one. I dropped the pen with a clatter and my head sank into my hands. I stared at the table. There was only one thing for it. I'd have to give up this place. The only way I could break even and look after Ivo properly would be to move in with Philly and accept a loan from Tom. The two things in the world I least wanted to do. Bugger, bugger, bugger! I screwed the paper up into a ball, threw it at the wall and burst into tears. I had a damn good bawl actually, felt well and truly sorry for myself. After a while, though, I felt a little tug on my sleeve.

'Mummy sad.' Ivo's worried little face peered up at me through the crook of my elbow. I hauled him up on to my knee and wiped my face with the back of my hand, smiling. 'No, not really, darling, Mummy's just being silly, that's all. Feeling much too sorry for herself and being ridiculous.'

'Dickylous,' he agreed, nodding sympathetically.

I blew my nose and stood up, hoiking him on to my hip. 'Come on, this won't do. Worse things have happened to millions of people, haven't they?'

'You got bogey on your face, Mummy.'

'Oh have I, darling? Thank you so much.' I reached for a hanky and wiped my nose. 'Now, you see? I'm much better now, so come

on, let's go and get it over with. You'd like to go and live with your
Aunt Philly, wouldn't you?'

'And you?'

'Well, of course, and me,' I said vehemently.

I bundled him into his snowsuit and put my coat on. As I went to
the door, I turned and looked wistfully round my small sitting room.
It glowed with light and colour now that I'd finally got it organised. A
couple of bright kilim rugs I'd brought from London completely
covered the tatty old carpet and I'd brought some table lamps from
home too, which gave off a soft, rosy glow rather than that horrid,
harsh, overhead glare; tapestry cushions lay scattered in the window
seat, faded rose-printed curtains I'd laboriously made by hand for
our London bedroom but which Harry had abhorred hung at the
windows; water colours, pastels and drawings covered the walls. The
ugly sofa with its rusty springs was transformed by Alice's glorious
patchwork quilt thrown over it and either side of the roaring fire the
shelves in the alcoves groaned under the weight of my books. All the
things I'd made and collected and loved over the years had come
together in this one small room to give an overall effect, which if I
might say so could quite easily have come straight out of the pages of
Country Living doing a feature on hideaway country cottages.

I sighed and shut the door behind me. 'Oh well, it's only bricks
and mortar.'

'You still got bogey, Mummy.'

'Thanks, darling.' I wiped my nose again and held out my hand.
'Come on then. Off we go.'

He took my hand and with Blinky Bill in the other together we set
off solemnly up the still icy hill to inform our landlord of our
imminent departure. And anyway, I thought staunchly, what was so
terrible about living with Philly? Plenty of single mothers would
dream of having a rich sister to move in with. God, I was bloody
lucky to have the option.

It was a beautifully crisp afternoon and the bare, dark trees that
flanked a softly gold Farlings were silhouetted dramatically against a
sailor blue sky. As we walked through the yard, a clutch of chickens
rushed out to greet us, clucking round our ankles, hoping we might
be bringing their afternoon feed. One cheeky bantam cockerel
chased me in zigzags all the way round the side of the house and up
to the front door. Well, what do you know, I thought as I reached for
the door bell, I've pulled a chicken. Something to boast to Tom
about anyway.

I rang, and as my finger left the buzzer, Joss instantly opened the door. He stood in front of me dressed in an old Barbour and boots. He blinked.

'Well, whaddya know. I was just coming to see you.'

'Well, here I am.'

He opened the door so I could pass through and I walked into the softly defused light of the flagstoned hall, the only room I'd ever actually seen in this huge house, and the only one I was ever going to get to see now, I realised with a pang. A log fire burnt in the grate just as before. Did he light it every day I wondered, or did he have servants to do that for him, just before they ironed the newspapers and warmed up the loo seats? Either way, it was the height of luxury and I made a mental note that one day, when my ship finally came in – which of course it would after this small, ephemeral financial hitch had passed – I too would have a fire in my Grade II Jacobean hallway. Might even have a pair of lurchers stretched out in front of it too, you never knew. He shut the door behind me.

'Drink?'

I sank into a leather wing chair by the fire with a sleepy Ivo on my lap. 'Oh God, why not? Thanks.'

He went to a mahogany dresser in the corner and poured a couple of fingers of whisky from a decanter. As he handed it to me he regarded me curiously.

'You're not your usual cowering self today. What's all this flopping down into my chairs uninvited and drinking my scotch?'

I smiled wryly. 'I suppose I've got nothing to lose any more. It doesn't exactly matter if I offend you and you chuck me out.'

'Ah, so the obsequious manners were calculated to ensure your continued survival at the cottage. Well, before you actually relieve yourself on my carpet, might I inquire why that no longer applies?'

I told him, skimming lightly over my horrendous debts and the state of the rented property in London, but I think he got the general idea.

He stood over me, listening, one elbow leaning on the mantel above the fire while his other hand swirled the golden liquid around in his glass. When I'd finished, he nodded.

'Okay. Well, prepare to hand back that drink, perch on the edge of your chair and resume tenant status, because the reason I was coming to see you is I have a message for you. It seems you have a job.'

'What?'

'The pub called ten minutes ago. Asked to speak to "the cook wiv the kiddie" – I take it that's you. My God, you've only been back a day and already I'm taking messages for you, thank Christ I had a phone installed for you down there if this is any indication of your popularity.'

'Oh no, no I'm not popular at all, I mean – what did they say?' I asked eagerly. 'The pub?'

'Well it appears you have a friend in Mrs Fairfax at the village shop. After you gave her your ad she rang her brother Bob who just happens to be the landlord at the Red Lion – this is the Pennington mafia for you – and it transpires he'd that minute sacked the chef down there. Caught him in a compromising position with one of the barmaids apparently.' He rubbed his eyes wearily with his hand. 'Please don't ask me to expand on that, Rosie, I can assure you that I got the lot in glorious, lurid detail from the outraged landlord but I'd rather not share it with you if you don't mind. Anyway, the long and short of it is that Bob and cheffy had a mutual fuck-off conversation and now Bob wants you to step in as cook.'

'Oh! Oh God how marvellous, what exactly would that mean? I mean, did he say what it entailed or anything?'

'I'm afraid not. Sadly I had to bring Bellowing Bob to an abrupt halt as my other line went, and I'm afraid I deemed my dealer ringing from Cologne with details of my next exhibition more important than inquiring whether the pub liked its eggs sunny side up or not, but he did leave a number for you to ring. Here.' He handed me a scrap of paper. 'His name's Bob Carter incidentally.' He frowned. 'He did mention something about him needing forty three-course meals for tomorrow night though.'

'Christ – you're kidding!'

He grinned. 'Correct. No, I swear, Rosie, I haven't the faintest idea what it involves, but take it from me, whatever you serve up in that joint is bound to be better than anything they've subjected us to in the past. Tatty old omelettes with bits of flabby bacon inside and soup that you daren't get to the bottom of for fear of what you might find.' He shuddered. 'Oh yes, you'll be doing Pennington one hell of a favour by taking over that stove.'

I stood up, delighted, hoisting Ivo on to my hip. 'I'll go and ring him now. Oh, this is marvellous, Joss, I can't believe it's all happened so quickly! I thought I was destitute, thought it was the poor house for me. I've got so many debts to pay and – yes, I must ring Mrs Fairfax too, you know, thank her and – oh,' I turned suddenly as I made for the door. I paused and beamed back at him. 'Thanks for coming to tell me, Joss. And for the drink too.'

'No problem, and to tell you the truth I was going to the studio anyway. If you can bear to hang on for just two seconds I'll get my stuff and walk down with you.'

'Okay.'

I waited while he knocked back his drink and reached across to his desk to gather up a sheaf of drawings. He tucked them under his arm, grabbed a couple of pencils and then opened the front door for me. I went through under his arm, and together we went out into the sudden blackness that had descended outside. As we walked down the icy slope towards his studio and my cottage, a silence fell. I swallowed. For some reason, I felt unaccountably tongue tied. Talking had been so easy just a minute ago, back there in the hall when we'd had the business of my cooking to discuss, so why now, walking alongside this giant of a man in the pitch dark, did I feel almost shy?

When we arrived at the workshop door I hesitated. I was about to say goodnight, but then, lingered. If he says, goodnight then, Rosie, I'll say the same, I thought to myself, and then I'll go. I waited. He didn't. Instead he wrestled with the padlock for a moment, shot back some huge bolts and flung open the door. He reached up and flicked on the light. As he stood aside, I stepped in. My hand flew to my mouth. I gasped. I stood for a moment, taking it all in, gazing around in wonder.

It was a huge cavernous barn, and from the high oak beams above spotlights shone down, picking out, almost individually, the most fabulous array of sculptures and statues I'd ever seen. To one side of the studio was a long workbench, and on it a row of sleek, dark bronzes. Most of them were figurative: girls, athletes, nudes and animals. Panthers, gazelles and racehorses reared up at me with arched necks and wide staring eyes. All were breathtakingly lovely and instinctively I wanted to touch them, but it was the pieces in the centre of the room that had originally made me catch my breath and which still arrested me now. I turned back and gazed. For under the glare of one huge spotlight, three gigantic, pure white figures stood like sentries before me. I walked to them – Ivo practically asleep in my arms – as if pulled along by a piece of string. In total contrast to the bronzes, these enormous twenty-foot statues were carved exclusively from huge slabs of white Carrara marble. They were so abstract in form it was almost impossible to tell who, or even what they were, but there was no mistaking their mysticism, their power and their beauty.

'Oh!' I reached up and touched one tentatively. 'God, they're beautiful!' I gazed for a moment, then swung round. 'What are they?'

Joss grinned and came up beside me. 'As some artists would nebulously tell you, they're whatever you want them to be, but as a matter of fact,' he looked up, 'these are my pagan gods. That's Apollo's arse you're stroking there.'

'Oh!' I snatched my hand back.

'And this is Persephone,' he moved on, 'and beside her is Icarus, sadly lacking a head at the moment.'

'Yes, yes I can see that now,' I said eagerly. 'There are his wings and – oh, I see, there are Persephone's seeds next to her! Gosh, is this what you sell then? What you put in your exhibitions?' I wandered round, marvelling at them.

'Hell no, that's my bread and butter over there,' he jerked his head towards the bronzes on the bench. 'Those beasts with the flaming nostrils and the fiery eyes and the girls with the bent backs artfully touching their tippy toes, those are the ones that pay the school fees. That sort of art is real fashionable now, it's what every self-respecting Conran trendy wants in his converted attic space in Docklands. Those are the pieces that bring in the dough and most of the ones on that bench are commissions for pretty wealthy individuals. But these . . .' he thrust his hands deep in his pockets and gazed up at Persephone fondly, 'these are my passion. These are the guys who make my heart beat faster, get the blood coursing through my veins.' He stared a moment longer then shrugged philosophically. 'Sadly though, they're not commercial which means they're not financially viable. I mean, let's face it, who wants a socking great lump of marble in their front room between the couch and the television, and of course I'm not good enough for museum status yet so—'

'Yet!' I interrupted staunchly. 'But by golly, you will be! My gosh, I've never seen anything remotely like these, and okay, so I don't know that much about art but if you ask me these things knock spots off anything you see in a fancy London gallery!'

'Why thank you, for that supreme vote of confidence, Rosie.' He smiled and gave a mock bow but I could tell he was pleased by my enthusiasm. He sighed. 'Who knows. Maybe one day I'll be hustling one of these guys into the back of a lorry bound for the Tate, but for the moment, no. They're not everyone's bag and they certainly don't line my pockets. But that's okay, it just means that in the daylight hours I do those,' he indicated the bronzes behind us, 'but in my own time, I work on these guys. I begin my late night love affair with my gods and goddesses.' He grinned down at me, and the lights from the ceiling made his hazel eyes gleam. I gazed into them, for a second almost dazzled.

A moment later though, he'd turned, wandered over to his workbench. I watched his back as he sorted out a chisel, put it down and picked up another. I took this as my cue to go and cleared my throat.

'Perhaps I'd better leave you to your love affair while I go and ring the pub. I suppose it's about time I embarked on *my* new relationship with the landlord of the Red Lion.'

He walked back across the room, tool in hand, eyes narrowed at his statues, and already, I felt, oblivious of me, lost to Persephone's charms. 'Sure, you do that, Rosie,' he said abstractedly. 'And don't take any crap either, take it on your own terms.' He began gently tapping away.

I turned and set off down the hill, Ivo fast asleep in my arms now. The cold night air hung around me like a dark cloak after the dazzling brightness of that room and the excitement I'd felt at the prospect of the job at the pub seemed almost forgotten. I felt strangely moved. It seemed to me that those figures had stirred my soul, spoken to me somehow, or was it . . . something else. Almost as abstracted as Joss had been, I wandered into the empty cottage, kicked shut the door behind me and perched on the sofa. With Ivo lying in my lap I picked up the phone. I punched out the number Joss had given me. Yes, I thought as I put the receiver to my ear, it was something about the spiritualism of those statues but also—

''Ello!' A rough voice broke into my reverie.

I jumped. 'Um, hello, could I speak to Bob Carter please?'

'Bob Carter speaking, who's that?'

I explained who I was and the message I'd received.

'Ah! Yes! Right. Well now look, luv, we heard you was a bit of a chef see, and between you and me we've got one hell of a problem on that front. It's all gone a bit pear-shaped down here, lost our main player as it were.'

'Yes, I did hear that your chef had gone.'

'Oh he didn't go or nofin', luv, didn't walk if that's what you mean, no one walks from here, I pay too well. No I sacked him. Well bloody hell, I had to!' His voice rose indignantly.

'Yes I—'

'Caught him giving our Kylie a good seeing to over the cold meat counter and that's not on, is it? Well you'd know that, being a chef an' that, it's not hygienic is it, not wiv food around. We're very hot on hygiene down here at the Red Lion, very hot indeed.' I felt him mentally straightening his braces.

'Yes, I'm sure you are.'

189

'And my sister Enid, you know, from the shop, well she says you do some lovely French stuff – not that we'd want any of that titchy nouvelle business mind – but if you could see your way clear to knocking up some honest to goodness English fodder – trays of lasagne, curry, that sort of thing – well then as far as I'm concerned we're laughing. The job's yours!'

I suppressed a smile at his description of English food. 'Yes I'm sure I could do some . . . indigenous fodder.'

'Steady,' he said nervously, 'we don't want nothing too digenous, we got a very straightforward clientele 'ere, and no offence, luv, but we don't actually want you to cook down here neither, orright? Not actually in our kitchen see, 'cos that's where we went wrong with the last bugger. Gave him the run of the place, and he gave us the bleedin' run around in return! No, if it's all the same to you, we want you to cook the stuff indoors, bring it down, and then me and the missus'll bung it in the microwave later, see? Piping hot we'll make it, mind, we don't have no truck wiv reheated rubbish down here, it's all freshly made on the premises.'

I smiled at this massive contradiction but my heart leapt too. Brilliant, so I could do it all from the cottage with Ivo at my heels, and I wouldn't have to explain away my two-year-old commis chef assistant which I'd been just about to summon up the courage to do.

'Oh that suits me fine,' I breathed, 'I'm happy to do it here. So – what would it be then,' I reached for a pencil and paper, 'trays of lasagne, casseroles – moussaka?' I suggested helpfully.

'Nah, we tried a mousse once but it went down like a cup of cold sick. What this lot want is stodgy puddings, see. Baked jam roll, treacle sponge – how's your spotted dick?'

'First rate,' I muttered faintly.

'Great, yer on. We'll say food's off for tonight and tomorrow night, but come Wednesday I'll expect you down here wiv about forty covers, okay? Let's say two trays of lasagne and two of shepherd's pie for starters, and then a couple of decent puddings. Bring them here about six and have a port and lemon on me.'

'Great, and um, how much would I get?' I said quickly. 'I mean, what are you paying?'

'Two hundred quid a week for providing food every night 'cept Sunday – we don't want no lunch neither, my missus just does sandwiches for them that wants it – and all your ingredients paid for too of course. How's that?'

I made a few quick mental calculations. That wasn't bad. In fact if I could do it all from home it was a damn good wage for the country.

'Yer on,' I said, slipping into Bob speak. 'I'll take it.'

'Good girl! Told you I paid well didn't I? That randy chef didn't know what side his bread was buttered, but it's his loss and your gain. See you Wednesday then, and not too much garlic or nofin' orright? Cheers.'

And with that he'd gone. I put the receiver down slowly and gazed at the sleeping child in my arms. I felt pleased, but also somewhat bemused by the sudden turn of events. It seemed to me that my life was lurching, not so much from the sublime to the ridiculous, but from the dismal to the not so dismal. I was hardly going to leap up and shout, Yippee! I'm a pub cook, but on the other hand, it meant my hands were closing round the reins of my life again. It may not be the job of my dreams, but it would give me independence from my family, and I could make something of it, I was sure. Yes, maybe that was it, I mused as I gazed down at Ivo's dark lashes brushing against his rosy cheeks. Maybe, after all, one's capacity for happiness was simply dependent on one's ability to make adjustments to changing circumstances. To make the euphoric, let us say, out of the not-so-dismal. I smiled at Ivo, pleased with myself. Still fast asleep, he went bright red in the face, pushed hard and – oh God, that terrible, familiar smell. So that was what he thought of my home-spun philosophy, eh? I moved my hand from his nappy area and sank back with a sigh. Oh well, whatever the answer was, at the moment it all seemed to be totally and utterly out of my hands, and all I could reasonably hope to do, was go with the flow. Just like my son.

Chapter Fourteen

Two days later I drove into Cirencester and bought every ingredient I could conceivably need to meet the Red Lion's requirements. I staggered back, dumped half of Waitrose on the kitchen floor, then mentally flexed my muscles as I prepared to squeeze it, tardis style, into my minuscule fridge. Funnily enough, it's amazing how much you can cram into a two-foot-square space if you've got the inclination, and luckily it was so cold anyway that anything I couldn't force in just sat on the freezing windowsill. Then with Ivo happily stuffing playdoh down the cracks in the lino, I rolled up my sleeves and set about frying batches of mince on one of my tiny electric rings and boiling up pounds of potatoes on the other.

After the restaurant kitchens I'd been used to in London it was a bit like being transported to Lilliput, but it was a challenge, it was manageable, and I began to feel remarkably cheerful as I went about my work. Humming away happily I zapped on the radio, flicked on the oven to heat up, flicked it on again . . . and again . . . oh hell . . . don't tell me . . . God *please* don't tell me. I crouched down and peered in, fiddling around with the switch, prolonging the awful truth that my sweaty palms had already confirmed. No light. Bugger. It was broken. There was no doubt about it, this oven was well and truly knackered and had probably been that way for quite some time. I sank back on my heels and stared into its dark empty space. Right. What now then, Rosie – get it fixed? Flip through the Yellow Pages and chew your nails until some listless mechanic arrives to confirm the fact that your 1930s' appliance has indeed given up the ghost and since all the parts are pre-war there's nothing he can do, or . . . yes. Yes – of course. Joss.

I raced to the phone. Joss had been supportive hadn't he? Joss had been enthusiastic, and anyway he was always working, probably never set foot in the kitchen except to clean his chisels, he was bound to say – for God's sake, woman, stop fannying around and bring it up here! I punched out the number and waited. A girl answered.

'Hello?'

Ah. This must be Martha. 'Oh, hello, is Joss there please?'

'Nah he's gone away.'

'Gone away? But – oh. I only saw him yesterday, he didn't say!'

'Why should 'e?'

'Er, well, no reason, I just thought—'

'Yeah he's gone to New York for a few weeks. SoHo he said, which I always faught was a strip joint, but 'e says it's work.'

'Oh! Right.'

''Bye.'

She put the phone down. I stared into the receiver. Bloody hell! He'd gone. Christ, now what? I thought for a second, took a deep breath, steeled myself and rang back. She answered immediately.

'Martha,' I breathed, 'I'm so sorry, I didn't introduce myself properly. I'm Rosie Meadows and I'm the new tenant down at the cottage. I'm sorry to be a bore but I wondered if you could possibly do me an *enormous* favour. You see, I'm supposed to be cooking forty covers for the pub tonight and the thing is my oven's broken. I don't suppose there's any chance I could borrow yours is there? The rings on the top seem fine so I could do most of the work down here but it's just cooking it through that's the problem.'

I waited, my heart in my mouth. Felt her hesitate.

'I could give you a hand with the children?' I went on quickly. 'You know, while I wait for it to cook? And I could make a bit extra for their tea too, if you like?'

That did the trick.

'All right,' she said reluctantly, 'bring it up.'

'Thanks,' I breathed. 'You're a star.'

'Yes!' I hissed as I replaced the receiver. I was about to shout 'Result!' and punch the air in a yobby manner, but my fist froze by my ear as an ominous smell caught my nostrils. I skipped the self-congratulations and scurried back to the kitchen to find the mince burning away merrily and Ivo carefully emptying the entire contents of the fridge on to the floor. I flew around providing damage limitation and had just about managed to get things under control and was back, stirring at the stove again, when a voice behind me made me jump out of my skin.

'That's a funny smell.'

Two blonde heads popped up under my elbows. I breathed again. My God these twins were stealthy, it was like having the Apache warriors on your doorstep. They were in their uniforms, fresh from school and they seemed to have brought their rather smelly terriers with them too.

'It got a bit too hot, that's all,' I told them.

'I fink it's burnt,' said the one with the freckle. Ah, Emma.

'Yes it may be a bit, but I've turned it down now,' I said, firmly extracting their noses from the hot pan and turning them around, 'and I'm sure I can retrieve the situation. Good grief, what on earth have you got there?'

I stared at the huge wicker basket they appeared to have dragged into my sitting room.

'That's our stuff!' said Lucy, running to it happily and dragging it over. Her sister raced to help her. 'We brought it down to show you!' she confirmed.

Oh deep joy, I thought as they proceeded to unpack the contents of their dressing up box on to my tiny kitchen floor. In seconds the place looked like a flamenco dancer's dressing room as out came one frothy dress after another. I fried away at the stove and watched out of the corner of my eye as they ripped off their clothes and shimmied in and out of outfits, chattering constantly. I couldn't help smiling as I realised they'd chosen to be the same character and instead of fighting, had settled on the happy coincidence of both being her.

'Come on, Barbie!'

'Coming, Barbie!'

'Let's go clubbing, Barbie!'

I blinked into my pan.

'Yes let's, Barbie!'

And so it went on. Endlessly, with absolutely no pauses for breath and much mincing up and down the room with handbags and feather boas. Of course, I reasoned as I watched them twirl, they were only dressing up like any other little girls, but I couldn't help wondering why there wasn't a clown's suit or a nurse's outfit amongst this designer collection. As I turned to put the finishing fork squiggles to the top of one of my shepherd's pies, I caught sight of Toby's red blazer out of the kitchen window. He was sitting on my garden wall with his back to the cottage, throwing stones over the other side. I watched his hunched back for a moment, then wiped my hands on a tea-towel and went outside.

'Hi, Toby.'

He half turned. 'Oh. Hi.'

'What you doing?'

He shrugged. 'Nothing.'

'How was school?'

'All right.'

'D'you want to come in and have some juice?'

'Not really.'

I sat beside him, facing the opposite way. After a bit I tried again.

'I hear Daddy's gone away for a bit. When's he coming back, d'you know?'

'Christmas Eve, so he says.'

'Oh, that'll be nice.'

'Yeah, terrific. And no doubt he'll appear loaded down with presents like frigging Santa Claus and expect us all to sing "Jingle Bells" round the piano.'

I was startled by his bitterness.

'Oh come on, don't be like that. I'm sure he doesn't want to go, it's just his work, that's all. Don't get upset.'

'Who's upset? I'm not upset, I couldn't care less!' He jumped angrily off the wall and ran away down the other side. I watched him go for a moment, narrowing my eyes into the distance as he raced towards the frozen river, shimmering in the limpid winter sunshine. I waited until he was out of sight then sighed and went inside. I hadn't known these children long, but as Michael had predicted, they popped down to the cottage quite a lot, and I was beginning to realise this sort of behaviour was pretty much par for the course. The twins were bubbly and lively and, as a pair, pretty much self-sufficient, but Toby positively eschewed company of any kind and slunk off to the river at a moment's notice. I felt for him actually. It must be rotten to be left by his father as much as he clearly was, but on the other hand, plenty of fathers travelled on business didn't they? It was just that there was usually a mother around to pick up the pieces and hold the home front together while he was away. I sighed. Happily for once this was not my problem.

'What d'you normally do about tea?' I inquired as I went back in the kitchen.

Lucy was balancing a tiara on Ivo's head who was loving every minute of it, entranced that two such huge children should deign to pass the time of day with him, and Emma was tying headscarves on the terriers, both of whom, I realised with a start, appeared to have blue nail varnish on their toenails.

'Oh we just rummage around in the larder. There's usually bread and cheese or something, but I mostly have Coco Pops.'

'I see.'

'Vera comes today though,' Lucy reminded her sister. She turned to me. 'She's our cleaner, and she sometimes makes yukky fish paste sandwiches, but we just give them to the dogs.'

'Really,' I said marvelling at this liberal regime, which seemed to go totally unchallenged. I watched as Emma squeezed herself into

195

a ludicrously tight, sequined body suit.

'D'you think Daddy will bring back presents from America? D'you think he'll buy me a Barbie ball gown?' she asked as she gyrated about, disco style.

'I've no idea. Who gave you that outfit?' I inquired innocently.

'Marfa, it was her sister's. Marfa's boyfriend Gary says I look sexy in it. What's sexy, Rosie?'

My blood boiled briefly but I let it come down to a rolling simmer while I shook out her normal clothes.

'I suppose it means looking nice for boys. Do you want to look nice for boys, Emma?'

She turned, aghast. 'Ugh, no! What, you mean like those vile yobbos who gob on the pavement in the village?'

'Exactly. Here, put your clothes back on and then come up to the house with me. I've got to get this food in the oven now and if you like,' I threw back over my shoulder as I went to the car, 'I'll make that bodysuit into a couple of Barbie ball gowns for you when I get a moment.'

'Would you! Great! Oh, Rosie, thanks!' they chorused, delighted.

I smiled as I loaded pies, lasagnes and puddings into the boot of my Volvo. Considering they seemed to have brought themselves up, they were actually very sweet, if a little exhausting. I got in, and with Ivo strapped in beside me, drove carefully up to the house, with the twins in my rear-view mirror slowly dragging their basket up the hill behind me. I parked outside the kitchen door and as I unloaded the car looked for signs of life. Seeing none I gave a sharp tap on the back door, pushed on through then stopped for a moment on the doormat as I gazed around in surprise. I was somewhat taken aback to find myself in a very tatty, old-fashioned, unfitted kitchen. Aside from a huge oak dresser that covered one wall, there was an ancient range, a floor-to-ceiling cupboard, a large formica table in the middle and very little else. The paint also appeared to be peeling off the walls. Over by the dresser, a very skinny girl with aubergine-coloured hair which grew vertically out of her head was talking on the telephone. She wore three earrings in each ear, a gold stud in her nose, a black jumper that covered her bottom and her fingers, leopard-skin leggings and huge platform boots.

'Yeah . . . yeah . . . I know . . . I know . . . yeah . . .'

I smiled as I went past her but she didn't acknowledge me. As I bent to put the pies in the enormous old Aga, she broke off and put the phone down. I straightened up and smiled.

'Hi, I'm Rosie, thanks so much for bailing me out like this.'

Her white face against the dyed hair was thin and pinched and she had huge dark circles under her eyes. Late night clubbing no doubt.

''Sorright,' was her hostile response. She eyed me warily and I grinned back. No, I would not be intimidated by a girl ten years younger than me however scary she might look. I opened my mouth to initiate a conversation but at that moment, the twins burst in through the back door.

'Marfa! This is Rosie, she lives in the cottage and she's going to make ball gowns for our Barbies!'

'Well bully for her.' She pushed past me, picked up a Diet Coke and a *Cosmopolitan* from the table and left the room.

I gazed after her, genuinely surprised by her rudeness. Although I could see at a glance that we might not necessarily be one another's cup of tea, as anyone who looks after small children for any length of time will testify, adult company in any shape or form and however fleeting, is usually a bonus. One must, of course, come to recognise that restless, uneasy look in the postman's eye if he's kept talking at the gate for more than the statutory two minutes, but the tenant from the cottage would seem to me to be fair game, and I'd have thought she'd relish the opportunity to meet someone over the age of eight who might consume quantities of Nescafe with her. But it was not to be.

I sighed as I busied myself getting treacle sponges into the oven, but when my next visitor arrived, she couldn't have been more different. All fourteen stone of Vera Hawkins complete with hairnet and string bag, breezed in just as I was crouched down at the stove.

'Oooh, look at that now, a lovely sticky pudding! Ooh and I know who you are then, luv, I said to my Vic, I said they've got a new cook down the Red Lion and she's livin' in the old cottage at the big 'ouse, so that must be you, luv, is it? I'm Vera by the way.'

'Rosie,' I said with a smile as she beamed down at me, shedding her Pakamac like a second skin and bustling over to the cupboard for a housecoat.

'Well it'll make a change to have some decent food down there, luv, I can tell you,' she said as she buttoned herself in. 'But if you don't mind, I'm going to get on and leave you to it. I've got my work cut out doin' my few hours an' then getting back to get 'is tea on, 'e's ever such a demanding old bugger 'e is.'

And with that she bustled away, duster in one hand, Mr Sheen in the other, ample behind following purposefully in her wake as she embarked on her Herculean task in this huge house. As I watched her go, I realised with a smile who she reminded me of. Of course,

John Prescott in drag with a very considerable bosom.

Remembering my promise to Martha I offered the twins a jigsaw or a book while the food was cooking but 'See our bedrooms! Come see our bedrooms!' was the insistent, shrill response. If truth be told I was dying to see the rest of the house so I staged a great sigh, let myself be dragged out of the kitchen, and then with a girl on each hand and Ivo at my heels, set off down the corridor to the stairs.

I glanced in all the open doorways as they dragged me along, and considering the elegant grandeur of the entrance hall, it was a revelation. And a huge disappointment. Everywhere paint was peeling off the walls, wallpaper was torn back to the plaster and carpets were either tatty and frayed or nonexistent, with most rooms relying on bare unpolished floorboards. The furniture was mostly old and good, but simply crammed into rooms any old how with no consideration for style or comfort, resulting in a somewhat temporary look, as if it had been plonked there by removal men to be rearranged later. I was staggered by the contrast. It could, of course, have been beautiful. It was a large, rambling house with lots of grand, high-ceilinged rooms many of which ran into one another via a series of double doors. The windows were arched and mullioned, the doors Gothic and the fireplaces, huge stone affairs with vast grates, but Joss and Annabel, it seemed, saw nothing of this. Some windows appeared to be permanently shuttered making the rooms dark and gloomy, and most fireplaces just served as extra bookcases, with stacks of books piled high in their alcoves. The only pictures I saw were likewise stacked in corners. When I asked the girls why they weren't on the walls they looked at me in surprise, as if it had never occurred to them, so I didn't pursue it.

We went on to the hall and up a staircase of which it transpired there were three. This, the main one, was shiny and lethal – Vera and Mr Sheen having evidently staked their claim – but the other two were equally perilous, being spiral and rotten with woodworm, so that you had to watch where you put your foot for fear of falling through. All of these assault courses were a source of joy to Ivo, who kept trying to give me the slip and clamber up and down the precipices, like some novice skier intent on sustaining multiple fractures on the black run on day one. Once we'd made it to the girls' bedrooms I dutifully ooed and ahhed as yet more pink-sequined froth appeared, but then seeing they were totally absorbed, I left them to it. As I walked back across the landing, I noticed a door was open. I peeped in and caught a glimpse of Martha, fast asleep on a bed. Blimey, that was pretty cool, wasn't it? Was there no end to her gall? Still, mine was not to reason why and all that was required of me was to collect my food and return, somewhat bemused, to the relative sanity of my cottage.

And so began something of a routine. Every day I'd cook as much as I possibly could at my stove, then take it all up to the house. Determined not to be cowed by Martha's sullenness I'd breeze in with a 'Lovely day Martha!' To which she'd turn her cold grey eyes on me and answer 'Is it?' In the icy silence that followed I'd flounder blithely on about how much I loved these crisp winter mornings, whilst what I really wanted to say was 'Well, Martha, and how would you like a good kick in the pants, you silly tart?'

The arrangement suited me fine though, so I just bit my lip and observed her with mounting astonishment. As far as she was concerned my arrival heralded her departure, and the moment I set foot in the house she'd pluck her bag from the table, grab her leather jacket from the back of a chair, and disappear. And not just into the bowels of the house either, not upstairs for a kip and a Diet Coke, but out, into her car, and away down the hill for a good couple of hours. I watched from the window as she roared down the drive in her ancient Mini. Crikey, she had a nerve. What happened if Joss or Annabel rang, I wondered? Asked where she was? And where on earth did she go for heaven's sake? Off to see Gary? Off for a quicky?

In fact it was a relief to be rid of her. The atmosphere lightened when she'd gone and the twins were surprisingly good company. I taught them some basic cooking as they jabbered like magpies around me, and even Toby would come and perch on the kitchen table, watching as I worked. Sometimes I chatted to him about the river; asked him about the wildlife down there, whether he thought there'd be much fishing this summer, if he'd seen the heron's nest down by the spinney, carefully drawing him out on a subject I knew he found irresistible. I noticed his face wasn't quite so thunderous of late, and I also found that if I tried hard enough, I could actually make him laugh. Once, when I'd popped back to get something from the cottage, I came into the kitchen to find him singing away to the radio I'd brought up.

'You've got a nice voice, Toby,' I said in surprise. 'Do you sing at school?'

'Don't be silly,' he snapped, jumping off the table. 'D'you think there's room for more than one artistic temperament in this house?' And with that he slammed out of the back door, armed with a packet of Jaffa Cakes.

I sighed and went back to my lamb à la Grecque. Yes, lamb à la Grecque. You see, as the weeks had gone by, I'd sneakily managed to foist all manner of haute cuisine on to the Red Lion, and all under the euphemistic guise of 'stew'. I'd go in armed with coq au vin and announce 'Chicken stew, Bob!' To which he'd rub his hands gleefully and say 'Ooh, good girl, Rosie! Yesterday's fish stew went down a treat!' I'd smile at this description of my bouillabaisse, but it was true, it was going down a treat, because contrary to what Bob had maintained, the locals had very good taste, appreciated decent food, and were lapping it up. Cooking with alcohol wasn't a problem because I picked it up free from the pub, and since I always stuck to seasonal ingredients, it wasn't expensive either, all of which meant that I got to cook interesting food, the locals ate well, and in the event, I became positively lauded. 'The New Cook at the Red Lion' was quite the talk of Pennington and the surrounding villages. Bob, of course, was delighted.

'It's packed!' he roared when I rang one night to remind him to chop some parsley on to the jugged hare. 'The only time we've been as full as this is when we had a bent barman who was giving away free drinks to all his mates!'

I was quietly thrilled. Everything I cooked was perfectly capable of being reheated in a microwave and I resisted the temptation to experiment. Spinach and crab soufflé might taste tremendous fresh from the oven at Farlings, but would taste like a tatty old slipper by the time Bob and the missus had finished with it. Yes, it was hard work – particularly with four children and two terriers in beads and sunglasses trailing me all the while – but I enjoyed it, and Ivo was learning quite a lot too, what with having the older children around. Mostly words like bugger. I couldn't imagine where they'd picked their language up from, but I supposed it must be Martha, although I have to say, I'd yet to hear her swear. I'd yet to hear her say anything much actually, except 'yeah . . . I know . . .' on the phone. As I walked in on this particular morning, she was at it again, presumably to Gary. I carried a brace of partridge I'd managed to get from a local gamekeeper over to the table and wondered for the umpteenth time why on earth Joss and Annabel kept her on. Strangely enough the children seemed to adore her and spoke very fondly of her, but I couldn't help thinking—

'No! Oh no!' she suddenly shrieked into the phone. I nearly dropped my birds. I swung round to see her collapsing into the receiver. 'Oh, Nan, I can't bear it! Not again!'

I watched in astonishment as, sobbing wildly now, she dropped the phone and hid her face in her hands. I dithered for a moment, then scurried over.

'Martha! What on earth's happened, what's wrong?'

She sobbed on, heartrendingly so. I put my arm tentatively around her shoulders. Her skinny body shook, but she didn't resist me, so I led her gently to a chair. Gary. Yes, that's it, it must be Gary.

'It's my dad,' she cried, her voice breaking. 'He's got cancer. It was all right for a bit, but Nan says it's come back!'

I sat down and gazed at her in horror. 'Oh! God, Martha, I had no idea!'

She cried into the table, her spiky head cradled in her arms now. 'He'll 'ave to go back to 'orspital, it'll kill 'im!'

I bit my lip, regarding her slumped form for a moment. Then quickly I got up and nipped to the fridge for a bottle of wine. I grabbed a couple of glasses, sat down and poured them out. When I was sure she'd had a bloody good cry and was getting to the catchy breath stage, I pushed one towards her.

'Here,' I said gently. 'Take a gulp of this and then tell me all about it, eh?'

She raised her head and blinked at the glass. Her watery eyes flicked up at me, then she reached out and took a slug. Her hand shook as she lit a cigarette. She took another swig of wine, another drag on her cigarette, but then gradually, haltingly, and with pauses for nose blowing, it all came out. About how her mother had died four years ago. About how she'd got this job on the strength of her father being the gardener here. About how her dad had suddenly been taken ill and how she'd become the breadwinner, about how there were three younger children at home to look after and how she was terrified they'd all be taken into care if she lost her job. About how scared they all were for her dad, how she had to rally the younger ones, keep their peckers up, make them believe he wouldn't die when all the time her heart was in her boots. Her face crumpled occasionally, and there were pauses to catch her breath, but she told me about the terrible pain her dad was in. Told me how she sat by his bed as he crushed her hand to bits, his face contorted with agony. She told me how terrified he was of going back to hospital, how he relied on her, how they *all* relied on her, and finally, how truly, terribly, exhausted she was by it all.

'And I know I'm not giving it my all up here neiver,' she sniffed, 'but I used to, I swear it. I'm fond of these kids and they're all right they are, I've seen they're all right, but it's just I'm so knackered now. And now that Joss is away and I'm stayin' up here, I'm up all night wiv Toby too. He 'as these terrible nightmares see when 'is dad's away, so by the time I start work in the mornin' I just 'aven't got the strength!'

I gazed at her. 'So . . . hang on . . . when you disappear every day—'

'I get back to Dad. That first chemo took it out of him, left him ever so weak, so I get him some lunch, get the kids' tea ready, make sure our Damien's not skiving school, then sit wiv Dad some more. Read to him an' that.'

'Oh!' I started guiltily. 'And I thought you were seeing your boyfriend!'

She stared at me. 'Boyfriend?'

'You know, Gary.'

She gave a hollow laugh. 'Gary chucked me months ago. Said he never saw me 'cos I was always up here or wiv me dad. And anyway, he's wiv that slag Dawn Pentergrast now isn't he. He don't know I know that, but I walked past his house last Saturday and saw them at it, in the back of his Mr Whippy van.'

'Oh!'

'And I wouldn't have him back now anyway,' she said fiercely. 'Not after where he's been. My dad says he wouldn't put his walking stick where he's been.'

'No, well. Absolutely.'

She sniffed. 'Don't matter, I was goin' off him anyway. Didn't like his friends much, all that black leather gear – I reckon he was into M and S.'

'Er, don't you mean—'

'And I didn't like the way he was wiv the twins, neiver,' she said hotly.

'What d'you mean?'

'Always coming up here and swearing an' that, and when they was dressin' up one day . . .' her eyes slid away. 'Well, 'e was out of order. That's all.'

I gazed at the dark spiky head, the shaky hand holding the cigarette, the dark circles under her eyes. My gosh. I'd misjudged this girl.

'So – do Joss and Annabel know about all this? About how it is at home?' I said gently.

'Yeah, and that's why Joss keeps me on. He's all right he is. Dead loyal to my dad. And I'm not useless neiver,' she said fiercely. 'I looked after the twins when Kitty died, did the whole bleedin' lot when Joss went to pieces. He was a shambling wreck for a year and I brought them up single handed when they came home from that neo-natal unit at the 'orspital. He was that cut up about Kitty he didn't know if he was coming or goin'.'

'Oh – so you knew Kitty then? Did you work here then?'

'She took me on a few months before she died, not as a nanny like, she didn't want that, just to help her out. Didn't turn out that way though did it. She was lovely she was,' she said gently. 'Lovely wiv Toby too. Never off her hip he wasn't, just like you and that little bugger,' she nodded affectionately at Ivo. She smiled. 'She'd have him on one arm and wiv the other she'd be stripping walls and digging the garden an' that, she did it all on her own. Old Joss, he didn't make much money then, wasn't famous like he is now, so they couldn't afford any help. They took this old wreck on when her gran died, no one else wanted it. They were going to do it up themselves. You know, gradual like.'

'But . . .' I looked around, 'they haven't exactly, have they?'

'No 'cos she died before she could get to grips with any of the fancy stuff. What she did is what you can't see, like got the damp sorted out and all the rot in them beams.' She dragged on her cigarette. 'She did that front hall though. She said, "Martha, I'm going to start at the front and give a good impression, then I can entertain the neighbours out there and hope to God no one wants to come through and use the lavvy!" ' She smiled. 'She'd just started to strip the walls with one of them steam machines – size of a house she was, wiv the twins – when she went into labour and died. Why d'you think it's all hangin' in tatters and everything's back to the plaster?'

'You mean . . . when she died, he left it like that? As it was?'

'He couldn't bear to finish it and her not see it. It was her project see, meant everything to her. She was going to have a beautiful house, lovely garden, lots of kids . . . but it all went wrong.'

'So why didn't he sell it?'

'He tried. He put it on the market but no one wanted it what wiv it being such a mess inside, and he couldn't bring himself to practically give it away, so—'

'So he just lived in it? Exactly as she'd left it?' I looked around at the tatty kitchen, then back at her in astonishment. 'Good God, he's done a Miss Havisham, hasn't he?'

'Miss what?'

'Well – you know, kept everything as it was, as if it never happened!'

'Yeah and you should see her sewing room upstairs an' all.' She jerked her head up. 'Beautiful room that is, right at the top of the house, through a trap door. Full of plans and drawings, half-made curtains and bedspreads – there's still a bit of stuff in her sewing machine, just as she left it. He ain't never touched it.'

'And no one ever goes up there?'

'Oh Toby does. Joss don't know he does, but I've caught him up there. Not doing anything, not playin' or nofin', just sitting up there, in her chair at her machine.'

'Oh!' My hand flew to my mouth. 'God how sad! Does he remember her then?'

She shrugged. 'Dunno. You know Toby, he don't say much. He probably just thinks about how it might have been. You know, if she'd lived an' that. I do that sometimes too.' She stared into her wine. Of course, she'd lost her mother too.

'How awful,' I murmured. 'Poor you. And poor Toby! But – doesn't he get on with his stepmother?'

She looked at me blankly. 'Annabel? Stepmother?' She snorted. 'Blimey, she don't know the meaning of the word! No, as far as she's concerned she's just their dad's wife and the fact that he's got kids is a blimmin' inconvenience.'

'But – how can he love her?' I blurted. 'I mean, if she's so uncaring, so different from his first wife?'

She gave a strange smile. 'Yeah, well you've not seen her yet, have you? She's enough to knock any man sideways she is, my Gary spat his beer across the room when she walked in, and she knocked Joss for six all right, he's mad about her he is. She's bleedin' mental though. All that chantin' and meditating and funny food, and all those wacko books she writes about how to live your life.' She snorted derisively into her wine. 'What does she know about life. She don't know nofink she don't, just does it to be famous. She likes all that see, that's why she went for Joss.' She sighed. 'Reckon she'd like to see the back of me though.' She picked gloomily at her black nail varnish. 'I 'ope to God she's not back for Christmas. Joss says she might stay with her mum in Boston. I bleedin' hope so. Sharon Fairfax down the Spa says she's out for me. Says the next wrong move I make I'll be out on my ear. Dunno what I'll do then.' She began to shake slightly. I closed my hand over hers on the table.

'Right, now listen to me, Martha, you're not going to be out on your ear because here's what we're going to do. You've saved my life by letting me use this kitchen, so now I'm going to help you. You let me cook everything up here which will save me traipsing up and down to the cottage, and I'll give you a hand with the children until Joss and Annabel get back. I've got Ivo so I may as well have the others and I want you to go and spend some proper time with your dad and then have a sleep. I'll come up here first thing in the morning so you can whizz off and come back about tea-time, all right?'

Her red-rimmed eyes gazed at me. 'Why would you do that for me?'

'I've told you, you've helped me, and actually, it suits me not to be working in two kitchens, so it suits both of us, doesn't it?' I smiled into her exhausted, grateful face.

A silence fell. God, she was so young to be coping with all this, I thought as I watched her pick her nails. And so frail looking too. As I drained the end of the bottle into our glasses I wondered when was the last time she'd had any fun.

'What do your mates do for a laugh around here, Martha?' I said at length.

She came back from her thoughts. 'Eh? Oh, they go down Cheltenham way. There's some new club down the mall, Saturday nights is happy hour so—'

'Right, you're going.'

She smiled. 'Nah. It's miles away and it'll be a late night and—'

'Nonsense, you're going. I'll baby-sit the children, I'll even stay the night if needs be, but you're going to get out and have a bop, okay?'

She gazed at me. Gulped. 'I faught you was going to be a right snotty cow. Faught because you had a kid you'd tell me I was doing it all wrong, but I could see you weren't like that after a few days, it was just . . . I couldn't get back then. Once I'd been rude an' that, d'you know what I mean?' She looked at me appealingly.

I grinned. 'It's okay, I misjudged you too, Martha. It was only later when I realised how fond the children were of you and how nicely brought up they were that I knew I'd got my wires crossed somewhere. I feel bloody guilty too if you must know.'

'So we'll start again eh?'

'I think that's a good idea.'

We smiled at each other over our glasses and I realised that, but for the purple hair and the body mutilation, she was really quite a pretty girl.

'Your husband died, didn't he?' she said suddenly.

'Yes, yes he did.'

'I'm . . . sorry.'

I smiled. 'Well to tell you the truth, Martha, we were never exactly soul mates.'

She looked at me in surprise, then grinned. 'Oh so it's good riddance, is it? My Aunt Dolly married someone like that, she hung the flags out the day a loose slate knocked his head off. Hangin' by a thread it was. Still, there's talk round here that you won't be on your own for much longer anyway.'

'Really? Why's that?'

She grinned. 'Don't give me that. You know damn well that vet's got the hots for you, seems he can't stop finding laminitis in the horses' hooves or some other flimsy excuse to get up here. Blimey, I nearly crash into him every time I go down the drive!'

I blushed, thereby admitting to a grain of truth in this. It hadn't entirely escaped my notice that Alex Munroe had taken an inordinate amount of interest in the horses of late. In fact, it seemed that hardly a day went by without him coming up here on some pretext or another, popping in to report on this mare's fetlocks or that gelding's withers. Yes, these past few weeks, the horses had surely never been so well looked after. Personally I had mixed feelings about this. On the one hand there was no denying the fact – as my family had been so quick to point out – that he was a very attractive man. Besides this, as I'd got to know him, I'd grudgingly come to recognise a ready wit, an easy, relaxed manner, an above average intelligence, and yes, a nice guy who was undoubtedly a lot of fun. On top of all this, if the gossips were to be believed, he was clearly rather taken with me. In other words, in the space of a few short weeks, he seemed to have fallen quite effortlessly into my lap. So pick it up and run with it you might say. Except there were other things to take into account here. Other things to consider. It was, after all, only a month or so since Harry had died, and although there was little love lost, there was still a husband lost, and I wasn't convinced I wanted the attention so soon, nor the local tongues to wag so vociferously. Having said that, it was also true that over the past weeks, all that had got me through the long days of solitary cooking was that tap on the back door, followed by his tousled head as he came in, stamped the mud off his boots, swore about the weather and asked if there was such a thing as a cup of tea going in this godforsaken place? Then he'd sniff the air, remark that something smelled good, and if it was one of my ambrosial casseroles simmering in the oven, was there any danger of some of it coming his way? Seeing that Martha was never there at lunch time, it had then seemed as natural as anything for him to pull up a chair and join me and the children for lunch.

Later, when the children had left the table and run off, he'd stay and watch as I put the finishing touches to my dishes. He'd dip his finger absently in pudding basins and pick at mincemeat as I chopped away at the table, asking me a bit about Harry, about my life in London. But he never probed, and because of that, I was grateful to talk. I told him about my unhappiness prior to Harry's death, and my mixed feelings and guilt about it after. He seemed to understand, and it seemed to me that, despite his jokey manner, here was a man who'd been hurt himself. I remembered Philly mentioning a girlfriend and when I dug a little deeper, I discovered that there had been someone; someone he'd lived with for two years but who'd never completely fallen in love with him, but whom Alex had hoped, rather desperately, to keep through the confines of a joint mortgage rather than love.

'Silly bitch dithered for two years then up and left me,' he said cheerfully, popping a raisin in his mouth. 'She wasn't quite cut out for the country. The dirt got into her nails and she got bored with scraping the cow pats off her Gucci shoes.'

'But you miss her?' I asked as I separated some filo pastry.

He smiled wryly. 'Not enough to become a city vet. Not enough to spend my time looking after old ladies' pekes and chihuahuas which is what she wanted me to do. She saw herself in a town house in Chelsea with a little mews attached for my surgery and a window box full of geraniums. She'd like me to have nipped home for lunch every day and then whisked her off later for cocktails and quails' eggs in Knightsbridge.' He shrugged. 'The truth is we were going in totally different directions when we bumped into each other in the first place, we just took a ridiculously long time to disentangle ourselves. Wish I'd never met her actually,' he said gloomily.

I eyed him as I assembled my strudel. 'You do miss her.'

He narrowed his green eyes into space, considering this. 'I miss having someone around,' he said finally. 'But I'm not sure if it's her I miss, or just the idea of her. D'you know what I mean?'

I did. Being alone night after night, the empty evenings stretching ahead of me and the silence echoing around me was not exactly a barrel of laughs. And the curious thing was, I hadn't felt that way in the beginning. Back then I'd relished the solitude, but I was beginning to wonder whether solitude had turned into loneliness. Whether I'd crossed the divide. Alice and Michael had come down once or twice and taken me out to supper, but somehow, being a threesome had just reinforced my status. When Alex had pointed this out, I'd just bitten my lip and avoided his eye, as I now avoided Martha's.

'Actually, Martha,' I said, clearing my throat, 'the horses have been rather unwell lately, what with all this snow. The cold gets into their joints you see, makes them seize up, and if Alex has had the odd cup of tea in the kitchen it's because he's frozen to death out there too. That's all.'

'Bollocks!' she scoffed expressively. She waited, but when it became clear I wouldn't be drawn, she sniffed. 'Well you could do worse, you know. He's got a bit of money he has, and what wiv a kiddie an' all, maybe you shouldn't look a gift horse in the mouth.'

God she didn't beat about the bush, did she? And I was just about to tell her so when there was a tap at the back door. It flew open and Gift Horse himself stuck his head round.

'Hi!' he announced cheerfully.

'Hello, Alex.' I reddened and sank into my wine.

Martha folded her skinny arms and nodded triumphantly. 'Talk of the devil.'

'Oh really? Should my ears have been burning then? Shall I pretend to go out again and listen at the door? Oh, I say, a bottle of plonk, an *empty* bottle of plonk what's more, and that can only mean one thing,' he looked thoughtfully at the two of us, then grinned. 'A thaw has taken place with young Spikey Spice here. You see, Rosie? I told you she'd come round sooner or later.'

At that moment Vera staggered down the back stairs, having come to the end of her exhausting few hours. 'Cor blimey I need a cup of tea,' she gasped, rubbing her back. 'Ooh look, a party and, good gracious, if it isn't you *again*, Mr Munroe!' She looked meaningfully at Martha. 'Off you go then, luv, the kids are wanting you upstairs and these young things will want to be alone!'

Martha slipped up the back stairs with a huge grin at Vera and a wink at me. God, it was a bloody conspiracy!

'Cup of tea, Mr Munroe?' said Vera bustling over to the kettle. 'Then I'll leave you in peace, eh?'

'No thanks, Vera, I can't stay, I just popped in to say – well, to ask actually, if you were doing anything on Saturday night. Only there's a jazz band playing in the pub. Should be fun.'

'Me?' I blushed.

'Well not Vera. I'm not tangling with old Vic.'

'Oh, right.' I blushed some more. God, what was I, sixteen? 'Well I'm not sure, that's the night before Christmas Eve isn't it and I promised Martha I'd baby-sit.'

'Oh, come on, Vera will baby-sit, won't you, Big V?' He threw an arm around her ample shoulders.

'Course I will, if I get 'is tea on first.' She jerked her head in the direction of her husband's ever-demanding stomach. 'Strewth, that reminds me,' her hand flew to her mouth. 'I want to get him a bit of brisket from the butcher's and then I've got to be home to catch the post.' She abandoned the kettle and hastened to the door for her coat. 'Our Beryl's sending me a knitting pattern,' she went on. 'She posted it yesterday, so like as not it'll come in the second post. If I don't get my skates on he'll widdle all over it.'

'On what?'

'On the letters, luv. Soaks 'em so I can hardly read them.'

'Vic? Pees on the post?'

'Lord luv us no, not Vic, although he's that incontinent I shouldn't think it'll be long, he only has to cough and he's had a tinkle – no, our Randy. The bugger.'

I stared, uncomprehending. Randy? The bugger?

'Our old Jack Russell,' she said patiently. ''E's only got to hear the postman coming up the path and the letters dropping through the door and 'e's widdling all over them, all excited like. Have to race him to the doormat every morning.'

'Have you never thought of a mailbox, Vera?' inquired Alex, his mouth twitching.

'A what?'

'A box,' I explained, 'on your front gate, like they have in America.'

'Gawd luv us, no, I don't want anything American, I'm too old for all that malarkey, so's my Vic.' She sighed and shook out her hat. 'He's never really been the same since he had 'is testicles off, poor bugger.'

I sincerely hoped we were back to Randy.

Vera tied her corrugated rainhat firmly under her chin and eyed me sternly. 'Now you mind you get out to that pub of a Saturday night, luv, you've been workin' far too hard. Do you the world of good.'

'Of course it will,' affirmed Alex.

I smiled. 'Sorry,' I said, scooping Ivo up from his high chair, 'but I really will have far too much to do. I'm cooking a Christmas special for the pub that night and I don't want to be caught with my trousers down just when this job's going so well.'

Alex raised his eyebrows. 'No trousers down. Just a quiet drink.'

'Idiot,' I said, reddening. 'But thanks for asking me anyway,' I added truthfully, finally meeting his eye.

I turned and headed for the back stairs, leaving two disappointed faces behind me.

'She'll come round, luv,' I heard Vera whisper hoarsely, 'just give 'er a bit of time.'

I smiled at this and went on upstairs, leaving them to their machinations, but actually, my mind wasn't really on Alex or Vera at that moment. What really intrigued me, and what I was going to try and find, was Kitty's room.

Chapter Fifteen

With Ivo in my arms, I went up the stairs two at a time. Up and up until it seemed to me I couldn't go any further. The room had a trap door, Martha had said. I walked back and forth along the top landing, staring at the ceiling, puzzled. I was just about to dash along to the girls' room and ask Martha for further and better particulars, when I suddenly spotted a small half-door, high up in the wall, which I'd always assumed was a cupboard or something. I reached up and pulled at the handle but it stuck fast. Damn, it was locked. I gave it one final irritated wrench when suddenly it swung back. A step ladder shot down in front of me, missing my head by inches.

'Christ!' I leaped backwards.

'Thteps!' shrieked Ivo excitedly, wriggling to get down and indulge his passion for mountaineering.

'Steps,' I agreed, 'and jolly steep ones at that.'

I peered blindly up into the darkness, felt around for a light switch, miraculously found one, and then, wondering how on earth Kitty had managed this assault course on a daily basis with a toddler in tow, somehow half carried, half piggy-backed Ivo up. We wobbled precariously to the top step where I lunged forward and dumped him thankfully on the floor in front of me.

'There – whoops!' We fell together, laughing in a heap. I sat up, brushing the hair out of my eyes, but as I looked around, my laughter faded.

'Oh,' I groaned with delight.

It was a long, airy, attic room with a huge, white, cavernous ceiling full of beams and rafters also painted a gleaming white, stretching away to an enormous round window which dominated the end wall and through which the light flooded. It was Swedish, American boathouse or even New England church-like in style, and full of glorious pale colours. Glazed lemon walls reached up to the white rafters, pale green drapes hung casually but artfully round wooden poles at the windows, dark pink sofas and creamy calico cushions contrasted with faded, antique chairs and all on a pale, stripped wooden floor. After the darkness and clutter of the rooms downstairs it was like stumbling into an Atlantis, a jewel of a room, oozing style both old and new, an oasis of calm, light and tranquillity but all sadly neglected now and covered in dust and cobwebs. I got up and moved hypnotically around, touching things, stroking chair backs.

At one end of the room, under the round window and behind one of the huge squashy rose sofas, was a long, fruitwood table. It was covered in a chaotically organised sort of way with all manner of papers, bills, fabric samples, swatches of wallpaper, stencils, paint pots, books and prints. In one pile was a large sheaf of drawings. I picked up the top one and saw at once that it was a plan for the drawing room. Windows, curtains, fireplace and furniture had all been carefully sketched in, swatches of wallpaper and fabric were pinned in the corner and it was covered with notes and diagrams in an artistic, italic hand. I studied it for a minute then put it back carefully. Beneath the table were vast square baskets, one stacked high with magazines – *Interiors, House and Gardens* – another with china, piles of old blue and white Asiatic Pheasant plates, all destined for a dresser no doubt. Further along was another basket with more fabric, sticking up in rolls this time, and then another, a jumble of antique lace, appliquéd muslins, embroidered silks and bits of hand-blocked wallpaper. I crouched down and let a creamy, soft damask slip through my fingers. At the far end of the table was a sewing machine, still, as Martha had said, with a length of fabric under its needle, and next to it a pile of neatly stacked curtains made up in the same, old gold material. On top of that pile was pinned a note which said, 'Dining room. To be hemmed.'

I moved along, round and down the other side of the table, looking at the piles of receipts and order forms, all neatly paper-clipped together, and across to a beautiful little Georgian writing bureau. It was open, with its mahogany flap down revealing the small drawers at the back, and in front of it was a balloon-backed chair with a yellow buttoned seat. I sat down. The desk was crowded, but still neat and orderly. In one corner was a pile of correspondence, in another bills, then writing paper, two notepads, envelopes and some letters in a bundle, tied up with a blue ribbon. From Joss? I wondered. I touched them briefly, then ran my hand over a smooth, sandstone paperweight in the shape of a heart. Had that been a present from him? An old black Bakelite phone sat on the corner of the desk and I picked it up, wondering if it was purely aesthetic, but no, it worked. As I replaced the receiver I wondered how often she'd sat here, talking away happily to family, friends, relatives; chatting, laughing. It brought a lump to my throat. No wonder Joss couldn't bear to do anything to this room, this happy, painful, labour-intensive workroom that was almost overpowering in its nostalgia. A beautiful, living collage of the former occupant.

My eye roved across the piles of papers on the bureau and snagged on a watered silk file. I picked it up and opened it. Inside were recipes. Hundreds of them, cut out of magazines, torn from newspapers or scribbled down in her own arty hand. A lot of them I knew, many were classics – Elizabeth David, Arabella Boxer – but some were more obscure. Next to them she'd scribbled her own amendments – 'cut out sugar', 'add some dill' – and there was nothing particularly unusual about any of it, except, except . . . I swallowed. It all looked so familiar. I snapped the file shut and put it down.

Right in front of me was her diary, open. I'd known it was there but up to now I'd been avoiding it. I scanned the entries. Under Monday was a list: 'Cook for freezer. Finish trimming crib. Buy present for babies from Toby.' Under Tuesday was, 'Lunch with Molly. Ring midwife.' Then the pages went blank. I flicked through and came across a big red star next to a Friday and underneath she'd drawn a pair of babies' faces with a question mark and an exclamation mark. I bit my lip. That must have been her due date.

I got up from the desk feeling very strange. Sad, naturally, but very shaken too. Unsettled. I gazed about the room again, taking in the arty clutter, the heaps of material, the tidy piles, the order she was attempting to give to domestic chaos. You see I knew this girl. I recognised her so well.

Then my eye travelled to the other end of the room, the end I'd been avoiding up to now. I'd seen the playpen when I'd walked in, but it had made me ache to look at it. But Ivo had seen it now, and he was tugging my hand, dragging me over, and when I wouldn't come, he toddled off on his own. I followed reluctantly. As I gazed inside, my eyes filled up. Over time it had clearly become a toy box and the bright, plastic mat was littered with cars, old teddies, soldiers, wooden trains, squashy balls, and above it, swinging from the high rafters, handmade mobiles slowly turning. Ivo rattled the bars eagerly.

'In!'

'No, Ivo.'

'In. IN!' he insisted. I ignored him as he gazed wistfully through the bars at toys left exactly as they'd fallen years ago. He hoisted his leg up, attempting to clamber over. I pulled him off the bars and made to carry him away but he squawked angrily and tried to nose dive back into it, out of my arms.

'MuMMY!!'

'NO, Ivo.'

Struggling with him, I made for the stairs, but suddenly he kicked out at me, catching my knee.

'Ow! You little—' I loosened my grip and in that instant he wriggled free.

'Ivo!'

He was off, dashing back to the playpen, but as he ran, his eyes lit upon something else, something far more exciting to his left. It was a tiny child's desk, with crayons, papers, colouring books and little pots of paint, all neatly arranged and ready for action. Ivo's joy was complete. He darted to it, dragged out the chair, sat down, and before I could stop him he had reached for the crayons and was scribbling furiously on the pristine white paper, tearing it in his determination.

'Ivo, don't!' I swooped and tried to pick him up, but he clung to the chair with both fists, determined that this new toy would not evade him even if the playpen had.

'Dwar!' he shrieked. 'DWAR!'

'No, no drawing, it's not ours. Come on, we're going now, I'll find you something downstairs.'

'DWAR! DWAR!'

'Yes, but downstairs, I'll find you some crayons and—'

'What are you doing here?' a shrill voice rang out behind us.

I swung round and to my horror saw Toby standing at the top of the steps. His face was clenched, very pale.

'Toby!' I gasped. 'I'm so sorry, Martha said – well, we came up to, well, just to have a look, and then – Ivo saw the toys!'

He stared at me and I realised he was trembling.

'This is my mother's room.'

'I know, I know it is, darling, and it was dreadful of us to come up without asking you first, I feel so ashamed, but I just felt I wanted to know her a little more, Toby, to understand her. And now I've seen the room I do, but I should have asked first, I'm so sorry.' I tugged desperately at Ivo who was clinging to the chair for grim death.

'He's using my crayons. That was my desk when I was little.'

'I know, I know – oh, come ON, Ivo!' I struggled to pick him up but the chair came too as the wretched child clung on. His feet lashed out in fury and he kicked the desk over. It fell with a mighty crash, spilling all the paints, the crayons and papers on to the floor.

There was a horrified silence. Then Toby flew at us.

'You stupid boy!' he screamed, pummelling at us with his fists. 'You stupid, interfering woman with your stupid little boy!'

'Toby, stop!' I turned to protect Ivo, then put him down and swung back, holding Toby's arms as he lashed out at the air, his face contorted with fury. He struggled with me for a moment, then to my relief went limp. He burst into tears. I held him tight, holding him against me, letting his sobs flow into my body, cradling his head.

'Oh, Toby, I'm so sorry,' I cried, distressed.

He sobbed loudly into my chest, great shoulder-shaking sobs that racked his little body.

'Toby, don't, we'll put it all back, I promise we will!'

'It's not that,' he gasped, 'it's not really Ivo, he can stay, it's just – it's *everything*!'

I held on to him as he cried and cried. Gradually his sobs subsided, and as they did, I sneaked out one hand and surreptitiously managed to set the desk upright, feeling around behind me for the chair and setting that straight too. Ivo, intrigued by a bigger boy's tears, toddled over and put his arm round him, patting him solemnly.

'Poor Toby.'

Toby raised his head and gave a watery grin. 'Thanks, Ivo.'

'All right now?' I peered anxiously into his face.

He wiped his nose with the back of his hand and nodded. 'Yes. Sorry. I didn't mean to – hit you or anything. It's just this room. Being here. Sometimes it makes me happy, but sometimes I'm sad.' He shrugged. 'Dunno why really.' He looked around.

'It's because it's where you were with your mother. It's bound to be full of happy memories but sad ones too because – Ivo, will you leave that ALONE!' I lunged after the little beast who was making for the desk again.

'Because she died,' Toby finished. 'I know. Leave him, I don't mind, really, and I don't think Mummy would have minded either.'

I cringed as together we watched Ivo thrust a brush into each of the paint pots, mix up all the colours and then splosh it joyously over the paper, getting most of it on the desk. Toby seemed to be positively enjoying watching him now.

'That must have been like me,' he said with a bemused smile. 'Same age, painting like Ivo. Look, those are mine on the wall.'

I looked up, and pinned to the rafters was a collection of child art, mostly scribbles and, as he'd said, not dissimilar to the ones Ivo was doing now.

'Do you remember anything?' I asked softly, kneeling down and drawing him cautiously on to my knee. To my surprise he didn't resist.

He sniffed. 'Only little bits. Like her hair when she kissed me goodnight. I remember it used to tickle my face. And I remember – sort of, smells. A soft jumper. And some bracelets jingling.' He shrugged. 'I wish I remembered more, but I don't.' His face buckled and a huge tear plopped down his nose. He struggled heroically with his face. 'I think that's what makes me sad sometimes.'

'Of course it is,' I said kissing the top of his head. 'It's bound to, but doesn't Daddy help you remember? Don't you talk to him about it?'

He glanced up at me in astonishment. 'Oh no, that would make him too upset. He doesn't want to remember, he wants to forget. And anyway,' he said bitterly, 'he's got her now. What does he want to remember Mummy for?'

'Well, just because he's got Annabel, it doesn't mean he doesn't still miss your mummy, and sometimes, by going back it's easier to go forwards again. If you both shut it out because it's too painful it won't go away, it'll still be there.'

I wondered why Joss didn't talk to Toby. Who was he afraid of upsetting? And how could either of them be reconciled to the pain if they were both locked in their hurt without comforting each other?

'It won't ever go away,' said Toby fiercely, 'however much we talk about it. That's stupid. It'll always be there. I'll always not have a mother and everyone else will and that's all there is to it!' He jumped off my lap and ran to the stairs. He turned and scrambled down the ladder, his face hidden as he disappeared down through the hole. There was a thump as he jumped the last few steps on to the landing.

I sat and listened as his feet ran away down the passage. I sighed. It was ever thus with Toby. Two steps forward, one step back. With another heavy sigh I picked myself wearily up off the floorboards and brushed down my jeans.

Ivo was still intent on his painting and, not wanting to risk another tantrum, I crossed to Kitty's desk to check I'd left it as I'd found it. I smoothed down the page of the open diary and as I did, saw Joss watching me. From a tiny framed photograph in the corner of the desk. I hadn't noticed it before. I picked it up. He was walking up a grassy hill towards the camera, only it didn't look like Joss. He looked about ten years younger, tanned, windswept, incredibly good-looking, and the clothes were all wrong too. I'd only ever seen him wear rather cool baggy black ensembles, which went with his dark, brooding moods somehow, but here he was wearing a white T-shirt and jeans with, good heavens, a backpack on. When I looked closer I realised it had a tiny baby inside it. Toby. That in itself was surprising enough as he didn't seem like the type to go hiking up hills with his offspring on his back, more of a pat them on the head in the nursery type, but it wasn't just that. It was his face. He was laughing, and his eyes – they were so merry. Dancing almost. I found myself staring for ages. When I finally replaced the photograph in the corner, the ancient frame fell apart in my hands and the whole thing came to bits. Bugger. I tried to fix it and as I did, I realised there were more photos in the back. I slid them out guiltily, feeling that my fingers were well and truly in the till now, but quite unable to retract them. There was nothing unusual about the pictures, just a few family snaps obviously taken on the same day on the hill, again with Joss looking young and carefree, again with Toby on his back, but this time some of Kitty too. I stared at the bright, confident face that smiled out at me and realised I'd never seen a picture of her before. There were none around the house. Was that at Joss's or Annabel's instigation? I wondered. She had short sandy blonde hair with a long fringe that hung in her eyes, a few freckles, bright blue eyes and a huge smile with a slight gap in her teeth. Very pretty, but not in a groomed, manicured sort of way, just in an utterly natural and impossible to achieve without the basic bone structure sort of way. I replaced the photos with Joss's at the front. Slowly I got up from the desk. I went over to Ivo and crouched down beside him as he painted.

'Come on, darling, we're going now.'

For once he sensed I meant it and didn't prevaricate. He put down his brush, took my hand and together, precariously, we manoeuvred the stepladder downstairs. As we went back down the main staircase, I chewed my thumbnail thoughtfully. He'd changed of course, that much was clear; in fact I'd hardly recognised him, but people didn't change that much, did they? That carefree young man must surely still be in there somewhere, underneath that grim exterior? And could he not still come back, given the right set of circumstances? Given the right . . . well.

I wandered through the hall, along the dark, oak-panelled corridor back to the kitchen, but stopped short outside the open drawing-room door. What plans she'd had for this dark, gloomy room, and how wonderful those curtains would have looked at those tall windows. Imagine how it would be without that revolting swirly red wallpaper too. Could still be. My heart was beating ridiculously fast.

Ivo was racing excitedly about the room now, this being an unexpected privilege since I'd usually shoo him back into the kitchen or the playroom, but in his exuberance, he knocked against a pile of books on the coffee table and sent them flying. As he ran off and I bent to pick them up, one of them fell open. It was a collection of Yeats's poetry and inside, on the fly leaf, was written: 'For the one that so nearly got away. For the one that brought me back. My darling Annabel, with all my love and gratitude, Joss.'

I stared at it for a moment. I felt cold. Then I swallowed hard. Of course. Yes, of course, he was married, for God's sake, to her. What was I thinking of? I touched my forehead. Was I going insane? You're the frigging next-door-neighbour, for God's sake, Rosie, that's all, and apart from anything else, that man in the photo doesn't exist any more. He's moved on. To something more – exotic. And who d'you think you are anyway; the second Mrs de Winter? Or maybe even the third?

I snapped the book shut, flung it aside and marched off down the corridor. Back to the kitchen. Back to my stamping ground, back to – yes, back to where a cook belonged. When I got there, all three children were at the table armed with spoons, digging furtively into a tray of my special fudge cake pudding I'd prepared for the pub. *Neighbours* blared from the kitchen television. They looked up guiltily as I came in, their faces covered in chocolate, poised with contrition, feeble excuses ready on their mendacious lips, then stared in amazement as I totally ignored them. Ivo, wide-eyed with wonder, slunk between Toby and Lucy and dug his hand eagerly into the tray, delighted to take advantage of this uncharacteristic aberration in his mother. I went straight to the dresser, picked up the telephone and punched out a number determinedly. It rang for a while, then he answered.

'Hello?'

'Alex? Hi, it's Rosie. Listen, are you still thinking of going to the pub on Saturday night? . . . Good, because I've changed my mind . . . Yes, I'd love to come.'

Chapter Sixteen

Saturday night turned out to be more fun than I'd bargained for. The village pub was positively heaving with people and you could practically smell the Christmas spirit and see the walls pulsating as we approached. As Alex and I pushed our way into the crowded, smoky bar, it became clear that the entire village was in situ. Most of them were wearing silly hats covered in mistletoe, holly and tinsel, and all, it seemed, were intent on one thing and one thing only. To have a riotously good time and get as rip-roaringly drunk as possible. Now in the normal run of things, bearing in mind my recent troubles and demeanour, this might have appealed about as much as colonic irrigation, but funnily enough, tonight, my demeanour was different. Tonight I was In The Mood. Sod it, I thought as I squeezed purposefully through the merry throng. It's Christmas, it's the first time I'd been out in weeks – I don't count late night shopping – and I'm too young to hide my light under bushels. I was also buoyed up by a fairly certain knowledge – affirmed by the twins' clasped hands and gasps of 'Ooh!' and 'Aah!' as they'd sat on my bed and watched me get changed – that for the first time in a very long time I looked, well, if not exactly glamorous, at least clean and solvent.

I'd swapped my habitual bobbly jumper and leggings for a snappy little Donna Karan red jacket that I'd hardly recognised in my wardrobe it was so long since I'd worn it, applied a modicum of make-up – not the usual London faceful, no point in frightening the natives – and even dried my hair with a hairdryer, which was a first since I'd moved to Gloucestershire. The size 10 – yes, *size 10* – jeans that I'd bought in Cirencester fitted like a glove, and together with a white top under the red jacket, I looked, if I say so myself, pretty passable. I wouldn't go so far as to say heads were actually rotating as we pushed our way through the Yuletide throng, but there seemed to be a certain amount of interest. Eyes were definitely trained my way – quite a few eyes actually, blimey, I must be looking better than I thought, I flicked back my hair – or hang on, was it . . . ah. I see. It was Alex.

Well, I have to admit I could see why. Having never previously seen him in anything other than Barbour, wellies and a fair amount of sheep shit, I have to say he scrubbed up rather nicely. His reassuringly broad shoulders sat snugly in a distressed brown leather jacket, his russet waves curled seductively on to the back of his collar and those magnetising green eyes, deployed with that fatal, sexy, tigerish grin, had all the Lucindas and Sophias of the hairband and skiing tan persuasion dribbling into their spritzers, reaching for their Marlboro Lights, tossing back their fringes and generally parting like the Red Sea as we made our way to the bar.

For the first time in a very long time I felt I was in the right place at the right time with the right sort of man. And why not? I thought throwing back my own recently washed blond tresses with the best of them. I can still do this. Oh yes, I can still flirt and smoulder, thank you very much. I'm not so old that I can't cast my mind back and remember how to do it. I think. Just.

Once we'd made it through the seriously well heeled, we reached the seriously hard drinkers on the outskirts of the bar.

'Gin and tonic?' asked Alex.

'Please.'

'Anything to eat?' He grinned. 'I hear it's not bad in here.'

'No, thanks. Funnily enough I can never face my own food when I've been making it all day.'

I waved to Bob who I could just about see behind the bar.

'This braised venison is going down a storm, Rosie!' he shouted. 'They can't get enough of it.' A couple of people in the restaurant area turned and raised their glasses to affirm this. 'Had to ban one cheeky git though,' Bob went on as he pulled a pint. 'He said the food in here was nearly as good as some river café, so I said it was better than any bleedin' caff and he could take his custom elsewhere! We're getting a bit low on that Ozzy Bocco though, luv, you might have to make two batches next time.'

He hurried off to serve someone and, with Alex at the bar, I suddenly found myself surrounded by red-faced, inebriated farmers, all pouring strong dark beer down their thick red necks and clutching pint mugs to their enormous paunches. There was no question of stepping aside to let me follow Alex either, they all leered openly and deliberately blocked my way to get a better view. One florid labourer with trousers up to his armpits leaned his huge beery face down to me.

'Young veterinary's gone public now, 'as he? That's going to set the cat among the pigeons. We knew 'e was keen on you all right but you can't come in here with 'im and not have 'alf the tongues in the county waggin', you know!'

I smiled politely. 'So it appears.'

Another one dug me hard in the ribs. ''E's got quite an eye for the ladies has that young lad, but only the very prettiest mind! 'E's that fussy like!'

'Really. Well then, I imagine I'm flattered.'

'And so you should be. There's enough young totty round here for a man like 'im never to have to get out of bed all day. Look at that lot over there makin' sheep's eyes at 'im. Strewth, if I was a younger man I'd snap a few of them up meself, but I reckon I'd look to you first, luv. Reckon 'e's got 'is head screwed on all right.'

'Shut your great big vulgar mouth, Albert Parsons!' admonished an apple-cheeked lady to my left. It was Mrs Fairfax from the shop. She swatted his shoulder. 'What would she be wanting with the likes of you? 'E's ever such a nice young lad though,' she confided to me, nodding towards Alex who was waving a tenner at the barman. 'But if you'll take my advice,' she leaned across and hissed in my ear, 'you'll not give it away, neither. Make 'im wait. There's too many young girls dropping their drawers for too little these days – our Sharon, the little hussy, for starters, and for what? Half a shandy and a packet of crisps, that's what! You hold out for a bit more, my luv. You go for a slap up meal in a Berni Inn and don't hold back on the Black Forest gateau and liqueur coffees neither. Pretty girl like you can make 'em wait for it, and they will, too.' She prodded my hips. 'You're sitting on a bleeding gold mine there, luv, and don't you forget it!'

'Thank you so much,' I muttered faintly. 'I'll bear that in mind.'

Alex returned with the drinks to catch the tail end of this.

'Half a shandy and a packet of crisps all right for you, luv?' he muttered as he steered me away. 'Then back to my place?'

I giggled. 'Dream on, mate, it's Black Forest gateau or nufink for me, and I wouldn't mind parking my gold mine somewhere neither.' I scanned the bar. 'Although I don't suppose there's much chance of that in here.'

Alex looked around. 'Not a hope with this multitude, except – hold on, there's a space over there.'

We began to squeeze our way through to a table until Alex abruptly stopped. He turned about. 'Er, no. Change of plan. Think we'll stop here actually.'

'Why not over there? There's an empty table, isn't there?'

'True, but sadly it's next to Flora and I'm not exactly flavour of the month with her at the moment.'

'Flora?'

'Ex-girlfriend.'

'Oh really? The one you lived with?' I peered behind him with interest and saw a pretty, fairly pneumatic girl, with long blond hair, shooting the filthiest of looks in our general direction.

'No, that was Amanda. Flora came after her, and it was never really serious, I only went out with her a couple of times. It came grinding to a halt on her birthday actually. She had a dinner party and threw a complete wobbler in the middle of it. Apparently I behaved badly. She hasn't spoken to me since.'

'Why? What did you do?'

'Ignored her, so I'm told, and talked to someone else during dinner.'

'Doesn't sound too heinous.'

'Oh, and I forgot to bring her cake in too. Apparently she kept shooting me meaningful glances which I totally ignored, so in the end she stalked out to the kitchen, lit the candles and brought it in herself.'

'What, to get some attention?'

'Oh, she did that all right. She'd taken her top off. She was stark naked from the waist up.'

'Blimey!'

'And unfortunately her hair caught fire in the candles, so just as we were all dragging contentedly on our mid-course ciggies, this extraordinary vision appeared in the doorway, hair ablaze, tits dangling in the butter icing.'

'Oh God!' I gasped, trying desperately not to laugh because I was suddenly aware of Flora's eyes boring into us and I just knew that she knew that I knew, etc.

'Rather heroically I punched the cake from her hands and rolled her up in a Casa Pupo rug, thus minimising the damage, but of course she's never quite forgiven me.'

'I can imagine,' I giggled.

'And she's been known ever since as Flaming Flora, which hasn't helped much either.' He shrugged his shoulders in an innocent what's a boy to do? kind of way. But the green eyes glinted and I knew better.

'I see. In other words she fell madly in love with you and you treated her shoddily.'

He opened his eyes wide. 'Lord, no, that couldn't be further from the truth. I had no idea she was even serious about me, honestly, Rosie.'

'Relax, Alex, I'm not about to spontaneously combust should you neglect to speak to me.'

He grinned. 'I'm delighted to hear it.'

'But does the entire village always take such an avid interest in your affairs?' I nodded towards the bar where Mrs Fairfax and her cronies still had their heads together, smiling and nodding and speculating in our general direction.

'Oh, all the old biddies round here have known me since I was a baby and they've been trying to marry me off since I was about eighteen. Can't wait to get their best frocks out of mothballs and dust off their hats. That's why they all got so excited about Amanda, thought she was the one. You could almost hear the collective groans of despair when she packed her bags and left and I became Sad Single Man again.'

I grimaced. 'I know the feeling. My mother began agitating for the champagne and the orange blossom the moment I hit puberty, and she wasn't happy till I was floating up the aisle in a sea of raw silk. She couldn't have cared less whose arm I was on, it could have been Bernard Manning's for all she cared.'

'Is that why you married him then? Bernard Manning? Family pressure?'

I giggled. 'Perhaps, but that's no excuse. The bottom line is it was my own stupid fault. I just didn't examine the goods thoroughly enough.'

He looked thoughtfully into his pint. 'So . . . it's a bit of a relief in a way then, is it?'

'You mean now he's dead?' I said sharply.

'Well, you know, I was just thinking—'

'Well, I didn't dance on his grave and give the sherry a good bashing, if that's what you mean.'

'No, I didn't mean that. I just thought – well, maybe it's about time you were honest with yourself. About how you really felt about him. I reckon it's the best way for you to get over all this, Rosie.' His eyes were soft and steady.

I looked into them. 'There may be something in that,' I admitted, slowly.

He raised his glass and held my eyes over it. 'Good. Let's drink to that then.'

'To what?'

'To honesty.'

I shrugged. 'Okay. To honesty.'

We drank, and then we drank again and, let's face it, we drank a whole lot more that evening. We danced too, to a staggeringly awful 'Hi Ho Silver Lining' style band, that was by no stretch of the imagination jazz, but such was the enthusiasm of the sweaty, raucous crowd that we couldn't help punching the air and joining in with the 'Brown Sugars' and the 'Nut Bush City Limits' with the best of them. The lead singer was energetic, overweight and about forty-five, with a toupee that kept slipping as he tried to have sex with his microphone. Alex and I fell about laughing and I have to say I felt ridiculously, absurdly young again. Carefree, almost. Then came the clinchy numbers. 'Lady in Red' was crooned so badly that the entire dance floor felt honour bound to join in the chorus in a drunken, dog-howling manner, and all the while, as we clutched each other and laughed ourselves sick, I was aware of his hands on my waist as we danced, stroking the small of my back. It wasn't unduly unpleasant.

Finally, to spectacular applause, the band played its last number, and we made our way with the rest of the world to the door. Except that no one seemed to be actually going through the door. Coats stayed slung over the backs of chairs, more cigarettes were lit, and an awful lot of pint glasses appeared to be filling up at the bar again, even though it was well past closing time. It made me wonder if this pub actually closed at all and – good heavens, wasn't that Ed Spire the local bobby knocking back a pint over there in the corner? In the crush, Alex and I got separated. He was accosted by a bucolic farmer with important calving news, and I by a florid woman in a squashed hat who appeared to know me intimately, and lest I was in the dark proceeded to fill me in.

'Your sister lives over yonder, down Tigg's Bottom!' she declared triumphantly.

'Yes, that's right.'

'She's married to Miles Hampton, Bill Markham's cousin!'

'That's it.'

'And you're rentin' that cottage, up at the big house, belongs to them Americans don't it!'

'Yes, it does.'

''E's a sculptor 'e is, that Joss Dubarry. Famous too, been on the telly!'

'That's right.'

'You've got a kiddie yourself, you have.'

'I have, yes.'

And so it went on. On and on, until I thought that unless I presented her with a cut-glass rose bowl and declared her the outright winner of the Rosie Meadows specialist subject category, it just wouldn't stop. I nodded and smiled gratefully as she imparted yet more details of my life to me, desperately casting about at the same time to find Alex and catch his eye. Instead I caught someone else's.

'Miles!'

I broke away from my would-be biographer and pushed my way through to my brother-in-law who was leaning against a wall, cradling a pint and watching me thoughtfully, with a half-smile.

'What are you doing here?'

'Well this is my local you know, and I am occasionally allowed out for a pint in it if I've been a good boy. Especially at Christmas.'

'Is Philly here?'

'Don't be silly, she'd rather stick needles in her eyes than join this common, marauding crowd. No she's on tree trimming and present wrapping duty tonight. I'll tell her I saw you though.' He gave a sly glance over in Alex's direction. 'She'll be most interested.'

I groaned. 'Oh God, Miles, no, please! Philly means Mum, and you know what that means.'

He smiled sadistically. 'Ah yes, Mum. Address book open, sweet sherry in one hand, telephone in the other. Armed and lethal. What's it worth?'

'All my worldly goods, frankly. As it is I'll probably have the local paparazzi snapping away on my doorstep tomorrow. God, if I'd known I was having a drink with Pennington's answer to Liam Gallagher I'd have curled up with Joanna Trollope and an Ovaltine.'

'Ah well you see, he's about the only red-blooded unattached male left in these parts who doesn't walk around in small circles and hold conversations with himself all day. They all feel duty bound to find him a mate.'

'Yes well it's not me, okay?'

'Sure? You could have fried an egg in the looks you two were exchanging on that dance floor.'

'God – bloody spy!' I spluttered. 'Miles, just do me a favour and keep your observations to yourself, will you? I don't want half of Gloucestershire speculating on—'

'Alex! Good to see you!' Miles stretched past me and shook Alex's hand as he came up behind me.

'Hello, Miles, I didn't spot you in here!'

'He was lurking,' I muttered grimly. The two men did a lot of hearty back slapping and hand pumping as men do when the lager's been swilling about with the testosterone and we chatted for a bit, or shouted rather, over the drunken carols that were now being bellowed at full volume. But when Oh-Come-Let-Us-Adore-Him reached fearsome heights, Alex jerked his head inquiringly towards the door. I nodded energetically back and the three of us pushed and shoved the final few yards to freedom. Finally we emerged into the welcoming, cold night air.

'Phew, thank God for that,' said Miles. 'That's enough Yuletide spirit to last me a lifetime. 'Night, Alex. See you on Christmas morning, Rosie.'

'G'night!' we called after him as he made off for the car park.

We peeled off in the other direction and set off up the hill to Farlings. Vera was baby-sitting while Martha had her girls' night out, but I'd promised to take over and stay the night when I got back from the pub. I snuggled down into my coat, pushing the collar up against the cold and enjoying the sensation of the freezing air on my flushed cheeks. We trudged through the snow in silence for a bit. Then I smiled at Alex sideways.

'You knew it was going to be like that, didn't you?'

'Like what?' he said innocently.

'Like a proverbial goldfish bowl. I felt like I was on display or something, one of my own dishes of the day. Do all those people have a vested interest in your personal life or something? Do they get free drinks when you appear at the pub with someone of the opposite sex? I've never seen so much winking, I thought some of them were in danger of dislocating their eyelids.'

He chuckled. 'I told you, it's nothing personal, they're just bored witless that's all, and if it looks like there's going to be a romance between the emotionally retarded vet and the beautiful young widow from London they'll all hold their breath. Anyway, they probably think I need fattening up and reckon you're the girl to do it. It's their chance to view a real-life soap opera, you see.'

I snorted. 'God they must be hard up if they think my life is going to entertain them. I'm only sorry to disappoint them.'

'Does that mean you're going to disappoint me, too?'

I looked up sharply. 'What d'you mean?'

He thrust his hands deeper in his pockets and gazed down at the snow. 'Only that I like you. Is that allowed?'

'Of course it's allowed,' I said quietly.

There was a silence.

'It's just—'

'No, me first,' he interrupted. 'Hear me out, before you start telling me it's too soon and you're not ready for anything heavy yet, etc., etc.'

I shrugged. 'Okay.'

We walked on a bit. At length he cleared his throat. 'The thing is, Rosie, you're the first girl I've met for a long time that I haven't – well, that I haven't compared to Amanda.'

'Is that good?' I ventured.

'Well, I think so. I think it means . . . that I'm getting over her. That I like you irrespective of her. I don't find myself thinking, is she as pretty, or as funny, or as clever, or as anything, as her? For what it's worth, the last few weeks that I've been coming up to the house and spending time with you have been the happiest I've spent for a long time.'

'Well, I've been happy too, Alex,' I said carefully, 'but that doesn't mean I want to – well, to leap into anything again.'

'Why not?'

'Why not? Well because I've only just buried my husband that's why not.'

He shook his head. 'Doesn't count.'

'What d'you mean it doesn't count? Of course it counts!'

''Fraid not. You didn't love him, did you?'

'Well, not at the end, no, but—'

'And not for a year or two before that, either. Not since just after you first got married, when the rosy glow of the wedding and the honeymoon wore off, am I right?'

'Well, maybe we did have a bit of a strained relationship but—'

'And then you discovered you were pregnant, which wasn't so bad because when Ivo was born you had someone else to transfer your love to.'

'I don't know about that, I—'

'And it was only later on that you woke up with a jolt and discovered you positively loathed the guy, and that you'd always loathed him, and then the dawn came up with a vengeance.'

I halted in the snow, rounding on him. 'You're very sure about all this, aren't you? I've only known you a few weeks, what makes you so convinced you know my life story?'

'I don't, but like I said in the pub, I'm just trying to get you to be honest. I think it'll help you.'

'Well I don't need help thank you!' I said warmly. 'I'm not looking for therapy.'

'I don't mean you *need* help, don't get in a strop, but I've observed you over the last few weeks, Rosie. You're not mourning this man, you're glad to be shot of him, but my God you feel guilty about that and it'll screw you up completely if you're not careful. And why should you feel guilty? It's not your fault he's dead and the fact that he *is* dead doesn't canonise him, you know. It doesn't make him a saint. God, you're the bloody saint for putting up with him for as long as you did.'

We were on the doorstep of Farlings now. I turned to look at him. His eyes were intent, persuasive.

'Forget him, Rosie, forget that life you had. Try something else. Try a little happiness for a change.'

I put the key in the lock and gave a wry smile. 'You mean try *you* for a change.'

His face creased into a grin. 'Well, maybe I do! Is that so dreadful? Is that such a crime? I like you, I've told you that, so are you going to leave me freezing to death on this cold doorstep or are you going to ask me in for a coffee?'

'Ah, coffee. That old euphemism.' I pushed on through the door.

'God, you're a suspicious old bag,' he chuckled, following me in. 'I said I liked you, I didn't say I fancied you rotten and wanted to shag you senseless on the – oh, hello, Vera.'

'Ah good, you're back.'

Vera, ensconced on the sofa by the fire in the hall on the grounds that it was the cosiest room in the house, happily didn't seem to have heard Alex. She began winding in her knitting like a demon.

'Thought you were never coming,' she grumbled, rolling up her *Family Circle* and stuffing it in her string bag.

'Sorry, Vera, I think we found the pub that never closes.'

'Ah well, that's all right. Does you good to have a nice time now and again, it's just that he'll be frettin' and wanting his Horlicks if I don't get back soon.'

'Well, thanks so much for coming over. You were right, it did do me good to get out.'

She paused, smiled as she buttoned herself up to the chin in her coat. 'You're all right, luv. I'm glad you had a good time. See you anon.'

'Yes, thanks. Goodnight.'

I opened the door for her, and in a flurry of overcoat, woollen hat, gloves and knitting bags, she was gone.

All of a sudden the hall seemed very quiet, very still and very empty. Alex threw his coat on a chair and moved across to the fire. He stood with his back to me for a moment, then turned, smiling slightly, watching me.

I moved over to the tree that Martha and the children had decorated that afternoon. I fingered a bauble.

'Right, coffee?' I said brightly, for some reason feeling unaccountably nervous.

'Not for me, thanks. Keeps me awake.'

'Oh. Right. Whisky then?'

'Puts me to sleep.'

'Ah.'

Our eyes met with a deafening crash.

'Come here.'

I didn't, but that didn't deter him. Two seconds later, and in the same number of strides, he was over the Persian rug and into my corner. The next thing I knew, I was in his arms.

'Look, Alex, the thing is, I'm not sure if I'm ready for – mmmmm!'

Down I went in a tango-esque, back-breaking embrace; mouth to mouth, head in the Christmas tree, pine needles up the nose. It was quite a while before I surfaced, and when I did, I appeared to be panting. It was a long time since I'd been kissed like that, but something inside me, something parched and withered, began to unfurl, remembering. Coloured fairy lights danced in front of me, but Alex's eyes seemed to be generating more energy than all of them put together. This was going to be hard to resist.

'Now look, Alex,' I gasped, rationally enough, 'let's just take this thing slowly, shall we? Let's not – whooops!'

Blimey, I was flat on my back on the sofa now – this man didn't wrestle pregnant ewes to the ground for nothing. His silken tackle had me prostrate and drowning in one lengthy, mesmerising kiss after another. On and on they rolled, and the terrible thing was that far from resisting, I appeared to be collaborating now. If my heart wasn't in it, something else was, and the more it went on, the more it seemed to be habit forming. My arms were wrapped wantonly around his neck, I seemed to be in the grip of a hormonal impulse – oh God, was I giving up the fight? No no, I'll fight again in a minute, I thought desperately, his tongue hypnotically warm in my mouth, really I will. I'm just mustering forces, playing for time, in a minute I'll—

'Ooaah!' I squeaked as a furtive hand snaked up my jumper. 'Alex wait!' I gasped. 'I really think—'

'Too much thinking, my love . . . listen to the old bod . . . that's better . . . now, if you just . . . there . . . God, you're beautiful, so mind-blowingly beautiful it's unbelievable . . .'

Well, that did it, that really did it. Back in the dark mists of time I suppose someone, somewhere, might just have referred to me as beautiful, but we're talking ice ages here. We're talking pre-Harry, pre-Rupert-the-lumberjack, pre-anyone of any consequence, and even then never mind-blowingly beautiful. And never followed up with the observation that this beauty was unbelievable. Truly. I'd have remembered. Well, I was putty in his hands. I went with the current. I went with all the arid, dried-up, pent-up emotions of the last few years and – ping! – so did my bra strap. Above his head the tree lights flickered, tinsel glistened, and baubles danced, but I shut my eyes as I caught sight of two large purple balls hanging pendulously together. I didn't want any lewd associations to spoil the moment. Instead, I settled back to enjoy it, because frankly it was all over bar the shouting now, wasn't it? My bodice was ripped and he was gaining ground like Stormin' Norman, marching across the plains, going into the foothills, except – oh God – wait! No, it *couldn't* be a total walkover, not here in the hall, not with the children just upstairs! Because what if they came down? Suddenly my mind flashed up an over-sentimentalised picture of a clutch of small, pyjama clad children on the stairs, clutching teddies. Emma, wide-eyed, lisped 'Rothie, why have you got no clothes on? Oooh, you rude girl!'

'No!' I shrieked sitting bolt upright. Then, 'Mmwmmwrm!' as I was jack-knifed down again, silenced by his lips.

Only this time he meant business. Although I was struggling now, he didn't seem aware of it and anyway he was bigger than me. In fact he was so huge and so all over me I thought I must be suffocating, and I didn't hear anything other than the roar of hot breath in my ears. Didn't hear the crunch of tyres on the gravel outside. Didn't hear the car door slam, or the footsteps crunch through the snow and on up the steps. Didn't hear the key turn in the latch or the front door open. All I felt was the sudden, sharp gust of wind in my face and on my bare midriff. Alex's head shot back. Over his shoulder, framed in the doorway in a long dark coat and with a face like stone stood Joss. Standing beside him, wrapped in full-length camel cashmere, and with bright, scarlet lips, was the most beautiful, dark-haired, doe-eyed creature I think I've ever seen in my life.

Chapter Seventeen

I leaped off the sofa in dismay, and not a little disarray. 'Joss!' Clutching desperately at my clothes I pulled down my jumper. 'I – we didn't expect you until tomorrow!'

'Evidently,' he said drily.

'I'm – I'm baby-sitting for Martha.'

'So all is revealed. Good evening, Alex.'

Alex, having eased himself upright, seemed about to hold out his hand, then thought better of it. He raked it through his rumpled hair instead and grinned sheepishly. 'Joss, Annabel,' he nodded to them as he tucked his shirt in.

'Alex just popped in,' I said quickly.

'So I see,' drawled Joss. 'Caught in flagrante delicto, you really should be more careful you know. Rosie, I don't believe you've met my wife. Rosie Meadows, Annabel Dubarry.'

Annabel held out her hand, her dark eyes dancing with amusement. 'I say, what a hoot! No, we haven't had the pleasure, I'm awfully sorry if we've put a stop to yours!'

'Of course not,' I muttered, blushing furiously. 'We were just, I mean we weren't flagellating or whatever Joss said, we were just—'

'Snogging,' finished Alex unabashed, with a grin. 'And very pleasant it was too. How was your flight then, you two? Good trip?' God, he was cool, wasn't he? Anyone would think we'd just been nibbling cucumber sandwiches or something.

'Pretty shitty, thank you, and I need a drink.' Joss made for his decanter on the desk. 'There are two ways to fly the Atlantic I've discovered. One is to drink nothing and arrive feeling lousy, and the other is to drink heavily and arrive feeling lousy. I chose the former this time which was a huge mistake. Will you join me or have you already helped yourself?'

'I haven't, as it happens, and actually I'd better be on my way. I've got to be up early tomorrow. G'night all, 'night, Rosie.' Alex turned to me, took my face in his hands and kissed me full on the lips before

I could move a muscle. I stood rooted to the spot, crimson with shame and embarrassment.

'Goodnight,' I muttered, thinking, just go. Just go, damn you.

A moment later he was gone. The door slammed and we heard his footsteps crunch away down the drive. Joss turned back to his desk to pour some water into his whisky. I could hear my heart pounding. I could also see a bit of grey bra peeking out of the top of my jumper. I quickly poked it back down, but not before Annabel had caught my eye and smirked. I turned to Joss, my face on fire.

'Joss, I'm so sorry, but Martha needed a break so I filled in for her.'

Joss turned back, swirled his drink around in his glass and regarded me levelly. 'Yes, well, sorry to surprise you, Rosie, but the airport called to say there'd been a cancellation at the last minute, so we took the tickets. I tried to get a message through this morning but there was no one here.'

'As a matter of fact we didn't think it would be a problem,' purred Annabel in a transatlantic drawl. 'After all, we do live here.'

'It's not a problem,' I mumbled, wishing the ground would swallow me whole. 'And it's not really what it looks like either. Alex and I had a drink that's all and – well, I don't know why he kissed me, I expect we'd both had too much.'

'Well that's understandable at Christmas,' she said, 'but you do see, don't you, that if the kids had come down and found you like that, clothes strewn everywhere, naked flesh romping around—'

'There was no naked flesh and I can assure you that was as far as it was going,' I said, trembling with humiliation and embarrassment.

'Oh, I'm pleased to hear it, because you know, Rosie, with small children around one has to be *so* careful. They really are so impressionable, and although it was kind of you to baby-sit you really mustn't use it as an excuse to christen our sofa you know.' She raised her eyebrows despairingly at Joss.

'All right, Annabel, take it easy,' said Joss quietly. 'I'm sure Rosie's got the message.' His face showed no emotion but I'd seen enough of the anger and irritation on his face in that fleeting second in the doorway to know how disappointed he was in me. My misery knew no bounds. I felt as if I'd run headlong into a brick wall. Thus far I hadn't been able to look him in the eye, but I knew I had to now, even though my face was flaming.

'I'm sorry, Joss.'

He looked at me carefully. 'It's okay. We'll say no more about it.'

'But don't let it happen again!' added Annabel in a schoolmarmy tone, wagging her finger. Her brown eyes were laughing at me. I wanted to kick her in her pert little pants.

She laughed merrily. 'Oh, don't look so embarrassed, Rosie, I know it's hard because, after all, Alex is terribly attractive, and in your position it must be awfully difficult to resist someone like that, but please, do try to keep a hold on your libido, at least while you're in our house, hmm? Lord knows, we couldn't give two hoots what you do in the privacy of the cottage, you can have him any which way you like down there, can't she, honey?'

'There's nothing happening in the cottage,' I spluttered. 'I told you, it's not like that, he just—'

'Oh save it, will you?' Joss interrupted angrily. 'I'm dog tired and this is all I need to come home to. Stop baiting her, Annabel, for Christ's sake. I'm off to bed.' He drained his glass.

I took this as my cue to go. 'Yes, well, goodnight.' I turned shakily and made for the stairs, but Annabel's husky voice stopped me in my tracks.

'Um, correct me if I'm wrong, but don't you live in the cottage, Rosie?'

I turned, my hand on the banister. 'Yes, I do, but my little boy's asleep upstairs. I'm just going to get him.'

'Oh, okay. Well don't hang around. It's awfully late and we want to get to bed, don't we, honey?'

I gritted my teeth and made to move on but she stopped me again.

'Just one thing, Rosie.'

I paused.

'Have you been smoking?'

'I don't smoke.'

'Ah, so it must be on your clothes. I can smell it at twenty paces. It's something I absolutely abhor.' She smiled. 'Just so's you know.'

I stared at her. She really was incredibly beautiful with her brown, almond eyes, pouting cherry lips, dark waist-length hair and tiny petite figure. I'd have given anything to look like that, she reminded me of a girl in Hot Gossip who I used to dream of looking like, lying on my tummy, chin in hands in front of *Top of the Pops*. And here she was hurling insults and casting aspersions when I'd been kind enough to baby-sit her children, and somehow, because of the way she looked, it didn't seem outrageous at all. I could quite see how beautiful people got away with so much. I cleared my throat and tried to think of a crushing response, but actually, I was too tired.

'Please don't wait,' I muttered as I mounted the stairs. 'I'll see myself out.'

233

Behind me I heard Annabel sigh, and then in a voice fully intended to travel, 'God, these single girls. Aren't they just the end? What is it about them these days d'you think? One sniff of trouser and it's – whooomph! Fasten your seatbelts!'

I didn't wait to hear Joss's reply. I just stumbled down the dark passageway to Ivo's room, picked up my sleeping child and raced down the back stairs, through the kitchen and out into the night. Oh God how awful. How desperately, horrendously, unbelievably *awful*! I was furious with myself. To be caught like a teenager in such a stupid, compromising position. Tears of rage and humiliation stung my eyes – God, I could kick myself! And her, Annabel, with her supercilious beauty, smirking nastily at me the while, delighted, it seemed, by my humiliation. I hugged Ivo to me as I slithered down the icy hill. But it was Joss that hurt the most. Joss's eyes, his obvious disappointment at my juvenile behaviour. I'd let him down. He'd trusted me, and I'd betrayed that trust. And I'd betrayed myself too, I knew that now. I'd let loneliness make me reach for the wrong kind of intimacy. Not the kind I'd wanted at all. And that in itself made me realise that my position here was untenable now. I had no choice. I couldn't stay in his cottage when – well. When he'd seen me like that. I'd go to him tomorrow, apologise, offer to give it up. It made my eyes flood to think of leaving this place, and leaving the children too who I'd grown so fond of, but I had to give him a way out of this. It was what he'd want. And it wouldn't work anyway, I thought as I let myself into the cottage, not now I'd met her. I went up and put Ivo down in his cot. No, not now I'd seen her. As I gazed at my son my eyes filled with tears. Yes, it had all changed now, it was all . . . so different somehow. I lay down on my bed, exhausted, and finally, I must have slept. Fitfully, but I slept.

The following morning I was woken by a sharp rapping at the cottage door. I looked at my clock. Seven o'clock. *Seven o'clock?* Bloody hell! Who could this be? Was it Joss coming to evict me already? I got dressed hurriedly and leaving Ivo sleeping peacefully, raced downstairs. Halfway down though I paused, my hand frozen on the banister. There, sitting at my little gate-leg table, looking absolutely immaculate in a cream Joseph Tricot ensemble, was Annabel, my fountain pen, I noticed, poised in her hand.

'Ah, Rosie,' she purred, 'I hope you don't mind but I let myself in. I was just through leaving you a note.'

'Oh?' I said nervously.

'Yes, you see Martha's just called, her father's had to go into hospital again. A secondary tumour's been diagnosed apparently.'

'Oh!' I sat down abruptly on the stair. 'Oh God, poor Martha!'

'I know, dreadful,' she swept on, 'but the thing is, Rosie, this is such an incredibly busy time of year and I did wonder if you might pop up and give me a hand. Martha mentioned how well you got on with the kids and I've got such a lot to do today. Of course I'd make it worth your while. Joss told me all about how your husband left you destitute, you poor, poor thing.' Her face was all consternation.

I reddened. 'Well I'm not exactly in the poor house if that's what you mean.'

'No no, of course not, but a little extra always helps doesn't it?'

I swallowed, and as I did my pride went down with it. I wasn't cooking for the pub now for a few days which meant my income dropped dramatically. She was right. Needs must, even if it was Christmas Eve.

'All right. I'll come up and give you a hand.'

She was instantly on her feet, business completed, smoothing down her cashmere. 'Excellent.' She made for the door. 'I haven't seen the kids yet but I imagine they're still in bed so if you wouldn't mind getting them up and feeding them and then clearing the kitchen – I simply must do an hour's meditation and yoga today if I'm going to feel even halfway human. I'll be in my room if you need me – but I'm sure you won't,' she added quickly.

I watched her go. Yes, well, how the mighty have fallen, eh? A lack of staff had almost made her grovel there. Almost. I sighed. Actually, after last night's fiasco I felt positively indebted to Joss, so once I'd got Ivo ready we went quickly up to the house. There was no sign of life so I got the children up and dressed and we made our way down to the kitchen. As we passed by Annabel's door on the landing I heard a low chanting.

'What's that?' I whispered to Toby.

'She's saying her mantra.'

'Oh!' I listened.

'Hummin-puu . . . Hummin-puu . . .'

'Human poo as far as I can make out,' he said with a perfectly straight face.

I suppressed a smile and then when we'd all had some breakfast, took them out for a walk.

When we burst back through the kitchen door about an hour later, the children glowing, their hats and coats dusted in a fresh fall of snow, Joss was sitting at the kitchen table in jeans and a black jumper. His tawny hair was wet and swept back and he looked about as attractive as a man can look whilst munching cornflakes.

He glanced at me. 'Thanks, Rosie,' he said. 'Annabel finds them one hell of a handful even at the best of times.'

Even as he spoke, Lucy and Emma launched themselves at him like an Exocet missile.

'Daddydaddydaddy!!'

'Hello angels!' He hugged them hard, snowy coats and all, and gave them both a smacking kiss on the cheek.

'Hi, Toby!'

'Hello.'

Toby inched forward, shyly almost, but Joss reached out and pulled him to him, squeezing him and kissing him squarely on the forehead. Toby smiled.

'Daddy, have you brought us presents, haveyouhaveyouhaveyou!' demanded his sisters, almost weeing with excitement.

'Certainly I have, but they're all staying firmly under the Christmas tree where they belong until tomorrow morning when,' his eyes grew large and mysterious, 'all will be revealed!'

This caused Emma to squeak hysterically and clutch anxiously between her legs.

'And anyway,' Joss went on, mercilessly building up the suspense, 'the real presents are up to Santa Claus, aren't they?' He frowned, looked perplexed. 'Now. Santa Claus. Any idea when he's coming?'

'Tonight, tonight!' shrieked Emma, twisting her legs into knots, clearly in grave danger now. 'And Rosie's made mince pies so he can have one and we're going to put a bucket of water out for the reindeer and all sorts!'

'A bucket of water, eh? Hope there's a large brandy for the man with the sack.'

'Yes! There is! And Rosie's made Christmas cake as well!'

'Really?' He looked over her head at me quizzically. I blushed under his gaze. Our first real encounter since the horrors of last night.

'Oh well, it's not much,' I said quickly. 'I was cooking it for the pub anyway so I just made some extra. I wasn't sure if Annabel would have time to do it all.'

Toby snorted with derision.

'Er, no, I guess not,' agreed Joss, his mouth twitching as he considered this. 'That's very kind, Rosie. Annabel will be . . . delighted.'

At that moment, Annabel herself swanned into the kitchen. I noticed she'd changed and was now wearing a crisp white shirt with black jeans, her dark hair flowing in waves down her back. She looked drop-dead gorgeous but far from delighted.

'Who the *hell* decorated that Christmas tree in the hall? It looks like someone's thrown up on it!'

'We did! We did it!' squeaked the twins.

'Which is precisely why I've told you not to. God it looks so hideous! And tinsel too, so unbelievably tacky! Rosie, when you're through cleaning up in here, would you please root around in the basement for the proper decorations? I think we'll have the white and gold theme this year, bows and stars, the box should be labelled. I have to go up and look for my damn lipstick now, *some*one has seen fit to remove it from my dressing table and I can't find it anywhere!'

She exited left, and at that point it occurred to me, as perhaps it did to everyone present, that this was the first time she'd set eyes on the children for nearly a month, and apart from barking about a naff tree, she hadn't even so much as acknowledged them. There was a small silence. Then a moment later, the thought clearly having crossed her mind too, she was back, smiling from ear to ear.

'*Dar*lings!' she breathed huskily, crouching down between them, 'how lovely to see you!' She kissed Toby's cheek who stood like stone and gathered the twins to her, who reluctantly left their father's side.

'Angel babies, have you been good? Did you miss us?'

'We thought you were staying in America,' said Toby sullenly.

'I was, darling, but at the last moment I felt so horribly homesick and missed my chickens so much I simply had to get on that plane and see you all!'

I raised my eyebrows into the washing-up at the sink.

'Did you bring me a present?' demanded Lucy shamelessly.

'I did, my chick, and the biggest, most gorgeous-ist pressie it is too, all bows and frills and – careful poppet, I've just ironed this shirt.'

'Really? Can I see it now?'

'No, angel, tomorrow.' She neatly disentangled herself and stood up, smoothing down her shirt. As she did, she gazed about her despairingly. She sighed. 'Joss, honey, we really *must* do something about this kitchen. I'd forgotten how totally grim it was in here. Look, even the plaster's coming off the walls now.' She picked away at the pink powder with a razor-sharp red nail. Joss didn't answer, his head deep in a newspaper. 'You know,' she went on, 'I was flicking through one of those dreary "wifey and homey" magazines out of sheer boredom on the plane on the way back, and as a matter of fact I did see something rather attractive. It's called a Shaker kitchen apparently, if one's sad enough to follow these trends. Lots of elegant cream wood with round, chocolate brown knobs on the doors.'

'Oh yes, I love those big brown knobs,' I enthused.

'Don't we know it, honey,' purred Annabel, quick as a flash.

Joss and Toby burst out laughing. I flushed miserably. Emma stamped her foot in the midst of the mirth. 'What?' she cried. 'What! Tell me!'

'A knob's a willie,' Toby informed the twins helpfully. 'So Rosie likes big brown willies.'

'Oooh, Rosie, you naughty girl!' Emma shrieked with laughter, clutched her mouth – then froze suddenly, legs crossed. 'Shit!' she squeaked. 'I've wet myself!' She gazed down aghast, as sure enough, a large puddle appeared between her feet. Then she burst into tears.

I grabbed a roll of kitchen towel, thankful for the diversion, and sank down and hid my flaming face in her knees as I set about de-bagging her, reaching out with my other hand to fish around in the laundry basket under the table for some clean pants and jeans.

'Shit, eh?' murmured Annabel, raising her beautifully arched eyebrows. She stepped round me to reach for the telephone. 'Some choice language you've picked up from somewhere since we've been away, young lady. Who's been teaching you words like that, I wonder?'

Down on the floor, down in my place among the stinking, soiled undergarments, I damn nearly sank my teeth into her elegant little ankle. I watched it hungrily like some rabid terrier as it stood next to me in its handmade shoe.

'Now,' she went on in her ghastly mid-Atlantic drawl, 'if everyone could just be quiet for one single moment while I ring this restaurant – Emma, do stop snivelling – I'll confirm the reservation for all of us tomorrow. Where in the hell has the phone book got to?' She began picking things up despairingly from the dresser, then dropping them down in a heap. 'Look at all this garbage!'

'It's there,' I said, pointing under her nose where it was always kept. 'You mean – you're going out tomorrow? On Christmas Day?'

'Sure.'

'Oh! Martha ordered a turkey for you.'

'A turkey?' She gazed down at me in astonishment, as if for all the world I'd said she'd ordered her a dog turd. 'Oh the silly girl. She must have forgotten, we always go out for Christmas lunch. I don't touch meat, processed sugars or animal fats and I have an absolute horror of preservatives, so we always go to Le Forbergère where I can at least get a decent nut rissole.'

'Oh, right. Sorry, I didn't realise, I'll cancel it, I just thought—'

'No no, don't worry, *I'll* cancel it.' She waved me away with her hand, sighing wearily, as if she had more than enough to do already. 'No doubt *some*one will want it.'

Oh yes, I thought grimly, tucking Emma's shirt into clean jeans and wiping her tearstained face. Someone will. Some poor, dreary fool who works their fingers to the bone in an effort to treat their loved ones to Christmas in the traditional style will pounce on that turkey delightedly. Hug it to their poor overworked breast. Some dull little wifey in their dull little homey.

'Now, what's that darned butcher called,' she muttered, riffling through the phone book.

'Parsons,' I muttered back.

There was a pause. 'Ah. Yes of course.' She turned slowly. Her dark eyes flickered briefly over the now immaculate draining board, then rested on me. 'Thank you so much for all your help, Rosie,' she purred, 'but I'd say you'd be wanting to get off soon, wouldn't you? Only this is very much a family time, isn't it?'

I gritted my teeth as I straightened up. Right, so I really had just been a convenient dishwasher hadn't I. 'Yes, I'm going back to my own family actually,' I said, turning my back on her. 'But I just wondered – could I have a quick word with you first, Joss.'

'Of course.' He got to his feet immediately, putting down his paper. He went quickly out to the hall.

I was startled. Oh, God, right. Well, he was obviously keen to speak to me too then. I scurried after him, as, damn it, did Annabel. He frowned at her as she scuttled into place next to him by the fire, but she didn't move from his side. Hadn't she got anything better to do? Wasn't there some antelope carcass she should be hovering over? Or even a nut rissole.

'Well,' I began, as I stood before them, feeling about fourteen, twisting my fingers about nervously. 'It's just that – in view of last night, I wanted to give you the opportunity of cancelling my lease. I sort of imagined that's what you'd want.'

Annabel pursed her lips and nodded. 'Very sensible. Yes, I think under the circumstances that might be the answer, don't you, darling? Although,' she puckered her pretty little brow, 'the trouble is if Martha's not going to be around . . .' she bit her lip, clearly torn between wanting to see the back of me and not wanting to be saddled with the children.

'Don't be silly, it's out of the question,' snapped Joss. 'There's no question of you leaving. What happened last night was regrettable but hardly outrageous. Your love life is your own affair, and as far as I'm concerned you're staying. I had a long talk with Vera on the telephone this morning and I happen to know you've been one hell of a help to Martha. Vera says you've really taken her under your wing and not just helped her out with the cooking but with the kids too. Frankly I'm worried sick about that young lady. She's got far too much on her plate at the moment, but I'm damned if I'm going to sack her if I can possibly help it, and if I know she's got someone across the way who she can turn to when the going gets tough then frankly that sets my mind at ease. Vera says the girls are crazy about you and even Toby gets on with you which is a first. No, I won't hear of it, Rosie, to tell the truth you're doing *me* a favour by staying put. Of course, if it's all been a perfect nightmare and you can't stand another moment living cheek by jowl with this godawful family then you have my sympathies and fine, you must go. But as far as I'm concerned you're staying.'

Oh God, was I? Blimey, talk about forceful. I gulped. 'No it hasn't been a perfect nightmare and I'd love to stay,' I heard myself whisper. Er, hang on, Rosie, what was all that last night about your untenable position? And how you'd have to go on principle? Oh, bugger the principle, I thought, gazing into his lion's eyes and thinking how unbelievably handsome he looked with that piercing stare and that sculpted jaw line.

'Good. That's the end of it then.' He glanced at his watch. 'Now, if it's all right with everyone I want to take a quick look at my studio and then I'm going to take those kids tobogganing. See you after Christmas, Rosie.'

'Righto,' I croaked, as he left the room.

That left me and Annabel. She folded her arms and smiled, pseudo-sweetly.

'Now then, Rosie, it seems you have a reprieve. Don't abuse it, will you?' And with that she turned haughtily on her heel, and exited the hall using the other door.

Which left me. I sighed, and choosing the front door as my own particular mode of exit, picked up my child and went home to pack, to load up the car, and thence to return to the bosom of my own, pretty peculiar family, for Christmas.

As I drove along the narrow lanes a short while later, banked up on either side with huge blue-white snow drifts, I felt both sad and relieved to be out of that house. Sad, because I'd had all the build-up of Christmas there – the children stirring the pudding, opening their Advent calendars, decorating the house with holly – and now I'd miss the big day, miss them opening their presents. I'd also miss the twins' birthday which was on Boxing Day – yet another obscene pile of presents was growing daily in the cellar – but on the other hand, part of me felt hugely relieved to escape. For all his medal pinning commendation of my services to Martha, I couldn't forget Joss's face the previous night and I wanted to distance myself from it, in the hope, I think, that by removing myself, he might forget it too. I also wanted to distance myself from Alex for the time being. I wasn't at all sure how I felt about that man, but it was something of a relief to know that for a few days, at least, he wouldn't be able to stick his head round the back door and walk into my life unannounced. And there was the charmless Annabel to consider too. I'd really have to bite my tongue if I was going to live next door to her, but if I was, and it looked very much as if that's what I'd decided on the spur of the millisecond back there, I needed to retrench and decide how I was going to deal with her. Decide whether I was going to chortle along with the rest of the gang the next time she slung gratuitous insults at me, or whether, in fact, I was going to up and biff her on the nose.

As I crunched into my parents' gravel drive, I couldn't help smiling at the frantic display of red and green fairy lights slung busily about the leylandii in the front garden. As I'd driven down their private road, slowing down for the sleeping policemen, it hadn't escaped my notice that the Christmas lights had got more and more competitive as I went along, and Mum had clearly spent a small fortune ensuring that she'd be buggered if her display wasn't the best. I have to say, sartorially speaking, I found myself reluctantly lining up with Annabel on this one. I was all for a bit of Christmas spirit, but this was like being in Regent Street.

Finding myself without a door key I pressed the bing-bong chimes and peered through the bevelled glass. A second later I heard humming, and Mum flung open the door. Her jewellery jangled merrily, her face was flushed from the oven, she had lipstick on her teeth and she was clearly slightly pickled already from her second sweet sherry.

'Rosie!' She held out her arms.

I grinned as I hugged her, reeling under the heady, familiar sensory onslaught of Je Reviens, Brussels sprouts and 'Carols From King's' playing in the background. Suddenly it was good to be back.

'Happy Christmas, Mum.'

'Happy Christmas, my darling!'

It was the usual, festive gathering at The Firs that year; Mum, Dad, Philly and Miles and their three boisterous children, and me and Ivo, but minus Harry of course. In this respect I think I'd been rather dreading it, thinking Mum might do a lot of sighing and breast beating, holding handkerchief to eye and wailing about how sad it was to be without the prodigal son wolfing down the whisky and the turkey as usual, but in the event it was quite the reverse. Mum was surprisingly perky for her, and if anything, it was the rest of the crew who seemed a touch *piano*. The children were as noisy and over-excited as ever of course, and Ivo was in his element with three big children to play with, but Philly looked tired and drawn and seemed to snap at Miles for no real reason, and he in turn resorted to skulking behind a newspaper. Dad was quiet and subdued, and took himself off to the potting shed quite a lot, all of which was perfectly normal, but it seemed to me that he'd aged dramatically in the last few months. He looked exhausted, and as he laid aside his paper and raised himself heavily from his armchair for the umpteenth time to answer yet another call for 'More logs, darling!' or 'Lay the table please Gordon!' it seemed to me that his teeth were well and truly gritted.

The reason for my mother's skippy excitement finally became clear when she cornered me in the kitchen after Christmas lunch. I was trapped in the sink – hello sink, fancy meeting you again – with all the choice, crusty saucepans, when she sidled eagerly up to me.

'So!' she declared portentously, whipping a tea towel round her waist by way of an apron and seizing another to dry up with. 'I gather you're seeing a vet!'

My Brillo pad paused mid-scrub. I turned slowly. Her eyes were shining.

'Who told you that, Mum?'

'Oh, it's all the talk, darling,' she breezed, picking up a pan to dry and polishing away with brio. 'Everyone knows, seems the whole of Philly's village is positively buzzing with it!'

'Well, you can jolly well get her to un-buzz it then. I am not *seeing* a vet, as in walking *out* with a vet, or even *dat*ing a vet, I just went for a drink with a vet, all right?'

'I hear he's ever such a nice young man, very respected in the community, and frightfully successful too. Got quite a large practice I believe.' I gritted my teeth. She liked that word, 'practice', it made him sound like a bloody doctor, which of course was Mum's idea of middle-class heaven. 'And by all accounts he's rather taken with you too, and good heavens, why not! So he jolly well should be!'

I leaned the heels of my hands heavily on the bottom of the sink. 'Mum, he's a friend, that's all. I'm not looking for a relationship with anyone at the moment, okay?'

'Not what I hear, my love,' she trilled with a deadly beam. She leaned sideways into my ear. 'From what I gather you were, ahem, rather interrupted last night.' She nudged me in the ribs. 'Having a little kiss and a cuddle, hmm?'

I froze, then turned to her aghast. 'Who on *earth*—'

'Oh, Philly said that Annabel Dubarry woman was in the village this morning. She was in the queue at the baker's apparently, giggling about it – not unkindly though, darling. I think everyone's genuinely very pleased for you.' She nodded earnestly, put her hand on my arm. 'Really. Especially after all your unhappiness, everyone's absolutely delighted you've found a, well, a new amour.'

'Mother, he is not a new amour! Jesus, Harry has just this minute up and died and—'

'Oh, it's all right,' she interrupted, jerking her head skywards. 'I've told him all about it, he knows.'

'Told who all about it?'

'Harry, of course.'

I stared at her in amazement. 'Harry!'

'Yes, darling. I had a little chat with him the other day. Honestly, my love, he doesn't mind at all. He completely understands.'

My mouth dropped open. Oh God, she'd really lost it now, hadn't she? She was barking. No wonder Dad looked so grim and witless.

I spoke gently. 'Mum, you've got me worried now. What are you saying? What d'you mean you spoke to him?'

'At Marjorie's, silly.' She looked at me, exasperated. I stared back. Suddenly her eyes widened. 'Oh! Lord – didn't I tell you?'

'Tell me what?'

'Oh, gracious, I must have forgotten!' Her eyes were huge now and full of portent. 'Guess what?'

'What?'

'Marjorie Burdett is psychic!' she hissed.

'Marjorie Burdett is . . .' I groaned. 'Oh God. Since when?'

'Since last month!' She folded her arms triumphantly. 'She discovered quite by accident and in the middle of the most unlikely setting. She was out on the golf course on her own, doing a little green practice on the eighteenth, vaguely thinking about a late uncle of hers who'd had a very nice putting action, when all of a sudden – there he was! Her late Uncle Terence! He appeared out of nowhere apparently, just as she was putting into the hole – held the flag out for her and everything!'

'Mum, hang on—'

'*Quite* extraordinary, it was. She said there he was, larger than life and as clear as you're in front of me now. Spoke to her too! Told her her grip was all wrong – well of course it always has been lousy – and that she wasn't keeping her eye on the ball. Well, you can imagine, Marjorie got herself in a right old state about it and went hurrying off to see one of those mystic medium types who held her hand and said, 'Yes, *yes*, my dear, you *are*! You're psychic, and it's a gift!' Well I have to tell you, Rosie, it *is* a gift and it's been absolutely marvellous! Given her a whole new lease of life, and us girls too because, frankly, between you and me, Jeannie and Yvonne and I were getting just a l-i-ttle bit fed up with all that pyramid jewellery stuff of hers. I mean there's only so much paste and diamante you can con your friends into buying, isn't there? But now, instead of looking at her ghastly old baubles, we have a little seance instead! *Such* fun. We cover the table with a darling red tasselled cloth that Marjorie picked up for next to nothing in Costco, and then we all hold hands – frightfully giggly to begin with, darling – and Marjorie sits at the head of the table and looks solemn, and then she mumbles a bit and her eyes go all squiffy, and her bosoms heave about a bit, but then suddenly, hah!' Mum clasped her hands, eyes huge. 'She's got someone! She's established a channel!'

'Well, bugger me,' I said drily.

'It's just like fishing really. She dangles a hook and up comes someone we know! Sometimes it's Jeannie's ex-husband who was an absolute rake and goes on and on about all sorts of risqué you-know-what, and sometimes it's Yvonne's aunt who was terribly well connected and is absolutely riveting on various members of the royal family – dead ones of course – and then the other day it was Harry!'

'Really.'

'Yes, and, oh darling, he's on *such* good form, I *wish* you could hear him! We had such a lovely long chat about how happy he is up there and about all the nice friends he's made – he's sharing a room with a frightfully nice chiropodist from Purley apparently, not top drawer of course, but then Harry says heaven is a much more classless society, and that actually quite a few of his friends are rather common now, which I thought showed he was really trying. Really entering into the spirit of the thing. Very illuminating on bunions, by all accounts.'

'Bunions?' I muttered faintly.

'The chiropodist, darling. Oh and he's joined the gym, lost quite a bit of weight, and—'

'The gym!' I groaned. 'Oh, for heaven's sake, Mum!' My God,

Marjorie was going to have to do her homework a bit better than this.

'Yes, and that's interesting actually, because I was thinking of joining the one in Banbury, but Harry says the facilities are far superior up there and I'd be better off waiting.'

I stared at her. She laid a hand on my arm.

'Until I get there, darling,' she said gently. 'We all have to go some time, you know. Oh, and he goes jogging now and plays badminton and—'

'Mum, are you sure you've got the right Harry? You haven't got him muddled up with some other Harry, Harry from Billericay or Harry from Croydon or something? You do speak to him, do you?'

'Well, indirectly, darling, through Marjorie of course. She's the medium. But I do get the most terrific buzz when he emanates, my whole body turns to jelly and I shake and tremble and get hot and sweaty – it's just as if he's a living orgasm!'

'I think you mean organism.'

'Whatever, but the point is I had a word with him the other day about your young man.'

'Ah.' I gritted my teeth.

'No no, now don't look like that, my love, he's absolutely delighted! Really thrilled to bits for you, says he knows the family very well – the father's on the same corridor as him apparently, just across the way – and he says his first cousin is related to the Earl of Suffolk!'

I moaned low into the soap suds. God, what had Marjorie conjured up here? A flying motel full of dead aristocrats and chiropodists?

'Anyway, the thing is, he says you're not to waste another moment shilly-shallying around on his account. He says he simply wants you to be happy and I told him that those were my sentiments exactly. And shall I tell you something *so* weird, Rosie?' Her voice lowered to a portentous whisper.

'I'm hungry with curiosity, Mother.'

'Well, on the way home from Marjorie's, I popped into Menzies for a bar of chocolate – summoning up ectoplasm is terrifically munchie making – and just as I was passing the magazine rack, guess what fell off the shelf? Slap bang at my feet?'

'What?' I said guardedly.

She drew her pearls warmly about her, raised her chin and regarded me with mad, important eyes. 'Guess!' she hissed.

'Mum, I can't, just tell me, for God's sake.'

'*Brides* magazine!' she announced triumphantly. She pulled open the kitchen drawer and produced it with a flourish. 'And do you know what *page* it fell open at?'

'Surprise me,' I muttered, feeling weak from the onslaught.

She opened it with a flourish. 'Suitable speeches, etiquette and bridal gowns for *second marriages*! Now isn't that *spooky*?'

I stared at her for a moment. Looked into her wide, pale blue eyes. Then I snatched the magazine from her, ripped it straight down the middle, and popped it into the bin beside me. 'Certainly is, Mum. So spooky that it can go straight back to the underworld where it came from. And now if you'll excuse me I must go and relieve Dad of Ivo, and *no*,' I swung round as she beetled after me, almost banging into me, '*no*, there will be no second marriage—'

'But—'

'And there will be *no* suitable speeches—'

'But, Rosie darling—'

'And there will be *no* mother of the bride outfits either, and do you know why?'

She pouted, petulantly. 'Why?'

'Because there will be no bloody second bride, that's why! Mother, I am not, repeat *not* getting married!' With that I turned on my heel and with a suitably extravagant flounce marched out of the kitchen.

Chapter Eighteen

Suffice to say, after all the festivities I wasn't too unhappy to leave The Firs. What with Mum cornering me at every opportunity and urging me to join hands with her and Feel The Vibrations, and Philly and Miles bickering constantly and Dad skulking off at a moment's notice, I felt I was in a madhouse. It did actually make me realise that having Harry around had given the sane members of my family – and I don't include my mother in this – a focus; some sort of rallying point, someone to join forces against and roll our eyes heavenwards about. Yes, I thought as I drove thankfully back to the cottage after breakfast, how extraordinary. Over the last couple of days I'd almost, *al*most, missed him.

I crunched up the main drive and round the side of the house, peering through the dark, mullion windows and looking for signs of life. Seeing none, I drove on through the stable yard and down the back drive to the cottage. It was absolutely freezing inside and that damp, almost reproachful air of being unloved and unlived in for quite a while hit me as soon as I walked in. I badly needed to get to the shops to replenish the larder but knowing I'd be loath to return to these Arctic conditions I dashed about zapping on radiators, collecting firewood from my little shelter outside and tried to get the fire going. I'd just about got it to draw by holding a sheet of newspaper in front of it when the telephone rang. I swore, dropped the paper which went up in flames, and reached for the receiver, gloves still on.

'Hello?'

'Ah, you're back.' I recognised Annabel's drawl.

'Yes, I've just got here.'

'Excellent, only Martha's father's still at death's door, damn it, so I'm up to my eyes here, and I was hoping you might be a real honey and go to the store for me.'

For a moment, I was stunned into silence.

She hurried on. 'It's just I've got a plane to catch in the morning –

I'm going back to the States to spend some time with my folks,' glory hallelujah! 'but the house is in total chaos and the kids are rampaging about like anything, they seem to have gone completely crazy since I've been away. Would you mind, Rosie? I'd be so grateful.' Her voice had taken on an unattractive wheedling tone.

I hesitated for a moment. 'Okay,' I said finally. 'I was going anyway, so—'

'Terrific.'

There was a click and I realised she'd put the phone down. I stared at my receiver in amazement for a moment, then quietly seethed. So, dishwasher *and* errand runner now, eh Rosie? You're not a pushover, are you? You just go down of your own accord. I did a few ante-natal deep breathing exercises to assuage the old temper – knew they'd come in handy one day – checked that the fire was going, and then with Ivo's little gloved hand firmly in mine made my way grim-faced up the drive to the house.

She'd obviously been watching out for me from a window because as I approached, the back door opened.

'Here you are.' She waved a piece of paper imperiously in my face.

Curbing the urge to say, 'Look here, Mrs Dubarry, is there any need to be quite so spectacularly unpleasant?' I regarded her with interest.

She was looking particularly young and dewy today, damn her, dressed from head to toe in some sort of kittenish, cashmere legging-and-top ensemble, which clung to her tiny figure and made her look as if she was entirely composed of a series of gentle, seamless grey curves. I felt she should be designated an area of outstanding natural beauty, whilst I, panting from the exertion of the hill in an old Barbour, a felt hat and dragging a toddler, could quite easily pass as a historic monument. I wondered how much younger she was than me, and gave what I hoped was a sophisticated smile.

'Thank you, Annabel,' I murmured as I took the list, hopefully demonstrating that I may be a desiccated old bag but maturity had at least taught me some manners.

'Rosie, do you happen to know if the kids have been getting any ease? You know, in food colouring. Candy and things.'

'Oh, Es!' I laughed. She didn't. I hastened on, 'Um, no, I don't think so, except, well, I've bought them the occasional packet of sweets from the village shop, I suppose.'

'Well, please don't give them the occasional *anything*, Rosie. It sends them totally haywire and makes them completely unmanageable. In future a piece of raw carrot will suffice or, if you must, a healthfood nutbar. Now, you should be able to get everything on the list in the village but if you can't, Waitrose will be open in Cirencester.'

I ran my eye down the list. I was tempted to tell her exactly where she could put her piece of raw carrot but heroically restrained myself. God, she'd be lucky. Herbal tea, organic oats, freshly squeezed orange juice, bagels – I wasn't convinced Mrs Fairfax's store could stretch to any of that – *Vogue, Hello, Harpers* – all vital consumables for the larder of course, essential I should go this very minute – pine nuts, condoms— I looked up sharply. Her dark eyes were watching me.

'If you wouldn't mind,' she purred. 'Only we've run out, and we won't be seeing each other again for quite a while. Here's fifty pounds, that should cover it all. Thank you so much.' And with that, she very sweetly shut the door in my face.

I stared at the paintwork for a moment, then turned, rather dazed, and went back down the drive for my car. Bloody hell, that was a bit rich, wasn't it? I'd never bought condoms in my life before, let alone for someone else; in fact the only time they'd made a brief, and rather hilarious, appearance in my life was so long ago they'd been called something completely different. Oh well, I reasoned, as I snapped Ivo into his car seat, it could be worse. It could be haemorrhoid cream or something, although I doubted if someone as glamorous as Annabel would be caught dead with piles. One of the perks of the childless, of course. How odd, though, I mused as I drove off along the snowy lanes. I could have sworn I'd spotted a look of triumph in her eyes as I'd read that list of hers. A sort of yes, deary, that's exactly what *I'll* be doing tonight, okay? smirk. Now why on earth would she want to pull that kind of one-upmanship with me?

I sighed and swung the car into the supermarket car park, joining a long queue of ordinary mortals without an ounce of cashmere between them, who were all bracing themselves to crowbar their way into an already overflowing store. It had been shut for two days, and it was a bit like entering the Gaza Strip. People were already three abreast in the aisles doing serious battle with elbows and trolleys, but I put my head down and went for it with the best of them. Finally I staggered out, exhausted but triumphant, a glowing Ivo – who always enjoys a scuffle – on one hand, four pints of fresh orange juice dangling from the other, and bundles of fresh figs, prunes and bran clenched firmly between my teeth. Either this woman had a huge problem with her bowels or she was going to have one soon, I decided, as I threw it all unceremoniously on the front seat. 'And may it keep you enthroned upon the lavatory for days on end!' I muttered, as I slammed the door shut. I dusted off my hands and jumped in. Right. Home. I headed off, but then spotted a chemist's on the outskirts of town and screeched, rather creatively, to a halt. Damn, I'd almost forgotten. I hadn't bought Annabel the where-withal to get her organic oats. Leaving Ivo sleeping peacefully in his seat, I hurried inside to acquire the more personal items on her list.

Ding-dong, went the 1950s-style door chimes as I stepped inside. I blinked in the gloom, as to my surprise I found myself in a dark time warp of a chemist's shop. It was the kind of old-fashioned place where dark mahogany drawers lined the walls, going right up to the ceiling, and one could almost imagine a white-coated apothecary lurking in the background, brewing up potions.

'Hi, Rosie.'

I peered through the gloom and made out, not an apothecary behind the counter, but Lenny, Mrs Abbot's son from the village store. He was tall and rather good-looking in a blond, loose-limbed sort of way. I had no idea he worked in here.

'Oh, hi.'

'Need any help?'

'Er . . . no. No, I'm fine, thanks.'

Damn. Lenny. That was all I needed. I prowled around the silent, empty shop looking for the bloody things, then approached the front counter, feeling his eyes on me as I scanned it. God, why weren't they here where they were supposed to be, among the cough sweets and the vitamins? I began to feel a bit hot and his eyes didn't leave me, so I wandered to the back of the shop and picked up a hairbrush. Oh, for God's sake, Rosie, you're not going to do the classic teenage thing of buying everything in the shop except what you actually want, are you? You're a grown woman, for heaven's sake, just go and ask. Right. Absolutely. I put the hairbrush down and marched deter-minedly to the counter, but at the last minute chickened out and grabbed some toothpaste. I waved it triumphantly.

'Found it,' I assured him confidently. 'Oh, and a packet of condoms too, please.'

'They're over there, bottom shelf in the corner,' he said, pointing. 'Here, I'll show you.'

Oh no, please don't, I thought hurrying after him, I'll find them, really. But it was too late, he was already crouching down, and I had no choice but to crouch – a little too chummily for my liking – next to him. I gaped in amazement at the vast range spread out before me.

Red ones, black ones, ribbed ones, gold spangly ones . . .

'Blimey, spoilt for choice,' I muttered.

'Yeah, I know, they come in different sizes too.'

'Really? Oh well, they're for someone else, I've no idea what size he takes.'

'Size of pack,' he said suddenly. He stood up, blushing.

I swivelled back to the shelf. Size of pack? My eyes confirmed this undeniable truth. Three, six, twelve, twenty-four, etc. – not, Rosie, small, medium, large, extra large, abnormally large, can't-tuck-it-in-your-trousers-it's-so-large. Ah.

Feeling a deep blush unfurl, I grabbed a pack of twelve and hastened to the counter where Lenny was already waiting, head bowed.

'I'm sure those will be fine,' I muttered, as I counted out my change. 'As I said, they're not for me, so . . .'

Lenny didn't answer. He was silent as he took my money, silent as he rang it up on the till, and he was very, very careful not to look me in the eye as he handed me the receipt, put my goods in a bag and completed the transaction. I turned and hurried from the shop to my car.

'Oh God!' I gasped as I flopped down with relief into the driver's seat. Ivo woke up with a jolt behind me. 'Oh, Ivo, what a nightmare!'

I crunched the gears and set off at speed, feeling faintly giggly now. I snorted. Rosie, you fool, who d'you think's going to go in and ask for the extra small ones then? Who the hell was that going to impress on the bedside table – ooh, great, a tiddler! No, no, they'd all swagger in asking for carrier bags, and then everyone would wonder why there'd been such a huge population explosion. I laughed to myself, and Ivo, delighted, joined in.

'Mummy laugh!'

'Yes, Mummy laugh. Is that so unusual, my darling? It's either that or I'll go completely bananas.'

'Bananas,' he decided firmly.

I grinned, and like a magician produced one with a flourish from Annabel's fibre-providing fodder beside me.

'Want one?'

'Yeth!'

I peeled it down and passed it over. He grasped it eagerly. I smiled as I watched him in my rear-view mirror. Oh, what the hell, I thought, watching him fondly. Whatever happens, whatever life wishes to toss at me, whatever people think of me, Lenny, Annabel,

251

Joss, I've still got him. I smiled as he unashamedly threw the peel on to the floor. I've still got my boy. He caught my eye and grinned back.

As I turned into Farlings' drive, I spun deftly round the side and parked at the back by the kitchen door. It was a wonderfully bright but chilly day, and aside from a few rolling clouds threatening from the east, the sky was clear and blue, throwing the dark green countryside into glorious relief. I wondered if the children would be out playing in the garden on a day like this, I'd have loved to have seen them.

Vera opened the back door as I got out. She bustled over and kissed me warmly.

'Merry Christmas, luv, and thanks ever so much for the soap, it was such a treat.'

'Merry Christmas, Vera. Are the children about?' I asked, peering in at the windows as she helped me unpack.

'Haven't strayed from the television set since she got back,' she said, jerking her head backwards. 'She bought a whole heap of them videos back with her and she's 'ad them plugged in ever since. Says it's educational but the plain fact is she don't want them running about making a racket.'

'Can I pop in and say hello?'

She made a face. 'Best not, my duck. She's got the hump over some video or other that's been turned down by them TV people again. She's on the phone nonstop giving them merry hell, ragin' and screaming an' that. She asked me to tell you to deliver the goods to the back door – and them were her words, if you please.'

'Did she indeed,' I said grimly.

'Oh, and she left you a fiver.'

'What!' I exploded, as she reached in her pocket. 'Vera, you can tell her to—'

'Quite right, luv,' she said stuffing it back hastily, 'but she'll be gone in the morning. It's best left.'

'You're right, Vera,' I said, giving her a hug. 'She's not worth it.'

When Ivo and I got back, the fire had warmed the cottage and the low sun was streaming in through the windows on to the patchwork quilt on the sofa. I threw another log on and a rosy glow seemed to prevail.

'Well, Ivo,' I said later, as we sat side by side on the sofa eating a late picnic lunch of ham sandwiches, crisps and satsumas. 'Another year.'

'Yeth,' he agreed solemnly.

'And it's New Year's Eve soon, did you know that?'

'Yeth, I did,' he affirmed, without the faintest clue what I was talking about but happy to have a conversation.

'And shall I be partying, d'you think? Shall I be boogieing on down till dawn?'

'Don't know, Mummy,' he replied gravely, picking a piece of fat off his ham and placing it affectionately on my knee.

I smiled. 'No, I'm not sure I do either.' I sighed. 'Still, no harm in having a little company, is there?' I wiped my knee and looked out of the window. Another year. And somehow I didn't want to see it in alone. There was Alex of course, I knew I could see it in with him, he'd made that much perfectly clear on the telephone, when he'd somehow managed to get hold of me on Boxing Day at my parents' house.

'Sorry for ringing over the holiday season, my love, but I wanted to apologise for pouncing on you like that. Hope you weren't too fearfully embarrassed in front of Joss and Annabel, but what can I do when you drive me wild with desire?'

I grinned. His unabashed lust was quite disarming in a way. 'Control yourself springs to mind, Alex,' I said sternly.

'Ah, but you see I can't, that's the problem! Tell you what, keep New Year's Eve free and we'll pick up where we left off, eh?'

'We'll see. I'm not quite sure what I'm doing yet.'

'Oh God,' he groaned, 'you're not going to go all coy on me, are you? Not going to play hard to get? You've no idea how that turns me on, Rosie! Keep this torture up and I'll be taking cold showers and chewing the curtains! I've got this thing about rejection, you see.'

'Idiot,' I giggled.

'I have! Oh, and incidentally, I loved it when you denied flagellating me the other night, gave me no end of a laugh on the way home. I had this wonderful vision of you astride me in leather, brandishing birch branches, giving it what for. Had to walk around in the snow a bit longer to cool off. I say, what did you think of old Annabel then? Quite a stunner, isn't she?'

'In more ways than one,' I said grimly. 'I feel like I'm seeing stars every time I have a conversation with her, she's got all the charm of a sledgehammer. What is her problem, Alex?'

He laughed. 'Well, I agree, she's not exactly a girl's girl. Not the sort to have a natter with over the *Daily Mail* and the Hob-nobs of a Monday morning, but she's okay really. Trust me, she'll grow on you.'

'Yes, like bindweed,' I said sourly. 'I can imagine her getting quite a stranglehold actually.'

'I can see you're not convinced,' he laughed, 'so enough of her, and back to me. Back to New Year's Eve.'

'I think not, actually,' I said firmly. 'Let's meet again on a less heady night of the year, shall we, Alex?'

There was a tremulous pause. 'You don't trust yourself with me,' he said, a note of excitement creeping into his voice. 'Oh God, this is too thrilling for words, you're frightened you'll get carried away! One sniff of my manly scent and you'll be putty in my hands!'

I laughed and assured him that this was not the case, but that should I have a dramatic change of heart, I'd ring and succumb to his manly whiff pronto. Finally I managed to put the phone down.

No, I thought looking out of the window as the skies darkened around me, no, I didn't want anything as fresh and thrilling and upfront as Alex. Not yet anyway. Come January, come a new beginning, well, who knew how upfront I might feel, but right now, at the end of the old year, I just wanted friends. Old friends. Would it be too much to ask for Alice and Michael to come for supper? I wondered. And maybe Philly and Miles? Yes, why not? Impulsively I reached for the phone and punched out Alice's number.

'Hello?' She sounded dispirited.

'Alice? It's me! Happy Christmas.'

'Rosie!' she rallied. 'Darling, how lovely, and the same to you, I've been trying to reach you.'

'I've been at Mum and Dad's.'

'I thought as much. Grisly?'

'Moderately, but Mum was quite amusing, if a little alarming.' I giggled. 'She's gone all psychic on us, Alice, summoning up spirits, tuning in to the Beyond and all that sort of wacko stuff.'

'No!'

'Oh yes, it keeps her and Marjorie frightfully busy. Apparently there's no end of ectoplasm on the Other Side demanding their attention, namely – and get this, Alice – Harry, who Mum claims to have an exclusive hot line to.'

She giggled. 'Oh God!'

'Yes, and by all accounts he's a totally new man. You and I wouldn't recognise him now. He goes to the gym, keeps fit, and simply *loves* common people, terribly caring and sharing and New Labour.'

'God, how killing!'

'I know, but it's keeping her happy and Dad thinks it's absolutely marvellous. Not only does she go to badminton on Monday nights, but she's off at Cosmic Marjorie's on Tuesdays too now. He's got the house to himself.'

'While she's off with another man. I always suspected she had the hots for your husband, Rosie.'

'Oooh, yuk,' I shuddered. 'That's too revolting to contemplate. Anyway, enough of them. New Year's Eve.'

'Oh yes?'

'Would it be too boring to come to supper? I thought I might ask Philly and Miles too.'

'Oh Rosie, you're sweet, but Michael's already going to a party. An agency do, would you believe, quite near you actually, in Cheltenham.'

'And you mean you're not?'

'Well, I'm *invited* of course, but you try getting a baby-sitter on New Year's Eve, and apart from anything else, do I really want to grin and bear it as I bop around the clock with Michael's colleagues? Knowing all the nubile young secretaries are thinking, golly, she's a bit fatter and frumpier than I thought she'd be. No, thank you. I'm looking forward to a poached egg on toast and a quiet night in with Clive James.'

'Well, why don't you come down anyway? Bring the girls,' I suggested doubtfully, realising I didn't have anywhere to put them.

'And put them where? On the roof? No, darling, you know as well as I do that cottage is simply not viable, and incidentally, apart from anything else, I know you mean well and want all the people you love to love each other, but with the best will in the world your sister and I have never seen eye to eye. I always feel like a scruffy schoolgirl when I'm with her, she's so scrubbed and efficient and apple-pie perfect. I always get the impression she looks down on me for being chaotic and messy and – oh, I don't know. You know what I mean.'

'No,' I said huffily, knowing exactly what she meant. Then I sighed wearily. 'Okay, maybe you're right. Perhaps I'll just see it in with Clive too. I don't fancy just having Philly and Miles on their own, they're a bit niggly at the moment.'

'Don't tell me the ice maiden cracketh?' she said sarcastically. 'Sorry, sorry,' she added quickly, 'I didn't mean that. I'll tell you what, we'll both make a determined effort to get absolutely plastered, and then if we're not being sick into our respective buckets at midnight, we'll ring each other and have a pissed and emotional confab and do our own rendition of "Auld Lang Syne", okay?'

I laughed. 'You're on.'

Chapter Nineteen

True to her word, Annabel left at the crack of dawn the following morning and I popped up to the house to see the children. They were a disaster area. Toby was zombified by too much television and walked around looking as if he was on drugs, and Emma and Lucy were spoilt and petulant, surrounded by far too many Christmas toys, none of which they seemed to play with. Sensing drastic action was called for, I surreptitiously sneaked most of the toys off to a cupboard to be rediscovered in the Easter holidays, and took the fuse out of the television plug. There. I brushed off my hands and looked around, just as Joss came in.

'Oh, Rosie, thank God. Martha isn't back yet, her dad's no better and I have this darn commission to finish – my dealer's going crazy. Would you do me a hell of a favour and take charge of the kids for a bit? Martha's promised to be back by the time I go to Cologne – and I hope to Christ she is – but even then I reckon she's going to need a hand. Would you help me out here? I know you've got your job at the pub but I'd pay you a decent whack and you could still do your cooking up here, couldn't you?'

I looked into his harassed, hazel eyes and found myself saying, 'Of course, Joss, it's not a problem. And actually I've been using your kitchen for weeks now, so I reckon I owe you something.' I grinned.

'Yeah.' He gave a slow smile. 'I figured as much. We'll call this the quid pro quo then, shall we?' And with that he disappeared to his workshop.

Still smiling at this little exchange and wondering about how much 'a decent whack' would be – churlish to ask – I in turn went off to get half a ton of beef bourguignon under way, and to take over the somewhat frayed and tattered childcare reins.

I didn't see Joss again until about four o'clock that afternoon, when he reappeared, looking grey and haggard, covered in dust, demanding to know how one went about getting some damn food in this place? 'Jesus, you're cooking for the multitude anyway, aren't you? One plate's not gonna be missed, is it?'

It didn't matter how much I told him, I'd sent Emma down at half-past twelve, Lucy at one o'clock and bellowed like a fish-wife myself out of the back door at half-past one that lunch was ready, he still didn't believe me. So the next day I took his lunch down to his studio and plonked it on a slab of marble. Dish of the day happened to be Hungarian goulash, and since he chipped away at the same time as absently picking at things, it proved disastrous. He burst back into the kitchen, bawling like a child that he'd got sauce all over his goddam wide-eyed nymph and where the hell was the Jif? In future, I decided, I'd give him chicken legs and sandwiches. 'Finger foods,' I muttered to Ivo as I shut Joss's workshop door softly behind me, having retrieved his empty plate. 'For babies like you, darling, who can't cope with a knife and fork.'

Actually, in spite of his tantrum, I had an idea we'd co-exist pretty easily, and of course I'd still have the privacy of my cottage, an escape from the bedlam of Farlings. At least, I thought I would, until I was bathing the twins later that evening and Emma promptly threw up in the bathwater, swiftly followed by her sister. When I'd finally got them into their pyjamas and tucked them up with buckets by their beds, I dashed down to the studio for a quick confab with Joss. He immediately began to tear his hair and look a bit wild about the eyes, so I quickly suggested I could move in and deal with whatever lurgy it happened to be. Cue one huge sigh of relief from the man with the chisel.

As a matter of fact, I didn't mind. For a start it meant more money for me, and actually when he wasn't engrossed in the Greek past or being demanding in the present, Joss was very good company, with a dry, almost deceptive wit, so that sometimes it was only later, maybe after I'd shut his studio door, that I'd laugh out loud at something he'd said.

I'd assumed he'd carry on working that evening, but was surprised when he suddenly joined me, as I sat having supper in the kitchen, plate balanced on my knees, glued to the little television in the corner. I felt rather embarrassed at being discovered watching *EastEnders* and reached for the flicker to switch over to something more cerebral, but he stopped my hand, saying, 'Hey, no, leave it. I'm intrigued!' He then watched in cynical, amused silence as I lapped it all up. I had the last laugh though when he suddenly cried, 'Hang on, I thought she was going out with Grant!'

A documentary and the News followed, and Joss settled down to watch intently, but not in silence. Television for Joss was not, I discovered, something to vegetate in front of, to let the brain off the hook and let the cathode rays take the strain. No, it was a two-way medium. He argued with it, took strenuous issue with it, swore at it, threw shoes, books, and on hearing the words 'the people's dome', one of my chocolate mousses, which took ages to wipe off all the knobs. He demanded to know why he was forced to pay a licence fee to view such insulting drivel, and when some art prize was announced he was almost apoplectic with rage.

'Bastards! Bastards!' he screeched, tearing his hair and reaching for a shoe to hurl. 'How could they give it to him! It must be a joke, it must be!'

'Doesn't look like it,' I remarked, watching the winner walk up to the podium to take his prize.

'But that painting is total trash! Total, unadulterated trash, even a moron could see that. You can see that, can't you, Rosie?'

'Thanks,' I muttered. 'Um, can't say I've seen it actually.'

'But you do like art, don't you?' he demanded. 'Most people in this country don't any more of course, they just play computer games or secretly watch pornography on the network, but you've seen the inside of a gallery, haven't you, Rosie? You don't just knit, or whatever it is you're doing there?'

I laid aside the name tag I was sewing into Toby's school shirt.

'Yes, Joss, I can and do appreciate art, and frankly I'd like nothing better than to wander around the Tate while someone else looked after my child, but sadly my leisure moments are few and I've got all these name tapes to sew on to your son's clothes. Tell me, do you ever do anything remotely practical, Joss? Do you live in the real world at all, do you decorate, do you put up shelves, do you dig the garden, do you clean your car, or do you just get someone in to do it for you? Because if I had someone to do all those things for me, I daresay I'd get a lot of culture in too.' A trifle cheeky, I'll warrant, but I was a little sick of playing the ignorant peasant to the arrogant lord of the manor.

Joss's eyes widened with delight. 'Jeez. Didn't know you had it in you, Rosie. You'll be telling me exactly what you think of me next!'

One of the twins cried from upstairs and I got up to deal with her. 'I would,' I muttered, 'but I'm not sure I'd have time to do your character justice.'

I flounced out of the room as Joss gave a hoot of laughter. Flounce, blush, flounce, blush, I thought as I stomped upstairs, why did I always do that? What was the matter with me? I was behaving like a bloody adolescent.

When I came back downstairs having mopped a fevered brow and administered copious amounts of calamine lotion and Calpol – the opiate of the infants – I sat down in my chair and picked up the shirt to carry on. The name tape was already sewn neatly into place. Startled, I glanced across at Joss who was watching television with a straight and innocent face. I suppressed a smile, and without saying a word picked up the next shirt and carried on.

The shirts were all part of Toby's new boarding school trousseau. I'd known of course that he was going to prep school, but the fact that he was going to board had come as a complete surprise to me and, frankly, I couldn't think of a more unsuitable candidate. I voiced as much tentatively to Joss over breakfast the following day.

'Are you sure? I mean, d'you think he'll like it?'

'Not at first, no, but he'll settle down. It'll be good for him, Rosie. He's stuck out here in the middle of nowhere with only his sisters for company – he needs a little action. Annabel's very keen for him to get involved in the sporty side of things, you know, have the camaraderie, whatever that means.'

I bet she is, I thought, privately knowing full well she wanted him out of the house and off her hands. Later I canvassed Toby as gently and tactfully as I could for his views on the subject, but he was tight-lipped and resigned.

'Dad wants me to go, so I have to go, that's all there is to it. What's the point of talking about it?' And with that he slammed out of the kitchen and stomped upstairs clamping his Walkman to his head. He knew better than to express a true opinion or show his feelings, and I knew better than to follow him.

The twins, though, were a different matter. They were dreadfully upset that he was going away and I found both of them sitting on their bedroom floor in their pyjamas, sobbing piteously and cutting all the hair off their dolls' heads with the kitchen scissors. I watched in amazement as Lucy began sellotaping the tresses on to an old bathing cap, crying inconsolably the while.

'Lucy, what are you doing?' I sank down in dismay next to her.

'I'm making Toby a wig,' she sobbed.

'What on earth for?'

'Because he's going to balding school,' she wailed, 'and all his hair's going to fall out!'

'Oh no, darling, no!' I hugged her hard. '*Board*ing school. It means you stay overnight, it doesn't mean your hair falls out!'

A pair of startled, tear-stained faces turned to me. 'Oh! You mean . . .' Slowly they turned back and regarded the row of poor, scalped dolls. 'Oh!' gulped Emma.

'I'll buy you some new ones,' I said quickly, before they had time to summon up a fresh flood of tears. 'In Cirencester. We'll go and choose them together.'

Emma shook her head. 'No, it's okay,' she said, wiping her eyes with the back of her hand and possibly feeling slightly foolish. 'We're too old for dolls now anyway, aren't we, Luce?'

'Oh, surely not!'

'Mmm, we are,' Lucy agreed, lower lip quivering bravely. She glanced at Emma and then down at the mutants before us and hesitated. 'Except . . . maybe one Barbie each?'

'One Barbie it is,' I said staunchly, 'just for old time's sake. And if we should happen to run into Ken, maybe we'll have him, too?'

'Ugh, no, not boy dolls, puke!'

I grinned, pleased to see that they'd recovered their equilibrium and that although they'd outgrown their dolls, they weren't quite into the 'Ken' side of things yet. They seemed much better though, and since no one had been sick for at least four hours, I said they could get dressed and come downstairs. We went down, hand in hand, just as Joss was coming out of his study into the hall. He was holding a sheet of paper in his hand, looking bemused.

'I've just found your school reports, girls.'

'Oh yes, I meant to tell you,' I said, 'Martha told me she'd put them on your desk. They probably got lost under all your papers.'

'Is mine good, Daddy?' Emma asked eagerly, hanging on to his arm and jumping up to see. 'Do I get a prize?'

'Not bad, but no prizes, I'm afraid, although I must say one entry intrigues me immensely in yours. Under "Music", your teacher, a Mr Cruikshank, has written, "Very good progress. Emma has mastered tonguing and fingering." '

I snorted. Joss raised his eyebrows at me. 'Precisely,' he murmured. 'Pray tell, Emma, what exactly does Mr Cruikshank mean by that, do you suppose?'

'Oh, that's for the recorder,' she said proudly. 'I can play "London's Burning" all the way up to pour on water now.'

'Excellent,' said Joss faintly, 'so all is revealed.'

I giggled. 'Gosh, poor old buffer, I bet he had no idea.'

'Oh, don't you believe it,' said Joss drily. 'These teachers are all there. They delight in a little mischief to razz up the parents. When Toby was little he came home from school once clutching a painting he'd done, lots of brown splodges in a green field, and underneath was written, "My daddy's bollocks".'

'Oh God!' I giggled.

260

'I'll never forget the gleam of glee in his teacher's eye when I dropped him off at school the next morning. Oh sure, it's these little moments that get the poor bastards through the day, it's their revenge for being imprisoned for hours on end with twenty-five revolting six-year-olds. Why else d'you think they get the class to write "My Weekend News" every single Monday morning, if not to have a good laugh at the poor old parents' expense? "On Sunday Pop was very very thirsty and then he was sick on his pants and fell asleep on the floor so Mom went to sleep with Uncle Hank." Hell no, the joke's firmly on us, I'm afraid. Along with the exorbitant school fees of course.' And with that he disappeared back into his study, shaking his head gloomily.

The peace was short lived. Two minutes later Lucy was in hysterics again, and this time with blood on her hands. She came running into the kitchen, emitting a piercing scream and looking as if a bottle of tomato ketchup had been emptied on her head. I nearly dropped the vast monkfish pie I was making for the pub, thinking she'd scalped Toby, or even Ivo this time.

'What?' I screamed. 'What's happened!'

'It's Darling-Heart!' she sobbed. 'He's dying! Smelly-Pig bit him on the bottom and he's got blood coming out of his hole!'

I sighed, wiped my hands, and quickly followed her out to the yard. Darling-Heart and Smelly-Pig were two of the three giant, lop-eared rabbits, the other being called Angel-Baby, who'd been given to the children by Annabel for Christmas (yeah, ta *so* much, Annabel, Martha had said, guess who has to clean out their cages?). They'd been greeted with rapture by the twins – 'Oh! How sweet! I'm going to call mine Darling-Heart!' – 'And mine's Angel-Baby' – and disgust by Toby. 'Yuk, a stupid tame rabbit. I'm going to call him Smelly-Pig.'

'You can't call him that!' Emma had wailed.

'Of course I can,' retorted Toby. 'I can call him anything I like. There's a boy at school with three guinea pigs called Hank, Spank and—'

'Toby!' I roared. I forbade him to reveal the identity of the third guinea pig but conceded that Smelly-Pig was indeed a softer option.

Unfortunately, from day one, all of the rabbits had loathed the very sight of each other. In fact they only had to get within spitting distance and they were ripping each other's ears off. Naturally we kept them apart, and a rigorous system of apartheid was created by pinning three pieces of chicken wire down the middle of their runs. Much of their leisure time was spent hurling themselves against this

261

wire in an effort to kill each other but it was too high for any real damage to be done. Until today, that is, when goaded, doubtless, by Darling-Heart's taunts, Smelly-Pig had clearly hopped just that l-i-ttle bit higher than usual, launched himself up over the wire and, pausing only to spit in his neighbour's lettuce, had bitten Darling-Heart's balls off. Blood was pouring from the poor castrated rabbit as I picked him up. I ran inside with him, seized a tea towel from the draining board to staunch the flow of blood and, with Lucy and Emma all the while screaming beside me – 'He's going to die! He's going to die!' – frantically wrapped it round him.

'No, he's not going to die,' I said, struggling to tie it on, 'but if he'd just bloody well hold still for a minute I might be able to bandage him up and – damn!'

The rabbit wriggled free, the blood-soaked tea towel trailing him around the kitchen.

'Use a nappy, use a nappy!' Lucy cried, seizing one from Ivo's changing bag. She waved it in my face. 'Oh, save him, Rosie, please!'

That didn't seem such a bad idea, and I'd just wrestled the bleeding rabbit to the floor and got him snapped into it when Joss appeared in the doorway to see what all the commotion was about. He frowned as he regarded me huffing and puffing in a pool of blood, then blinked as he saw a rabbit in Pampers.

'Let me guess,' he said drily. 'You're desperate for another child and even a rabbit will do. I hope you're not breast-feeding.'

'Wrong,' I said grimly. 'Smelly-Pig bit his testicles off.'

'Balls.'

'No, it's true.'

'No, balls, not testicles. I detest genteel words when perfectly good Anglo-Saxon ones will do.'

'Must you be so pedantic at this precise moment?' I muttered. 'He's haemorrhaging all over the place here.'

'Well, take him to the vet, for heaven's sake. Let's spend a small fortune sewing him up when he would probably heal perfectly well of his own accord. That's what vets are for, isn't it?' And with that he stalked out again.

Swearing and cursing, I found an old grocery box, popped the rabbit inside, taped it up and punched a few air holes in the top for luck. Then, this not being Vera's day – or mine, come to that – and with Joss apparently incapable of looking after even one child while steeped in Greek mythology, I bundled Ivo, Toby, the hysterical twins and the rabbit into the car and hurtled off to the vet.

Naturally the traffic into Cirencester was very heavy, naturally it was pouring with rain, and naturally, when we finally got there, the queue at the vet's stretched all the way round the waiting room, out of the back door, and on to the pavement. Bugger that, I thought, pushing my gang ahead of me through the door. We muscled our way into a crowded reception area, packed to the gunnels with a motley assortment of Christmas hamsters, pale looking goldfish, mournful dogs and eczema-ridden cats. Amid the hostile glares of their owners I hustled my party through this animal lasagne and into a tiny square foot of space that I'd managed to create with my elbows. The twins were still sobbing quietly, but the boys were horribly interested in all the invalids, and I spent my time sounding like Joyce Grenfell as I tried to restrain them.

'Toby, please don't touch the snake . . . because I'm sure its owner wouldn't want you to . . . you don't mind . . . but he's a bit unpredictable . . . Toby, *please* don't touch it! . . . No, Ivo, it's a tortoise . . . no, you can't take its lid off . . . because it doesn't *come* off, darling. Look, a nice doggie instead . . . oh dear you're very worried about him, are you? . . . Silver and gold diarrhoea? No, I don't think I've ever seen that . . . ah, he ate the Christmas decorations. Ivo, pat the other end if you must . . . no the *other* end, darling, because he's got a bad tummy and – there, you see, that's why! Oh God, it *is* a funny colour isn't it – *don't touch, Ivo!* . . . Alex! Jesus, what a relief.'

The door to the surgery swung open and there stood Alex, looking like a veritable angel of glory in his long white coat, and an attractive one at that. He was clearly under pressure here, but nevertheless the eyes continued to sparkle, the smile was still disarmingly crooked, and the auburn locks contrasted beautifully with his white collar. I'd never seen him in his consulting rooms before and for a moment I felt a touch of my mother's Harley Street-itis coming on. Not now, Rosie, not now, old girl. For a moment he didn't see us, then as I waved frantically from the back of the room, his face cleared. He looked surprised.

'Sick rabbit,' I mouthed, pointing down at the box.

He came towards us, squeezing with difficulty through the rain-soaked, steaming throng. 'Sorry, so sorry. Excuse me.' He crouched down next to us and peered in the box.

'What's wrong with it?'

'Nasty bite. Bleeding heavily.'

'Ah.' He glanced around, then, 'Come to the cinema with me next Saturday and you can jump the queue,' he muttered out of the corner of his mouth.

'You're on,' I muttered back.

Alex straightened up. 'I'm so sorry, everyone,' he said with a charming smile to the assembled company, 'but we've got a very sick rabbit here. Bit of an emergency, I'm afraid. Won't keep you a moment,' and with that he ushered us towards his surgery, amidst cries of, 'Yeah, an' I've got a very sick gerbil an' all,' and, 'Bleedin' nerve, I've been here all morning!'

'So sorry . . . excuse us . . .' I muttered as we made our way through the mutinous, glaring throng. Finally the door shut mercifully behind us.

'Thanks, Alex,' I gasped with relief, 'I was getting a bit desperate out there.'

The children and I clustered anxiously round the table as Alex set the box upon it. He carefully lifted Darling-Heart out in his nappy. His mouth twitched in amusement.

'Groin injury,' I informed him.

'Ah.'

He removed the nappy, laid him down on the table, felt for his heart, then looked up at the assembled faces. 'Well, I'm awfully sorry, folks, but this rabbit is dead.'

A shriek went up from Lucy. She did a brief stagger, then a swoon, and then promptly collapsed in a heap on the floor. I hurried to pick her up but she pushed me away, clearly beside herself with grief and needing a floor to prostrate herself upon.

'No, no! It can't be!' she wailed.

'Oh, Lucy darling, don't! I'll get you another one, I promise!'

'I don't want another one!'

'You can have Smelly-Pig if you like,' Toby offered gallantly.

'I don't want Smelly-Pig! He's a murderer bastard!'

Alex sidled up to my ear. 'Er, shall I dispose of the body?' he inquired quietly.

'NO!' shrieked Lucy, suddenly jumping up. 'No, I want to bury him.'

Sobbing and sniffing, she carefully picked up the limp rabbit and placed him tenderly in his box. Then she tucked the box under her arm and out we all trooped again, into the grim, hostile crowd that was waiting ominously for us in reception. One old fellow raised his eyebrows inquiringly. Toby shook his head grimly and made an eloquent, throat-slitting gesture with his finger. All at once hostility turned to sympathy, and a collective 'Ah . . .' went up from the crowd. A gangway was made for the small weeping girl and her dead bunny. Silently the procession made its way out to the car park, with Lucy leading the way and even Ivo, it seemed, silenced by the solemnity of the occasion. I drove slowly home in the rain, wind-screen wipers slapping.

'I want to bury him in the garden,' said Lucy, in a barely audible whisper from the back.

'Of course, my darling. And so you shall. We'll make a nice little grave for him.'

'With a headstone.'

'Yes, my love.'

'And flowers.'

'Naturally.'

'And lots of mourners, everyone's got to come. We'll ring Martha and Vera. Even Daddy's got to come, and we'll sing hymns.'

'Er, yes, I expect so,' I said doubtfully. That last bit made me slightly nervous. Daddy *and* hymns? I had a feeling Daddy was less than pious.

In the event, I needn't have worried. I knocked softly on the workshop door, shut it behind me and quickly explained to Joss exactly what had happened and how upset Lucy was. He rose magnificently to the occasion, left the pagan gods standing in gigantic splendour behind him, and out we all trooped into the garden for the funeral. Vera was duly summoned and came hurrying up the hill from her cottage and even Martha whizzed over from the hospital, glad of a reprieve from bedside duties. Huddled under macs in the pouring rain and ankle-deep in Flanders mud, we all looked on, as Joss, under close instructions from Lucy and Emma, dug what looked to me like a sodding great hole.

'Bigger!' Lucy kept calling. 'Bigger, Daddy. I want to bury him in his hutch and blankets and everything so he doesn't get dirty!'

'Okey-doke!' gasped Joss, sweat pouring off his brow. 'Shan't keep you a moment, my darling.' He turned to me in an aside. 'Does this come under "digging the garden" in your practical book then? I seem to remember I've only got to clean a car and I'm a New Man, aren't I?'

'Nearly,' I grinned. 'Just a few more shelves to put up and it'll be welcome to the real world, Joss.'

The grave finally dug, we all stood about solemnly as Lucy, our chief mourner, officiated at the ceremony. First we had to hold hands round the grave and privately remember Darling-Heart, then we all sang 'Away In A Manger', and then, it being the only prayer Lucy could remember, we all said, 'For what we are about to receive may the Lord make us truly thankful. Amen.' I couldn't look at Joss during any of this and kept my head well and truly bowed. Lucy then nodded importantly to her father, the undertaker, who with due ceremony and *gravitas* picked up the box and walked slowly towards the hole.

He was just about to lower it in when Lucy suddenly cried, 'One last kiss!'

Joss turned. 'Oh Lucy, sweetheart—'

'Yes, Daddy, I just want to give him one last kiss!'

Joss sighed and came back. He removed the lid. 'All right.'

We all clustered obediently round to watch Lucy administer the last rites, when suddenly . . . the rabbit opened one eye.

'ARGHHHH!' shrieked Vera.

'Holy shit,' murmured Joss.

'He's alive!' screamed Lucy. 'Darling-Heart's alive!'

After that it all got terribly giggly. Lucy rushed Darling-Heart inside, and under Vera's instruction put him in a box in the low oven of the Aga to warm up.

'Funny if she cooked him now,' remarked Toby, peering in.

For some reason Joss and I found this unaccountably amusing, but Lucy didn't, so we hurried outside to hide our faces and ostensibly to fill in the hole. We kept having to stop though, and hold our sides and collapse on our spades from laughing so much; in fact at one point Joss nearly fell in the grave.

Happily, Darling-Heart didn't cook, and half an hour later was out of the Aga, hopping about, and tucking into some rather pricey rocket leaves Martha had found at the bottom of the fridge. I rang Alex.

'No! That's not possible. He had no pulse.'

'Well, he's got one now,' I said eyeing Darling-Heart as he crapped on the kitchen table. 'Either that, or we've got the second coming.'

'Good God. Well, I suppose it must have stopped briefly, that can happen, you know. I'm so sorry, Rosie, it seems I made a mistake.'

'Don't worry, I'm just glad we didn't bury him.'

As I put the phone down, Joss looked up from reading the newspaper in the corner. 'Damn vet doesn't know his arse from his elbow. Too busy looking at you to diagnose the patient, I suspect.'

I blushed, predictably, and busied myself with clearing up Darling-Heart's mess on the table. I let my hair fall over my face as I did it.

Joss grinned. 'Thought so.' He shut the paper. 'You'll be spending tomorrow night with him then, I take it?'

I looked up. 'No, I'm not actually.'

'Really? Don't tell me he hasn't asked you to the New Year's Eve shindig down at the Red Lion?'

'Certainly he's asked me, but I don't particularly want to go.' I met his eye, aware of Martha's inquisitive gaze.

He looked at me for a moment. 'Oh okay.' He got up, stretched widely, yawned and threw his paper down on the chair. 'Well, if you're going to be on your own at the cottage you might just as well come up here.'

'Oh, I don't know,' I muttered.

He shrugged and made for the door. 'As you wish.'

'Although,' I said quickly, 'I suppose I could cook supper for us both, or something?'

'Why not? Or something.'

With that he left the room, leaving me standing in the middle of the kitchen feeling slightly foolish and more than a little confused.

Chapter Twenty

I found myself going to a great deal of trouble preparing a simple little supper for New Year's Eve. First I sat down and planned my menu, then I tore into Cirencester clutching my list of ingredients. In vain, as it happened, because asparagus, quails' eggs, guinea fowl and fresh peaches are elusive at the best of times, but in mid-winter they're downright invisible. I was determined not to be beaten though, and doggedly drove further and further afield in an effort to track them down. It was only when I found myself bouncing down an unmade-up track in the middle of nowhere because someone had suggested there might just be a farmer down there who'd be happy to kill a couple of guinea fowl for me that I began to question the logic of all this. What's this all about then, Rosie? I wondered as I hit the main road again with a bump, my freshly slaughtered poultry safely stashed in the boot. Why are you scouring the countryside searching for palpably unobtainable out-of-season goodies when you could be slapping a couple of steaks in a pan and opening a tin of Libby's fruit cocktail? Who's it all for then, eh?

It's for me, I said firmly, as I swung the car back into Farlings' drive. I'm doing it for myself, to prove to myself that when I was picked by Jean-Phillippe all those millions of years ago out of scores of young hopefuls to train under him in his kitchen, there had actually been a reason. I'm attempting this culinary extravaganza purely for my own self-esteem, okay? Okay, I agreed doubtfully, somewhat unconvinced as I staggered through the back door laden down with shopping. Just then I caught a glimpse of Joss's black jeans as he exited left to his study and my knees went a bit weak. I had to sit down. Must be carrying all those groceries I thought, panting a bit. And no breakfast too, of course.

Even so, as I ranged all my ingredients around me later that afternoon, it occurred to me that ulterior motives or not, this feast was certainly going to put my skills to the test. It was a long while since I'd attempted anything as complicated as this and certainly not with three beady-eyed children watching from the tea table and an old-style country cook at my elbow.

'I'd take them diddly little chickens straight back where they came from if I was you,' sniffed Vera, peering over my shoulder. 'Blimmin' nerve. Fancy selling you scrawny little buggers like that.' She poked one in disgust.

'They're guinea fowl actually and yes, you're right, they do tend to be a bit lean but they taste delicious,' I assured her, hurriedly measuring the marinade into a jug.

'Guinea fowl? Oh, Daddy likes those,' piped up Emma, putting her plate in the dishwasher. 'And you've got those titchy little eggs, and sparrow's grass too, how clever, Rosie, those are all Daddy's favourite things!'

'Really? Gosh, how extraordinary, I'd no idea,' I murmured.

Vera flashed me a sudden, curious look and I hid behind my hair, concentrating hard on extracting some giblets. Why couldn't everyone just go away and leave me alone? I still had loads to do and I was beginning to feel a bit hot and flustered now – Jesus, was that the time? Five o'clock already! Vera seemed to have taken root under my feet.

'What's that then?' She narrowed her eyes as I began smearing the breasts.

'It's a sort of saffron mixture, with herbs and butter. Um, Vera, I don't mind holding the fort for a bit if you want to pop out and get something nice for Vic,' I suggested tentatively. 'I mean, I expect you'll want to cook him something special, won't you, seeing as it's New Year's Eve?'

'Ooh, no, luv, I shan't bother to cook. I've got a nice bit of tinned salmon for 'is tea and that brother of his is coming round to drink our rum and talk nonsense at us all night. It'd be wasted on him. 'E's never been quite the same since he had that plate put in his head, poor bugger.'

'Yes, well, I can see how that might send one a little . . . off beam,' I murmured, eyeing Emma as she popped her finger into a bowl of cream. 'Emma darling, if you've finished your tea why don't you – where d'you think you're going, Toby?'

Toby stalked past me into the hall, carrying his plate of untouched food.

'I can't eat this, it's disgusting.'

I'd noticed that as the end of the holidays drew near, Toby's behaviour was getting more and more unmanageable.

'Don't be silly, it's just lamb and vegetables. The girls ate it, it's delicious.'

'It's not delicious and I hate these sprouts. They make everything smell farty.' He disappeared round the corner into the loo. 'And there's only one thing to do with farty sprouts . . .' There was a splash, then we heard the loo flushing. He reappeared with a clean plate. 'All gone.'

Emma snorted with laughter.

'Toby!' I stormed.

'Sorry, but I just couldn't eat it. It was too vile for words.' And out he went into the garden, slamming the back door behind him.

I banged down my carving knife. 'God, that boy just gets worse and worse!'

'Needs a bloody great rocket up his backside if you ask me,' remarked Vera. 'How are you placed for rockets?'

'Not too well at the moment,' I said miserably, watching him through the window and wondering if I should follow him.

'Exactly, me neither. Leave him alone, luv, and have a chat with him later. He'll come round, you'll see. It's this school business what's worrying him.'

I sighed. 'I know.'

'And meanwhile we'll get out of your way and get the dusting done. Come on, you two.'

I smiled gratefully as she led the twins and Ivo away, clutching a duster apiece. 'Thanks, Vera.'

My next visitor was Joss. I'd just legged it to the loo for an emergency pee, but on flushing had discovered that the sprouts were still bobbing about merrily. The S bend, it seemed, couldn't swallow them any more than Toby could. I flushed again, and again, then cursing vilely fished them out with my hand. I was just on my way to the kitchen bin with them when Joss appeared. He peered into my hands.

'Ah, dinner is served, I see. Gone vegetarian, have we?'

I laughed. 'No, it was the children's tea actually. Toby wouldn't eat them.'

'Bloody boy doesn't know what's good for him,' he remarked, and so saying took a sprout from my hand and popped it in his mouth. 'Mmm . . . delicious.' He looked at my stunned face. 'What's up?'

'Nothing!' I hurriedly took aim and chucked the rest into the open bin.

He shook his head. 'You're terribly wasteful, you know, Rosie. Those sprouts are full of fibre.'

Too right, I thought weakly as I washed my hands. Thank God he didn't know how much.

Finally, our meal was prepared. All three courses had turned out beautifully and all it needed now was some immaculate timing. Quails' eggs and asparagus sat in puff pastry baskets with a hollandaise sauce just waiting to be warmed through; guinea fowl breasts with saffron and a julienne of vegetables were all poised to be steamed; peaches baked in red wine with homemade vanilla ice cream sat chilling in the fridge. Perfect. All I had to do now was cajole the children into bed, get myself ready, and lay the table.

It all went like clockwork. The children, for some reason, were tired and amenable and fell into their beds, and I ran excitedly off to my cottage to change. I'd already planned to wear a rather chic little navy blue dress that I hadn't worn for ages because of being much too fat, but I was pretty sure that after all these months of stress it would be fine. I had a quick bath and slipped it on. It zipped up like a dream. I put on some dark tights, some low-heeled pumps, brushed my hair, and then with a surprisingly shaky hand applied my make-up. Very carefully I outlined my eyes, mascaraed my lashes, added just a smidgen of blusher, some pale pink lipstick and – I stood back to admire my handiwork. There. Just a squirt of Chanel here . . . and here . . . some pearl earrings . . . and I was ready.

I dashed back to the house, my heart pounding. Now. The kitchen. I frantically cleared up books, papers, magazines, children's toys, shoving them all into a cupboard and squeezing the door shut. Then I set about laying the table. Earlier in the day I'd polished some silver I'd found in a drawer so I set that out instead of the usual stainless steel. Then I carefully arranged the tiny bunch of snowdrops I'd picked earlier in a little vase and set that in the middle. I stood back. Now, candles. I'd bought some beeswax ones in Cirencester which smelled delicious so I ran into the sitting room, pinched some candlesticks and lit them. What else? I wondered, looking around, my heart pounding. Ah, yes, the lighting. Terrible, really dreadful; that overhead strip would have to go and – oh yes, I know, I could borrow a table lamp from the hall. I dashed out and found one with a red shade which gave off a rosy glow, came back and plugged it in. The effect was amazing, instant atmosphere.

Now, music. A radio stood on the dresser. I flicked it on and a worthy, female Radio Four voice droned on and on about the relentlessness of the menstrual cycle. No, that wouldn't do at all. Hastily I twiddled the dial until I found something moody and – ah, that was more like it, 'Strangers In The Night' – how apposite! Giggling to myself I twirled round the kitchen with an imaginary partner, humming along. I glanced up at the clock. Ten to eight, surely he'd be in soon? Needing a drink? Ah, yes, drink. I took a couple of glasses from the cupboard and poured myself some wine from the bottle in the fridge. I sipped it pensively. Leaning back against the dresser I smiled around at the softly lit room, admiring my handiwork. He'd still be working of course, but any minute now he'd put down his hammer, wander in here, take one look at the moody lighting, the elegant table, the flowers, the candles, hear the music, see me all dressed up and think, blimey, is she hot for me, or what?

The roundabouts slowed to a shuddering halt. My glass froze in my hand. My mouth fell open. I gasped in horror and clutched the dresser behind me. Oh my God, Rosie, what have you done? Have you gone completely mad? Have you taken leave of your senses? Are you clinically insane? You might just as well have written READY AND WILLING on your forehead and erected a banner announcing TONIGHT'S THE NIGHT! Perhaps you should have propped a mattress against the wall, just in case. I clutched my mouth. Oh-my-God-oh-my-God, what on earth would he think, and what if he comes in right this minute, sees all this seduction paraphernalia and – shit!

Horrified, I leapt into action. I blew out the candles, flicked on the overhead strip light, turned off the rosy glow, zapped off 'Strangers In The Night' – *strangers in the night, Jesus!* – and pausing only to fling the snowdrops in the sink, flew down the hill like a terrified rabbit. Frantically I tore off my dress, my tights, my shoes, found my old jeans, my sweatshirt, my woolly socks, my tatty loafers, threw it all on, and with as shaky a hand as I'd applied my make-up frenziedly scrubbed it all off again. Sensibly I stopped short of actually flaying myself, but by golly the end result was well-scrubbed. Oh God, I moaned as I tore back downstairs again, oh God, you idiot, Rosie, you total, utter, idiot! I did the 500 metre dash back into the kitchen clocking the time – twenty past eight, help! Quickly I swapped the silver for the grubby old stainless steel, glancing around and wondering what else I could do.

My eyes flew to the food. All that effort, all his favourite things which over the weeks through careful, sneaky listening I'd gleaned like a mole, like an FBI agent, and now here they all were, following one another in quick succession. What would he think? Well, he'd either think it was an incredible coincidence or he'd think I was passionately in love with him, that's what. Oh God, was I? I went hot. Was I in love with him? I sat down for a moment. Felt my forehead. I didn't want to answer that question. I was his tenant, for heaven's sake, and he was married, it was unthinkable that he'd even consider me of course but even if he did it was such a betrayal of trust and – oh, bugger the trust, what was I going to do about the sodding food! I wrung my hands miserably over the asparagus and quails' eggs. I could, I supposed, squirt tomato ketchup over the lot and douse the guinea fowl in vinegar to put him off the scent, but somehow I couldn't bring myself to do that. Professional pride wouldn't let me. I swallowed hard. No, the food would have to stay immaculate but I, mean- while, had to look as dishevelled and undesirable as possible. That was my penance. I had to look as if absolutely nothing could be further from my mind than a romantic little evening *à deux*. Hastily I messed up my hair till it stood on end, found some chewing gum I'd confiscated from Toby, popped it in and chewed hard. Yuk. I knew I had a spot brewing on my forehead so I gave it a quick pick – there, that should flare up nicely. Then I zapped on the television, turning the volume up sky high, and flopped down in front of it, swinging one leg over the arm of the chair in an attitude of oikish nonchalance. I was just wishing I could fart to order like Toby to pep up the ambience when in walked Joss.

'Hi. Sorry I'm late. Hope you weren't waiting for me.' He went to wash the dust from his hands in the sink.

'Eh?' I turned bleary eyes on him, chewing gormlessly, as if totally brain-damaged by *Brookside*. I blinked.

'Oh, hi, Joss. No, not at all.'

'Mmm, that's a smell I recognise. Chanel, isn't it?'

My rotating jaws froze. I flushed to my rumpled roots. 'Um . . . yes. Yes, it is.' Bugger.

'Very pleasant. Are we eating in here then?'

'Er, yes. I mean, where else?'

'Well, why don't we take it through to the hall? It's so unbearably grim in here with this God-awful overhead light. Here, grab one end and I'll take the other.'

He pushed open the side door with his bottom and stood poised at one end of the table. Dumbly I stood up and took the other end. Together we carried it through. He'd lit the fire, I noticed, and as we set the table down in front of it, all at once, with the golden walls, the red carpet, the books and the antiques, it became a rather cosy dining room.

273

He looked around, frowning. 'D'you know, it's funny, I could have sworn there was a table lamp on that chest over there, I wonder where—'

'Oh, I know where it is, I was – borrowing it!' I flashed back into the kitchen and returned with it triumphantly.

'Excellent. Now. Candles d'you think?'

'Why not?' I gasped, feeling a bit of knee tremble coming on and smoothing my hair down a bit.

'I wonder where—'

'I know!' I almost screeched, and scampered off to retrieve the candles like an eager old spaniel on the scent of his master's slippers. I found them in the kitchen drawer where I'd flung them. They were still hot. Bit like me. Calm down, Rosie, calm down. I breathed deeply. And don't pant.

I hastened back. He took them from me and lit them. 'That's better.'

'Yes, much!' My voice was squeaky. I cleared my throat. 'Much,' I growled. I looked around. Blimey, this was an even more seductive atmosphere than the one I'd created in the kitchen.

'Kitty and I used to eat in here when we could be bothered,' he explained matter-of-factly as he sat down.

'Ah. Right.' I dithered stupidly for a moment, then hastened off to the kitchen to get the food. 'But – you don't with Annabel?' I ventured bravely as I came back in.

He grinned and poured the wine. 'It might have escaped your notice, Rosie, but Annabel doesn't exactly eat. Oh, she might nibble a raw lentil if she's bingeing, but that's about the extent of her calorific intake.'

'I wish it was mine,' I sighed as I put the starter down in front of him. 'I don't think I've ever nibbled anything, as my hips will testify.' Oh, well done, Rosie, really, well done. Did you really want to draw attention to your bottom so early on in the evening? And of course he glanced down.

'Looks all right to me.' I cringed and sat down smartly. 'You're designed like a woman, that's all. If you didn't have hips you'd be a man.'

I wondered momentarily where this left the twig-like Annabel, but Joss was raising his glass, so I seized mine, anxious not to be left behind.

'Your health. The New Year, a new beginning, whatever takes your fancy.' He took a sip and winced. 'Oh God, this is poison, Rosie, where in the hell did you get it?'

'Oddbins,' I said defiantly. 'I'm afraid I couldn't quite run to the claret.'

'Oh okay, don't tell me, I haven't paid you enough for your help. Well, there's no need to run to anything as a matter of fact, we've got a cellar full here, crazy not to use it.' And so saying he got up and disappeared. He returned a few minutes later brandishing something that at least had a cork, and which he declared infinitely more drinkable.

And so the evening progressed. We ate, we drank, the conversation flowed, and on the odd occasion when it did fall winded to the table on account of one or two of my more nervous efforts, he picked it up again, carrying it forward smoothly, effortlessly. He talked about the exhilaration of suddenly becoming sought after, after years of struggle, and of the pressure he felt to always produce good and innovative work. But he didn't just talk about himself. Without getting too personal he asked me about myself, how my business was going, whether I enjoyed being in the country, if I was lonely, or if I was secretly relieved to get out of London. I found myself telling him about Harry, too, about the dreadful time when he'd threatened to take Ivo away from me, and I discovered it helped to talk, to get it off my chest. Gradually, by the time we got to the pudding, helped by the wine, the food, and the heat from the fire, I'd learned to relax. I sat back, replete, and looked around, wiping my mouth.

'This is a lovely room.'

'You've said that before.'

'Have I? God, how moronic.'

'No, but surroundings matter to you, don't they?'

I thought this over. 'Yes, I suppose they do. I certainly couldn't live in a complete tip like you do.' Clearly I was emboldened by the wine. 'But then I suppose you don't notice things like that,' I said with a slight smile, 'being on a higher intellectual plane than the rest of us earthlings and all that.'

He laughed. 'Kitty used to say that.' He looked around. 'She was happy with this room too. Felt she'd accomplished something here. Yes, this room and her attic.'

'I've been up there,' I said quietly.

He looked up sharply.

'I – thought I'd better mention it,' I said nervously, watching his face darken. 'Only Toby found me up there, so I thought he might say something. I suppose – well, I suppose I just wanted to look.' I flushed. 'Nosy, you might say.'

He shrugged. 'You might.' He played with the stem of his glass. 'So what did you think?'

'Well, I . . .' God, what did I think? What did I think of a man who kept a room virtually untouched since the day his wife died? Privately I thought he still mourned her, and was still deeply in love with her, but I didn't say so.

'I think it's a way of keeping her spirit alive. Of hanging on to her memory. And that's nice. I certainly got a sense of who she was.'

He nodded. 'You think I'm a sad old git.'

'Of course I don't.'

He sighed wearily. 'Last summer, Annabel chivvied and bullied me about it to such an extent that I damn nearly got around to clearing it out. But then I mentioned it to Toby and he didn't speak to me for three days.' He shrugged. 'Somehow it never happened.'

'Toby's still very young. In a year or two he'll come round. Maybe you could do it together.'

He smiled. 'Maybe.' He set his spoon down and looked bleakly into his empty pudding bowl. 'Well now, Rosie. That was really very, very disappointing.'

I started.

He grinned. 'Don't be silly, it was absolutely delicious. The best meal I've eaten in years, and let me tell you I've parked my backside in some so-called swanky places recently. You don't need me to tell you that you are one extremely talented cook, so why aren't you doing anything about it?'

'What d'you mean?'

'Well, Martha tells me you trained with that pan-chucking, enfant terrible of the cookery world, Jean-Phillipe Whatsisname. You don't suffer for your art like that unless you've got some kind of end in your sights, so what's the end?'

'Oh, I don't know,' I said vaguely, getting up and clearing the plates. 'There's the pub, of course, and I thought I might cook a few dinner parties while I'm here, make up batches of lasagne for harassed housewives, that kind of thing.'

'That's it?'

'Well, it is now, yes. I mean years ago, hell no, I had all sorts of plans, but I've got to cut my cloth accordingly. I've got Ivo, I'm a widow, I—'

'What sort of plans?' he cut across me.

'Oh well, *then* it was to have my own restaurant of course.'

'What kind of restaurant?'

I stared at him.

'Don't you know?'

'Yes, of course I know,' I said slowly. 'I know exactly. I know down to the design of the menu, the colour of the tablecloths, the paint on the walls, the type of flour I'd use to bake the bread, the sort of pastry, the flowers – of course I know. It's been my dream, my sanctuary, since I was eighteen. We all have a place to go in our heads to hide, that's always been mine.'

He took the plates from me. 'Leave those. Sit. Tell me.'

And so I did. I sat down and told him exactly. About how it would be a country restaurant attached to a farm shop and how fresh produce would go from there into the restaurant every day and how anyone coming to eat in the restaurant would be encouraged to visit the farm shop to buy for themselves. I told him that in order to get to the restaurant, diners would have to walk right through the kitchen, along a glass partition, so they could see the food being prepared. I told him that having gone through this ultra modern, state-of-the-art preparation area, they'd find themselves in a light, airy, traditional dining room and not the operating theatres so beloved in London, all chrome and glass, and ghastly overhead spotlights. Its deep, parchment walls would be lined with oil paintings, water colours and groaning bookcases, a log fire would be blazing in the grate, and mahogany tables, set not too close together, would lead to two sets of French doors, thrown open in summer and issuing on to a terrace. Here there'd be a few more tables, and around them cottage garden plants would spill out of ancient urns. The herb garden would come right up to the terrace, the sun releasing its heady scent in the summer, and beyond that would be a vegetable garden sloping down to an orchard and then up the other side to a vista of hills beyond. I told him how only the very best, the very freshest ingredients would be used in the restaurant and how the emphasis would be on home-produced English food like hare, pheasant, fish and seasonal vegetables, and not the tarted up pasta and polenta that was so fashionable in restaurants nowadays. It would be back to our roots, but without the overcooked heaviness so often associated with English food. I told him about the wine list, about the prices I envisaged, I even told him my idea of getting a string quartet, perhaps from a local music college, who might be persuaded to play in the evenings for some pocket money. In short, I told him my dreams. I must say, he listened very politely. When I'd finished, he cleared his throat.

'So why haven't you done all this?'

'What with, chocolate buttons?'

'Well, I'm not suggesting the money's going to fall out of the sky, but I believe the received wisdom is to go to one's bank manager with a business plan, pretty much like the one you've just presented to me, borrow the money and gradually pay it back.'

I gave a hollow laugh. 'Oh, Joss, have you got any idea how many aspiring restaurateurs do that every year? How many people borrow, open, cook, struggle, fail, close, go bankrupt, collapse, get therapy and end up at the funny farm? I just can't afford to take risks like that!'

'Okay, so don't.'

I stared at him. 'Oh, it's all right for you, isn't it? All your dreams ever involved was fiddling about with bits of rock, or torturing a lump of iron with a blow torch. Not much outlay there, not much loss of sleep on the loan repayments, not many salaries to pay at the end of the month, not much loss of face either really, because who's to know if your Greek gods don't come up to scratch in the privacy of your own studio?'

'Is that what bothers you then? Loss of face?'

'No, it isn't actually and – my God, you're beginning to sound just like my brother!'

'Ah, so I'm treading a well-worn path, am I? With the famous film director, who I gather knows my wife, incidentally.'

I glanced at him quickly, but his face was impassive. I nodded. 'Yes, well, Tom says much the same. About how I'm afraid to compete, afraid to stick my head above the parapet. Fear seems to be the number one driving force in my character actually,' I said cheerfully. 'My main asset.'

He smiled. 'Not fear. Just lack of confidence.' He got up and went to the bureau. 'Glass of Madeira?'

'Please.'

I thought this over. Yes, I supposed I did lack confidence. I watched as Joss poured the drinks at the sideboard and caught sight of a photograph of his wife at his elbow. Unlike her, of course. It was a black and white studio shot, chin resting on hand, mouth full and pouting, moody eyes straight to camera. Oh yes, she had confidence, she had it in spadefuls. Bucketfuls, in fact. I looked into her direct, smouldering gaze and wondered if you were born like that, came out of the womb zinging with self-assurance, or whether you became that way because everyone just fell at your feet the moment you entered the room. Beauty was so easy, wasn't it? It made life so incredibly simple. A bit like falling off a log.

'I hope she hasn't been giving you too much of a hard time.'

I came to, sharply. Joss was sitting opposite me again, following my eyes.

'N-no. No, not at all,' I faltered, reaching for my glass.

'It's just her way, I'm afraid. You mustn't take it personally.'

'I don't,' I said, thinking yes, well, rudeness could be my way too, but clearly I don't have the 'confidence'.

I picked up my spoon and idly smeared the last traces of ice cream around my plate with the back of it. Suddenly I felt miserable. 'She'll be back soon, I imagine.'

'Tomorrow morning, first thing. She could only get a night flight, unfortunately.' He grinned ruefully. 'I mean for us. I'm afraid the Red-Eye tends to make her a bit irritable.'

So what's new? I thought bleakly. 'Is she . . . very successful?' I heaved this up from somewhere, wondering how on earth I'd managed to steer the conversation so disastrously around to his wife.

'Oh, sure she is, in her field.'

What's that, anything with a dollar sign in front of it? I wondered bitchily.

'Which is why she sometimes comes across as being rather,' he hesitated, 'well, difficult. It's the stress that comes with success, I'm afraid.'

'Must be dreadful.'

He laughed. 'It's just her way, Rosie. She's used to being something of a star and there's a tendency to overstep the mark without really realising it. I gather she summoned you up here to run errands at Christmas. I'm sorry about that.'

'That's all right. I don't mind doing a bit of shopping for her, although I might draw the line at buying your contraceptives in future.'

'Sorry?'

'Oh – nothing.'

'What contraceptives?'

'Oh, it's just – she asked me to get some condoms.'

He frowned. 'We don't use condoms.'

I stared at him. I think it dawned on us simultaneously.

'Well, well, well,' he drawled, 'so that's her game now, is it?' He gave a hollow laugh. 'Well, whaddya know.'

I gazed down at my plate. Jesus Christ, they hadn't been for him. She was having an affair. Felt the blood rush to my cheeks. Oh God, how *awful*. How could I have said that? And I must look like the arch bitch too, just casually dropping it into the conversation, but it simply hadn't *occurred* to me they might not be for him.

There was a terrible silence. Above the fireplace the clock ticked slowly. A log shifted in the grate. I glanced at the clock. In a few more seconds it would be midnight. Joss's eyes swept up just as the hands met vertically.

'Twelve o'clock,' he said grimly. 'Happy New Year, Rosie.'

'Happy New Year,' I muttered.

He raised his glass. 'To auld acquaintance,' he said bitterly. 'Lest they be forgot.' He knocked his wine back in one and set the glass back on the table. Stared at it bleakly. 'For the sake of auld lang syne . . . yeah, auld lang syne . . .'

I stared at him. He seemed to have gone into a trance, staring fixedly at a spot on the table just beyond his wine glass. I bit my lip. He was clearly devastated. And I'd wreaked that devastation. I remembered his inscription in the poetry book and I remembered Alex telling me how crazy they were about each other. We sat there in tortured silence. Then a cry rent the air.

'That's Ivo!' I got up with a jump, knocking my chair back.

I fled from that room and up the stairs two at a time, along the corridor, glad to get away, my heart pounding. Ivo was standing up in his cot, bright eyed and grinning from ear to ear. I picked him up and instantly smelled a filthy nappy. Damn. I'd have to go back down to the cottage to get some more. I hesitated with him in my arms. Should I put him back in the cot to scream while I was gone – I could hardly hand a smelly baby to Joss – or, yes, why didn't we both go back together? He was wide awake now and it would be an excuse to get out of the house, otherwise what would I do? Bring the nappy back, change him, go back downstairs and sit opposite Joss again? Or just sneak back to the cottage like an informer who's done her work? Done her damnedest? My yellow streak won. Yep. Sneak back. I wrapped a blanket round Ivo and went downstairs. Joss was still at the table. With one sentence, it seemed, I'd immobilised him. Turned him to stone.

'Um, look, didn't bring any nappies, so I'm going to take him back to the cottage.'

He didn't look up. I moved towards the door. Put my hand up to the latch.

'Don't be ridiculous,' he snapped suddenly. 'Just go and get the lousy diaper, you don't have to go back yet.'

Oh, but I do, I thought, lifting the latch. 'I may as well,' I muttered. 'He's wide awake anyway now so . . .' I bit my lip. Turned. 'Look, I'm so sorry, Joss. I honestly didn't mean to . . .'

I stopped, almost overwhelmed by the depth of feeling on his face.

It was taut, pale, and a muscle was going in his cheek. I had a sudden, ghastly realisation that he was struggling with tears. I felt a huge lump of horror in my own throat and without another thought hastened out, shutting the door behind me. I stood for a moment in the darkness, shaken, then ran to the car. I slipped Ivo into his seat and jumped in. Down to the cottage we sped, my heart hammering. Once inside I hurried him up to his room, changed him, and popped him smartly down to sleep under a pile of blankets, for once deaf to the outraged cries that followed. I went to my own room, undressed and got into bed, pulling the duvet up over my head. I brought my knees up to my chin and hugged them hard, shivering as I lay there curled up in the darkness. Oh God, what a mess. What a God-awful mess I'd made of that! It must have looked as if I'd planned it all too, the supper, the chat, the subtle turn of the conversation around to his wife – and then the *coup de grâce*. The unshakable, irrefutable evidence of Annabel's adultery. And with nowhere for him to run and hide. He'd just had to sit there and take it. I'd had him pinned like a fly under a rolled-up newspaper and I was perfectly poised to watch him squirm.

I remembered the look on his face, startled at first, then pained. I shivered. A rogue thought came into my head that he could be shot of her now, now that he was enlightened, available to me, but I suppressed it with the memory of his ashen face. Don't kid yourself, Rosie, in his eyes you couldn't hold a match to her, let alone a candle. I imagined him still there, draining his decanter, drinking the dregs in front of a dying fire, imagining her miles and miles away. In someone else's bed. Whose? I wondered. Torturing himself, longing for her, hating me. I began to cry silently, I longed for sleep to shut it all out. Next door Ivo's cries had abated and I shut my eyes, willing the same oblivion for myself. Finally Morpheus must have taken pity on me, I must have drifted off, because the next thing I knew, I woke up with a start. A tremendous thumping was coming from below.

I sat up, startled. What was that? For a moment I couldn't remember where I was. Had I imagined a noise? Was it in a dream? Then, *thump-thump-thump*, there it was again, and shouting too. It was someone outside, someone was at the door! I leapt out of bed and ran to the window. It was pitch dark outside, but down below, just to the left of the porch, I could make out a shadowy figure, in a long dark coat, and hat. Definitely a man, but it was too dark to see who. Oh God, was it Joss? Had he come to accuse me of lying, of self-seeking treachery to promote myself at Annabel's expense, or perhaps he'd come to – I didn't know what, but I grabbed my dressing gown and ran downstairs.

'Rosie! Let me in!' called a voice. It was hoarse and I didn't recognise it, but I knew in a flash it wasn't Joss.

I crept to the door, my heart pounding.

'Who is it?' I whispered.

'For pity's sake, let me in!'

I hesitated for a moment, then reached up, and shot the bolt across. Without me even turning the handle, the door flew open. The next moment I was smothered, as someone fell on top of me, reeking of alcohol. Whoever it was was wrapped in an enormous overcoat, a hat over his eyes. At first I didn't recognise him, but as I staggered back under his weight – 'Michael!'

Chapter Twenty-One

'Michael! What the hell are you doing here!'

'Well, thank bloody Christ for that,' he gasped, hanging on round my neck. 'I thought I was going to have to die of hypothermia on your bloody doorstep! Shagging New Year's Eve, and the bastard hotel locks me out. It was only three o'clock in the morning, for God's sake – shagging New Year's Eve!'

He swayed alarmingly and I just about managed to stay upright. 'Jesus, Michael, get off me, will you!'

He was clearly catastrophically drunk. His face had that totally unbuttoned look, his eyes were pale and glassy, he stank of booze and stale scent and his bow tie was up around his ear somewhere. The remains of a party popper hung from his hat and he had lipstick on his cheek. I dragged him in like a dead man, but before I kicked the door shut behind him, I spotted his car.

'Christ, you didn't drive here, did you?'

'Had to. Some bastard took the last taxi, but I tell you what, Rosie, I shouldn't have done,' he shook his head gravely. 'Really shouldn't have done, and it's not that I'm not shit hot when I've had a few pints, fucking Ayrton Senna I am, but those bastards in blue are out there in force tonight. The place is crawling with pigs, waiting in lay-bys, hiding in hedges, bastards – Christ, bloody New Year's Eve and you can't even have a shagging drink! Had to dodge 'em,' he demonstrated with a drunken weave of his hand, 'had to duck and weave, slip and slide – lost 'em though, lost them in the lanes.' He winked broadly. 'See, I know these lanes.'

'I take it it was a good party then,' I said drily, still staggering under his weight.

He steadied himself and held me at arm's length, hands on my shoulders. 'Oh-oh,' he said warily, 'I know that look.' He wagged a finger in my face. 'Alice gets that look at parties, and I say, fellers! I can tell by the look on my wife's face that I'm having a good time!' He roared with laughter. 'Always goes down well, that one, always

283

gets a laugh, 'cept from Alice of course.' He sighed, frowned with deep concentration. 'What did you ask me?'

'It doesn't matter, Michael. Look—'

'Ah yes, bloody good,' he said nodding hard, as it all came back to him. 'Bloody good party. Good company too, in fact I seem to remember forming a splinter group with one rather luscious little creature at some point in the evening. Off we crept,' he demonstrated with crawling fingers, 'up the stairs, just the two of us – or was it three? No, no, I'm boasting, don't boast, Michael, it's not nice, it was definitely the two of us, and it's no good looking at me like that, Rosie, Alice wouldn't come with me, so what's a chap to do?' he wailed.

'I can't imagine.'

'YOU'RE JUST NOT TRYING!' he roared happily.

'Michael, d'you think you could just get off me for a moment?' I gasped. 'Only I think I'm going to collapse!'

'Sure, sure,' he said in injured surprise, 'anything to oblige. Should have said so, Rosie, wouldn't want to throw myself at you, delectable little morsel though you are.' He tittered drunkenly and tried his legs. 'Perfect balance,' he muttered, 'should have been in the circus. See?'

They just about supported him, albeit unsteadily, and I slipped away and rubbed my sore shoulders. As he swayed dangerously in the middle of the room, he suddenly looked sombre.

'Anyway, Rosie, I've got an announcement to make. And since you're the only one here, I may as well make it to you.'

'What's that?'

'I'm not drinking any more.' He paused. 'But then again, I'm not drinking any less!' He roared at his laboured wit, nearly cried actually. 'Ah, dear me,' he sighed, wiping his eyes, 'you've got to laugh, haven't you? If you don't laugh, I'll tell you what, you'll fucking well weep. D'you know what I always say about life at this time of night, Rosie? Do you?'

I glanced at my watch. Four o'clock in the morning and I was about to get drunken philosophy. I folded my arms wearily. 'What?'

'I say a man's got to have beliefs. And I believe I'll have another drink.'

This almost crippled him, he buckled up with a great whoop, slapped his knees, then tottered unsteadily towards the sideboard where I kept the whisky. 'Ah, Michael, you old dog, you old devil you!' he gasped, pouring himself a hefty one. 'You're a bad boy, you know that, don't you? A really bad boy.' He knocked it back in one and smacked his lips hard. 'Ahhh . . . nectar. Pure, unadulterated nectar. Another one, Michael? Why not, my good man, just to the top please, garçon.'

He went to pour another but I nipped across and intercepted him. 'I think not actually, Michael.' I took the glass from his hand, turned him round to face me, and gave him a little push in the chest. It didn't take much. He toppled, like an obedient skittle, flat on his back on the sofa. He lay there for a moment, blinking up at me in astonishment. Dumb and inert. Then his blue eyes gleamed.

'You saucy old she-devil, you! Seducing me now, eh? Come on then, get yer kit off, I can take it, I can handle another one, plenty more where that came from!' He struggled with the button on his trousers.

I threw the patchwork quilt over him. 'Oh, just belt up, Michael, and get some sleep, would you? I'm bloody tired and I'm going to bed now, and I don't want to see or hear from you for the next six hours, got it?'

He squirmed with delight. 'Oooh, strict! I always knew you'd be strict, you scrumptious little creature. Black mortar board and black stockings, eh? And I'll call you Miss, shall I? I can't wait,' he groaned, shutting his eyes in ecstasy. 'Come on, help me up and we'll finish this off in your bed, much more comfortable.'

'What an attractive proposition,' I muttered, wrapping my dressing gown firmly round me and making for the stairs.

'Aw, come on, Rosie,' he wheedled, puckering his lips. 'You know you've always fancied me, especially in black tie – look!' He opened his overcoat to reveal a filthy dress shirt, stained with wine. A hairy stomach sprouted through a gaping button. 'Sexy or what, eh? A sort of cross between Tom Jones and a certain thrusting young Cabinet minister, wouldn't you say?' He gave what I imagine he thought was a smouldering wink and a quick shunt of the hips.

'Funnily enough, Michael, I'm finding the combination relatively easy to resist.'

He dropped his jacket and blinked in genuine astonishment. 'Well, stroll on down!'

'No, straight up actually, and if you don't mind I'd like to go to bed now. It's ten past four and I'd like to get just a couple of hours of shut eye at SOME POINT TONIGHT!'

'Oooh, lovely temper,' he murmured as I went upstairs. He moaned low, shutting his eyes. 'Lovely bendy rulers . . . lovely rubbers . . .' He sniggered dirtily. 'Lovely navy blue knick-knacks . . . lovely garters, lovely, lovely detentions . . .' I slammed the door smartly on his Lolita fantasy and climbed back into bed.

'Jesus!' I muttered as I flopped back heavily on to my pillow. What a bloody night. And what a *state* he was in, for heaven's sake! How often did he get like that? I wondered. And with how many women in how many flats or hotel rooms? Because there was no doubt about it, Michael Feelburn was not just an outrageous bottom-pinching flirt, oh no, he was a serious philanderer. An ageing Lothario with an unguided sex drive, and the more I thought about it, the more I realised I'd always known. There were too many public displays of affection in that marriage. Too much kissing on the doorstep, patting Alice on the bottom, telephoning her at all hours of the day to assure her he loved her, and then too many late meetings and unavoidable delays. I wondered if Alice knew. I turned over, bunching my pillow up in half. No, she couldn't possibly know. She was so strong, so brave, she'd never stand for it, not in a million years. I doubted if she even suspected, and that was probably what he feared most, because there were no two ways about it, at the merest sniff of a rat Alice would be up and out of that house with a daughter under each arm, her easel on her back and her moccasins on her feet. Alice was not a woman to take infidelity lying down, as it were.

As I gazed at the dark wall, I suddenly wished to heaven I didn't know about it either. Alice was such a forthright person, she made it hard for you to dissemble in her company. You automatically wanted to lay all your cards on her stripped pine table and give it to her straight down the banks. Not that I would, of course. No, that wouldn't help anyone.

I pulled the duvet miserably over my head and sighed. God, as if I didn't have enough problems of my own without this one as well. I thumped the pillow and turned over, wondering if Joss was asleep yet. I hoped he was. Like time, it was one of the greatest healers. I shut my own eyes without much conviction, but strangely enough I drifted off again almost immediately, exhausted probably, slipping easily down the dark lanes of sleep.

As I slept, I dreamed of Joss. I saw him standing by a fire, but not the fire in the hall, this was a huge fire, outside – yes, a bonfire, and on the other side of it someone was calling to him. Someone was yelling to him to come round the bonfire and – oh, it was me! I could see myself now on the other side, trying to run round to him, but the fire was spreading, catching the grass like a tinderbox, licking along it in streaks. I saw Joss running as I ran, trying to outstrip it. We ran together, the fire between us, but all the time the fire licked faster and faster and I couldn't get across, couldn't reach him, and I was being suffocated by the smoke, too. It was in my eyes, my mouth, I couldn't open my mouth, I couldn't breathe, I – Christ, I really *couldn't* breathe now, there was a terrible weight on top of me and— I opened my eyes. Jesus Christ, *Michael*!

Except I couldn't say it. Couldn't scream it either, because his mouth was pressed hard on to mine as he lay on top of me, suffocating the life out of me.

'MMmmmmmm!' I squealed in horror.

I froze as a ghastly, sickly-sweet smell of stale alcohol and unwashed skin zoomed up my nostrils. I shot terrified eyes down – all I could move – and saw that but for some pants – shit, he was naked! Panic welled within me. He had my wrists pinned back to the bed and I had an awful, cold realisation that he was serious. Paralysed with incredulity that this was happening to me, I must have been inert for long enough for him to shove his tongue in my mouth. Suddenly I snapped to. I bit it hard. His head shot back.

'Ouch! You little bitch!'

'GET OFF ME!' I shrieked, bucking my hips to shift him.

'That's it, fight me, fight me!' he panted, bucking me back with his groin. 'But you want me really, don't you! You've always wanted me!'

'I bloody don't!' I shrieked. 'Michael, I'll bloody kill you for this, I'll—' but down I went again, under another, hard, debilitating mouth crush, fighting for breath. Oh God, why the hell had I pushed him on to that sofa? It had clearly got his blood up and now he was determined to have his way. Suddenly I was frightened. Michael wasn't a big man, not much taller than I was, but he was strong, nippy and extremely deft. Squash was his game and he took pride in thrashing bigger, burlier men than himself, and he also boasted hockey colours from his very minor public school. I began to realise that his ability to bully-off should not be underestimated. I couldn't move. I struggled under him but he had me pinned and his hips were grinding into mine. Suddenly I found wisdom. I stopped fighting and went limp, flopping back on the bed. Sensing my lack of resistance, he relaxed his grip and I was able to wrench my head to one side.

'Michael, wait!' I gasped. 'You're right, you're right but not like this!'

His head shot back, his hands were still holding my wrists, but his eyes gleamed.

'Oh Rosie, you little darling, it's true, isn't it? You've always wanted me, haven't you?'

'Yes, yes, I have!' I gasped.

'I knew it! I've seen the way you look at me, undressing me with your eyes. You've fantasised about me, haven't you? Panted for my manhood!'

Bloody hell. 'Yes! Yes, that's it!'

'Well, now you're going to get it!'

'Great!' I gasped. 'Excellent, couldn't be more pleased – but listen, Michael, not like this, okay?'

'Like what?'

'Well, like this, in my ghastly old winceyette.'

He glanced down at my spriggy Laura Ashley nightie. 'Get it off,' he panted, 'get the bloody thing off!' He began tugging it up.

'I'LL DO IT!' I screeched, perhaps a little too forcefully. I gulped. 'I mean, I'll do it,' I insisted, more gently. 'Really, Michael, I'd like to, I – I'd like to undress for you, seductively. You see, it's all part of my fantasy about you, that you watch me take my clothes off.'

'Oh God,' he groaned. 'Oh God I knew it, I just bloody well knew it! You're all the bloody same, you're all gagging for it! Oh Jesus, I can't bear the suspense, take it off! Take it off, you little sexed-up weasel!'

He didn't entirely take his weight off me, but he loosened his grip and rose, press-up style, to accommodate my undressing beneath him. It was enough. With one superhuman effort, I jerked my knee up hard and – boomph!

'AAARGH!' He gave a shriek of pain, his eyes bulged, then he reeled sideways, clutching between his legs in agony. I rolled deftly the other way, off the side of the bed, and grabbed the first thing that came to hand. Happily it was a brass lamp base. I jumped up, brandishing it furiously.

'Come near me again, Michael Feelburn, and I'll bash your bloody brains out! I swear to God I'll kill you!'

Michael lay, curled up and green, gasping on the other side of the bed.

'You little bitch,' he spluttered. 'You treacherous little—' Suddenly he lunged, throwing all his weight at me, seizing me round the waist and sending me flying backwards in a rugby-style tackle. As we crashed back into the wardrobe together, I brought the lamp base smartly down on his head – crack! – just as a large china potty filled with dried flowers toppled and fell from the top of the wardrobe. It flew down and landed with a crash on his head, smashing into a thousand pieces. There was a deathly hush. I was still under him. Scared witless, I frantically wriggled free of his weight. He rolled over and began to groan.

'Oh God . . . Oh Jesus, Jesus . . .' he moaned.

I sprang up, panting. Then I jumped clear, up on to the bed. He was lying with his head at an awkward angle in a jigsaw of china and dried flowers. The brass lamp base was at his ear. His eyes were shut and his mouth was open. His face was very pale against his body, and going greyer by the minute. A trickle of blood began to gush steadily down from his forehead. He started to groan again, this time louder, and he moved his head to one side, raising his hand feebly as the blood flowed down his face. He was down, but he was by no means out, and I had a horrible feeling he could come to at any second, find some superhuman hidden reserves and avenge himself with another spectacular dive at my person. I didn't need any prompting, I had to get out of there.

Seizing my dressing gown from the back of the door I edged round him, terrified a hand might shoot out and grab my ankle, then fled across the landing into Ivo's room. Despite the noise he was still fast asleep in his cot, oblivious of everything. I picked him up, grabbed his snowsuit from a chair, and ran downstairs with him in my arms. In the relative safety of the sitting room I plunged him into the suit, all the time glancing up to the top of the stairs.

'Quick, darling, quick, arms in,' I panted, my heart pounding away somewhere near my oesophagus.

Ivo gazed at me with bleary, startled eyes as I zipped him up. Any minute now I expected to see Michael, naked, covered in blood and gore, bursting out on to the landing, and then with a mighty roar plunge downstairs to finish his business. I was pretty sure a man like Michael would not like to be thwarted. I hoisted Ivo on to my hip, and pausing only to thrust my feet into my boots, opened the front door and ran out into the snow, nightie and dressing gown flapping.

A cold blue dawn was breaking over the distant hilltops as I fled to the car. My hands were shaking uncontrollably as I bundled Ivo into his seat. He'd already had one moonlit drive this night and he gazed at me now in wide-eyed astonishment. What, in the car? Again? All the time I struggled with his straps I glanced back over my shoulder at the open front door. Shit, why hadn't I shut it, for God's sake? Locked it even? And why did I frigging well insist on strapping my child into his car seat when there was a madman after me! There, he was in. I ran round to the driver's seat, dived in, slammed the door, shoved the key in the ignition and . . . for an awful, heart-stopping moment, the engine failed to turn over.

'Oh, come on, come on!' I pleaded.

It whinnied miserably. I glanced back in terror, quickly locked my door, rammed in the choke, gave one last desperate pump of the accelerator – and it roared into life. Crashing the gears I shot off up the drive, wheels spinning.

As we sped towards Farlings, it occurred to me for a second to drive past and go on to Philly's. Should I go there, should I? My mind was spinning. I felt in dire need of a shoulder to sob on, a hug, some sympathy, but on the other hand Philly would be absolutely horrified. And furious too, quite rightly of course, and then there'd be the most almighty fracas. Mummy would instantly be summoned and Miles and Daddy would be instructed to get every able-bodied man in the village out of bed, and then armed with pitchforks and shovels they'd surround the cottage, ambush Michael and frogmarch him ceremoniously through the village to the police station where he'd be clapped in irons to await God knows what. Was that what I wanted? I bit my lip. I had to think fast but rationally about this, decide exactly who I was going to tell. And I had to think of Alice. I clutched my mouth but a sob seeped through my fingers. Oh God, Alice! My poor, poor, Alice!

No, I couldn't, I thought as I swung the car decisively up to Farlings' back door. I couldn't do that to her. Nor to the girls. I'd creep in here where at least I knew I'd be safe, and then I'd think about what to do in the morning. I had a key so I could steal through the back door and up the back stairs without waking Joss or the children. He'd had a late night so he wouldn't stir for ages anyway. It was almost light now, must be nearly six o'clock. I'd borrow one of Vera's pinnies, give Ivo some breakfast and then carry on a normal day's work without anyone being any the wiser. I could think what to do about Michael later. Right now, I just wanted to get away from him.

I stole in through the back door and locked it firmly behind me. The house was dark and silent. Dram the border terrier had already smelt me arrive and came wriggling to greet me. I patted his head, whispering softly to him, and moved silently through the kitchen. There was no sign of Truffle, but presumably Joss had locked him in the study to stop him chewing the kitchen chair legs, as was his current wont. But as I crept down the passageway towards the stairs, he started barking. Bugger, he *was* locked in, and now he was pretending to be a guard dog! Quickly I nipped along the passage with Ivo on my hip and opened the study door.

'Truffle, you stupid berk, it's me!' I hissed.

He instantly shut up and greeted me enthusiastically, wagging his fat behind and snuffling gleefully.

'Get back to bed, you fool!'

He turned obligingly, thumping his tail, and lay down behind Joss's desk where he would no doubt resume the secret chewing of its back legs.

I shut the door on him and crept back down the passageway in the pitch dark, feeling my way along the walls for the gap where the back staircase would be. There were no windows down this end of the house and I couldn't see a bloody thing. I was tempted to turn a light on. That wouldn't wake anyone, surely. I was just feeling along the wall for the spot where the light was when instead of the switch I felt – human flesh.

'AA-A-ARGH!' I shrieked, jumping a mile.

At the same time an arm locked round my neck from behind. Something hard and cold pressed up against my cheek. Oh God. It was Michael.

'Take another step and I won't hesitate to use it,' said a reasonable and familiar voice.

'Joss!'

There was a pause, then the light snapped on.

'Rosie! What the hell are you doing!' He was in his dressing gown, shotgun in hand. My heart was pounding.

'Jesus Christ, you scared the hell out of me!' I gasped.

'Well, I wasn't too relaxed about it myself! What the blazes are you doing creeping round the house in the middle of the night? I thought you were a goddam burglar!'

'I went home,' I muttered, clutching the wall for support and feeling rather faint now, ready to die actually, 'and then I decided – to come back!'

'Why?'

'Why?' I stared at him.

'Yes, why did you come back?'

'Because – well, because I couldn't sleep! So I thought – I'd get the breakfast ready, wash up the supper, do something useful.'

'Really? How very keen.' He eyed me suspiciously. 'I'm impressed, especially since it's New Year's Day and the kids won't be up for hours. Hey.' He peered a bit closer. 'What happened to your head?'

'My . . . ?' I reached up and touched my forehead, which now I came to think of it hurt like hell. My fingertips came back red.

'Oh God, I'm bleeding!'

'Damn right you are and you've got a socking great bruise coming up there too. What happened?'

I gulped. 'Nothing,' I whispered.

291

He led me by the arm into the hall and flicked on the overhead light. He stared into my face. 'You're as white as a sheet and you're trembling. What the hell's been going on, Rosie?'

I stared at him for a second, then suddenly cracked a smile. 'Oh! Oh yes, I know, it must have been where I fell against the wardrobe! I was getting undressed, you see, to go to bed, and I think I was still a bit pissed from supper – I had a few drinks when I got back to the cottage too, and I slipped and fell! It's nothing really, Joss.'

He stared at me for a long moment. 'Who did this to you?'

'No one, really, no one. I . . .' His face wouldn't wear it. My eyes slithered away.

'Come on, Rosie, tell me.'

I swallowed. 'Someone . . . got the wrong idea,' I muttered finally.

'Who got the wrong idea?'

Suddenly my knees went. I sank on to the sofa, put my face in my hands and burst into tears. 'Michael Feelburn!' I sobbed.

'Michael Feelburn? What, you mean my old tenant at the cottage? That smug, self-satisfied little snake-hipped, womanising bastard?'

'Yes, but Joss, he was very, very drunk, I really don't think he meant it!' I wiped my face with the back of my hand and noticed it was shaking. Foolishly I just couldn't stop crying. 'He came back drunk from a party, you see, and he got shut out of his hotel, so he drove down here and knocked me up in the middle of the night and crashed on my sofa, but then he jumped on me while I was asleep!'

'Charming.'

'I bashed him with a brass lamp and then a chamber pot fell on him. He's probably still out cold!'

'Well, let's find out, shall we? If he's not, he soon will be.'

He took his Barbour from the hat stand, shrugged it on over his dressing gown, pushed his feet into his boots and, still holding his gun, walked to the door.

I grabbed his sleeve. 'No!' I shrieked. 'No, Joss, wait, think of Alice, think of the children!'

Joss turned. 'Rosie, I'm not going to blow his brains out, I'm simply going to scare him witless, okay? Meanwhile, perhaps you'd like to ring the police.'

'Oh no, I can't!' I gasped, holding on to him very tightly. 'You see, I don't know if I want to! I mean – press charges. He is a friend, after all, and he was very drunk, Joss, very drunk, and Alice is my best friend and—'

'And he'll get drunk again. And he'll do it again. D'you think he would have raped you?'

I stared at him. 'Well, I – don't know.'

'That's a "yes" if ever I heard one. Very well, let's play it your way. We'll get him up here first and then you can decide if you want to call the police. But I'd like the pleasure of waking him up with a shotgun in his mouth first, okay?'

He prised my fingers off his arm and reached up for the bolt. But just at that moment, as he was about to pull it open, there was a tremendous banging from the other side. Someone rapped the knocker hard.

'Shit!' I leaped backwards. 'It's him! He's come back to get me!' I scuttled behind Joss.

'Well then, he'll get a little surprise, won't he?'

Joss undid the bolt and swung back the door with a flourish. There, standing on the doorstep, silhouetted like statues in the hard, early dawn, was not Michael Feelburn but two men in overcoats. Their collars were turned up against the cold and their faces were grey and grim.

'Morning, sir.'

'Good morning.' Joss stepped back in surprise.

'Mr Dubarry?'

'Yes, that's right.'

'Sorry to bother you at such an ungodly hour, sir, but it's rather important.' The man in the hat reached inside his coat and pulled out a warrant card. 'Police. We'd like to speak to a Mrs Meadows, who I believe is a tenant of yours. We came to ask if you knew where we could get hold of her.'

'I'm Mrs Meadows,' I whispered, stepping out from behind Joss.

'Ah. May we come in then?'

'Sure.' Joss stepped aside, looking somewhat dazed. They moved to the middle of the hall as Joss shut the door behind them. There was a silence. One of the men turned very deliberately to face me.

'Mrs Meadows, we'd like to ask you a few questions and we wondered if you'd be kind enough to come down to the station with us.'

'To the . . . but why? What for?'

'We're conducting a murder inquiry and we believe you might be able to help.'

'A . . . Oh God!' My heart stopped beating. I clutched it. 'Is he dead?'

'I don't think there's any doubt about that, Mrs Meadows.'

I went cold. Fear shot through my body. My eyes turned to Joss. 'Oh Joss, my God, I've killed him!'

I remember the horror in his eyes as he looked at me. I remember touching my head, feeling blood on my hand. It was still warm. My head throbbed strangely, like a muscle. I also remember that I had to stand with my legs apart, to stop myself from fainting.

Chapter Twenty-Two

When my legs wouldn't support me any longer I sank down on the sofa. My head dropped into my hands. There was a creak of shoe leather as the two policemen moved towards me in unison. Joss sat down beside me, Ivo was at my knee. I felt a bit like Custer at his last stand, totally surrounded, except I didn't even have any wagons. Slowly I slid my face up out of my hands and looked at their faces. The two above me were grim and uncompromising. Joss's was pale and taut.

'I didn't mean to,' I whispered. 'It was self-defence! I swear to God, I thought he was going to rape me!'

The sergeant frowned. 'In the kitchen?'

'No, in the bedroom, it happened in the bedroom. That's where I hit him, but I had no idea – oh God, I just grabbed the first thing that came to hand, it wasn't my fault it was a brass lamp! I suppose it must have been very heavy, but I didn't realise it could—' My voice broke and I clutched my mouth in horror.

'You hit him with a brass lamp?' The sergeant took off his hat and scratched his head. 'But the pathologist's report said he died of fungal poisoning.'

My jaw dropped. 'Fungal . . .' Slowly it dawned. 'Oh!' I gasped. 'Oh no, that was Harry!'

'That's right. Your husband, Harry Meadows.'

'Oh God, I thought you were talking about Michael!'

'Michael? Who's Michael?'

'Oh, *Harry*! Oh God, no, I didn't kill Harry, that was just a mistake, just an accident! I thought you meant I'd killed Michael when I smashed him over the head, I thought—'

'Er, never mind, Rosie,' said Joss quickly. 'I'm sure these gentlemen don't want to be dragged into a silly little domestic incident. It was just a minor scuffle, officer, with a friend of ours. He got a bit overexcited, too much New Year's Eve spirit and all that.' He squeezed my shoulder. 'No real harm done, eh Rosie, just a tiny cut.'

'Tiny cut, you must be joking, there was blood everywhere! I gave him a hell of a bash – THWACK! – right on his temple! God, I wouldn't be surprised if there weren't still bits of brain clinging to the carpet, splattered on the walls even – oh God, I thought you meant I'd *killed* him!'

'Ha ha!' Joss laughed nervously. 'A little thing like you? Don't be silly, you couldn't hurt a fly!' He gave my shoulder a slightly more dislocatory squeeze. 'As I said, officer, no real harm done.'

'Really,' he said eyeing me doubtfully and pulling out a notebook. He licked the end of his pencil. 'Well, let's hope not. I must say this is all very confusing, Mrs Meadows. Where is the unfortunate gentleman now, do you suppose? The one with the crater in his skull and half his brains on the carpet?' He looked around, as if half expecting to see a bowed and bloodied man stagger in through the door with a brass lamp base sticking out of his head.

'He's legged it,' said Martha, coming through from the kitchen where she'd clearly been listening for the last few minutes. 'I saw him as I come in just now on my way back from the 'ospital, comin' up the back drive. He was staggering about a bit, clutching his head and swearin' an' that, but there weren't much blood. When he saw me he leapt in his car with his tail between his legs and drove off like a bullet. He'll have a headache, I should think, but there ain't much wrong with him other than that.' She sniffed. 'Nothing that taking a meat cleaver to his todger couldn't sort out, anyway.' A palpable wince went round the assembled males.

'I see,' said the sergeant faintly. 'Good. Well, I'm . . . delighted to hear it.' He looked bewildered. Clearing his throat, he said, 'Now, Mrs Meadows, leaving aside for one moment this Michael fellow, could we perhaps get back to the little matter in hand? That of your husband?'

'Oh yes, Harry,' I said springing happily to my feet. 'Yes, I can help you all you like with that, officer, although I have to warn you, I've already spoken to the Gloucestershire police so there probably won't be much that isn't on file somewhere anyway. Just hang on a tick and I'll go and get changed and then I'll come with you. I'm still in my dressing gown, you see.' I gave a quick twirl just to prove it, then froze. I clutched my mouth. 'Oh God, you really put the wind up me there though, I thought you'd come for me – thought I'd bloody killed him and someone had tipped you off. God, I honestly thought—'

'Excuse me.' Joss suddenly took my arm and hustled me from the room, marching me down the back passage. He swung me round to face him at the foot of the back stairs. 'Will you shut up!' he hissed. 'They're going to slap a double murder charge on you if you're not careful!'

'Oh, don't be silly, Joss, Michael isn't dead and I didn't kill Harry so I've got nothing to worry about! I'm innocent!'

He sighed. 'I'm sure you are, but I still wish sex and violence didn't conspire to dog your innocent footsteps quite so determinedly. Jesus, Rosie, it's one thing after another with you. If you're not being raped on my sofa you're being raped at the cottage, and if you're not murdering your own husband you're murdering your best friend's husband!'

'I know, I know,' I said incredulously, 'it's extraordinary, isn't it? I just can't think how it happens! I'm such a quiet, home-loving girl really, but it'll all be fine now, Joss, you'll see.'

He rubbed his eyebrow wearily with the heel of his hand. 'Well, let's hope so. The problem is, though, that fascinating though this crypto-saga of serial rape and annihilation is, I've actually got to get on a plane to Germany in precisely,' he glanced at his watch, 'four hours' time. I've stupidly promised to do a week of lectures there to promote my new exhibition in Cologne, which despite taking its theme from man's inhumanity to man doesn't even begin to compare with your everyday life in terms of lurid shock horror. But the point is, Rosie, I won't be here, and with bodies falling around you like flies, that bothers me somewhat.'

'Oh, don't you worry about me, Joss, I'll be fine, really I will. Now that I know they're not about to clap me in irons – God, I could almost hear the cell door clanging shut behind me! I had visions of Martha and the children coming to see me at Holloway, holding my hands through the bars, sobbing copiously. God, I thought I was going to be sick!'

'Keep your voice down!' he hissed, glancing nervously back towards the hall. Through the half-open door we could see the two policemen warming the backs of their legs by last night's still smouldering fire. They glanced over at our raised voices, then down at their boots again.

'Go on,' muttered Joss, giving me a little push, 'go get changed before they get us for conspiracy as well.'

'Will do,' I grinned. Still feeling wonderfully euphoric, I rather daringly reached up and gave him a little kiss on the cheek. Without pausing to gauge the effect it had had, I turned and ran to the cottage, dressing gown flapping, giggling to myself as I dashed up into my bedroom. You see, I thought happily, that's what adrenalin does for you. Gives you the courage to be totally brazen.

When I returned, Joss had gone off to pack. The twins and Toby had woken up and come down in their dressing gowns, wide-eyed with wonder at having real policemen in the house. Having kissed them both and hugged Ivo I left them all in Martha's hands. 'How is he?' I whispered as I gave her a hug.

'Much better,' she said. 'You know what, Rosie, I think he's over the worst.'

'Oh, thank God.'

'So don't you worry. I'll look after Ivo while you're gone – you're all right.'

'Thanks.' We hugged each other again and I went outside and got in the back of the police car. The children were enthralled and insisted on seeing me off.

'Are you really going to a police station? Can't we come too?' asked Emma gazing wistfully at the car.

'Sorry, darlings, but I'll be back soon and I'll tell you all about it then.'

'Could you put the siren on?' asked Toby.

I leaned forward to the sergeant in the passenger seat. 'Would that be too much trouble?' I whispered. 'Just down the drive? They'd really love it.'

'Certainly not,' he muttered grimly.

I shook my head at them. 'Sorry, darlings, it's for official business only I think but – oops, here we go. 'Bye!' We were off.

As we sped down the drive, I waved to them all standing there at the front door until they were out of sight. Then I grinned and relaxed back into the seat. 'Rather nice actually,' I raised my voice above the engine. 'I mean to be sitting down for a change and not charging around getting breakfast. It's always absolute mayhem in there at this hour of the morning.'

No answer from the boys in the front. God, they were sour, but then again, working on New Year's Day couldn't be much fun, I supposed. I tried again.

'I expect you were busy last night.'

'Why's that then?'

'Well, you know, New Year's Eve. Drunken revelry and all that?'

The sergeant turned round in his seat and regarded me levelly. 'This isn't *The Bill* you know, madam, we're in homicide.'

'Oh, right.' Gosh, I'd offended him. 'I see, so you mean you're more like the *Prime Suspect* detectives then. More the sort of gritty plain-clothes types, debriefs in smoky rooms, walls covered in gruesome pictures of the victims, poring over your files till midnight with your ties askew and plastic coffee cups, that sort of thing!' I was rather pleased with this little thumbnail sketch, but it fell on stony ground. An icy silence prevailed as they declined to answer. I stared at the backs of their necks. Gosh, they were a humourless couple. Still, I decided it might be prudent to keep quiet until we got to the police station which, incidentally, was the other way.

'Cirencester's that way,' I said, turning round in my seat as we sped past the turning.

'Really.'

'We're not going to Cirencester?'

My friend performed another one hundred and eighty degree turn in his seat. 'We're from the Oxfordshire constabulary, Mrs Meadows. We're going to Oxford.'

'Oh! Gosh, what a long way. You mean you've come all this way at the crack of dawn just to . . .' I tailed off. Pick me up.

Suddenly I felt a bit nervous. A bit – hot. Right. So we weren't just popping into town for a friendly chat over a cup of cocoa, and they weren't just a couple of local bobbies. So what exactly was going on here? I wondered. As we sped along the road I gazed out at the increasingly unfamiliar landscape. Dank, lustreless winter fields with the occasional smattering of sheep, heads bowed and huddled in corners, flashed past, and on the horizon, wet, black trees spread their bare branches against a pale grey sky. I felt a mounting sense of unease, of foreboding.

Eventually we swept into a car park – correction, swept *through* a car park – and straight up to the front door. It was as if we were really rather . . . important. The sergeant leapt out and opened my door. I got out and smiled nervously, but he didn't look at me, just turned and propped open the swing door to the station. I went through under his arm and waited, my heart pounding. He overtook me and set off at speed down a long, bleak corridor. I scurried after him, with the thus far silent driver of the car at my heels. We came to a halt outside a pale blue door with a tiny, reinforced window. The sergeant pushed it open and jerked his head for me to go through. I walked in cautiously and looked around. It wasn't actually a cell but it might just as well have been. It was cold and dark, and aside from a table with two chairs on either side, totally bare. The walls were painted in regulation grey gloss. I wondered if gloss was more resistant to wall punching or something. Right up by the ceiling was a long, shallow window, but so high you couldn't possibly see out.

'Wait here.'

I swung round to answer, but he'd gone. The door clicked firmly shut behind him. I swallowed hard and after a moment's indecision went tentatively across to one of the chairs. I sat down gingerly. Which one was mine? I wondered. Was this one all right? I glanced at the door, my mouth as dry as sandpaper now. God, this was awful, what were they trying to do, frighten the living daylights out of me or something? If they were, they were blinking well succeeding, that was for sure, but then again, why on earth should I be frightened? After all, I hadn't done anything wrong, had I? Suddenly I wished I had a packet of cigarettes to fiddle with. I didn't smoke but it would give me something to do with my hands, I could have shunted the box around a bit, read the health warning on the side, flicked out a couple of snouts. I knew from years of telly viewing that this was one of the few environments where cigarettes were allowed, indeed positively encouraged. I picked my nails nervously instead.

Finally the door swung open with a flourish. I jumped as in marched – yes, *marched* – good grief, it was Helen Mirren. Well, it wasn't of course but I swear to God it could have been. If ever there was a dead ringer, this was it. She had the same no-nonsense grey-blonde hair tucked efficiently behind unadorned ears, the same ruthlessly scrubbed face with those cool steely eyes, the inquisitive nose, the thin, pinched lips and the same, crisp white shirt under the sombre, androgynous dark suit. This was a woman who'd never painted her toenails, woken up with cake crumbs in her bed, or danced to Agadoo. This was a woman whose knickers never went grey in the wash and whose house plants never died. In fact she looked as if she ate glass for breakfast. I instinctively sat up straight as she took the chair opposite me.

'Good morning.' Her voice was level. Not hostile, but only by a whisker.

'Morning,' I muttered, resisting the urge to add, 'ma'am.'

She took some papers from a plastic file and shuffled them efficiently. Just then the door opened softly and in slid a WPC in uniform. She was fatter and fluffier than her boss and looked as if she could even have a couple of kids at home, along with some rather messy drawers. I smiled hopefully at my potential ally, but she sidled into a corner and stood stock still, eyes trained on a spot above my head. Bloody hell. I swallowed hard and turned back. The Ice Maiden, meanwhile, had taken a tape recorder from her case and set it on the table. She flicked it on and snapped in two tapes. Then she raised her pale, untinted lashes and fixed me with sharp grey eyes.

'I'm conducting this interview with Mrs Rosie Meadows on

January the first, at,' she consulted her watch, 'eight thirty-two a.m.'

I gazed at her in horror. 'You're taping this?'

She gave a thin smile. 'It tends to be the accepted thing these days. It's for your own protection as much as anything else.'

Heavens. My own protection. 'Should I – should I, you know, have a brief or something then?' I asked hesitantly, slipping crassly into *Bill*-speak.

'You're entitled to a solicitor, of course.' She waited, hands folded.

'Well, I . . . well. I mean I've got nothing to hide, so . . .'

'So shall we go on?'

'Yes. Fine,' I muttered. 'Go on.'

She folded her arms and leant forward, suddenly adopting what I imagine she thought was a benign expression. But I wasn't fooled, oh no, not likely. This woman was about as benign as a polecat.

'Now, Mrs Meadows . . .' she consulted her file, 'Rosie.' She looked up. 'I believe your husband died on the night of the sixth of November, thirty-six hours after eating a poisonous mushroom commonly known as the Panther Cap, is that correct?'

'Yes, that's right,' I whispered.

'I have here,' she reached into a plastic bag, 'just such a mushroom.' She drew out a white-stemmed fungus with a brownish cap. 'I also have,' she delved into another bag, 'a field mushroom, a cep, and a chanterelle which I believe are the types your late husband had ostensibly been collecting.' She drew out three more mushrooms and put them beside the Panther Cap. She looked up at me. 'All quite different, wouldn't you say?'

I cleared my throat and dug deep for courage. No, I would not be intimidated. 'Yes, but if I might say so you have some very extreme examples there. That Panther Cap is particularly small and rather spotty, whereas there are, in fact, some much larger, pure brown specimens, and your cep is pretty big. Small fresh ones straight from the woods can be quite mottled and about the same size as a largish Panther.'

'I see.' She paused. 'So the two could be confused?'

I gauged this. 'Well, they could be, although to my eye they're still jolly different.' Pays to be honest, I thought.

'Quite. But then you do know rather a lot about fungi, don't you? I gather you studied with Antonio Carluccio?'

'Well, I did a four-day course, yes.'

'Which makes it all the more extraordinary then, don't you think, that you didn't spot the difference as you cooked them?'

I sighed. 'Yes, except that as I've said before, I really only gave

301

them a cursory glance in the pan. I was distracted at the time, thinking about something else, and he'd collected all sorts of other mushrooms too, not just the ones you've got there, but oysters, parasols, so it was quite a mixture.'

'Even so, this one,' she persisted, picking the Panther Cap up, 'is still remarkably distinctive, wouldn't you say?'

'Yes, I would,' I agreed, 'and it's a mystery to me how I missed it, but I did, and I'm sorry. I've already said so.'

'You're sorry you missed it or you're sorry your husband's dead?'

I flushed. 'Look, I've been through all this once already with the Gloucester police. I answered all these questions then, is there really any need to interrogate me like this?'

'I'm afraid there is, Mrs Meadows. You see, since your earlier interview and the routine interview your family gave, certain facts have come to light. The coroner's office have therefore passed the inquiry over to us for full investigation.'

'Oh, really? Why?' I tried to make this sound merely curious, but it came out as a bleat of alarm.

Silence. She turned a page in her file, reading, or pretending to read, ignoring me. I could feel myself burning up now. My hands were clammy and sweat was beginning to prickle my forehead. Finally she raised her eyes. Her look was impenetrable.

'Mrs Meadows, you mentioned in your earlier interview – and you've said as much again just now – that you were distracted at the time your husband showed you the mushrooms. That you were thinking of something else. Would you mind telling me what?'

'Well, I – can't remember exactly.'

'Would you have been thinking about divorcing him, for instance?'

'Oh! Well, yes, yes, I suppose I might.'

'You were planning to divorce him?'

'Yes, I was.'

'And you'd informed him of this?'

'Yes.'

'And what was his reaction?'

'Well, he wasn't . . . very keen.'

'He wasn't very keen. He resisted, in other words.'

'Yes.'

She leaned forward intently. 'Isn't it true to say that he resisted to such an extent that he said he was prepared to fight you in court? And not only that, but, to quote your sister, that he'd fight you for custody of your son? Something which, it seems, he was confident he'd get?'

'Yes, he did want Ivo.'

'And didn't he say he'd lie, cheat, blacken your name, brand you an unfit mother – in short, stop at nothing, be it reasonable or unreasonable, to take him away from you?'

'Yes, he did, but—'

'Quite convenient then, wouldn't you say, that he died before events could come to such a head?'

I looked at her in horror. 'You're surely not suggesting I killed him to stop him taking Ivo away?'

'I don't know, Rosie. Why did you kill him?'

'No – I didn't! I didn't mean it like that, I just meant – God, no, of course I didn't kill him!'

Her eyes bored into mine and it seemed to me they probed right through to the back of my head. I felt a kind of rushing pressure in my brain. The silence was unbearable. I dug my nails deep into the palms of my hands under the table. Keep calm, Rosie, keep calm. Eventually she lowered her eyes and slowly turned a page in her file. She folded her hands.

'Tell me, did your husband make a habit of collecting mushrooms for breakfast?'

'If we—' my voice sounded high, unnatural. I cleared my throat. 'If we were staying at my parents' house, yes, he did. He was very keen on his food and fungi grow pretty abundantly there. It was a bit of a treat for him.'

'So, it would have been as easy as anything to pre-empt this, wouldn't it? To pick a particular mushroom, say the day before, pocket it, bide your time and then when no one was looking simply add it to the pan?'

'I did no such thing!' I stood up, knocking my chair backwards. My heart was pounding.

'I merely hypothesised that it would be easy,' she said evenly. 'Please sit down, Mrs Meadows.'

With a trembling hand I picked up my chair and sat down again.

'Mrs Meadows stood up in anger, she's now seated again,' she said for the benefit of the tape. I stared at her, feeling damp, clammy now, scared to death.

'Tell me, does the name Timothy McWerther mean anything to you?'

'No, it doesn't. Why?'

'You're sure?'

'Yes, I'm sure.'

She pursed her lips and drew from inside her file a photograph.

She passed it over to me. I knew she was watching my face. I prepared to hand it straight back, but then – 'Oh! It's Tim.'

'So you do know him.'

'Well, yes, but only as Tim, not Timothy Whatever-you-said.' I passed it back to her. 'He works in the Wandsworth Sainsbury's, as a packer. I knew him vaguely and we just sort of chatted a bit. Had a laugh.'

'Did you have an affair with him?'

'No!' I gasped. 'Certainly not!'

'And yet your husband, returning home unexpectedly one day, surprised you with him in your bedroom.'

My mouth fell open. 'How did you—'

'Know that? We're detectives, Mrs Meadows.'

I flushed, bit my lip. 'Look, I know it sounds – peculiar, incriminating even, but it wasn't like that. He helped me home from Sainsbury's once with some shopping and while I was on the telephone he took some soap and bubble bath and things upstairs to the bathroom.'

'And then into the bedroom.'

'Yes, but—'

'Where you followed him a few moments later and where your husband later discovered you both. Quite familiar, don't you think, for a housewife and a young lad from the local supermarket? One wonders,' she mused, puckering her brow and tapping her pencil thoughtfully, 'what might have happened had your husband not arrived home at that particular moment. One wonders how that scenario might have unfolded. One wonders, too, how often this lad made a habit of helping you home with your groceries, popping upstairs to put the soap in the bathroom, tissues in the bedroom, pausing by the bed, sitting down—'

'Never!' I yelled, choked by angry tears now. 'That's not true, any of it, it wasn't like that. God, *ask* him if you don't believe me!'

'Oh, we have, Rosie.'

'And?'

She paused before delivering her trump card. 'And he admits to having had an affair with you.'

I stared. After a long moment I sank back in my chair, aghast. 'He admits to . . . no, he *can't* have done! It's absurd, you're lying, it's simply not true, ask anyone!'

'We have. The staff at Sainsbury's confirm that he made a bee line for you, your neighbour has seen him enter your house, and friends of his confirm that the two of you were something of an item.'

I gazed at her, almost unseeing. 'Where is he?' I whispered at last. 'Let me see him. Let me speak to him. You'll see then, you'll see by his reaction that it's not true!' My hair was pricking my head, I was terrified.

She shook her head. 'I'm afraid that's not possible. Not only is it illegal for suspects to corroborate evidence, but since Mr McWerther is currently being detained by us in conjunction with another matter, he is, as such, unavailable for comment.'

When I'd interpreted this spiel of police jargon, I stuttered, 'You mean you've arrested him? What for?'

'Rosie, I'm going to ask you again. Were you, or were you not, having an affair with Timothy McWerther?'

'Not!' I rasped loudly. 'I was not!'

'I put it to you that you were, and that the two of you collaborated to kill Mr Meadows on the assumption of collecting the inheritance due to him from his uncle, Sir Bertram Meadows.'

I blinked. 'Good God. That's absurd!'

'Is it?' Her smile was thin, disingenuous. Then quick as a flash it disappeared. She raised her chin, challengingly, waiting.

My mouth opened but I seemed to have neither wind nor words to draw on. I sat, immobilised, gazing at her stupefied as she calmly looked back. Finally I found my voice. 'L-look,' I stuttered. 'I've changed my mind. I'm not saying any more. I want a lawyer.'

She nodded. 'And I fully advise you to get one. Personally, I think you're going to need one. I'm therefore terminating this interview with Mrs Meadows at,' she shot her watch out of her sleeve, 'nine twenty-one precisely.' She snapped the tapes out, pocketed one, gave me the other, then stood up and tucked her papers under her arm. I looked up at her.

'Wh-where are you taking me? Where am I going?'

'Home, I imagine.'

I swallowed. 'B-but . . . you said . . .'

'We're not charging you. Not yet anyway. There are one or two details to fine tune yet, but rest assured, Rosie, we shall be meeting again. In fact, it's only a matter of time before we'll be seeing a great deal of one another. Good day.'

And with that, she swept out of the room.

Chapter Twenty-Three

Needless to say, I didn't exchange much merry banter with the policeman who drove me home that morning. In fact it was as much as I could do to keep myself from throwing up in the back of his car. As we drove into Farlings I directed him, in a halting whisper, past the main house and then down to the cottage. I didn't even recognise my own voice. As we came to a stop outside, he looked at me in the rear-view mirror.

'You all right, luv?' His brown eyes were kindly, concerned. He must have been about my father's age, probably coming up for retirement.

I nodded but did not trust myself to speak. I fumbled for the door handle and got out. I shut the car door and stumbled up the path, knowing he was watching me. He waited until I'd let myself in, then as I leaned back heavily against the front door, I heard the car purr slowly up the drive. I shut my eyes for a moment, feeling the blood rush to my head. I took a deep breath and let it out slowly. As I opened my eyes, they lit upon the gin bottle on the sideboard on the other side of the room. I stumbled across, fell on it, and with a hand that shook so much I had to pause for a moment to regard it with awe, poured myself a giant slugful. Recklessly I knocked it back. My nose wrinkled in disgust. God, it was vile, like taking medicine, but I was determined to numb the pain instantly without the namby-pamby diluting effect of tonic. I took another gulp, and this time it didn't seem quite so putrid. Clutching the glass possessively, I turned, and nearly made it to the sofa, but my knees gave way just short of it and I sank to the rug in front of the fire in a heap. Still in my coat, I put my head in my hands and had a bloody good cry.

After a few minutes I blew my nose, wiped my eyes and finished off the gin. There. That should start to reach the vital organs soon enough. I sniffed hard and stared at the old Turkish rug I was sitting on. It was so worn in places that the brown threads underneath were laid bare. Oh yes, threadbare. How strange that I should suddenly see the point of that word at a moment like this. I stared bleakly at it. Oh God, what was I going to do? Was this really happening to me? Had I really just been interrogated, intimidated, accused of – Jesus – of murder? And not just any old murder but pre-meditated, plotting and scheming Machiavellian sort of murder, in cahoots with a toy-boy sort of murder, my *lover* supposedly, some flipping shop boy of about nineteen and – oh hell, it was no good, I needed another slug of that gin and then I needed to *talk* to someone, I needed to talk to someone right now.

I knew in an instant I yearned for Joss. I longed to hear his irritated, authoritative voice say oh, don't be ridiculous, Rosie. If you didn't do it then that's the end of it, it's as simple as that. They can't *make* you confess for God's sake, the whole thing's utterly absurd – or some such other, similarly dismissive riposte. But of course talking to Joss was out of the question. In the first place he was probably still on a plane, and in the second place, even if he wasn't, I was pretty sure Annabel had joined him at the airport and if she answered the phone she might not be too thrilled to hear me demanding to speak to her husband regarding a little matter of a murder charge I was on, and oh, incidentally, *so* sorry I dropped you in it over the condoms, Annabel, do hope I haven't wrecked your marriage.

No, Joss was definitely out, at least until such time as he rang Farlings when I might be able to race Martha to the phone and apropos of absolutely nothing, slip into the conversation that by the way, I've had a *slight* problem with the homicide boys over in the next county. Nothing I couldn't handle of course, but they are attempting to reel me in, the bastards. I shivered. Homicide. Murder. *Me* – shit! I damn nearly did, but instead I leapt up and grabbed the phone. I sank to the floor with it and stared at the dial. Who then? Philly? No, not Philly, she'd worry herself into anorexia in seconds and she'd also be pathologically incapable of keeping it from my parents which wouldn't do a huge amount for Daddy's angina and would have Mummy committing hara-kiri on the spot. 'You'll go to jail!' she'd shriek. 'Oh God what will the Burdetts say!' And with that she'd seize the pearl-handled cake knife and plunge it into her breast, falling headlong into the pavlova she'd just lovingly assembled. No, it had to be Alice. Dear, strong Alice who could always be relied upon to keep her head in a crisis. I punched out her number and nearly dropped the phone when Michael answered. Christ, I'd forgotten about him! He recovered first.

'Rosie. A happy New Year to you,' he said with forced civility.

In a flash I realised Alice must be listening. 'A-and to you too, Michael,' I croaked.

'I take it you want my wife?'

God, he was cool. But if he could be cool so could I.

'Please.'

There was a long pause, then, 'Rosie!' Alice's voice came on, happy and relaxed. 'A *very* happy New Year to you, my dear. Gosh, we completely forgot to ring each other last night, didn't we? Actually I was asleep before half past eleven I was so exhausted and the telly was such crap, wasn't it – hang on a moment.' She broke off and I heard her talking to the children. ''Bye, my darlings! Be good, give my love to Granny!' And then she was back. 'Michael's taking the children to my mother's for the day,' she explained. 'Giving me a break since I didn't get to go out last night and he did.'

'Ah. Yes. How was his . . . party?'

'Oh, pretty dull, by all accounts, although some drunken idiot managed to smash a beer glass over his head, poor darling. There was a scuffle at the bar apparently and Michael just happened to be in the way. He's got a hell of a lump on his forehead and he's still got a rotten headache.'

I bet he has, I thought grimly.

'Anyway, how are you?'

'Well not so good actually, Alice. I've got a bit of a problem. You see,' and with that I burst into a fresh flood of tears, and to the dramatic accompaniment of sobs, shrieks and pauses for nose blowing, I gave her a lurid, graphic account of the last few hours. When I'd finished, there was a horrified silence on the other end of the line.

'Good God,' she muttered faintly.

'I know!' I wailed. 'Oh Alice, what am I going to do?'

'Do nothing,' she said firmly. 'Just stay right there and sit tight. I'm coming down.'

Well I literally sat and waited. I felt almost numb with shock, and I didn't feel I could possibly do anything other than sit in a heap in my coat and stare into space. Now and again I tried to grasp the full implications of what was happening, but at the last minute my mind would scuttle away in terror and retreat to that comfortable, numb sanctuary of nothingness again. The only thing that disturbed my vigil as I waited the hour and a bit it took for Alice to come down, was the telephone ringing. I stared at it for ages, counting at least twelve rings before I finally picked it up.

'Hello?' I whispered.

'You all right, Rosie?' It was Martha.

'Martha!' I said with relief. 'Yes I'm fine, well, sort of fine . . .' I broke off, struggling with my voice.

'Ah. Thought so. Bit more serious than we thought then was it? Think you bumped him off, do they?'

'Yes!' I gasped. 'Yes, they do, isn't it dreadful?'

'Course it's dreadful, silly sods, it's blimmin' ridiculous. But don't you worry, they can't touch you, they haven't got a leg to stand on.'

'Sadly they seem to have quite a few, but listen, Martha, would you do me a favour? D'you think you could possibly hang on to Ivo for me for a bit? It's just – well I don't want him to see me upset, and I am . . .' I wrestled with my face muscles, 'I am rather – at the moment.'

'Course I can, he's fine with me. He can stay up 'ere for the night, wiv me an' the kids and then you can 'ave 'im back in the morning when you feel a bit better.'

'Oh, Martha, would you do that? But what about your dad? What about going to the hospital?'

''E's turned the corner,' she breathed. 'That's why I was in so early today, wanted to come and tell you. It wasn't a secondary tumour after all and they reckon 'e's clear of the last lot! 'E's coming home soon!' She tried, but couldn't keep the excitement from her voice.

'Oh, Martha, that's wonderful. Oh, I'm so pleased for you.'

'Yeah, well, forget about 'im for the minute,' she said quickly, 'let's just get you sorted out, eh? Blimey, you've done enough for me, you can leave Ivo wiv me as long as you like.'

'Thanks,' I whispered. 'You're a star.'

'You're all right,' she said, returning the compliment with her own, ultimate accolade.

When I put the phone down I found my legs had gone to sleep underneath me so I simply pulled myself up from the floor on to the sofa, like a seal slipping out of the sea on to the rocks, and curled up in the corner waiting. Finally Alice arrived. I heard the car door slam outside and then her footsteps on the path. I hurried to open the door before she knocked.

'Oh Alice!' I fell into her arms, sobbing.

She held me for a moment, then gently but firmly disentangled me and led me back to the sofa. She sat me down and picked up the gin bottle.

'I see we've been hitting the hard stuff already.'

'Had to,' I sniffed. 'I might not get cocktails in jail.'

'Now listen, Rosie,' she said, shifting sideways so she could see my face. 'I've been thinking about all this on the way down and the more I think about it, the more bloody ridiculous I can see that it is. You're getting yourself in a complete state about nothing here.'

I stared at her. Her blue eyes were shining with conviction and her red hair glowed around her head like a halo, making her look like a blazing heretic.

'Am I?' I said in surprise.

'Of course you are! Listen, did they arrest you?'

'No.'

'And did they charge you?'

'Well, no, but—'

'So they just questioned you, right?'

'Well, yes, but fairly aggressively, Alice!'

'Of course, because they're trying to put the frighteners on you! It's a classic case of manipulation by fear, my love. They've got absolutely nothing on you, but because lover-boy has for some reason claimed to have had a tempestuous affair with you, they've put two and two together and thought, aye aye, her husband's just died hasn't he? Kind of convenient if she was having a ding-dong with someone else, perhaps she bumped him off. So what do they do? They bring you in, give you the once over, scare you witless, then let you stew for a bit to see if you take the bait, see if you confess.'

'But what if they just pin it on me anyway? I mean the cap more or less fits doesn't it?'

'They won't, Rosie, I promise you. Give them time and they'll realise they're barking up the wrong tree. In fact, I'd put money on it they know that already, just from interviewing you this morning. I'll bet you anything you like old Steel Knickers went back to her colleagues down the corridor and said, "Uh uh, no dice, boys. She simply isn't the type." They can tell, you know, they get a nose for this sort of thing – it's like me spotting a great painting in someone's house, or you happening on a terrific new recipe. These people can sniff out a villain at twenty paces, and let me tell you, my love, that ain't you. You're simply not the calibre.'

'Oh, Alice, I wish I could believe you but you didn't hear the dreadful things she said to me! I'm sure she thinks I'm bitter and twisted and she knows I loathed Harry, and I mean, let's face it, ninety per cent of murders happen within the family don't they? I read that somewhere. It's the little things that send people over the top, like not screwing the tops on jars and forgetting to put the rubbish out, and Christ, let's face it, I had far more reason than that to kill him, didn't I? She was right about that, he was going to take Ivo away from me and, oh God, shall I tell you something really, really dreadful, Alice?'

'What?' she said, looking fearful for a moment.

'No, I can't,' I said seeing her face.

'Oh, for God's sake, go on!'

'I – I used to fantasise about him dying!' I gasped. 'I did, Alice, I used to imagine him walking past a conveniently loose roof tile and being decapitated, or – or being knocked down by a runaway milk float or eating a dodgy mussel or a prawn or something, getting salmonella and – oh God, that's how he died, Alice, don't you see?' I wrung my hands. 'I might actually have done it, I might have done it subconsciously!'

'Don't be such an idiot, Rosie, have you any idea how many women fantasise about their husbands dying?'

I blinked. 'No.'

'Every other sodding one of them! God, if they locked up every woman who offered up a little prayer that the ladder might topple sideways just as hubby was cleaning out the gutters the prisons would be heaving! For heaven's sake, Rosie, it's perfectly natural to wish your husband was dead, but there's a world of difference between fantasising and actually *doing* the dirty deed. The trouble is, they've *got* to you now, and you're trying to persuade yourself that you *did* do it which is precisely what they want! Get a grip, for heaven's sake. You're innocent!'

I gazed at her. She was right, I had to keep calm. I bathed in the fierce light in her eyes, hanging on to her conviction. Suddenly the light in them flashed to an idea. 'What about Tim?' she said suddenly, seizing my hand. 'What do you know about him? Why d'you think he's implicated you like this?'

'I haven't the faintest idea! I don't know anything about him!' I wailed.

'Well, for some reason he's using you as an alibi, isn't he? He's claiming to have had an affair with you to help himself – and incidentally, they'll soon find out that that's a load of old tommy rot. She said they'd asked all his friends – well, what about asking your friends? They haven't asked me, have they? They haven't asked *your* nearest and dearest about this man-cub you're supposed to have been trailing around on a chain for months. I'm quite sure one or two of us would have spotted him. No, Rosie. He's using you for some reason and you've got to try to think why.'

I stared at her, trying to digest all this. Then I clutched my head in despair. 'Oh God, I think I'm going mad. I mean, I know nothing about him! What d'you think he's done?'

She compressed her lips. 'I don't know, but he's obviously a shady character. You don't get many stunningly good looking ex-public schoolboys shelf-stacking in Sainsbury's, do you? The GTC perhaps, or even Thomas Goode, but not Sainsbury's. Perhaps it's a front for a huge undercover operation, perhaps he's injecting lethal bacteria into the Ambrosia cream rice, popping Semtex in the Coco Pops, smuggling caviar out by the bucketful – God, I don't know, the possibilities are endless!'

'But what's it all got to do with me?'

'Oh, absolutely nothing. As far as he's concerned you're just a desperate, last-ditch attempt at some cover, but they'll soon find out that's all bollocks and you don't even really know him.' She frowned. 'Didn't you say you saw him recently?'

'Yes, in the street, and he walked straight by.'

'Hmmm . . . interesting.' She narrowed her eyes thoughtfully. Then she got up. 'Oh well, never mind.' She sighed and brushed down her skirt. 'Now.' She looked around purposefully, hands on hips. 'Let's see about getting some lunch organised, shall we? I'm starving and, God, it's cold in here. I tell you what, you light the fire and I'll scramble some eggs or something. I thought I'd stay, incidentally,' she said, sailing through to the kitchen. 'I rang Michael on the mobile and he's going to stay at Mum's with the children for the night. Where d'you keep your eggs, in here?' She peered in the fridge.

I stared in disbelief at her retreating back. Then I got up and scurried after her. 'But – what are we going to do, Alice? I mean, shouldn't I be ringing solicitors, beetling off to barrister's chambers, that sort of thing?'

'Hmmm?' She took her head out of the fridge and gave me a vague look. 'Oh no, the last thing you want to do is get a solicitor. He'll only charge a fortune and for what? For listening politely to your story and then telling you to sit tight and do absolutely nothing before handing you a socking great bill. Well I can do that.' She smiled. 'Without the bill of course. Look, Rosie,' she said patiently, 'you haven't been arrested and you haven't even been charged, so you don't actually need professional advice. Honestly, you just wait, in a few weeks' time it'll all have died down and you'll have forgotten all about it, I promise. Ah, I've got them. Slightly past their sell by date, I see, but never mind. I'll put three in, shall I? And a bit of cheese too?'

I wandered back to the sitting room, biting my nail. I perched on the edge of the sofa, watching her bustling about. Could she possibly be right? Were they just putting the frighteners on me, testing the water in case I coughed? In case I admitted it? Suddenly I thought of something.

'We still haven't had the inquest yet of course,' I called to her. 'I mean Harry's inquest.'

'When is it?'

'Well, the police said it can take anything up to a couple of months.'

'Well, there you are.' She broke an egg into the pan with a flourish and turned, smiling confidently. 'The coroner's bound to bring in a verdict of accidental death and then everything will be fine! You wait Rosie, the truth always outs in the end, all you have to do is keep your chin up and lie low for a bit. Don't let the bastards grind you down.'

I bit my thumbnail a bit more. Chin up, keep cool, sit tight, lie low – God there were so many bloody inert things I had to remember to do, but I could do them all right. I could lie so low they'd have to take the floorboards up to find me. There I'd be, huddled in the foundations, cool, tight, and low, but with my chin well up. And with Ivo snuggled in beside me too, of course. With any luck they wouldn't find us for years and we could come up for – ooh, his eighteenth birthday or something. Have a nice little celebration.

As promised, Alice stayed, and actually played a blinder. She refused to indulge my tendency to lapse into sudden hysteria and then convalesce in a heap on the sofa, and bullied me relentlessly into carrying on as normal. First we trailed around the fields for 'a breath of fresh air', and then when we came back she insisted on clearing out all the kitchen cupboards. Well, actually it was me who cleaned them out because she insisted on mixing up some filler to mend the cracks in the kitchen wall, an apparently crucial job which needed seeing to instantly. Then of course, having mended all the cracks, we had to paint the wall. It wasn't exactly what I felt like doing on the day I'd been accused of murdering my husband, but I have to admit it took my mind off things and I felt totally exhausted afterwards, which I imagine was the general idea.

After that we sat in front of the fire, listened to music and chatted a bit, but she refused to discuss my predicament further, dismissing it as ludicrous and not worth wasting our breath on. Gradually some of her bravado rubbed off on me and I was able to relax a bit, but I was never able to forget. I was also aware of Alice's deliberate ploy to distract me and that worried me somewhat. She was almost too determined, too single-minded in her mission, as if actually she, too, was secretly worried sick. Now and again I'd catch her looking at me, but if my eye snagged on hers she'd prattle on again, about the children, about how lousy it was living in London, about her painting, about anything uncontroversial, and occasionally I'd find myself actually listening to what she was saying without permanently being in a state of blind terror. But it was always there. That ghastly black cloud, lurking ominously and threatening to roll in from the back of my mind.

She stayed the night, sleeping in Ivo's room, and the next morning got up early and left for London before I was up. I found a note on the table downstairs.

'Stop worrying! Everything's going to be absolutely fine – you'll see! Love and kisses, Alice. PS – Read these, v. good for stress!'

Underneath the note was a book called *Learning to Breathe Again* and another called *Yoga for Life*. There was also a packet of herbal tea and a cassette entitled *Relaxation Made Easy*. I smiled. All very alternative, and all very Alice. The hearts and flowers approach to the gritty reality of life.

Nevertheless, as I flicked through the books while I ate a piece of toast, I found that my tummy wasn't churning quite so dramatically as it had last night. Twenty-four hours and a good night's sleep had helped to distance that ghastly interview and cast it, almost, into nightmare realm, so that it seemed to me, as I sipped my tea in my sunny little kitchen, that it might never have happened. Gosh, perhaps Alice was right, I thought as I stared out of the window at the dew-soaked fields, cradling my mug. Perhaps I was getting my knickers in a twist over nothing here and perhaps they did pressurise people on a routine basis just to see if they squealed. Well if they did there should be a law against it, I thought angrily. It was not only highly unsociable but extremely upsetting and I had half a mind to write to my MP. Yes, the more I thought about it the more outrageous it became – harassing a grief-stricken widow? It shouldn't be allowed! I'd write to him this morning, or her of course, no need to be sexist.

I finished my toast and was just about to jog up the drive to Farlings with a slightly lighter heart when I remembered the milk-man wasn't delivering over New Year and we'd need milk. I'd have to pop to the village first. I grabbed the cassette Alice had given me to listen to in the car and as I did, her note dropped on the floor. When I picked it up, I realised she'd written something on the back.

'PPS – It's just possible they may be watching you to see if you try to get in touch with Tim or any of his cronies, so just be aware and act perfectly naturally. Above all, *don't panic!*'

I dropped the note in horror. Christ! Watching me? Where? I ran to the window. A snowman stared back at me. I recoiled in horror. Was there someone in there? I crept forward. Oh, don't be stupid, Rosie, you made that with Ivo for heaven's sake, she's just warning you to be careful, that's all. I took a deep breath and for a moment considered not going out at all, just staying in my nice cosy cottage with my thumb stuck firmly in my mouth. But then I rallied. I seized the car keys, stuck my chin out and strode off down the path. Admittedly as I got in the car I glanced about furtively, but then again, what was I looking for? Undercover agents posing as rhododendron bushes?

I drove off, humming 'Greensleeves' slightly hysterically, and trying to keep my spirits up, but at the same time wondering melodramatically if I shouldn't be savouring these moments. Driving a car. Going to the shops. Were these to be my last days of freedom? I looked up at the vast expanse of sky as I entered the village. That's what everyone said they missed in prison, wasn't it? Seeing huge skies. As I gazed at it wistfully I suddenly had to brake hard to avoid crashing into Ted Parsons the butcher, as he parked outside the post office. Sorry! I mouthed through the window with a grin as he got out of his car. He caught my eye but turned and hurried away. Oh well, I thought as I got out, perhaps he hadn't really seen me. Or perhaps he thought a near miss wasn't all that hysterical. I slammed my door and made my way along the frosty pavement to the Spa.

It was buzzing as usual, crowded with old women in headscarves busily popping Carnation Milk and Rennies into their wire baskets. I smiled to myself. These days practically every shop opened whether it be a Sunday or even a bank holiday, but anyone born before 1960 still acted as if the world might stop turning at any moment and the doors clang shut. There was certainly some panic buying going on over there by the fridge, it was three deep with yakking Vera look-alikes, and I waited patiently for a few tweed coats to clear before I could reach in for my own few pints of milk. But as I loitered, a couple of heads turned, and suddenly all the women stopped talking. A deathly hush fell. I glanced over my shoulder disconcerted. What? What was happening? When I looked back, I realised they were all staring at me. I flushed, confused, then in a second all was back to bustling normality again, except that my way to the milk was clear because the women had suddenly found business elsewhere. The fridge, it seemed, had lost its appeal. Slowly I took my cartons. I turned and walked to the till. The shop seemed to go quiet. I swallowed hard. No, I must be imagining this, this was surely nothing to do with me. Old Miss Martin, a great buddy of Vera's, was dithering over the Weetabix as I passed down the cereal aisle.

'Morning,' I murmured.

No answer. But then I had said it very softly, hadn't I? She can't have heard. My heart was pounding as I joined the back of the queue for the till. Mrs Fairfax was smiling and chatting behind the counter as she packed people's bags, and I relaxed a bit. She was so nice, a mate almost, and a great fan of Ivo's. On the counter was the usual box of cut-price items which had passed their sell by dates and were being sold off cheaply. When it came to my turn I picked out a bar of chocolate and a few old Christmas cards.

'May as well get well ahead!' I said cheerfully as I handed the cards to her.

'Looks like you might have to,' she said grimly.

Everyone stopped what they were doing and stared. Mrs Fairfax had now made it a very public humiliation. Very, very slowly she packed my bag, taking an inordinately long time to ring up four pints of milk, a bar of chocolate, and a few Christmas cards. Long enough, in fact, to give everyone time to witness me flushing from my toes to my fingertips and right up to the top of my fringe. Only when I was well and truly burning with shame did she let me go.

'That'll be two pounds eleven pence then.' She held out her hand and met my eye defiantly. No cosy dimples, and no apples in the cheeks either.

I handed her the money and with as much dignity as I could muster walked from the silent shop, aware of a dozen eyes burning into me. My hands shook as I got in the car. I turned the key in the ignition and drove off at speed. As I did my tummy flipped over and my hand flew to my mouth. Oh God, they knew! Everyone knew and what's more they believed it too, they thought I was guilty! Guilty. It was as if it had been branded on my forehead with a red-hot iron, and before I'd even had a chance to plead my innocence. And here, in a village I thought I knew, in a place where I was beginning to feel I belonged and was among friends! Oh God!

As I swung round a bend, desperate to get away from all those censorious eyes, I spotted Alice's relaxation tape on the seat beside me. I seized it. Yes, that's what I needed, some deep-breathing exercises. Perfect. Just don't panic, Rosie, don't panic, and remember – this is village life, that's all. It's just small-minded, parochial people with nothing better to do than gossip and snipe, and you heard what Alice said, don't let the bastards grind you down. Well that includes this bunch of peasants too! I glanced down at the tape. 'Learning to Relax Again' – perfect, yes, I'd like to do that, I really would, but very difficult to get into, particularly with one hand, and particularly when the sodding thing was hermetically sealed in snug-fit cellophane wrap plastered with Annabel's smug face. God it would have to be one of hers, wouldn't it? I dug at it with my nails, then went for it with my teeth, swerving all over the road as I bit into the wrapper. Finally I managed to rip it open, but as I flipped the box open with one hand, it promptly broke and the tape fell on the floor. Veering dangerously, I lunged down at my feet. Where was it now? There? No, that was the brake. Ah, here – bugger – WATCH THAT CAR, ROSIE! Swerving out of the way of a blue Audi but determinedly clutching my tape, I rammed it into the cassette player. I gripped the wheel and waited – as a high-pitched, constipated groan was emitted from what was palpably a broken tape. Furious, I punched it out, but its entrails were stuck in the mechanics of my cassette player and reams of tape came with it.

'Cow!' I shrieked. 'Call this bloody relaxing? Do you? DO YOU CALL THIS BLOODY RELAXING!'

In a fit of fury I buzzed down my window and flung it out as hard as I could. Unfortunately, I just happened to be passing Miss Martin's cottage where her sister, another Miss Martin, was standing at the garden gate, no doubt anxiously awaiting the arrival of the Weetabix. It caught her a glancing blow – crack! – right on the temple.

'Oh shit!' I gasped, staring in my rear-view mirror at her stunned, white face. Horrified, I sank down low in my seat. Oh God, don't let her die. Please don't let her die! Please don't let me have struck that spot that literally takes no more than a tap to send an octogenarian reeling into her grave. I couldn't stand any more dead bodies!

I could still see her in my rear-view mirror, dazed and rooted to the spot, staring after me. I quickly swung a left off the main road to get out of her line of vision. At some point, somewhere down that dark, tree-lined, shady lane, I drew into the side of the road. My whole body was shaking with the sheer accumulation of disasters and I simply couldn't drive any further. Apart from that, I didn't know where I was going. Actually, I thought I was going to faint. I bent my head forward on to the steering wheel and moaned low. Then I breathed deeply. In . . . out . . . in . . . out – you don't need a frigging tape to teach you how to breathe – in . . . out . . . in . . . out.

Gradually I felt a bit better. A bit calmer. And when I did finally raise my head from the wheel, I realised that actually, I did know where I was. Oh yes, this was Alex's lane wasn't it? I blinked my blurry eyes. In fact there was his rather racy green Mercedes down there, outside his cottage at the end of that row. How odd that he should be at home and not at his surgery although – no, of course. He wouldn't be working today. Suddenly I brightened. Oh for a cheery face. Oh, for an unconditional hug, an unquestioning smile, a friendly greeting. Yes of course, Alex! Why didn't I think of him before? Eagerly I sat up and started the car. I plunged into first and purred the few hundred yards up the lane to the row of beautifully converted, workmen's cottages with the stream running through the gardens behind. I pulled in behind his car.

Alex had knocked the end two cottages together so that they made quite an impressive pad. They were detached from the rest of the row, separated by a narrow alleyway that he'd lined with terracotta pots and urns which were spilling over with herbs and variegated ivy. Yes, it was really rather idyllic, and as I approached, I felt a bit better.

I knocked at the green front door and waited. Nothing. I waited a bit longer, then rang the bell. I stared up at the house. Damn, he must have popped out. Disappointed, I pressed hard on the buzzer, just to get rid of some irritation. After a few moments I moved across to the bay window and shaded my eyes with my hands, peering in. An anglepoise light was on at the desk in the corner, papers were scattered on the floor along with a coffee mug, and a fire was burning in the grate. I frowned. Wouldn't he have put a guard up? I went back to the door and rang once more. Perhaps he was in the bath, or on the loo or something.

Finally, I had to give up. Disappointed, I started back to the car, but as I passed the bay window again I suddenly saw movement. Yes, there he was, bent double, right under the window seat. What the hell was he up to? I rapped on the window.

'Alex! It's me!'

He popped his head up in surprise. 'Oh! Hi! Hang on.'

A second later the front door opened. 'Sorry, I dropped a contact lens. Were you ringing?'

'For ages! Didn't you hear me?'

He grinned. 'Must be going deaf. I had some music on too.'

'I can't hear any.'

'I turned it off as I came through.'

'Oh, right.' I smiled. He smiled back. But he didn't seem to be forming the words 'Come in', and he was standing squarely in the doorway.

'I – just wondered how you were,' I said brightly.

'Me? Oh fine! Fine!'

I nodded, 'Good. Haven't seen you for a while.'

'No, well, I've been terribly busy, Rosie, it's been absolutely horrendous actually. I've been up to my eyes.'

'Really? Over New Year?'

'Well, animals don't stop being sick just because it's a holiday, you know.'

'No, I suppose they don't.'

There was a pause. Well he obviously was very, *very* busy or he'd ask me in. I hesitated. I wasn't sure I could spill the murder inquiry beans right here on the doorstep.

'Oh well,' I said cheerily, 'I'll see you next Saturday then.'

'Saturday?'

'The cinema. Remember you asked me at the surgery? You let us jump the queue.'

He clapped his hand to his forehead.

'Saturday! God I completely forgot! I'm so sorry, Rosie, something's come up.'

'Oh?'

'Yes, my – my sister's coming over.'

'Oh! Oh right. I didn't know you had one.'

'Yes, she's – been away.'

'Oh really. Where?'

He stared. 'Peru,' he said finally, nodding hard. Then he scratched his head sheepishly. 'Can't really get out of it, I'm afraid, it's been so long since I've seen her. Sorry.'

'That's okay. Some other time then?'

'Oh, definitely! Definitely. Um listen, Rosie, I'd love to stand and chat but I've just put some bacon under the grill. Shall I give you a ring?'

'Oh, er, right, yes, I've got to go anyway. Got masses to do. See you!' I leaned forward to peck his cheek but somehow, caught his ear instead.

'You moved!' I laughed.

'Did I? Sorry. 'Bye then, speak to you soon!' And with that he shut the door.

I gazed at the green paintwork for a moment, then walked thoughtfully back to the car. How odd. He'd seemed . . . strange, somehow. Distant. And fancy forgetting he was taking me out on

Saturday when he'd literally blackmailed me into it. I got in the car and drove off slowly. Was this the same man who'd lusted after my body so very recently? Who'd practically lived in my kitchen, telephoned me at all hours, wrestled me on to sofas, hustled me into corners, begged me to succumb to his burning passion and appeared to be beside himself with desire for my very person? I shook my head, bemused. And the funny thing was, I reflected as I drove along, I couldn't ever remember him wearing contact lenses, or glasses. Suddenly I went hot. My hands gripped the wheel. He'd been hiding. He'd seen me all right, he'd seen me the moment I'd walked past the sitting-room window and he'd lunged for cover under the window seat. He'd heard me ringing the bell, ringing and ringing, and he'd hoped I'd go away. He hadn't wanted to see me because . . . he knew. The gossips had already got around to his picturesque neck of the woods and he'd discovered I had a nasty little habit of poisoning husbands. He'd decided not to swell the ranks. He thought I was a liability and wanted nothing more to do with me lest I slip something into his cocoa. He thought I'd done it. They all thought I'd done it.

With a pounding heart I drove home, sick to the stomach, and feeling very, very alone.

Chapter Twenty-Four

Somehow, the days passed. To a casual observer it might even seem as if my life went on as normal, but I knew better, the telltale signs were there. There was the way my anti-perspirant no longer did the trick, for instance, and the way it took half a bottle of wine and a generous slug of Night Nurse to get me to sleep at night, and the way I was getting through loo paper like there was no tomorrow. Alice, loyally, rang every day, and on hearing my voice would say triumphantly, 'You see!'

'See what?'

'Well, you're obviously still there, aren't you?'

'Yes, well, I haven't actually been clapped in irons and dragged to a prison cell if that's what you mean.'

'Precisely! There you are then.'

Yes, here I was then. Intestinal malaise worsening by the minute, hysteria mounting daily, branded as a murdering witch by all and sundry but still here, still breathing. So that was all right. But actually, as I nervously watched the days pass on the calendar and still no imperious knock came at the door, still no black-gloved hand gripped my shoulder to steer me to the police station, I did begin to wonder if Alice wasn't right after all. Perhaps all I did have to do was go to ground and keep stumm, and then miraculously it would all just go away, like some hideous dream that had no bearing on reality.

Reality soon reared its ugly head though, in the form of Bob. He rang to give me my marching orders.

'I'm sorry, Rosie, but it's the missus. She says you've gotta go. No one's eating see, and she says she don't like the way you never touch your food neither. Keeps banging on about not knowing where you get your ingredients . . . What can I do, luv?' He was clearly distressed.

'It's all right, Bob. I'll go quietly.'

Like most ebullient, overblown men, Bob had a shrewd little woman behind him, with her thumb well over him.

And so I was unemployed again, but in the general scheme of things that didn't actually seem so cataclysmic, and apparently life went on. Joss and Annabel were still away, Martha took over the reins again at Farlings, and the children went back to school. Martha took the girls, but on the day Toby was due to go came white faced and tearful to my cottage.

'Poor little bugger, what do they think they're up to, bloody boarding school.'

I sighed, reached for my coat and handed her Ivo. 'All right, Martha, I'll take him.'

'Oh, would you, Rosie? I reckon he's better wiv you.'

And so it was that half an hour later I drove Toby, pale faced but otherwise betraying no emotion, to the huge Gothic pile in seventy sprawling acres which was to become his home for the next five years.

We drove silently up the long gravelled drive. I parked, Toby got out wordlessly, then together we walked up the stone steps and through the open doorway into a flagstone hall, where the reception committee was waiting. Mr Archer, the steely-eyed but consciously avuncular headmaster, bore down on us beaming and patted Toby on the back with such brio that the poor child's cap flew off. By his side his twin-setted and pearled wife was equally eager to please, and clasping my hand in both of hers did an extraordinary sort of bob, so that for an awful moment I thought she'd curtsied. They couldn't have been nicer actually, if a little obsequious, but then, at £2,000 a term, who could blame them?

I hugged Toby hard but he felt like a statue. He wouldn't even kiss me goodbye, just turned, stony-faced, and walked down a passageway with his new housemaster, like a prisoner going to his execution. As he disappeared round a corner, I fled with a choking heart, hoping, pretending even, that he'd be happy, but knowing full well that the odds were against it.

I went home wearily and kept to myself. Aside from Martha and Vera, I saw no one. They both stayed as staunchly loyal as ever, assuring me that they hadn't said a dicky-bird to anyone in the village and that all the old busybodies had heard through Mrs Fairfax's brother who was desk sergeant at the Cirencester nick and who had 'quite a mouth on him'. Vera declared herself outraged at the reaction of her friends, most of whom, she said, if the truth be known 'had skeletons in their cupboards like you wouldn't believe and were nothing but a load of bloomin' hypocrites!' She promised me she could tell me a thing or two about that lot all right, but it didn't really help.

I avoided shopping in the village and used the out of town,

anonymous Waitrose, and I spent most of the time alone in the cottage with Ivo. Another cheery call had come from Mr Mendleson (I've-done-my-level-best) to inform me that despite spending an enormous amount of time showing countless people round the London properties there were no bites at the cherry. Right. Excellent news. All the time I longed for Joss to come back, longed for the sane, sensible slant he seemed to put on everything, but Joss was now in Italy and couldn't possibly be hassled with this. All he wanted to hear was that the home fires were burning brightly and that the children were okay, so when he rang the first day and asked how it had gone at the police station, I said fine, just some routine questions, and left it at that. It had been on the tip of my tongue to blurt out, 'Come back, they think I did it, I'm going to bloody swing for it!' but I never did.

I couldn't help thinking, though, that despite Alice's advice to do nothing, I should be doing *some*thing other than sitting by the fire reading *Spot the Dog* to Ivo and sucking wine corks. Shouldn't I be hiring a team of crack criminal lawyers, trawling through the best legal minds in the country? Finally my nerves got the better of me and on an impulse I flipped through my address book and rang Boffy. Crack criminal lawyer he certainly wasn't, but he was a solicitor of sorts and he had, after all, been Harry's best friend and therefore, by rights, one of mine.

His secretary put me straight through, even though he was apparently in a meeting, and relief flooded through me when I heard his voice, as jocular and hearty as ever.

'Rosie my dear! How the devil are you?'

I relaxed. 'Fine, Boffy. How about you?'

'In peak condition, my love, and all the better for hearing your dulcet tones. It's been far too long! Just because poor old Harry's left us for happier hunting grounds doesn't mean you have to be a stranger to your old muckers, you know. Charlotte and I were just talking about you the other day, saying how much we missed you and wouldn't mind dragging you out for a spot of sups, so how about it some time, eh?'

My heart creaked gratefully. 'I'd really like that, Boffy, I've missed you both too.' I crossed my toes guiltily in my loafers. Only half a lie really, because actually, talking to him now made me realise that on his own he wasn't such a bad old stick, it was just en masse with the rest of the tribe that he could be so obnoxious.

'So what can I do for you, my dear, or is this just a social call? Jolly nice if it is.'

'I'm afraid it isn't, strictly. You see, I'm in a spot of bother, Boffy, and I wanted your advice.'

'Ask away, my love, that's what I'm here for, in loco husbandis, as it were, if you'll excuse my Latin!' I could almost hear him puffing up importantly, braces straining on the gut as he no doubt settled back in his chair and prepared to advise the little woman on blocked drains, trouble with the tradesmen, or some such other piffling trifle.

'The police think I murdered Harry.'

'Wh-what?'

There was a clatter, and I think he actually dropped the phone, but then he was back to me in an instant. 'Don't be ridiculous, I've never heard anything so absurd!'

'It's true. They think I deliberately slipped him a dud mushroom and then rubbed my hands in glee as he nose-dived into his soup in front of you at the club.'

'Good Lord, this is preposterous! I'll tell them so myself, Rosie. This is totally absurd and what's more it's extremely distressing! Good heavens, how dare they suggest such a thing! Which Mr Plod at which particular Toytown Yard has come up with this little fairy story then?'

'Well, it's the lot over in the next county, down at Oxford. They seem to think I had a vested interest in Bertram's house and that's why I did it.'

Boffy snorted. 'That old mausoleum! You didn't even want it, did you?'

'Well, quite, but try telling them that. They think I was in league with my lover, you see.'

'Your love— Oh, Rosie, it gets more and more outrageous! Who exactly is in charge of the investigation?'

'A Superintendent Hennessey, but watch it, Boffy, she's barely human.'

'Hang on, my pet, I'll get a pen. Superintendent . . . Hennessey. Okay. Well, don't you worry, I'll haul her right over the coals for you, tight knickers and all. Harassing a young widow like that, it's unreal! They're so bloody desperate for convictions these days, you see, the police force is in such a hopeless mess they'll grasp at anything, but this is just farcical, and as Harry's best friend and your solicitor I shall tell them so in no uncertain terms. A lover indeed, and who, pray, is he supposed to be?'

'It's too ridiculous, Boffy.' I sighed. 'Some check-out boy who used to work at Sainsbury's. I hardly even knew him.'

The line went quiet.

'Boffy?'

'What's his name?' he asked quietly.

'Timothy McWerther. Why?'

There was no answer. I frowned at the mouthpiece. 'Boffy? Are you still there?'

His voice, when it came, seemed to come from far away. 'Rosie, I'm so sorry, something's just come up . . . going to have to fly.'

'Boffy? What's the matter, d'you know him or something? What's going on?'

'Of course I don't know him, but – listen, Rosie, I'll be frank. I really don't think I can help you here. I have, after all, got my reputation to think of. Let's face it, I am a professional man and, well, I'm sorry, but I just don't think I can get involved.'

I stared incredulously at the phone. 'Involved in what? Boffy! Tell me, please, do you know something? Look, I'm desperate. Please, I—'

There was a click and the line went dead. He'd gone. Slowly I replaced the receiver. I stared at it, stunned for a moment. Involved in what? Was I being awfully thick here? Was this Mr McWerther a notorious gangster, a drug smuggler or something? Had I not been reading the newspapers properly? Was I missing something that was apparently common knowledge? The phone rang again and I snatched it up instantly – thank God for that, he'd obviously had a change of heart.

'Rosie?' said Martha in a quavering voice. 'Toby's school's just rung. They said there's been an accident.'

'Oh God,' I whispered, 'what sort of an accident?'

'Well, she said it's not too serious, but a boy's in the san with concussion.'

'Toby!' My heart lurched.

'Oh, no, it's not Toby. They said 'e did it!'

'What? Oh, nonsense, Toby wouldn't hurt a fly!'

'I know, but try tellin' them that. Oh, what am I going to do? She sounded ever so cross and she wants me to go up there and I don't know how to talk to people like that!'

'It's all right, Martha, don't worry, I'll go.'

With my heart in my mouth I dropped Ivo off with Martha and roared off to Stowbridge House. Oh God, what had he done? Walloped someone with a cricket bat? Felled a small boy with a golf club? My mind flew round in crazy circles like a child manically swirling a sparkler in the dark. One minute I was wondering who the devil Timothy McWerther was and why Boffy had backed off quite so dramatically, and the next, what on earth a quiet, sensitive boy like Toby was doing knocking seven bells out of a child in his first week of term and putting him in the sanatorium? I glanced in the mirror and frantically raked my hand through my unbrushed hair as I swung a dangerous left at some amber lights – Christ, just missed that lorry. Oh God, what was happening to my life! If it would only slow down for just two minutes then I could at least get it into perspective. I felt as if I was on some crazy out-of-control roundabout, unable even to put a foot down.

When I arrived, the headmaster and his wife had clearly been waiting in the hall because the moment my finger hit the buzzer, the door opened.

'Ah, you must be Miss Garfield, we spoke on the phone.'

'Er yes, that's right.' I wasn't about to admit I wasn't in charge of Toby's welfare.

'I'm *so* sorry to have dragged you up here,' Mr Archer bore down on me, resplendent in a tweed, three-piece suit. 'I'm sure it was just an accident, but we *did* wonder if you might have a little word with Toby—'

'—just to set him on the right track,' continued his wife, smiling thinly at me through her powder. She took my arm and guided me through the hall and on up the sweeping staircase. '*So* hard to settle in immediately, we *do* appreciate that, and some boys do get more upset than others, leaving home, the family—'

'—loved ones, creature comforts,' purred her husband behind her. 'But all the same, unruly behaviour simply *cannot* be sanctioned here, and although we don't want to discipline him too severely, we *did* wonder if a quiet word from you might do the trick.'

I was being propelled expertly down an upstairs corridor by this smooth-talking double act now, one on either side.

'*Too* sad his father's not around, and I gather Mummy died when he was tiny, so naturally all sorts of behavioural problems there, but if you *could* just explain that civilised behaviour *is* encouraged, nay, expected at Stowbridge House, we would appreciate it.'

They stopped, breathlessly, and flung open a door. There on a bed, at the far end of an empty dormitory, with his *Toy Story* duvet and his teddy on his pillow, sat a little white-faced boy. His knees in his grey flannel shorts were pale and goose bumped and his mouth was taut.

'Toby!' I ran to him and put my arms round him. 'What happened, darling?' I whispered, sitting beside him and holding him close.

'He took my pictures,' he gasped, trying not to cry. 'Called me a

326

wimp for having them by my bed, then he threw them round the room, and look . . .' In his hand, tightly clasped, were some photos of Kitty. One of them was crumpled.

I looked up at the two faces above me. They were smiling but the eyes were grim. 'It's his mother,' I explained.

'So I gather,' the headmaster purred, 'but then boys will be boys and it was just a prank, I'm sure. No real harm came to the photographs but sadly,' he feigned a whinny of a laugh, 'I have a ten-year-old boy in the san with concussion and a set of worried parents halfway up the M5, who, by the wonders of modern technology and mobile telecommunications, have already conveyed their displeasure to me and are threatening to withdraw their son forthwith!' The smooth tone evaded him and he snapped this last word out like a Rottweiler.

'Rosie, I'm not staying here,' muttered Toby. 'Take me with you, please. I can't bear it, please!'

'Ooh now, come come.' Mrs Archer quickly sat down beside him, no doubt seeing another set of fees evaporate in front of her eyes. 'We're not as bad as all that, surely!' She went to put an arm round him but he flinched so violently she retracted it.

She looked over his head at me, and as if he was deaf, or not quite normal, murmured, 'This is all perfectly natural, Miss Garfield, please don't worry. Boys *do* take a few weeks to settle in and when temperaments *are* a little wayward and backgrounds unfortunate, as is the case here . . .' she nodded meaningfully at Toby.

'He's not a case,' I muttered. 'Could I use the telephone please? I'd like to ring his father.'

'Certainly, certainly!'

At the mention of Joss, they were all smarm and obsequiousness again, bowing and scraping as they ushered me from the room. Despite the Uriah Heep act, I saw them exchange a meaningful glance. As I got to the door, I looked back at Toby sitting on his bed.

'Back in a mo,' I promised.

He nodded, eyes fearful.

I was shown downstairs and into a study. As I sat down at the huge leather-topped desk and reached for the telephone, I paused. The dynamic duo hovered in the doorway. I cleared my throat.

'D'you think I might have a moment alone?'

'Of course, of course!' Hands were thrown up as if they were amazed it hadn't occurred to them before, and then out they backed, smiling and nodding, closing the door softly behind them. I grimaced. Actually it made very little difference because I was convinced they were either still on the other side, ears pressed firmly to the door, or on another extension. I looked in my diary and with a sinking heart dialled the current hotel in Italy. I was pretty sure he wouldn't be there, he was bound to be at the gallery and I was merely going through the motions to give me time to work out what to do next, when to my surprise Annabel answered.

'Oh! Oh, I wasn't really expecting – um, Annabel, it's Rosie.'

'Rosie.' She said my name slowly as if she was considering it carefully, mulling it over, getting ready to truss it up and toss it around the room.

'Um, is Joss there?'

'No. No, he isn't, Rosie.'

I felt her settle down, cross her sheer stockinged legs and prepare to deliver a mighty piece of her mind, so I rushed on dramatically, 'Annabel, it's Toby. He's in trouble I'm afraid.'

She sighed expansively. 'Oh, what now? And anyway what's that got to do with you? Where's Martha?'

'Er, out shopping, but the point is—' I hurried on, giving a long impassioned plea on Toby's behalf, and when I'd finished I could have sworn I heard her exhale a cigarette.

'So what d'you expect me to do hundreds of miles away? Spank his bottom?'

'No, it's just – well, he's begging to be taken away. He says he can't bear it here and to be honest,' I lowered my voice, 'I can quite see why. The head's a bit of a cold fish and I think Toby's being bullied, which is bad enough at a day school but at a boarding school, away from home—'

'Oh Rosie, don't be silly, it's just teething trouble, these things happen! They're bound to, especially in the first week. You surely don't expect Joss to take him away because of a silly little fight, do you? It's an absolutely marvellous school, I chose it myself and the headmaster is a darling man, a big fan of my books, incidentally, and so keen to please. No, it's out of the question, Rosie. We worked very hard to get Toby in there, it's terribly academic – and let's face it, Toby's not the brightest pixie in the forest – and it's got a terrific sporting record too, quite the best feeder around for Eton. God, he doesn't know how lucky he is, there are parents out there who'd kill to have their children at Stowbridge House. The trouble is, that boy's been spoiled, and a little discipline is just what he needs. Do him the world of good, show him he can't go around bashing other kids' heads in. Good heavens, I'm *appalled* actually. That *poor* little boy! *Do* send my sincere apologies to Jerry and Simone, it's *too* distressing for them to have to deal with this in the first week of term.'

'I don't think he's a poor little boy so much as a great big bully who deserved to be slugged. He's at least two years older than Toby, and yes, I know boys are always unhappy at the beginning of boarding school, it's just that I don't think Toby will ever be happy here. He'll just retreat further and further into his shell, even more than he does at home. He doesn't have the emotional resources to draw on to get through a school like this, he—'

'Rosie, how *dare* you. How *dare* you tell me Toby's emotional status and what's right and wrong for him! It's none of your damned business.' There was a silence. 'He stays there and that's final.'

I swallowed hard. 'Right,' I croaked. 'Sorry.'

'I should think so! Now, have Martha call me the minute she gets back. Goodbye.' She hung up.

I sat for a second staring dazedly at the blotter on the desk. Then I got up and went out to inform the headmaster and his wife, who were waiting in the hall, of what they already knew. Their eyes were gleaming confidently, faces smug. Actually, I didn't even bother. I just said, 'I'd like to see Toby again.'

I went slowly upstairs, followed just by Mrs Archer this time, Simone to her friends. Mr Archer, sensing the battle had already been won, hastened away to attend to more important business, like preparing his apologetic spiel for the M5 travellers, no doubt. Toby was still sitting on his bed, staring at a space on the floor somewhere between his black lace-up shoes. I sat down beside him.

'Annabel says you have to stay.'

'Did you talk to Dad?'

'He wasn't there.'

'You can't leave me here, Rosie, I'll kill myself.'

Simone gave a tinkly laugh. 'Oh, believe me, dear,' she winked at me, 'we've heard that one before!'

Well, that's nothing to be proud of, *dear*, I thought, but I didn't utter.

'I should go now, Miss Garfield, if I were you,' she said in a low, cajoling voice. 'He'll be fine. I'll see he's all right.' She raised her voice shrilly. 'Say goodbye to nanny, Toby, there's a good boy!'

He looked up at me, pleading silently with his eyes. I hugged him hard but knew better than to kiss him. The Judas kiss. ''Bye, Toby, see you at half-term.'

'No you won't,' he muttered.

I didn't answer, just got up quickly and walked from the room. I didn't look back and ran down the four flights of wooden stairs with

Simone prattling away behind me about the awesome responsibility of looking after *so* many boys and 'Gosh, if you'd only heard *half* the empty threats I have in my time!'

I shook her cold, heavily ringed hand at the door and looked into her calculating, pale blue eyes. Then I turned and walked to the car. As I got in, I shivered. God, I'd thought boarding schools like that had gone out with the Dark Ages. I thought they were all cosy bedtime stories and relaxed uniforms and jolly housemasters and weekends at home now, but trust Annabel, with all her hypocritical pretensions to enlightened education, to find one that was still firmly entrenched in the cold shower tradition of the nineteenth century. To find one that, quite simply, allowed Toby as little freedom as possible.

As I drove to the end of the drive, I suddenly stopped the car. I turned round in my seat and stared through the rear window. High up, behind the bars of a top floor window, was Toby, watching me. He looked frail, pale and very young. I turned back quickly and put the car into gear again, but as I did, I suddenly remembered a story of my brother Tom's. I hadn't gone to boarding school, but Tom had, and he'd told us about a boy called Parsons who every day for a whole term had tried to run away from school. He always stuffed his pockets full of fried bread before he went – for some extraordinary reason the boys were given this to eat at break time – and then he'd pound up the long drive, half a mile apparently, through a wooded area, across a stream, and try to get to the gates. Every time, though, the headmaster would drive slowly up in his car, wait for him, and bring him back. It was a bit of a laugh, by all accounts, because the word would get about, 'Parsons is making a break for it!' and all the boys would rush to the windows, cheering him on up the drive, then booing the headmaster as he brought him back. But one day, Parsons fell out of a fourth-floor window and died. No one ever really knew whether it was an accident, but his pockets, which every day were stuffed full of fried bread, were found to be empty.

My hands rested on the wheel. I looked back. He was still there. Slowly I got out of the car. At first I walked, calmly, and then it seemed to me I was running, running fast, the huge Gothic building bearing down on me, until I reached the front steps, leapt up them, and burst through the huge oak door. As I ran through the hall, Simone popped her head round an adjacent door. 'Miss Garfield, can I hel—' but I'd gone. Up the stairs, one flight, two, three, four, then down the empty corridor, coat flying, and into the dorm. Toby was standing now, waiting for me, eyes shining.

'Pack your things,' I panted. 'Quick! Where's your trunk?'

'In the basement,' he sang, 'but I don't need it, just my books and pictures!' He had those in his hand. I grabbed the other one.

'Come on!'

Together we clattered back along the corridor, then down the flights of stairs, making a hell of a racket. Jerry and Simone were waiting for us at the bottom.

'You have no right!' Simone screamed as we reached the landing above them. 'His mother—'

'She's not his mother and I'll take full responsibility while his father's away. Send his trunk on, please. Come on, Toby!'

We had the advantage of the stairs and a flying start, and together we jumped the last few steps and flew between the pair, scattering them in our wake, bursting through the front door, down the steps and out into the sunlit drive.

'Freedom!' squealed Toby. 'It's like *Escape From Colditz*!'

'And there's the wooden horse!' I cried as we ran for my beaten up Volvo at the end of the drive. We arrived panting, glancing back over our shoulders, and piled in, laughing hysterically now, very high on adrenalin and full of emotion. I plunged the car into gear and we roared off, whooping away. I threw back my head and laughed out loud, glancing across at Toby. His happy, shining eyes and pink cheeks were enough for me, and at that moment I cared about nothing. Not about the police, not about Harry, Tim, Boffy, Joss, Annabel or the shit that now must most surely hit the fan – nothing, save that Toby and I had made it, and that in my heart I was sure I'd done the right thing. I gripped the wheel. The blood was storming in my veins and I felt very much alive, very ready to take on anybody. Toby was still bouncing around beside me, squeaking gleefully about the looks on the Archers' faces, but gradually, as we ate up the miles and got nearer to home, we both grew silent. As the fields became more familiar and we whizzed past the road leading to the twins' school, reality began to rear its ugly head. Toby slipped Fauré's *Requiem* into my cassette player. We sat in silence and let the wistful, mournful arias wash over us.

'You know, you still have to go to school, Toby,' I ventured at length.

'I know.'

There was a silence.

'If you could have chosen, where would you have gone?'

He shrugged. 'Dunno.'

'Where have your friends gone?'

'Dunno. Don't have any really.' He stared out of the window. This was classic Toby.

'Well, where's Sam gone?' Sam was a quiet, shy boy who'd come for tea once or twice.

'Westbourne Park. It's just back there.'

'And?'

'And what?'

'Well, does he like it?'

'How should I know?'

I bit my lip but persevered doggedly. 'So why didn't you go there?'

He shrugged again. 'Dad quite liked it but Annabel said it was for pansies. Said I'd grow up all arty-farty and poofy.'

Ah, right. As opposed to emotionally crippled and anally retentive.

'But Sam goes there?'

'Yes, I said so, didn't I?'

I studied him sideways for a moment, then drew into the side of the road and stopped the car.

'Don't do this to me, Toby.'

'Do what?' His face was blank.

'This don't know, don't care routine. This clam up and then no one can get to me act. You owe me, mate. I've just rescued you from that horrendous school and it's pretty inconceivable they'll have you back now, so you owe me, and I want you to talk to me.'

'What about?' His voice was still truculent, but quieter. More subdued.

'About you. About what makes you tick. About what you want to do, what you *like* doing, about what makes your heart beat faster. Come on, Toby, give us a clue, for God's sake!'

He turned his head away from me and stared out of the window.

'I know you love animals, nature, birds, but is there anything else?'

Silence.

'When I was about your age,' I persevered, 'we went on holiday once, me and my family, and we stayed with some friends in Cornwall. They lived in a beautiful old house, perched on a cliff top overlooking the bay, and they ran a restaurant there. Every day, while all the other children were playing outside, I hung around in the kitchens, persuading them to let me watch, even occasionally to let me help. It was just polishing the knives and forks, stirring the odd sauce, that sort of thing, but I loved it. I loved the hustle and bustle, the excitement of the customers arriving, the glorious smells, the fresh vegetables coming in from the garden, a fisherman coming through the back door with his catch, the rabbits hanging up, the smell of the herbs, and then afterwards, when the food had been served and eaten, relaxing in the kitchen and chatting about how the day had gone, which recipes had worked, which hadn't. I vowed that one day I'd have a restaurant like that. Well, I haven't got it and I probably won't have it now, but it gave me a direction, Toby. I saw at once that this was something I wanted to do, something I could aim for.'

He stayed staring out of the window, gazing into space. But after a while, he began to speak tentatively. I had to strain to catch the words.

'I'd like to learn the clarinet. I'd like to learn to play that concerto in A by Mozart and I'd like to meet other people who like music.' There was a long pause.

'Go on,' I said softly.

'I'd like to play in an orchestra. Maybe even . . .' he frowned.

'What?'

'Maybe sing in a choir.' He blushed.

'And do they do all that at Westbourne Park?'

'Sam's going to learn the flute *and* the viola.'

I turned the key in the ignition, glanced over my shoulder and with a certain amount of aplomb performed an astonishingly immaculate but highly illegal U turn in the middle of the road. As we roared back, Toby looked amazed.

'Where are we going?'

'Need you ask?'

Two minutes later we swung into the gates and up the drive. Well, let's face it, I had to have some sort of alternative plan of action available to Joss, even though he was bound to shoot it down in flames, and this at least was a start. I looked up at the building in front of me. Westbourne Park was a modern, purpose-built school with a large playground at the front and playing fields behind. We drove up and parked at what I assumed was the main entrance.

'Come on,' I said cheerfully, getting out.

Toby sat still and licked his lips.

I popped my head back in. 'Toby. Come on, you've got to go somewhere, let's at least go and see,' I coaxed.

He got out. I took his hand and we walked up to the double swing doors, but as we attempted to open them, they rattled and my heart sank. They were locked. I looked up at the plate-glass windows and the empty classrooms above us. 'Doesn't look like they've even started yet, Toby.'

'Not till Tuesday week,' said a voice behind us. 'We're quite a bit later than all the other schools around here.'

I swung round. A middle-aged woman with curly brown hair and tortoiseshell glasses smiled. 'It all comes out in the wash though, just means we finish term a bit later. I'm Anne Perkins, the headmistress here, and although work might have stopped for the children, it doesn't seem to have done so for me!' She indicated the huge stack of papers in her arms. 'Just popped in to see to this little lot. Can I help?'

I took a deep breath, and began. She wasn't gushy, and she didn't beam with delight as I outlined the reasons for Toby being so swiftly disenchanted with his previous school and so keen to become a member of hers, but she listened carefully, looking from me to Toby, and no doubt taking in the tearstained little boy in his flannel shorts and the somewhat frazzled-looking woman beside him. When I'd finished, she nodded.

'Well, obviously it would be up to his father, but as it happens we do have a place in the first year because one little boy's family has just been posted to Germany. I'd be delighted to offer it to Toby, but as I say, I'd have to speak to his father.' She frowned. 'But haven't we met before, Toby?'

'Yes, I came round with my dad. He liked it but my – my stepmother wanted me to go to Stowbridge.'

'Ah.' She frowned. 'Well, if that's the case, we may not suit, I'm afraid. We're two entirely different schools, you know, and your stepmother may think us a mite too relaxed in comparison.'

'It's not her who counts,' said Toby hotly. 'It's my dad's decision.'

This was said with feeling, and she could easily have exchanged a grown-up raised eyebrow with me, but she didn't. She regarded him solemnly.

'Well, I'll tell you what, Toby. Why don't you speak to your father this evening and ask him to give me a ring, and then we'll see if we can't sort something out.'

'He's all over Europe at the moment, I'm afraid,' I explained breathlessly, sensing a ray of hope here. 'He's the sculptor, you see, Joss Dubarry,' I threw in shamelessly, 'and he's travelling around a bit. I may not be able to get hold of him for a few days.'

She smiled. 'Doesn't matter, there's no rush. I won't fill the place now seeing as it's so close to the beginning of term, so we'll hold it open for Toby for, what? Say three weeks? How would that suit?'

'Perfect,' I beamed, 'just perfect. Thank you so much!'

'Not at all.' She smiled and walked with us back to the car. As we got in, she looked thoughtful. 'I really must stress that you'll find us very different to Stowbridge. We're co-ed, you know, and we only weekly board and we don't spend quite so much time on the playing fields as they do. We also ask that right from the word go you take up at least one instrument, did you know that?'

'Yes,' breathed Toby. 'I'm going to play the clarinet.'

She smiled. 'Perfect. We could do with another clarinettist in the orchestra.'

Toby and I drove home in companionable silence. He was rather like me in that respect. Didn't always feel the need to talk. But as we came into the village, I glanced at him sideways and suddenly realised he was on the verge of tears.

'What's the matter?' I said, aghast.

There was a silence as he struggled with his face. 'I want to say something to you,' he gasped eventually, 'only I can't!'

We were drawing up to some red lights. As we stopped, I took his hand and smiled. 'That's all right. I know what it is, and actually, as long as I know, it doesn't really matter whether you say it or not, does it?'

He turned brimming eyes on me. I saw them widen with recognition. I smiled. So that was all right then. As we took off from the lights, I hunted around beside me, then snapped a rather joyful concerto into the cassette player. It just happened to be Mozart's clarinet concerto in A. I glanced at Toby slyly as his mouth opened in astonishment.

'Oh, you'd be amazed, Toby. I'm full of surprises.'

He threw his head back and laughed delightedly.

A few minutes later we drew into Farlings and Toby couldn't wait to get out of the car and run and tell Martha and the twins, who would be home from school by now. It was then that I realised, with a jolt, that Martha would be shocked. Horrified even. And if Martha would be horrified by my precipitate action, what the hell would Joss and Annabel be? As I slowly got out of the car, the enormity of what I'd done hit me. I, the next-door-neighbour, had taken these people's son away from his school within a week of term and tentatively signed him up for another without even consulting them. No, correction, *with* consulting them, but just totally ignoring their instruction. Right. Unusual decision, Rosie, really rather unusual. As I followed Toby into the house, my heart sank even further into my boots as I realised that in actual fact what I'd probably done here was far worse. I'd probably raised Toby's hopes sky-high, only to have them dashed to the ground when Annabel returned, worked her charm on Jerry and Simone, and insisted he be reinstated at Stowbridge. Yes, well, let's see how much he loves you then, when he's dragged screaming and kicking back to that pre-war institution, shall we, Rosie? I took a deep breath and let it slowly hiss out through my teeth. Oh God, what a mess. What a God-awful, bloody mess.

As I walked through the back door into the kitchen, the mess loomed larger. Martha dashed towards me looking grim. Ah, he'd told her, and she *already* thought I was mad, and not only mad but totally irresponsible. I steeled myself.

'You've got visitors,' she said, jerking her head sideways.

My heart stopped. Oh God. This was it then, was it? They'd come for me.

'Where?' I whispered.

'Front hall. Went to the cottage then came up here. Been hanging around since ten o'clock this morning.'

I nodded. 'Right. Thanks, Martha.'

I took down a glass and had a quick drink of water. I set the glass down shakily on the draining board, stared at it for a moment, then turned and walked through to the front of the house, trying to keep my head high. As I went along the corridor I wondered what sort of expression Marie Antoinette had had on her face as she went to the guillotine.

I turned the corner into the hall, but as I did, I stopped in my tracks. I was confronted by, if anything, a far more terrifying sight than a couple of police officers poised with handcuffs at the ready. Because arranged around the hall, on the sofa, chairs and standing in front of the fire, looking grim and in some cases extremely tearful, was almost the entire cast of my immediate family. Philly and Miles, Mum and Dad.

Chapter Twenty-Five

'What's this?' I said lightly. 'A council of war?'

'Rosie darling!' My mother lurched across with a sob and fell on me. She was swaddled as usual in her old mink coat which smelled of stale scent and she was gripping a lipstick-covered tissue. 'Oh, my poor darling, my baby, you'll go to prison!' Her eyes widened and she drew back in horror as another terrible thought struck her. 'Oh my God,' she gasped. 'We'll have to move!'

'Not necessarily, Mum,' I said disentangling her and depositing her in the nearest chair. 'We'll tell the neighbours I've emigrated, if you like. Either that or I've had a sex change.'

'Why didn't you tell us?' demanded Philly, looking white and tense, perched primly on the arm of a chair. 'We had no idea until Miles came back from the pub and said the whole world was talking about it!'

'Ah, so you've heard the verdict already then, Miles. The village Tricoteuses were clicking away busily, were they?'

'I didn't stay to chat, Rosie,' he assured me. 'I put my pint down and came straight home.'

'No casual gesture, I can assure you,' remarked Philly snidely. 'It takes a lot for Miles to leave a pub, but the point is, we feel so stupid, Rosie!'

'Well, gosh, sorry for the inconvenience, folks. Sorry to be so *shaming*, Mummy, and for you to feel so *uninformed*, Philly. Just the eighteen years at Her Majesty's pleasure for me of course.' I went to the desk and poured myself a shaky drink from Joss's decanter. May as well go the whole hog on the brazen hussy front and drink the landlord's Scotch, I thought, and it wasn't as if it was the first time either. Good morning, decanter, I greeted it silently as I replaced the stopper, we're seeing rather a lot of each other these days, aren't we?

My father crossed the room and put his arm round my shoulders. 'We're just concerned, love, that's all,' he said gently. 'Tell us what's been going on, eh? We feel a bit sort of – in the dark.'

Oh God, this was much worse. I shrugged brusquely, knowing I was close to tears. 'Nothing much to tell really, Dad. The Oxfordshire police had me down for a chat and asked me some rather probing questions, that's all. Pointed out that since I hated Harry's guts I might have had a bit of a motive, but then again, they haven't actually charged me so there's probably nothing to worry about. Drink, anyone?' I waved the decanter airily.

'That doesn't mean anything,' said Philly grimly. 'That's just their softly-softly approach, and meanwhile they're quietly shoring up more and more evidence, so that when they do finally drag you in, there'll be so much ammunition levelled against you you won't be able to stand up. You'll go under, they'll submerge you with it.'

'A cheery little thought,' I murmured into my glass. 'Thanks, Phil.'

'I'll get my man O'Sullivan on to it,' said Daddy importantly. 'He's a damn good solicitor, O'Sullivan, known him for years.'

'Well, of course you have because he must be about a hundred and four years old,' scoffed Philly. 'And he does conveyancing, Dad, which is hardly going to help Rosie on a murder charge. No, no, she doesn't want an old provincial hack like O'Sullivan. I'll have a word with a friend of mine, a partner at Clifford Chance. A real City hotshot.'

Dad looked suitably crushed. 'Of course, my love, whatever you think's best. If you've got some fellow who's more suitable—'

'It's not a fellow, it's a woman,' she said tartly. 'She was at Cambridge with me. Got a starred first actually, terrific forensic brain.' She sat up straight. 'Yes, if anyone can get her off, Gillian can.'

I stared at her, perched authoritatively in her cashmere overcoat and silk scarf, eyes bright, cheeks burning righteously.

'When you say "get her off",' I said mildly, 'you do realise I didn't actually do it, don't you?'

'Well, of course you didn't, darling,' said Philly soothingly, 'it's just a figure of speech. I just meant that she'll get to the bottom of it, that's all.'

'And I've sent for Tom of course,' put in Mum with a sniff.

I swung round, aghast. 'Oh Mum, you haven't!'

'Oh yes I have, this is a family crisis! We must all band together, fight them on the beaches and all that, and we need a real man about the place now that Harry's gone. Tom will know what to do.'

I wondered where this left Daddy and Miles if all the real men had gone. Neatly emasculated I supposed.

'He wasn't in his office when I rang,' Mum went on, dabbing at her eyes, 'out on location apparently, but a frightfully sweet girl took a message, must have been his PA, I suppose. She couldn't have been nicer. I explained that his little sister was facing a murder charge and that things were looking rather bleak, and she said that she was sure he'd want to come straight back, and incidentally if it wasn't too much of a personal question, what exactly was the murder weapon? Well, I explained about the mushrooms being poisonous and everything and then – bless her, she was so concerned – she asked if you were a sympathetic sort of character and whether you were pretty or not and I said that you *were* a sympathetic character but in a bit of an underdog sort of way, and *quite* pretty but understandably a little jaded at the moment.'

'Thanks, Mum,' I muttered. 'So I'll be a jaded underdog in a TV drama directed by my brother before I've even made it to the courtroom, will I?'

'Well, d'you know, I *wondered* if that's what she was getting at!' she said, turning shining eyes on me. 'And actually, Rosie, it would be rather marvellous, wouldn't it? I mean it's bound to sway public sympathy your way, particularly if they get some gritty individual to play you, someone rather plain and unknown but with bags of integrity, and Michelle Pfeiffer to play Philly of course, and I *did* wonder if Sophia Loren might be persuaded to come out of retirement to play me. It's often been said that there's an uncanny resemblance.' She rested her chin on her finger and presented us with her profile so we could admire the uncanny resemblance. 'And I thought Edward Woodward for your father, and Harry's terribly keen for James Fox to play him—'

'Harry!' I stared at her.

Her eyes widened in surprise. 'When I talked to him the other day, darling. You know, with Marjorie.'

'Ah, right,' I muttered, sinking down into a chair and feeling rather weak suddenly. 'Yes, I'd – forgotten about Marjorie.'

'And he agrees with me that it should be played entirely from your perspective, with you as the wronged wife and him as the out-and-out rotter, because actually he doesn't blame you at all, my darling. He says he was a dreadful husband to you and drank far too much and can quite understand why you were glad to see the back of him.'

'Sweet Jesus, keep her out of the dock,' moaned Miles, rubbing his eyes with the back of his hand.

'And he wants you to know that although he's missing you and Ivo like mad, he's having a lovely time up there.' She folded her hands happily on her lap and leaned forward confidentially. 'I must tell you,

Rosie, he's terribly excited at the moment. He's just started a decorative napkin folding course which he says is absolute heaven!'

I gazed at her in wonder. It suddenly struck me that her eyes, which were always a trifle wild, were slightly madder than usual today. When I looked closer, I saw that under her fur coat she was wearing a rather eccentric embroidered shawl, and that hanging round her neck were not the usual clinking array of gold necklaces, but strings of coloured beads.

'It's all part of a table-laying course he's doing, but Harry likes the napkin bit best because he says that the way you present your table linen plays a significant part in expressing the real inner *you*.' She pursed her lips. 'I think he's absolutely right.'

'She's lost it,' muttered Miles, shaking his head sadly, 'she's really lost it, I'm afraid.'

'He says it doesn't matter,' she went on emphatically, mistaking her dumbstruck family's silence for encouragement, 'whether it's elegant peach damask or crisp Irish linen tumbling from a crystal glass, napkin-folding is a further expression of *self*. Harry says we shouldn't be afraid to experiment either, folding into symbolic or representational shapes like the rising sun, or the butterfly in the circle of life.'

Miles snorted uncontrollably at this and gasped in my ear, 'She's got her lines crossed, Rosie, she's tapped into Barbara Cartland's dead butler by mistake!'

'And he's even learning to embroider them too,' she said dreamily. 'He's doing a darling little cross-stitch on red gingham at the moment, the sort of thing you might want to go with for an informal fork supper.'

'Sounds like the sort of thing you might want to go with to the lavatory!' hooted Miles.

'I'll make some tea,' said Philly hurriedly.

'I'll give you a hand,' I said, hastening after her to the kitchen. The kitchen was empty, Martha and the children had obviously gone upstairs.

'Oh God, she's barking, Phil!' I said in horror. 'She's absolutely doo-lally!'

'I know,' said Philly wearily, filling the kettle. 'I've tried to keep it from you, Rosie, but it's these wretched seances, and it's not just once a week now, it's every night.'

'No!'

'Oh yes, and always round at our house too. Marjorie's changed the venue, claiming it's more atmospheric at The Firs, but I reckon it's to save her pocket. Dad says she appears bang on drinks time and then off they scuttle to the dining room to summon up the ectoplasm together. And of course Mum never actually hears these celestial voices, it's all filtered down through Marjorie The Medium, who as far as I can make out just guzzles one gin and tonic after another, bolts copious amounts of smoked salmon sandwiches – she can't get extra-terrestrial, it seems, without half a side of smoked salmon inside her – then shuts her eyes solemnly, lays both hands portentously on the table and makes it up as she goes along.'

'Well of course she does!'

'And when Mum says eagerly, so what's old Harry up to now Marj? all she has to do is open one eye, look furtively round the dining room, spot a pile of napkins and say, ooh, well, he's having ever such a lovely time folding napkins, Liz, and Mum's absolutely transfixed!'

'But why on earth doesn't Dad put his foot down?'

She made a face. 'Dad? Come on, Rosie.' She sighed and got some mugs down from the dresser. 'Actually, I think he gives in to her because he feels she's been so stressed recently. What with Harry dying and now you in trouble, he probably thinks it's a harmless little diversion for her, and of course she absolutely went to pieces in the hospital.'

'What hospital?'

'Oh!' She flushed. 'Nothing, it was . . . where's the Earl Grey kept?' She gazed around.

'Philly, what hospital?'

She bit her lip and turned to face me. 'I wasn't supposed to tell you. Dad made me promise. He didn't want you worried with so much on your plate at the moment. He had another angina attack the day after Boxing Day.'

'Oh God!'

'But he's fine now,' she said quickly, 'absolutely as fit as a fiddle. They just kept him in overnight for observation, that's all.'

I sat down abruptly on a stool. 'Oh Philly, everything's going to pieces suddenly, isn't it?' I said hollowly. 'Everything's collapsing around me like a house of cards and somehow I feel . . . it's all my fault.' I put my head in my hands.

'Don't be silly, of course it's not!' She seized my hands and pulled them away from my face. 'You mustn't think like that, Rosie, everything's going to be fine! Dad's going great guns now and we're going to get you sorted out, I promise. Honestly, Gillian Cartwright's a marvellous trial lawyer and if anyone—'

'Can get me off, she can. Yes, I know.' I raised my head. 'Philly, you think I did it, don't you?'

She blanched. 'Don't be ridiculous! Of *course* I don't!'

I nodded. 'Yes you do, I can tell. You think because he was fat and alcoholic and unpleasant and wouldn't give me a divorce I bumped him off.'

'No! No, I—'

'Oh, you don't *blame* me because you think that actually you might have done the same thing yourself if you'd had the misfortune to be married to a pig like that, but you definitely think I did it, don't you?' I fixed her with my eyes.

'All I think,' she began in a low voice. She stopped, licked her lips and started again. 'All I think, Rosie, is that you've got to stop sitting around doing nothing. You've got to stop waiting for the axe to fall and *do* something. God, they interviewed you days ago and you've told no one, not even your own family, for heaven's sake! It's this wretched inertia and hiding yourself away that looks like an admission of guilt, nothing else!'

I stared over her shoulder into the distance. 'Alice says I should just keep cool,' I said slowly. 'She says—'

'Oh, Alice!' Philly slapped both hands angrily on the counter in despair. 'What does she know? She hasn't got a single brain cell in her alternative little head! All she knows about is stirring her brown rice and making corn dollies out of reconstituted oats. She wouldn't know prosecuting counsel from mitigating evidence, she couldn't fight her way out of a paper bag, let alone a murder inquiry!'

'She's my best friend,' I said fiercely, 'and just because she hasn't got an Oxbridge degree, it doesn't mean she's a simpleton! I don't know why you've always been so down on her, Phil, you've never liked her and she's been marvellous throughout all this, if you must know!'

'Well, *I'd* have been bloody marvellous if you'd just have let me in, but it's one thing to be marvellous and do bugger all, and another to wade in at the eleventh hour and try to pull the cat out of the bag, which frankly is what we've got to do now!'

'Need any help, girls?' Miles stuck his head round the door. 'Shall I take the tray?'

'Oh, for heaven's sake stop calling us "girls" and treating us like bloody fairies! We can actually manage a tray without our arms snapping, you know!'

It was said with such venom I blinked.

'Sorry.' Miles withdrew hastily, probably clutching his balls. There was a pause.

'Bit strong, wasn't it?' I said.

'Oh, he just gets on my tits,' she said angrily, throwing her head back and scratching it energetically. I blinked again. Tits? Since when did Philly even admit to bosoms?

'He thinks he's so flipping macho, striding around the farm all day with his gun under his arm, popping pheasants and then appearing at the kitchen door rubbing his hands and saying, mmmm, something smells good! I'd like to boff him on the nose. I'm sick of it, Rosie. I will not play the domestic little woman any longer just to satisfy his sexist, chauvinistic pride!'

I opened my mouth in wonder but Philly had already banged the cups down violently on the tray and stalked off into the other room. Well, I thought as I followed her through. It's all coming out now, isn't it?

Back in the hall I encountered the twins holding court to my family. They'd obviously escaped from Martha and were enchanted to happen upon some strangers to entertain downstairs. Lucy was perched prettily on one of my mother's knees and Emma on the other, playing with her beads and both flirting outrageously.

'What delightful children,' murmured my mother as I came in.

'Martha told us to come and get you,' said Lucy quickly. 'She's just tidying the bedrooms but she wants to go and get her dad now.' She fingered Mum's tasselled shawl with wonder. 'I didn't know your mummy was a Gypsy lady, Rosie.'

Mum laughed softly. 'Not exactly a Gypsy, my love, more a psychic time traveller.'

Dad moaned, barely audibly, and shook his head.

'Come on, Lucy, Emma,' I said holding out my hand. 'Let's go and relieve Martha. Sorry you lot, but I've got to go. Martha's collecting her father from hospital and since it's his first night home, I'm staying over. Right now I need to go and bath the children for her.'

'You mean – we're going?' asked Mum in surprise.

'Well, you can finish your tea,' I said generously, 'no rush. Come on, you two.' I went towards the stairs, grateful for the excuse.

'How old are you?' asked Lucy, staying put on Mum's lap and peering up into her eyes.

'Oh goodness,' Mum tinkled nervously and patted her hair. 'I believe I've lost count!'

'Really?'

'Yes, my pet, one does, you see, when one's had as many birthdays as I have.'

'Let's have a look in your pants.'

'Lucy!' I gasped.

'Well, look,' she twisted round and hoiked her pants out of the back of her jeans, 'mine say five to six years, see?'

I seized her hand and pulled her firmly off Mum's lap. 'Come on,' I said grimly, 'we're going now.' I grabbed Emma as well. 'Say goodbye to everyone, I dare say you'll see them all again very soon.' We headed for the stairs. 'Oh, and don't forget to bang the front door shut behind you when you go, will you?' I threw back pointedly over my shoulder.

'But we haven't even discussed anything yet,' protested Philly, coming to the foot of the stairs. 'I wanted to get a copy of your statement on Gillian's desk by first thing tomorrow if possible.'

'Don't think we'll manage that, Phil. We've missed the last post, I'm afraid.'

'Fax it up.'

'Does rather, doesn't it?'

There was a startled pause. Miles sniggered. 'No!' Philly said angrily, sensing I was being deliberately obtuse. 'Use the fax machine. Joss has got one, hasn't he?'

'Oh.' I smiled. 'Yes, he has. Righto.'

She sighed wearily and folded her arms. 'Okay, Rosie, what's the matter? Don't you want me to help you?'

I paused and turned to look at her at the bottom of the stairs. Her cheeks were pink and her eyes bright with indignation. She looked hurt, baffled no doubt by my refusal to take advantage of her considerable intellectual ability and recourse to people in high places. But sister or no sister, I wasn't at all sure I wanted anyone in my camp who didn't believe in me.

'Not right now,' I said truthfully. 'I'm sure a time will come when I'll be begging you to bail me out, Phil, but for the moment, let me do this my way, okay?'

I turned and went on up the stairs, leaving her open-mouthed and flummoxed at the bottom.

That night I slept fitfully. I tossed and turned in Martha's bed at Farlings and had a terrible dream that I was being hustled down some stone steps and thrown into a dungeon at the bottom. Just as the door slammed shut behind me, I turned to see Harry, dangling the key through the bars, smiling nastily.

'Harry!' I ran and gripped the bars. 'It wasn't me, I didn't do it, I swear to God I—'

'Save it for the parole board, Rosie,' he snarled. 'And meanwhile, twenty years' hard napkin folding for you, young lady!'

With that, he thrust half a hundredweight of peach linen through the bars.

'Come on!' he cracked a whip. 'Get folding!'

'But Harry,' I bleated, seizing the top one and folding frantically, 'I didn't do it, I—'

'Call that dainty?' he roared. 'I've seen better efforts from these mass murderers!'

I glanced into the neighbouring cell where, sure enough, my fellow inmates – huge, burly, tattooed men – were pleating away nimbly, humming happily as they tucked here and fanned out there, creating the most marvellous birds of paradise and tropical sunsets.

'I can't do it!' I wept. 'I can't. I'll never be able to do it – just kill me now!'

I flung the napkin away and opened my eyes to find I was sitting up in bed, furiously pushing my duvet off, absolutely drenched in sweat. My hair was plastered to my head and the morning sun was streaming in through a gap in the curtains. I sat stock still for a moment, trying to get my bearings. Where was I? In prison? In London? At the cottage? No, Farlings. Martha's bed. I turned and seized her alarm clock. I stared. Half past eight. Half past eight!

'Bloody hell!'

I leapt out of bed in panic. Half past eight and, oh God, it was term time now, no breakfast telly for the children to lounge around in front of in their pyjamas, I had to get everyone up and dressed! Had to get the twins to school. Where were they? And where was Ivo? Where was everyone?

Hurriedly I dashed to the basin and splashed some water on my sweaty face, then I flung off my nightie and threw on a bra, pants, jeans and a sweat shirt. I briefly caught sight of myself in the mirror and recoiled in horror. God, I looked like an Old Master drawing or something. Pausing only to rake a comb through my hair, I flew out of the room and raced down the back stairs, only to be ambushed at the bottom by the urgent demands of my still very irritable bowels. Damn! Cursing their terrible timing, I dashed quickly into the downstairs loo. Once enthroned, I realised that the house was ominously quiet. I listened. No, not a peep, they hadn't even switched on the television. Oh God, they must all still be fast asleep in their pits and the twins had to be at school in – I glanced at my watch – precisely ten minutes!

'LUCY, EMMA!' I roared.

No answer. Hell. And oh *bloody* hell, there was no flaming loo paper! Typical! With my trousers down around my ankles I shuffled to the kitchen where I knew there was a box of tissues on the dresser, but as I burst through the door I met a quite terrifying sight. Round the table, fully dressed, wide-eyed and silently dipping soldiers into boiled eggs, were Toby, Lucy, Emma and Ivo. At the head of the table, looking grim, exhausted and very stony-faced, sat Joss. His eyes travelled down to my large white bottom, then up again.

'Rosie. Good of you to join us,' he drawled. 'I gather you're making very free with my son's education.'

Chapter Twenty-Six

Quick as a flash I pulled up my jeans. Probably not quick enough though.

'Joss! I – didn't know you were—'

'Coming back?' he inquired. 'No, neither did I, it came as a complete surprise to me too, Rosie. Up until last night I imagined I was working in Europe for another two weeks, but then a scurrilous rumour regarding the future of my son's education reached me and I suddenly found myself at the airport desperately trying to negotiate a flight. You could have knocked me down with a feather. I thought I was meeting up with my dealer to go over next year's plans, but it was not to be, and here I am, home on the range.' He reached for some toast, his face impenetrable.

'Look, I can explain,' I croaked, shuffling towards the table and surreptitiously doing up my flies.

'Good, I'm glad to hear it,' he said, calmly wiping his mouth with a napkin. 'In fact I'm keen to be enlightened.' He turned to face me for the first time, hazel eyes blazing. 'Because imagine my surprise, Rosie, when, having been told by Annabel of a "minor incident" at Toby's school, which had apparently rendered both you and Martha "panic stricken and hysterical", I abandon my work, move heaven and earth to get back here, and stagger exhausted into my own home to find that it looks like the *Marie Celeste*! *My* children are nowhere to be seen, *your* child is screaming in a cot and instead of Martha, I find *you* fast asleep in *her* bedroom. When I finally run the children to ground watching unsuitable television in the sitting room, I am coolly informed by my son that yes, the rumours are perfectly true, and on account of him knocking a fellow pupil unconscious he's ditched one highly expensive private school in preference for another.'

'No, no, it's not quite as simple as that. He hasn't actually been signed up yet, all we did was pop over to Westbourne Park yesterday and talk to the head but—'

'Oh good, *good*,' he interrupted with ill-disguised sarcasm. 'I'm pleased to hear it's just a *little* bit more complicated than that, because for a moment there I was thinking I didn't have any choice in the matter! I was thinking it was all cut and dried and that all I had to do was get my cheque book out and sign on the dotted line, and I have to say, Rosie, that if that *had* been the case I might legitimately feel that although I asked you to give Martha a hand and assume a little responsibility while I was away, you might have overstepped the mark and assumed just a little too much!' His voice rose dangerously.

The children, having clearly been read the riot act at an earlier stage in the morning, were still diligently dunking their soldiers, but the toast wasn't quite making it to the mouths. Their eyes were out on stalks.

I spread my hands on the table. 'Look,' I said in a low voice, trying to keep calm, 'I know it seems like an extreme reaction, Joss, but seeing the situation at first hand as I did yesterday, I really couldn't see any other option open to me but to take Toby away.'

'Well, you could have left him there!' he spluttered incredulously. 'That was the other option surely.'

'Yes, I could, but I was genuinely concerned for his safety and I thought it was far better to run the risk of incurring your wrath than to have an altogether different scenario on our hands.'

'Oh really?' He leaned back in his chair and regarded me with wide-eyed bafflement. 'Like what? Like Toby committing hara-kiri with a pair of compasses perhaps? Or maybe turning himself into a human pyre with a bunsen burner maybe?'

'Well, these things do happen, you know! You read about it in the papers all the time!'

'Oh, come on, Rosie, you panicked and you overreacted!'

I nodded, trying to keep my temper. 'Quite possibly, yes, I'm willing to accept that I was very emotional, but it's easy to be dismissive in retrospect, isn't it? Because we don't know what would have happened if I'd left him there, do we? All I *do* know, Joss, is that you and Annabel disappear for weeks on end to pursue your precious careers at a crucial stage in your son's life – like when he's starting *boarding* school, for God's sake, when most parents would be sobbing into their pillows at night wondering if they were doing the right thing – and you expect Martha to cope with every eventuality that comes her way. Well, she couldn't and so she asked me and this is how I cope with it. This is *my* reaction to a young boy's cry for help, and I've no doubt your reaction would have been to dismiss his distressed face and shaking knees as utterly shameful and tell him to brace up and knuckle down and rah-rah-rah along to the school song etcetera, but it wasn't mine *and you weren't there and I was*! Now I'm sorry if you think I made a monumentally bad decision and I'm sorry that I didn't stop to consider which school would take Toby away for the longest period of time and get him out of yours and Annabel's hair, but at least my decision came from the heart with Toby's best interests to the fore, which is more than I can say for some of the absentee parenting around here!' I was trembling with rage now.

He regarded me stonily for a moment. 'Have you finished?'

'Not quite.' Oh, I was well away now, blood up and shooting straight from the hip. 'Because what I suggest you do now, Mr Dubarry, is get in your car and take your son back to whichever school takes your fancy. I'm quite sure if you cross their palms with enough silver Jerry and Simone would welcome him back with open arms, and the head at Westbourne Park is waiting to hear from you, so instead of blaming me, why don't you just get out there and *sort it out for yourself*!'

'That would be all right, would it? If I had a say in the matter?' He stood up, his eyes boring into mine. I glared back. In the stony silence that ensued, Toby got down and crept round the table to me.

'Do I have to go back to Stowbridge House?' he whispered.

'I don't know, darling,' I muttered.

'Get in the car, Toby,' snapped Joss, still staring at me.

'But Dad, you won't take me back to Stow—'

'JUST GET IN THE GODDAM CAR!'

Toby fled obediently.

'And I'll take you to school too, girls,' he said, 'since it's on the way.'

Lucy and Emma slipped down from their chairs and, unusually silent, followed Toby out to the car, for once intimidated by atmosphere. Joss turned to look at me before he went out.

'Don't tell me,' I quipped sardonically. 'You'll speak to me later.'

'Don't bank on it,' he spat, before slamming the back door.

I watched it reverberate in its frame for a moment. Then the house plunged into eerie silence. I turned to look at Ivo who was still wide-eyed at the breakfast table.

'Well, darling,' I whispered. 'Things really couldn't get much worse, could they?'

'Don't know, Mummy,' he said in an awe-struck tone.

With a lump in my throat, I tidied up the kitchen. I threw cereal bowls in the dishwasher, slammed the door shut, wiped down the surfaces, then flung the wet dishcloth miserably in the sink. I stared at it as it sank into the plughole. Don't you bloody cry, I told myself fiercely. You've got enough on your plate without crying about this. One arrogant bastard in a foul humour is nothing to snivel about, okay? I blinked back the tears determinedly. Okay. And don't start thinking it wasn't so long ago that you entertained foolish ideas of appealing to the arrogant bastard either, because that'll really set you off. That'll really open up the floodgates. I gritted my teeth and nodded hard at the plughole. Right. I won't think about that either then. No foolish ideas.

Just as I was blinking away like a demon, the door flew open behind me. Vera breezed in on a blast of cold air.

'Sorry I'm late, luv, his spastic colon's playing up again. I had ever such a tussle wiv him in the lavvy this morning trying to get him out of 'is braces in time, it's a wonder I got here at all today.' She took off her headscarf and glanced at Joss's suitcase still sitting in the middle of the floor. 'He's back then, I see.'

'He is. And he's not a happy man either.'

'Why's that then?'

I gulped. 'Just . . . this and that.'

'Ah. Like that, is it?' She bustled off round the kitchen, her back stiff, clearly offended that she wasn't going to be privy to any secrets. But Vera couldn't stay silent for long.

'Did you get that note I left 'bout your brother then?'

I turned, still hanging on to the sink. 'What note?'

'I left it by the phone. He rang last night. I popped up to get me knitting bag I'd left behind and the phone went just as I was goin' out the back door. Said he'd got some funny message that you was on a murder charge and wanted to star in his next film, but your Mum thought your breasts might need liftin' first.'

'Oh God!'

'Wanted to know if it was a joke.' She eyed me beadily.

'And?'

'I told 'im it was.'

'Oh, thanks, Vera,' I breathed.

''Sorright. Don't want any nasty rumours starting, do we?'

I smiled my appreciation, but as I did she stopped strapping herself into her pinny and stared.

'Lord luv us, you *do* look a sight this morning!'

'Do I?' I put a shaky hand to my hair and realised it was still plastered to my head from my nightmare.

'Never seen you look so rough. Have you got your monthlies or something?'

'No, I haven't actually.'

'Well, you look like you have. Our Eileen used to go a bit green and pasty-faced like that when she had hers. I tell you what, you go up and have a bit of a power shower like wot they've got up there, make a change from that rusty old bath of yours, and come back down when you're feeling better, eh?' She chuckled as she reached up into the cupboard for a duster. 'I don't suppose that did much for 'is humour this morning, did it? You lookin' like that? You know what Her Highness looks like in the morning, all bronzed and made up and manicured up to the whotsits, I expect he took one look at you and went right off his breakfast!' She bustled out to the hall with her duster, chuckling away, but not unkindly.

I stared bleakly at the dishcloth in the sink. Ah, right, so you're putting men off their boiled eggs now, are you, Rosie? Excellent. Couldn't be more pleased.

'Mummy! Out!' Ivo was clenching and unclenching his hands demonstratively in his high chair behind me. As I went across to release him, I received a dazzling smile. The pure beam of unconditional love. I kissed him passionately as I scooped him up.

'So he likes nail varnish and seamless tans at the breakfast table, does he? How shallow can you get, eh, Ivo?'

I hoisted him brusquely on to my hip, but nonetheless made a quick detour to the mirror in the hall just to see what the fuss was all about.

'Jesus!'

I recoiled in horror, then peered a little closer. Crikey, it didn't even *look* like me. Who was that sad creature with the dark blonde dreadlocks and the slitty little eyes peering out of the white face? I swallowed. Yes, well, perhaps I could just go up and wash my hair. Then at least when the Looks Fascist returned he could beat me without flinching. I turned and trudged gloomily up the stairs with Ivo in my arms, but as I got to the landing window I paused. Something had caught my eye. The first-floor window offered the most marvellous view down the back garden to the hills beyond and out to the open countryside, but somewhere to the left of the vista, through some trees, a blue light was flashing. It was outside my cottage. Yes, outside my cottage a blue light was flashing . . . on top of a police car. I stared. Then Ivo spotted it too. He jabbed his finger on the windowpane.

'Peeth car!' he said, overjoyed.

351

'Yes. I know, darling.'

I got closer to the window and narrowed my eyes. The car appeared to be empty. Well, of course. Its occupants were clearly inside the cottage, looking for me. I watched for a moment longer, then slowly turned and retraced my steps downstairs. At the bottom I encountered Vera, rolling up the rugs, mop and bucket poised to wash the flagstones. She stared at me as I went past.

'You all right, luv? Looks like you've seen a ghost.'

'Yes, I'm fine. Fine.' Oddly enough, I did feel fine. I felt quite calm. You see, in a way, it was a bit of a relief. Put an end to all that nervous anticipation. 'I'm just popping down to the cottage, Vera.' I paused. I almost said, I might be some time. 'Won't be long. I think I've got some visitors.'

She didn't answer, just watched as I went calmly out of the front door and shut it softly behind me. I stood on the top step for a moment, gazing at the landscape, breathing in the crisp morning air. Its coldness was heady somehow. I raised my eyes to the vast, cloudless blue sky. Big skies. Then I turned and set off down the hill.

As I approached the cottage, I realised the front door was wide open. I crept up as quietly as I could and peered cautiously inside. Yes, well, if they were hoping to surprise me, I'd surprise them. Instead, what I saw made me draw my breath in. I almost didn't recognise my own sitting room. The whole place had been turned upside down. Drawers had been pulled out and thrown on the floor, papers were strewn everywhere and books had been wrenched haphazardly from the bookshelves, leaving the shelves bare. Cardboard boxes chock-a-block with stuff I didn't even recognise had been plonked in front of the fire, presumably brought down from the attic because there was a gaping hole in the ceiling and the trap door hung open. Glancing into the kitchen I saw that all the china, pots and pans, and even the food from the larder was spread about the floor. Potatoes had been shaken from their bag and were rolling around; in fact everything, it seemed, that could be turned over or taken out had been. It looked as if I'd been burgled.

'Ah, Mrs Meadows.'

Out of the gloom stepped a familiar figure. Her mouth was set in its habitual thin line, her eyes were cold, the colour of winter skies, and her face was white against the upturned collar of her navy coat. Superintendent Hennessey showed her teeth in a cruel approximation of a smile.

'What the hell's been going on here?' I whispered.

'We're searching your cottage, Mrs Meadows. We do have a

warrant, of course.' She whipped a paper out from inside her coat. 'Happily we didn't have to break the door down since you'd rather conveniently left it open, but it's perhaps not a terribly wise thing to do on a regular basis. Then again, that's the country for you, I suppose.'

I went in past her, staring at the mess. 'But – what are you looking for?'

'Hard to say really until we find it. Perhaps you could give us a few pointers.'

I turned. She fixed me with her eyes.

'Well, I haven't the faintest idea!'

'No?'

'No! But I know one thing's for sure, you can't just walk in here and ransack the place for no reason, it's outrageous! And you must have known I was up at the house, why didn't you come and get me? I mean, what were you going to do, leave a note saying, turned the place over, see you soon? God, you've even tipped the potpourri on the floor. What were you looking for in there? Drugs? Diamonds? Human remains?'

'You tell me, Mrs Meadows.'

I gazed at her. Without taking her eyes off me, she inclined her head sideways and threw her voice up the stairs. 'How are you getting on up there, Bill?'

'Still looking!' came a voice.

'Well, make sure you go through it with a fine-tooth comb. I want all those drawers and cupboards emptied and the beds stripped, duvets out of the covers. The kid's room too.'

'Righto, guv.'

She lifted her chin defiantly at me and thrust her hands deeper into her pockets.

I nodded slowly in realisation. 'Ah, right. Yes of course. This is intimidation, isn't it? You're not looking for anything at all, you're just doing this to break me down, aren't you?'

'Call it what you will,' she said softly.

'Well, it won't work,' I said hoarsely. 'Because I didn't bloody do it, okay?'

I turned and with Ivo in my arms blundered past her, outside into the cold. One other thing was for sure, I thought, as I stumbled round to the tiny patch of garden at the back, I wasn't giving her the satisfaction of having me as her audience as she devastated my home. I lifted Ivo up on to the little flint wall that divided the garden from the fields and sat down beside him with my back to the cottage, hugging him hard. I stared out into the misty blue distance.

After a while, though, Ivo got bored with my tight, trembly arms and clambered down the other side. He found an icy puddle to slide on. I watched as he skidded on it. The ice was thin and he cracked it easily with the heel of his boot, squealing with delight as the water splashed up. Tears pricked my eyelids, but happily they were tears of rage. Fury was mounting fast and I welcomed it, because I knew as long as I could stay good and angry and not cowed and frightened, I could beat them, and actually, by turning my cottage inside out they were going the right way about making me absolutely bloody livid. Sorry, Superintendent Hennessey, I thought savagely, but if you think this is going to make me sink to my knees and blurt out a false confession, you're wrong.

I took a deep breath and waited. I could hear banging and crashing coming from inside but I ignored it, knowing it was purely for my benefit. I concentrated instead on the way the icy water left little white trails on Ivo's boots as it froze. Like snail trails. Finally, after what seemed like an age, Cold Lips herself came round to see me.

'We've finished here,' she said briskly.

'Found anything interesting?' I asked bitterly.

'Not yet, but we'll be searching your house in London next.'

'My . . .' I shook my head. 'Fine. Fine, go ahead,' I said wearily.

'You still have the keys, I take it? Only it saves the embarrassment of breaking the door down in front of the neighbours.'

I looked at her pinched face and wondered when she'd ever been sensible to people's feelings, embarrassment or otherwise. Wordlessly I got off the wall and went inside to fetch the spare keys for her. Ignoring the total chaos that confronted me, the clothes – even my *underwear*, for God's sake – strewn over the banisters, the papers littering the floor, plates piled high on the kitchen floor, I reached into my handbag.

'Here.'

As she went to take them, I held on to them for a moment, forcing her to look me sharply in the eye. 'I've said this before, but I'll keep on saying it. You're making a big mistake here.'

'Really,' she said drily, yanking the keys from my hand. 'I wonder if Harry would agree with you. But then conveniently for you he's six feet under and can't actually comment, can he?'

And so saying she turned on her heel and walked out. As she got in the passenger side of the panda car, I caught a glimpse of the driver. I realised it was the same, vaguely sympathetic older man who'd driven me home from the police station that day. I thought he flashed me an apologetic look as they drove off, but then again I couldn't be sure, and to be honest I didn't really care.

I sat down on an upturned box in the middle of the floor and stared around me. Havoc had most surely been wreaked here. Ivo toddled in from the garden and looked about in astonishment.

'Methy!'

'Just a bit, darling,' I croaked. I gulped hard. Because now that they'd gone, anger had turned to dismay, and seeing my possessions strewn about me like this, my clothes hanging over the banisters, almost made me feel as if I'd been raped. Thankfully Ivo was blissfully diverted by the chaos and moved from one pile to the next, playing happily with electricity bills here and saucepan lids there, and didn't seem to notice that his mother was quietly dissolving on an upturned box and weeping silently into her hands. It was only when my face was so wet and my nose running so hard I had to look up to wipe it, that I realised there was someone standing over me. I glanced up in alarm.

'Joss!'

'What's going on here, Rosie?' he said quietly.

'Oh Joss,' I sobbed shamelessly, 'I'm in big trouble!'

'So I see.' He sat down beside me in his overcoat.

'It wasn't just a few routine questions at the police station,' I gasped. 'You know, that time when they took me there after New Year, when you went away. They grilled me absolutely rigid and – oh God, Joss, they think I killed him, they really do!' I fought with my breath and wiped my face with the back of my hand. Joss handed me a hanky.

'I know, I thought as much. I spoke to Martha on the telephone yesterday and she more or less told me the worst. It was one of the reasons I came back, aside from seeing to the schools of course.'

'Oh.' I suddenly remembered. 'How did it—?'

'He's fine at Westbourne Park, Rosie. You were right, he'll do well there. He's much more suited to that kind of atmosphere and I liked the head. I went to Stowbridge first but the Archers were remarkably unpleasant and threatened all sorts of lawsuits before I could even open my mouth. It seems the other boy's parents have already removed their son, which is naturally Toby's fault. In fact they seemed to think the whole damn episode is everybody's fault but their own. It's extraordinary how when the chips are down people show themselves as they really are. He's a pompous ass if ever I saw one and she's a really cold fish. You were right to take him away, Rosie.' He paused and gazed about him, looking genuinely appalled.

Suddenly, though, he rallied. 'Anyway, enough of that.' He stood up, rubbing his hands together briskly. 'Let's see about clearing this place up, shall we, and then you can tell me about the God-awful mess you seem to have gotten yourself into. Look at all this garbage, is this all yours?'

I blew my nose miserably on his hanky. It was clean and white. A lovely handkerchief, I almost couldn't bear to spoil it. I couldn't help noticing, too, as he stood over me, how beautifully square his hands were as they hung at his sides and how kind his golden eyes as he looked down at me. He was a powerfully built man, tall with broad shoulders, not the type you'd expect to be artistic, more of a sportsman or something but then sculpting was, I suppose, pretty physical work. Physical – now why did that make me feel a bit hot . . . ? Oh God, if only things weren't so ghastly, I thought miserably, wiping my nose again. If only I'd met him ten years ago, if only I'd met someone like him instead of Harry, if only Annabel could be run over by a truck, if only—

'Rosie?' He broke into my reverie.

I tried to remember what he'd asked me. 'Oh, yes,' I sniffed. 'It's all mine, I expect.' I looked about. 'Well, no actually, these cardboard boxes aren't mine. They've all come down from the attic. I thought they were yours but if they're not they must belong to Alice and Michael because I've never even been up there.'

'Doesn't look like they've even looked in them,' he said, peering at the neat pile of books and clothes, 'just brought them down so you have the hassle of taking them back up.'

'Quite! They just want to harass me, the bastards!'

'Okay, okay. Take it easy. Come on, let's shunt them back up. One of these days the Feelburns might even have the courtesy to stop by and pick them up instead of just dumping their crap in someone else's attic, but for the moment it can go back where it came from.' He tested the little ladder that came down from the loft. 'That's steady enough. You go up and I'll pass them up to you, they look darned heavy.'

I obediently climbed up and we set about humping the boxes back to the loft, him passing them up and me studiously avoiding touching his hands as I took them from him. They were mostly full of files, papers, books and old clothes, and as Joss repacked one that had fallen to bits, I riffled idly through the one he'd just passed up, mostly to try to avoid staring at his golden-brown head below. It was dark in the attic but as I peered in the box I realised . . . how odd. There was something remarkably familiar about some of these things. I picked up a faded Paisley scarf and then an old blue jumper underneath. I knew these bits of clothing. Recognised them. They were Philly's. I delved deeper. A couple of old cassettes that could have been anybody's, but then – an old velvet slipper, tatty, but very distinctive, with frayed embroidery on the front. Philly's again, because I remembered she'd brought them back from Nepal. There were a couple of Jane Austen paperbacks and as I flipped them open – yes, on the inside covers there were the Ex Libris stickers that Philly always plastered in the front of her books, and in her black italic handwriting, Philippa Jane Cavendish. I frowned.

'Joss?'

He straightened up from his packing below. 'What?'

'Something . . . a bit odd here.'

He came halfway up the ladder. 'What is it?'

I looked up from the book. 'These things belong to my sister, Philly.'

He peered in the box. 'Oh. Do they?'

'Well, don't you think that's a bit odd? I mean, what on earth is her stuff doing here? In my attic? Or your attic, come to that?'

'Or even Michael's attic,' he said drily.

I frowned. 'What?'

He shook his head. 'Nothing. Beats me, Rosie.' He made to go down again.

'It does not!' I said suddenly. He stopped on the ladder. 'What d'you mean, Michael's attic? What's going on here, Joss?'

Slowly he came back up the rungs until his face was level with mine. 'Ah yes. I'd forgotten you were probably the only person left in Pennington unaware of your sister's infidelity.'

I stared at him. 'My sister's . . . Oh, don't be ridiculous! Infidelity with who?'

'With whom,' he corrected instinctively. 'With Michael Feelburn, of course.'

I stared, gormlessly. 'Michael!' My jaw dropped. 'That's not true!'

'Well, maybe not any more, but it was, I can assure you. Your friend and mine, the very same Tricky Mickey, and frankly, much as I liked Alice, it was one of the reasons I wanted the Feelburns out of here and was pleased to see you installed instead. It was quite a relief to put an end to all the late night shenanigans that went on down here as he hustled your sister backwards and forwards. I felt pretty bad for poor old Alice too.'

I stared in horror. 'No! *Philly!* God, I just don't believe it. Philly – and with *Michael,* of all people!'

'I know, defies belief, doesn't it? But then again when you think about it, it was all pretty convenient really. What with him being down here on business mid-week and Alice living up in town and your sister being in the next village. Oh yes, it was a regular Wednesday-night fixture. The rumour in the village was that the poor old cuckolded husband – Miles, is it?'

'Yes,' I whispered.

'That he thought she was out doing an evening art class.' He laughed softly. 'Life studies, apparently.'

'Well, yes, that's right,' I said slowly. 'She did do that on Wednes-days. She did a course at the local pol—'

'Bullshit! She didn't do any damn course anywhere, Rosie! The only nude she studied with any intensity on a Wednesday evening was Michael Feelburn!'

I clutched my mouth. 'God, that makes me feel sick!'

'Well, you introduced them apparently.'

I stared. 'I *did*?'

He shrugged. 'So I heard. Some dinner party.'

I blanched. Oh God, yes, I *did*. I did introduce them, at that ghastly supper party, ages ago, when Philly and Alice had hit it off so atrociously. I'd been so busy worrying about the bad vibes between the girls that I hadn't even noticed Michael. Had he been shooting Philly hot looks all the while, playing footsie under the table? Was that how it had started?

'Oh God,' I groaned, 'that was years ago. It must have been going on for ages then!'

'So it appears.' He looked around at the boxes. 'I mean, she certainly moved a heck of a lot of stuff in, didn't she?'

I shook my head in mute astonishment. Philly. *Philly*, of all *people*! I looked up sharply. 'So – did everyone know?'

He scratched his head. 'Well, you know better than I do what these English villages are like, Rosie. You can't scratch your butt without word getting about. I certainly knew because it all went on in my own back yard, right outside my window. Oh, they thought they were being terribly clandestine and discreet as they arrived back late, no doubt from dinner in Cheltenham, with her slumped down in the passenger seat, complete with big hat and dark glasses – summer only naturally, the darkness did the job in the winter – and then she'd leave in the same disguise an hour or so later, but I keep erratic hours and I was usually still in the studio in the window as they passed in and out. You could set your watch by them. I'd think, ah, Philly and Michael, it must be ten o'clock on a Wednesday evening, and then, ah, Philly and Michael again, it must be half past eleven and he must have shagged her senseless.'

'Don't!' I snapped my hands over my ears. 'I can't bear to think about it!'

'And I certainly caught enough glimpses of her to recognise her that day she turned up on my doorstep with you, asking if there was any room at the inn.'

My hands left my ears. 'I remember you staring at her,' I said slowly. 'I thought you fancied her, like most people do.'

'I'm sure they do, she's a great-looking girl but she's not my type. No, I was just starry-eyed at the magnitude of her gall. It seemed pretty rich to me to be asking to rent the cottage when she'd been testing the bedsprings for the past couple of years.'

'The past couple of . . .' I lapsed into silence, staggered. Suddenly a thought struck me. 'Oh God, d'you think Miles ever found out?'

'Funnily enough, I never asked. Never actually approached him in the pub, slapped him on the back and said, hey Miles, old buddy, you must be Philly's husband! Did you know she was being slipped a length on a regular basis by that Feelburn guy?'

'Oh yuk.' I shuddered. Then I shook my head in bewilderment. 'And I mean, for heaven's sake, why?'

He shrugged. 'Why does anyone have an affair? For the excitement, the danger, the release it brings from their mean, mediocre little lives?'

'Yes, but Philly's life isn't mean and mediocre! She's got everything! A beautiful manor house, a loving husband, three gorgeous children, money to burn – and with *Michael* of all people. He's so pleased with himself, so smug, and God, I thought she loathed the Feelburns!'

'Just one of them. The one that was married to her lover.'

I stared. Of course. Suddenly it all made sense. It would explain all her unprovoked attacks on Alice, her snide remarks about her alternativeness, her bean bags, her brown rice. She was jealous of her being with Michael.

'And then he tried me,' I said bitterly, remembering.

'Perhaps he figured it ran in the family.'

It was said lightly but I wasn't in the mood.

'Sorry,' he said quickly, seeing my face, 'just a joke.'

I let it pass, because suddenly I remembered something Michael had said that terrible night. Something about us all being the bloody same. Was he being a little more specific than I'd imagined? Had he just got the push from Philly? Had he finally been scorned? And had he moved on to me thinking he'd try something in the same vein? Was that why he'd been so aggressive? So determined to have his way, to wreak some sort of vengeance perhaps? I was so lost in my thoughts that I didn't hear Joss whistle through his teeth. It was only when I heard him say 'Jeez' in a low whisper that I looked up. He was flipping through one of the books.

'What?'

'Well, bugger me backwards, as they say round these parts.'

I craned my neck to see. 'What is it?'

He snapped the book shut. 'Okay, well, this one is called *The Mycologist's Handbook*.' He held it up for me to see. 'And this little beauty,' he held up another, 'is entitled – *A Passion for Mushrooms*. And d'you know who they both belong to?'

'Who?'

He flipped open to the title page. 'One Philippa Jane Cavendish.'

Chapter Twenty-Seven

I stared at him. 'What are you saying, Joss?'

'Well, it's a bit unusual, isn't it? Not one, but two – no, wait on – *three* well-thumbed tomes on the humble art of mycology. I mean, how many mushroom manuals d'you have in your collection?'

'One or two actually,' I said defensively.

'Yes, but you're a cook. Your sister was an anaesthetist and is now a housewife. I think it's pretty peculiar if you must know.'

We met each other's eyes for a long moment. Finally I gave a slight smile. 'By "pretty peculiar" I take it you mean you think she poisoned my husband,' I said lightly.

'Well, is it possible?'

'Of course it isn't bloody possible!' I stormed. 'My sister Philly? She wouldn't hurt a fly! And I mean that quite literally! God, when we were little she used to provide a matchbox ambulance service for ants or spiders found stranded in our kitchen, taking them outside in case they were trampled underfoot! The whole reason for her going into medicine was because she felt she'd been "called", for heaven's sake, like some kind of latter-day Florence Nightingale. Of course it's not possible, she's a healer, Joss, not a killer!'

'I didn't mean characterwise,' he said calmly, 'I meant practicably. Could she feasibly have done it? Forget her sensibilities, Rosie. Where was she at the time of Harry's last breakfast? Where was everyone, for Chrissake?'

'Well, she was – with everyone else. In the drawing room. I think.'

'Were you there too?'

'No, I was in the hall. I remember going out there to get myself a drink while the mushrooms cooked and just sitting down on the stairs to drink it.'

'So you don't really know if anyone quietly left the drawing room, slipped into the kitchen and popped the killer fungi in the pan?'

'Oh, don't be ridiculous! You're talking about my family here, a normal, sane, middle-class family!'

'And since when has sanity or class ever precluded murder?'

'Oh, excuse me, but class would most certainly preclude my mother! What? Blood on her hands at the Conservative bring and buy? Or at the Cancer Research monthly meeting? God, she'd rather stick pins in her eyes, and sanity would certainly preclude my father – along with honesty, decency and downright integrity too, if you must know!'

'So that's your folks out of the frame then.'

'They were never in it,' I seethed.

'And Miles?'

'Oh God, Miles doesn't have strong feelings about anything or anyone. Ask him about Myra Hindley and he'll probably say she's a basically nice person. He's far too placid to do anything remotely aggressive. It's as much as he can do to open *Country Life* and slip a malt whisky down his throat. It certainly wouldn't occur to him to kill anyone.'

'Which leaves Philly.'

'Well, only by a process of elimination!' I spluttered.

'Who hated Harry.'

'Well, yes, but—'

'Loathed him in fact.'

I paused. 'Okay.'

'And who, despite her fey, winsome ways, is in actual fact an extremely forthright, trouser-wearing girl. Who takes the lead at all times – certainly in the sisterly field. Who's always protected you, could never imagine why you married Harry, loves you with a passion, loathes him with a vengeance, hates to see you being trampled underfoot like those poor little ants and desperately wants to rescue you but sees you slipping more and more into his clutches. Naturally she's delighted when she hears you're going to divorce him, she's jubilant that you're finally going to get shot of the bastard. But then Harry plays his trump card. A few days later, in front of the entire family, in his usual, bullying, inimitable style, he declares that he'll never let you go and that if you dare to take him on he'll perjure himself in court, proclaim you an unfit – nay, *abusive* mother – and take Ivo away from you for ever. To her horror Philly sees you begin to cave in. She sees you capitulate before her very eyes in a way that she would never dream of doing, so that to her utter frustration it seems that her little sister will *never* be free of this boorish, pugnacious, alcoholic bully unless . . . And it would be so easy, wouldn't it? Because as a matter of fact she knows where they grow. And she knows what they look like. She's read all the books, you see. All she has to do is slip down to the bottom of the garden early one morning, harvest her booty, bide her time and then a little while later, when the fry-up begins, slip quietly into the kitchen and pop something she'd prepared earlier into the pan.'

I gazed at him in horror. 'No,' I whispered. 'No, she wouldn't!'

'Wouldn't she? Why? Because she hasn't got the balls?'

'No, it's not that—'

'Or the brains?'

'No.'

'Or the determination? The guts? The tenacity? All those qualities, Rosie, that you so envied her as you were growing up? All those qualities that drove her to the top of the medical field, the social field, and any other field you care to mention, those qualities which you lacked and which, frankly, make her capable and you not?'

I paused and met his eye squarely. 'She wouldn't have the duplicity,' I said firmly. 'Yes, she's got all those other things, she's got them in spadefuls, but Philly's as honest as the day. She's simply not capable of deception in any shape or form.'

'Even in the form of Michael Feelburn?'

I stared.

'You wouldn't have believed it, would you, Rosie? Your beloved Philly, mother of those gorgeous children, chatelaine of one of the most beautiful houses in the Cotswolds, Lady Many-Acres, pillar of the community, school governor, tireless charity worker, your childhood idol, your big, beautiful indomitable sister – to cheat on her *husband*? To have an *affair*? And not, mind you, a falling-in-love affair, a head-over-heels can't-help-themselves-poor-bastards affair, but a sneaky, sordid, organised little Wednesday night sex romp with, of all people, that smooth-talking trouser-snaked Lothario Michael Feelburn? Is *that* in her character?'

There was a silence. I held his eye grimly, determined not to waver – but then suddenly jumped like a rabbit when the phone rang. I snatched it up.

'H-hello?' I whispered into the receiver.

'If 'e's down there with you, you can tell him from me 'e'd better get back 'ere sharpish. I can't be doing wiv any more of this upstairs downstairs malarkey from her ladyship. I'll ave 'er up for 'arassment if she's not careful!'

I passed the phone to Joss. 'It's Vera.'

'Vera, hi . . . Oh God. Oh Jesus, all right. Okay, Vera, yes, I get the message. Yes I will, take it easy . . . yes, I'm on my way.' He put the phone down wearily. Then he rubbed his face with both hands and

363

sighed. 'It seems Annabel's been calling every five minutes to speak to me. There's some lousy book deal her agent's let her down on and she wants me to throw some kind of weight behind her and sort it out.' He looked across at me. 'I'll have to go up and call her, Rosie. She's driving Vera crazy with her "just get hold of my husband for me or you're fired" routine.'

'Charming,' I muttered.

He didn't reply. I bit my lip. Was that bitchy? Yes, okay, probably, but actually I didn't care, because suddenly what I wanted, I realised with a huge surge of jealousy, was for him to sort *me* out. To drop everything and give *me* the benefit of his undivided attention, to calm *me* down, not her.

He stood up to go. I watched his tall, broad back and sat there on my upturned box, marooned in my misery. As he went to the door, he turned. His gaze settled on me again.

'Now listen to me, Rosie. You do nothing, okay? You stay here and you see no one and you *speak* to no one about this. Just quietly sort this place out and go about your business, but don't actually do anything until I get back, because although I may be otherwise engaged for some time I *will* be back, and I'm going to darn well get to the bottom of this one. Okay?'

He must have taken my dumbstruck gaze for agreement, because with those explicit instructions he went, leaving me to wonder, as I sat in the middle of my chaotic sitting room, if it was simply his six foot two of all-American maleness that made me go weak at the knees, or the fact that I was a rather pathetic female with a secret passion for dominant men. 'I'm going to darn well get to the bottom of this one, okay?' Lovely. I allowed myself a brief swoon over that. God, I'd like to have it on tape to listen to in my darkest moments, or even my brightest ones, come to that. Eat your heart out, Annabel, I thought smugly, he's going to sort me out too, see? I sniffed. I just happen to be second, that's all.

I sat there dreamily, gazing into space and hugging my knees, lost in a glorious reverie that somehow, amazingly, everything was going to be absolutely fine now, simply because he'd said it was going to be. Because he was determined to get to the bottom of it. Suddenly, though, I snapped to. I dropped my knees with a jolt. Oh God, and why was it going to be fine? Why did I have to do nothing, say nothing, sit tight? Because – because he meant to implicate my sister, that's why! I went hot. Philly! Great Scott, he must be mad. Did he really think I was going to sit around filing my nails when I knew the way his mind was going? When I knew what he intended to do?

Quickly I scooped up Ivo who was happily chewing final demands on the floor and made for the door. I poked my head out cautiously. Joss's footsteps were just crunching up to the top of the gravel drive, and then I heard the back door slam. He was in. Seizing our coats, I crept out to the car. Fumbling with the straps, I tried to immobilise Ivo in his seat, who, sensing I was in a hurry, instantly began to wriggle and be difficult.

'Biscuits,' I breathed, 'chocolate ones, at Aunt Philly's house!'

'Thmarties!' he demanded.

'Ooh, yes, lots of Smarties, darling, and lollies too!'

He caved in dramatically and I snapped him in, got in myself, and then wishing to God I didn't have to pass Joss's house every time I wanted to go out, drove guiltily up the drive with my head well down. As I did, I had a sudden vision of Philly doing exactly the same thing as she went past with Michael so I threw my head up defiantly and sped out of the gates. So what if he saw me, I was my own woman, wasn't I? I could do what I liked. I hurtled down the narrow country lanes much too fast, as if somehow, the faster I drove, the less time I'd have to think about it all. My head was spinning. Of course it wasn't true, of course his assumptions were ridiculous, he didn't know Philly, for heaven's sake. He didn't have any idea just how wide of the mark he was, but somehow – somehow I just wanted to see her. If only to remind myself of how outrageous his supposition was.

Five minutes later I turned down into her valley, swept through her stone gateposts and into her gravel courtyard. I came to a halt, turned off the engine and sat for a moment, just taking in the sheer, heart-stopping beauty of the place. The majestic old house loomed benignly over me, crawling with ancient gnarled creepers which snaked around generous, floor-to-ceiling sash windows, like lots of wide open friendly eyes with shaggy eyebrows. Snowdrops and crocuses were just sprouting from the tubs by the front door and around them a little squad of bantams pecked busily in the shrubbery. I felt better already. I took in the calm, tranquil scene a moment longer, then got out and went round to lift Ivo from his car seat. He squeaked with excitement when he saw where he was.

'Philly's!'

'Yes, my darling, did you think I'd lied to you as usual?'

'Yes!'

I grinned and kissed him hard on the forehead. 'You want to watch it, Ivo, you're getting to know your mother far too well.'

I carried him round to the back door and shouldered it open. A black cat shot out like a rocket.

'Hell-o!' I called. 'Anyone at home?'

'—and you can stop that bloody grizzling too!'

I paused on the doormat. 'Philly?'

Her flushed face shot round the playroom door into the kitchen.

'Oh! Rosie, sorry, I didn't even hear you. This ruddy child hasn't stopped caterwauling all morning, I can't even hear myself think!'

'I know the feeling,' I said, shutting the back door with my bottom and picking up a sobbing Chloe as she ran to me. I put Ivo down and hoisted her on to my hip. 'Ivo gets like that sometimes, it's as if nothing you can do is right for them.'

'Nothing I *ever* bloody do around here is right,' she declared savagely. She banged the kettle down hard on the Aga hob. 'Instant all right?'

'Er, yes, fine. I prefer it.'

'Just as well.' Philly reached up for the coffee jar, her face hot and flushed, her eyes angry. She brushed a strand of hair from her face in irritation.

'Why isn't she at school?' I asked, settling down at the kitchen table and cuddling my snivelling niece on my knee.

'She *says* she's got an earache, but it's amazing how it disappears the moment Teletubbies starts.'

'Ah well,' I said soothingly, 'these things flare up and down all the time with children, it's just like temperatures.'

'Evidently it's just mine that seems to keep on rising.' She banged the lid on the coffee jar. Then she sighed. 'Oh, I'm sorry, Rosie, ignore me. I'm in a filthy mood this morning. Everything seems to have got on top of me at the moment, that's all. The bloody decorators are still here – well, let's face it, they've taken up residence, I'm going to file for adoption soon – and they've cocked up the wallpaper in Bertie's room *yet again*. I mean, how easy is it to put up a Thomas the Tank Engine border *upside down*? *Twice!* And the builder's just cheerily informed me that there's yet more damp in the breakfast room – although I wouldn't put it past that crook to have thrown a bucket of water at the wall – which means another army of tea-swilling, foul-mouthed, cigarette-puffing builders in my home for months on end and – oh, for heaven's sake, Chloe, leave Ivo alone! He doesn't want to be your blinking little polar bear!'

I disentangled my wailing son tactfully from Chloe's affectionate grasp and hoisted him up on to my knee. 'Well, that's life in a big house really, isn't it?' I remarked.

'Yes, I know it's life, that's exactly the problem. It's the whole mind-numbing process of getting through one tedious, itch-making day only for another one to sodding well dawn on the back of it.'

I smiled. 'So you're stressed.'

'Just a bit.'

Ivo wriggled off my knee. I gazed up at my sister. 'Is that why you had an affair with Michael?'

She paused as she poured the kettle. Set it down and turned.

'Ah. So that's why you're here. I wondered.' She regarded me for a moment, then turned back and resumed her pouring. 'Oh well, I suppose it was inevitable you'd find out sooner or later. Which charming little bird whispered in your shell-like then?'

'No one. The police came to search the cottage. They brought everything down from the attic, including your things. Your clothes and everything.

She swung round. 'They searched your cottage?' she gasped. 'What the hell for?'

'Who knows?' I watched her closely. 'Looking for something, I suppose.'

'Oh, Rosie, I'm so sorry, how *ghastly* for you. Is it a mess?'

'It's not too bad. I was more shaken by how intimidating I found the whole thing, it's a bit like being strip-searched, I imagine. There's a female superintendent in charge who's distinctly charmless and intent on having my guts for garters. Anyway, after they'd gone I realised some of the junk in the boxes belonged to you. Joss was there, he told me the rest.'

'Ah. So there was a little bird.'

'Well, as you said, I'd have found out sooner or later.'

'I dare say.' She turned and began unloading the dishwasher, her back to me, ignoring me. I watched her for a moment. I could feel myself simmering up inside.

'Philly, how could you!' I blurted out.

'How could I have an affair, or how could I do it with Michael?'

'Well, both!'

She paused in her unloading and straightened up, cradling a cup. She sighed. 'Oh, I don't know. I just wanted to escape, I suppose. To get away from all this,' she waved her hand around.

'All what?' I looked around at her beautiful farmhouse kitchen with its brand new terracotta floor, its shiny red Aga, the huge circular pine table, the butcher's block – well-scrubbed of course, no BSE lurking there – the vase of white pansies set just so, the hanging copper pans, the neat bunches of dried flowers, the Bridgewater pottery sparkling on the dresser, the spriggy curtains with matching napkins stacked neatly in a wicker basket, the elaborately decoupaged jugs and watering cans sitting on the windowsill which overlooked her very own rolling acres – all a little contrived, I grant you, but God, who's being picky? I for one wouldn't turn it down for the world.

'All what?' I echoed again, incredulously.

'Well, it's all so neat, isn't it? So perfect. In fact it's so bloody perfect it makes me want to puke sometimes, Rosie, and I know that makes me sound like a spoiled bitch, but now that I've got it all, what am I supposed to do with it? Sit and admire it? Applaud my good taste? Fiddle with my dried flowers, contemplate my good fortune? They're just *things*, you see, they don't *do* anything.'

'Well, how about bringing your children up amongst these Things?' I said, a trifle piously perhaps but with mounting irritation.

She gave a hollow laugh. 'Oh yes, childcare. It's all so wonderfully glorious, isn't it? Or so Penelope Leach and Miriam Stoppard would have us believe as they get on with their own sparkling careers, and so *boring* too, and don't you dare tell me it isn't, Rosie, because you know it is. There's nothing remotely stimulating about potty training, or carrot blending, or reading *Elmer the Elephant* for the umpteenth time, or having "Does the Queen poo, discuss" conversations all day long.'

'No, okay, it's not stimulating, but it's, well, it's—'

'Don't you dare say fulfilling,' she pounced. 'Or satisfying. Or any of those other rosy-glow feel-good words we read in the women's pages of the *Telegraph* as we scrape the Weetabix off the wall or get the Playdoh out of our pubes or share a cup of tea with dolly, because none of those words actually touch on the mind-numbing monotony of it all, do they?'

'Well, go back to work!' I snapped crossly. 'Get a nanny, for God's sake, swallow your pride!'

'I *can't*, Rosie, and believe me it's got nothing to do with pride. It's got nothing to do with the fact that I gave up work in a blaze of mother-to-be, luminous glory, pledging myself wholeheartedly to breast-feeding for a minimum of eighteen months and taking the high moral ground with all those heartless souls who pursued their own ends and ran guiltily out in their Armani suits the moment the nanny arrived. It's got nothing to do with that, the point is I physically *can't* go back now.'

'Why not?'

'Well, for one thing I've left it too late. I've been out in the wilderness for six years now and I don't care how terrific everyone said I was then, no one wants to know now, but it's not just that either, Rosie. The bottom line is I'm too highly qualified. I'm an anaesthetist, goddammit, not a secretary, or even a GP or a solicitor. I can't just slip back into an office or a general practice. I work in an operating theatre in a hospital, and if I went back to it I'd have to work flat out, nights too, and not necessarily even in Gloucestershire. I can't just pick up the phone to Cheltenham General and say, oh hi, look, I live down the road and I've got a window of opportunity somewhere between the school run and ballet and tap so how about I nip down and give someone a good gassing? Positions like that are fought over, people kill for them, and yes, if I *really* wanted it badly enough I might just get a job again, but miles away, somewhere like Skegness General if I was lucky, and how would I square that with being a Gloucestershire farmer's wife and mother of three children?' She stared out of the window at the sheep grazing beyond the post and rail fence in the field.

'It's all a big con, you know,' she said quietly. 'And we're all foolish and naive enough to believe it. At eighteen, bright-eyed and armed with a stash of A levels and bags of optimism, we think, yeah, right, I can do that. I can be a surgeon or a barrister or a nuclear physicist if I want, and so we can. And we do. Until suddenly, just when it's all going swimmingly and we're doing terrifically well, we get fat. And we have a baby, and then something strange clicks in and makes us want to look after the little wretch but we hastily ignore that and say, no, no, I'm buggered if something as primeval as maternal hormones is going to come between me and being a consultant, or a QC, or whatever, and so we go on. We go on pretending we're still the same thrusting, ambitious people we were a year or so ago, but we're not. We've got this thing, you see, this baby, which the guys in the trousers with the facial hair haven't. And make no mistake about it, Rosie, from then on in we're doing it with one arm tied firmly behind our backs. Six-month post in Paris? Sorry, there's little Johnny to think of. Consecutive late-night meetings? Sorry, but I always get back in time for the bath. I *insist* on getting back for bathtime. Call them small, those differences, but they're there.' She paused and picked a sprout out of the sink. Threw it in the bin behind her. Then she sighed.

'So either we accept those differences and go at it half-cocked, which didn't appeal to me, or we abandon the whole thing in mid-stream, like I did. All that work, all those exams, all that shinning up the greasy pole but never actually making it to the top, all the effort with none of the glory, and for what? To say that we've done it? To say that we could have got there? To prove a point, satisfy our egos? What a waste!'

'Okay,' I said quietly, 'so what's the answer?'

'I don't think there is one. I just think we should be more prepared for reality, that's all. I shall certainly prepare my girls, encourage them to be secretaries or beauticians.'

'Philly! You don't mean that!'

She swung to face me. 'Why not? Sammy, who waxes my legs periodically, has two children and works four mornings a week. Well, that's more than I do, isn't it? She talks to people, gets out of the house and earns money. That's certainly more than I do in this godforsaken rural idyll! Oh yes, if Anna and Chloe come running home from school telling me they want to be bishops or airline pilots, I shall say, fine, darlings, highly commendable, but do you want to have children? Because if you do, how are you going to square it with flying your 747 to Istanbul five times a week, or administering to your flock? No, no, my chickens, put away those university applications and do a nice little hairdressing course instead, because that way you really *can* have it all!'

'You're bitter.'

She smiled. 'Undoubtedly. But not twisted. I'm bitter because I'm bored witless, Rosie, and that's because I'm clever. I was good at what I did and I'm not doing it now and other people less able than me are. But I'm not twisted because I have no grudges to bear, no axes to grind. I made the choices, the decisions, no one else did. It's my fault they happened to be the wrong ones. Wrong science A levels, wrong degree course, wrong career, wrong . . .' She paused.

'Husband?'

She sighed. 'Oh, I don't know. Yes. No. Who knows? Let's face it, if it hadn't been Miles, it would have been someone like him, wouldn't it? I was programmed from birth to marry a rich, good-looking personable chap like Miles and you know me, I always run true to type.'

'And what's wrong with that?' I squeaked, thinking, God, some people would give their eye teeth to run according to that sort of type, including me!

'Nothing,' she said patiently. 'There's nothing wrong with Miles, he's lovely. Solid, dependable, amiable, jocular Miles. It's *me* that's wrong. I just feel so constricted, so – frustrated, and sometimes I just want out.'

'But with Michael? Why *Michael*, for heaven's sake?'

She shrugged. 'He's like-minded. He feels it too, the stultifying niceness of it all. The bide-a-wee home-sweet-hominess of going back to stripped pine doors and spaghetti bolognese and two point four children.'

'But he's such a—'

'Prat?'

'Yes!'

'True, but he's terrific between the sheets.'

'Oh!' I blinked.

She smiled. 'Sorry. I've offended your middle-class sensibilities, haven't I? Nice girls like us aren't supposed to think like that, are we? And anyway, he's probably not all that terrific at all, not with Alice. It's just the naughty, clandestine nature of an affair that brings out the beast in one.' She raised her chin at me defiantly. 'Brought out the beast in me too, if you must know.'

'Oh. Er, good.' I wasn't sure I must know that at all.

She turned, threw back her head and scratched it energetically, gazing out of the window. Her eyes, I noticed, looked very bright. Ablaze. I cleared my throat.

'And was Michael the only one that you . . . you know . . .'

'Had an affair with?'

'Yes.'

'No.'

I gasped. 'Oh Philly!'

'Oh Philly!' she mimicked. She turned and smiled. 'It's all right, I wasn't that promiscuous, I don't need to be carted off to the AIDS clinic or anything, but there was one other, before Michael. But he was much too young, too lovestruck, and he got far too close. I didn't want that. He demanded too much of me. Logistically he had to go too because it was crazy, he lived miles away and I was forever on the motorway driving two hours to London for a quick ten-minute bonk with a toy boy. No, Michael was perfect. He was on the spot but not all the time, he didn't want me to leave Miles like the other one did, and I don't think he even really fell in love with me. He was pretty upset when I finished it of course, but it had gone on too long. It was getting boring. No,' she mused, 'what Michael liked was the sex.'

'Which is what you liked too.'

She smiled. 'Not really. I mean it was okay, but what *I* liked – loved, actually – was the danger. The total recklessness of it all. The thrill that one false move and it could all end in tears. One slip and all of this,' she swung her arm round the room, 'could be gone. It could all go up in smoke. Home, husband, children even – it was like playing Russian roulette with my life. I felt . . . vital. Alive. It wasn't unlike being back in the operating theatre actually, with your finger on the button, your hand in total control, knowing that one false move and you could have a corpse on the table. Either that or a vegetable.'

I stared at her. Christ, she was cool. I shuddered. 'God, I'd hate that.'

She swung round and almost – almost – smirked. 'Of course you would. But then you've always lacked that killer instinct, haven't you?'

I gazed at her. 'Yes, I . . . suppose I have.'

'I've always envied you that actually. Your placidness, your anything for a quiet life approach. You'd rather live with a man like Harry, a man you hated, than rock the boat, wouldn't you?'

As I stared at her, I felt myself begin to tremble.

She shook her head. 'I couldn't do that. At least I've never hated Miles. We get on pretty well, it's just that it's not wham-bam-capow any more.'

I cleared my throat, which seemed inexplicably dry. 'Philly,' I faltered, 'about Harry. Could you ever – I mean, did you ever—'

'Shit!' She lunged, but too late, the cup slipped off the table. 'Oh, for God's sake, Chloe, that's the second glass of Ribena you've had over this morning!' She seized a cloth and began frantically mopping the floor. 'You stupid child, you just don't look, do you! Too busy getting in everyone's way!'

'Here, I'll do it.' I cuddled a distraught and sobbing Chloe with one arm and grabbed another cloth from the Aga.

'No! That's pure Irish linen, for heaven's sake, not a floorcloth!'

'Sorry!' I dropped it.

At this point Ivo began to wail in sympathy with Chloe and in the middle of all the mayhem, the telephone rang.

'God Almighty, give me strength,' Philly hissed. 'I'll take that in the hall, I won't hear myself speak in here.' She marched off, slamming a soggy tea towel on the floor before she went.

Chloe whimpered and hung round my neck and Ivo attached himself firmly to my bended knees. With both of them clinging on like limpets, I mopped up. I felt numb, shocked, and as I mopped, I had a terrible sense of realisation that I didn't want to have at all but that wouldn't go away.

'Shh, Chloe, shush, it's all right. Here, let's find the biscuits.'

I settled them down at the table again with more juice and biscuits, and gradually the crying subsided. As they sniffed into their mugs, I sat opposite them, watching the door, waiting dumbly for Philly to come back, unable even to look a Jaffa Cake in the face. She did come back, a few minutes later, but as pale as anything, as if she'd seen a ghost. She stood still in the doorway, staring somewhere above my head.

'What?' I said in alarm. 'Philly, what's happened?'

'That was Mum.'

'And? What?' My heart lurched. I felt afraid.

'It's Dad.'

'Oh God!' My hand flew to my mouth.

'He's about to drive down to the police station. Hand himself in.'

I stared at her. Couldn't speak. Slowly her eyes came down and met mine. 'It was Dad, Rosie. He's just admitted it. He killed Harry.'

Chapter Twenty-Eight

I stared at her. 'No. No, that can't be true! Dad wouldn't – he can't have done!'

'Of course he can't have done it,' she said sharply. 'You and I both know that.'

Our eyes locked like magnets.

'He's covering up,' I breathed. 'Protecting . . .' I couldn't say it.

'Exactly.' Philly paced round the kitchen, then paused at the window, staring out, drumming her fingers on the work surface, her back to me.

'Has he actually gone to the police?'

'Not yet. He can't, Mum's got him locked in the potting shed.'

'Oh!' I smiled in spite of myself.

'She says she's not letting him out until he stops all this silly nonsense and she's been pushing little notes and ham sandwiches under the door, pleading with him. But you know Dad when his mind's made up.'

'Oh God, poor Daddy, but you'll talk to him, Phil? You'll talk him out of it?' I said anxiously.

'I'll try. But if I can't . . .' she swung round. 'What will you do?'

'Me?'

'Oh, come on, Rosie, you know what Dad's up to! He's convinced his angina will see him off in a year or two anyway, so he's making the ultimate sacrifice!'

'Yes, but – for you!'

She stared. 'What did you say?'

'For you,' I whispered.

She squinted incredulously at me. 'What the hell d'you mean?'

I gulped. 'I found your books, Phil.'

'What books?'

'Your mushroom books,' I said, hating myself. 'Three of them, well-thumbed and well-used, with your name in them. They were with all the rest of your stuff in the boxes from the attic.'

She gazed at me for a long moment, then her eyes slithered away. Philly's eyes never did that. She shook her head. 'I don't know what you mean,' she said softly.

'Philly,' I was trembling now, 'I *found* them.' She was silent. I licked my lips. 'Look,' I said beseechingly, 'you can talk to me, you can trust me, I know you did it for me and we can work this out together. I'll help you, I promise, but you've got to trust me, talk to me!'

'I don't know anything about any books,' she said. Then she walked to the dresser and calmly lifted her car keys off a hook. She tossed them in the air and as she caught them she turned and gave me a strange smile. 'I can't quite believe you're doing this, Rosie.'

'Doing what?' I shrieked. 'I'm not doing anything! I just found them, that's all. Now if you just happen to be a closet mycologist but thought you'd better not mention it in case anyone thought it a hideously suspicious coincidence in the light of your brother-in-law's demise, well fine, let's chuck them all away, we'll burn them together, but tell me, Phil! Let me in, please!'

'I haven't the faintest idea what you're talking about, but right now I'm more worried about Dad. And I've got to go to Mummy. She's in a terrible state, weeping hysterically, understandably.'

'I'll come too,' I whispered, getting up.

'I hardly think that's a good idea, do you?' Her eyes were like flints. 'Mummy's bound to think you're the reason Dad's doing this and she won't be far wrong either. She may not be totally overjoyed to see you.' She walked to the door.

I was shaking now, couldn't believe this was happening. Philly, my darling sister whom I'd looked up to all my life, identified with, believed myself to be so like only not quite so magnificent, whose opinion I'd waited for on everything before making up my own mind accordingly. My deepest held belief had always been that our differences were just superficial – looks, intelligence, confidence – but that beneath all that, we were the same. That we were just like each other. But that wasn't so, I could see that now. I felt, with a startling, breathtaking realisation, almost as if I didn't know her at all. It was unbearable.

When she got to the door she paused. Turned. 'Look,' she said in a low voice. 'I know this isn't you talking, Rosie. I know you're – upset. You're frightened and confused and I don't blame you, I can understand that, and I can forgive you too because, well, you're not really in your right mind, are you?' Her eyes met mine momentarily, then darted away as she turned for her small daughter. 'Come on,

375

Chloe.' Taking her by the hand, she went, closing the door softly behind her.

I sat there, shivering, staring after her. I felt a sudden surge of bile in my throat. The revulsion of what we'd just said to each other, which could now never be unsaid, made me feel physically sick. It would always be there. Those hostile, accusing words. I felt hot and then went very cold. I put my fingers to my eyelids. Tears. I swallowed hard. She'd forgive me, she'd said. *She'd* forgive *me*. For what? I shook my head, then thumped it hard with the palm of my hand in frustration. Oh, come on, think this through, Rosie, stop feeling sorry for yourself and just get some grey cells working up there! Oh God, why was it that I couldn't think at all at the moment? I just seemed to be drifting faster and faster through a horrific sequence of events as they carried me further and further on, until I'd surely just be swept over the rapids at the end.

I flopped back in my chair. So why not bail out now? I thought suddenly. Why not just give in, hop off the roundabout, give a full confession to the police and satisfy everyone? Go directly to Jail, do not pass Go, do not collect £200. It would certainly satisfy my sister who clearly thought I'd done it, and my father who, God bless him, was intent on playing the sacrificial lamb, so sure was *he* that I'd done it, and my mother who, persuaded by those around her, must now surely think I'd done it. So why not just hold up my hands? Why not present myself at Cirencester police station saying, 'Yep, it's a fair cop, guv, I did hate the bastard and everyone knew I did and that's why I finally did for him.' Was that what everyone wanted? Was that what was required of me?

I gazed out of the window. It would certainly put an end to all this ghastly suspicion and speculation within the family, stop us tearing at each other's throats, and instead everyone could breathe a monumental sigh of relief and say, well, *quite*. And who can *blame* the poor girl? He was a perfect *brute*! I might even get off, I thought in surprise. There was always that possibility. Yes, I might get off scot-free on the grounds of diminished responsibility or – yes, I know, I could say I had PMT or something. It was amazing how many women were killing their husbands these days and running that defence. Just a twinge of a curse pain and, oops, good heavens, the next thing I knew the knife was in his chest, Your Honour, or, good gracious, did I really tamper with his brakes? No, Your Honour, no, I don't remember doing it, must have crept out to the garage in the middle of the night when the cramps were pretty bad. Of course, I reasoned, it wasn't so easy for a father-in-law to explain away something like that, or even a sister-in-law come to that, but for me, the wife, with a small son in tow and no previous form and *heaps* of provocation, well, it could be a breeze. Yes, okay I'd probably go to prison, but not for long, and not a ghastly Holloway sort of place, more of an open prison, more of a university campus type thing, with lots of libraries and tennis courts – a bit of a holiday camp really. And I could use the time wisely, take a geography degree, pitch and put. Who knows, it could be the making of me.

And meanwhile, of course, on the other side of the wire, after the initial shock horror of 'Oh my God, how could she have done it!' – yes, after all that, and seeing as I was a nice girl from a nice middle-class family, the *Daily Mail* would probably take up my story and do a feature on me. Out would come the years of psychological torment, the suffering at the hands of an alcoholic, brutish husband, and there'd be pictures of me as a sweet young thing at Pony Club camp, or in a swimming costume on a Cornish beach, and pictures of Ivo too, looking terribly forlorn and sad and holding a framed photograph of his mummy in prison, and then there'd be an absolute *tidal* wave of sympathy for me.

Yes, and then Mummy could appear at press conferences, weeping copiously, supported by Daddy looking grey and drawn, and then Philly would start campaigning tirelessly for my release. She'd storm Parliament, go on the ten o'clock news, get up petitions, become a sort of Jill Morrell figure. She'd like that, it would give her a sense of purpose. Make her feel 'alive' or whatever it was she wanted to feel. Vital, that was it. And then when I was released – which, believe me, wouldn't take long with Philly at the helm – we could all stand together on the steps of the Royal Courts of Justice as the triumphant Cavendish family, arms raised in a victory salute. 'Freedom for the Gloucestershire House-wife!' the tabloids would proclaim, and there'd be photos of me punching the air and grinning wildly, and then we could all go home and have a nice cup of tea and it would all blow over and within, ooh, a couple of weeks probably, Mummy would be out foraging around for a new husband for me.

Off she'd go, nose to the ground, like a ferret after a rabbit, a bargain hunter at a car boot sale, round and round the Gloucester-shire circuit, a word here, a dinner party thrown casually there, a divorced accountant here – right next to me, in fact, right beside me at the dinner table. He'd be grey-suited, brown-shoed, a bit bald, a bit paunchy but terribly respectable, and my heart would sink, but then again, crikey, beggars can't be choosers and after all I did have 'form'. So I'd smile and I'd grit my teeth and later on I'd think of England, and then before you could blink I'd be hustled down that aisle again with Mummy and Philly in peach and lilac respectively, beaming at each other with relief over the orange blossom. Then in nine months' time I'd doubtless be in an interesting condition again, and that, as they say, would be that. Happy ever after for all concerned, except – *except* . . . I stared down at the stripped pine table . . . that it wasn't going to be like that. Because I didn't do it. I didn't . . . bloody . . . do it. My hand closed round my car keys on the table, and as they did, my resolve hardened like Superglue. No, I didn't do it, and since that was the only, single, solitary thing I *was* sure about at the moment, I wasn't going to swing for it. Sorry, everyone, but no. You can find some other scapegoat.

I stood up, knocking my chair over backwards in my determination. Without bothering to pick it up, I scooped up Ivo, marched out of Philly's terribly tasteful kitchen, banged her terribly tasteful Gothic door behind me, and scattering a few startled bantams in my wake marched smartly out to my filthy old Volvo.

I beetled back down those narrow lanes thinking dire and bitter thoughts. Of course, I reasoned grimly, it was only natural, given my permanent status of doormat in this family, that I should be expected to lie down completely one day and let everyone trample all over me. In fact, the more I thought about it, the more it occurred to me that prison, with a roof over my head and three meals a day, was beginning to look a bit aspirational. Surely a Siberian labour camp was more the ticket for me? A nice spot of starvation in a freezing cold wasteland, like that Solzhenitsyn book about poor old Ivan Denisovich who was so cold at night he had to trap his farts under his blanket to keep warm. Shouldn't that be my fate? Wasn't that more my natural milieu? I ground my teeth manically. Was it heck as like, as my father would say, they could all go to hell! Steam pouring from all orifices now, I screeched to a halt in front of the cottage and marched up to the door. On it was pinned a note. I snatched it off and read it.

'I said *don't* do anything, *don't* talk to anyone, and *don't* go anywhere. Why can't you bloody well listen? Ring me the moment you get back. Joss.'

Oh, *did* you say that? I seethed. Yes, well, I'm sorry, but while you were chatting to your dear wife across the Channel about some poxy book deal, excuse me if I did just toddle off to try to clear my name, only I've got this little matter of a murder charge hanging over my head! I screwed the note up, barged through the front door and flung the ball of paper at the opposite wall screeching 'ARRGGGHHHH!' as I did so. Ivo was most impressed.

'Mummy cross,' he said in awe.

'Yes, well, it's either that or I go to pieces entirely, darling, so best to keep up the aggression, eh?'

'Yes,' he agreed solemnly. 'More biscuits?'

'Oh my gosh, will you ever give up! No, Ivo, I'll make you a nice cheese sandwich instead, we'll try a spot of nutrition for a change, otherwise you'll end up with rickets and then they really will take you away from me. They'll have you listed as a malnourished child and the Social Services will come down on me like a ton of bricks.'

I flopped on to the sofa and stared into space. I didn't want to ring Joss. Not just yet, not after the conversation I'd just had with Philly. I didn't want to add more grist to his mill. Didn't want to admit to him that even I was suspicious of her now. I bit my thumbnail and gazed miserably round the room. It was still, of course, in the same chaotic state my friends in blue had left it, and at some point I supposed I ought to get round to clearing it up. It was just that I didn't really feel like doing anything right now. All I actually felt like doing was lying in a cool, white bed in a Swiss clinic in the mountains somewhere, sipping beef tea. I sighed. On the doormat across the room the morning's post lay abandoned and unopened. In fact yesterday's was probably still there too, I was sure I hadn't got round to opening that either. I got wearily to my feet and picked it up before it got lost in the general confusion. I stood on the mat, flipping through it. There was nothing much there. A couple of clothes catalogues, an envelope informing me I might have won a super-duper star prize if I could just be bothered to open the envelope. I couldn't. Then there were one or two bills and then a more interesting-looking pale blue Basildon Bond affair. It was addressed to me in a neat, round hand. I opened it and smoothed out the paper.

'If you want to know more about Tim McWerther, meet me at your house in Meryton Road at 2.00 p.m. on Tuesday.'

It wasn't signed. I stared, and then read it again. For a moment I couldn't think who the dickens Tim McWerther was, then suddenly I could. I dropped the note on the mat like a hot coal and jumped back in alarm. God Almighty, an anonymous note! Whatever next? This was like wandering into a Robert De Niro film – any minute now I'd open the door and find a dead dog on my doorstep, or a horse's head in my bed! I gazed at the sheet of paper lying there on the mat. Oh no, I didn't like the sound of this at all. What, meet some stranger in an empty house and end up with a silk scarf round my neck or something? No thank you.

After a bit, though, curiosity got the better of me and I inched forward, peering down. Who was it from? I wondered. Whoever it was was clearly highly suspect, because why on earth hadn't they signed it? Very gingerly I reached down and picked it up again. I turned it over. There was something written on the other side. 'Come alone.'

'Bloody hell!' I dropped it again smartly and nearly leapt up on the sofa. God, you must be joking!

I gazed at it in horror, then paced around the room a bit, my heart hammering. Right, this is simple, I thought. You know what to do now, don't you, Rosie? You know what any sane, sensible, intelligent person would do? Exactly. You ring the police. You tell them about this strange missive, you give them all the information, all the details, and you get them on your side for a change. Let them see that you're trying to help. After all, they've got Tim McWerther in custody, haven't they? That's what the superintendent had hinted anyway, so they must be itching to find out more about him. Well, tip them off, do them a favour, and then let *them* go and meet the mystery guest. Yes. Absolutely. Without wasting another moment, I picked up the phone and rang Superintendent Hennessey in Oxfordshire. She wasn't there, she was in London apparently, but the desk sergeant, on hearing who I was, instantly gave me her mobile number. VIP treatment, you see, I thought darkly. I rang it and she answered immediately.

'Ah, Mrs Meadows, I've been looking forward to having a little chat with you.'

'Oh, really?' My heart began to thump again.

'Yes, I'm in London at the moment, just left your house.'

'Ah. Oh yes, of course.' I'd forgotten she'd gone off to search that. 'And?' I said warily. 'Found anything interesting?'

'Yes, very. May I share it with you?'

'Do I have any choice?'

'Not really, no. We found a note in your bedroom. Under your pillow, actually. It reads as follows.' She cleared her throat. ' "I won't go quietly, my love. Don't imagine I will. We're in too deep for that. Come back to me. Love and bunny hops, Tim." '

There was a pause. I boggled into the receiver.

'Any views on that?' came her voice.

'Could you repeat that please?' I whispered.

'Certainly.' She did, but this time with a little more feeling. Then she added, 'We've checked the handwriting, by the way. It's genuine.'

Silence.

'Mrs Meadows?'

'Yes?'

'You're still there?'

'Yes.'

'Have you anything to say?'

'Nothing at all.'

'Nothing at all, eh?'

This woman had a fine line in sarcasm which consisted of repetition followed by question mark. Simple but surprisingly effective. I took a deep breath.

'Nothing at all, except to say that it's quite clearly been planted there. Like I told you before, I know Mr McWerther very vaguely. I've met him once or twice. He's certainly never been my lover. For some reason he's trying to imply that he was.'

'I'd like to agree with you, Mrs Meadows, but my problem is that we've had him firmly under lock and key these past few weeks. It would be nigh on impossible for him to get that note into your house.'

'Someone else then.'

'Ah, I see, someone else. Now why on earth d'you think anyone would want to do that?'

'I don't know.'

'You don't know, eh?'

There she went again, with the withering irony. It was beginning to get on my nerves.

'Well, I suggest you come up with some ideas pretty soon because frankly it's not looking good, is it? You deny all knowledge, carnal or otherwise, of this boy and then lo and behold we go and find notes of an intimate nature in your bedroom. What am I to think?'

'Well, quite, and I have to agree that if I were you I'd find it hard to resist coming to some dodgy conclusions. It's more than a little circumstantial, isn't it, so why not charge me? Why not arrest me? Why all this shilly-shallying around? Why don't *you* have the courage of your convictions, Superintendent Hennessey, or is the truth that actually you're far from convinced yourself?'

There was a long pause. I quietly marvelled at myself during it. Interesting technique, Rosie. Calling the bluff of the officer in charge of your very own murder inquiry, very bullish, very bullish indeed. If a little foolhardy perhaps.

I was somewhat relieved to hear her finally murmur, 'All in good time, Mrs Meadows. All in good time. Now, you rang.'

'Sorry?'

'You rang me.'

'Ah yes.' I paused. 'It was . . . nothing actually. I just wondered how you were . . . getting along,' I finished lamely.

She snorted derisively. 'Oh, we're getting along just fine. I'll be seeing you soon, Mrs Meadows.' There was a click, and our conversation, for the moment anyway, appeared to be at an end.

Slowly I replaced the receiver. Then I stared down at the note on my lap. Why hadn't I told her about it? Was it simply for fear that she might turn up at the house, sirens blazing, car doors slamming, in which case our mystery guest would do a runner and she'd write the whole thing off as an elaborate hoax on my part and accuse me of penning the letter myself? Or was it more? I wondered thoughtfully, getting up and walking to the window. It occurred to me that if someone was planting fictitious notes in my bedroom, might they not also be sending me anonymous letters? And hoping I'd tell the police about it? Might it not be one and the same person, and might they not be hoping that I would indeed bring the police along, and thereby lure me into an even bigger trap? Stitch me up quite comprehensively? Yes, I thought, heart hammering, that was it. Whoever it was would be assuming I wouldn't have the guts to come alone and would reach for the phone, as I'd just done. Drag along old Steel Knickers. I snatched up the note. Two o'clock, it said, on Tuesday. That was today. I looked at the postmark on the envelope. Two days ago. Someone must have put some blind faith in the vagaries of the postal system and hoped it would arrive, but arrive it had and right now – I glanced at my watch – it was ten to twelve. If I hurried, I could just about make it. I wavered for a split second, then, bugger it! I'd had enough of this. If I ended up with a knife in my back for my pains then so be it, but I was damn well going to London and I was going to find out once and for all what was going on.

I raced around the cottage grabbing coat, money, keys, handbag and at the last minute dashed upstairs and found – a hatpin. One of the things my mother had always impressed upon Philly and me was the importance of carrying a hatpin when travelling on public transport or anywhere where undesirables – anyone in a slightly grubby mac, in my mother's book – might loiter. It was apparently absolutely essential. Quite where one was supposed to stick it, should the occasion arise, I've no idea, but I was in no doubt that today was definitely a hatpin day.

I ran downstairs again, picked up Ivo and put the poor bewildered child back in the car. Then I drove very, very cautiously up the back drive and stopped just short of Farlings. I crept up to the kitchen with my son in my arms and tapped on the window, at the same time glancing nervously up to the bedrooms. I couldn't see him, but that didn't mean he wasn't glaring out of a turret somewhere.

I tapped again. 'Martha!' I hissed. 'Thank God you're back.'

She sprang round from the stove. 'Oh, there you are,' she said, opening the window. 'He's been looking everywhere for you.'

'Where is he now?'

'Upstairs,' she jerked her head, 'yellin' obscenities across the ocean again.'

'Martha, I have to go to west London. Are you staying for a while? Would you have Ivo for me?'

She sighed. 'Course I will, Rosie. Blimey, you've done enough for me.' She held out her arms and I passed him through to her.

'And listen, do me a favour, don't tell Joss where I'm going, okay?'

'Okay,' she said doubtfully. 'You all right then? Not in any more trouble? Not doin' private espionage or anything?'

'Course not, and I'll be back this evening, I promise.' I tiptoed away.

'Well, you be careful,' she called after me.

'I will!' I gave her a cheery backward wave as I hopped back in the car, then I sped away down the drive hoping to goodness Joss's beady eyes weren't trained on me from an upstairs window. I had absolutely no doubt that he would not approve of this little excursion, but then, it wasn't his bacon we were saving here, was it? It was mine, and I was damned if it was going to be cured, smoked, chopped up into tiny cubes and flambéed without me doing a single thing about it.

I roared up the M4 much too fast, the steering wheel shaking violently, the whole car throbbing alarmingly. My poor old Volvo was already well past its prime, poor thing, and recently too many bumpy country lanes had begun to take their toll. It was hissing ominously now and I could tell it was voicing strong objections to me re-enacting *Miami Vice* on the motorway and playing fast and loose with its rusty old undercarriage. Just don't break down, I begged under my breath. I don't mind if bits fly off you, but just don't break down. I'll give you a service soon, I promise.

Happily it held together and eventually I was ploughing my way through the heavy London traffic. I stopped, started, and crawled my way through Fulham, out to the more leafy environs of Wandsworth, and then instinctively swung the car this way and that down to Meryton Road, a route I could almost do in my sleep. Slowly I crawled up my old road and came to a halt outside number 63. I turned the engine off and looked at my watch. Ten to two. I'd made good time and by rights I should have ten minutes alone in the house before my visitor arrived.

I got out and looked up. My house. Where I'd started my disastrous married life really rather hopefully, if not totally joyfully. The street itself was quiet, empty, as it always was mid-week and in the middle of the day. I opened the little iron gate with its familiar rattle and walked up the path. The tiny front garden was covered with rotten leaves and an old Twix wrapper had blown in and impaled itself on a bare rose bush. It waved mournfully to me in the breeze. I snatched it up, feeling guilty that it was all so neglected now when once I'd laboriously planted the tiny bed, sown the grass, tended our few square feet so religiously and done my wifely duty. I turned the key in the front door. Inside was similarly reproachful. When I'd finally managed to push the front door open against the junk mail that had accumulated behind it, that awful musty, dank smell that uncared for houses have shot up my nostrils. I wanted to rush around opening windows and dusting every piece of furniture in sight, but I limited myself to hastening down the passage to the kitchen and throwing open the back door, letting in a rush of cold, damp, January air.

As I turned and walked back through the house, it suddenly struck me that perhaps I wasn't alone. I stood very still and listened, my heart pounding. Perhaps my friend was already here, had jemmied a lock, forced an upstairs window, and was even now waiting for me, crouched behind an armchair, wedged behind a door, poised to jump out.

My heart hammering now and my hand clenched firmly round the hatpin in my pocket, I crept cautiously from room to room, going upstairs, peering in cupboards, looking under beds like I did when Ivo had had a nightmare, only this time I didn't feel brave enough to shout, 'Come out, Mr Grizzly Bear, wherever you are! You've got Mummy to contend with now!'

When I'd peered and prodded extensively, and finally satisfied myself that I was indeed alone, I went downstairs. I bit my thumbnail nervously and looked around. It struck me that considering this place had recently been searched by the police, there really wasn't a cushion out of place. It made me realise, with a surge of anger, that the devastation at the cottage really had just been for show. Just another way of putting the frighteners on me. The bastards.

I paused in the hall and with my finger wiped the dust from the photograph that stood on the hall table. It was of Ivo's christening. I picked it up and gazed for a moment at the supposedly happy family group. My mother was at the front looking pleased and proud in eye-searing yellow, and I was next to her looking pink and rather fat, but happy with Ivo in my arms. Daddy was behind, pale as usual, but with a definite smile, and next to him Philly, looking glamorous and chic in cream linen with a navy hat. Beside her was Miles, looking not at the camera but adoringly at Philly, and then Tom, bronzed and beautiful in a pale blue Brooks Brothers shirt, fresh off the flight from LA. Next to him was Alice, the godmother, looking fey but stunning in antique lace with a tapestry jacket, and Michael beside her, very aware of the camera, very slick, very smooth, very man at C&A. Then came Boffy, the godfather, pinstriped and beaming, and Charlotte beside him in a claret suit, and then next to her Uncle Bertram, leering roguishly into the camera. Back along the front row again, and next to me, of course, was Harry. He was fairly busting out of a ten-year-old suit, which must have been an optimistic purchase at the time but which he'd clearly had to be poured into for this occasion. He was florid-faced, probably the worse for a couple of snifters, but he was beaming broadly at Ivo, and obviously as pleased as Punch.

I stared at the photo. It brought a lump to my throat. Because when all was said and done, and whatever else had happened since, this was undoubtedly a happy group on a happy day. It had certainly, I thought with some surprise, trying hard to be fair and not to over-sentimentalise – yes, it had certainly been one of the happiest days of my life, anyway. My darling son's christening day.

The doorbell rang violently. I jumped out of my skin, and as I did, the picture slipped from my grasp, clattered to the stone floor and the glass smashed into a million pieces. For a moment I froze. Then quickly I ran, scuttling into the drawing room, darting behind the curtain at the bay window. I crept along the wall behind it and peered out. My heart was hammering. God, and I'd meant to be so *ready*, so *prepared*, so much in a position of advantage, like at an upstairs window perhaps, ready to see whoever it was coming down the street and up the garden path, and now all I could see – I craned my neck – was a red Mercedes parked in the road behind mine. I didn't recognise it. Inching round the curtain a fraction more I saw on the step the extreme side view of someone. Whoever it was was wearing a long coat, and a brown felt hat, and standing so deliberately close to the front door that I couldn't make out any more.

I cringed back into the curtain, panic rising. My throat was dry and I felt very sick. What the hell was I doing here, for God's sake?

Oh Rosie, you fool, why did you come? For a moment it occurred to me to make a run for it. To dash down the passage and go out through the open back door, but then, steeling myself, I crept back through the sitting room and down the hall. Stealthily I tiptoed up to the front door. Wishing to goodness I'd had the nous to invest in one of those little spy holes that Harry had always banged on about, I slowly raised my hand for the knob. As it closed on it, the bell rang again. Urgently, right in my ear.

'Aargh!' I squealed inadvertently, then 'I'm coming!' I bleated in a pathetic little squeak.

I waited. Nothing. Oh God, how I wished some friendly voice would respond, 'Jolly good! No rush, only the milkman here with your extra pinta!' But no. And so my hand went back up again, and this time I turned the knob, opened the door and peered round it. There on the step, in a long black coat, and with an old felt hat pulled down over her eyes, stood Charlotte.

Chapter Twenty-Nine

'Charlotte!' I opened the door wider.

'Hello, Rosie.'

'Good grief!' I stared at her like a moron, mouth hanging open.

'May I come in?' she ventured eventually.

'What? Oh! God, yes, of course – sorry, yes, come in! How lovely to see you!'

I stood aside delightedly. Charlotte! Good heavens, what on earth was she doing mixed up in all this, but crikey, what a blessed relief she was! I mean, she was hardly going to de-bowel me with a Stanley knife or knee-cap me with a Kalashnikov, now was she? As she stepped inside she proffered her cheek. So eager was I to peck it, I tripped and fell against her, damn nearly snogging her.

'Steady,' she muttered nervously, backing away.

'Sorry!' I gasped. 'Tripped over the doormat. Come in, come in! Sorry about the mess, by the way,' I added as she stepped gingerly over the broken glass. 'Had a bit of an accident. Here, through here.' I ushered her into the sitting room, all gushing hospitality now that I knew it wasn't the mad axeman.

She stepped inside and stood uncertainly in the middle of the room, looking about her, hands in pockets. One hand shot up to fiddle with her silk scarf and I realised, with surprise, that she was nervous, an emotion I hitherto would not have associated with Charlotte.

'Here, let me take your coat and hat.'

'Thanks,' she muttered. She quickly slipped out of them and handed them to me. She smoothed down her navy blue skirt and touched her pearls.

'Drink?' I offered. 'Or, if it's too early, a coffee or tea or—'

'No, I'd like a drink. A gin and tonic, please,' she added, her eyes going quickly to the sideboard, clearly in piteous need.

I rushed around getting flat tonic and gin and no ice because the freezer had been defrosted, and no lemon, and apologising all the time, but actually very glad to have something to do. Something to say.

'Gosh, I can't tell you how pleased I am to see you, Charlotte,' I burbled on while I rattled bottles. 'You've no idea how worried I was. I thought some balaclavaed maniac was going to force his way in here and drag me bound and gagged to the cellar and do God knows what to me with blunt instruments. I really wish you'd signed that letter though, it would have saved me an awful lot of angst.'

'Sorry, it was a bit cloak and dagger, but I couldn't be sure if I did that that you wouldn't tell someone. The police maybe.'

I glanced at her quickly. So she hadn't wanted the police. Well, that was one thing I'd been wrong about then. I handed her a drink and took a seat opposite her, watching as she sipped it quickly. She was beautifully dressed as usual, all navy-blue pleats and cashmere, but much thinner than I recalled. She'd always been a well-built girl with whacking great thighs, but her skirt was almost falling off her now and her cheeks looked sunken, falling away from the bones and making her eyes look dark and tired. She was also heavily made up, which was unusual for her during the day. It occurred to me that Charlotte and I had never actually been on our own together like this. She'd always been at the helm of a loud and intimidating gang and we generally only met round the dinner table, having always had a tacit agreement that we weren't exactly one another's cup of tea during daylight hours. I felt distinctly encouraged to be doing this on my patch, and with her clearly ill-at-ease.

'So,' I said cheerfully, brushing down my jeans as I crossed my legs jauntily. 'Tim McWerther. I'm all ears.'

She regarded me over her gin for a moment, then set her glass down. 'I wouldn't look so eager, Rosie. You're not necessarily going to like this.'

'Try me.' I smiled, but suddenly I felt much less gung-ho.

'Well, frankly, I'm amazed you don't know all this already. I thought that's why you killed Harry. I remember being totally shocked when it happened but quietly very impressed. I thought, my God, that girl's got guts. Who'd have thought she'd have had the balls to see old Harry off.'

I stared at her. 'Well, you're quite right,' I said slowly. 'I wouldn't have had the balls to see him off. Which is why I didn't. So come on, Charlotte, stop casting aspersions and just spill the beans, okay?'

She pursed her lips for a moment. Then she looked up with a brisk, defensive air. 'You didn't come with us the weekend we all went away to the Camerons', did you? I think you were about to have Ivo.'

I blinked, wrong-footed. The Camerons? Who the hell were the Camerons, for heaven's sake? I quickly slung my mind back to when I was pregnant with Ivo. God, in those days there'd been so many grand house parties that Harry had eagerly scurried off to, his Barbour in one hand, his Purdey in the other, and I'd been so preoccupied with morning sickness and tiredness that I'd been glad to see him go. One less meal to cook, as far as I was concerned. Where he'd actually gone and the names of the people he was staying with had all rather gone over my head. This one certainly didn't ring a bell.

'No, I don't remember them. I know Harry went away for the weekend when I was practically in labour, which didn't over-impress me, but I can't think where.'

She nodded. 'That was to the Camerons. They live up at Alsworthy Hall, in Shropshire. I don't know if you know Shropshire, Rosie, but not a great deal happens there. Lots of grass, lots of sheep, lots of hunting, but that's about it. Consequently people tend to make their own entertainment, create their own brand of fun.' She smiled ruefully and lit a cigarette. 'And they're a wild bunch, those Camerons,' she said softly, exhaling the smoke in a thin line. 'All six of them. The youngest, Mickey, is the worst of the lot. A totally mad bastard. He was about nineteen then and he was down from Oxford that weekend, brought some of his Piers Gaveston club pals with him. One of them was young Tim.'

'Oh! Really? Gosh, how strange. So . . .' I frowned. 'Hang on, you mean Harry met him too? He met Tim?'

'Oh, we all met Tim. And we all took to him too. This crazy, beautiful, angelic looking boy with the big blue eyes and the floppy blond hair, oh yes, we all fell for Tim. And we all played his games too. Up to a point.'

'What games?'

'Oh, you know. After-dinner games. You must remember how stupid we all were, Rosie, couldn't wait to get pissed and take our clothes off, throw bread rolls, dance on the table – all that immature sort of stuff. I remember your eyes over the dinner table, bored and censorious. I seem to remember you usually went up to bed at that point.'

'Ah yes. Well, maybe I was a bit of a kill-joy but I'm afraid it just wasn't me.'

She gave a wry smile. 'Unlike me, eh? Everyone knows what I'm like, don't they? Good old Charlotte. Game for anything. Won't catch her being a party-pooper, oh no.' She took a great slug of her drink. 'Yes, good old Charlotte,' she said softly. She glanced at me. 'Well, I'm afraid even I couldn't put on a brave face for some of the entertainment young Tim dreamed up.'

'Like what?'

'Well, let's just say that it wasn't enough for Tim to get everyone stark bollock naked with strip poker. He had to see them perform too.'

'Blimey.' My eyes boggled. 'You mean—'

'So I excused myself and went up to bed,' she went on, 'and missed out on all the fun, no doubt.' She gave me a beady look. 'I'm a great believer in what the eye doesn't see, etcetera, etcetera. Anyway, I woke up the next morning to find that Boffy wasn't in my bed so out I stumbled, bleary-eyed, down the corridor to find him. I went next door to Harry's room to see if he'd crashed out in there, but it was empty, so I opened the door opposite, which happened to be Tim's room, and there they all were. Half the house party, in bed together. So sweet.'

'You mean—'

'Tim, Boffy, Harry, two Cameron sisters and Lavinia.'

'Good God. Harry! And Lavinia! Golly, I always thought she was so prudish!'

'Didn't look very prudish with a peacock feather stuffed up her backside, I can tell you.'

'You mean they were naked?'

'Not exactly. In various stages of ridiculous undress really. Anything from women's underwear to lampshades to jock straps to bunches of grapes and feather boas. All very grey and unshaven and all fast asleep and spread-eagled, mouths wide open, gin bottles everywhere.'

'Christ.'

'When they saw me, they came to in an incredibly sheepish manner. Boffy staggered out in a pink nightie and stumbled down the corridor after me, swearing blind it had been totally innocuous, hilarious but innocent horseplay. He insisted nothing had happened and was absolutely lamb-like in his contrition. He was so earnest and distraught and so sweet to me for days afterwards that eventually I gave in and forgave him. I decided that it probably had just been a one-off and obviously under the influence of drink and God knows what else, so I decided to forget about it, although privately I vowed that we wouldn't be visiting the Camerons again for some time.'

'But I thought you liked all that. The high jinks, the silly dressing-up games. Actually, I thought you instigated most of it.'

'Did you? Just goes to show, doesn't it?' she said ruefully. 'I obviously played my part pretty well. No, I didn't much care for it in public, but Boffy adored it and he loved me to join in, to be one of the lads. He always said he felt sorry for Harry because you wouldn't. He didn't know I respected you for it.'

'But you were always so down on me, so patronising!'

She shrugged. 'Because I was jealous that you didn't have to lower yourself, I suppose, and I did. I mean, I'm quite happy to have a lark in the privacy of my own home but I don't actually enjoy making an exhibition of myself.' Blimey, you could have fooled me, I thought. She sighed. 'Anyway, after that we didn't go out for some time. We kept ourselves to ourselves, had a few quiet bridge suppers and that was the end of it. Or so I thought.' She stubbed out her cigarette and lit another one immediately. 'But then the gambling started.'

'At the Claremont Club? You knew about that?'

'I thought I knew about it, Rosie, but I didn't, because in actual fact they weren't gambling at all. There was no Claremont Club. No losing at the blackjack table. It was all a cover for something else.'

My heart slipped a bit. 'What?'

'For seeing Tim. For going to fancy dress parties at his house.'

I stared at her. 'What d'you mean?'

'They used to go there to dress up, to act out fantasies. You know, Squirrel Nutkin, Fireman Sam, Angel Gabriel, that sort of thing.'

I stared at her. 'They're not gay, are they?' I breathed.

'I knew you'd say that. And I swear to God I think the answer is no. At least,' she hesitated, 'Boffy swears to God the answer is no. He says it was all just a bit a fun that got out of hand.'

'Oh, for heaven's sake,' I exploded. 'Angel Gabriel? That's women's clothes!'

'I don't think Angel Gabriel was a woman, Rosie.'

'Well, all right, maybe not, I don't want a theological debate about it, but we're still talking white nighties and halos here, aren't we? I mean I don't necessarily need my men to play rugby and sink ten pints a night but I quite like them to wear trousers!'

She sighed. 'It's just a way of playing out repressed fantasies that's all. Lots of Englishmen do it. Look at Lily Savage and Harry Enfield, they're always strapping themselves into pinnies, doesn't necessarily mean they're woofters.'

'Bit dodgy though, isn't it?' I said nervously, reaching for the gin.

'I mean, they're comedians, doing it for a living, they're not property developers and solicitors.'

'I know, I know, and believe you me, even by my standards young Tim kept an extremely strange house, stuffed full of exotic young things – and not all boys, incidentally.'

'But what did they do there?' I squeaked. 'I mean, what went on? If they're not gay and they weren't doing, well, gay things, what were they doing?'

'Apparently it was all rather childish. There was an awful lot of drinking to begin with and everyone got as tight as ticks, and then Tim brought out the fancy dress box and everyone just delved in and took a character. So for instance if you were Fireman Sam you might be in a uniform ringing bells and waving your hosepipe around, or if you were Baby Bunting you could just gurgle away happily in the corner with your dummy. It was that sort of thing.' She said it as casually as if she'd said they'd just slipped down to the pub for a game of darts.

'Good grief,' I said faintly. I had a sudden vision of Harry in a nappy with a dummy in his mouth. I felt horribly sick, but also mightily relieved that he was dead and that I didn't have to deal with this.

'Did Boffy tell you all this?'

'He did because I made him. I knew something was going on and I said if he didn't tell me I'd leave him. But he's terrified I'll say something to someone. He doesn't know I'm here, of course.'

'No, no, of course,' I said quickly. 'What else did he tell you?'

She shrugged. 'Not much. Just a bit about the outfits. Apparently Harry quite liked to be Anthea Turner and Boffy was always that blonde woman, Bunny Thingamygig off the *Antiques Road Show*. He said he just put on a blond wig and fondled ashtrays, pretended they were antiques and burbled away into an imaginary camera about eighteenth-century rococo gilding. I suppose it's all pretty innocuous if you think about it.' She looked at me beseechingly.

My jaw was down by my chest, my eyes out on stalks. Innocuous!

'Oh, and Boffy liked to be Suzanne Charlton too,' she rushed on, getting it all out. 'I think he just sort of stuck cushions in his suit for shoulder pads and spoke in a shrill voice. Tapped weather maps with pointy sticks, apparently.'

'Pointy sticks!' I echoed faintly, reaching for the bottle again. I poured myself a slug with a shaky hand. 'And Tim presided over all this?'

'Oh, absolutely. He provided all the equipment, you see, and then he just let them get on with it.'

'Just like playschool,' I breathed, 'with a dressing-up box!'

She nodded. 'Totally. Small boys playing out their sad, repressed little games. I blame cold mothers and uniformed nannies and boarding school actually, they all had to learn to be "little men" by the time they were about six and they never got to do any of this. Lots of stiff upper lips, no teddies and no crying in the dorm.' She crossed her legs and brushed some dust off her skirt. 'And of course it doesn't come as a complete surprise because Boffy and I do quite a bit of dressing up at home.' She glanced up at me defensively.

I boggled. 'You *do*?'

'Well, in the privacy of our own bedroom, of course. As married couples do, you know.'

'Oh! Oh, yes, of course.' I stared at her, fascinated. 'Er . . . as what?'

'Sorry?'

'What d'you dress up as?'

'Oh, nothing madly original. Just, you know, rabbits, with bits of cotton wool stuffed here and there. Chickens perhaps.'

'Chickens!' I breathed. I dug my nails into my hand to stop myself guffawing and nodded knowingly. 'Oh yeah, right. Chickens.'

'I mean, it's not unusual, is it?'

'Heavens, no!'

'It's just we've never actually,' she hesitated, 'crossed gender before.' She frowned into her glass.

'Not even as chickens?'

'Oh no, I always laid the eggs.'

I fought hard with mounting hysteria, in serious trouble now. When I'd finally gulped it down, I gave a bright smile. Gosh, it was a relief to give those face muscles an airing.

'Well, to be perfectly honest, Charlotte, if I were you I wouldn't worry about this one little bit! In fact, I'd throw myself right into it!'

'Really?' She looked up doubtfully.

'Absolutely! Be Hugh Scully to his Bunny Whatserface, be Michael Fish to his Suzanne Charlton! Golly, if you can lay eggs, I'm sure you can get used to a few bits of old porcelain lying about the bedroom and the odd weather map being pulled out from under the bed.'

'You think so?'

'Lord, yes, it'll be a breeze! Gosh, before you know it, you'll be tickling his rain clouds with your isobars and rubbing your warm fronts against his ridge of high pressure!'

She glared at me. 'We're not kinky, you know, Rosie,' she snapped.

'Oh no!' I said hastily. 'No, of course you're not! Sorry, it was just a suggestion, got a bit – carried away.'

'Yes, well,' she said huffily. She reached across and helped herself to more gin. We were silent for a moment. She, no doubt, contemplating a new wardrobe full of pinstriped suits, boxer shorts and ties, and me contemplating my erstwhile marriage. It made me feel sick to the stomach to think of Harry in women's clothes or bunny suits, but at least, I thought with some relief, our marital liaisons had finished long before then. There'd been virtually no hanky-panky after Ivo was born, so at least he wasn't coming back to me after he'd been nibbling carrots with the other Flopsy Bunnies. I shivered. That would really have made my skin creep, and I wondered it didn't Charlotte's. I looked across at her now. She looked sad, Savile Row perhaps having lost its appeal.

'Of course you never had my problem, did you?' she said sadly.

'Sorry?'

'Well, you never really loved Harry, did you?'

I thought this over. 'In the beginning perhaps, but . . . no. Not later on.'

'That makes it so much harder.'

'I can see that,' I said quietly.

She sank into her gin again. Another thought struck me.

'So, I suppose they had to pay for all this then?'

'Hmmm?' she came back.

'This fancy dress malarkey.'

'Oh yes. More and more, that's the whole point. You see, it got to the stage where Tim would double the price at each session, and then he'd start to charge them if they missed a week. And then when there was no money left and Boffy and Harry had both drained their accounts dry and remortgaged their houses and stopped going, he charged them anyway.'

'For not going?'

'For him keeping quiet. For not sending the photographs he'd taken of them in drag to Boffy's family, to his partners at the law firm, to me, to you, to Uncle Bertram.'

'Blackmail,' I breathed.

'Exactly.'

'So . . .' I thought back quickly. 'So that time when Tim came here, befriended me in the supermarket, carried my bags home, that was a trick to get into my house, wasn't it? Yes, of course,' I went on slowly, my thoughts keeping track with my words, 'he came here to leave the note. The one the police found. "I won't go quietly, my love . . . we're in too deep . . ." Yes, that's it, he ran upstairs while I was answering the phone and tucked it not under my pillow but under Harry's!'

'What note?' She frowned, but I was well away, my mind racing.

'And then by the time I got upstairs, he'd already planted it, and was back in the bathroom busy putting Badedas in the cupboard, and then—' my hand flew up to my mouth – 'Oh God, yes! Then Harry came back!'

'What are you talking about, Rosie?' Charlotte leant forward.

'Yes, Harry came back and – oh God, I remember now! The look of absolute *horror* on his face! I thought it was because he'd caught me with a man in our bedroom, but it was because it was Tim! And Tim went into some ridiculous charade about pretending to be a plumber or something, but all the time he must have been laughing up his sleeve at Harry. Because in a way it was even more effective to be seen talking to his wife in his bedroom, wasn't it? Because, how much had he told me? The threat was so implicit, wasn't it? How much had he divulged? How much did I know? Harry went very pale, I remember that, and Tim said, "Haven't we met before?" Oh Lord, he was teasing him, playing with him. God, he must have loved it. And when Tim had gone, Harry accused me of having an affair with him, but all the time, yes, all the time he must have been worried sick, wondering how much I knew.'

'And that very day,' said Charlotte, catching on suddenly, 'you threatened to divorce him, didn't you? It was that day, wasn't it, Rosie? Boffy said you were on your way to your parents' house.'

I stared at her. 'Yes, that's right, but – that was just a coincidence. I'd been planning that for ages, that just happened to be the day I snapped.'

'Yes, but Harry didn't know that, did he?' she said eagerly. 'He'd just interrupted you having a cosy chat with Tim and he wasn't to know Tim had just popped in to leave an unpleasant note under his pillow. For all he knew, Tim had spilled the entire can of worms! Because suddenly, here you were, apropos of absolutely nothing, demanding a divorce. What was he to think?' She narrowed her eyes and stared beyond me. 'And so his life and his reputation must have trickled away before his very eyes. He saw a messy, vindictive divorce with pictures of himself dressed as a fairy godmother all over the tabloids—'

'I wouldn't have done that!'

'—and everyone finally seeing him for what he really was. A sad, mixed-up fat boy who liked to wear funny clothes.' Her eyes swung back to me. 'And how would he cope with that, Rosie? Someone like Harry? You know how he was, reputation was everything to him, wasn't it? What would they say at the club? At the royal enclosure? At his shooting parties? More to the point, what would Uncle Bertram say? That hot-blooded old heterosexual? Well, he'd be changing his Will pretty damn sharpish, wouldn't he? So let's see what Harry's lost, shall we?' She held up her hand and ticked off her fingers. 'He's already lost all his money to Tim, but now he's lost his wife, his son, his reputation, his friends, his social life and, finally, his inheritance. Knowing Harry as you do, Rosie, is his life worth living?'

I stared at her for a long moment. 'He committed suicide,' I breathed.

She nodded. 'I'd say that's a pretty shrewd assumption.'

We gazed at each other for a while, then I slumped back in my chair, my eyes still fixed on her. 'He slipped the dodgy mushroom in.'

'Precisely.'

'But he asked me to check them, Charlotte. Why bother if he knew he was going to add one himself?'

She shrugged. 'Who knows? A final act of vengeance to implicate you perhaps, or maybe just to cover his tracks. He didn't *want* people to know he'd committed suicide, did he? He didn't *want* that final stain on his character, that's why he didn't leave a note. He wanted it to look like an accident, or perhaps murder, but certainly not suicide.'

I gazed at her. 'But how can I prove all this?' I said slowly. 'The police still think I did it.' I sat up. 'You're the only person who can help me, Charlotte. You must go to them, you must tell them all this!'

'I can't!' she said, recoiling in horror. 'You know I can't. Tell them about Tim's house, the dodgy dressing-up sessions? Boffy would lose everything if it all came out! He's a solicitor, for God's sake, he'd never work again! His family would cut him off and, God, he'd never forgive me, that's for sure.' She got up and paced about, shaking her head vehemently. 'Oh no. No, I can't do it, Rosie.' Suddenly she turned, sat down again. 'And it's not just because of us,' she went on in a low voice, 'there are other people involved too, other people who went there.'

'Like who?'

'Oh, you know, civil servants, company directors, the odd Cabinet minister even.' She gave a hollow laugh. 'My godfather apparently, the one who's a High Sheriff – or Maid Marian, as Boffy tells me he's known at Tim's house. Tim's very well-connected, you know, his uncle is a duke. The press would have an absolute field day if all these names came out, he runs a very upmarket establishment.'

'Good grief. And he works in Sainsbury's during the day?'

'Well, he's got to do something in the daylight hours. He doesn't need to work at all, of course, he's loaded, but it's quite a good cover and it probably gives him a thrill to see the wives of all his clients squeezing the grapefruits when he knows what their husbands will be squeezing later.'

'What a bastard.'

'Who, Tim or the husbands? I don't think you can really blame Tim, Rosie, he's just providing a service. He's clearly getting something out of their emotionally crippled systems which might otherwise be taken out on people like us, their wives.'

'There's nothing very attractive about blackmail though.'

'True, and that was his big mistake. He got greedy, and it may well be his downfall. Harry topped himself. Tim's got blood on his hands now and he's also being questioned by the police, although I suspect they're not getting very far because he hasn't been charged yet. I imagine he must be very nervous though.'

'Which explains why he's been so keen to pin it on me,' I said slowly. 'To convince the police that he and I were the ones having the affair, to pretend that the note was to me, to pretend he was simply a young guy having an affair with an older woman he met in Sainsbury's, a woman who got too involved and killed her husband in order to be with her lover. He's claiming all this to take the heat off him.'

'No doubt. And from what you say, it seems to be working.'

I stared at her as gradually everything began to slot into place. 'Oh God, Charlotte, it all makes perfect sense now! You've got to help me, you've just got to! And you must have intended to, otherwise why come here? Why ask me to meet you here? Why not just keep quiet and hope that—'

The doorbell rang, stopping me in my tracks. We both leapt to our feet.

'Who is it?' Charlotte gasped. 'Is it the police, did you tell them you were coming here?'

'No, of course not!'

'Well, who is it then?'

It rang again. Two short beeps, then a long, chilling, insistent ring. We gazed at each other in horror.

'It is the police,' she muttered. 'I'm going out the back way, through the garden.'

397

As she made to go, I caught her arm. 'Don't be silly,' I hissed. 'If it is them they'll probably have someone posted round the back and you don't want to be caught running away, do you? For heaven's sake, just sit down and act perfectly naturally. Good grief, this is still my house, why shouldn't I have a friend round for a drink?'

Her face was very pale as she stared at me. 'Okay,' she whispered, 'but don't let me down, Rosie. Promise me you won't say a word!'

I swallowed hard. God, it would be so easy, wouldn't it? And why should I promise?

'I promise,' I muttered finally, praying fervently it wasn't the police, because if it was, I might be sorely tempted to point the finger at her and Boffy and subject them to the shame and ignominy of the tabloids and thereby save myself from the gallows.

I went slowly through to the hall. Oh, let it not be the police, I prayed as I got to the door. The mad axeman, yes, Tim with the Flopsy Bunnies and Angel Gabriel in tow, fine, but please God not the police or I might just fall into temptation and deliver myself from evil.

I reached for the doorknob, took a deep breath, swung it back and – oh, thank you, God, thank you, Thou art an absolute star. It was Joss and Alice.

Chapter Thirty

'Oh, how marvellous,' I gasped. 'I thought you were the filth!'

'Filth?' Joss frowned.

'Pigs, coppers, you know, that's how us fugitives tend to refer to them.' I glanced hastily up and down the street to check all was clear. 'Come in,' I hissed, dragging them into the hall, 'but quickly. How did you know I was here?'

'I put Martha on the rack and tortured it out of her,' said Joss, stepping inside.

'She promised not to say!'

'And very heroic she was too. I shone bright lights in her eyes and pulled her fingernails out and she wouldn't budge an inch. Then I threatened to lock her in the house so she wouldn't be able to slip home and get her dad some tea. She sang like a canary.'

'Ah yes, she would.'

'And even then all I had to go on was "up west somewhere", so I hurtled up the motorway like a lunatic and went straight round to Alice's, who hadn't the faintest idea where you were but insisted on coming with me. Together we must have knocked on every conceivable door in London before she realised you must be here. What the devil's going on, Rosie? I told you to stay put, for heaven's sake, and I've had the police on the phone every five minutes asking if I know where you are.'

'Oh God! You didn't tell them?'

'I didn't damn well know! And now I find you holed up in an empty house like something out of Custer's last stand. I fully expected to find furniture against the door and sandbags up against the windows.'

'Nice idea,' I said admiringly, 'but actually there's no need for any of that any more because I've just found out something simply marvellous. I don't know why it didn't occur to me before!' I clasped my hands ecstatically.

'What?'

'You'll never guess!'

Joss ground his teeth. 'Correct.'

'Harry committed suicide!' I squeaked. 'Isn't that wonderful!'

Two faces looked at me blankly.

Alice frowned. 'Are you sure?'

'Quite sure, only,' I grimaced, 'slight technical hitch. I can't actually prove it. But anyway, never mind all that, come and meet the genius who planted the seed in my brain in the first place – here, through here!' I hustled them joyfully through to the sitting room. Charlotte stood up uncertainly, hands twisting together.

'Charlotte, this is my – well, my landlord, I suppose, Joss Dubarry, and Alice Feelburn who you probably remember from Ivo's christening.'

A few hellos were muttered and Alice and Charlotte exchanged the mutually incredulous looks of women who inhabit different planets. Charlotte stared at Alice's swirling Indian skirts and Alice at Charlotte's navy blue pleats and pearls.

'I gather you think Rosie's husband committed suicide,' said Joss politely, for all the world as if he was inquiring if she grew her own vegetables or something.

'Well, it's just a hunch, of course.' She looked nervously at me.

'Oh, absolutely,' I said quickly. 'We've got no proof, no proof at all.' I smiled at her reassuringly. 'But if you think about it,' I said, turning eagerly to the others, 'it all makes perfect sense, doesn't it?'

'Does it?' Alice looked perplexed. 'I don't think so. I mean, why on earth would he want to do that? Take his own life?'

'Oh, because – because I was going to divorce him, of course!'

'Well, yes,' she said doubtfully.

'And,' I cast about wildly, 'and because he was so fat!' I added triumphantly.

She stared. 'Bit extreme, isn't it? I mean we all get depressed about our weight, but to resort to hara-kiri by way of a crash diet is—'

'Absolute rubbish, I agree.'

The funny thing was that no one's lips moved when that was said. I swung round in the direction of the voice and to my horror saw – oh my God – Superintendent Hennessey, in her habitual blue overcoat, hands in pockets, collar turned up, walking up behind us from the kitchen, her trusty, uniformed sidekick on her heels.

'You'll have to do better than that, I'm afraid, Rosie. Oh, and incidentally, this isn't rural Gloucestershire, you know, you really can't go around leaving the back door open, you'll get all sorts of odd-bods wandering in. I say, what a splendid gathering, do I know everyone? Rosie, perhaps you'd do the honours?'

I gaped at her for a moment, thinking that actually what I'd much rather do was faint clean away on the spot. Why wasn't she beetling back to Oxfordshire? What was she doing loitering in London still?

'Righto,' I croaked. God, she had a hideous knack of turning up at precisely the wrong moment, didn't she? Perhaps that was what had attracted her to the force, the fact that everyone would always be so utterly dismayed to see her.

'Um, well, this is Joss Dubarry, whose cottage I rent, and Alice Feelburn and Charlotte Boffington-Clarke. Superintendent Hennessey,' I muttered with a brief nod in her general direction.

'Delighted, delighted,' she purred with what purported to be a smile but bitter experience had taught me better. 'And all having a nice little afternoon tincture, I see,' she said, eyeing the gin bottle. 'I won't, thank you, Rosie, got to keep a clear head about me. Now,' she rubbed her hands gleefully as if she really had just wandered in on a drinks party. 'Let's see. You were hypothesising, I think, before I so rudely interrupted, about a suicide, Rosie, is that right?'

'Well, it's possible, isn't it?' I muttered.

'Oh, anything's possible, but I'm afraid we need a little more than Harry's weight problem to convince us.'

'Oh well, of course!' I laughed nervously. 'I wasn't suggesting that was the only—'

'And since we don't,' she snapped suddenly, 'have any more to go on than that fatuous suggestion, and since we do, on the other hand, have an overwhelming amount of evidence against you,' she paused and I caught on her sharp eyes like barbed wire, 'I'm afraid it's my unpleasant duty to arrest you, Mrs Meadows. For the murder of your husband, the late Mr Harold Meadows. You do not have to say anything, but it may harm your defence if you do not mention, when questioned, something which you later rely on in court. Anything you do say, may be given in evidence.'

There was a stunned silence. I stared at her.

'You don't mean that,' I breathed. 'You surely don't believe I did it.'

'As I said,' she said carefully, 'an overwhelming amount of evidence suggests—'

'Suggests,' spat Joss. 'That pretty much exposes the poverty of your situation, doesn't it? You've got no real proof, no evidence, but so desperate are you to drag someone triumphantly down to the station and press charges that you'll throw the book at anyone! Oh yes, time is marching on, isn't it, Superintendent? This man died weeks ago and you've got to get a conviction under your belt pretty damn quickly or someone higher up the ladder is going to want to know the reason why, so you'll make the cap fit just about anyone, including someone who you and I both know to be innocent!'

'Mr Dubarry, I'll ask you to hold your tongue!' she snapped. 'This is outrageous, you're interfering with a murder inquiry and—'

'No, *you're* outrageous,' interrupted Joss, stepping forward and pointing a finger in her face. 'In fact, you're way out of line. You're doing your damnedest to force a false confession out of someone who you know is liable to crack with the right sort of pressure. You're deliberately and callously instigating a miscarriage of justice.'

'And *you* are deliberately obstructing police business! One more word out of you and you'll be down at the station with her.' She gave a curt nod to her friend in blue. 'Cuff her, Jenkins.'

'Cuff her?' Joss said incredulously. I gave a little yelp of horror and shot behind him. 'You're out of your mind. I'll have you up for false arrest, I'll—'

'OH ALL RIGHT!' Charlotte's cry cut through the proceedings like a knife.

We swung round to see her pale and trembling by the window, nearly as pale and trembling as I was, in fact, as I offered my puny little wrists up to the sergeant.

'All right,' she repeated softly.

There was a silence.

'Thank you, Mrs Boffington-Clarke,' Superintendent Hennessey said, after a pause. Suddenly I realised she'd been waiting for this.

Charlotte walked back from the window, arms tightly folded over her chest. She sat down on the arm of a chair and licked her lips.

'It's true,' she muttered. 'Harry did commit suicide. He told Boffy he'd done it, told him he'd added the mushroom to the pan.'

'When?' I said, aghast. 'You didn't tell me that!'

'When they had lunch together at the club. On the day he died. He'd eaten it the day before, you see, but it takes at least twenty-four hours to get into the system. Boffy said he sat down as usual and ordered lamb cutlets and claret as if it was a perfectly normal Monday. He didn't touch his food but while Boffy ate, he told him what he'd done. He said he couldn't live with the ignominy and shame that Tim was threatening him and Boffy with, said his whole life had been a sham anyway but now that the precious little he did have – you, Ivo, Bertram's house – was going down the plughole too, he'd lost everything. He said he realised he'd implicated you in his death but he'd done it in a moment of spite and he asked Boffy to see that you were vindicated.' She looked at me. 'Harry wanted him to undo the damage, you see, tell the police he'd taken his own life, but Boffy was too scared. He knew it would all come out if he did, his own involvement with Tim.'

'You mean Boffy sat having lunch with Harry knowing he was going to collapse?' I whispered.

'Oh, no, once it came out, Boffy was going to get him to hospital. And Harry wanted to go. He was scared stiff by this stage, pale and trembling and in pain. You see, he'd thought that the moment the mushroom had passed his lips, he'd drop down dead, like something out of an Agatha Christie book, he hadn't realised it could take up to three days. Boffy had just stood up to call an ambulance when Harry collapsed. Actually, Boffy said later that Harry wouldn't have minded going like that.'

'In the club, over the port,' I breathed.

'Exactly.'

'Mrs Boffington-Clarke, you will of course be able to give a full statement with regard to your husband and Mr Meadows's involvement with Mr McWerther?'

'I can't,' she whispered. 'Boffy would kill me.'

'I don't think so,' she said quietly. 'At the end of the day, I don't think he could have lived with Rosie going to prison just to save his own good name, do you?'

Slowly I turned to view this icy-cool police woman. 'You knew about all this, didn't you? You've known all along.'

'Not quite all along. We've certainly had our suspicions and we've been following Tim McWerther for some time now, but we were never able to find out where he operated from. To this day we still haven't discovered the exact location of the house because he rarely went there himself, just pulled the strings from a distance, and although we knew he had quite an impressive clientele, again, we had no specific details. No doubt Mr Boffington-Clarke will be able to enlighten us, give us a list of names.' Charlotte went a bit green. Superintendent Hennessey turned to me. 'We also had a feeling Tim might have pushed your husband over the edge, Rosie. I'm quite sure the note under the pillow wasn't the first threat he received, just the first one Tim had brought to the house. I imagine there were plenty more through the post to both gentlemen. Am I right, Mrs Boffington-Clarke?'

Charlotte nodded miserably.

'So you *knew* he committed suicide then?' said Joss.

'Only for sure since ten o'clock this morning. When we searched this house. We found something rather interesting on the back of the bedroom door, you see.'

'Oh?' I gazed at her. 'What was that?'

'A Paisley dressing gown. Your husband's Paisley dressing gown, the one he was wearing when he collected the mushrooms at your parents' house?'

I thought back, remembered him flapping down the lawn in it, his big bottom swaying from side to side. 'Yes,' I said slowly. 'Yes, I think you might be right.'

'Oh, we know we're right, because in the pocket we found tiny spores. The minutest flakes of fungus. We've just had the results back from the lab, that's why I was coming to find you. The spores are undoubtedly from the Panther Cap. There's no doubt about it, the mushroom came out of his own pocket.'

'So you weren't coming to arrest me at all!'

'Quite the contrary, but I'm afraid when I saw Mrs Boffington-Clarke here I couldn't resist taking the opportunity of forcing her hand for the extra information we needed. Having you all assembled here together was really rather convenient. Sorry to have scared you like that, Rosie, but it was all to the good, I'm sure you'll agree.' She went towards the door. 'I'll be in touch with you soon, by the way, to take a statement, but it's just a formality, nothing to worry about.' She paused at the door, looking back. 'This way then, Mrs Boffington-Clarke, if you please.'

Charlotte looked startled. 'Oh, y-you mean we're—'

'Off to take your statement, yes, that's right.'

God, she didn't mess about, did she? We all watched dumbly as poor old Charlotte, white-faced and trembling, stood up and retrieved her coat and hat from the back of a chair. She wasn't exactly frogmarched out of the room but she was certainly escorted from it rather closely. We held our breath as the front door closed behind them. There was a stunned silence. Joss, Alice and I looked at one another.

'Well, bugger me,' said Alice at last, with feeling.

'Is that it then?' I whispered. 'Am I free?'

'Certainly looks like it,' said Joss. He began to smile. I shot a look at Alice, and the next thing I knew we were all rushing together, laughing and hugging each other. It was a bit like a rugby scrum actually, except that Alice and I were both crying a bit and I was very aware of Joss's arm round my shoulders, so warm and so tight I wanted it to stay like that forever. I was also aware that much as I loved Alice I couldn't help wishing she was in Dar-es-Salaam, or somewhere equally far flung at this precise moment. A second later, however, we all broke away laughing and sniffing.

'God, the relief!' I gasped, wiping my nose attractively on my sleeve. 'Oh God, I really thought that was it for me, thought my number was up – you know, come in Rosie Meadows, your time in the free world is over and your stay at Strangeways is about to begin! Oh, the joy, the *relief* and – gosh, I must ring my mother! Yes, I must ring Mum, tell her to let Dad out of the potting shed, tell her to ring Philly and – oh Christ, *Philly*!' I clutched my head. 'Heavens, I simply must speak to Philly because – God, how awful, to think I actually *accused* her! Accused my own sister! And all because she had a few poxy books in my attic. Remember, Joss? Those mushroom books! How strange,' I said slowly, 'it must just have been a complete coincidence, she must have bought them and forgotten all about them. Don't you remember how we thought it was her, Joss?'

'I do,' he said slowly. He was looking at Alice. Alice had turned a bit pink.

'What?' I said, looking from one to the other. 'What is it?'

'You know, don't you?' she muttered, raising her pale blue eyes to his.

'I had a fair idea,' he said quietly.

I stared at them, dumbfounded. 'What?' I demanded.

Alice turned to me. 'I put them there,' she said calmly. 'That time you were first accused by the police. You know, when you rang me in a complete panic and I dashed down to be with you, stayed the night. On the way down I bought those books in a second-hand book shop in Burford. When you'd gone to bed that night I went up to the attic to get some of her old books, steamed off the Ex Libris labels that Philly had written her name on and slapped them into the mushroom ones. Actually I was going to put them prominently in the bookcase downstairs so that someone would find them pretty damned quickly, but at the last minute I chickened out. I didn't quite have the nerve, so I just shoved them back in the attic on the off chance that the police might search the place and find them, which of course they did, but they didn't have the nous to look in the boxes.'

'But . . . why?' I stared at her incredulously. 'Why on earth would you want to—'

'Incriminate your sister? Oh come on, Rosie, I loathed her, for God's sake. I *hated* her. She stole my husband, for crying out loud – she ruined my life!'

I gazed at her in astonishment. 'You knew,' I breathed.

'Well of course I bloody knew, we all knew, didn't we? It's an absolute classic, a regular little modern morality tale.' She walked to the fireplace, then turned, a pained expression on her face. 'I surely don't have to fill you in, do I, Rosie? You do know the story? The one about the flirtatious, bottom-pinching husband who meets a beautiful, intelligent girl at a dinner party – yours, incidentally – and is absolutely astonished when she not only returns his oafish, hot looks over the salmon mousse but actually arranges to meet him the following week at a motel?' She laughed quietly. 'He couldn't quite believe his luck, the poor bastard. Never had such a steaming success. So off he scurries, and they duly have a sordid little bunk up, and then blow me if it isn't swiftly followed by another one the following week, and then another, until it quickly becomes a regular little Wednesday-night fixture at – guess where? Not the nasty sordid motel any more, but my very own rose-clad weekend country cottage!' She threw back her head and rasped out a hollow laugh. 'Yes, my cottage,' she breathed at the ceiling. Then her blue eyes came back at us, blazing. 'Oh, she's not in *love* with him of course, this beautiful, intelligent girl, she's just amusing herself. And why not? She's bored, you see. Bored with being top dog at the PTA, bored with being chairwoman of Cancer Relief, bored with growing her own vegetables and winning all the prizes at the village show, bored with her perfect house, her perfect garden, her perfect pillar of the community lifestyle, and what she needs now is a bit of knobbing. Yes, that's it, she thinks, knobbing! That'll make a nice change from *Countdown* and *Ready Steady Cook*. Now, who shall I have? Ooh yes, I know, I'll borrow dowdy old Alice's husband. He'll do, he looks keen enough and he pops down here once a week on business. Yes, that's it, I'll have hers. So what if Alice has two small children? So what if she's my sister's best friend? So what if it'll leave her life in tatters, I'm Philippa Hampton, for heaven's sake, I can do whatever I like!' Her voice rose shrilly here and she stopped for a moment. I realised she was struggling for composure, breathing hard. Poor, brave, strong Alice. I gulped.

'I hated her,' she hissed through her teeth, 'loathed her with a passion that was almost frightening. I really think,' she added with some surprise, 'that at one stage I could quite easily have killed her. She had everything, it seemed, everything she could possibly want, but she wanted my husband as well.' She shook her head in dumb disbelief. 'And then when she'd finished with him, when she'd sucked him dry and got all she wanted out of him, d'you know what she did? She threw him back to me like a limp rag. Tossed him back to where he came from but where he no longer wanted to be. He'd tasted forbidden fruit, you see,' she said ruefully. 'Boring old home life simply couldn't match up.' She swallowed hard. 'Poor old Michael. He almost went mad with the rejection, and I'm pretty sure he went out searching for anything in a skirt for a time, just to make himself feel wanted.' I stared down at my feet, recalling my own little debacle with Michael. Mad was how I would have described him too.

'And of course,' she went on softly, 'I was pretty mad myself. Mad with grief. And that's why I planted those books. I saw it as the perfect way to get you off the hook, Rosie, and implicate her at the same time.' She raised her chin defiantly. 'And it *was* perfect. It fitted in beautifully with the over-dominant way she had of protecting you – too much, I'd always thought. Poisoning Harry could quite easily have been her ultimate act of big-sisterly protection, her way of saving you from that big, bullying husband of yours. And it also fitted in beautifully with her unflinching arrogance. She would have imagined she'd get away with it, wouldn't she? She's always considered herself invincible, I knew that from the way she'd handled Michael.' She smiled. 'Yes, she could quite easily have done it, don't you think? Killed Harry?'

'But – you wouldn't have gone through with it, would you?' I said, gazing at her in disbelief. 'Framing her like that?'

'I don't know. I like to think not, but as I said, I was mad. I like to think that had she actually been led to the dock I'd have held up my hands, but who knows?'

'I know you would have, Alice,' I said warmly.

She shrugged. 'Well, we'll never know now, will we?' She turned to Joss who'd been listening quietly the while. 'How did you find out?'

He cleared his throat. 'About the books? Well, I had another look at them before I came up here and discovered that two or three perfectly ordinary novels in the box had had their labels torn out. It struck me as something of a coincidence, that's all. I couldn't help wondering if someone who had a grudge against Philly had done it deliberately, and then I fell to wondering who that person might be. Your name seemed to fit alarmingly well.'

She smiled. 'Yes, I can see that it might.' She turned, stared out of the window. I watched as she stood with her arms folded, very straight, very rigid, but very vulnerable too.

'So . . . what are you going to do, Alice?'

She turned, coming back from far away. 'Hmmm?'

'I mean, are you going to stay with him?'

'With Michael?' She sighed. 'He wants me to, but I'm going to see how I feel when I get back.'

'Get back from where?'

'From America. I'm going for a month, taking the girls.'

'Oh! Oh, Alice, what a good idea! That's it, go away, get away from it all. Where are you going?'

'To Los Angeles.' She flushed. 'To stay with Tom.'

'Tom?'

'Your brother. He invited us.'

'No! *Really?*' I sat down abruptly on the arm of the chair. 'Crikey, when?'

'When he was over for Harry's funeral. Kept banging on about the lack of real people out there and how nice it was to see me and did I remember him coming to see me in *The Tempest*. I did. I'll never forget it.' She smiled ruefully. 'A standing ovation at a university production and your gorgeous brother clapping like mad in the front row. It was my finest hour. Sad, but true.'

'Not sad at all,' I said slowly, 'just amazing to think that after all these years . . . So, d'you think – you know, you and Tom?'

She shrugged. 'Who knows? I don't even want to think about it. I'd like to think I could find it in my heart to forgive Michael, come back in four weeks' time and for everything to be fine and dandy again, for the girls' sake more than anything. But if I can't . . .' she bit her lip. She gave herself a little shake. 'Anyway, I'm sure Tom's only invited me out as a friend, his life must be pretty much wall to wall with beautiful women. He probably felt a bit sorry for me.'

Don't be too sure, I thought privately. The more I thought about it, the more I could see Alice being right up Tom's alley. I stood up and gave her a hug. 'Whatever you do will be right, Alice. Just follow your instincts, that's what you always used to say to me.'

'I know,' she said, suddenly getting a bit sniffy and digging a hanky out from up her sleeve. 'I was as bad as Philly in a way, bossing you about, wasn't I? There I was, doling out the matrimonial advice over the kitchen table, thinking I had the perfect husband and the perfect little domestic set-up and all the time . . . Oh well.' She wiped her nose and smiled. 'Poor old Joss,' she said glancing sheepishly at him. 'All these emotional, weeping women, must be wishing he'd stayed in Gloucestershire.'

'You're kidding,' he said, scratching his head in bewilderment. 'This is the most insight I've had into the grey and hazy subject of women for a long time. I'm totally enthralled.'

She grinned. 'Well, I'm going to stop being enthralling now because I must go. I've got to go and pick up the girls from my neighbour.' She blew her nose noisily. As she tucked the tissue back in her sleeve, she gave me a watery smile. 'Rosie, I'm so happy for you, I really am. I'm so pleased that all that ghastly suspicion has lifted and,' she looked from me to Joss, 'and, well, I'd just like to say that I *do* so hope—'

'Yes, thank you, Alice!' I breathed hastily, giving her a sudden bear hug, crushing the breath out of her and hopefully preventing her from saying what I think she'd been about to say. I could almost see the cogs in her brain working feverishly, right along the lines of, okay, so what the devil's this attractive man doing beetling up and down motorways, defending Rosie against over-zealous police officers, if not for some romantic reason or other? And shouldn't I, as Rosie's best friend and ally, be the first to offer my warmest congratulations?

I put her in an arm lock and frogmarched her smartly down the hall to the front door, just about letting her say a brief goodbye over her shoulder to Joss, but that was it. Because if truth be told, I was as keen as she was to see a joyous conclusion to all this, but if it was all right by her, I wanted to be the first to know. The first to experience it.

I hugged her again at the door. 'See you in a month's time with a seamless LA tan then, Alice!'

She smiled in surprise. 'Golly, I suppose so. I can't quite believe I'm really going actually.'

'Of course you are,' I said warmly, 'and you're going to give it your best shot too. Go for it, Alice, and if it doesn't work out, come back and try again with Michael, but keep your options wide open, you deserve it. I have to say that on a purely selfish level I'd like to see you firmly at my brother's side. If you ask me, you're just what he's been waiting for all these years.' Suddenly a thought struck me. 'Blimey, just think, Alice, we'd be sisters!'

'Good grief.' Suddenly she looked rather horrified. 'Heavens, would I have to call your mother Mum? I find Elizabeth hard enough, keep wanting to revert to my Mrs Cavendish days!'

We giggled and I kissed her goodbye.

'Good luck,' was all she mouthed to me as she went down the path, but there was no disguising the huge wink and jerk of her head back towards the sitting room and the Unknown Quantity.

My heart was pounding with excitement as I shut the door. I paused for a moment, willing myself some composure, some coolness, but finding absolutely none I turned and went back into the sitting room.

Joss was standing at the fireplace with his back to me, staring down into the empty grate. Any minute now he'd turn round. Our eyes would lock, a slow smile would spread across his face. He'd walk towards me, slowly, gazing all the while. I felt giddy already, my knees were going weak with the tension. I grabbed hold of the back of the sofa for support. Turn round, I willed him desperately, quick, or I'll have to sit down. He did. He turned, his tawny eyes heavy with passion. Now, I thought hungrily as he came towards me, now, yes, for sure, something so right after so many years of wrong, yes . . . yes . . . *yes*! I held on tight to the back of the sofa and lowered my eyes seductively. That's it, Rosie, not too pushy, play it cool. He was within inches of me now and I could almost feel his breath on my face. A collapse into his arms must surely be imminent because I could feel the rough tweed of his coat, could almost sense the warmth of his body as he – brushed past me.

'Well, come on,' he snapped irritably. 'Let's get out of here. We've got the lousy M4 to contend with yet. Thanks to you I feel like I've been on that road the whole damn day!'

And with that seductive little *bon mot* hanging in the air, he marched through the hall, out of the front door and down the path to his car.

Chapter Thirty-One

Half an hour later I was speeding feverishly down the motorway after him, sticking to his Range Rover like Superglue. I stared straight ahead, wide eyed, shocked and uncomprehending. Blimey, how on earth could I have got it so wrong? Had I totally misread the signs? Had I quite comprehensively misjudged his intentions? Well, evidently I had, because what better chance had he had than back there in that empty house, with me explosive with joy at clearing my name and panting to celebrate in an appropriate manner? What more excuse did a man need to stride purposefully over the Axminster, take a girl in his arms and kiss the living daylights out of her? Instead of which he'd affected the demeanour of a man who frankly, would rather have unblocked my lavatory with his bare hands than come within inches of my person.

My heart, which latterly had been pattering away somewhere near my tonsils, was sinking now with every second, every mile that my battered old Volvo was eating up. I gripped the steering wheel, gazing longingly at the number plate in front of me. I knew it by heart. I murmured it aloud, rolling the letters around on my tongue. What a totally glorious number that was, and so far out of my reach! Suddenly my eyes filled with tears. I thumped the steering wheel hard. Oh, for God's sake, this was so unfair, I should be so happy now! I shouldn't be snivelling, I shouldn't be crying, I'd just cleared my name, this should be a day for celebration! I no longer had to slink around under an old mac and a cloud of suspicion, I could hold my head up high and the world – well, my world, such as it was, the village of Pennington – would be forced to recognise this. This, by rights, was my moment of glory, my moment to ride back into town with my conquering hero by my side, the man who all along had proclaimed my innocence, stood by me, rooted through boxes of second hand books for me, flown back from Europe to help me, lingered over candles and rabbit graves with me, swum in a sea of mutual affection with me – or so I'd thought – and not just thought, actually, but sensed, yes, sensed, with every nerve and sinew in my body. So what the dickins were we doing dashing back to Gloucestershire in separate cars in such a premature manner? This, to me, seemed an entirely retrograde step. There were children in Gloucestershire, wagging tongues, responsibilities, ties, whereas surely in London we could have found somewhere quiet and private to confess our secret love, to unburden ourselves, before heading back to reality to do our duty?

Joss suddenly pulled out of the middle lane and shot off into the fast lane away from me. I instantly made tracks after him but swung out with such an astonishing lack of care that I was immediately beaten back by a blare of horns behind me. A lorry swept by, missing me by inches. Shaken, I crept sheepishly over to the slow lane. The storming excitement I'd felt in the house had curdled now, gone sour, and I felt the bitterness of rejection seeping in. I recognised it, you see, because I'd felt it once or twice before. It was nothing new.

You're a fool, Rosie Meadows, I told myself bitterly. And you've got a very short memory. You're his tenant, remember? Why is it I have to keep telling you this? He came to help you out of a tight spot because you're living in his cottage, that's all. Of course he wanted to see you were all right, but as for any romantic notions, forget it. In the first place, as you might recall, he's married. Married to that beautiful, talented, pencil-thin, yoghurt-eating, yoga-practising she-devil to whom he's clearly devoted or why else would he suffer her absences, her tantrums, her indifference to the children, her infidelity, with such fortitude? Why else would he spend hours pleading with her to come home? Why else, unless he was eaten up with that totally irrational all-consuming passion, that same one that you have for him, that thing called love?

I slowed right down to 50 mph and let him out of my sights. A hot flush of embarrassment washed over me. God, how stupid of me, what a fool I'd been. All he'd been doing was being kind, looking after me in the absence of anyone else. I was, after all, a helpless widow and he'd felt sorry for me, providing at most an absorbent shoulder to cry on, but that, categorically, was that. How could I have even thought he'd be interested in someone like me? I put my hand to my forehead and went even hotter. You go out with sidekicks, Rosie, remember? People who wear glasses, people with no hair, people who look like doors, troglodytes, and you marry people like Harry, fat people, people who wear bunny suits, people with personality disorders, okay? Joss is none of these. Joss is a main man, a deliciously handsome, famous sculptor, way, way out of your league, the stuff that dreams are made of, but even then beyond any of *your* wildest fantasies. And you're more than likely embarrassing the hell out of him with your wistful, devoted, puppy dog eyes. I went even hotter and fanned my face with my hand. Oh God, why was I so hot? Crikey, this wasn't the menopause coming on, was it? That was all I needed. I reached forward and turned the cold blower on full blast, then gagged as a few dead leaves and a mouthful of stale air hit me. Hastily I turned it off. And what, incidentally, had you been hoping for back there anyway, Rosie? A bended-knee declaration of passion perhaps? Or just a quick grapple on the sofa? What sort of erotic little tapestry did you hope to knit yourself into, hmm?

I retreated into misery now, holed down well beneath the surface. I slunk low in my seat and crawled the rest of the way home, eventually creeping into Pennington a good hour and a half later. I stopped at the garage in the middle of the village for petrol, sank back in my seat and sighed. Here I was again then. Hello, Pennington. As I got out and walked bleakly round the back of the car to the pump, two elderly women across the street spotted me. They stopped and waved. Surprised, I forced a smile back as I filled up the tank, not actually feeling like smiling at anyone at this precise moment and not quite sure who it was at this range either. As I peered, I realised that one of them was looking left and right and bustling purposefully across the road towards me. It was Mrs Fairfax from the shop.

'I want to apologise,' she gasped, clutching her side from the exertion. 'We've heard the good news, Dot and I, Vera telephoned us ten minutes ago like, when Mr Dubarry 'ad rung, and I don't know that I've ever been so ashamed of myself. I said as much to my Horace just now as I fixed his tea, and he said he never knew how I could have thought as much in the first place. He always said you never done it, nice slip of a girl like you, and I'm that vexed with myself for giving in to all that gossip. There, I've said it.' Her face was pink and a bit trembly, and it was such an honest, fulsome apology that I couldn't help but smile.

'It's all right, Mrs Fairfax. I'm sure if I'd been in your position I'd have thought much the same.'

''Ere, luv,' she pressed something into my hand. It was a small bunch of snowdrops, their stems tightly wrapped in silver foil. 'Fresh from the garden. When I put that telephone down from talking to Vera, I went straight out and picked them for you myself. Good luck to you, my dear, and the little nipper.'

At the mention of the little nipper, tears, unaccountably, pricked my eyelids. I nodded. 'Thank you,' I whispered.

I watched her turn and beetle back across the road to Dot, duty done, then paid for the petrol and got back in the car. I sat for a moment staring bleakly out of the windscreen. Good luck. Now why should that make me feel so empty? So low? Was it because it implied I was starting again, setting out on yet another journey, when actually, I felt pretty travel weary already? Pretty much all in? I sighed and turned the ignition, swinging the car back out into the village. It was quite clear that Joss had telephoned Farlings from his car and then Martha and Vera had lost no time in spreading the word, bless them, because as I drove along I was startled to see people stop and smile. One woman who I didn't even know, paused from raking her leaves to wave, and another actually swung open her sitting-room window and waved her duster. If only I didn't feel so deflated, I thought, I could have indulged in a lap of honour round the village. Could have slung a laurel wreath round my neck and had a bottle of champagne bubbling in my hand, like a victorious Grand Prix hero. As it was I just smiled faintly, nodded my thanks and drove on through the village. On and out, up the hill to Farlings.

As I crunched up the gravel drive, I noticed Joss's car wasn't there. He'd probably taken Toby to get the twins from school, which would just leave Martha and Ivo. Well, that was a relief anyway, I thought, getting out and slamming the door. I didn't particularly want to bump into him so soon after he'd spotted that predatory light in my eye, that wanton, come-hither flicker of abandonment. Instead I could just look forward to hugging my son, couldn't I? Yes, exactly. Oh the joys of simple, straightforward, maternal love. Why on earth did we women ever aspire to anything more complicated? I smiled at the thought of young Ivo. Maybe he'd heard the car, maybe he was wriggling excitedly from Martha's arms even now, toddling to the door to greet me.

I pushed open the back door into the kitchen, all prepared to scoop up a running two-year-old and smother him in kisses. But as I went in, I stopped. Stared. Because a rather different tableau greeted me. For there in the kitchen, presiding over the most immaculate but sterile nursery tea complete with wholemeal sandwiches, grated carrot, vegetarian sausages and celery sticks, as yet untouched by any children, was not Martha with Ivo, but Annabel.

'Rosie!' she purred, hurriedly stubbing a cigarette out and chucking a copy of *Hello!* in the bin. 'What marvellous news! May I be the first to offer you my warmest congratulations?' She smiled, flashing her perfect teeth.

'Annabel! I – thought you were still in Europe.'

'Well, I flew back this morning. There didn't seem much point in topping over if Joss wasn't there, and it's only a few hours away, you know.' She smiled. 'I know people round here think twice about driving to the next village, but I've been travelling round the world all my life. It's absolutely nothing for me to hop on a plane and come home.'

Well bully for you, I thought bleakly. I sank down exhausted in the wheelback chair by the Aga, then automatically sat up, wondering if that was presumptuous. Perhaps I should ask to be seated or something while her cosmopolitan highness was still standing. But no, she didn't look too put out and, good grief, she was still smiling at me. She came across and hovered over me.

'You must be real tired, Rosie,' she said in concern. 'I mean, emotionally. Pretty much drained by all this, I imagine. Cup of tea?'

'Um, please. Yes, I am rather tired.' God, she was being suspiciously nice.

'But glad it's all over?' She bustled over to the kettle.

'Well, relieved, yes. Where's Ivo?' I looked around.

'With Martha, outside on the swing, and Joss is fetching the kids from school.' She put the kettle down. Turned. 'So I guess this is probably quite a good time.'

Suddenly I smelled danger. 'Good time for what?'

She came over, perched her pert little backside daintily on the edge of the table and clasped her manicured hands. She smiled. 'Rosie, I think it's about time we had a little chat, don't you?'

I caught on her pseudo-sweet voice like Velcro. She was looking particularly drop-dead gorgeous today, I noticed, in bright red jeans and a tiny white T shirt that hovered somewhere around her navel. Blimey, it was no wonder the central heating blared in this house if she insisted on showing off her brown tummy in January. I considered standing up for this little exchange but then thought better of it. I always felt like the Incredible Hulk when I lumbered around next to her.

'Oh yes?' I inquired brightly.

'Well I'm sorry, Rosie, but I'm afraid there are going to have to be some changes round here.' She glanced down at her nail varnish, then back to me. 'You see, unfortunately I'm going to have to ask you to go.'

'Go where?' I said stupidly.

'Elsewhere, I'm afraid. Find somewhere else to live.'

'Oh! You mean, you're evicting me?'

415

She smiled. 'I hardly think eviction is the word when you've been living in our cottage practically rent free, do you? I'm aware that Joss lets you have it for a fraction of the price, but we're not running a charity here you know, and the thing is, I've got the opportunity to get a proper rent for it now. Some friends of mine rang, they're Buddhists as a matter of fact, I met them through the ashram and right now they live in Islington, but they're dying to get out to the country and be true eco-warriors. They're lovely, warm, caring people and I can't wait to have them on my doorstep, but they must have vacant possession within twenty-four hours or the deal's off.'

I gulped. Crikey. How warm and caring.

'And frankly we need the money, Rosie. Now that we're both travelling so much I've insisted we take on a proper, trained nanny. Joss is adamant we keep Martha, but he agrees she needs some back up, and let me tell you, honey, back up in the form of one of those uniformed girls doesn't come cheap.' She gazed around at the shabby kitchen. 'So there's that, and then of course we have to find the money to do this place up . . .'

'Oh! You mean, Joss wants to—'

'It's time, Rosie,' she said portentously. 'He's ready now you see. He's had a block about it before, and understandably, but he's had his space and now he's cool.' She fixed me with her deep liquid gaze. 'I gave him that space, Rosie, see? I knew he needed it, but he's ready to turn all that negative energy into something more positive.' She sighed contentedly and crossed her slim, red-jeaned legs. 'Yep, Joss and I had a long, long talk on the telephone yesterday.' She paused considering. 'I wouldn't say he's needy exactly, but he wants me to be there for him more, you know? Wants me around more. He also said it's high time we had a baby of our own.' She grinned. 'You know what Joss is like, he's like – Annabel, it's high time we had a baby. Well aye aye sir!' She laughed. 'He's right though, and funnily enough I've felt these real strong primitive urges in my own body lately, and of course motherhood's very fashionable now. Frankly, the days of the working woman thinking she can have everything are over.'

'Really,' I muttered drily. I couldn't help wondering what would happen to the child when motherhood became unfashionable again. Personally I'd give her about two weeks. 'And – and Joss?' I managed. 'I mean,' I cleared my throat, 'he wants me to go?'

'Why, yes of course he does, otherwise I wouldn't be standing here telling you all this, would I?' She gave a tinkly laugh. 'He asked me to tell you, actually, left me to do his dirty work, I guess.' She gave me a

416

wry, conspiratorial, look. 'You know what men are like, Rosie, and Joss is the world's worst, can't bear to upset anyone. He's a bit of a coward in that respect, so he slipped out with Toby to get the girls from school instead. I wouldn't be surprised if he takes them to the park or something totally out of character, just to make sure he's out of the house long enough for me to get this little interview over and done with!' She laughed, but as it died away, she sighed. Pursed her lips. 'You see, the point is, Rosie, he finds it all a bit embarrassing. I didn't want to mention this before, but it appears you've made something of a fool of yourself one way and another. Am I right?'

I felt a blush unfurl from my feet. 'What d'you mean?' I breathed.

'I think you know,' she said gently.

I gazed at her. Couldn't speak.

She helped me out. 'Mooning around after him? Making a bit of a play for him? Cooking him scrumptious candlelit suppers on New Year's Eve, making goo-goo eyes – that type of thing. You've fallen for him, haven't you, Rosie?'

I went about the colour of her jeans and felt about the size of her T shirt.

'Oh, it's okay,' she went on with a chuckle, 'don't look so chastened, it's not that heinous a crime. After all, he's a very attractive guy and you're, well, you're alone.' She smiled kindly. 'And obviously quite desperate, especially with a little kid in tow. It's only natural for you to have a crush on him.'

'I am not desperate!' I spluttered.

'And it's certainly not the first time it's happened either,' she swept on. 'God, if I had a dollar for every girl who's ever fallen for Joss I'd be a very rich woman indeed!' She sighed. 'And you know I blame myself in a way. I can see now how it happens. Because I'm away so much he probably seems like the vulnerable, abandoned artist, beavering away in his studio night after night without the love of a good woman to inspire him, but I can assure you that's not the case. Shall I tell you something, Rosie?' Her brown eyes suddenly trained on me like headlamps. 'We make love every single night. Even on the telephone.'

I gazed at her. She seemed to demand a response. 'Really,' I gulped eventually.

'Oh yes, we're at it for hours, and sometimes it gets so passionate I have to put the phone down and call him back. And then when we *see* each other – boy!' She threw back her head ecstatically. 'There's just no stopping us. We're at each other like a couple of tigers, ripping each other's clothes off – we can't control ourselves. We've just done

it, as a matter of fact. Right there on that chair you're sitting on.'
I shot up like a rocket. 'Christ!'
She smiled fondly at the space my bottom had just vacated. 'He's
never been able to resist that chair. It's one of our very special places.
It rocks a bit you see, gathers a momentum all of its own . . .' She
coiled a strand of hair dreamily round her finger, staring into space.
'Daddy bear's chair . . .' she murmured. Suddenly she snapped to.
'But the point is, Rosie, three's going to be rather a crowd, isn't it?
You do see that don't you? We simply can't have you mooning
around us in a lovesick manner, it's just too embarrassing. I'll give
you back your deposit of course . . .' She delved into her handbag for
her chequebook and as she did, a Mars bar wrapper fell on the floor.
She snatched it up quickly and began writing. '. . . here we go, it's
not much, but my goodness you're going to need every penny you
can get now that the pub's sacked you, aren't you?' She glanced up,
pen poised over her signature. Bit her lip. 'You know, Rosie, I hate to
sound disloyal but I did kinda sympathise a bit with Bob over that.
That whole ghastly business with your husband shook Joss and me
rigid and I have to say we were never entirely happy about you being
around the kids so much. Not that we thought you'd actually spike
the fish fingers or anything crass, but as Joss said, there's no smoke
without – Rosie!' She broke off as I exited smartly by the back door.
I ran down the lawn into the garden leaving it wide open.
'Rosie, you forgot your cheque!' She waved it after me.
'Keep it!' I yelled back in a strangled voice.
'Oh don't be silly, there's no need to go off in a huff! You might be
glad of it a bit later when you haven't got a job and—'
'—And I'm desperate?' I swung round, tears stinging my eyes.
'Keep it,' I yelled. 'Keep your sodding money, I'll never be that
desperate, I don't want any of it!'
Her eyes hardened. 'Ah. I see. It was just my husband and my kids
you were after then, was it?' She glared at me for a moment, then
slammed the door.
I turned and ran on, stumbling round the garden to the swing at
the back where Martha was pushing Ivo. He jumped off and ran to
me when he saw me. I swept him up in my arms, burying my face in
his cold pink cheek and blond curls. Martha hurried towards me.
'Rosie! I'm that chuffed for you, really I am! I knew all along you
didn't bloody do it but – hey, what's up?' Her smile dropped when
she saw my face.
'Nothing,' I muttered, kissing Ivo's forehead fiercely and blinking
hard. 'Nothing. Um, look, Martha, I'll ring and explain, but I can't

talk now. I'll be at my parents' and – well I'll ring you later, I promise.'

Choking back sobs, I turned and ran with Ivo down the hill to the cottage. Shakily, and almost in a dream, I dashed in and out and loaded the back of the car with as much stuff as I could manage, and then when the boot was full to bursting, slammed it shut and belted Ivo in. As we lurched back up the hill again I could hardly see for tears, but was aware that Martha was standing at the back door, her dark spiky hair standing to attention, gaping after me as I sped past. As I flew towards the gates I heard a familiar crunch coming the other way and knew that I was about to pass Joss. I swerved off the gravel on to the grass, put my foot down and shot past, just catching sight of Lucy and Emma's astonished faces in the back. I clutched my mouth in anguish. Oh God, I'd miss those children, more than I cared to think about. I'd miss him, but I'd miss them too, and I hadn't even said goodbye!

Perhaps it was better that way, I thought a few minutes later, calming down a bit as I drove along the lanes to my parents' house. Less embarrassing for Joss and much less emotionally upsetting for the children. Crikey, what must he think of me though, throwing myself at him like that? Perhaps in the long run it was better that Annabel had told me, otherwise I could have gone on making a prat of myself indefinitely. Oh yes, it was entirely possible that given time I could have gone the whole hog, prostrated myself ready and waiting in the boy-next-door's bed perhaps, clad in a minimal amount of black lace and waving a champagne bottle, making 'goo-goo eyes'. I shuddered, hoping to goodness that had been her expression and not his.

As I came to a halt in my parents' drive I noticed Philly's car was there. A second later the front door flew open and down the steps came the pair of them, my mother and my sister, running out to meet me, clearly having heard the good news. Mummy was waving both hands wildly in the air, tottering dangerously in high heels, and Philly, arms outstretched, was beaming widely, benevolent as ever. I got out wearily and fell into their arms.

'Oh, my baby!' sobbed Mummy. 'I've just put the phone down to Alice, she rang to tell us and – oh thank God! After all you've been through!'

'Well, it's all over now,' I said soothingly. I raised my head from her shoulder and found my sister's face. 'Philly, I'm so sorry,' I whispered. 'What must you think of me?' My eyes ached with strain but hers were warm and kind.

'What I always think, that you're my sister and I love you. I don'
blame you for thinking what you did, Rosie. I had a word with Alic
and she told me what she'd done and why. I can't say I really blam
her either.'

Our eyes met in understanding.

'What?' demanded Mummy, swooping like a hawk. 'What ha
Alice done and why, what?'

'Nothing,' said Philly. 'It doesn't matter now, it's all forgotten
Come on, let's go inside.' She kept her arm round me and squeeze
my shoulder. 'Rosie, I'm so happy for you,' she whispered.

'Me too.' I swallowed. 'If only—'

'What?'

'Oh, nothing. I'm just tired that's all.' I opened the back door an
got Ivo out of his seat. 'Mum, I've sort of lost my cottage. Joss an
Annabel have taken on some new tenants with a bit more money. I
it all right if Ivo and I stay here for a bit?'

'Of course you can, my darling, stay forever!'

'Er, well we'll see,' I said nervously. 'Where's Dad?' I looke
around.

'Oh!' Her hand shot to her mouth. 'Lord, I forgot to tell you
father! He's still in the shed!'

'Mum!'

'Oh Gordon, Gordon, I'm coming!' She ran off round the hous
and then down the back garden, flapping her hanky in distress
'Gordon, Lizzie's coming!'

Philly and I watched her go for a moment, then went inside. Iv
pottered off and we sank down in opposite sofas on either side of th
fire in the sitting room. I rested my head back. 'Well, I'm glad that'
all over.'

'So am I,' she said with feeling.

I raised my head and looked at her. 'Thanks, Philly. You've bee
an absolute brick throughout all of this and I've been a selfish
ungrateful cow.'

'No, you haven't. No one can blame you for thinking what yo
did, Alice saw to that. The awful thing was, though,' she mused, 'tha
I really thought it was you who'd put those books there. Couldn'
believe my ears when you came and told me about them in my
kitchen. I thought, blimey, here she is, my own sister, my own flesh
and blood, sneaking around and implicating me to get herself off th
hook. Just to save her own precious hide.' She smiled wryly. 'So yo
see, we both believed the worst of each other. Both thought the othe
was capable of treachery.'

I shivered. 'Don't remind me. God, just think how horribly it could all have ended.'

'Except that it hasn't,' she said firmly. She got up and walked to the window, arms folded. Then she turned and smiled. 'And you know, the funny thing is, Rosie, that believe it or not, something amazingly good has come out of all this.'

I glanced over at her. Her cheeks were flushed and her eyes bright. Really? I thought wearily. Well, why the devil can't some of it filter down to my neck of the woods then? I frowned. 'What?'

'Well after I left you in the kitchen this morning and came here to be with Mum, Miles came home and couldn't find me. He rang and discovered I was here, so he came across. We've had a long talk, Rosie. We've been upstairs in Mum's bedroom for ages actually, thrashing things out. He's just gone, had to get the children from school.'

'Oh? And?'

'And I told him everything.'

I gaped. 'What – about Michael?'

She blushed. 'Well, actually he already knew. It didn't come as a surprise to him at all. In fact,' she bit her lip, 'if I'm honest, I knew that he knew all along. Even while it was happening.'

I stared. 'You mean he knew and he didn't say anything?'

'No, he didn't, and that's what spurred me on,' she said urgently, coming back and sitting down. 'Kept me seeing Michael! I kept thinking, oh, for God's sake, Miles, be a man, *fight* for me or something, but he didn't. Wouldn't. He just sat back and took my lies, week after week, let Michael whisk me off to hotels and secluded cottages right from under his nose.'

'Good grief. Why?'

She shrugged. 'He wanted it to run its course he says. He knew it was an aberration and I'd come out at the other end, and he said he didn't want to confront me and risk losing me.'

'Blimey. He loves you all right.'

'I know,' she said ruefully. 'And now that it's over, now that I can't even bear Michael's name to be mentioned any more, I know he was right to do that. I love him too, you see, Rosie, but the thing is, I do need more. We talked about that upstairs and we both recognise it. It's not enough for me to be stuck at home, the farmer's wife, the mother, the gardener, I'll always want something more stimulating at the end of the day, and because I was so angry and bitter it resulted in a fling. But not any more. I know what's right for me now, and adultery it certainly ain't, but I can't do this homebody bit any more. I'm going back to work.'

421

'Really? What, as an anaesthetist?'

'No, that would be impossible with a family. No, I'm going to retrain as a GP.'

'Oh! Can you do that?'

'Of course,' she said calmly.

'But how long will it take?'

'Oh, a few years, but it'll be worth it. I can work shorter hours and not necessarily every day and I can also work locally. It makes perfect sense.'

I looked at her. Of course it did. Everything Philly ever did always made perfect sense. Philly never really fell on her face did she. Or if she did, she never came up smelling of poo, always of roses. Husband discovers she's had a torrid affair? Not a problem. She clearly needed the stimulus. Wrecks my best friend's family life into the bargain? Never mind, it wasn't her fault, she was frustrated, poor thing. Now me, if I'd done that, I'd be an old dog, an old trollop, but Philly? No, she just needed to go back to work. There was something missing in her life. I smiled bravely. Don't be a bitch, Rosie.

'That's marvellous, Philly.'

'Isn't it just.'

'And Miles doesn't mind?'

'Mind what?'

'You going back to work.'

'What's it got to do with Miles?'

'Well, I just thought . . .'

'Oh no, I'm sure he's delighted.'

Yes, well, he would be, wouldn't he? Better than shagging, I thought uncharitably. I got up quickly and went to the window to hide my jealous face. Oh God, what was wrong with me? Was I so bitter and twisted that I couldn't even be happy for my own sister any more?

'It's extraordinary how everything's turned out so well isn't it,' she went on behind me. 'Most of all for you, Rosie. I'm *so* pleased, you must be *so* relieved to be off the hook!'

I pressed my forehead on the glass. I didn't answer but privately I thought, yes, well excuse me, Philly, for not being too ecstatic because actually I didn't do anything in the first place. I was wrongly accused. I didn't 'get off' any hook because there was no hook to get off. And look at me now. Back home with Mother. No job, no house, no man and still expected to be grateful. And look at Philly. Plays fast and loose, shits on just about everyone in sight, goes home to her forgiving husband, prepares to become a GP and juggle her job and her children magnificently, and in a few months' time everyone will be saying how marvellous she is and how well she manages everything and up will go the Hallelujah Chorus and sometimes *it just made me puke.*

I shut my eyes tight and rolled my head on the cold glass. Stop it, Rosie, just . . . stop it. This is what happens to failures, of course. They become horrible, spiteful people.

When I opened my eyes again, I blinked, then smiled, in spite of myself. For coming up the back lawn, arm in arm, were my parents. That was strange enough in itself, but then something even more peculiar happened. My mother suddenly reached up and kissed my father's cheek. Dad looked surprised, but then a slow smile spread across his face. I realised I hadn't seen them kiss since I was quite small. It brought a lump to my throat. I went out to the hall to meet them.

'Daddy.' I held out my arms and he slipped away from Mum to hug me.

'Hello, love.'

'Thanks, Dad,' I gulped. 'Nice try and all that.'

'Don't thank me, darling,' he whispered as Mum went off to the kitchen, 'it's the best rest I've had in years. I haven't been near the sink, chopped any wood, topped and tailed any beans or scrubbed any carrots, and what's more I've pricked out all my dahlias!'

I giggled. 'Oh good.'

'More to the point,' he took my elbow and led me away conspiratorially, 'my isolation seems to have had a curious effect on your mother.' He glanced through the door at her as she bustled around putting the kettle on. 'She's been acting decidedly frisky, I shall have to get her to lock me in sheds more often!'

I laughed. He turned my shoulders around to face him. 'And what about you, love? Are you all right?'

'I'm fine.'

'Good. I'm sure it was a fairly futile gesture of mine, but I had this strange notion that by pretending it was me, I might force someone else's hand. And I had to do something. I couldn't stand by and let them accuse you when I knew you hadn't done it.'

I smiled. 'Thanks, Dad, for that single, supreme vote of confidence, and it wasn't a futile gesture at all. It galvanised me into going to London to find out what was going on.'

'Where I gather your friend spilled the beans.'

'Charlotte, yes, she did.' I paused for a second, and then decided on balance not to go into the nature of the beans. The big dressing-up box of beans. I wasn't sure my father could take all that on an empty stomach and several hours of dahlia pricking. Instead I gave his arm another quick squeeze and watched as he ambled off quite happily to the kitchen to be bossed and fussed over by my mother as she made him and Ivo go off and wash their hands before sitting down to a ham sandwich and a glass of milk.

'Go on, the pair of you,' she scolded, 'you're both filthy. And make sure you get right under those nails, Gordon. Heaven knows what you've been doing in that shed!'

As grandfather and grandson disappeared sheepishly into the downstairs cloakroom together, she turned and caught my eye.

'I know all about that business, you know,' she said quietly.

'What business?'

'About Harry. What Charlotte told you. I caught him once, trying on that pink bed jacket of mine. The one with the ostrich feathers round the neck.'

My mouth fell open. 'No!'

She nodded. 'Oh yes I did. And then when he decided to do that aromatherapy course, I asked him if it wasn't a bit, you know, effeminate. He came clean. Told me all about it.'

'Harry never did an aromatherapy course!'

'Oh yes he did, my darling. Up there.' She rolled her eyes skywards. I gazed at her, stupefied. 'Now come along, you two,' she raised her voice as Dad and Ivo reappeared. 'Come and have your tea. And, Gordon, eat up those crusts, please, you're getting as fussy as Ivo. There's nothing like a bit of roughage to get those bowels moving. I happen to know you haven't been ponky-poos for days.'

I gazed at her in wonder for a moment, then drifted, dazed, back to the drawing room, shaking my head. I sank down in a stupor. 'Good God,' I muttered.

'What?' Philly looked up over her *Harpers*. 'What is it?'

'She says she knew about Harry!'

'What about Harry?'

'You know, the shoulder pads, the pointy sticks . . . Suzanne Charlton . . .'

She frowned. 'Who the hell's Suzanne Charlton? What pointy sticks?'

Suddenly I realised she didn't know anything at all about any of that. I wasn't sure I had the energy to go into it now. Some other time perhaps. I sighed. 'It doesn't matter,' I said flatly.

Philly frowned at me for a moment. 'Are you all right, Rosie?'

'Fine, fine,' faintly.

'It's the shock, darling,' she said gently, reaching out and patting my hand. 'You'll probably feel a bit, well, strange for a while.'

I nodded. She went back to her magazine and I let her go, let her think I was still a bit shell shocked, a bit deranged. I turned my head slowly back towards the kitchen though, to Mum. Suddenly I couldn't help it.

'Philly, you don't think there's anything in all this mediumistic lark, do you?' I blurted. 'Only, Mum seems to be awfully well-informed about Harry's movements up there.'

'I doubt very much if he's Up There at all,' she said witheringly, flicking over a page. 'If you ask me, he was hustled straight into the "going down" lift.'

'He wasn't all bad, Phil, you know,' I said quietly. I thought back to what Charlotte had said, about Harry asking Boffy to clear me, to tell the police it was suicide.

She glanced up in surprise. 'Well, if you say so,' she said grudgingly, 'but in answer to your question, no. I don't think there's anything at all in Mum's latest obsession, she's just rambling as usual, and if she rambles enough, she occasionally strikes lucky, that's all.'

'I wouldn't be so sure,' I said darkly, glancing nervously out to the kitchen again. 'I've always said there's something very peculiar about our mother. I wouldn't mind betting she's got a hot line to—'

'Shh!' Philly looked up sharply, cocking her ear.

'What is it?'

'Nothing.' She got up. 'I'll be back in a mo.'

She hastened out to the kitchen and sure enough was back a moment later. With Mum at her side. They stood over me, the pair of them. Two pairs of shining eyes gleamed down at me.

'Rosie, buck up! Here – brush your hair!' Mum began attacking me with a spiky hairbrush.

'Ow! What – why?' I ducked, then got up and backed away.

'And quick, tuck that dreadful baggy shirt in, smarten yourself up a bit, for heaven's sake! Philly, where's your lipstick?'

'Get off will you!' I said as they tried to tuck me in. 'What's happening?'

Suddenly Mum lunged for the air freshener on the windowsill and blasted me with some disgusting lavender squirt as if I was a fly.

'Oh, yuk. Stop it, Mum!'

'I just knew I should have washed these chair covers,' she muttered, abandoning me to smooth down the covers, bustling round the room straightening ornaments, plumping up cushions. 'They're dreadfully stained, and if I'd just thought to get some fresh flowers I could have made a nice little arrangement on the piano and—'

The doorbell went. The pair of them froze.

'He's here!' hissed Mummy.

'Who?'

'You know!' She gave me a little push. 'Go on. Go and answer it!'

I stared at their flushed, excited faces. Their shining eyes. Slowly I turned and went to the door. My heart was racing, pounding away like crazy. He'd come. Yes of course he'd come, why on earth had I thought he wouldn't?

As I got there, my hand closed on the doorknob and I shut my eyes for a brief, giddy second. Then I swung it back. Giant white lilies, the type that look as if they've been grown anywhere except in a garden, were thrust into my hands. The heady scent rocked me backwards. I gasped, then took another step back. Because behind the flowers, looking impossibly handsome and grinning from ear to ear, was Alex.

Chapter Thirty-Two

Oh!'

'For you,' he beamed, thrusting the bouquet into my hands. He was wearing his old blue Guernsey and his extra special tigerish smile, the one that made his green eyes crease up at the corners. They twinkled seductively. 'I wanted to be the first to congratulate you, Rosie, I just can't tell you how pleased I am for you.'

'Try,' sprang ironically to mind, but I resisted, thinking again how odd all these congratulations were, as if I'd won a prize, or had a baby.

'You must be absolutely thrilled.'

There he went again, as if it was 9lbs 2oz and very definitely male.

'I'm relieved,' I said firmly. 'I think thrilled would be putting too fine a point on it. We are, after all, talking about the death of my husband here.' I staged a sombre expression.

'Of course, of course,' he said quickly, instantly dropping the twinkles and adopting something a little more suitable. He lowered his eyes decorously and somehow got them stuck on my chest. They wouldn't budge. He sighed deeply. 'All the same, Rosie, inappropriate as it may be, I have to say I'm absolutely dying to celebrate with you. I passed a charming little pub as I came along, and I thought why don't we nip down there and have a quick snifter? You know, catch up on all the news?'

I raised my eyebrows. 'And then?'

He laughed. 'Oh okay, I'll come clean. I thought I might whisk you out to dinner too, seeing as how you're looking absolutely gorgeous and I still find you utterly irresistible. There, how's that for cards on the table.'

I moved the flowers so they obscured his objects of desire. It was quite clear he was a tit man, in fact I'd suspected as much all along. That night he'd grappled me on the sofa in Joss's hall, his hands had found their mark pretty damned quickly and one gets to recognise these traits when one is the owner of outsized anatomy.

'You resisted me fairly easily the other day,' I said lightly. 'In fact seem to remember you hid under a window seat to avoid me.'

He laughed nervously and ran his hand through his russet curls 'God yes, I'm sorry about that, I've been meaning to apologise actually, it's just I was so unbelievably busy. I remember now, I had heaps of paperwork that day and I was avoiding all calls, even my dear old mum who rang to wish me a Happy New Year!' He grinned 'It was nothing personal, Rosie, I just got totally snowed under. You know how it is.'

'Ah, right. I thought perhaps you imagined I was the Pennington Poisoner, on the prowl around the village for her next victim Sniffing out succulent young men, looking for tasty morsels?' I gave quick, teeth-sucking impersonation of Hannibal Lector.

'Oh, don't be silly, of course not!' He laughed even more nervously and did some more hair-scraping.

'And I thought perhaps you were wondering if you were next or the list.'

'No! No, nothing like that, good heavens!'

'Spot of arsenic in the tea perhaps? Deadly nightshade in the soup Then before you know where you are, another one bites the dust.'

'Ah ha ha! Ridiculous!'

'Of course it is, I'm so pleased you agree. I just wanted to clear that up. And I'm so sorry I haven't got time to nip to the pub and have a quick snifter with you but I've got to get supper ready. Oh and the flowers are lovely, by the way, I shall give them to my mother. She was just saying she needed something to brighten up the sitting room. She'll be thrilled.' I beamed and plonked a very unromantic kiss on his cheek. 'Goodbye then, Alex.' I went to shut the door, but quick as a flash he stuck his head round. Short of decapitating him, I had to pause.

'Oh, er, well, you're obviously a bit busy right now but—'

'Totally snowed under. Up to my eyes and avoiding all calls. You know how it is.'

'Er, yes, yes I do, but I just wondered – tomorrow night? If you're not too busy? There's a new wine bar opened up in Cirencester, they've got a reggae night on, sounds rather fun Thought we might have a bit of a bop, a bite to eat and . . .' he ground to a halt. Good God, man, get your eyes off my chest Somehow he managed to hoist them up, crease into a smile, and ooze out some more charm.

'Come on, Rosie, what d'you say? Why don't we let sleeping dogs lie and start again, eh?' He reached out a finger and stroked my arm.

adding a spot of smoulder to the eye contact. 'What d'you say, hmmmm?'

'I say, hmmm . . . no. I say go and play sleeping dogs with someone else. I say, sorry, Alex, but the truth is I find you totally, and utterly, resistible.'

With that I shut the door in his astonished face. Then I turned and walked straight into my mother, who just happened to be polishing the banisters with her hanky. As one does.

'Where's he gone?' she squeaked in alarm.

'How should I know.' I pushed the flowers in her direction, glanced nonchalantly at the headlines in the *Telegraph* on the hall table and walked into the kitchen.

'But – what did he want?' She hastened after me, hanky flapping in one hand, flowers in the other.

'He wanted to take me out.'

'*And?*' she shrieked.

'Oh, *and* – whisk me back to his place to fondle my breasts I shouldn't wonder.'

'Rosie!' She dropped the hanky.

'Sorry, Mum, but he's a bit of a lech. And a doubting Thomas to boot. The first I might have been able to entertain, but the two together,' I shook my head, 'uh uh.'

I plucked an apple from the fruit bowl, tossed it in the air, caught it and sauntered through the kitchen. My, that had felt good, very, very good. *I'd* said goodbye. *I'd* shut the door. *I'd* said not today, thank you. In fact it had felt terrific. No wonder people did it to me so often.

'You little fool!' My mother's voice carried after me. 'You'll never do better than that, he's a vet, for God's sake!'

'Well, look at it this way, Mum,' I said opening the back door and pulling on my wellingtons, 'he could have been a doctor. Imagine if I'd passed *that* up.' I gave a mock shudder and exited into the garden as she snorted in despair behind me. Then on an impulse I stuck my head back round the door again.

'Hey, Mum?'

'What?' she hissed furiously.

'I've never told you this, but once, years ago, you'll never guess what?'

'What?'

I glanced about furtively to check no one was listening, cupped my hand round my mouth and whispered, 'I turned down an ortho-paedic surgeon!'

429

She gazed at me, horrified for a moment, then, 'Get out!' she shrieked. 'Out!'

I grinned and shut the back door behind me. I stood for a moment on the back step taking in deep breaths of the cold, biting air, then set off down the garden, munching my apple as I went. Out of the corner of my eye I saw Philly packing up her car, preparing to leave. The front door flew open and my mother joined her in the drive, ranting, raving, waving her arms demonstratively, rattling her jewellery, despairing of me no doubt. Philly stopped her packing to listen, folded her arms, head on one side, sighing, nodding, sympathising. I clearly was The End. What *would* they do with me? This dreadful problem child who just would *not* lie down with the first man they found. Lots of head shaking, arm folding, shoulder shrugging. I walked on. On and on, down the brick path that snaked through the copse at the end of the lawn, down past the pond where I'd lain on my tummy and gazed at the fish for hours on end as a child, and on to the sanctuary of the potting shed.

I lifted the latch. Two guilty and extremely dirty faces swung round. My father and Ivo sat side by side at the potting bench.

'Oh good,' sighed Dad. 'I thought it was your mother. We've had a bit of a session in here, nothing serious, but you know how she carries on.'

I smiled. Ivo was covered in mud, as was his grandfather, and before them were rows and rows of overflowing flowerpots.

'Always a tricky job, watering the seedlings, and Ivo can get rather carried away,' admitted my father, as Ivo, kneeling up on the bench, wobbled dangerously with a huge watering can before sloshing half a gallon of water into a two inch pot.

'Twicky job,' he confirmed gravely as the bench flooded.

'Oh, Ivo, be careful! All Grandpa's seeds!'

'No, no, love, let him be. I can sort it out later,' Dad said. 'He's enjoying himself.'

I smiled gratefully. 'Making work for you, you mean.'

I sat down in the corner, watching them work. Happy, quiet and diligent, the silence punctuated just occasionally by Ivo's 'Like this, Grandpa?'

'That's it, laddie.'

The peace, the earthy smells, the tangible contentment of the pair of them was comforting. I basked in it. Then after a while I picked up a seed catalogue beside me. I flicked through it idly. At length, Dad spoke.

'Who was that at the door then?'

I put down the magazine and told him. And the outcome. He chuckled. 'Oh, Rosie, that'll take your mother months to get over, months and months! And it'll be dragged up every time you put a foot wrong, how Rosie blew her last chance, you mark my words.'

I sighed. 'I know. I shall undoubtedly live to regret it, and the worst of it is, she's probably right. My judgement *is* so appalling, I probably don't know a good thing when I see it.'

'It's got nothing to do with judgement, love. You'll know, the moment you feel it. You just haven't felt it yet that's all. You don't weigh these things up, Rosie, it's instinctive.'

I gazed into his kind brown eyes. 'Yes,' I said quietly, 'yes, I do know that actually.' I gulped. Picked some dried Ready Brek off my jeans. Then I looked up quickly, narrowing my eyes. 'Dad, why did you marry Mum?'

'Why?' He laughed, put down his trowel. 'Well she was everything I wasn't, I suppose. She had a posh southern voice, she drank sherry like a lady, she could dance, she could chatter away sociably like, she was pretty and cultured. Or so I thought. And I was just a loutish yob from the North.'

'So you weighed it up?'

He paused. Glanced across at me. 'Yes, I see what you mean. I suppose I did in a way.' Quickly he picked up his trowel again, then just as abruptly set it down. 'I was ambitious, Rosie,' he went on quietly. 'I'd made a deal of money all right, but I didn't have anything to back it up. Didn't have the class. Your mother wore the latest Paris fashions, made them herself from *Vogue* patterns, played tennis in proper whites. I thought she was the bee's knees. I thought she was everything I needed to put the cherry on the cake.'

'And she wasn't?'

He paused. 'I've no regrets, Rosie. But let's just say I hadn't reckoned on her being even more ambitious than I was. And you can't make a sow's purse out of a pig's ear. She thought she could and she's been thwarted in her attempts ever since. Whichever way you look at it, I'm still a pig's ear.'

I squeezed his arm. 'Well, you're the nicest pig's ear I've ever seen,' I said warmly.

'Why, thank you for those kind words, oh daughter of mine,' he said, grinning, 'but if you could just see your way clear to taking your left elbow out of my azalea pots I'd be even more grateful . . . thank you.'

He carried on pricking out his plants for a bit. Then after a while he spoke, but he didn't look up. 'I've been thinking, Rosie, about

431

building a cottage at the end of the garden.'

I glanced up. 'Oh yes?'

'Well we've had planning permission for four years now and it runs out next year. Seems a shame not to use it. Thought you and Ivo could have it. I'd build it down by the stream so you'd have that in your front garden, make it the boundary to the house. Might be a bit of a hazard for a bit, but it's not deep, and Ivo would love it later on, building dams, that sort of thing.'

A lump came to my throat for various reasons. Firstly, how sweet of my father to use all his savings to provide a roof over my head, knowing full well that if I shared one with my mother we'd end up killing each other, but also – oh also because there was such a dismal sense of finality about it. This was it then, was it? The spinster daughter, at home with her parents. Now and – what, forever more? I sighed. In the distance I heard tyres crunching on the gravel drive. That would be Philly probably, back off home to her house, her family, her husband. I cleared my throat.

'Thanks, Dad, I really appreciate the offer. Can I – well, can I think about it?'

'Course you can, lass. There's no rush, you take your time.' He looked pleased that I hadn't turned it down flat. He turned to help Ivo, who was struggling to separate terracotta flowerpots. One cracked as he finally pulled them apart but Dad ignored it, sweeping the pieces on the floor and giving him the whole one. It occurred to me that if I couldn't provide Ivo with a father, the least I could do would be to provide him with a resident grandpa.

'What does Mummy say?'

'What does Mummy say about what?' My mother suddenly stuck her head round the door. She looked cross. Dad and I both jumped like naughty children.

'Nothing, my love, nothing at all,' soothed my father. She clearly didn't know.

'Really,' she said drily. 'I know you, Gordon, and I know the pair of you when you get together. So this is where you all are. Back in here getting filthy again. There's a cup of tea waiting in the kitchen if anyone wants it.'

'Thank you,' we both muttered dutifully in unison.

She went to go then popped her head back. 'Oh, by the way, that was your ex-landlord calling to see you, Rosie. I told him where to go in no uncertain terms I can tell you.'

There was a silence. I gazed at her. 'Joss?' I whispered.

'Yes, flaming cheek, having thrown you out of your house. I sent him away with a flea in his ear all right, gave him a piece of my mind. Now come along, Ivo – oh good gracious, look at the state of those trousers! Leave all that mucky earth now and come and wash your hands with Granny, come on!'

It hadn't been Philly. Those had been Joss's tyres on the gravel. My father's eyes left his workbench and came round to meet mine.

'There's roadworks down at Markham's Corner,' he said quietly. 'He's bound to get stuck there. If you ran through the woods and across the stream, like as not you'd catch him.'

I stared at him for a moment – then needed no further prompting. I jumped up, pushed past my mother in the doorway and dashed down the garden.

'Where on earth d'you think you're going!' Her voice carried after me but I raced on, on and on until I reached the stream. Ignoring the bridge which was further upstream I leapt across. One foot slipped back and I felt water seep into my boot, but I caught hold of the reeds on the other side and pulled myself through them, panting up the bank and staggering across to the little wood beyond. I plunged into it, breathlessly dodging round the thickets as one after another they reared up at me. There was no real path running through here, just a clump of brambles here, some saplings there, bigger, more mature trees to race round and then more clumps of brambles. I put my head down and went for it, shielding my eyes with my forearm and pushing on through. Oh please, please let me catch him, my heart was pounding, please let me be in time!

Eventually I made it to the clearing. I raced across the wet grass, down the bank, tumbling over and over at the bottom. I picked myself up and threw myself at the fence that marked the end of our land. Ignoring the fact that it was laced with barbed wire and panting hard now, I clambered over, tore my jumper, yanked it free and jumped down the other side. Then I raced off on the last leg, through some scrubland, across some rough pasture and then finally, finally out on to the verge of the main road. The fast road that led back to Cirencester.

I stood at the side of the dual carriageway gasping, covered in mud, clutching my side, looking desperately about. Cars were coming thick and fast, flying along in both directions, but no green Range Rover. Oh God, I was too late, he'd already gone, except – yes! Yes, here it came, hurtling along much too fast, definitely defying the speed limit, and with a very grim looking Joss at the wheel.

'STOP!' I shrieked at the top of my voice, stepping out into the main road Anna Karenina style. I waved my arms frantically then at the last minute, thinking better of being squashed to a pulp on the tarmac, hopped back on to the verge. He shot by me and for a moment I thought he wasn't going to stop, but then I saw the brake lights flash and he screeched to a halt a few hundred yards down the road. A swarm of angry motorists swerved to avoid him, blaring their horns, shaking their fists madly.

I squinted into the distance. The car door opened. He jumped out and turned towards me. He shut the door and stood there, waiting. My heart stopped for a moment – then bounded on again. Oh! He was waiting for me! I must run to him, this was my big moment, it had come at last, yes, I could sense it! Delirious with happiness, I set off at a gallop, charging up the road like a demon. I ran and ran, but still he seemed so very far away. If only I wasn't so desperately unfit, I thought, panting hard, and if only I hadn't just run a marathon through a wood already. But no matter, on and on I puffed towards the tall dark figure on the horizon, standing legs apart in a pose somewhat reminiscent of Clint in *A Fistful of Dollars*. A rogue thought entered my mind that he could at least have broken into a walk and met me halfway, but I dismissed it instantly. No, no, that wouldn't have been cool, men like Joss didn't run, and this way was so much more romantic. Why, I was like one of those girls running through a corn field, arms outstretched, racing towards her lover; I'd fly into his arms, he'd swing me round, I'd kiss the living daylights out of him, oh yes, I would – I stopped for a moment, clutched my side, felt rather sick suddenly. I gulped down some air. Come on, Rosie, just a stitch, get going. Oh yes I would, I thought, setting off again at a trot – well, a limp – the moment I . . . God I felt ill . . . the moment I sodding well reached him, I'd kiss the living – Jesus did he have to park so shagging far away! Finally I staggered up to him, wheezing, gasping, willing myself not to throw up on his black jumper. He reached out and grabbed my arm.

'What the hell d'you think you're doing? You nearly got yourself killed!' He looked furious. 'And I nearly had half a ton of metal up my backside!'

'Sorry!' I gasped. 'Wanted to catch you – heard you'd been round – Mum said – wanted to—'

'Get in.'

'Eh?'

'Get in, for God's sake!' He marched me round to the passenger side, bundled me in and slammed the door behind me. 'D'you want to die on the freeway or something?'

I watched, dazed, clutching the upholstery and gasping for breath, as he strode round and got in the other side. He started the car and we crawled along the hard shoulder with him glancing in his rear-view mirror for a gap.

'Pillock,' he muttered.

Presumably that was meant for some other motorist, except – the road was now clear. I frowned. Pillock? Who, me? I boggled. Surely not, where was the romance in that? He joined the road at such a speed it practically gave me whiplash and I clutched the seat as he roared up to a roundabout, spun round it – all the way round, it seemed to me, and on two wheels too, but then again I was probably still in shock – and back down the road again.

'So,' he said, shooting me a surprisingly venomous look for one who I'd been planning on sharing a special harmony with, 'you moved out. Nice one, Rosie, and perfect timing too. The children are delighted, can't stop crying, in fact.'

My mouth fell open. 'I did not!' I managed to squeak. 'Who told you that?'

'Annabel.'

'Annabel! Is that what she told you? God, no, she told *me* to go, said you were embarrassed by me!'

'Embarrassed by what?'

'Oh, you know, hanging about and . . .' I fell silent as my mind offered me a glimpse of me 'hanging about'. Like a devoted spaniel, lying at her master's feet, slippers in mouth. I bit my lip. 'Nothing. She just said, well that she'd got some new tenants. Eco-warriors or something.'

He rasped out a laugh. 'Eco-warriors! God that's a heroic, last ditch attempt.'

'It's true, Joss, she told me to go, told me to eff off. Just ask her if you don't believe me,' I said petulantly.

'I can't do that, she's gone.'

'Gone where?'

'Who knows? To London I presume. Before making her way back to the States.'

'She's going abroad again?' Blimey, and I thought she was going to be there for her 'needy' husband, have a baby, get the decorating done. 'How long for?'

'For good.'

'For—' I glanced over in surprise.

He sighed. 'Rosie, it appears to have escaped your notice that Annabel and I do not live like normal married couples. In fact we

435

tend to live two thousand miles apart, and when we are in the same house, albeit briefly, we fight like banshees and tear each other limb from limb. Has this completely passed you by?'

'Er, no, I suppose not.'

'And so she's finally agreed to the divorce. She's resisted it for two years now and I haven't had the heart to push it, but I think even Annabel knows when she's beaten. Knows when she's outclassed.'

'The . . . divorce? Outclassed? What d'you mean?'

He bit his lip, staring straight ahead. 'Nothing. If you don't know then . . . maybe I'm wrong.'

I swivelled round in my seat to face him. 'No, Joss, hang on. Just tell me, please, in plain English. You're getting divorced? I thought you adored her!'

'You did? Why?'

'Well, everyone said so!'

'Who's everyone?'

I thought back, tried to remember. 'Well, Alex actually.'

'Really,' he said drily. 'Alex. Yeah well he would, wouldn't he? Didn't want anyone queering his own pitch with you, I imagine.'

I stared stupidly at him.

'Look, Rosie,' he went on in the tone one normally reserves for very small children, and the educationally subnormal, 'the first time we met was outside a solicitor's office in London, am I right? Both seeing the same type of people? Divorce lawyers?'

'But – I thought that was a social call. Seeing your brother-in-law you said, Annabel's brother.'

'I was seeing my brother-in-law. Kitty's brother. He's handling my divorce.'

'Oh!'

'And call me old fashioned if I didn't spell it out at the time, but I didn't think it gentlemanly to tell the world, particularly since Annabel was resisting the action. Didn't think it was fair on her to blab. Especially since you went on to become the tenant in the cottage.'

'N-no, of course not.' The tenant. I sat on my hands.

'She was still so desperate to make a go of it, you see, tried to keep up a show of marital bliss to everyone. God she even took Martha and Vera in, but it had never been like that. Not even at the beginning really. Apart from anything else, she's incapable of having a proper sexual relationship, she can't form an intimate bond with anyone but herself. Lately she calls it celibacy because that's trendy, but it goes much deeper than that. She went off the boil soon after we got married, trotted out one lame excuse after another.'

I gaped in wonder at all these illuminating revelations tumbling out. 'But – I thought she was having an affair! When she asked me to go shopping, to buy those—'

'She was warning you off. Figured you were getting too close. I knew what she was up to.'

'Oh!'

'It just wouldn't occur to her to have an affair, Rosie, not unless it could further her career. She's not interested in sex you see. Some people are like that you know.'

Blimey. No, I didn't. 'So – crikey, why on earth did you marry her?'

He sighed. 'Because I didn't know all this at the beginning. She covered her tracks pretty well. I met her when she was a student at Harvard and I was over there giving a lecture. She made a bee line for me. Seduced me, as a matter of fact, and went through all the sexual motions in what I now realise was a fairly calculating manner. I was immensely flattered because she is, I think you'll agree, extremely easy on the eye, and she was incredibly sought after by all the young bloods there. At the time, Kitty had been dead for almost a year and for some reason that milestone loomed ominously. Made me fearful. Made me think I should be getting on with my life instead of sitting by the fire night after night crying into my Scotch, never going to bed, burying myself in my work – or the bottle – shutting myself away in the studio with my bits of stone.' He shrugged. 'I guess I was vulnerable and I clutched on to what I thought was a good thing, but looking back I don't think I actually loved her.'

'So then why did you—?'

'Because I figured the kids needed a mother and I thought that in her homespun, alternative way, she'd be kind to them. She wasn't. She wasn't interested in home life or kids, she had a totally different agenda. She was interested in my name and using it to promote her own as a budding young writer – or guru, as she likes to think of herself. She's a hypocrite you see. She likes to tell people how to bring up their kids and what to eat and how to give up smoking and how to have sex but she doesn't do any of it herself. It's just a money-making exercise. And of course that's another thing she liked about me, my money, what there is of it.' He sighed. 'And d'you know, stupidly I think I believed it would work because she was so unlike Kitty. I think that's what attracted me to her. She was so tough, so driven, so ambitious, so totally different from Kitty, and I

437

couldn't bear to be with someone similar because I feared the comparison. But I was so wrong. It just made me miss Kitty more.'

'So how come she's finally gone then?'

'This afternoon she was officially served with a decree nisi from Jonathan, Kitty's brother. I didn't want it to be like that, but in the end she left me no choice. She's finally got to get out of my house.'

'You mean you've wanted her to leave before?' I said in surprise.

'Certainly I have. But I wasn't going to chuck her out and I wasn't going to move either, which was my only other option.'

'But I thought – well I thought you were so in love with her!' I blurted. 'On New Year's Eve, you went so maudlin suddenly, as if you couldn't bear to be without her!'

'Hell, no. I guess I went quiet because you telling me she'd sent you off for condoms reminded me of what she was like. Not just ice cold but manipulative too. And it reminded me of what I'd lost. Four years to the day.' He paused. 'Kitty died on New Year's Eve.'

'Oh!' I gasped in horror.

'It's the first year in four I've seen a moment of it sober. That was thanks to you, Rosie. And that's how Annabel knew she was beaten. She knew I'd spent it with you and she knew I wasn't comatose in a heap on the floor either. And it made me realise something, too. Made me realise I could spend that night with you and not just bear it, but enjoy it. Somehow, I also knew that Kitty wanted it too. That it was time now. That she'd approve.'

I held my breath. Gazed out of the windscreen at the fields whistling past. 'You . . . loved her very much.'

'More than words can say.'

I fell silent. Tried not to breathe. It seemed I suddenly had far too much breath, all noisy and gassy and intrusive. More than words can say . . . oh God . . .

'And I didn't say those words enough. Which probably explains why I find it so hard to express myself to you, too. I'm all right on paper, Rosie, give me a pen and paper and I'll tell you how much I love you, but leave it to my vocal chords and—'

I swung round. 'How much you—'

'I don't believe you don't know,' he said quietly.

'No!' I gasped. 'At least – well I'd hoped, of course, prayed – but it seemed so much, *too* much, and – yesterday in London, you seemed so distant, so cool!'

'Yes, well, forgive me if I didn't take you in my arms in your marital home just after the police had given a morbid account of your husband's last few hours. It seemed to me the metaphorical chalk mark of his body was still outlined on the sitting-room floor. It seemed somewhat tacky.'

'Oh! Yes, right.'

'Just as flying into your arms on the hard shoulder of the highway also seemed inappropriate and, frankly, downright dangerous.'

'Oh! Well, yes, I suppose it might have been and – gosh what a supremely practical man you are, Joss!'

He smiled. 'Only comparatively. Well?'

'Well what?'

He gripped the wheel hard, driving faster than ever now down a rather familiar lane. 'You're not exactly making this easy for me, Rosie. Here am I, a jaded and emotionally battered man with two wives behind me already, three mixed-up kids in tow and damn all to offer you except my feelings and I'm doing my best to see if you feel the same way.' He flew over a sleeping policeman, then suddenly swung a left and skidded to a halt on some gravel.

I felt dizzy, all I could see were his eyes, which as he turned to me were heavy with meaning. I gazed into them.

'Oh yes!' I breathed. 'Yes, I see what you mean and I do, I *do* feel the same!' I went to fly into his arms but the bloody seat belt garrotted me.

'Here,' he snapped it open and finally – finally I was there. Where I belonged. He bent his tawny head to mine and kiss after kiss unfolded on my lips, each one, I thought as I shut my eyes, more gloriously, deliciously sweet than the last. I realised with a pang that I was turning to jelly. At last, I thought joyously, at last after so long, after so many years in the wilderness, after so many years of arid, dried-up emotions, it seemed the thaw was finally taking place. As he lifted my chin to gaze into my eyes, kiss my cheeks, the side of my mouth, my hair, I basked blissfully in the glory of it all, slowly opening my eyes to feast on him. But as I feasted, something else came into my line of vision. My mother. Peering through the sitting-room window. I froze.

'Shit!' I squeaked sitting bolt upright. 'This is my house!'

He looked around. 'Yes, I know.'

'I mean, my parents' house!'

'Sure, I know that,' he said patiently.

I gulped. Rearranged my clothing, patted my hair. Heavens, I'd never actually snogged in my parents' drive before, not even as a teenager, and I was surprised this eminently practical man found it such an appropriate location. Why had he driven here? Surely there were miles of lovers' lanes back there just waiting to be grappled in,

439

what the hell were we doing at my parents'?

He sat back, his arm along the back of the seat, watching m
'Well, go on then.'

I gaped at him, mystified. 'Go . . . on . . . where?' I panicked. O
God, had he changed his mind again? Was he taking me home t
Mother? What was wrong with this man?

'Go and get Ivo. I presume you come as a package, don't you? Ju
as I do? Apart from anything else, I've got pretty attached to the littl
guy.'

I stared. 'Oh!' I groaned ecstatically. 'Oh yes, of course! Is tha
why—'

'We've come back? It is, as a matter of fact, unless you'd like to pu
him up for adoption?'

'No! No, I wouldn't!' I leapt out of the car and ran up the drive.
stopped short of the front door. Turned. Two seconds later I wa
back, rapping on the car window. 'Joss!'

He opened his door. 'What?'

'Get out! I want you to meet my father!'

He grinned, got out and ran his hands through his hair. 'Meet th
parents, eh? Sure, but I have to warn you, I haven't done this fo
years. Not since I was in the Ivy League. Hope I don't use the wron
fork or fart as I sit down.'

I giggled as we held hands and walked up to the door. 'Well, you'v
already met my mother. She was the one with the blue hair who tol
you to bog off.'

'Ah yes, charming woman, delightful. How will she feel about m
marrying her daughter, I wonder?'

I stopped dead in my tracks on the top step, my hand on the doo
handle. 'You – want to marry me?'

He turned. Took both my hands. 'Yes, didn't I mention that?' h
said gently. 'Yes, I do. I want to marry you more than anything else i
the world.'

'Crikey!' Crikey, Rosie? Was that a mature response? Cool even? '
– I mean—' I struggled.

'I know, I know,' he interrupted hurriedly, 'you've just buried
husband and I'm rushing you, and I know you have other plans too
other dreams, like your restaurant, but I've thought it all through
Rosie, really I have. I thought you could convert the old hay barn
you know, the one way across the meadow. It's huge and it's got
gallery in it and heaps of old beams and character, I reckon with a bi
of work you could transform it, have it just exactly as you planned
herb gardens, herbaceous borders, the works. Hell, you can have

nude flying circus in there for all I care, and I thought—'

'Stop, stop!' I laughed. 'No, it's not that! It's not the restaurant – God, just you and the children are more than enough for me – it's just, well, I didn't know! Didn't know you felt so strongly!'

His eyes melted over me. 'I can't remember when I first fell in love with you, Rosie, I just know it got worse and worse. Almost from the day when you appeared on my doorstep with all your possessions and your ridiculous pride and your courage and your small son in tow, all I could think was, if only. If only I hadn't rushed into marrying Annabel. If only I'd waited, but then I couldn't be sure you'd come along, you see. And when you did, I felt as if I'd been kicked smartly and smugly in the teeth. I thought I'd have to sit by and watch, helpless, as you sailed off into the sunset with that smarmy goddam Alex Munroe but thank God you didn't, because yes, I do want to make you my wife but if you're going to turn me down, please tell me now and I'll go and get quietly hammered in the pub and we'll forget all about it.'

I was trembling now. 'Don't get hammered,' I whispered. 'I love you so much and yes, *yes*, I'll marry you, right now if you like! Oh Joss, I must be the happiest girl alive. I—' Suddenly I stopped. Listened. 'Just a minute.' I put my hand on the front door and pushed it gently. My mother shrieked and nearly toppled over backwards. She was crouching down with her ear to the keyhole, duster in hand.

She struggled to her feet, covered in confusion and delight. '*Mister Dubarry*,' she beamed, 'or may I call you Joss? Might I say how delighted I am to see you again and how sorry I am about our little contretemps earlier. I *do* apologise. Good gracious, whatever was I thinking of, whisking you away like that! Now of course you *have* both been married before so a white wedding is probably out of the question, but cream can be awfully nice, or even lemon yellow. I know Marjorie's son married a divorcee and she looked absolutely sweet in yellow, if a little fat, and it's amazing what some avant garde vicars will let you get away with these days. Why, Cynthia Parker's daughter was six months pregnant and she went sailing up the aisle in ivory, the little hussy, so I really don't think there'll be any problem there and . . .'